BERTRICE SMALL

A
DISTANT
TOMORROW

HQN™

Recycling programs
for this product may
not exist in your area.

ISBN-13: 978-0-373-77652-8

A DISTANT TOMORROW

Copyright © 2006 by Bertrice Small

Printed in U.S.A.

**Also available from
Bertrice Small
and HQN Books**

Lara

Watch for more titles in the World of Hetar series,
coming soon!

The Twilight Lord
The Sorceress of Belmair
The Shadow Queen
Crown of Destiny

For Tom and Megan with love from Ma

A
DISTANT
TOMORROW

THE PROPHECY

From the darkness came a maiden.
From the golden light came a warrior.
From a distant tomorrow will come
Hetar's true destiny.

Prologue

VARTAN, LORD OF THE FIACRE and head of the Outlands High Council was dead. Treacherously slain in his own hall by his jealous younger brother, Adon, who coveted the lordship.

"Now I am the ruler over the Fiacre!" Adon boldly declared, his gaze sweeping the hall. "My brother was a weak fool, but I am not."

Adon's wife, Elin, smiled by his side, proud to have encouraged her mate to murder.

The lady Bera, mother of the brothers, fell to her knees cradling her firstborn, glassy-eyed with shock as she stared at the blood staining Vartan's tunic. She began to wail her mourning. But Vartan's wife, the half-faerie woman, Lara, called silently to her sword. Andraste flew from its place above the great hearth and into her waiting hand. Her fingers closed about the sword's hilt, and the weapon began to sing in its deep voice a song of death.

"I am Andraste, and I drink the blood of the betrayer and his ilk!"

Adon's handsome head was immediately severed from his body. Elin's quickly followed. Each face wore the same stunned look of astonishment as it tumbled to the floor. Greedy and stupid, they had believed a swift surprise attack on Vartan would quell any opposition. For years afterwards the Fiacre would wonder why neither Adon nor Elin had not considered what Lara would do to avenge her mate. To protect their two children.

But on that terrible day, as Bera's bitter keening filled the air with its deep sorrow, Lara walked from the hall, her blade, dripping blood, still in her hand. Andraste was now singing low of vengeance satisfied. Suddenly all was darkness about her. Lara stopped, able to see nothing but shadows surrounding her. And then she heard Adon's voice speaking to her from the gloom.

"Do you really believe that by killing me you have stopped it? Hetar will come, no matter. Your children will be enslaved, and the legend of the Outlands, of Vartan and Lara, will be expunged, and cast into the very darkness in which you now stand frozen."

"I have a destiny," Lara told the invisible voice.

Adon laughed. "To fulfill it you must leave your children. You must give them up to others, and go. I do not believe you have the courage to do that, Lara, daughter of Swiftsword, widow of Vartan. You have become soft living among the Fiacre. You are no more now than an ordinary mortal."

She felt a new anger racing through her veins. "I will do whatever I must to protect Vartan's son and daughter!" she cried.

He laughed again. "We will see," he said mockingly.

"How typical of you, Adon, to hide yourself from me in this darkness," Lara said scornfully. But silence greeted her words as the darkness that surrounded her began to fade away. As it did she was filled with deep sadness. Lara realized that her time with the Fiacre was almost over.

Chapter
1

A MAN HAD RUN from the hall crying the terrible news. Lara walked on. The children! She had to get to her children. Dillon, at four, was old enough to know what had happened to his father. The Fiacre would keep his memories of his sire alive. But her year-old daughter, Anoush, would not even remember Vartan. What in the name of the Celestial Actuary had possessed Adon to commit this terrible act? She struggled to remember everything that had happened just a short while ago.

Liam, Vartan's cousin and best friend, ran up to her. "What has happened?" he asked her, his gaze going to Andraste's bloody blade.

"Adon killed Vartan," Lara managed to answer him. "He walked up to him, smiling, his wretched wife at his side. And then without warning or provocation he plunged a dagger into Vartan's heart. I suspect the tip was poisoned, for Vartan died instantly. When Adon declared himself Lord of the Fiacre, I slew them both where they stood. I must get to the children, Liam! Dillon must not learn of his father's murder from anyone but me. And you—you must now take the lordship of the Fiacre."

"That is the Fiacre elders' decision," Liam answered her. His father had been given the lordship when Vartan's father had died many years back. When his father had gone to the Celestial Actuary to settle his debts the elders had offered the lordship to him, but he had refused it in favor of his cousin, Vartan. Liam had not wanted the responsibility of the clan, but he knew now there was no choice.

"You are the logical choice," Lara said, and then she hurried on. Her children would be with Liam's wife, Noss. Dillon was best friends with their son, Tearlach. Entering her friend's house she called to her. "Noss! Where are you?"

Noss, heavy with her second child, appeared. She smiled. "Have you come for Dillon? Sit with me a while, and have some frine. The boys are having such a good time." Then her eyes grew wide at the sight of Andraste. "What has happened?" She had not seen the sword bloodied since the great Winter War, when she and Lara had fought with their men to take back the lands of the Piaras and the Tormod clans that had been illegally confiscated by the Hetarians. Noss saw how pale Lara was, and she now led her to a seat. "Tell me."

"Adon murdered Vartan," Lara said, and then explained to Noss exactly what had happened.

Noss's hand flew to her mouth to still her cry of horror. How could this have happened? And to Lara? Lara had always been so fortunate, and so filled with magic. Murder did not happen to people like that. "You do not weep," Noss finally said.

"Ethne weeps for me," Lara said, raising the crystal up to show Noss. The crystal was dripping tears. "I have no time to weep. I had only a brief time in which to slay Adon and his foolish wife before he would have attacked me and my children. And soon I must leave the Fiacre," Lara said softly.

"It is time?" Noss whispered.

Lara nodded. "It is time. I am glad I followed my mother's advice and gave Vartan children. But now I must tell Dillon that his father is dead, and his mother is leaving. Will you and Liam raise my little ones, Noss? This new journey I am about to undertake is not yours. You have found a home, a husband and a good life among the Fiacre. This is your destiny. Mine still awaits me, though I know not what it will be."

"Of course we will take Dillon and Anoush, but do you not want Bera to have them?" Noss ventured. "She is their grandmother."

"And they must never forget that," Lara replied. "But Bera will have to take her other grandson as Elin's family is dead, and I will not have Vartan's children raised with his murderer's son. Cam may be only two and a half, but he is already a sly and spoiled little boy. Bera will have her hands full with him. Dillon caught him pinching Anoush at the Gathering last autumn. My daughter was black-and-blue all over her tiny arms from that little monster."

"Anoush was just a little baby last autumn," Noss said indignantly.

"Yes, and when Dillon saw what Cam was doing he ran to his father. But Elin would not allow Cam to be punished. She said Cam was innocent, and that it was Dillon who had hurt his sister out of jealously. That her son was just looking at the baby."

"Dillon adores Anoush, and has since her birth," Noss cried.

Lara nodded. "Yes, I know. But Cam has no one but Bera, and her heart is too good. She saw Adon as a fool, but little else. It was a mistake." She sipped at the frine in the cup Noss had given her. "Will you fetch my son now? I must tell him the news."

Noss nodded, but then she said, "The elders will choose Liam to take the lordship, won't they?"

"Yes, they will," Lara answered. "He is the right choice."

Noss sighed. "He never wanted it, you know."

"I know," Lara agreed, "but now he must accept the responsibility as his father accepted it when Vartan's father died years ago. Liam is a strong man, and his marriage to you has settled him. He is ready. And so are you, dearest Noss."

Noss arose. "I will fetch Dillon," she said, and hurried off.

Lara sat silently. Instinctively she reached for the crystal about her neck. It had been a long time since she had sought Ethne's advice. *What am I to do?* she asked silently. The crystal was still wet with Ethne's tears.

You know what you must do, Ethne answered her

softly. *You have already begun to prepare yourself, and the Fiacre, for your departure.*

I could have lived the rest of my life in contentment here, Lara told her guardian crystal.

It is not your destiny. The queen told you that you would have but a few years. Five of them have now passed. You are strong. You are ready. And it is time. The flame in the crystal flickered. *I have wept your tears, Lara, that you not be weakened. But you must weep for Vartan, too. He has brought out the best in your human nature, my child.*

"Mama." Dillon stood by her side. He was his father's image in miniature. "Noss said you would speak with me?"

Lara felt the first tears for Vartan begin to slip down her cheeks.

"Mama! What is the matter?" the little boy asked.

And she told him as her tears poured forth, clasping him to her breasts as he grew pale with the realization of what she was saying. Her hand absently stroked the dark hair on his small head. And they wept together, mother and son.

Finally Dillon's sobs slowed, and looking into his mother's beautiful face he said, "I will kill Adon! I will avenge my father, Mama!"

"Adon is already dead, and his wicked wife as well," Lara told her son. "See!" She drew her sword forth, and showed him. "This is their blood that Andraste wears."

"What will happen now, Mama?" Dillon asked her.

"The elders will chose a new lord, Dillon, for that

is our way. I believe they will choose your father's cousin, Liam," Lara told her son.

"You are going away," Dillon said quietly.

At first Lara was startled by the adult tone in her child's voice, but Dillon had been intuitive since his birth. "Yes, soon," she replied. She would not lie to him.

"This house is not fit for the Lord of the Fiacre," he remarked. "Liam and Noss must have the hall, Mama. This place will suit grandmother and me. Anoush is too small to have a voice in this decision." He sounded so like his father that Lara almost began to weep again.

"Yes, this will be a good home for your grandmother," Lara agreed. "But you and Anoush will not live with her. You will remain in the hall with Liam, Noss, and Tearlach, my son. Your cousin, Cam, has also been orphaned by this tragedy. His mother had no family left. Bera will want to raise him, but I will not have you or Anoush living in the same house as the son of Adon and Elin. You will accept Liam as your lord. He will stand in your father's stead. And Noss will care for you as I would. She owes me a great debt, though I would not remind her of it. I do not have to for she knows it in her heart. And you, my son, and your sister will treat her with the same respect that you would show me. You will honor her and you will obey her commands."

"I will, Mama, and I will see that Anoush does, too," he promised. Then the small boy in Dillon said, "You are not going right away, Mama, are you?" His anxious face looked up at her.

She smoothed his soft hair beneath her hand. "No, not right away," she promised. "Now go and find Tearlach, my son, and ask Noss to join me."

The little boy ran off to do her bidding. Lara reached for her goblet of frine, but Noss was quickly there, and stayed her hand.

"We need wine," the younger woman said, uncorking a decanter, and pouring a fresh goblet of the strong red brew. "Here, I will join you." She filled a second goblet. "Dillon seems all right."

"We cried together," Lara replied. "He knows I'm leaving."

"You told him?" Noss was surprised.

"No," Lara answered with a small smile. "He just knew. Don't discourage his instincts while he is with you, Noss. I know such things tend to unsettle your nerves, but you must let whatever powers Dillon has grow and thrive."

"I will," Noss promised nervously.

Liam entered the house, and came to join the two women. "I could not remain in the hall," he said. "Bera's keening would awaken a statue. The word is spreading. I've dispatched messengers to all the Fiacre villages. The elders will gather in three days' time to choose the new Lord of the Fiacre."

"It must be sooner," Lara said. "The clan lords will know as soon as our own people. A new head of the Outlands High Council must be chosen as well."

"I'll take the lordship of this clan, though reluctantly," Liam responded, "but I am not the man to lead the Outlands. That you cannot ask of me."

"Vartan was the one man the others trusted, and

admired," Lara spoke thoughtfully. "He was strong, and he had my counsel. Roan of the Aghy is ambitious and will seek the post, but he is too hot tempered. The best man would be Rendor of the Felan. He has a cool head, and I can advise him without his wife, Rahil, becoming jealous."

"You will go to the Felan then?" Liam asked her.

"Only on my way to the Coastal Kingdom in Hetar," Lara replied. "I sense that is where I am meant to be at this time."

He nodded. Then he asked, "Did you know what would happen to Vartan?"

"No!" Lara paled, surprised and shocked by Liam's query. "Why would you ask me such a thing? I would have given my life for Vartan as he would have for me."

"Did you love him?" Liam pursued.

"I should not have given him children otherwise, Liam. Faerie women, even half-faerie women, only bear offspring for the men they love," Lara said quietly. "When the war ended my mother advised me to stop trying so hard to live up to my faerie nature, and follow my heart. She said I had time. Yes, I loved Vartan. Not as much as he loved me, I know. But I did love him."

"Forgive me, Lara," Liam said, and bowed his head in apology to her.

"I had forgotten what it is like to be mistrusted by humans," Lara responded. "I have been so happy here among the Fiacre. I have even felt as if I were fully human, and one of you. Until now. Now I am forced to remember who I am, and that I have a destiny to fulfill. Noss has agreed to take my children, and I hope you will concur. She can tell you why."

"I will take Dillon and Anoush gladly," Liam said. He was ashamed of his question, and knew that Vartan would have been angry with him for asking it. "They shall be as my own, Lara. I swear it."

"But they must not be allowed to forget Vartan," Lara said. "Anoush will remember neither her sire or me, I know. She will think of you and Noss as her mother and father. If she is safe and happy then I am content. Dillon, however, will remember us. My son has magic in him, Liam. It must not be discouraged."

"I understand," Liam answered her.

"We will speak on this again before I leave," Lara told him. "Now I had best return to the hall and give what comfort I can to Bera. Will you keep the children a while longer?"

He nodded, watching as she turned away from him and left his house. His wife now came from the shadows where she had been standing and slipped her small hand into his big one. "Well, lass," Liam said with a small attempt at humor, "did you ever think you would one day be the Lady of the Fiacre?" He put his other arm about her.

Noss sighed. "Seven years ago I was sold into slavery by my parents. No, Liam, I never considered I should attain such a place in this world of ours. But then I could never have imagined the adventures that I shared with Lara, or a love such as the one I share with you, my husband." Her free hand went to her distended belly where the child within moved strongly.

"You are certain the elders will select you?" Noss asked him.

"Aye, they will," he told her. "Now I wonder if I had accepted the lordship when they first offered it to me if Vartan would still be alive." Liam sighed.

"He had his fate to live out," Noss counseled. "You have yours."

"You are becoming wise with age, wife," he teased her gently.

"Well," Noss said pertly in reply, "I am almost twenty." Then she grew serious. "Poor Lara, to lose her husband so cruelly. To leave her children behind. I do not envy her, despite her beauty and her faerie magic."

"I do not envy her because she must calm Bera," Liam said with a grimace. "The woman was in a terrible state when I finally left the hall. I think she has gone mad."

"Lara will calm her," Noss said with assurance.

But entering the hall and seeing the state her mother-in-law was in, Lara wondered if anyone could ease Bera's sorrow. The older woman paced up and down the hall muttering, her long gray hair swinging with each step she took. But her eyes were blank, without emotion of any sort. The three bodies were still upon the floor where they had met their end. Lara signaled to a male servant. "Fetch some others, and remove the dead," she ordered. "And clean Andraste before returning her to her place of honor." She handed her weapon to the serving man.

"No!" Bera screeched, and ran to Lara. "You

cannot take them from me. The bitch, yes! But not my boys. Not my boys!"

"Go," Lara said sternly. Then she took Bera by the hand, and sat her down by the hearth. "Listen to me, Bera. You cannot dishonor Vartan by leaving his body on the stone floor. His departure ceremony must be celebrated. He was the Lord of the Fiacre as was his father before him. The elders will demand Vartan be honored properly. As for Adon and Elin, they will be put into the earth unsung."

"From the moment he sprang forth from my womb Adon competed with Vartan," Bera said. Her eyes were now filled with her pain. "But Vartan never complained. He treated his younger brother with kindness. It is not our way to murder our own, Lara. How could he have done it? How? It was his mate— that wretched, wretched girl! I never wanted him to wed her. She was greedy and wicked, Lara. And now because of her actions her son is orphaned. What will become of little Cam, Lara? What will happen to the child?"

"You will raise him, of course," Lara comforted the woman.

Bera's sorrowful face looked into Lara's. "Yes," she said. "I will take him."

Lara considered telling her all that had transpired in the short time following Vartan's brutal murder, but she decided Bera was not yet ready to hear it. "You must rest now," she told her mother-in-law, helping her to her feet. "I will do what must be done." She signaled to a female servant. "Take the lady Bera to her chamber and give her a small goblet of wine." She reached into the pocket of her robes and drew out a small gilded pill. "Put this in the wine. It will aid her sleep."

"Yes, lady," the serving woman said, and led the grieving Bera from the hall.

Lara now turned to the servants who had entered the hall. "Six of you take the bodies of Adon and his foul wife out onto the plain," she instructed them. "Bury them deep in a single grave, and do not mark it. Have it done before the sun sets on this day. The rest of you are to build the lord's funeral pyre. His departure ceremony will take place in two days time at the hour of the sunset. Have his body brought to the bathhouse that I may begin the preparations."

She watched the servants lift the body of their lord. Vartan had built the bathhouse for her when they had returned from the Winter War. The Fiacre were used to bathing in small round tubs. But Lara wanted a bath such as she had enjoyed in her time with the Shadow Princes, a large bath in which she might submerse her entire body. A bath she might share with her husband. So Vartan had surprised her with the small bathhouse after telling her he was building a new cattle shed. He had imported the marble tub from the Coastal Kingdom, along with several carved stone benches. A small sob escaped her. Had she loved him? Oh, yes! With every bit of her human heart. Now she could feel that part of her hardening again as her faerie nature took over. To be strong, to follow her destiny, she knew she had to be faerie.

Hearing a familiar clap of thunder—considerably softened, she noted—Lara looked up to see her mother, Ilona, the queen of the Forest Faeries. Ilona held out her arms to her daughter, and rising from her seat by the fire Lara rushed into them. "What has happened?" Ilona said to her daughter, and Lara told her. "Then it is time," the queen replied.

"I know," Lara responded. "I have already begun making arrangements for Dillon and Anoush."

"I will take them!" Ilona said imperiously.

"Nay, I want Liam and Noss to raise them. They are Fiacre, Mother. One day Dillon might be chosen lord of his people, like his father and grandfather before him."

"Or Liam and Noss's lad might be chosen," Ilona said softly.

"If that is the will of the Fiacre then so be it," Lara answered her mother. "But you must visit them. Promise me! Dillon has been exhibiting certain instincts that must not be stifled. Anoush is too young for me to know. Tell me, how are Thanos and Cirilo?" she asked after her mother's consort, and her half brother.

"Thanos is Thanos," Ilona said dryly. "As for Cirilo I must admit he is everything I could want in a son, Lara. He will be a fine king one day. For now he is a typical faerie lad, getting into all kinds of mischief. He particularly enjoys teasing the Forest Lords. They have lost some of their territory on the border with the Midlands. Gaius Prospero is buying up the smaller farms and blending them into great ones. It allows him to control the price of the crops he grows. The rumor is growing again that he would be emperor of Hetar."

"I am going to the coast," Lara told her mother. "I feel it is where I should be now. But it has been so long since the voice within spoke to me that I am not certain I am hearing it correctly. Could I be wrong, Mother? Should I remain with the Fiacre and my children? I am suddenly unsure."

"I am not surprised," Ilona remarked. "It has been but hours since your husband was murdered before your eyes, since you slew his murderers. You are suffering shock, but your first thoughts are always the best ones, Lara. It is time for you to leave the Fiacre. If the voice says the coast, then that is where you must go. Do not be afraid, my daughter."

"When you said I had time," Lara began, "I never thought it would end this way. I expected that when the knowledge came to me, Vartan would fuss at me and try to prevent my going, no matter he said he wouldn't. I did not expect him to die. Am I responsible for that, Mother?"

"Nay," Ilona replied. "Vartan's fate was his fate. His jealous younger brother was destined to slay him, for that was Adon's fate. That you gave your heart to Vartan for a brief time, that you gave him children, had nothing to do with his end, Lara. You may believe that I speak the truth to you.

"Now I must go. Your faerie family will be here for Vartan's departure ceremony. What did you do with Adon and his wife?"

"The ultimate shame for Outlanders. I had them buried in a secret and unmarked place," Lara explained. "They will have no funeral pyre, or family and friends to sing their souls to the Celestial Actuary's kingdom. They will lie beneath the earth until the flesh rots from them, is eaten by maggots and beetles, and finally their bones dissolve into the earth itself. Their souls will wander in the Limbo forever. Even Bera dare not mourn them publically. I am just sorry they have left a child."

Ilona put a hand on her daughter's hand. "For whatever reason, it is the will of the Celestial Actuary that they did." She arose. "Goodbye, my daughter." Then she was gone in her puff of purple mist, leaving a scent of flowers behind her.

Looking to where her husband's body had lain Lara saw it was gone. She arose slowly and went to the little bathhouse where their servants had set Vartan upon a long stone bench. But for the stain of blood upon his tunic he looked as if he were sleeping. Lara bent and kissed the cold lips. "Oh, my dear love," she whispered to him. "I am so sorry. So very sorry." And the tears came again. When they finally stopped Lara sat down next to her dead mate, and began to assemble her thoughts.

Liam had sent word to all the Fiacre villages, but what of the other clan leaders? She would send for them by faeriepost, and transport them to the departure ceremony herself, for she knew they would want to honor Vartan. Several serving women crept into the bathhouse and looked to her for guidance. Lara rose, and working with them they stripped Vartan's body of his bloody garments, and washed it tenderly. When the task was almost done Lara fetched the garments in which her husband would be displayed on his funeral bier. At the end of the departure ceremony the bier would be taken outside to the funeral pyre, where Lara and Dillon would light the fire that would burn Vartan's body to ashes as all sang his soul to the kingdom of the Celestial Actuary. For an Outlander to be buried in the earth was anathema.

On his lower body they fitted him with a pair of brown leather trousers Vartan kept for special occasions. They drew his finest boots, highly polished, onto his feet. A soft linen shirt came next, and over it the tunic of his office as head of the Outlands High Council. Lara had embroidered it herself, having brought the fine material and silk threads back from their first visit to the Coastal Kingdom. The tunic was deep green in color, and the long sleeves of the garment were folded back to make a cuff that displayed the deep blue lining. She had embroidered the cuffs with silver and gold stars. On the chest of the tunic Lara had embroidered a large gold circular wheel divided by spokes. Within each segment were symbols representing the eight Outlands clans. Cattle for the Fiacre. Horses for the Aghy. Grain and flowers for the Blathma. Grain and vegetables for the Gitta. The Piaras had gold and silver rocks. The Tormod showed multicolored gemstones. The Felan displayed sheep, and the Devyn a harp for they were the poet's clan. In the center of the wheel was a single blue star. Vartan had loved the tunic of office Lara had made for him.

"What shall we do with his hair, lady?" one of the women ventured.

"It will be tied back as he always wore it," Lara answered her.

"Shall we fold his arms over his chest, lady?" another asked.

"No, leave them by his side," Lara said. "He would want his tunic of office well displayed, and so do I. I want no one to forget what we have accomplished these past years in our efforts to keep Hetar in its place."

When Vartan's body was finally dressed, and ready to be displayed, Lara called for the Fiacre men to come and return the lord to his hall. The body was transported by means of a stretcher decked in white silk and decorated with summer flowers. The men from Vartan's home village of Camdene took turns bearing their lord. In the hall the bier awaited. A ring of candelabra flanked it at either end. The stretcher was set in its place, and then Lara commanded them quietly to leave her. She brushed back into place a small lock of her husband's hair that had come loose from its binding. She critically eyed the disposition of his tunic, smoothing a barely discernable wrinkle from his chest.

It was all so terribly unreal. Just a short time ago Vartan had been a vibrant, living being. Now he lay cold and silent, his big body seeming to stiffen before her eyes. His spirit had flown from him—surely it no longer inhabited his great frame.

How could this have happened? Why had she not seen Adon's perfidy before he had the time to strike? She silently cursed her husband's brother and Elin. Had they had any thought for what they were doing? Did they really believe that the Fiacre would accept a fratricidal murderer as their lord? That Lara would not avenge her husband to protect her children? Did they not think of their own son, Cam? She sighed. Obviously they had not.

There was still much to do. Outside the summer's long twilight was deepening. The men sent to bury Adon and Elin returned, reporting they had done her bidding. She thanked them, and then went to the chamber she had once shared with Vartan. Taking her writing box up she wrote messages to the six other clan lords. Then she summoned six faeriepost messengers, told them where she wanted them to go, and that they were to wait for a reply. Each message said the same thing. It told of Vartan's death, and asked that they prepare to be transported by means of her magic on the day of the departure ceremony. A new head of the Outlands High Council must be chosen before Vartan's departure pyre was gone to ashes. The messengers flew off, and Lara, putting her writing box away, went to the kitchens.

She found the cook and the kitchen staff in various stages of weeping. Drawing a deep breath she said in a firm voice, "You must begin preparations for my husband's departure ceremony. As many of the Fiacre as can come will be here in another day. The lords of the other clan families will be here. Would you have it said that the hospitality of the Lord of the Fiacre is poor? You cannot stand about in mourning. You have work to do!" And then turning on her heel she left them.

"She has a cold faerie heart," one of the kitchen maids said.

"Perhaps," the cook replied, "but it is a broken

heart, I fear. Let none doubt that the Lady Lara loved our Lord Vartan with all her being."

Lara returned to the hall to find the bier now surrounded by flowers. She smiled, and with a small incantation, made certain that the flowers would remain bright and fresh until Vartan was brought to his pyre. Gazing down at him she was again astounded at how cold and lifeless the shell that had once housed his spirit was. It had been a great spirit, which was perhaps why having gone, Vartan's body looked so empty.

"He is not there." Lara heard Bera's voice in her ear.

"No, he is not," she answered. "You should be sleeping."

"I didn't take the pill," Bera said.

"She was supposed to mix it in your wine," Lara replied with a small smile.

"Where is Adon?"

"Out on the plain with his wife," Lara said quietly.

Bera's eyes filled with tears, which she attempted to swallow back.

"It had to be done," Lara told her.

"I know," Bera agreed, "but he was my son, too."

"He killed Vartan," Lara responded.

"And you killed him," Bera remarked softly.

"Aye, and I have not a moment's regret that I did," Lara answered her mother-in-law. "I just wish I had seen into his black heart before he murdered Vartan. Perhaps none of this would have come to pass, Bera."

"What will happen now?"

"Liam will be chosen by the elders to be the new

lord. He will come into this house, the only one in Camdene fit for a Lord of the Fiacre. You will have his house in which to raise Adon's son, Cam."

"What of Dillon and Anoush?" Bera asked.

"I will not have them living in the same house as Adon's spawn. Liam and Noss have agreed to take them," Lara told the older woman. "I cannot remain here now. I feel the pull of my destiny once again."

"Would this have happened if Vartan had not married you?" Bera wondered aloud, and then hastily said, "I am sorry."

"My mother says his fate was his fate," Lara answered. "I expect that is true."

Bera nodded. "Do your children know what has happened?"

"I have told Dillon. Anoush is too small to understand," Lara responded.

"I think I will return to my chamber and take that pill now," Bera said. "I am suddenly very tired, Lara. You should get some sleep, too. The next few days will be very busy, my daughter."

"I know," Lara agreed. "I will rest soon." She walked the older woman to the staircase that led to her chamber. Then she returned to the hall and stood by Vartan's bier. "I did not know it would end this way, Vartan," she said softly. "I swear I did not know."

THE ELDERS of the Fiacre arrived to hold their meeting and choose a new leader of the clan. Their first instinct was to delegate Lara, but she refused, explaining to them why she could not accept the honor, and asking if they wanted her counsel. They did, and she named Liam before departing to let them debate the matter. Finding her own bed she did not even bother to undress, and falling into it slept until the next morning.

The day dawned bright and warm. Lara arose and washed her face and hands. Smoothing the wrinkles from her gown, she went out into the hall, which was already filling with clansmen and women. Vartan's cousin, Sholeh, headwoman of the village of Rivalen, had arrived. As she stood taller than many men, Lara saw her immediately. The two women hugged wordlessly.

"Where is Bera?" Sholeh asked.

"It was too much for her," Lara answered.

"You have done it all yourself?"

"He was my husband, Sholeh," Lara said.

"You have done well, and Vartan would be proud," Sholeh replied. "Where is that snake, Adon?"

"I slew him and his wife while Vartan was yet warm," Lara replied.

Sholeh nodded. "It was well done, Lara. And they are buried?"

"Out on the plain in an unmarked place," Lara said.

"I curse them both!" Sholeh said fiercely. "You will lead the Fiacre yourself now. It is your right, and you were half my cousin's wisdom, I know."

"Thank you," Lara said, "but no. Liam shall be the new Lord of the Fiacre. You cannot be dissatisfied with him. The elders in their usual way wanted to meet in three days and debate the succession, but I saw they met last night instead. Liam was the natural

choice. I will not remain with the Fiacre much longer.
I am being called from the Outlands."

"I will be sorry to see you go," Sholeh told her
companion. "But Liam is not the man to lead the
High Council, I fear. Who will you put your influence behind? Roan of the Aghy? He would take it in
a minute, you know."

Lara shook her head. "Roan is too hot tempered.
Rendor of the Felan would be my choice. He is a wise
and thoughtful man. The responsibility will cause him
to rise to the challenge of being head of the High
Council. He will not fail the Outlands."

"Roan will not be pleased," Sholeh noted.

"We need a military leader as well," Lara said with
a smile.

"Damn!" Sholeh exclaimed. "We are losing a valuable advisor in you, Lara."

"I will not leave the Fiacre forever," she said. "My
children will remain here with Noss and Liam. Bera
must raise Cam. I won't have my children in the same
house as the son of their father's murderer."

"You're right," Sholeh agreed. "Now, if I can help
you in any way—"

"You are family. I welcome your aid," Lara responded.

The Fiacre clan came and went from the hall,
paying their respects to their fallen lord. No one
would be sent away. Every structure in the village
was filled with the mourners, and many bedded down
in the fields surrounding Camdene. One by one, Lara
brought the other clan lords to her hall to pay their

respects to Vartan. They would be guests within her home until the departure ceremony was concluded.

Roan of the Aghy at once noted the need for a meeting of the clan leaders. To his surprise and pleasure, Lara agreed with him.

"You cannot leave this matter for another day," she told them. "Tonight when all have gone to their beds we will meet. Liam will stand in my husband's place, but I will be at his side as I was at Vartan's."

The clan lords nodded.

"Word of this will spread quickly to Hetar. Before Vartan's pyre is ashes you must send word to Hetar's High Council that you have a new leader," Lara continued.

Heads nodded in agreement with her. The day passed. The house of the slain leader fed all in Camdene. It was their responsibility to do so although the cook fretted that they were going to run out of supplies before it was all over. Lara assured him that if it became necessary she would call upon her magic to keep their larders full. Finally, the dark came. Fires burned on the plains surrounding Camdene indicating the campsites of many mourners. It was time.

"My lords," she said to the clan heads who were sitting by the hall fire, "I believe the time is now come to open the discussions. No one can replace my husband's leadership, but you must choose a new head of the High Council now, and send word of your choice to the City. You cannot allow Hetar's government to believe the Outlands are in disarray, or weakened by Vartan's murder."

"I would put forth Roan of the Aghy," Floren of the Blathma quickly said.

"Perhaps we should first ask the lady Lara if she has a preference," Accius, the clan leader of the Devyn said. He was certain that she did have a choice, and he was curious to know who it was.

"I thank the great bard lord of the Devyn for his courtesy in soliciting my opinion," Lara began, and several of the men smiled for they knew her well enough by now to recognize that she was about to surprise them with her own ideas. "Given what has transpired over the last five years it is obvious to me, nay, necessary, that we need both a head of our council, and a war leader as well. I have heard disturbing rumors of late that Gaius Prospero will soon crown himself emperor of Hetar. This man is no friend of the Outlands. Roan of the Aghy is a great warrior, equal to my own husband," she flattered the horse lord. "It must be he you choose for your military leader. For head of the High Council, however, I will put my faith in Rendor of the Felan. He is not easily brought to anger. He is thoughtful, and his advisement wise. He is more than equal to the challenge of dealing with Hetar," she concluded, her gaze sweeping them all.

"But he is not the warrior Roan is," Floren said.

"Nay, he is not," Lara agreed quietly. "And if there is war again, Roan will lead the Outlands, with your approval. But you need a man with a knack for diplomacy in treating with Hetar. Rendor made friends with the Coastal Kings years ago, and that friendship has never wavered. Indeed, it has grown stronger with the passing of time." She arose from her place among them. "Let me go and fetch you refreshments while you discuss this among yourselves," Lara told them. She glided across the room to prepare a tray of wine.

"You are silent, Rendor," Imre of the Tormod said.

"I am astounded," Rendor answered him.

"She said nothing of this to you beforehand?" Torin of the Gitta asked.

Rendor shook his head. "Nothing. I am as surprised as you are."

"What think you, Roan?" Accius of the Devyn queried the horse lord.

"I think I have been neatly and nicely outmaneuvered," Roan chuckled. "I do not like to admit it, but Lara is right. I am the man to lead you in war, but I am not the man to lead you in or to peace. Rendor of the Felan is that man."

"My cousin would find it amusing that it takes two of you to replace him," Liam told them with an engaging grin.

His companions laughed heartily, nodding in agreement.

"Can we agree upon this solution then," Accius asked them. "Rendor for peace, and Roan for war?"

"I will call the roll," Lara said returning with a tray of nine goblets. Passing them about she took the last cup, and began. "Rendor for peace. Roan for war. Petruso of the Piaras—aye or nay?"

Petruso, who was a mute, nodded vigorously his aye.

Lara called the others in sequence. "Imre of the Tormod?"

"Aye!"

"Floren of the Blathma?"

"Aye!"

"Torin of the Gitta?"

"Aye!"

"Liam of the Fiacre?"

"Aye!"

"Accius of the Devyn?"

"Aye!"

"Roan of the Aghy?"

"Aye!"

"Rendor of the Felan?"

"Aye!"

"Then it is settled," Lara said.

"Not quite," Rendor told them. "You have not given us your vote, Lara."

"I am not a member of the council," Lara replied.

"Nay, you are not," he agreed, "but you are the founder of this council, and in a matter as important as this one I believe you should have the right to vote."

The other lords murmured in agreement with Rendor.

Quick tears sprang up behind her eyelids to sting her eyes. Lara nodded her acknowledgment of the honor they were giving her. "In the matter of Roan and Rendor, the founder of the council votes aye," she said. Then she raised her goblet. "To the Outlands," she toasted, and they raised their goblets to join her, their voices strongly echoing hers.

"To the Outlands!"

The meeting broke up, the lords going to their sleeping places, but Rendor remained behind to speak with Lara.

"You might have told me," he said dryly.

"If I had you would have refused me," Lara answered him. "Your genuine surprise at my choice proved to the others there was no collusion between us. Given what has happened, Rendor, my friend, there was no time for the clan lords to debate and argue over this matter. We needed to settle the succession quickly. I have soothed Roan's ego, and believe me that none of the others wanted the position themselves."

"Sometimes you frighten me, Lara. You know each of us far too well, I think."

"I will be leaving the Outlands soon," she told him quietly. "I am called once again by my destiny."

"But we need you!" he exclaimed.

Lara shook her head. "You flatter me, Rendor, but I will not leave you defenseless, I promise. Whatever mischief Gaius Prospero is brewing up I will counter."

"How?" he wanted to know. "If you are not here how can you help us?"

"I am only going to King Archeron. Gaius Prospero is not as powerful as he believes. In the City and the Midlands, aye! But the Shadow Princes scorn him, and the Coastal Kings will not cooperate with him because it would not be in their interests to do so. As for the Forest Lords, they have their own difficulties. They may agree to support the Master of the Merchants, but their support will amount to little or nothing. Your friends and mine will protect the Outlands from any trouble."

"Will you remain with Archeron?"

"I don't know, but I do not think so," Lara answered.

"Where will you go?"

"I cannot say. All I can tell you is that for now I must go to the coast," Lara said. "But I will not go until autumn. I still have things to do to help ease the transition between Vartan's rule and yours, and between Vartan and Liam."

"Your children?" he asked.

"Are Fiacre, and will remain here," she told him.

He nodded. Then he said, "Rahil will be overwhelmed by this."

"I will speak with her when I visit you," Lara assured him.

"Lara, I am so sorry," Rendor told her.

"I am sorry, too," she replied, putting her hand on his. "I never imagined an ending like this. Oh, I knew one day I would be called again, but I thought when that time came and I prepared to go, Vartan would grumble and complain, but in the end he would keep his promise to me for he was not a man to break his promises. My mother says it was his fate to die at Adon's hand. I do not understand such a fate, Rendor."

"Nor do I, Lara," Rendor said.

"I suppose that lack of understanding is my human side," Lara told him with a small smile. "But my heart has become cold and faerie again. If it had not, I should not be able to do what I must."

"I will lead the Outlands to the best of my abilities," Rendor promised her.

"I have great faith in you," she replied. "So did Vartan."

The lord of the Felan began to weep softly. "I cannot believe my friend is gone," he said. "Just weeks ago we met on the plains and spoke of the autumn's Gathering. He wanted me to bring my finest wool cloth for you to choose from so he might have a new cloak made for you for winter."

"He was thoughtful that way," Lara replied. She had to get away from Rendor. If she did not, she knew she would collapse in a fit of weeping. "It is late," she said. "I must find my bed, Rendor. Tomorrow will be a busy day for me, and Bera is quite helpless now." She patted the hand in hers, and pulled free. "Good night, my friend." Then she hurried from the hall to her own chamber.

Safely locked within the room she had shared with Vartan, Lara did give way to a small spell of weeping, but only to release the tensions that had been building up within her ever since Vartan's death two days ago. Two days! The time had gone so quickly. She bathed her face and hands, and kicking off her slippers, lay down. She had done what she needed to do with regards to the Outlands. Rendor did not have her husband's stature, but he would be respected by Hetar in time. She had been surprised to find an ally in Accius of the Devyn. She suspected her job to turn the clan lords from Roan's candidacy would have been more difficult without him. She must remember to thank him.

Now all that remained was to plan more carefully for the children. She would leave them at summer's end, before the Gathering. It would give her time to prepare Dillon, and guide Liam as Vartan would have had him guided. And Noss must understand that from time to time Ilona would visit her grandchildren. She must not be fearful of the queen of the Forest Faeries. Lara smiled to herself at the thought of trying to forge a friendship between her mother and Noss. Her eyes began to grow heavy. Tomorrow would be a long, important day. And at its end she and Dillon would light Vartan's funeral pyre at the very moment of the sunset, thereby ensuring her husband's journey from the light into the light. She felt the tears beginning to come again.

"Vartan," she whispered to the night. "Why did it have to end this way?" But there was no answer. Lara wondered if there would ever be. She sighed, resigned. She should know better than anyone, she thought, that the lines between the worlds were firm once a soul had crossed into the next life. Vartan might look down on them from the realm of the Celestial Actuary, but Lara would never again hear his voice.

Chapter 2

IT WAS THE LONGEST DAY of the year in the Outlands when Vartan of the Fiacre was sent off to the kingdom of the Celestial Actuary. Not a cloud spoiled the clear blue sky. The sun shone down the day long as Vartan was feted, feasted and toasted. There were almost as many people as at the yearly Gathering in the autumn, and Lara realized that many members of the other clan families had somehow managed to come to pay homage to her husband. The day long she moved among them with her son, Dillon, speaking to those she knew, accepting condolences from strangers who approached her with tales of Vartan's kindness to them once, seeing to everyone's comfort. That they had food, that they had drink, that they had shelter from the hot summer sun.

Many spoke of the grave maturity of Vartan and Lara's young son, Dillon, especially when he had walked from the hall leading those bearing his father's body to the funeral pyre. He had accompanied his mother the day long, his demeanor almost protective of her. She spoke to him in low, quiet tones, pointing out certain members of the various clans; introducing him to the men who might someday be of help to him. Dillon gave his hand to these men, and looked directly at them with Vartan's eyes. Many were startled by the adult behavior of such a young boy. But Dillon, son of Vartan, knew on the day of his father's departure ceremony that he would never again be a child.

A delegation of Shadow Princes led by Kaliq, Lara's former lover and mentor, had arrived in early afternoon. Lara had come close to weeping when she saw them. She let Kaliq enfold her in his tender embrace, and heard the words of comfort he silently offered her without speaking. The words were for no one else but her. Ilona, queen of the Forest Faeries, came with her consort, Thanos, and their son, Lara's half brother Cirilo. Lara had never seen this sibling before, and she was enchanted by him. He was very faerie, but more her mother than Thanos. He greeted his much older sister with a smile and a kiss that was like being brushed by butterfly wings.

Lara recalled at that moment that she had two half brothers. She wondered how Mikhail was doing. It had been seven years since she had seen him. He would be almost eight years old now, but he would look nothing like the golden-haired Cirilo.

As the sun began to sink toward the horizon the final preparations were quickly executed. The Outlanders gathered about the funeral pyre in an almost completed circle; the circle broken only to leave clear a view of the setting sun. The sky was a magnificent panorama of colors. Blue, pink, mauve, purple, red, orange, pale green and gold played over the faces of the assembled mourners. Lara and Dillon, escorted by Liam and Rendor, stood before the pyre. Bera, her face haggard with her grief, handed widow and orphan their lit torches. All was absolutely still, and not a breeze stirred. As the sun began to make its final descent below the horizon Lara and her son lit the funeral pyre. As the flames sprang up to engulf Vartan's body the sun disappeared. But in the skies above a comet streaked over the Outlands, trailing a shower of silvery stars. A gasp of wonder arose from the mourners.

Lara caught Kaliq's gaze. *Thank you,* she told him silently. His magic had but added to the legend that had already begun to grow surrounding Vartan of the Fiacre, who had found his half-faerie wife wandering on the plains one day, and brought her home where she became a blessing to all Outlanders. The tears began to slip down her beautiful face as the flames leaped higher, the fire crackling, hissing and roaring with its growing power. Dillon stood by her side, his small hand in hers. They did not leave the pyre until it finally collapsed into a pile of glowing coals and gray ash. When the fire was gone entirely a wind sprang up, scattering the ashes across the plains of the Outlands until nothing was left but a blackened spot where the pyre had once stood. And Lara knew she had her mother to thank for this final act of mercy.

Liam and Rendor, who had remained by her side now escorted her back into the hall, Liam picking up the exhausted Dillon, carrying him. The boy was asleep by the time they entered the house.

Thanos and Cirilo came to bid Lara farewell, but Ilona would remain a while longer with her daughter. The Shadow Princes had gone, but for Kaliq. The rest of the clan lords had each joined their own people. Bera was nowhere to be seen. Food had been set upon the high board, and Lara, dismissing the servants, now invited her remaining guests to table. There were roasted meats and poultry, summer vegetables, bread, butter, cheese and fresh fruit. And there was wine and ale aplenty. They ate in silence, but finally, when there was nothing left to eat, the queries began.

"When do you mean to leave Camdene?" Ilona asked her daughter.

"Before autumn," Lara responded. "I will not leave my children so quickly since they have just lost their father. Anoush will not understand, but I must prepare Dillon more. He understands, but he does not really understand. He must before I go."

"Where will you go?" Kaliq wanted to know.

"To the sea," she said.

He smiled, and caught Ilona's eye. "It is time now."

Lara could not help but chuckle softly. "Do not act so mysterious with me, Kaliq. You surely remember how I dislike it."

"You have lived too long among ordinary mortals, Lara," he told her gravely. "No offense, my lords," he nodded to Rendor and Liam.

"I am an ordinary mortal," Lara told him.

"Your mortal half is hardly ordinary," he said, "and you have a magical half as well in the faerie blood that runs in your veins. You did not just decide that you would depart the Outlands for the coast. And you knew that to remain here was not your fate. Your destiny is once again calling to you, and you will fulfill that destiny. Even if Vartan had not died you would have followed the voice within. You have no other choice."

"And when I reach the coast, what am I supposed to do?" she demanded.

"You will know what to do when the time is right to do it," he responded.

Lara threw a grape at him. "Kaliq, you grown more annoying with each word you utter." And then she laughed. "But the last time you pushed me out the door to follow my fate I found Vartan. I wonder what is in store for me this time?"

"Wherever you go," Ilona said, "you are always protected, and your magic will aid you, my daughter. You must remember that although there may be times when your fears will overcome you, push them back, and remember the words I speak to you now. You are protected, Lara."

"I would return your horse to you," Lara suddenly said to Kaliq. "Dasras cannot come where I must eventually go."

"No," Kaliq replied. "He cannot go with you, but leave him among the Fiacre in your son's care, Lara." Then he turned his gaze onto Liam. "Roan will seek to gain the beast from you, my lord. Do not let him have Dasras, no matter how tempted you may be by the gold or other inducements he may offer you. I will know if you betray me in this matter, Liam of the Fiacre, and my judgment will be swift and harsh. Do you understand me, my lord?"

"The horse will remain among the Fiacre, and we will protect him from any who would seek to gain him," Liam promised, not in the least offended by the Shadow Prince's threat. The prince was a magical being and thus to be respected.

Kaliq turned back to Lara. "Keep Andraste and Verica with you always," he told her. "Verica will advise you, and Andraste is your protection. Never be parted from them, but if you are, just call to them when you need them, and they will come to you. They are both made so that no one else can either use them, or keep them from you."

"Now you are beginning to intrigue me," Lara answered him. "This will not simply be a visit to the Coastal Kings, will it, Kaliq?"

He smiled his beautiful smile at her, but said nothing.

Lara laughed. "My destiny must unfold in a certain manner," she said. Then she grew serious. "Tell us, Kaliq, what is happening in the City. I know you have your representatives there in the council."

"Indeed," Kaliq replied. "In the five years since the Winter War," he began, "Gaius Prospero has worked diligently to regain his popularity among the people, and his influence among the guilds, and magnates. It has cost him a great deal of gold, I would imagine. But then, he stole a great deal from the Outlands. The City is growing, and expanding. For lack of conflict the Mercenaries and the Crusader Knights sit idly in their respective quarters. The wealthy continue to live comfortably, the wiser among them discreetly, while the foolish waste their considerable resources in vulgar and conspicuous consumption and the poor barely subsist.

"Gaius Prospero has managed to avoid an all-out famine so far. He feeds the people with grain from his own granaries and diverts them with lavish entertainments. He does what he must to keep order, and to further his own ambitions."

"I have heard that the Midlands is now expanding into the territory of the Forest Lords," Lara said.

"Aye, 'tis true," Ilona answered her daughter. "It was subtle at first. A few trees here and a few there as the Midlands folk sought to cultivate new fields to replace the worn and tired soil of their lands. Without these new fields they cannot feed the City. If this happens, anarchy is bound to erupt. People will tolerate much, but starvation is a cruel spur to those already discontented."

"They have also expanded into the edges of our desert realm where the soil is still able to sustain some small growth," Kaliq told his listeners. "But it is difficult for them, for they must irrigate the land there, and that means water from the Forest Lords."

"And they have cooperated?" Lara was surprised.

"Gaius Prospero seems to have some hold over them that he did not previously have," Ilona said.

"He has learned, then, of my grandmother's curse upon the Forest Lords," Lara reasoned. "That has to be it, for Enda would not give either an inch of forest

soil or his water unless he felt that the illusion the
Forest Lords built up was threatened. To reveal to
Hetar that their bloodlines are no longer pure is tan-
tamount to their destruction. What of the Forest Faeries, Mother? Are you not also threatened by this
incursion into the forest?"

"We live in the deepest part of the wood, Lara,"
her mother said. "And we live on another plane of
existence from the mortals of Hetar. You could walk
through our palaces and never know you were there,
for you would not see them. Well, perhaps *you* might,
but then you are faerie. But if one day the forest that
sustains us is taken away we, like so many others in
the magic realms, will be refugees. Pray the Celestial
Actuary it never comes to that," Ilona said.

"The continuance of the status quo within Hetar
depends on the people being content," Kaliq said.
"This means they must be fed, and kept busy. Without work there is no coin to purchase even the cheap-
est goods. This affects not just the poor but the rich as
well, for their wealth comes from the goods and services they make, manage and provide. And there are
more without than with," Kaliq noted. "Unless something is done they will rise up against their masters.
The Master of the Merchants, Gaius Prospero, lob-
bies hard to be made emperor. He says that times are
changing, and Hetar must change with the times. That
an emperor will renew Hetar, and that he can solve
its problems, but only if he is emperor, and fully in
charge. Hetar must expand its borders to avoid chaos,
and while the City has eaten into the borders of two of

its own provinces, the most logical place for Hetar to come is into the Outlands with its vast tracts of land."

"We will fight them!" Rendor declared.

"They are many, and your clan families few," Kaliq said pragmatically. "They will overcome you with the might of their Mercenary Guild and Crusader Knights. They will enslave your peoples, and take all you possess for themselves. Those of us who are of the magical realm cannot allow that to happen. A great war would bring more problems than it would solve, for all of us, both magic and mortal. We helped you in the Winter War, and now we will help you before another war begins. But we cannot protect you forever," he said quietly. "Lara came to you for a purpose. To alert you to the danger. To show you that the magic world was not to be feared so we might help you when this time came," Kaliq continued. "But it is not enough that we do so. Lara must now leave you so that she may follow the destiny that will one day bring peace to all of Hetar."

"But how can that happen," Rendor asked, "if Hetar has too many people, and not enough lands, and we have lands but too few people? If we were willing to share some of our lands with Hetar they would probably accept, and then seek to take more and more until they had it all. They do not respect us, my lord prince. They call us barbarians although they surely know better, especially after the Winter War. They seek to wipe all vestiges of our clan families from history, leaving only themselves."

Kaliq smiled. "You are wise to understand that,

Rendor of the Felan, head of the Outlands High Council."

"Then how can you help us?" Rendor persisted.

"We will place magical barriers about the Outlands so that none with wicked intentions may pass through those gates and into your lands."

Rendor nodded. "And what are we to do then?"

"You will live your lives as you always have, in peace, going about your daily business," Kaliq said.

"And Lara? Where will she go, and will she come back to us?" Rendor asked.

"Do not ask him questions he cannot or will not answer," Lara chuckled. "He will speak to you in riddles as he does to me when I inquire of him that which he does not wish to impart. Such answers will only hurt your head as they do mine. I am content to go, Rendor, knowing that my beloved Outlands will be safe in my absence. I will not leave you forever. I will be back. After all, my children are Outlanders."

"I think we have concluded our business here," Kaliq said to those about the board. "Ilona, have you anything you wish to say before we take our leave of Lara and her friends?"

"Rendor, because you now stand in Vartan's place, and you, Liam, because you will care for my grandchildren, I give you permission to call my name should you need me. This is my gift to you, and a privilege allowed few, especially mortals."

The two Outlander lords bowed low to the faerie queen and thanked her for her generosity.

Ilona then embraced her daughter. "I will see you before you leave Camdene, for I intend that my grandchildren know me well before you go that I may help to comfort them when you are gone. Is your Noss competent to care for Dillon and Anoush? I seem to recall she was a girl afraid of her own shadow."

Lara smiled, and stroked her mother's delicate cheek. "She is grown now, the parent of one son, and another soon to come. Her marriage has given her confidence, Mother. My son and daughter will be safe with her, and loved, too. Having to leave them is what I feared when I gave Vartan children, but I always thought their father would be here with them." She sighed. "But they will have you, Bera, Liam, Noss and a whole clan of Fiacre who will watch over them, for they are Vartan's offspring."

"Beware Bera," Ilona advised.

"Why?" Lara wanted to know. "She has always been good to me, and she adores Dillon and Anoush."

"The death of her sons, the manner in which each died, remains with her, and always will. She cannot forgive Adon for his murder of Vartan, Lara. But neither can she forget that you slew Adon. She will appear to recover eventually, but she will never quite be the same again. What has happened to her has brought a madness into her soul. It lies beneath the surface of her sanity. She will raise Cam to be every bit as heroic as Vartan, but there is evil in that child's blood that cannot be extinguished. One day he will have to be slain, too, for the sake of the Fiacre. It would have been better if he had never been born," Ilona declared vehemently.

"Then teach my children to be wary of him," Lara said.

Ilona nodded. "I must go. I will be back before you leave here."

The two women embraced, and the men with them marveled that they looked more like sisters than mother and daughter, such was the faerie blood. There was a small thunderclap, and Ilona, queen of the Forest Faeries, with a wave of her hand disappeared into her cloud of purple haze.

Lara now turned to Kaliq and kissed him on the cheek. "Thank you, my dear friend, for coming on this day of days. Will I see you again?"

"If it pleases you," he told her.

"Do you still love me, Kaliq?" she asked him, curious.

"I will always love you, Lara, daughter of Swiftsword," he told her. And then he was gone, seeming to evaporate into the very shadows that had suddenly arisen to surround him.

Lara was now left with but two companions. She turned to them saying, "I am tired, and will find my bed. Rendor, pray do not leave Camdene until we have spoken in private again." Then she turned away from them and was gone from the hall.

Rendor and Liam now found seats by the hall fire that they might speak privily. A servant appeared, bringing them cups of wine, and was then gone again.

"I am almost frightened by what has transpired here this night," Liam said. "It would appear great changes are coming to all of us. What part we are to play in those changes I cannot tell." He sighed. "I have never wanted to lead the Fiacre, I should have been content being Vartan's cousin and friend, Noss's husband, and father to my children."

"The elders would not have chosen you had they not felt you were the right man," Rendor said. "Remember that once before they asked you."

"They asked because my father had been lord of this family after Vartan's father died," Liam answered him. "It was a matter of pure courtesy. They knew Vartan was the man who should lead us, and so did I."

"And yet they have chosen you now," Rendor noted. "I think, Liam, that you underestimate yourself and your abilities. As for the great changes to come, and what should be done, I believe we should follow the Shadow Prince's advice. We will live as we have always lived."

"Do you think that magic can really protect us from Hetar's greed?" Liam said.

"I do," Rendor replied. "Prince Kaliq would not have said it otherwise." Of course, Kaliq had also said magic could not protect them forever. But perhaps it would serve long enough for Lara to find the destiny that would save them all from disaster. He emptied his cup. "It has been a long day, my friend," he said to Liam. "I think I shall find my bed now."

Liam stood up. "I had best be getting home," he responded. "Noss is near her time, and she likes me with her."

In her bedchamber behind the hall Lara lay sleepless. Vartan was gone. Every vestige of him was gone, burned in the fire that freed his soul from his body.

He would be remembered in the oral history of the Outlands by the Devyn bards who were already singing of him. Once his generation had departed this world there would be few remaining who would remember the man, but they would know the legend of Vartan, Lord of the Fiacre. She wept silently again in the darkness of the night for the man who had been her mate. He had been a good man, a great leader. He had made a safe haven for her among the Fiacre. She was angry that fate dictated his demise, and yet had he lived, he would have resisted her going. And had he lived, would she even have heeded the calling of the voice within her? Ilona might claim that her daughter was not responsible for Vartan's death, but Lara was not at all certain of that. She was beginning to realize that this destiny she had put from her mind these last five years was bigger than even she could imagine. And she was still not certain of what exactly it was. She turned onto her side, punching at her pillows, and tried to sleep.

She had the summer ahead to consider, long days of warm sun and gentle breezes to spend with her children. Days in which she would prepare Dillon for life without either of his parents. She most regretted that her daughter was so young. Anoush would not really remember either her mother or her father, and that was a tragedy. But Dillon could tell his little sister of their parents as long as he could remember them. Vartan's face was already receding from her. Would her son's memory be any better? And what of Cam, Adon's son? They had never been friends to begin with, but Bera would surely try to foster a relationship between the cousins. Lara was not certain what to do about that. It seemed sad to deny Cam his place among them, but had not her own mother warned that Cam would be a troublesome child, and a dangerous man?

AT SUNRISE, Lara awoke surprised, for she had not remembered falling asleep the night before. Stretching she considered the day ahead. Rendor would want to leave today, and she must speak with him before he did. And she, Noss and Liam must decide the time for the new Lord of the Fiacre to move into the lord's house. It should be soon, for until Liam had made the house his there would be those who would always consider it Vartan's house—such was the nature of the Fiacre. She sat up, swinging her feet over the edge of the bed. First she wanted a bath. Slipping a house robe over her nakedness she slipped through a small door that led outside to a pergola thick with flowering vines that shaded the path to the bathhouse.

In the hall the servants were already at their daily tasks. With the old lord buried and gone, they returned to their comfortable routine. As they worked they gossiped with one another for they had heard that the new lord would be moving into the house shortly. Was it really true? When? But no one knew, and then Rendor, the lord of the Felan, and new high council leader was coming to the high board, and needed to be fed. Lara joined him shortly afterwards, fresh from her ablutions.

"You look tired," Rendor noted as she sat down next to him.

"I am," Lara admitted. "I don't think I have slept well since Vartan's death."

"But now you have the summer ahead with your children," he remarked.

"I will come to you before the Gathering," Lara told him. "Will you escort me to King Archeron's palace?"

"Of course," he said, "but what of the Fiacre?"

"When the day comes I will leave quietly. It is always best to leave quietly," Lara said softly. "I will use my magic to come to you. But I would ride to King Archeron's palace as we once did when Vartan first met him."

"You have entrusted me with a great responsibility, Lara," he said changing the subject.

"You were the perfect choice, Rendor. You have dignity and you have presence, which will be crucial in dealing with Hetar. First impressions are important with them. If you show them a strong leader they will respect you if for no other reason than the way you appear to them. But you are also wise, and will not be easily fooled by them. If they manage to get through the magic barriers that the Shadow Princes erect around the Outlands, be wary, and put off dealing with them as long as you can. Do not allow them to press you into any quick decisions, my friend. Hetarians are crafty folk," she concluded with a small smile. "Do not allow their charm and exquisite manners to lull you in a false sense of security. They are not to be trusted."

"If the magic barrier is strong, will they be able to get through?" Rendor wondered.

"The princes said those with no evil intent will pass between the two lands easily. Those who wish to treat with you first will be harmless. And it is better that Hetar not know of the magic that will protect the Outlands from them—at least not right away," she chuckled. "What the princes have done is to protect the Outlands from a military attack, Rendor. But there are different kinds of invasion. You must beware of a more subtle incursion by Hetar."

"You have given me much to consider," Rendor said.

"You will have to tell each clan lord before they leave today of the prince's gift to the Outlands so they will not be afraid. And so that Roan may not frighten them into a war that need not be fought at all," Lara advised.

Rendor chuckled. "Roan would be most distressed to learn how well you know him."

"Then perhaps it is better we not tell him," Lara replied with a small smile.

"If you had not this destiny of yours to follow I think you would have made the Fiacre an excellent clan leader, Lara," Rendor told her. "You are truly an amazing woman, and it is the Fiacre's loss that you must leave them."

"I have given the Fiacre my counsel for five years now, and I have given them Vartan's son and daughter. I cannot imagine being here without Vartan. But one day I will return, for this is where I mean to live out my days, Rendor. Keep the Outlands safe for me."

"I will try," he responded, and then he arose. "I

must go now. The journey home will not be nearly as easy as it was coming here." He grinned at her.

"I suppose I could transport you all back to your lands," Lara said thoughtfully.

He laughed. "You would frighten those of my clan who came to pay Vartan homage, and are not used to your magic. No. We will ride home." He took her hand in his, and putting it first to his heart, then kissed it, bowing to her as he did so. "Farewell, Lara. Rahil and I will look forward to your coming in early autumn."

"I will send word before I come," she promised him as she walked outside to see him off. And then she went to each of the clan lords, bidding them and their clan people farewell, and thanking them for coming to honor Vartan's life and last journey. Bowing to each group she said the same words. "I appreciate the homage you offered my husband as he departed for the realm of the Celestial Actuary." She stood as each group departed. Finally, Camdene was as it should be on a midsummer morning. The streets were quiet. The men in the fields tended to the crops and the clan's herds of cattle. The women went about the business of childcare, housework and gardening. Lara returned to the hall to find Bera awaiting her.

"We must talk," her mother-in-law said calmly. But the calm surrounding Bera was so fragile that Lara could almost see it.

"Come, and sit," Lara invited the older woman. "Have you eaten?" She brought Bera to the high board, and signaled to a servant to bring food.

"Everything tastes like sawdust now," Bera remarked.

"I know," Lara agreed as she poured a goblet of wine for Bera.

Bera drank slowly, and then she set the goblet down. "What is to happen now, Lara?" she asked the young woman in a plaintive tone. "You were Vartan's wife. These decisions are yours to make now."

"I think it best that Liam have this hall that has been for so many years the center of Camdene. I know his father did not rule from here, but both Vartan and his father did," Lara began. "Now that our people must deal more with Hetar it is important that the clan lord have a fine dwelling. And frankly, Liam and Noss will need a larger house with four children to raise."

"Four?" Bera looked confused. "I thought there was but one, and another to come soon. Has my poor mind gone entirely?"

"Liam and Noss will be raising Dillon and Anoush for me," Lara said. "I cannot have them living in the same house as Adon's son, Bera. I am sorry. That is why my children have not been here these past few days, but have remained with Noss. You will be moved to Liam's house with Cam. You will continue to be respected as Vartan's mother. You will lack for nothing. But my children will eschew Cam."

"But they are cousins," Bera said.

"Cam is Adon's son. Adon killed my children's father," Lara replied.

"And you killed both Adon and Elin," Bera re-

sponded. "You slew Cam's parents without mercy."
She looked directly into Lara's green eyes.

"Aye, I did, and I have not a single regret," Lara
answered, returning the look even as she remembered
her mother's words regarding Bera. "Cam is his parents' child. Their tainted blood runs in his veins. He
will never be free of their curse."

"You have a faerie's cold heart," Bera said cruelly.

Lara smiled softly, and nodded. "I do," she agreed,
"but it is for my children. If I did not, I should not
be able to do what I must do. Do not trifle with me
in this matter, Bera. I will not allow your sentimental heart to endanger Vartan's son and daughter. If it
were up to me I should take Adon's spawn far out on
the plain and leave him there to die. Indeed, it might
be better for all concerned if I did. But against my
better judgment I will give him to you to raise. Just
keep him away from my children." Then Lara left her
mother-in-law at the high board while she went to find
Noss and Liam to discuss the moving arrangements.

Several days later the transfer of households was
completed. Despite Noss's protest, Lara had moved
from the lord's bedchamber into a bedspace in the
little hall that had once been Bera's personal domain.
She found that she slept far better in the enclosed
place than she had in the large bed she had once
shared with Vartan. And her children were close by
in the nursery chamber. But Bera had hardly spoken
to her after their last conversation, and she had not
seen Cam at all.

The summer days seemed longer than she had ever
remembered them being. She sloughed off the respon-

sibilities of the lord's wife like a snake shedding its skin. Noss was now the lady of the Fiacre, and while Lara was happy to advise her, she was glad to see Noss pick up the duties and obligations that belonged to her high office. She spent much of her day with her two children. Anoush was toddling, and seemed fearless. Dillon kept to Lara's side like a small burr, full of questions and mischief. He made her laugh as no one else ever did.

One afternoon they sat beneath a tree in the grass. Anoush had fallen asleep in Lara's lap, and Dillon, leaning against his mother, demanded a story from her. It was time, Lara realized, to tell him her story. She began.

"Once a beautiful faerie girl ensorcelled a handsome Midlands farmer lad. She took him away to her bower in the forest where they made love for days on end. And in time she birthed a beautiful daughter whom she loved dearly. But when the baby was just a few months old the beautiful faerie girl had to leave her child, and her lover. She sent them back out into their own world."

"Why?" Dillon wanted to know.

"Because the beautiful faerie girl had certain obligations to her own mother, and family," Lara explained. "The lad she loved could not live in her world, nor could she have lived in his. Sometimes, my son, you must place your family duties above all else, and so it was with the beautiful faerie woman." She caressed his dark hair gently.

"What happened to the farmer's lad, and their child?" Dillon asked.

"He took his daughter and returned to his parents' house. But, alas, his father had died in the time he had been away, and his older brother was now the head of their family. The brother did not want the child in his house. He said her faerie blood would bring bad luck on them all."

"That's silly," Dillon said scornfully. "Everyone knows that faeries bring good fortune, Mama. I think this farmer was a fool."

Lara grinned. "I think so, too," she said.

"So what happened next?"

"Dorjan, the foolish farmer, said his brother must go, and take his child with him. But Ida, his mother, protested, and said if Dorjan sent his brother and the child from their house she would go with them. Dorjan would not relent, and so Ida, her younger son and the infant went to the City. There the son became a famous mercenary, and Ida raised her granddaughter. But when the child was ten years of age the grandmother died.

"The girl kept house for her father until he found a fine wife, Susanna, the daughter of a Midlands farmer. They wed, and Susanna gave her husband a son whom they called Mikhail.

"But the Mercenary was sad, for he wished to better his position in life. The only way he could do that was by becoming a Crusader Knight. He very much wanted to enter the tournament that was held once every three years to choose new knights, but he had not the means. And then he realized he had one valuable possession—his beautiful half-faerie daughter. If he sold her to Gaius Prospero, the Master of the

Merchants, he would have everything he needed for the tournament. A fine warhorse, new weapons and the best armor. His battle skills, he knew, would gain him the place he sought. And when he became a Crusader Knight his wife and son would be moved to the beautiful Garden District into a beautiful house with slaves of their own. His son would receive the finest education. But only if he sold his daughter into slavery. There was no other way for him, and besides, he had not even enough coin to give his daughter a dower portion. And so he sold his eldest child, but she was happy to be the means by which her father might advance himself. And she was very proud when he won his place among the Crusader Knights."

"What happened to her then?" Dillon asked eagerly.

"She was sold again, this time to the Forest Lords. But the Forest Lords were cruel masters, and so with the aid of a small giant named Og, she escaped the forest. She and Og traveled to the desert of the Shadow Princes, and there she learned how to love properly, and how to fight well, for she had inherited her father's warrior skills. And after a time the Shadow Princes sent her away into the Outlands where she met a handsome clan lord. She wed him, and they had two fine children."

"Mama!" Dillon exclaimed. "This is your story, isn't it?"

Lara laughed, and ruffled his dark hair. "You are such a clever boy, my son," she told him. "Yes, this is my story."

"Tell me more," he begged her.

"I will, but another day," she promised him. "You must remember all I tell you, Dillon, for when I am gone you will have to tell Anoush so she will know who her mother was, and is."

And in the days that followed she filled in what she had not told him in that first telling. Bit by bit, piece by piece, Lara fleshed out her story. First she gave him his grandfather's name. John Swiftsword. Next he learned that in order to become a Crusader Knight a man must look as if he were worthy. As young as he was, Dillon scorned such an attitude for his father had always said a man's worth showed in what he accomplished and did. Not how he looked. Hetar, he declared, was an odd place.

Lara told her son of her own childhood. How her grandmother had taught her all her own skills of housewifery, medicine, the art of bargaining and how to tell a good fabric from a bad one. And how she had had no friends among children her own age, for they feared her faerie blood. Yet she could not recall ever having seen her mother. And later she learned that her father and grandmother had forbidden the beautiful faerie woman who had birthed her to see her. But her mother had put the crystal Lara always wore about her neck with its guardian spirit, Ethne, within to keep her safe.

Lara explained how Gaius Prospero had let her remain at home until her father won his place. And at the urging of her elderly neighbor Lara had on her last night of freedom asked her father to tell her the story of his involvement with the beautiful faerie, Ilona, and how she had come to be born.

The Master of the Merchants had taken charge of his new slave the morning after her father's victory and his acceptance into the Crusader Knights. But the beautiful slave he thought to profit from was forbidden from being sold into one of the City's Pleasure Houses by the Head Mistress of the Pleasure Mistresses' Guild.

"Why?" Dillon asked his mother. "Did they not think you beautiful enough?"

"I was thought too beautiful," Lara explained to him. "After I had been displayed for sale to a very elite audience of Pleasure House owners, quarrels broke out over who should purchase me. The Head Mistress, in order to keep the peace, forbade Gaius Prospero to sell me in the City. So I was sent off with a Taubyl Trader to be sold into the Coastal Kingdom."

As the days passed, and Lara told her son more of the story, the boy learned how she had ended up being purchased by the Head Forester and his brother. And Lara told him of how Og had explained the secret of the Forest Lords to her. That Maeve, the old queen of the Forest Faeries, had cursed them with great cause. That Lara, because of her faerie blood, would not birth any child unless she loved the man involved with all her heart. And since she did not love a Forest Lord, Lara and Og had devised an escape plan.

"Then you loved my father with all your heart," Dillon noted.

"I did," Lara answered her young son. She was amazed by his understanding of her story for he was scarcely out of babyhood. But she could see in his eyes that he did, and as the days went by she added more detail to her tale. She told him how she and Og had fled the forest, and arrived in the land of the Shadow Princes. How Prince Kaliq had taken her for his lover, but knowing her destiny was greater, educated her and saw that she learned to fight. Kaliq had realized her mother, Ilona, was the heiress of the old queen of the Forest Faeries. He had engineered a reunion between the three, and Lara had learned the truth of her mother's desertion. Maeve had needed her. Ilona had had no other choice but to return to the faerie kingdom.

And on certain days Ilona herself would join them beneath the tree in the grass, and add her own voice to Lara's tale. On other days she would arrive with Lara's young half brother, Cirilo, who was but a year older than his nephew. The two women would watch as the boys played games together in the meadow, Anoush trailing after them.

"They are forging a close relationship," Lara noted to her mother one warm afternoon. "When I first began my story Dillon thought Hetarians foolish for thinking faeries brought bad fortune. He said faeries only brought good luck."

Ilona laughed softly. "So my grandson believes we are only good. Well, why not? In time he will come to see that faeries have at least two sides, as do mortals." Then her voice grew even more serious. "How much longer?" she asked.

"A few more weeks," Lara replied. "I want to be here when Noss has her new baby, and for a short while afterwards so I may help her."

"Has she not servants to help her?" Ilona wanted to know.

"Of course, but better a friend, and it gives me more time with Dillon and Anoush, Mother. I do not know when I shall ever see them again once I have departed the Outlands. I ache already with my loss." She sighed deeply with her sadness.

"At least your children will know that you love them, and did not leave them willingly," Ilona said, her tone bitter. "It will not be like when I was forced to leave you behind to obey the dictates of the faerie world. Your mortal grandmother was a cruel woman, Lara. She was jealous that I should have any influence over you."

"She did not know that I had a destiny, Mother. She raised me to live entirely within the mortal realm, for she knew nothing else herself. She loved me in her own way, but like you, I, too, regret the years we were separated. Still, we have each other now, and I am glad for it." She took up the faerie woman's hand, and kissed it. "I do love you, Mother," she told Ilona.

"You have the mortal knack of taking something dark and making it light," Ilona said with a small smile. "Perhaps mortals do have a certain magic about themselves after all." She kissed the hand in hers. "No mother could have a better daughter."

NOSS DELIVERED her child, a second son, early one late summer's morning. The child was born healthy, howling his arrival, and with a head full of bright red hair like Liam. He was named Alroy, and his mother almost fainted seeing the size of him, for his birth had been quick. Alroy was a large infant with a prodigious appetite when put to his mother's breast several hours later. His hands with their thick fingers kneaded Noss's flesh demanding it give forth the nourishment Alroy needed. Noss was enchanted by her second son, and very proud.

All the children in the house were brought to look at the new baby.

"He has hair like Da," Tearlach noted.

"Big," Anoush remarked sagely.

"He's going to be a great warrior," Dillon said.

They all looked to the boy, curious.

"I see it," Dillon continued. "I can't help it. I just do."

"A useful skill to have," Lara said.

"It's his faerie blood," Asta, Liam's mother said.

"Yes, it is!" Lara confirmed, "and isn't that wonderful? I have told my mother, and she will see he is trained properly. My son will be quite a valuable asset to this clan family with such a talent."

"Aye, he will be," Liam replied. "But he must not be brought along too quickly lest his skill be harmed."

Lara looked to the lord gratefully. Now she knew for certain that her children would be safe.

The days were shortening again. Lara could linger no longer, and she knew it. She could hear Ethne, her crystal guardian, urging her to go as she lay in her bed each night. It would get no easier, she realized, as each day passed. It would soon be time for the Gathering of the Outlands clan families, and she had promised herself she would go before then. Noss was up from her childbed, and managing the household well. The boys were at their lessons daily. Anoush, fascinated by Noss with her new son strapped about her body, trailed her as she went about her duties each day. It seemed to Lara that she had no place left in the hall that had once been hers and Vartan's.

"You are going, aren't you?" Dillon said to her as she put him to bed one evening.

"I will be gone when you awaken tomorrow," Lara heard herself saying to her son. "Do not forget me, or that I love you dearly. Do not allow Anoush to forget me, or doubt that I loved her, too. I go because it is my destiny now. Do you understand, Dillon?"

"Yes, and no, Mama," he told her.

She nodded. "I would wish it otherwise, my son. I believed that when this time came for us your father would be here. Yet I seem to have no choice in this matter."

He nodded. "Will we ever see you again?" he asked her.

"Yes," she assured him. "I just don't know when, Dillon."

"Do not forget us, Mama," Dillon said to her.

"Never!" Lara swore. "My blood runs in your veins, Dillon, my son."

He reached up, and touched her cheek with his small fingers. "You will be back, and before we are grown," he said with assurance. Then he closed his eyes, and Lara sat by his side until his even breathing indicated that he had fallen asleep.

Standing, she went to the cot where her daughter lay sleeping. Anoush had her dainty form, but like her brother she had Vartan's coloring. She would be beautiful one day, Lara thought. Bending, she placed a kiss on her daughter's smooth forehead. Then leaving her two children, Lara returned to the hall where Liam and Noss were sitting.

"I must go now," she told them.

"Wait till the morrow," Noss begged her friend.

"If I do not leave now," Lara said, "I do not know if I can. Dasras is now my son's horse. I have spoken with him. Teach Dillon to ride him immediately," Lara told Liam. "And remember your promise. Roan may not have Dasras, no matter what he offers you."

"Will you find a way to communicate with us?" Liam wanted to know.

"I will try," Lara promised. She went to Noss, and kissed her on both cheeks. "I trust you, dear friend," she told her. "Do not let my children forget me."

"I will be worthy, I swear it," Noss declared.

Lara then walked from the hall and out into the night. Above her the sky over the Outlands was ablaze with stars. "Aral change!" she said, and in her temporary form as a great plains owl she arose into the air to circle Camdene just once. And then, its great wings flapping, the night bird turned and flew toward the coastlands.

Chapter
3

THE PLAINS OWL flew steadily through the night sky. On the earth below the grazing cattle gave way to grazing sheep. The invisible barrier between Fiacre lands and those of the Felan had been crossed. The owl flew on until it saw below the village of Adrie where Rendor, Lord of the Felan, made his home. Some few miles beyond the village lay the waters of the great sea of Sagitta. The great bird was tempted to fly out over the sea, but it was beginning to tire. With a whir of its wings the owl dropped to the land below. As its clawed feet touched the ground Lara said, "Aral change!" and was immediately restored to her own form.

"I thought you would come tonight," Rendor's voice said from the open door of his house where he awaited her. "Welcome to Adrie, Lara. Come in!"

"How did you guess?" Lara asked him, smiling as he led her into his hall.

Rendor's deep laugh warmed the hall, and he pointed to his high board where Andraste, her sword, and Verica, her staff, lay. "I knew if you sent them ahead that you would not be far behind," the Felan clan lord chuckled.

Lara laughed in return. "I might have come on the morrow," she said.

"You would never leave the sword and staff alone long," he replied wisely. "Their sudden appearance quite startled a young maidservant clearing the evening meal from the table. She shrieked with her surprise, and the staff spoke quite sharply to her, causing her to faint dead away. I cannot recall when Rahil and I have laughed so hard," he finished with a grin.

"Oh, I am sorry!" Lara apologized. "Verica dislikes magical travel, but as I did not choose to ride, it was the simplest and easiest way to transport him. He wanted me to fly the whole distance carrying him in the owl's claws."

"Come and sit by the fire," Rendor invited her. He walked to a sideboard and poured two small goblets of wine, handing her one.

"I will stay with you but a few days," Lara said. "I know you must soon depart for the Gathering."

"My men and I will personally escort you to King Archeron," Rendor said. "The king must be reminded that Lara, widow of Vartan, daughter of Swiftsword, is greatly honored among all the Outlands clans. For all his scorn of the City and Hetar's government, Archeron is still Hetarian, and appearance is everything to him."

"Is he aware of how well you understand him?" Lara asked Rendor.

"I doubt it," Rendor replied. "He knows I am not a barbarian, but deep in his head, the doubts linger. If I were to come into his hall in furs, waving my sword, with helmeted warriors at my back he would not, I believe, be in the least surprised." The clan lord chuckled. "I always feel he is just waiting for me to reveal my true colors and prove Hetar right, that Outlanders are savages."

Lara giggled at the thought of Rendor in furs waving his sword. Then she grew serious. "We are far more civilized here in the Outlands than in Hetar with all its rules and mores."

"Then why do you return to it?" Rendor asked her.

"It is that damned destiny I seem to have been given," Lara told him. "I knew, and Vartan knew, too, that one day it would call me from the Outlands. I have no idea why I am going to the Coastal Kingdom, but that is where I am meant to be now. In the night I have asked Ethne, my crystal guardian, and she agrees. But Archeron's realm and that of his brothers is not my final destination, Rendor. I do not yet know where I will go, but when it is time I will."

He sighed. "I am sorry for it. We need you in the Outlands."

Lara shook her head. "You are protected, and you are capable of managing the Hetarians, dear Rendor, that I know. Though I have taught you all, you learned the lesson best next to Vartan. The Outlands will be safe under your guidance."

Rendor's wife, Rahil, came into the hall. "Ah," she said, smiling, her warm brown eyes lighting with her pleasure at seeing their guest, "you have arrived, Lara. I bid you welcome. Did my husband tell you of the poor maidservant?"

"He did, and I am so sorry to have frightened the girl," Lara apologized.

Rahil laughed. "Our people are not used to such magic," she said. "Are you tired? I have prepared a guest chamber for you."

"I am tired," Lara admitted. "I have not shape-shifted in some time now, and I flew the distance between Camdene and Adrie without stopping."

"And I do not doubt you have not slept well, if at all, since…" Rahil hesitated.

"No," Lara replied. "I have not slept well since Vartan's death."

"Then come along," Rahil said. "I will show you to your chamber."

"Good night, Rendor, and thank you for your hospitality," Lara said as she rose, and then followed Rahil's comfortable shape from the hall.

Her chamber was inviting, with a small fire to take the chill off the night, and a comfortable bed. Lara bid her hostess good-night and, stripping off her gown, climbed beneath the coverlet. To her surprise she was asleep almost immediately, and she did not awaken until half of the next day had passed. She probably would have slept a few more hours but that Rahil entered the chamber bearing a tray of food.

"I have decided that you must be cosseted," she told Lara. "For the moment you have no responsibilities but to yourself. You must regain your strength if you are to continue on your journey." She took a bowl from the tray, plunked a spoon into it and handed it to Lara. "Eat," she commanded the younger woman.

Lara did not argue. The truth was she was still tired, and felt weak. The bowl contained a delicious stew of meat and vegetables, which she savored slowly. When the bowl was half-empty Rahil tucked a slice of bread and butter into a corner of the bowl. Their eyes met, and Lara smiled. "Thank you," she said, and then she continued eating.

"I have three daughters, and like their mother none knows when to rest. I see you are much the same," Rahil noted. "Did Bera not see to your welfare in the days following Vartan's murder?"

"Bera lost her reason after what she had seen. She could do nothing more than weep, and curse fate over what had transpired."

"Then you did it all? The preparations for the departure ceremony? For all the guests? You sent the messengers out?" Rahil was surprised, and a little bit shocked.

"Noss looked after my children," Lara said. "And Bera recovered enough to move from Vartan's hall into a smaller house with Cam. I saw her settled before I left."

"Liam now rules in that hall?" Rahil nodded almost to herself. "It was a wise and generous thing to do, Lara."

"Our home was the finest in Camdene, and should

be the lord's house," Lara replied. "He and Noss have taken Dillon and Anoush to raise with their sons. And Noss has had another boy, Alroy. He was born with red hair like Liam."

Rahil smiled as she took the empty stew bowl from Lara and replaced it with another dish containing a baked apple swimming in rich golden cream. "So Noss will have three lads and a little lass to bring up. I have been told she is a good wife to Liam."

"They are fortunate in each other," Lara said. She spooned up the apple, licking at the corner of her mouth to catch a stray bit of the sweet.

"When you have finished you are to go back to sleep," Rahil told her. "I have brought you a cup of wine into which I have mixed a sleeping draught. You should sleep until the morning." She took the empty bowl that had held the apple, noting with pleasure that Lara had eaten every scrap. Setting the bowl on the tray she handed her guest the cup of wine.

Lara sipped it slowly. She was sated with the good meal, warm, and actually beginning to relax. "You are so good to me, and I thank you," she told Rahil. "When I arrived last night I felt drained of all my strength. I am yet weakened by everything that has transpired in these last few months."

"Whatever it is you are meant to do," Rahil said, "it is for the good of us all, Lara. Whatever I may do to ease your burden, I will do." She took the now empty cup from the younger woman, bending to kiss her on the forehead as she might a child. "Go to sleep now," she said, and picking up the tray, hurried from the room.

Lara slept, as Rahil had predicted, until the following morning. She awoke to see through a small paned window to one side of her bed the sky colored with the coming sunrise. A gentle breeze slipped through the slightly open window. Lara stretched herself. For the first time in weeks she felt good. Her body no longer ached with sorrow and tension. She felt a faint excitement as she considered what might lie ahead for her. And she realized that she was looking forward to going into the Coastal Kingdom.

"Hetar." She said the word softly. A place carefully divided into Forest, Desert, Coast and Midlands. A place where all roads led to the City at its center. Hetar, where appearance and possessions were everything; where each citizen's life was lived by careful rules that dictated his or her place within society. And yet there were ways to advance if one followed the rules. She had not realized until she had begun her travels how stifling it had all been. She might have never known, had she not been sent from the City on that early morning over seven years ago.

She might now have been a Pleasure Woman in one of the City's great Pleasure Houses. A creature of beauty, skilled in all the amatory arts, whose sole reason for being was to give and to receive pleasure. But if that had been her fate she should never have learned how to love, or to be loved. Or that her faerie blood allowed her to practice good magic. Or that her sire's blood had given her the ability to be the great warrior she had become. She often wondered what John Swiftsword would think of his daughter now.

Did he know she had played an important part in the Winter War?

Lara swung her legs over the edge of the bed and stood up. Yes! She was beginning to feel like herself again. She walked to the window, and pushing it all the way open, she breathed in the soft air, smelling the tangy salt of the sea on the breeze. Tomorrow. She would leave for King Archeron's palace tomorrow! And then she heard Ethne, her crystal guardian, quite clearly. She reached for the crystal that hung from the gold chain about her neck.

No, Ethne said. *You need more rest, my child. Here you are safe. You will never really be safe in Hetar while Gaius Prospero and his compatriots hold power.*

But Rendor and his people must leave soon for the Gathering, Lara protested in the silent discourse they had always used to speak with one another.

The Gathering is over a month away, Lara. Take this time while you have it, my child. You must be strong for what lies ahead.

Very well, Lara agreed, and the tiny flame in the crystal flickered. "Why," she muttered softly to herself, "do the magical beings surrounding me always speak in riddles?" Her ears pricked at the faint sound of laughter.

But Ethne had been right. Lara discovered that she was still tired, and very worn.

She enjoyed having Rahil fuss over her, plying her with tasty meals and making her sleep early, and rise late. Her strength began to return, and after two weeks had passed Lara decided it was now time to leave the Felan. "Tomorrow," she said that evening to Rendor as they all sat at the high board.

He nodded. "Is dawn too early?"

"Rendor!" Rahil protested.

"It is perfect," Lara agreed, and put a comforting hand on Rahil's hand. "I am well and strong again, thanks to you," she told the woman. "But it is now time for me to go, dear friend. I sense it."

A tear slipped down Rahil's sweet round face. "You have suffered so much," she said. "It doesn't seem fair to me."

"You should see her with that sword of hers," Rendor told his wife. "If you did you would not be fooled by her delicate face and form, wife." And he chuckled. "Each time I hear Andraste sing it sends icy ripples through me."

"She is a very fierce battle spirit," Lara agreed.

"And will you appear before King Archeron as you did the first time?" Rendor wanted to know. "All beautiful and faerie in a flowing white gown?"

"No," Lara told him. "I will appear as the warrior I am so Archeron will not be mistaken in his opinion of me. I have a destiny to fulfill, and I can allow none to stop me, Rendor."

Rendor nodded. "Then I am reassured," he said with a broad smile.

It was a full day's ride to reach the palace of King Archeron. They left just before sunrise, and reached the sea as the sun pushed up over the horizon. As they rested their horses briefly Lara was suddenly assailed by a thought as she looked out over the blue waters. Where did these waters come from? Where did they end? Did the Coastal Kings know? Would they tell her? And why had she not considered this before, when she first saw the Sea of Sagitta?

Lara knew that her destiny had something to do with this great sea whose waves rolled onto the sandy beach she now traveled. But what? Archeron would surely know more about it. She would ask him. The sea had to end somewhere, didn't it? Was there a sandy beach like this one on its far side? And if there was, were there people, too? Was it possible Hetar and the Outlands were not all there was to this world which they inhabited? The closer she got to Archeron's palace the more questions seemed to flood her mind.

"You are quiet," Rendor noted as they rode along.

"Do you know where the sea ends?" Lara asked him.

The Lord of the Felan look puzzled, and then he said, "The sea just *is*, Lara."

"You have never considered what might be on the other side of this sea?" She could see she was confusing him, but perhaps he had heard something that she could coax him to recall by questioning him.

"The sea is the sea," he answered her. "It is there. It has always been there."

"Think, Rendor. Yours are the only lands among the Outlands clans to border this water. The Coastal Kings are the only ones in Hetar to border this water. The sea must begin in one place, and end in another. There must be something on its other side."

"What other side?" Rendor asked now looking seriously befuddled.

He didn't understand. And truth be known, Lara wasn't certain she understood either. So many questions filling her head, brought about just by looking upon the Sea of Sagitta again. "I am being foolish," she said to him, and when she saw the relief in his eyes she knew she had been wise to end the conversation. Rendor hadn't the least notion to what she had been referring, or what she had meant. But she would wager that King Archeron would understand. The exquisite fabrics, the unique and beautiful jewelry the Coastal Kings brought into the City did not come from their hands. She had seen no manufactories on the coast. So where did the luxury goods come from?

As the morning became afternoon, and then late afternoon, they saw a troop of horsemen coming toward them. Lara was surprised until she realized that Archeron had sent an escort to bring her to him. "How did they know we were coming?" she asked Rendor.

He nodded his head toward the heights that bordered the beach. "Watchtowers. Discreetly placed, I will grant you, but there. You don't notice them because they look like piles of stones. And they have developed some sort of silent code using flags so that one tower may signal to another."

"How clever, and how very Hetarian," Lara chuckled. "I did not notice them the first time we came. That was careless of me."

"Nay," Rendor said. "You were coming as Vartan's wife, to help make peace between the Outlands and Hetar. The mystical faerie woman." He grinned.

Lara laughed. "Yes, I seem to remember I wore

a gown that certainly gave weight to my legend. I carried it to Adrie in a small carved wooden fruit. Vartan was very impressed by a woman who packed so lightly, and looked so beautiful nonetheless."

"The gown was concealed in a wooden fruit?" Rendor roared with laughter. "I had not heard that before." Then he grew serious. "He loved you very much, you know, Lara. He said he could not have accomplished what he did without you."

"He always underestimated himself," Lara said softly. "He had such greatness in him. I am still angry that fate let that greatness be silenced. My heart is broken, yet I felt nothing at all, Rendor. I feel no guilt for the lives I took. The sorrow consuming me is for Vartan, and for the Fiacre. But I have no pity for Adon and Elin."

"I regret Vartan's death is taking you from us," Rendor said.

"Vartan's death was but the catalyst. He and I both knew I would leave the Fiacre one day when my destiny called to me again." Lara sighed deeply, but said nothing more on the subject. What else was there to say?

The escort from the Coastal Kings reached her, and Lara was not surprised to see that it was King Archeron himself who led them. He was a tall, handsome man with silvery white hair and eyes the deep blue of the sea. Sliding quickly from his mount he looked up at Lara and kissed her hand. "Welcome back, widow of Vartan, daughter of Swiftsword," he greeted her. And then he lifted her from her mount. "Let us walk a ways along the shore, my friend." Archeron tucked her hand in his arm.

"You are sad," Lara noted astutely. "What has happened, my lord king?"

"Like you," Archeron answered her, "I have recently lost my mate."

"Alina is dead? We had not heard this in the Outlands," Lara said.

"We sent her out to sea just a few days ago. It was sudden, and very unexpected," Archeron replied. His jewel-like eyes were bleak with his mourning.

"You put your dead in the sea?" Lara was fascinated.

"We come from the sea," Archeron said. "And so when our mortal bodies die we return them to the sea. They are sent out into the waters with all the goods that they will need to live in the realm of the Celestial Actuary. Alina's vessel was beautifully decked, and I did not stint my queen. What do you do in the Outlands?" Now it was the Coastal King who was curious.

"Vartan was set upon a great bier within his hall for two days. It allowed all who wished to pay him honor to do so. The mourners are housed and fed at the family's expense," Lara explained. "On the third day the body is brought out of the hall to be placed upon a great funeral pyre, which is then set alight at the hour of the sunset. My son and I remained with him until all that was left were ashes. A wind then sprang up, and blew the ashes away, spreading them throughout the Outlands. This is the custom of the Outlands. It is called a departure ceremony. Criminals, however, are buried in the earth to rot while their souls suffer the torment of the damned. Vartan's murderer and his wicked wife were so disposed of after I slew them," Lara responded.

Archeron nodded. "I was told his brother killed him," he said.

"Aye," Lara answered him. "Adon had always envied his elder sibling, but I would have never thought he would do something like this. His wife, of course, urged him to it. I always knew Elin was ambitious, but her actions orphaned and endangered her only child. Now his grandmother will raise him alone, and the child will be held responsible for his parents' actions by many among the Fiacre."

"Did you ever consider that there was more to this?" King Archeron asked Lara.

Lara stopped suddenly. "What is it you are saying to me, my lord king?"

"Vartan was a powerful voice for the Outlands, Lara, and with you advising him, who knew what heights he might have reached? I have heard a rumor, faint, but very distinct, that there were certain men among the powerful in the City, who considered him a great threat to Hetar and to their own ambitions. And, too, a violent death that Vartan's faerie wife could not prevent might easily contribute to lessening your own authority."

Lara was stunned by his quiet words. For the tiniest moment she felt dizzy, as if she were going to collapse. Then, as a growing anger caused new strength to flow through her, she said, "And has any name emerged from among these certain powerful men, my lord king? Could Gaius Prospero be among them?"

"He has never forgiven you for the loss of prestige he suffered in the Winter War. It has taken him five years to regain his popularity, and to come within sight again of his goal to be made emperor of Hetar, Lara," King Archeron responded.

"And will he be made emperor?"

"We will have a better idea of what is happening in the City when Arcas returns. He is serving as one of our representatives on the council right now."

"So my husband's murder was an assassination," Lara said quietly. "Gaius Prospero, clinging to his belief that the Outlands is peopled by savages, thought that by removing Vartan the alliance between the clan families would collapse." She sighed bitterly. "His ignorance is terrifying, my lord king. The clan families are more determined than ever to remain strongly united. Rendor was chosen head of the council to replace Vartan. And they have made Roan of the Aghy their war leader. An incursion into our lands, an attack on any of them by Hetar, will be met with military action. This would-be emperor will set our world aflame with his ambitions. But how did Gaius Prospero get to Adon, or was it Elin to whom he appealed? Of course! It would have been Elin. That poor foolish woman with her pitiful dreams of her husband leading the Fiacre. Even had Vartan died a natural death, the Fiacre would not have chosen Adon to lead them."

"What will you do now?" the Coastal King asked

his beautiful guest. They began to walk along the beach once again.

Lara shrugged. "My destiny is calling once more."

"And it called you to come to me?" He smiled down at her. "I am flattered."

"It called me to the coast, but for what reason I do not yet know, my lord king. But I have many questions to ask you."

"I will answer those I can," he promised her.

"You must answer them all," she told him.

Archeron looked sharply at Lara. "Indeed," he murmured.

She laughed up at him. "I found the nearer I came to your kingdom the more curious I became. I know you possess the knowledge I seek, my lord king."

He smiled. "I will deny you nothing, Lara. I, too, know you have a destiny. There is a prophecy, known only to a few, in the Book of Hetar, which can be found in the temple of the Celestial Actuary in the City. I believe you are the one meant to satisfy that prophecy. And so does Gaius Prospero or he would not be so intent on destroying you."

"How many others know of the prophecy?" Lara questioned him.

"Only a handful of the high and mighty. Possibly the High Priest, but he is very old, and under Gaius Prospero's thumb, I fear."

"Tell me what the prophecy says."

"From the darkness came a maiden. From the golden light came a warrior. From a distant tomorrow will come Hetar's true destiny," King Archeron recited.

"I was a maiden who came forth from the darkness and squalor of the City. I became a warrior in the golden desert light of the Shadow Princes' kingdom," Lara said. "But where, I wonder, is that distant tomorrow?"

"Wherever it is, Lara, you are meant to find it," Archeron said quietly. Then he said, "Let us seek our horses now, and ride on to my palace."

Mounting, they rode along the shoreline again, King Archeron leading the way. Rendor moved his horse up next to Lara, murmuring so softly only she could hear him.

"What did he say?"

"Vartan's death may have been a cleverly planned assassination, conceived by my old friend Gaius Prospero," Lara replied as softly. Rendor's face above his short brown bread darkened with outrage, and she noted that his men were pressing in about them, shielding them from the coastal men-at-arms.

Lara put a warning hand on Rendor's arm, cautioning him to silence. "This is not the doing of the Coastal Kings, my friend," she said low. "We never expected our relations with Hetar to be what they once were, given the result of the Winter War. But they have struck at us in a way we did not anticipate. Speak of this to the other lords at the Gathering, Rendor. Warn them in as strong terms as you can that they cannot permit Hetar to lure them into any action against one another. If something untoward happens, and it appears to be the deed of another clan family, be suspicious. The Outlands have not fallen into chaos, as I am quite certain Gaius Prospero thought they would when he saw to my husband's murder. Instead another clan lord was chosen to lead us. Gaius will now consider other ways of causing difficulty for you and the Outlands. Beware, and be suspicious of Hetar no matter their soft words. They are desperate and have no place to go, no way to feed their growing population, no way to make new profits. You are protected for now, but you will not be forever. The clan lords must plan for that day."

"I wish you were not leaving us," Rendor said once again.

"I will not be gone from you forever," Lara promised.

Shortly before the sunset they arrived at the palace of King Archeron. The entire household was in mourning for his queen, Alina. There would be no banquet tonight to welcome the visitors. Rendor's men were led off to be fed and shown to their sleeping spaces. The king led Lara and the new head of the Outlands High Council into a small dining chamber overlooking the great Sea of Sagitta. Servants brought silver basins of perfumed water with which to wash the journey from their faces and hands. Then they stretched out on the three dining couches and the meal was served.

Lara's appetite was small that evening. She could not take her eyes from the sea beyond the palace. The sky above it was clear blue, and stained with streamers of rich color from the sun setting over the Outlands beyond the waters. A thin gold crescent moon was rising out of the sea, and above it the great star, Beltair, glistened brightly. It had been a long day, but she was not yet tired. Rahil's care had helped Lara regain her strength again, and soon, soon she sensed, something was preparing to set the course of her life on another path once again.

"You are quiet," King Archeron finally said to Lara.

"You have given me a great deal to consider this day," she answered him.

The king turned to Rendor. "She has told you?"

"Aye," Rendor replied.

"Good!" Archeron answered him. "The Outlands must be on their guard."

"You are Hetarian, and yet you do not agree with your own government," Rendor said. "Why?"

"The government has been corrupted by greedy men," King Archeron replied. "And these men will bring sorrow to Hetar. I but attempt to delay the inevitable."

Rendor nodded. "You will guard Lara from harm, my friend, will you not?"

"I will, for she has a destiny to fulfill." He smiled.

Lara and Rendor laughed.

Then Rendor said, "I shall leave early in the morning. We will depart for the Gathering in a few days. It should be a most interesting time this year."

"Give my regards to the lords," Lara told him. And then she arose. "My lord king, will you have someone show me to the chamber that is to be mine?"

Archeron called a servant, and gave the woman her instructions.

Lara walked to where Rendor was now standing. Rising up on her toes, she kissed him on both cheeks.

"Until we meet again, my Lord of the Felan," she said. "The Celestial Actuary guide you in all that you undertake, and keep the Outlands safe from evil men. Farewell!" Then turning to her host, she bid him good-night and followed the servant from the little dining hall.

The chamber to which Lara was brought was not the same one she had once shared with Vartan, and she was grateful for Archeron's sensitivity. But like that room, it had a single large arched window with an almost hidden door that opened onto a marble terrace overlooking the sea. The servant showed Lara the bathing pool, which was on that terrace, and not inside her chamber. Then she bowed, and left the king's guest to herself.

Lara dipped her hand into the small square pool. The water was warm and scented with yellow primrose. With a smile Lara pulled off her boots and stripped off her leather pants, her vest and her shirt. Not even bothering to pin her hair up, she stepped naked into the pool with a deep sigh of pleasure. There was nothing like a warm bath. Finding the seating ledge she sat down, and just enjoyed the sensation of the water lapping against her skin. There was an alabaster jar of soft soap on the side of the tub, and a large sea sponge. Lara filled the sponge with soap, and washed herself in the lavishly rich cleansing agent. Then she washed and rinsed her golden hair, wishing that she had a lemon to squeeze into it in a final rinse. No sooner had she thought it than there was a cut lemon on the edge of the bathing pool.

Laughing, she squeezed it into her hair, laving clean water from the curved shell faucet over her head.

But then the pool was swiftly draining itself. Sprays of water shot from small recessed spigots in the pool wall, rinsing her off. She bent to let the water cleanse the last of the lemon from her head before the bathing pool refilled itself with scented water. Lara relaxed as she watched the golden coastal moon rising higher, and was lulled by the sound of the waves below the great palace.

When the sky was finally dark she walked back into her chamber to find the lamps had been lit, and a small fire was burning in the little hearth opposite her bed. Drying herself with the large drying cloth she found warming on a rack by the fire she slipped on a loose night robe. Her pack had been brought to her chamber, and opening it she drew out the beautiful gold brush that Kaliq, the Shadow Prince, had once given her as a lover's token. Seating herself on a small velvet hassock by the fire she brushed her hair dry. She was finally beginning to feel sleepy. Lara climbed into the large comfortable bed draped in coral and gold silk curtains. What would tomorrow bring, she wondered? And how long would she remain here in Archeron's palace? Her eyes closed slowly of their own volition.

She awakened with the dawn, and rose to see the sunrise from her terrace. She had slept a sound and dreamless sleep. For the next few weeks Lara's days were relatively the same. She awoke, ate her morning meal upon the marble terrace and then walked about the town belonging to King Archeron's palace. The lords of the coastlands had long ago decided that each of their leaders would be a king with his own palace and village. It saved a great deal of debate, and the oldest of the kings was always recognized as their High King, no matter the family from which he came.

The palace was white marble, with soaring towers and gold-leafed domes. The town into which it blended was much the same. The windows of the houses overlooking the streets were bright with flower boxes holding blooms of every size and hue. The stalls in the market square were clean and filled with goods being hawked from beneath multicolored awnings.

Lara had no need of coin. If she saw something she admired it was pressed into her hand. She returned the kindness with a faerie blessing, which she learned was far preferred to silver or gold. And everyone knew who she was. The daughter of the great Crusader Knight, John Swiftsword, and a faerie mother, although her mother did not matter to the Hetarians. Nor did her sojourn in the Outlands where it was rumored she had mated with, and given one of the men there children. She was still the great beauty that she had been reputed to be.

In the afternoons Lara would ride along the beach with King Archeron, and in the evenings they would dine together. Often their evenings were spent in conversation. Other times they would play a board game similar to the one she had played with Vartan.

And then one evening Archeron announced to his guest that his son and heir, Arcas, would soon be returning from the City.

"No one travels the old-fashioned way any longer," he told Lara. "The representatives are now all transported to and from the City by means of magic."

"With whom has he served?" she asked, curious.

"King Balasi," Archeron answered. "His is an old and very respected family. But I find him easily led, and perhaps a bit foolish. When it is his turn to serve on the High Council in the City we always see he is sent with someone strong who is able to direct Balasi without his being aware of it. He is unable to cause difficulties then, for he is a pompous, self-important man. My son has never forgotten you, Lara."

"I did not say it when I was last here, but Arcas offended me deeply," Lara told her gracious and kindly host. "But perhaps it was just his enthusiasm that caused him to act in the manner in which he did."

"What did he say?" Archeron was distressed by her revelation.

"He made reference to my slavery, and then he touched me in an intimate manner," Lara said quietly. "I did not speak gently to him."

"I am sorry," Archeron replied. "But then, as you have considered, surely it was just his enthusiasm at meeting you that caused his breach of manners."

Lara nodded in seeming agreement with the king, but she knew Arcas's behavior had been caused by little more than his lustful nature. She was not looking forward to meeting him again. "There is a question that I have wanted to ask you ever since I saw the Sea of Sagitta again," she began.

"I will answer your query if I can," he said, glad to be off the subject of Arcas.

"What is on the other side of your sea? And why is naught said about it?" Lara looked directly at King Archeron as she spoke.

He chuckled. "No one has ever asked that question of me," he began. "How clever of you, Lara, to consider such a thing. Hetar believes it alone exists, but for the Outlands, which Hetar has declared a savage place in order to make itself seem more civilized and important. It is a very narrow view. But on the other side of the sea is a land its inhabitants call Terah. It is ruled over by the Dominus of the Terahn Dominion. It is from there our luxury goods come—the fabrics, the jewelry, the fine china and pottery, the objects of gold and silver. We trade the salt we produce, the pearls we harvest from the sea, and the coin we earn by selling Terahn merchandise in exchange for more of their goods. Gaius Prospero is unconcerned with where we obtain these things. He only desires them to gain more profit for himself. He assumes we manufacture these goods ourselves, and few from the City or any other part of Hetar have ever come to the Coastal Kingdom. All of us keep much to ourselves, and the City is the only place where we meet and mingle. Those across the sea are our secret. Now you know it, and you must keep that secret. We should lose our great advantage over the City if this was known to them."

"I will keep your secret," Lara said. "Have you ever been to Terah, Archeron?"

"No," he replied. "The Terahns do not permit strangers into their lands. We meet these fellow traders in the middle of the sea and there we exchange our goods."

"How did the Coastal Kings find the Terahns?" Lara wanted to know.

"That is the odd thing about our relationship," Archeron responded. "No one knows how it all began. There is nothing in our history to explain it, yet for centuries we have traded with them, and they with us. I remember asking my grandfather when I was a child, and he just shook his head, and told me that it had always been, and would always be. And the Terahns' knowledge of this partnership is no greater than ours."

"How strange," Lara remarked. "Haven't you ever wanted to know more about the Terahns, Archeron? Haven't you ever wanted to see their land, and if it is as beautiful as here? Haven't you ever wanted to meet them face-to-face?"

"Oh, I have met Terahns," he told her. "When I was younger I often captained one of my family's ships to the meeting place, and did business with their captains. I even met on several occasions the man who is now the Dominus. I met him as a boy. He is Magnus Hauk. A serious lad as I recall, and I am now told, deeply passionate about keeping the Dominion strong."

"It is interesting that these Terahns have never considered invading Hetar, or the fertile plains of the Outlands," Lara mused.

"Their own lands are said to be gloriously beautiful, but of course we have but their word for it as they have ours." Archeron smiled. "Actually, we know little of them, for they keep very much to themselves as do we. I do not believe they are an aggressive people. And they have never evinced any real interest in Hetar."

"How curious," Lara noted. "Perhaps these people are much like us."

"I could not tell you, for we do nothing more than trade. Prices are set for the goods in advance. We exchange cargos and go our separate ways. Sometimes, however, we might share wine or a meal together," Archeron said. "Not often, but now and again. It depends upon the captain with whom our own captain does business."

"So Terahns are not unfriendly," Lara said. "I wonder why it is you have never really made friends with them, Archeron."

He shook his head. "Trade is our only link, Lara."

As she lay in her bed that night Lara said to her crystal guardian, Ethne, *I am curious as to the land on the other side of this sea.*

Then go there, Ethne replied.

Should I? Lara wondered. *And since when have you begun to give me direction again? You have been insisting I make my own decisions for some time now.*

But this is a new direction for you to take.

Will I be protected if I go to the other side of this sea? Does magic function on that side of the sea, Ethne?

Magic acts everywhere, Ethne responded dryly. *How many times have I told you, Lara, daughter of Ilona and Swiftsword? You are protected. Wherever you go, my child, you are protected.*

Because I have a destiny. And Lara chuckled aloud.

Ethne laughed softly, but agreed. *Aye, because you have a destiny.*

But what is that destiny? Lara demanded once again.

Follow your instincts, my child, and you will learn it. Then the flame in the little crystal flickered and banked low. Ethne had no more to say.

Follow her instincts. Her instincts were not telling her a great deal these days, and she was becoming bored living in King Archeron's palace. She was accustomed to being useful, and she was not useful here. But she was now extremely well rested. Four months had passed since Vartan's murder. The Gathering was now over, and the clan families of the Outlands were preparing for winter. Did the Fiacre miss her? Did her children miss her?

Dillon would, Lara knew. But her daughter? Anoush would have probably forgotten her by now, and would be looking to Noss as her maternal figure. Noss was a good mother. *But I miss my children,* Lara considered. *Sometimes I hate this mysterious destiny that has taken them from me.* She cried softly for a short time, and then slept restlessly.

The next few days she spent most of her time out of doors, for she suddenly could not bear being confined within the palace. She walked the beaches for miles, and then walked back again. But for the waves and the seabirds soaring above her, all was quiet. The grassy dunes above the beach were golden with the cooler weather, but it never became truly cold here along the sea.

One day Lara had ridden several miles from the

palaces and towns of the Coastal Kings when curiosity directed her mount up into the dunes. She rode on as the dunes gave way to a wide swath of green land, and saw beyond it gently rolling hills. All of it was empty of domesticated animal, or people. There wasn't a house or a field to be seen in any direction. Here was certainly land enough for Hetar's burgeoning population. She wondered why it was not being utilized. *Another question for Archeron to answer,* she thought, stopping to gaze all around her. She turned her horse back toward the sea, and rode back to the palace. The day was becoming gray with an impending storm.

Why was it, Lara wondered, that as each day passed she was finding far more questions than answers? She asked Archeron about the fertile lands beyond the beach.

"We do not choose to allow strangers to inhabit our land," he answered her.

"But they are your fellow citizens of Hetar, my lord king," Lara said.

"They are people of the City and the Midlands," Archeron replied. "Hetar's provinces are almost equal in size. If we allowed the overflow from the City and the Midlands to come here we would lose our lands. They would crowd us out. They would want to enter our towns, and they do not understand us so they would cause difficulty. Eventually someone would learn the secret of our trading custom. They might even want to build their own boats, and sail upon the Sea of Sagitta. No. We will not allow our open land to be exploited by the folk from the City."

"The land lies useless. Why not farm it yourselves, and sell what you do not need to the City?" she suggested.

Archeron shook his head. "The land has always been just the land," he told her. "We are not farmers, Lara. We are traders."

Lara was astounded by his attitude. The Coastal Kings possessed great riches, and yet they had never shared these riches, nor did they want to share them. In the years since she had left the City, much had changed if the gossip was to be believed. The government was beginning to encroach upon the forest and the edges of the desert, yet here was all this unused land going to waste. She wondered if all the Coastal Kings felt the same way that Archeron did, but then, he was High King, and perhaps he was right. But it was a question she was going to ask Arcas when he arrived home.

Chapter
4

GAIUS PROSPERO looked across the table at his guest. His thick fingers closed about the stem of the jeweled goblet by his right hand. He lifted it to his lips, and sipped the wine within appreciatively. "So, you depart tomorrow, Arcas."

The young Coastal King nodded. "In the morning."

"And you will not forget your promise to support me in the vote before you go?" Gaius Prospero's cold dark eyes narrowed as he looked at Arcas.

"You have my vote, my lord," Arcas said. "Though the council is disbanding for a recess, I will return when it reopens again."

Gaius Prospero nodded, satisfied. "I am told that the widow of the Outlander, Vartan of the Fiacre, is visiting with your father. It is said he is quite taken with her beauty. Lara is an ambitious girl, and now that her little orgy among the savages is over with,

I suspect she looks to wed higher. The passage of years makes it impossible under our laws to enslave her again. She would even be safe in the City now. But perhaps living by the gentle sea suits her better. An old man could be tempted by such faerie beauty, and her magic could make an elder potent again. If she loved him, she might even give him a child." He smacked his lips appreciatively. "I would have liked to have her, but I could not bring myself to squander half her value just to satisfy my lustful cock." He chuckled.

"Do you have spies everywhere, my lord Gaius?" Arcas asked his host dryly.

"Everywhere," Gaius Prospero agreed with a smirk. "I hear your father and Lara ride each afternoon along the beach. The soft earth would certainly make a good bed."

"It does," Arcas answered, not showing his irritation. "I've taken many a girl in the dunes by the sea, my lord Gaius." Was the smug and power hungry Master of the Merchants suggesting that his father was Lara's lover? The thought that his father might have gotten what he could not have infuriated Arcas. A long time ago Lara was meant to be his personal Pleasure Woman, but that the Head Forester had seen her and paid an obscene sum to possess her. When Arcas had learned of Vartan's death several months back from the ubiquitous Jonah, Gaius Prospero's valued right hand, he had begun to consider the possibility of having Lara for his own again. Once he had told her he would never have kept her as a slave—but that had been a lie. If he could have her, he would imprison her in his apartments and never let her free. She would be only for him. For his pleasure. For his eyes alone.

To consider that his father had gotten there before him was a thought not to be tolerated. Archeron was newly widowed of Arcas's mother. Could he have loved Alina, and been so quick into another woman's bed? Yes, he could, if the woman was Lara! And Gaius Prospero knew it or he wouldn't have said it. Arcas thought the Master of the Merchants had actually enjoyed imparting the information to him. Damn Gaius Prospero to Limbo, he who intended packing the new High Council with his adherents, and having himself elected emperor of Hetar! But the pleasant smile Arcas wore never faltered. Finally he arose.

"I should be getting back to the Council Quarter," he said. "King Balasi and I want to depart early. I will see you in a few weeks, Gaius Prospero. My felicitations to your two wives, the lady Vilia and the lady Anora." Then with a bow he left Gaius Prospero. He did not look back, or raise his hand in farewell.

The Master of the Merchants smiled to himself as his guest departed. He had been unable to resist taunting King Arcas with thoughts of his father and the beautiful half-faerie woman. He knew how very much the younger man desired Lara. When the Winter War of five years ago had ended, and Gaius Prospero had gathered all the information he needed to learn how he had failed to annex the rich mountain region of the Outlands, the Master of the Merchants had discovered that the daughter of the Crusader Knight known as Swiftsword was responsible in great measure for his defeat. It was she who had advised the Outlanders against him. At first he could not believe it. He had been amazed that the exquisite creature he had bought from her father to sell into one of the great Pleasure Houses of the City had become such a skilled warrior and strategist. Once he had lusted after her himself, but now he considered her his enemy. He would have his revenge on her for that earlier defeat, and engineering her husband's death was just the beginning. And yet he wondered, if she came into his life again, would he still desire her?

It had taken five years to regain his popularity among the people. Five years to quiet the outcry against him by his fellow magnates, to calm the leaders and men of the Mercenary Guild. Seven carts piled high with Hetarian dead driven into the heart of the City was not a memory easily erased. And though they had buried those unfortunate dead quickly in mass graves, the stink of their rotting bodies had lingered in the air for days, reminding everyone of just what had happened—and who was responsible.

It hadn't been his fault, he convinced himself. But he had been unable to ride out in the streets for weeks afterwards. On the rare occasions he had ventured out, surrounded by mercenaries paid to protect him, people had cursed him and thrown refuse at him. He could never forget that, nor would he forget those who had turned away from him in those wretched streets, or refused to return his messages. He knew they plotted against him, but most were still fearful of his wealth, which could yet buy death for Gaius

Prospero's enemies. They might hate him, but he still wielded some small power.

The Head Mistress of the Pleasure Mistresses' Guild owed him a great favor for having sent Lara from the City to be sold. She had come to him some months after the Taubyl Trader had taken the faerie girl away and told him so. He had not wanted to see her, but Jonah had convinced him otherwise, reminding him that to lose the lady Gillian's favor was an error he did not want to commit.

"You do not want to lose her allegiance, my lord. There will come a day when you can hold her to account, but now is not the time."

So Gaius Prospero had welcomed the lady Gillian, and offered her refreshments and listened while she apologized to him.

"I know you are angry, Gaius, and disappointed by my decision in the matter of the faerie girl, Lara, but she really would have been too dangerous a possession for any of our Pleasure Houses to hold."

"You have cost me a fortune," he had grumbled at her. "I had to buy Vilia a new cart and horses to match. I had promised her, and had I not purchased them she would have complained, and many would have believed I couldn't afford them. And the girl ended up escaping from the Forest Lords, and in the end has led this Winter War, which has almost destroyed me, Gillian. The monetary loss is bad enough, but worse, my prestige has been threatened."

"Gaius, Gaius," she murmured soothingly. Then she had come and sat in his lap and begun kissing him with slow, hot kisses. Her tongue slipped into his mouth to play with his. One arm curled about his neck, while her free hand found the opening in his robes, and began to fondle his sex. When it was rigid the lady Gillian positioned herself so that she might absorb his fleshy cock into her body. "There now, Gaius, isn't that nice?" she purred at him. "I know taking pleasures cannot really make up for your loss, but I want you to know that despite everything that has happened I still consider you my dearest friend, and I will always ally myself with you in whatever endeavor you pursue. And I will advise the Guild of the Pleasure Women to follow my lead as well." Her arms wrapped about his neck, and she tightened the muscles within her sheath around him.

Gaius Prospero groaned with pure delight. When she leaned back he reached out and fondled her large breasts beneath her gown. "Gillian, you are an amazing woman," he told her. "Now ride me to ecstasy, you delicious bitch, and I will consider forgiving you."

And so she had, and while she did Jonah watched with both amusement and interest. The Head Mistress was a powerful friend to have, and Gaius Prospero would have been foolish to make her an enemy. After she had gone, Gaius Prospero had admitted as much to Jonah. With her allegiance assured, Gaius Prospero set about rebuilding his alliances.

He soothed the Guild of Mercenaries and the Order of the Crusader Knights with promises for the future. They would take the Outlands, but first they must rebuild their forces. It would take time and careful preparation, Gaius Prospero told them. Hetar would not fail again. They had moved too quickly before. This time, he would put all his own personal resources at their disposal, and Hetar would triumph.

With Jonah by his side, Gaius Prospero had worked out just how the acreage belonging to the Outlands would be divided up. Jonah cleverly divined just whose aid was most needed by his master. They were given their choice of land or slaves. And of course, the Midland farmers must be given land as well. Each year the old farms produced less, for the earth was tired, and this condition was causing a scarcity of foodstuffs. New farms needed to be opened up, new orchards planted, new pastures sown for grazing.

It had been difficult for Gaius Prospero in those early days following Hetar's defeat.

But Gaius Prospero had managed to keep his head above the water in those dark days. And much of his success was due to his former slave, Jonah. Jonah was clever, and he always looked ahead. Although he prided himself on his own mental skills, Gaius Prospero was not above using the abilities of others, and in Jonah he recognized an ambitious man. Better to have that man on his side. He had offered Jonah his freedom on the condition he remain with him for a term of ten years. It was not a verbal agreement, but one that was written down, and signed by both parties. Jonah even insisted on paying his former master the price of a sturdy male slave in order to make certain the transaction was completely legal and could not later be challenged. Two copies were made, one to be held by Gaius Prospero, the other by Jonah— although the Master of the Merchants did not know where his former slave kept his copy.

And so, working together they had struggled to rebuild Gaius Prospero's reputation. It had taken longer than the Master of the Merchants had thought it would, and it had certainly cost him a great deal more in hard coin than he had thought to spend. He had opened his storehouses to feed the many poor in the City during the winter months. He had given free entertainments in the public stadium, and held races open to the public with prizes that while unimportant to him were considered generous by the people. And he had taken a second wife in a public spectacle that delighted the City and had capped his return to favor.

Usually a magnate wanting another woman to wed divorced his current wife. But Hetarian law allowed a man to have three wives at one time. When Gaius Prospero had married Vilia he had divorced his childless first wife, Hedda. Vilia was quite adamant in that she would not play second wife to another woman, and Hedda was more than willing to accept a generous settlement to let him go. Only later did he discover she had been cuckolding him with a younger man. But Vilia, beautiful and already burgeoning with their first child, soothed his ego with caresses and kisses.

Gaius Prospero knew, however, that Vilia would not divorce him so he might wed another woman. And divorcing Vilia who was the mother of his four children would have been a ruinous proposition. Particularly given the expense involved in regaining his reputation. When he had told her he planned on taking a second wife she had, to his great surprise, laughed.

"Do so," she said to him.

She loosened her gown, revealing her wonderful breasts. He had always been fascinated by her bosom, and he could not take his eyes from it now. "You do not mind?" Unable to help himself he reached out and began to fondle her two full breasts.

"No," she told him. Her tongue snaked out to moisten her lips.

Suddenly he was suspicious. "Have you taken a lover, Vilia?" he demanded, his fingers digging into her flesh.

Again she laughed. "I am not Hedda, Gaius. You are all the husband I want. But if the truth be known your appetites are too great for me to satisfy. I am happy to let another woman carry some of the burden. It is your Pleasure Woman, Anora, is it not?" She smiled as his hands became gentle again. "I imagine you are tired having to constantly go to her only to find her engaged with another, when it would be so much simpler to have her here with us."

He nodded, amazed at the depth of her understanding.

"You must make the wedding a great public entertainment. To take a Pleasure Woman, buy her freedom and then wed her will but cap your return to popularity, husband. I shall welcome her before the masses, and we will provide a celebratory feast for all in the City," Vilia said. "At the end of the evening I shall lead her myself to the bridal chamber, and we shall offer gifts to all the children who are born nine months to the day of your wedding to Anora."

Gaius Prospero had been astounded by Vilia's

cooperation and her clever suggestions. He had rewarded her by putting her on her back then and there and using her lustily. He would never divorce Vilia now, he decided. She was a perfect first wife—and far too valuable an ally.

Vilia had been true to her word, arranging a great public celebration of his marriage to Anora to welcome this new wife. The Master of the Merchants had never known such utter bliss in his home life. The two women even conspired to entertain his lusts together now and again. He was amazed, and more than pleased by their cooperation. He had gold. His lustful desires were constantly and well satisfied. There was nothing left for him to desire but complete power, and it was now within his reach.

His clever plan to assassinate Vartan of the Fiacre had been genius. He had learned of the jealousy harbored against the Lord of the Fiacre by his younger brother. The brother was, if his spies were to be believed, unfit to rule. He was a young man filled with a sense of his own importance, which was based on naught. The Master of the Merchants secretly contacted Adon's ambitious wife, Elin, having first sent her a faeriepost to arrange a meeting place with her in the Outlands. He had flattered and cajoled her until the stupid creature had been convinced to do his bidding. She, in turn, persuaded Adon that the lordship of the Fiacre should be his and not his brother's. She prevailed upon her husband to do Gaius Prospero's will, assuring him that he would be both rewarded and supported by this powerful man. And then she gave her husband the dagger with the poisoned tip that he was to use to accomplish his task. When he hesitated, Elin nagged Adon until finally he acceded to her wishes.

Now with Vartan dead, Gaius Prospero's first order of business when spring came again would be to invade the Outlands once more. Vartan and Lara had been the heart of the Outlands' resistance. With the Lord of the Fiacre dead and his wife driven away by Adon, the Outlands would fall into Hetar's hands. Oh, there had been a message to the High Council that an Outlands lord named Rendor was now their council head, but this fellow, whoever he was, would not have Vartan's influence. And he would be the first of the lords to be executed when Hetar claimed the Outlands.

In the meantime, it but remained for Hetar's High Council to make Gaius Prospero their emperor once the winter recess was over. Emperor Gaius I—he liked the sound of it, the Master of the Merchants considered with a cold smile. Once, long ago in its very distant past, Hetar had been ruled by a line of emperors. It had been one land then, and not divided into the four provinces. It would be one land again, and the Forest Lords, the Shadow Princes of the desert, the Coastal Kings, and the Midlands governor, Squire Dareh, would pledge him fealty and do homage to him. The Crusader Knights would be his personal army, and the Mercenaries would fight under them and police the land for their emperor. And they would all obey his will, for what Gaius Prospero desired was for the good of Hetar. The emperor would be Hetar incarnate.

The touch of a gentle hand on his sleeve startled him. "What?" he demanded.

"It is late," the lady Vilia said. "Your guest has gone, Gaius, and yet here you sit while your two wives eagerly await your coming. Anora says you must be punished for your neglect of us. She says your bottom must be whipped most thoroughly, Gaius. Come." She drew him up, and led him from the dining chamber.

Gaius Prospero's heart began to thump with excitement. He had first been drawn to Anora because of her skills at punishment, and she had taught Vilia some of her art.

"Will you both beat me?" he asked hopefully. He loved it when together they plied their custom-made whips on his bare flesh. Each of the dozen thin strands of leather flowing from the carved wood handle was tied with several knots. The knots bit into his tender skin, arousing him greatly.

"Yes," Vilia said to his delight. "You are deserving of both of us tonight, Gaius. I hope you will be up to the task ahead," she murmured with distinct meaning.

Gaius Prospero's breath was already coming in short bursts as his emotions were hotly kindled. Could his life be any better? he thought happily. Everything was happening as he had planned it. Vartan was dead. He would soon be emperor. And tomorrow, Arcas would return to the coast to do battle with his own father over the beautiful Lara, who would then be forced to seek refuge elsewhere. Arcas was doing his bidding, and he did not even realize it.

And while the Master of the Merchants gloated

with the success of his schemes, Arcas lay awake in his bed in the Council Quarter considering all that Gaius Prospero had said that evening. Alone, his emotions cooling, he considered that the wily Gaius could very well have been baiting him. He was a very manipulative man who did nothing not to his own advantage. Arcas's father, Archeron, was an elder. Surely he was not truly interested in Lara as a lover. Yet Lara's faerie magic could possibly convince Archeron that he did love her. Was his father potent enough to create another son? Would Lara's faerie heart give him that son? Arcas tossed restlessly. The dawn could not come quick enough.

In the years since the Winter War the Shadow Princes had made an arrangement using their own magic that allowed the diplomats from the other provinces to go and come from the City immediately. Times had changed, and these representatives could no longer spend long days of travel between their own homes and the City. Each of the council members was assigned a time, and then transported to his own province on the assigned day. The last to go were the Shadow Princes, and the transport was closed by the final traveler. This prevented misuse of the Shadow Princes' magic.

Arcas and his fellow king, Balasi, arrived shortly after dawn. They would enter the transport together, but each would reappear in their own home. With a nod of thanks to the Shadow Prince in charge Arcas stepped within the conveyance, and a moment later found himself in his father's Great Hall. He nodded pleasantly to the servants sweeping the hall. "Good morning," he said.

"Welcome home, my lord king," they chorused.

"Where is my father?"

"It is his custom of late to break his fast with the lady Lara, my lord king," a servant answered. "You will find him in her apartments in the guest wing."

So, Arcas thought, irritated, *he eats the morning meal with her. Is that after he has spent a night of passion in her arms?* He hurried to the part of the palace to which he had been directed. An attentive servant flung open the door to the apartment. Arcas followed the sound of laughter through the chamber and out onto the terrace.

"Arcas!" His father arose from the table smiling, and embraced him warmly.

"Father," he said, but his eyes rested upon Lara. She was even more beautiful, if such a thing was possible. He returned his father's embrace, then releasing him said, "Greetings, widow of Vartan." He quickly caught her hand and kissed it.

Lara withdrew her fingers from his grasp. "Welcome home, King Arcas," she replied. "I know how very much your father has been awaiting your return."

"Sit down! Sit down!" Archeron invited his son. "Eat! If I know you, Arcas, you rushed to get home, and have had nothing since last night's dinner."

"Which I ate with Gaius Prospero," Arcas volunteered. He reached for the bread, and tore a large piece off the loaf on which he spread fresh butter. A servant put several hard-boiled eggs, a bunch of grapes and a slice of salted meat upon his plate. Another servant filled the goblet by Arcas's hand with sweet frine.

"And how is the wily Master of the Merchants?" Lara inquired.

"Soon to be created emperor," Arcas said softly.

"Your High Council is made up of fools that they would give Gaius Prospero such power," Lara replied bluntly. "He will abuse it, for he cannot help himself. His ambition knows no bounds, my lord king."

"She is right," Archeron spoke up now. "If we must all answer to Gaius Prospero as the supreme ruler of Hetar then what will happen to us, my son? Will our secret remain safe then?" The older man looked very concerned.

"You have told her?" Arcas demanded. Then he laughed. "Of course you have told her. You are bewitched by her. All men are."

"Your father told me because I asked what was on the other side of the sea," Lara explained. "Any stranger remaining in your kingdom for a time would wonder, Arcas. There are no manufactories here, so from where do your luxury goods come? You are the most distant province from the City. Few except the Taubyl Traders have ventured here, and they remain but long enough to sell their goods and purchase yours."

"You are clever as well as beautiful," Arcas replied.

"And you are as bold as you ever were," Lara noted. She then concentrated upon her meal. This young Coastal King had irritated her the first time she met him, and it would seem that nothing had changed.

"Hetar will be stronger under a single ruler," Arcas told them.

"I think you are wrong," Lara said. "A High Council with all the provinces represented gives a greater voice to the people of Hetar. And there is no danger to us."

"The Outlands presents a danger," Arcas quickly said. "They must be subdued."

"The Outlands present no danger to Hetar," Lara snapped. "That is Gaius Prospero's excuse to take what is not his. Do you think we have not heard that the City is riddled with poor? That the soil in the Midlands no longer produces enough crops to feed the people? The farmers have pushed into the forest, felling trees and clearing the land to plant. That must sit well with the Forest Lords. And Gaius Prospero has even dared to venture into the sandy grass of the desert as well. Do not tell me that his nefarious plans for war are because Hetar is threatened, for it is not!"

"How can you know these things?" Arcas wanted to know.

"Do you think Gaius Prospero is the only one with spies?" Lara taunted him.

He laughed. "I suppose not," he said. "This is a high-stakes game that is being played. The future of Hetar depends upon who wins."

"You have land here in your own kingdom that lies fallow and unused," Lara said to him. "I have ridden across it on many an afternoon. Why will you not share your lands with those who feed Hetar? You would not have to give it away, or even sell it. You could lease it to the farmers, and those who did not produce would not have their leases renewed. And the purpose of the land would not be for settlement, but only for growing. The Midlands farmers coming here could not bring their families. They would only work the land. They would pay their leases yearly, and then from their profits give Hetar's government a quarter share."

"Lease our land?" Arcas looked horrified. "It is ours. We do not want strangers coming onto it."

"You would rather involve Hetar in another war to try and take land from the Outland clan families?"

"The Outlands are populated by savages," he said. "They do not deserve the land. It should belong to Hetar."

"You know you speak foolishness, Arcas," his father said. "You are more aware than most on Hetar that the Outlands are populated by peaceful people who simply wish to be allowed to live their lives as they see fit, and as their customs dictate."

"I will grant you Rendor is a fine fellow," Arcas admitted, "but as for the others—" He stopped.

Lara was shaking her head. "Did you find my husband a savage, Arcas?" she asked him. "I found more civility and kindness among the Fiacre than among the good people of Hetar. Did not the mercenary Wilmot tell the High Council the truth of the Outlands when he spoke before them? For Gaius Prospero to persist in the fantasy of savagery, and to use it as an excuse to invade the Outlands, is just wrong!"

"You speak treason," he said in a threatening voice. "You are Hetarian."

"No, I am Lara—widow of Vartan, daughter of

Swiftsword, half-mortal, half-faerie. I was born in the faerie realm and raised in the City, but I found my greatest happiness in the Outlands," she told him. "I use the small magic I possess only for good, Arcas. I will speak against intolerance and injustice while there is breath in my body."

"How can someone so obviously meant for pleasure debate on such things?" he asked her.

"You are hopeless," she told him.

He did not understand her, Arcas thought irritably, but he found he still wanted her. Yet in the days that followed she grew no warmer toward him despite his many compliments. But her sweetness toward his father seemed to grow. And as Gaius Prospero had told him, Archeron and Lara rode out together almost every afternoon. They did not ask him to join them, and on one or two occasions he had suggested going with them his father had said no. Arcas had been amazed by the refusal. Was Gaius Prospero right? Was his father Lara's lover? Still, Arcas could find no other evidence of such a relationship. And he had easily learned that his father spent his nights in his own bed, and not in Lara's arms. This knowledge made him want her even more. Perhaps she was one of those women a man must force to his will. Of course! That would have been the way the Fiacre lord, Vartan, obtained her. Lara was a strong woman. She needed a strong man to tell her what to do, and how to do it. Then she would melt with passion.

IN THE DARK of an early winter's night Arcas made his way to Lara's chamber. He entered quietly, making

his way to her bedside. Flinging off his chamber robe
he gazed down at her sleeping form. She was exquisite. Perfectly made with lovely breasts, and just the
faintest swell of belly. Her skin was like white silk.
Her golden hair like thistledown. His male member
was hard with his deep longing for her. He was about
to climb into her bed and take her for his own when
suddenly her eyes opened. Even in the dimly lit room
he could see the icy green glare.

"Get out!" she said quietly.

Arcas was about to bluster a refusal when he
became painfully aware that his male organ had suddenly gone limp, and was shrinking at a most alarm-
ing rate.

"Get out," Lara repeated, "or do you wish me to
make it disappear entirely, Arcas?" Her cold voice
matched her cold eyes.

The Coastal King turned and fled, not even bothering to gather up his robe. Looking at it, Lara pointed
a finger, and the garment disappeared. Then turning over she went back to sleep again. But when the
morning came, she found she was very angry. She
would not tell Archeron of his son's breach of good
manners. It would hurt the man who was sheltering
her so generously, and drive a wedge between father
and son. She could not do that. *It is time for me to
move on,* she thought. But where? She listened to the
roaring of the waves as they pounded upon the beach
below.

To Lara's surprise Arcas sought her out that morning. He knelt before her.

"Forgive me," he said quietly. Then he sighed. "I

cannot help but desire you, Lara, and I have presented my case badly. When we first met I offended you, and now I have done it again. I apologize."

"What is it you want of me?" she asked him quietly. "I only share pleasures with those whom I choose, Arcas."

"And I am not one of those fortunate, am I?"

"Vartan is gone from me but six months, Arcas. I am not ready yet to love again, or even share my body again. I am sorry," Lara told him. "Get up now."

He arose. "Do you deny that you are my father's lover?" he asked half-angrily.

"Yes, I do," Lara told him. "Your father is my dear friend, but he is not my lover, nor is he ever likely to be. Is that why you did what you did, Arcas? Because you were jealous?" Her tone with him had softened.

Hearing it he nodded, lowering his head as if in shame. The bitch had refused him twice now. He would have his revenge on her. He had but to find a weakness in her character he might exploit. "Will you forgive me?" he repeated.

"Yes," she told him. He could never know she did it for his father's sake, and not his. Arcas was a fool. She had known it the first time they met, and he had but confirmed her belief with his behavior last night. "It will please your father we no longer quarrel."

"Yes," he answered her. "We should be friends, and allies. My father tells me that you are interested in our trading partners from the Dominion." He smiled.

"I am!" she said enthusiastically. "Tell me what they are like, Arcas? What do they look like? Do their women travel with them? Are there faeries in the sea?"

He laughed. "Would you like to see for yourself, Lara? I had planned to captain one of my ships to the meeting place while I was home. Travel with me, and you can meet some Terahns for yourself. And I swear to behave myself," he concluded with a rueful smile.

Could she trust him? she wondered. Her instinct warned her no, but instinct warred with her curiosity. "Perhaps another time," she said. "I have never traveled upon this sea of yours, and I am quite in awe of it. It is a powerful force, Arcas. I don't think I am yet ready, or even brave enough to sail upon it."

"Then another time," he responded. "I will take a second voyage before I leave again for the City. Mayhap you will come with me then, Lara. It is not because you are still angry with me, I hope."

"Nay, of course not," she lied facilely. And she even gave him a smile.

He departed the following day, and returned ten days later. She enjoyed the time Arcas was away. She did not like the man, and he had obviously become an ally of Gaius Prospero, which did not please Archeron at all. They had quarreled the night before Arcas had gone to sea. Archeron feared a more centralized authority could endanger the monopoly the Coastal Kings had on the secret of their sea trade. But Arcas had assured his sire that he was not that big a fool.

"Do you think I want us powerless?" he demanded of Archeron.

"Of course not, but if the secret is made known we may have no choice, Arcas."

"We are the only ones who can build sailing vessels or man them," Arcas responded. "The magnates in the City have no talent for that, nor a way to accomplish such a task, my father."

"The wood we need to build new ships we have always purchased from the Forest Lords," Archeron said. "Now the City allows the Midlands to encroach into the forests.

"Gaius Prospero plans a new invasion of the Outlands. Once he has accomplished that what is to prevent him from invading our lands, building his own ships and launching them into the sea? My brother kings and I will not cooperate in this planned incursion into the Outlands, Arcas. And do you truly believe that the Shadow Princes will allow an army to cross their territory? So your powerful friends must either push into the mountains once more, or go through us. Given what happened last time what do you think they will do, Arcas? And will you help them?"

"The clan families in the mountains of the Outlands were weakened by the Winter War. They were easy to subdue the first time, and will be easy once again," Arcas answered his father.

"The Outlands will not be easy to subdue this time, Arcas, and if you think they will be you are badly mistaken," Lara joined the discussion.

"What do you know of it?" he asked her.

"What I know is not for your ears, Arcas, for you would immediately send off a faeriepost to Gaius Prospero. You have, I note, kept in touch with the City since your return." She smiled sweetly, teasing him,

"Unless, of course, your correspondence is poetry being sent to a favored Pleasure Woman."

He laughed aloud, but neither confirmed or denied her suspicions. And then he had gone the following morning, and Lara had been glad to see him go. But Archeron was yet concerned by his son's attitude, and fretted to Lara.

"If only he would choose a wife. But each year on his birthday he admires the young women presented to him, but chooses none to wed. He is older than I was when I chose Alina. If he does not marry, and beget children our line will die out," Archeron said. He looked at Lara. "My son admires you greatly."

"I know, but he is not the man for me, my lord king," Lara answered him quietly. "And I yet mourn Vartan. Faerie women, even half-blooded ones, do not love lightly."

"But he does respect you, Lara. Perhaps if you would remind him of his duty to the Coastal Kings he would see reason. He told me that he invited you on this voyage, but that you refused him. I thought you were interested in the sea, and the Dominion beyond it. That cannot have changed."

"I was fearful of traveling upon those rolling waters," Lara lied.

"You need not be. I will take you out in my own small boat rather than riding out this afternoon. You will see you have nothing to fear," Archeron said.

That afternoon Lara took her first voyage upon the Sea of Sagitta, in a small boat with snow-white sails that King Archeron manned himself. She found the motion of the sea, the wind on her face and in her hair, exhilarating. And by afternoon's end, to her utter amazement, she was controlling the small vessel herself. Each day after that Archeron and Lara sailed his small boat together. She realized that she could no longer use the excuse of her fear of the sea to avoid a voyage with Arcas, yet still she did not trust him. But Archeron pleaded with her to accompany his son when he sailed forth again. Arcas was happiest, his father said, out upon the sea. She would remind him of his obligations to his own kind, and he would hopefully choose a wife and forget Gaius Prospero's great ambitions. Nothing must change. The Coastal Kingdom must remain the way it had ever been.

And Lara agreed because she could not offend this man who had been such a gracious host to her. She could not tell him that his son was a lustful and ambitious man who would do only what was best for Arcas. Besides, it was a short voyage, Archeron explained. She would sail to the meeting place, the cargoes would be exchanged and they would return. Archeron would tell his son to invite the Terahn to a meal so she might speak with him, and learn firsthand of the Dominion. Then they would return home.

Arcas returned with his ship's hold filled with luxury goods. He would make another voyage in a week's time.

"Lara will go with you this time," Archeron told his son.

"You are no longer fearful of the sea?" Arcas asked dryly.

"I have taught her to sail," his father replied.

"I find the sea beautiful, and I very much like

riding upon it," Lara said. "I shall enjoy meeting the
Terahns, my lord king." And as she spoke, Lara realized her concerns had vanished. Besides, what could
Arcas do to her out at sea? She would travel with
both Andraste and Verica as always. She wished she
had her horse, Dasras, though she could only imagine Dasras's opinion of the sea. It would not be a good
one, Lara thought with a small smile. She had been
wise to leave him with the Fiacre.

Several days later they prepared to depart. Arcas
had turned over the master's cabin to her although
he told her he would join her for meals there. The
quarters were spacious, located in the rear of the
vessel with a large window overlooking the sea. The
ship itself was sturdy, and built of a fragrant wood
that perfumed the air most pleasantly. It was fitted
with large square creamy silk sails, and flew multicolored pendants from its masts. Each of the flags
flying indicated whose ship it was, and the cargo it
carried, Archeron explained to Lara as they watched
the vessel being loaded with large baskets of salt and
silver boxes of pearls. Finally he escorted her aboard
his son's ship, and bid her farewell.

"You are bringing your sword and staff with you?"
Archeron asked her, curious.

"I would never leave them alone," Lara told him as
she lay them on a table in the great cabin. "They are
a part of me."

Archeron kissed her on both cheeks. "I will see
you when you return. I shall be interested to hear your
opinion of the Terahns you meet." He bowed, leaving
her, and went ashore.

Lara went out upon the deck as they set sail. Being upon this large ship was very different from the smaller one in which she had first traversed the sea. She felt much safer. She reached for the crystal about her neck. *Well,* she told Ethne, *we are off upon a new adventure, my friend.* The tiny flame in the crystal flared up.

Now the real adventure begins.

Do not speak to me in riddles. You know how much I dislike it.

Look upon Hetar well, my child, Ethne responded.

Will I not see it again? Lara asked. Her heart was beginning to beat rapidly.

One day, but not soon, Ethne said. *There are other places you must be to accomplish what you need to accomplish, my child.*

Riddles again, Lara chuckled. *I have a destiny. I am protected.*

I am glad you remember it, Ethne murmured mischievously.

I cannot forget it, for you will not let me, Lara told her guardian.

Trust only yourself, Ethne warned her, serious again.

I do not trust Arcas, Lara answered. *But I could not find a way to avoid this voyage. I did try. Should I leap from this vessel and swim ashore while I can?*

This journey is meant to be, but Arcas will betray you, Ethne said.

Lara nodded.

Arcas now joined her as Lara stood leaning against

the rail, watching the coast slowly recede. "Are you getting your sea legs?" he asked her.

"Sea legs?" She turned a puzzled glance to him.

"Are you becoming used to the motion of the ship?" he repeated with a chuckle.

"Yes," she answered him. "It is very different, however, than sailing your father's little boat along the shore."

"He taught you to sail the boat?" Arcas was interested.

"I wanted to learn. Your sea is so different from anything I have ever known. I would wager that most who live in the City have no knowledge of the sea," Lara told him. "It is quite magnificent. I hope we will have no storms. The storms I have seen roll into your coast from this sea can be frightening."

"My ship can weather any storms," he assured her. "I quite enjoy riding out the fierceness. To outmaneuver the wind and the waves is exhilarating."

"I will accept your word for it, Arcas," Lara told him with a small smile.

But the weather around them remained fair. Her first night at sea Lara slept surprisingly well. On her second day she watched great fish who escorted their ship through the waves, leaping gracefully alongside the vessel. At dinner that evening she asked Arcas a question that had been in her mind all day.

"Where are the men who sail this ship with you? I have seen few."

"The ship sails itself," Arcas explained. "Did my father not tell you?"

"It is alive?" Lara queried him.

Arcas nodded. "Each of our ships is imbued with a powerful sea spirit who guides it, and keeps it safe. The few men you have seen with me are here to keep the vessel company, and to load and unload the cargoes. And I have a single steward who cooks and serves us. The ship does everything else. I tell it where I wish to travel, and it takes me there. Of course the Terahns are not aware of this. I do not believe they have magic, or if they do, we have seen no evidence of it."

"Are they not suspicious that there are so few men aboard your ships?" Lara asked him. "Surely they must have noticed."

"The ship knows how to protect itself," Arcas explained. "When we reach our meeting point it works its magic, and the Terahns see a full complement of sailors aboard. Some of these magical creatures even help with the cargo transfer so the time involved is exactly what it should be. If I am familiar with the captain who meets us I will ask him to join us for a meal. This way you may meet a Terahn for yourself. I believe my father told me that was the purpose for your accompanying me."

"Yes, I should like to meet a Terahn," Lara said.

On the third day of their voyage Lara again sat out upon the ship's deck and watched the waves and the iridescent fish who accompanied them, leaping and arcing from the sea. She found them very beautiful. Again that night she peppered Arcas with questions.

"You say the ship is inhabited by a powerful sea spirit. Are these other beings who live beneath the waters? Are there Sea Faeries like our Forest Faeries, our Mountain Faeries and the Peris of the desert? And how did you get a powerful sea spirit to take your vessel upon itself? Do you know its name? Is it a male or female spirit?"

"There has always been a compact between the Coastal Kings and the sea spirits," Arcas explained. "We do not know how it came about as we do not know how our trade with the Terahns began. It has just always been. When a ship is built it is then set upon the waters, and we invite one of the sea spirits to come inhabit it, and make the vessel its home. They have never rejected us. Our people are blessed by the sea. As for faeries, I do not know if any exist beneath the sea. There are ancient tales claiming a civilization there, but I have no knowledge of such a thing."

"Magic is everywhere," Lara told him.

"We will reach the meeting ground early tomorrow," Arcas told her.

"I will be up early," she assured him, relieved that his behavior had been good during their voyage. He had not touched her even casually, or made suggestive remarks to her. He had behaved well, and yet Lara sensed her instincts about Arcas were correct. He was absolutely not to be trusted. Given the opportunity, he would betray her. But to whom? And how?

She was up and dressed early. Out upon the deck she watched as the Terahn ship, quite similar to that on which she stood, approached. Their vessel already had what Arcas called a sea anchor out to keep them in place, and their white sails had been lowered, rolled and tied to keep them from blowing in the wind. The Terahn ship reached them, and took the same measures. Two wide planks with wooden handrails were placed between the two vessels, and immediately the cargo began being transferred between them. Lara watched fascinated as sailors from the Terahn ship unloaded their cargo onto Arcas's ship, and an equal number of men from their ship hurried back and forth across the second gangway with cargo from the Hetarian ship.

By midafternoon the transfer of cargo had been completed and one of the gangplanks removed. Arcas did know the captain of the Terahn ship, and, as promised, had invited him to dine with them. He arrived in the hour before the sunset. Arcas welcomed him, and drew Lara forward to introduce her.

"This is the lady Lara, a famed leader of our world," Arcas said. "Lara, this is Captain Corrado of the Dominion."

The captain bowed and kissed Lara's hand.

"I am pleased to meet you, Captain Corrado," Lara told him.

"I had been told Hetarian women spoke," the Terahn said. "Our women do not." He then turned away from her, and began to speak with Arcas.

Lara was very surprised, but she had wanted to meet a Terahn. Their women did not speak? How odd. Perhaps that was why he had been so dismissive of her. Women were obviously of little importance in the Dominion. Yet without women, who would birth men? She wondered if anyone had ever considered asking a Terahn male that pertinent question.

The meal was served, and the two men continued to converse. Lara had to admit that Arcas did try to include her in the conversation, but Captain Corrado would each time answer Arcas while ignoring Lara. She wasn't learning anything about the Terahns except that the men were horribly rude. She almost signed aloud with her relief as the meal came to an end.

"Captain Corrado has brought us a fine Terahn sweet wine to complete our meal," Arcas said, and he pointed to indicate a little stone bottle.

The steward uncorked the bottle and poured the liquid into little silver goblets, setting them upon a tray and passing them about. First to Captain Corrado, then to Arcas, and finally to Lara.

"Let us raise a toast to the friendship between Hetar and the Dominion," Arcas said, and he raised his goblet. "To friendship, and continued trade!"

"To friendship and trade," his companions echoed.

Lara sipped from her goblet.

"No, lady, with this particular wine one must drink it down immediately," Captain Corrado spoke directly to her, and then he demonstrated by quaffing his goblet.

He had actually addressed her. Lara was surprised. Perhaps she had misjudged him. Arcas had downed the contents of his goblet. Good manners required that Lara do the same, although she found the vintage a bit too sweet for her taste. It was her last memory for some hours to come.

The two men looked at the girl who had collapsed upon the floor of the cabin. Arcas looked to his steward. "Carry her across to Captain Corrado's vessel. His steward will tell you where to put the lady." He then turned back to his companion. "You will tell the Dominus that she is a gift from King Archeron, Corrado."

"Not from you, Arcas?" The Terahn was curious.

"She is fond of my father. When she is told he betrayed her it will give her pain. I want her to feel that pain," Arcas replied.

"You hate her, don't you?" the Terahn said.

"I wanted to love her," Arcas admitted.

"But she rejected you, and this is your revenge. Well, the Dominus enjoys women with spirit, and I imagine this one will give him great pleasure. She is incredibly beautiful."

"She's not a virgin," Arcas felt he should say.

"Of course not," the Terahn replied. "No one that beautiful would remain a virgin. Who is she, Arcas? Tell me her history. The Dominus will be interested."

"Her father was a mercenary who became a Crusader Knight. Her mother is faerie. She was sold as a slave to advance her father's career, but escaped into the Outlands, a lawless area, and married one of their leaders. When he was killed she returned to Hetar. As her husband was respected by his kind, so was she," Arcas told the Terahn captain. "There is little else to tell."

"It's enough of a story," Captain Corrado replied. He arose from the table. "I will be on my way now. What do you intend telling your father, Arcas?"

"I have not decided yet," came his answer. "Perhaps I shall say the weather grew rough and she fell overboard. Despite our efforts she was lost to the sea.

It is a plausible excuse, Corrado. My father is a simple man and will accept such a tale."

The two men went out onto the deck, shook hands, and the Terahn crossed over to his ship again. No sooner had he stepped from the gangway than it was drawn back to the Hetarian vessel. He turned, but Arcas had already disappeared back into his cabin. Captain Corrado wondered what had induced him to leave the deck so quickly.

Entering the master's cabin Arcas looked about for Lara's sword and staff. They would be valuable to him, and she would certainly have no use for them now. But both of the objects that he sought were gone. He called to his steward. "Where are the sword and staff belonging to the lady?" he asked the man.

"Why they are there in that corner, my lord king," the steward said. He walked to where he had directed his master, and his glance was puzzled. "They were here. I saw them when I passed by to take the lady to the Terahn ship, my lord king."

Arcas swore under his breath. "They have followed her," he said. Why had he not thought to enclose them in a cabinet this morning? The damned staff and sword were magic, but if they had not seen her taken away they would have been his. He swore again, but then he said to the steward, "Tell them to raise the anchor. It's time for us to return home."

"Yes, my lord king," the steward said.

"It is unfortunate that the lady Lara tumbled over into the sea during a bout of rough weather, isn't it?" Arcas told his servant.

"Yes, my lord king. Most sad," the steward answered meekly, and he backed from the cabin bowing.

She could have been his queen, Arcas thought. Now she would be a pleasure slave for the Dominus of Terah. And the Terahns were not known for indulging their women. But it had been her choice. She could have been his queen!

Chapter
5

UPON AWAKING, Lara knew she was no longer on Arcas's ship. She lay on her back in a small enclosed space no bigger than a cabinet. She could feel the motion of the sea all around her. She reached for her crystal and was comforted by the feel of it between her slender fingers. *The adventure has begun,* she said silently to Ethne.

As her green eyes grew used to the dim enclosure Lara was able to make out a narrow door. Fumbling about she found a door handle and jiggled it. To her surprise the door immediately sprang open to reveal a large cabin well lit by the sunlight outside its bow window. Sitting up Lara swung her legs over the bunk where she had been lying, and stepped into the cabin. She quietly closed the cabinet door behind her. She needed no one to tell her that she was on the Terahn vessel. For now the best choice she could make was to remain exactly where she was. Captain Corrado would come eventually, and she would learn what she needed to know.

Spying a tray upon a small table she walked over to it. It held a short squat decanter of liquid, two small carved stone cups and a bowl of fruit. Lara uncorked the decanter and spilled some of the liquid into a cup. Putting it to her lips she smiled and drank it down. It was a light and fragrant wine. She filled the cup and, taking a peach from the bowl, settled herself in the cushioned seat that was built into the bow window. From the position of the sun it was obvious she had slept many hours into the morning of the next day. And there was nothing but blue sky reflected in the deep blue waters of the sea around them. Now and again she saw groups of the arcing jumping fish that she had seen from the deck of Arcas's ship, but nothing else. They were alone upon the sea.

Why, she wondered, had Arcas betrayed her into the hands of the Terahn captain?

Because, she reasoned to herself, she was meant to enter the Terahn Dominion. But to what purpose? It would be so much easier to live out her destiny if she knew what that destiny was. She had never liked riddles, and yet it seemed her whole life, from the moment she had departed the City, had been one riddle after another. She turned as the door to the cabin opened. A young boy scurried in, giving her a quick look with his wide dark eyes. He handed her a plate upon which was a thick slice of bread and a wedge of cheese. Then, turning, he hurried off.

"Thank you," Lara called after him.

The boy stopped and turned a face to her that was rigid with surprise. Then without a word he ran from the cabin.

Lara shrugged, and, after pouring herself another cup of the wine, began to eat the bread and cheese. When she had finished her meal she looked about, and saw a basin and pitcher stowed carefully in a small cranny. She poured water from the pitcher into the basin, and washed her hands and face using a small cloth she found by the ewer. Then she went back to her seat in the bow window and continued to watch the sea sparkling in the afternoon sunshine. There wasn't a cloud in the bright blue sky.

In midafternoon the door to the cabin opened again, and Captain Corrado entered. "How long have you been awake?" he asked her.

"Since morning," Lara said. "The wine was drugged, but how?"

"The servant was instructed to pass the tray to Arcas and to me first. We knew which goblet contained the sleeping draught," he explained.

"Of course," Lara answered him. "'Twas cleverly done, Captain Corrado."

"Are you not afraid?" he asked.

"Of what?" Lara replied.

"You have been betrayed by King Archeron, and sent into bondage across the sea to another strange land," Captain Corrado said.

"Archeron did not deceive me, Captain. He has always been a friend to the Outlands. And Arcas is foolish to believe that by telling me, I should lose all hope. Hope of what? I am here upon your ship now because it is meant that I be here. What lies did he tell you about me? But no matter—I shall tell you my history myself. Will you not sit down and allow me to offer you some of your most excellent wine?"

He was fascinated. He nodded his agreement, watching her closely as she poured the wine and handed him the cup. Then he listened as she quietly and succinctly told him her tale. She was the most beautiful creature he had ever seen. Her voice was clear and sweetly mellifluous. It was a bewitching sound that caressed his ears. He was not used to hearing a woman's voice. He found Lara's enchanting. And her story fascinated him. She was the daughter of a great warrior, and a faerie queen. Arcas had not quite put it that way. If he had to trust either of them, he realized, it would be Lara's truth he accepted, and not the wily Coastal King's.

As she finished he heard her say, "I hope you do not mind, but Andraste and Verica have come with me. They are quite harmless when not wielded, Captain."

"I did not see the servant carrying you bring anything else," Corrado said.

Lara laughed. "No, he did not, but my weapons came nonetheless. I told you that I am magic, and I am surrounded by magic."

"If you have such power then why are you here?" he asked her.

"I have already told you that, Captain. I am here because I am meant to be here at this time," Lara explained gently as if she were telling a child.

"What is your purpose in being here? Have you

come to spy for Hetar? Arcas talks a great deal and much too freely. There are changes coming to your world, lady.

"Your people will take new territory. After they have taken the Outlands they will surely turn their eyes to the sea. The Coastal Kings will no longer be able to keep their secrets to themselves, and once Hetar learns of Terah and our Dominion they are sure to seek to conquer it. Or has Arcas already betrayed his own kind?"

"The Outlands are protected from he who would be emperor, Captain Corrado," Lara said. "Gaius Prospero cannot know that yet, and he will strive mightily until he figures it out, if indeed he does. Hetar believes that its provinces and the Outlands are all that there is of the world in which we live. I know it is not, but does your Dominion take up all the rest? Or are their other places, and peoples? How much more is there? Have you not ever wondered that?"

Her curiosity fascinated him. "I do not know if there is more," he admitted.

Lara smiled. "But do you want to know?" she asked teasingly.

He shook his head. "I don't know," he said.

"Is there magic in the Dominion?" she queried him.

He nodded in the affirmative. "Aye, there is."

"Good," Lara told him. "I shall look forward to learning all about it."

"You are being given to the Dominus Magnus Hauk," the captain said. "You will live in his castle, and your freedom will be greatly curtailed, for you will be considered a slave, lady."

Lara laughed. "I was once before considered a slave by men, for all the good it did them. I am not a slave, and your Dominus will soon learn that. If all he wishes of me are pleasures he may have them, as long as I am free to follow the path set out for me."

Captain Corrado shook his head in wonder. "Lady, I had never seen or heard your like before. But because I see no evil in you I must warn you to tread carefully. Magnus Hauk is a very strong, and extremely determined man. He will not tolerate disobedience, especially from a woman."

"I thank you for your kindness and your advice," Lara responded.

"We will be arriving tomorrow," the captain said.

"Tomorrow? Arcas said each ship met three days out from their home port in the center of the sea," Lara exclaimed.

"Lady, you slept two days," came the answer.

"Two days!" Lara was astounded.

"The brew we gave you was potent," he said.

Lara laughed softly. "Aye, it must have been."

"I could not be certain you would not object to your current circumstances, and resist violently," Captain Corrado told her. "Had I known your disposition I would have permitted myself to enjoy your company more. Terahn women are not at all like you."

"If that is so, can you be certain that I will appeal to your Dominus?" Lara asked.

The captain smiled. "A man would be a fool not to want you, lady."

She smiled at him. "You flatter me."

"Tomorrow when we prepare to enter the fjord, would you enjoy being on deck?" he offered generously.

"What is a fjord?" Lara wanted to know.

"It is an inlet that leads to the Dominus's castle. There are many such inlets along our coast that you can take to reach our villages."

"Have you no central place of authority?" she inquired.

"The castle of the Dominus is that place. You will see," he told her.

The following morning the young boy came to the cabin and said, "The captain invites the lady to view the entering."

"Thank you," Lara told him, and then she said, "Why do you look so fearful?"

"I have never before heard a woman speak," the boy responded.

"Do you not have women in the Dominion?" she asked him.

"Aye, but our women do not speak," he answered her.

"Your women cannot or do not speak?" She was again very surprised.

He nodded. "They cannot."

"Give me a moment to prepare myself," Lara told him. "Wait outside, and then you will escort me."

"Yes, lady," he said obediently, and left the cabin.

The gown she wore was thankfully tailored with a long narrow pleated skirt, and long fitted sleeves. The neckline was cut straight across her collarbone and

slightly draped. It was a silvery gray in color. Lara
went to the sleeping cabinet, and slipped Andraste
in her leather scabbard over her head. She picked up
Verica and walked from the cabin. Glancing briefly
at her, the boy led Lara up onto the high open deck
where Captain Corrado was awaiting her.

"There is our coast," he said, pointing.

Lara was overwhelmed by the beauty of the green
cliffs and steep hills that flowed into taller mountains.
It was beautiful, and quite different from Hetar or
the Outlands. And then she saw the opening between
those cliffs. The ship was sailing toward it. "Is that
the entrance to your fjord?" she asked the captain.

"You have a sharp eye," he said. "We will reach it
shortly."

"And be done with this infernal rocking to and
fro?" a voice demanded to know.

"Verica!" Lara giggled for both Captain Corrado
and the boy by his side looked horrified. She hastened
to reassure them both. "This is Verica, my companion staff. He is most outspoken, I fear, but he means
no harm."

"Stop looking so terrified, lad," Verica said to the
cabin boy. "I am the spirit of the tree from which this
staff where I now reside was made. You have, I take
it, never seen my like before."

"N-no," the boy stammered.

"And you are unlikely to see my like again," Verica
told him.

"This is great magic," Captain Corrado said.

"My magic is used only for good," Lara replied.

"Will we soon land, and be off this rolling vessel?" Verica asked again.

"Yes," Captain Corrado said. "We are almost ready to enter the fjord now. Once we are inside you will find the waters calmer."

"I am relieved to hear it," Verica. "Look at my wood. It has a green tinge to it."

"I cannot believe I am talking to a staff," Captain Corrado said.

"The staff but houses my spirit," Verica told him. "Can you not see my face? I am told that it is quite a handsome face. Is that not so, Mistress?"

Lara turned her staff slightly, and the captain found himself staring into a long stern face with sharp eyes, a long, narrow nose, thin lips and a long curling beard. It was a beautifully carved face of a certain elegance.

"Ah, now I see you," the captain said. "And, yes, you have a most impressive visage, Verica. I am pleased to make your acquaintance."

"As I am to make yours, Captain," Verica replied in his most courtly manner.

The vessel began its turn into the fjord, and after a few moments of rough water where the inlet and the sea met they found themselves sailing upon what appeared to be a silken river. The green of the cliffs around them was so vivid it almost hurt Lara's eyes.

"Just a few miles upriver, and you will see the castle of the Dominus upon the heights," Captain Corrado said.

"May I remain on deck?" Lara asked him. "It is all so beautiful."

"I will have the boy bring you something to sit upon," he replied. "I must now see to our landing and the unloading of the cargo. I will not take you to the castle until that is done. My first duty is to my ship."

"Of course," Lara agreed. She was quite content to sit in the leather sling chair the cabin boy brought her and observe her new surroundings. The air was fresh with a mixture of both the sea and the land now. She saw no cattle, or horses, or sheep grazing on the hillsides. There were no villages, but Corrado had said there were. Perhaps this entry to the castle of the Dominus was all private land. And then their ship sailed around a sharp bend in the fjord, and Lara saw it.

The great castle was built half into the rock of the hillside. It was dark stone, massive in size, and yet it was not ponderous. It had soaring graceful towers with peaked roofs of gray slate. She could see greenery trailing over its wall in some places, and thought that there might be gardens behind those walls. There was nothing at all like it in Hetar except perhaps in the province of the Shadow Princes. Gaius Prospero would be pea-green with envy if he saw this magnificent castle. She smiled to herself. She could scarcely wait to learn all she could about the Terahn Dominion. And especially why did the women of this land not speak—a most curious mystery.

Their vessel nosed itself toward the shore where a long stone quay pushed out into the fjord. The ship was tied firmly to the quay, a gangway lowered, and then the unloading of the cargo began. Each box, each container, was quickly removed down the stone way through an entrance in the cliffs. Captain Corrado stood directing his men. As the ship grew emptier it began to float more lightly at its mooring. Finally the last of the cargo had been removed from the ship, and Captain Corrado came to fetch Lara.

"You are ready?" he asked her.

"I am," she said. "Will I meet the Dominus now?"

"Probably," he replied. "I am always expected to present myself to him immediately when I return from a voyage. He and I are kin."

"It is a steep climb," Lara noted as they walked down the gangway, and began to traverse the quay.

"We need not climb," he told her. "You will soon see."

He led her to the entry in the stone cliffs. Inside he took Lara's hand, and they stepped through a wooden gate onto an open platform enclosed by a railing. Almost at once the platform began to rise up through the interior of the cliff. Surprised, Lara watched as the platform passed by several open gates in the stone walls. As they approached the top of the cliff, she could see through to corridors, each one a bit grander than the one before it.

"How is this done?" she asked the captain.

"The conveyance is drawn up and lowered back down again by a mountain giant. We employ them for this purpose. They are not very intelligent, but they are quite strong and good-natured," he explained. "You mentioned that you have known giants."

"Only one, and he was considered small for his breed," Lara replied.

"These are big fellows," Captain Corrado said. The platform stopped, and a servant was there to open the gates for them. They stepped into a well-lit corridor. "Lady, our men are not used to the sound of a woman's voice. Try to remain silent. And be warned that the Dominus is a stern man. Please be discreet, for your own safety."

"Thank you," Lara responded, touched by his concern. Then she followed him down the corridor accompanied by the servant who had helped them into the hallway.

"The master is in his private quarters," Lara heard the servant say to Captain Corrado. "He was not certain you would arrive today."

"The weather was good, the seas fair. I have a surprise for the Dominus," Captain Corrado answered the servant.

"The woman?" The servant cast a quick glance in Lara's direction.

"She is half-faerie, and Hetarian," the captain said. "She is a gift."

"And a fine one!" the servant responded enthusiastically. "I wish someone would gift me like that, my lord Captain." And the two men chuckled, sharing the jest.

At the very end of the corridor were a pair of double doors fashioned from bronze. There were no guards before the door, Lara noted. Clearly the Dominus was entirely secure in his castle. The servant opened one of the doors and ushered them into a large chamber. To their left were great tall windows overlooking the fjord. Before them was a massive hearth with great andirons holding several large logs that burned brightly.

A man who had been seated in a large high-backed chair by that fire now arose to meet them. He was very, very tall, and his frame was large, yet in perfect proportion with his size. The face was handsome but severe, with a long nose, high forehead and cheekbones and thin lips. His hair was short and deep gold in color, with lighter gold highlights here and there. Thick gold eyebrows above turquoise-blue eyes matched his hair. He wore a single garment, a long dark blue robe with a round neckline. The look he gave Captain Corrado was a warm one.

The captain fell to a single knee, and taking one of the Dominus's big hands pressed it to his forehead, his lips and then his heart. "My lord."

"Welcome home, Corrado," the Dominus said. His voice was deep and musical.

"Now get up, kinsman, and tell me how the voyage went." He appeared to show no interest whatsoever in the woman by Corrado's side, but Lara had seen the quick flick of an eye that he shot in her direction.

"It was an ordinary journey but for one thing, my lord. Have you the time to listen to me?" Corrado asked the Dominus.

Magnus Hauk nodded.

"King Arcas wished to dispose of a political enemy, and so he has sent her to you as a gift. She is half-faerie, and she speaks with the sound of nightingales," the captain said. "Her name is Lara. She is intelligent. I have learned her history, but it is better told by her. I hope she will please you so I may tell Arcas when I see him again that she has."

"Does Arcas think we have no women in my Do-

minion? Or perhaps he believes Hetarian women sur-
pass Terahn women," Magnus Hauk said.

"I believe it is just that he wished to rid himself
of me, and thought to curry favor with you, my lord
Dominus," she said boldly.

The Dominus turned his gaze to Lara's. His was a
most powerful glance, and she almost looked away,
but she did not. "Her voice is indeed sweet to my
ears," Magnus Hauk said to his kinsman as if Lara
were not even there. "And she is beautiful, I will
admit." He reached out as though to grasp the neck
of her gown, but Lara stayed his hand.

"My lord, I have but this one garment to my name,"
she said.

"Remove it then so I may fully see what the Coastal
King has sent me," he told her. "You may remain, Corrado."

"My lord, with your permission I should prefer to
withdraw. What lies beneath that gown is a sight that
should only be for your eyes," the captain said.

The Dominus laughed. "Always the man of perfect
discretion," he answered. "Go then, my kinsman. We
will speak tomorrow, and I will tell you if I gained
pleasures with this woman and mean to keep her, or
if I will give her as a reward to another."

Captain Corrado looked horrified. "My lord," he
cried. "You must not allow another to have her. She
has great magic, and will be of much use to you. Do
not allow anyone else to gain the advantage over you."

Now the Dominus was intrigued, and his lust was
put aside for the moment. "Tell me of her magic," he
demanded.

The captain turned to Lara. "Show him, please," he begged her.

Lara laughed softly. "My lord Dominus, I ask your permission to show you my sword, Andraste. She is a most unusual weapon, but I should not unsheathe her without your permission."

"You have it," he answered quietly. "Are you an assassin then?"

"No, my lord Dominus. I am warrior-trained by the Shadow Princes of Hetar. When I completed my training the sword was a gift from the great sword master Lothair. It possesses a victory spirit who is called Andraste." Lara carefully drew her weapon from the sheath on her back. Holding it flat upon her two palms she displayed it to him.

The Dominus reached out to take the sword, but jumped back startled as a deep and powerful woman's voice warned him off.

"Greetings, Dominus Magnus Hauk. I am Andraste, and I permit only my mistress's hand to touch me. I drink the blood of the wicked."

"What magic is this?" Magnus Hauk asked suspiciously.

"The magic of Hetar, my lord Dominus," Lara answered him. "The staff I carry also has a name, and a voice." She turned Verica to face the Dominus.

"Greetings, Magnus Hauk. I am Verica," the staff said.

The Dominus stared hard for a moment, and then he said, "Your face is a noble one, Verica. I greet you."

Andraste began to hum low. The Dominus had not greeted her.

But then he turned back to the sword, saying, "You are every bit as beautiful as your mistress, Andraste."

"And far fiercer, Dominus," Andraste replied tartly, and Lara knew her weapon was slightly offended by Magnus Hauk's patronizing compliment.

"With your permission again, my lord Dominus," Lara said, "I will resheathe Andraste." She quickly did so, and at the same time set Verica aside.

"I will not take your weapons from you," Magnus Hauk told Lara. "You have my word on it. But I would have you put them aside now. I cannot take pleasures with an armed woman."

"I will leave you now," Captain Corrado said, bowing to his kinsman.

"Thank you, Captain, for your courtesy and kindness," Lara said quietly.

The sea captain bowed briefly to her, and hurried from the chamber.

"You have obviously impressed him," Magnus Hauk said. "I have never known him to bow to a woman. Our silent women are hardly worthy of such respect."

"All women are worthy of respect, my lord Dominus," Lara told him.

"Even in Hetar?" he asked her softly.

"What do you know of Hetar?" she countered.

"Very little," he admitted. "And other than the Coastal Kings, Hetar knows nothing of us. Are you going to remove your gown, or must I rip it from you, Lara?"

"Are you always so impatient, my lord Dominus? I learned long ago that patience leads to greater pleasures than a hasty coupling." She undid her gown at a shoulder, and shrugged it off. The silvery fabric slid to the stone floor of the chamber with a faint hiss.

Lara now stood quietly, and very still.

Magnus Hauk stared at the beautiful woman before him. She was the most perfect female he had ever seen in all his days. "Are all Hetarian woman as beautiful as you, Lara?" he asked her, genuinely curious.

"No," she replied honestly. "I am unique by virtue of my faerie blood, my lord Dominus. I expect women, like men, wherever they are from, come in many shapes and sizes. Some are always fairer than others. Some are plainer than others. Will you remove your robe so I may view your nakedness as you now gaze at mine?"

Magnus Hauk didn't know whether to laugh or remonstrate with this bold woman. Terahn women were silent and obedient. They always did as they were bid. But this beautiful female could be an interesting puzzle to solve. She intrigued him in spite of himself. A quick smile touched his lips. He undid the frog closures holding his garment shut, and shrugged it off. His eyes were fixed on hers.

Lara held his gaze for a long moment, and then breaking it, she looked him up and she looked him down, walking around him slowly as she did so. "You are a man of impressive attributes," she finally told him.

Reaching out he drew her against him. His hand began to slowly caress her heart-shaped face, the tips of his fingers brushing lightly against her skin as he traced the delicate structure. His turquoise eyes caught her green ones in a mesmerizing hold. His dark gold head bent as he murmured softly against her lips, "And you, my faerie beauty, are intoxicating."

His touch on her face, on her lips, set her heart to racing. She had cared deeply for Vartan of the Fiacre, but she was ready to love again. Yet something about this man cried danger! Instinct warned her that this was a man who could capture her heart, and break it. She shivered with the knowledge. He smiled wolfishly down at her as if he understood her very thoughts. It was a mistake on his part. Lara toughened her softening heart. To give this man an easy victory would be a great mistake, and she had no intention of erring where Magnus Hauk was concerned.

His mouth brushed hers. It had been months since she had experienced a warm mouth on hers. It felt wonderful, but her own lips remained cool and uncommitted to him. This was a battle that the Dominus was not going to win. His kiss deepened, becoming fierce and demanding. His body was hard against her. His tongue forced its way into her mouth. Lara briefly lost control of herself as the hot wet digit brushed her tongue. But then she recovered and firmly pulled her head away from him.

"You are bruising me," she complained to him. "My skin is delicate, and I will be marked by your roughness."

He stifled the groan that threatened to explode from within him. Women did not complain to or deny Magnus Hauk. Nor would they, had they been able to speak. Women yielded to the Dominus and were grateful for his attention. He grasped one of her beautiful breasts and squeezed it hard. "You," he said with emphasis, "belong to me. You will obey me as your master."

"Will you beat me if I don't?" Lara asked him. The look in her eyes was wicked.

"You belong to me!" he repeated.

"My lord Dominus, let us settle this matter immediately. Arcas of the Coastal Kings has done a stupid thing by sending me to you. I am Lara, daughter of Swiftsword of the Crusader knights, and Ilona, queen of the Forest Faeries. I am the widow of Vartan, Lord of the Fiacre and head of the High Council of the Outlands. I am no man's slave. Arcas is a fool, and he cannot know that his behavior was but a means for me to cross the sea, to come to Terah. I have a destiny to fulfill, and believe me when I tell you it is not to be your Pleasure Woman.

"You are a means to an end for me, Magnus Hauk. But until my instincts tell me otherwise I am content to remain here with you. And I will share pleasures with you. I find you handsome and virile. I even think I might desire you a little bit." She smoothed a hand up his bare chest. "Yes," she purred moving closer to him again. "I desire you."

"I may kill you," he growled at her. In his wildest imaginings he had never thought to hear a woman speak, let alone speak the words she had spoken to him. She was a defiant creature, but she challenged him to conquest. He would tame her, and she would be his as long as she continued to please him.

She laughed into his face. "How will you kill me, my lord Dominus? Tell me it will be with pleasure, with your hands, your tongue, that great weapon hanging between your legs." Reaching out she began to stroke him, fondling the seed sack beneath his rod.

Fiery heat suffused his big body, and he felt suddenly weak with his need for her. Taking her face between his hands he began to kiss her. Her lips now responded to his, parting slightly, moist and inviting, luring him onward. Magnus felt the strength filling him once more as she seemed to yield slightly to him. The tips of her breasts were like hard little nubs against his chest, her mons hot against his groin. He was backing her toward the hearth, and then suddenly he kicked her legs from beneath her, and lowered her to the floor.

Lara had regained control of herself. Her faerie heart had learned to be icy cold again. It would protect her. But she was also beginning to enjoy the man making love to her. She could tell he was skilled at it. He would give her pleasure, true, but she would give him pleasure such as he had never known in return. She would bind him to her, Lara knew. He would not realize it at first. He would just appreciate the physical sensations she offered him as their bodies met. But before long, he would be hers. He moved to mount her, but Lara held him off. "Not yet, my lord Dominus," she whispered, pushing him over so that he rolled onto his back. "Let me offer you sweetness beyond measure."

His need for her was desperate, but something in her voice caused him to lay back. Kneeling next to him Lara began to place feathery little kisses over his torso. She did this for some minutes. Then she began to lick the flesh she had previously kissed. Her tongue was warm and slicked across his torso, lighting tiny fires as it traveled. He was burning up as she climbed onto him, pushing a nipple into his mouth. "Suckle!" she commanded him.

He obeyed, drawing on the nipple strongly over and over again while his hand kneaded her other breast. After a time he released the nipple and turned his head to its twin. He sucked on it, even grazing the tender flesh with his teeth briefly. When she took her breasts from him and slid her body down his, he almost cried out like a maid.

"Does all this please you, my lord Dominus?" she asked him in a now husky voice. Her eyes had gone sloe with their growing desire.

"Aye." His voice almost cracked beneath the raging fire of his lusts. "Now it is my turn to pleasure you, Lara." Somehow, and he wasn't certain how, he managed to position himself between her legs. He felt weak with his desire. Lowering his head he spread her nether lips open. She was already moist, and he smiled, pleased. His tongue began to slide across the pinkish flesh. She was almost sweet to his taste. Before him the tiny nub of her sex beckoned him. He touched it first with just the tip of his tongue, and heard a small moan from her lips. He teased the nub gently at first, and then unable to help himself flicked his tongue fiercely back and forth over it until she was almost screaming. The sound was music to his ears. His strength returned, flowing into his big limbs as she sobbed and began to thrash beneath the marauding digit.

"Tell me what you want," he growled into her ear.

"Tell me what you want!" she demanded back.

"You!" he said.

"You!" she returned. It was time to give him the victory. She had already proven she was his equal in this game.

"Do you want me inside of you, Lara?" he teased her, placing a deep kiss on the now swollen nub before he gave it a final nip with his teeth that sent her into a sobbing frenzy of desperation.

"Yes! I want you inside of me," Lara whispered. "I need you, my lord Dominus! Hurry, please! Do not torture me any longer."

"You deserve nothing more for your bold defiance," he said cruelly.

"Please!" she begged him. He was a worthy opponent. She felt him moving on her, the tip of his great manroot preparing to take its revenge. She opened herself to him. "Please, my lord Dominus! Give us the pleasure that only you can!"

He thrust hard and deep, struggling briefly to prevent his juices from filling her too quickly. She cried out with his advance as he pushed all the way to the mouth of her womb. She was hot and tight around him. He had never known a woman's body to be like this. He could feel her juices already bathing him. Slowly he withdrew almost all the way from her, only to plunge within once more. Her slender body matched itself to his movement as he began to surge back and forth upon her.

She could not control herself—his deep well of passion had caught her unawares. She had never known its like. He filled her even as Vartan had filled her, and yet it was different. She felt different. She didn't understand what was happening, but she knew men enough to know that her unfettered response to his passion was giving him the greatest pleasures either of them had ever known. Understanding she could no longer manage the situation Lara gave into it. She flew. She burned. She melted into a helpless creature lost among the stars. And as the most incredible pleasure she had ever known consumed her, Lara screamed with her rapture, and then fell into a warm and dark chasm that reached up to enfold her.

His juices exploded with such violence that Magnus Hauk thought Lara would be rendered asunder. Surely there would be nothing left after this lustful bout. Blood thundered in his ears as her scream of delight reached him. His heart was pounding wildly, and for the briefest moment he thought he was going to die from the sweetness that consumed him. With the last of his strength he pulled away from her, rolling onto his back. When he could see clearly again and his heart was beating at a more normal rate he said to her, "I have never known pleasures like that."

"Nor I," Lara admitted softly.

"Why did you refuse the Coastal King?" he asked her.

"He is not my fate," Lara replied. "Why would I waste pleasures on him? I am not some Pleasure Woman who is paid for her services. Nor am I your slave, my lord Dominus."

"Nay," Magnus Hauk admitted. "You are not my slave, Lara, but then what are you to be to me?"

"Your guest?" Lara teased him gently.

He roared with laughter, sitting up, and turning to look down at her. "Aye, you are my guest," he agreed humorously. "And you are my lover."

She sat up, nodding. "It is fair," she said. "But what if I wish to take pleasures with another, my lord Dominus?"

"I will kill you," he replied. "You are mine!"

"Nay," she said. "You are mine!"

"A man cannot be ruled by a woman, Lara," he told her seriously.

"And I cannot be ruled by any other, man or woman," Lara responded, looking him directly in the eye.

The Dominus paused, surprised by her words. "I see," he said, "that we already have differences between us. We will have to negotiate them, will we not?" The blue eyes twinkled at her.

What an interesting man, Lara thought. He is strong, and he is arrogant, but he has a sense of humor. "I am said to be very good at the art of negotiation, my lord Dominus."

"Are you hungry?" he asked her.

"Ravenous!" she told him.

He arose and pulled her to her feet. "Let us get dressed, and then we will eat before this fire where we have already temporarily satisfied our other appetites. Then I intend making love to you again. All night. And after I shall take you to the women's quarters in the castle where you will meet my sister, Sirvat. She is in charge of the women here."

"You have no wife or mate?" Lara asked him.

"No," he said shortly, pulling on his dark robe again. "Just women."

Lara picked up her gown from where it had dropped. She slipped it on, and finding her sandals slid her feet into them again. It had been a most interesting day, and already the sun was sinking toward the horizon. Toward Hetar.

The Dominus called for food. When it arrived Lara was pleased by the variety offered. There was roasted meat, rare as she liked it, and as the Dominus obviously liked it. There was a fat, stuffed capon that sat upon a platter amid a sauce of stewed plums and apricots. There were long thin yellow bean stalks that had been steamed tender. A salad of mixed lettuces, some purple and orange leaves as she had never before seen mixed with the greens. The salad had been tossed with a tangy dressing, the ingredients of which she could not easily identify. There were two cheeses, one soft with a delicate creamy flavor, and the other hard, very sharp, and golden in color. Yet there was only one small loaf of bread. It was fresh and warm, however, but its flavor was unfamiliar to her.

They both ate heartily, and drank an intoxicating wine Lara suspected had been well laced with herbs to encourage their evening's activity. And true to his word, Magnus Hauk spent the hours that followed making slow sweet love with Lara. When morning came, however, he escorted her through the castle and placed her in the care of his young sister, Sirvat.

The rooms in which she had spent the night with the Dominus were elegant, but spare in furnishings. His chamber held only a large bed and a plain wooden chest. The corridors through which she now traveled were also simple. The walls were a smooth stone of a neutral color, lit by crystal globes filled with what appeared to be fireflies. The floors were dark slate. Lara was therefore surprised when the Dominus opened the doors at the end of a long hallway and ushered her inside.

The Women's Quarters of the castle were more luxurious than anything Lara had ever seen. The rooms were spacious, yet not overlarge. The walls were painted a warm golden yellow, and hung with exquisite tapestries woven in clear reds, blues, greens, purples and creams. The tapestries told stories, probably of Terah's history, Lara thought as she admired them. The furnishings were feminine—low couches upholstered in soft fabrics of various hues, plump silk and velvet pillows decorated with gold and silver threads, with tasseled edges. There were delicate tables of inlaid woods and mother-of-pearl. Little velvet stools. Hanging lamps of amethyst glass. There were heavy soft rugs covering parts of the floors.

As they entered, a lovely girl with golden-brown hair came forward, smiling. She bowed to Magnus Hauk, taking his two hands in hers and pressing them to her heart in a pretty gesture of welcome. Then her curious turquoise glance went to Lara.

"This is Lara, my Hetarian guest," Magnus Hauk said to his sister. "Will you see she is well cared for, Sister?"

The young woman nodded, and turned her smile on Lara.

"My youngest sister, Sirvat," the Dominus said to Lara. "Like all our women she hears, but is unable to speak." He turned to his sibling. "Sirvat, do not be afraid, but the women of Hetar have voices with which they speak and both Corrado and I have heard."

Sirvat raised a curious eyebrow, but nodded to her brother.

"I will leave you now," the Dominus said to Lara. "You will be safe here."

"When will I see you again?" Lara asked him.

"When you do," he replied with a grin.

Lara smiled back mischievously. "You will lust for me soon enough, my lord Dominus. And if it pleases me I will come to you."

Magnus Hauk laughed aloud. Then turning, he left her.

Lara felt a tug on her sleeve.

"Come along, woman of Hetar," a soft voice said to her.

Lara spun about. Were her ears deceiving her? "You speak!" she exclaimed. "Why does the Dominus think you do not?" Were her ears deceiving her?

"Come," Sirvat said, "and I will tell you." She led her guest into a lovely large room with arched windows opening out into a walled green garden, and a tiled marble fountain in its center. Taking Lara's hand Sirvat brought her to a pillowed bench. "It's that wretched curse that was placed upon us several hundred years ago," she began. "A powerful sorcerer who called himself Usi had come from the North, seeking

to control Terah. And he did for several years. But
he was cruel, taking women for his pleasure, which
more times than not was for the purposes of torture
and not passion. He hoarded wealth, impoverishing
the people. No one knew what to do to stop him. He
was, it was said, a ruthless being.

"Finally a woman called Geltruda decided that
something must be done if our people were to be
saved. She went out of her way to catch the eye of
Usi. They say she was the most beautiful woman in
all of Terah. The sorcerer lusted after her, but she kept
him at arm's length until he could no longer bear his
desire, and she agreed to come to his bed willingly.
Before she did she covered her body with poison
so that no matter where Usi might kiss her, his lips
would absorb it. By the time he realized what she had
done it was too late, and Geltruda herself already lay
dead of the poison.

"She had told her brothers of her plans, and now
they burst into the chamber where their dead sister
and the dying sorcerer lay. They sat watching his
agony. He cursed them with his last breath; because
they had accepted her counsel and allowed her to kill
him, the men of the Dominion would no longer hear
the voices of their women. And so it happened as Usi
said. But as the men of the Terahn Dominion could
still hear everything else, they decided that it was the
women who could no longer speak, and so they believe to this day. No one has ever been able to lift the
curse."

"Has anyone tried?" Lara asked Sirvat.

"Oh yes. But the magic of Terah is not strong

enough. I wish it were. There are so many things we would say to our men if they could hear us," the young woman said with a chuckle. "Will you tell my brother?"

"I don't know. Would you mind if I did? I am curious to learn more about this sorcerer. Perhaps I could lift the curse."

"Have you magic, then?" Sirvat inquired politely.

"I am half-faerie," Lara explained, "and aye, I do have magic."

"Who is this?" a voice demanded.

Lara looked up to see a woman with dark red hair. Behind her were two others, both dark-haired.

"Lara, these are my brother's women, Uma, Alcippe and Felda. This is Lara, a woman of Hetar. She is Magnus's guest."

"His new lover, you mean, Sirvat," the red-haired woman said sharply. She glared at Lara. "You are, aren't you?"

"And are you?" Lara said haughtily.

"I am Uma, the Dominus's favorite of his favored women," came the reply.

"No longer, I think," Lara said softly.

Uma looked outraged. She tried to speak but no words came out.

The two brunettes, one tall and slender, the other petite with a sweet face, giggled. They seemed pleased that Uma was upset. Interesting, Lara thought.

"You are being rude, Uma," Sirvat said. "Who my brother takes pleasures with is not your affair. Consider yourself fortunate to have attracted him, and to be living in the castle of the Dominus. You could find yourself back on the auction block."

"Ohhhh," the two brunettes gasped in unison.

"You are not my mistress!" Uma snapped.

"No, I am not," Sirvat said. "I am the sister of the Dominus, and run his household. If you persist in your rudeness I will speak with Magnus."

"Hah!" Uma said. "He cannot hear us. How will you communicate such a complex request to him?"

"He hears Lara," Sirvat said with a wicked smile. "She is not Terahn, but Hetarian. We have never known a woman from Hetar before, but she is now here, and he can indeed hear her voice." She laughed at the look of surprise on Uma's face.

"I hate you!" Uma said, and she ran from the chamber.

"Can the lord Dominus really hear your voice? I am Alcippe," the taller girl said.

"Yes, he can," Lara told her. "Both he and Captain Corrado were very surprised."

"Uma is very haughty," the smaller girl noted. "I am Felda. She thinks she has such favor with the lord Dominus that she can do what she wants."

"But she cannot," Sirvat said with emphasis. "Felda, dear, will you see a servant prepares a comfortable chamber for Lara? The empty one next to mine is suitable."

"Of course, Sirvat," Felda replied, and hurried off.

"Felda is very sweet-natured," Sirvat said. "And Alcippe is very intelligent, are you not? Poor Uma has nothing but her lush body with which to attract my brother."

BERTRICE SMALL   165

"She has been successful so far," Alcippe said with a chuckle.

"Beauty is both a blessing and a curse," Lara said.

"Yes, I can see you would know that," Alcippe said with a wry smile. "I do not think I have ever seen anyone as fair as you are."

Lara sighed. "It has been said of me many times," she admitted.

"Are you a slave?" Alcippe wanted to know.

"No," Lara told her, and then she explained her history to her two companions concluding with, "The Dominus has agreed that I am a free woman, which is fortunate since there is much I wish to learn of Terah. I hope some of you will be able to accompany me when I travel outside of the castle precincts."

"We do not go outside of the castle or its grounds," Sirvat said. "No woman leaves the environs of her village in Terah. And we do not leave the castle."

"Have you no capital city?" Lara asked Sirvat.

"What is a city?" the younger woman wanted to know.

"It is a place of many buildings, and districts. There are merchants and lords, common folk, and markets selling all manner of goods. A capital city is from where the government rules," Lara explained.

"We have no such place," Sirvat replied. "It is here from the castle that the Dominus rules. And it is here that many in my brother's service dwell. In the castle depths there are shops where the villagers may purchase any goods we need. We have but to request an item, and one of our women servants will fetch it. All the shops that a woman might patronize have women to serve. There is no need for us to leave the castle."

"But how did Alcippe and the others get here? They are slaves, are they not?"

"Yes, they are," Sirvat said. "Now and again my brother goes to the villages. Sometimes women are offered to him for his pleasure. And sometimes, if they please him, they are given to him."

"Your men are afraid for their women because they think they cannot speak," Lara said. "This curse has made it very difficult for your society. Before the sorcerer did you interact, one village with another?"

"There are tales of festivals, and fairs, and holidays celebrated as a whole," Sirvat replied. "But such things were done long ago, and even we are not certain in the truth of these tales. If not for the books we should not know at all."

Lara nodded. "But the Dominus in his castle remained your ruler."

"Yes," Sirvat responded.

Lara wondered how large the Terahn Dominion was. Was it possible for Magnus Hauk to control an enormous territory where only the men fraternized with one another? How far did his lands extend? None of it, to her knowledge touched Hetar. Were there other seas? Other lands? There was so much to learn, so much she needed to know. Did Magnus Hauk have the answers she sought? Why was she here?

Felda returned and said to Sirvat, "The chamber next to yours is being aired, but it is ready to receive an occupant. Have I missed anything?"

"Shall I repeat myself?" Lara asked them with a smile.

Sirvat nodded eagerly. "It is such a fascinating story, Lara. Tell us again, and let Felda hear. And then we will show you our gardens. Have you ever had a garden of your own? We grow the most beautiful flowers."

"Aye, I have had a garden," Lara told them. And then she again commenced a recitation of her history for them. "I am the daughter of the Crusader Knight, John Swiftsword, formerly a Mercenary, and Ilona, queen of the Forest Faeries..."

Chapter
6

LARA SOON LEARNED that Sirvat and the others had not exaggerated. The women who lived in the castle did not venture away from its precincts. But looking from a tower window Lara was stunned by the beauty she saw, and she wanted to see more. She longed to ride out into Terah although she did understand why Terah thought their women too helpless to travel.

Helpless? Lara almost laughed aloud at her own thoughts. Sirvat and the other women were far from helpless. They managed the Dominus's household and all that went with it very capably. And Lara assumed it was much the same in the rest of the castle, and in the villages beyond. But there seemed to be two separate societies in Terah. The men did what they had to do, and the women the same. They interacted very little except in the bedroom. And as long as the two factions could not act as one, Terah would remain as it was, and it would be vulnerable to Hetar sooner or later. She had considered when to tell the Dominus what she had learned. She needed to understand Terah more before she spoke with him.

Finally Lara approached the Dominus one late afternoon as they sat together in his own private garden. They were, after several weeks, on a first name basis. "Magnus, are you aware that your long-ago sorcerer placed his curse not upon your women, but upon the men of Terah?"

"What?" He looked very surprised, as well he might. "I do not understand, Lara."

"Your women speak," she told him. "It is you men who cannot hear them. That is exactly what the sorcerer wanted. That you no longer hear the voices of women, for it was a woman who had overcome him."

"The women speak," he repeated in a slightly bemused tone. "You actually hear the sound of their voices? It is not something in your head?"

"It is not an imagining, Magnus. The women have voices, and they speak," Lara told him. "Uma, who is unfriendly and unpleasant of temperament, has a particularly sweet voice. She sings sometimes in the evening when she is not needed by you. I am sorry you cannot hear her voice, for it is lovely."

"Can your magic undo this curse?" he asked her.

"I don't know," Lara told him. "I will ask Ethne."

"Who is Ethne?" He had never heard her mention that name.

Lara lifted up the crystal from the narrow gold chain about her neck. "Ethne," she said aloud, "please show yourself to the Dominus."

A flame within the crystal flickered brightly.

"What is it?" he asked.

"She is the guardian given to me by my mother, Queen Ilona, when she left me with my mortal father," Lara explained. "We speak a silent language, she and I. I will ask her how I must go about lifting the curse placed upon you. I have never before lifted a curse, but I believe I can do it." She looked down at the crystal between her two fingers. *Ethne, I would help the men of Terah. Can I break this curse?*

You must know the words of the curse before you can confound it, and make it yield to you, Ethne said. *Will they be remembered after all these many years?*

"Magnus," Lara said to him, "how long ago was this curse laid upon Terah? And did anyone record the words of the malediction?"

"It was over five hundred years ago," he answered her. "As for the words of the curse, if they are anywhere, they are recorded in the Book of Terah, which is kept in the Temple of the Great Creator."

"Then let us go there and find out," Lara said. "I am becoming very bored in the Women's Quarters. There is nothing to do. I am not used to being an ornament for mere pleasure, my lord Dominus."

His turquoise eyes twinkled. "Is that what you are? A pleasure ornament?" Grinning, he reached out for her, but Lara quickly jumped back.

"Oh no," she said, laughing and wagging a warning finger at him. "First we must settle this matter, and then we will discuss entertaining your wicked lust once more."

"I agree. We will leave tomorrow," he said. "We

found the most beautiful golden stallion outside of the gates this morning. He reminds me of you. He is yours if you think you can ride him. Now come here, my faerie love."

"A golden stallion? With a cream-colored mane and tail?" Lara said excitedly.

"Aye," the Dominus replied.

She jumped up from the pillows where they had been lounging. "Take me to him, Magnus!" She seemed suddenly galvanized by this knowledge.

"Very well," he said arising. "But afterwards…"

"Aye, afterwards," she promised. "How can I resist a man who is so vigorous?"

Taking Lara's hand the Dominus led her to the stables.

The head groom came forward to greet them.

"Where is the beast found this morning?" the Dominus asked.

"We have groomed him, fed and watered him, my lord. He was very thirsty," the groom said, bringing them into the stone building. "I felt the beast needed some quiet to restore his strength," the head groom finished. "Ah, here he is, my lord."

The stallion looked up at his visitors, making eye contact with Lara immediately.

"Dasras!" Lara cried. "How did you get here? I left you with the Fiacre for your safety." She opened the door of the stall, and stepping in, put her arms about the horse's thick neck. "I have missed you!"

"And I, you, Mistress," the stallion replied. "Your mother, Queen Ilona, thought you might have need of me, and so she gave me wings with which to cross the Sea of Sagitta to find you. She said you would be here."

Both the Dominus and the head groom had jumped back at the sound of the horse's voice. Now they stood very surprised looking at Lara and the animal.

"This is serious magic," Magnus Hauk said.

"Dasras, this is the Dominus of the Terahn Dominion," Lara introduced her horse to her lover. "Magnus, this is Dasras, my horse."

The stallion extended a leg before him and nodded his head. "Greetings, my lord Dominus," he said. "I am Dasras, sired by Hudak, born of Ronalda, from the herd of Kaliq of the Shadow Princes."

The head groom collapsed on the stable floor in a dead faint.

But the Dominus was made of sterner stuff. "And you flew across the sea from Hetar to reach your mistress, if I overheard you correctly."

"Actually, my lord Dominus," Dasras said, "it was the Outlands. When I told Liam, Lord of the Fiacre that I must go, he personally escorted me to Rendor of the Felan, whose lands border the sea and that of the Coastal Kings. I did not bother to enter Hetar. I departed from Rendor's sands."

"And you flew?" Magnus Hauk said.

The horse nodded. "I did. A most exhilarating experience, I must say."

"Where are your wings now?" the Dominus asked.

"I don't need them now," Dasras said.

"But where are they?" the Dominus persisted.

"I have absolutely no idea," Dasras answered him. "Queen Ilona told me when I need to fly to just think of my wings and they would be there. So I did, and they were. When I didn't need them, they wouldn't be there. It seems quite simple to me."

The Dominus looked slightly befuddled, and at his feet the head groom began to moan as he regained consciousness.

"This kind of magic is often startling to those who are not familiar with it," Lara said quietly. "Should we not help him up, Magnus?"

The Dominus bent, and pulled the groggy man to his feet. "It is all right, Peter," he said. "The horse does indeed talk, but his magic is good magic. Treat him well."

"Y-yes, my l-lord Dominus," the head groom quavered.

"Ho, Peter!" Dasras called to the man. "The young lad who took care of me when I was brought into the stable, I should like him to be assigned to my well-being. A lovely boy, and he knows well how to use the currying brushes. What is his name?"

"Jason," Peter said, surprised to find himself having a conversation with a horse. "He is my son. I taught him how to use the brushes."

"He has a lovely touch," Dasras replied.

"I shall see he has your care," the head stableman said. Then he hurried off to calm his frazzled nerves.

"Never fear, he will soon be used to me," Dasras said.

"How long will you need to recover from your trip?" Lara asked him.

"I will be fine by morning," Dasras assured her. "Where are we going?"

"To the Temple of the Great Creator, and you will have to ask the Dominus for I have absolutely no idea where that would be. But tell me, how are my children? What is happening in the Outlands? I know you have heard the gossip, Dasras."

"Dillon learned to ride me, but I did suggest to the lord that for now a smaller horse might be better. Anoush grows prettier each day, and toddles everywhere after Noss. Hetar has not yet invaded, although the rumors are rife," Dasras reported.

Lara nodded.

"This seems a vast land, Mistress," the horse noted.

"I would not know, for I have not yet explored it," Lara responded. "There is a curse on these people I must attempt to break, Dasras. The men cannot hear the voices of their women, and for centuries have believed the women don't talk, but they do. The men simply cannot hear them." Then she went on to explain.

"What are we looking for?" Dasras wanted to know.

"The words to the curse, for I cannot begin to untangle this web until I know them," Lara told him.

"He is a fine figure of a man, Mistress," the horse noted with a toss of his head toward the Dominus.

"Dasras!" Lara blushed.

The great beast snorted humorously, his dark eyes alight with mischief. Then he said, "Let me rest so come the morning I will be ready to carry you once again upon my back, Mistress. It will be good to go adventuring together again." He turned his head to Magnus Hauk. "As long as she gives you her fealty, you will have mine as well, my lord Dominus. But remember that my first loyalty is to Lara, widow of Vartan, daughter of Swiftsword of the Crusader Knights, and Ilona, queen of the Forest Faeries."

"You are an honorable beast," the Dominus said. "I understand, Dasras. Sleep well, for we have a long ride tomorrow." He gave the horse a friendly nod of his head, and then said to Lara, "Are you ready to come now?"

Lara hugged her animal again, kissing his muzzle. "Rest," she said. "I will see you on the morrow." Then she took Magnus Hauk's hand, and they departed the stables. "It is almost time for afterwards," she murmured, and he chuckled.

They returned to his private garden. It was a beautiful green place and walled with a small pool and waterfall. The hour had grown late, and above them the sky was blue and pink and gold with fragments of narrow clouds trailing lazily across the firmament. In the stone wall facing out there were several round openings through which one could look down into the fjord below. Across it the mountains climbed gently. And outside the castle, there was no sign of life that she could see.

He stood behind her, and now his big hands clasped her two breasts. "You did not tell me you had two children," he murmured in her ear. His hands fondled her. "Even I know faerie women give children only to those they love. Who was he?"

"Vartan of the Fiacre, my husband," Lara said. "I told you I was his widow, and Dasras greeted me as such. My husband desired children of me. He loved me deeply, and I cared for him in return. I gave him a son and a daughter, even though we both knew that one day I would leave them. What I did not expect was that he would not be there to care for our children."

"You do not say you loved him," Magnus Hauk said.

"I cared enough for him to let him seed me and bear him children," Lara replied.

"You will love me without reservation when you bear me a son," the Dominus said in a suddenly hard voice. "I will accept nothing less of you."

"I cannot promise you I am capable of loving a man," Lara told him.

"You will love me!" he repeated. "If you cannot, you are no better than my Pleasure Women."

"Find husbands for Uma and the others, and dower them generously. Nay, very generously," Lara told him. "It is unkind to keep them when you do not love them, my lord Dominus."

"How do you know I do not love them?" he demanded of her, his hands kneading her breasts, his fingers toying with her nipples beneath the fabric of her gown. His lips were nuzzling the back of her neck, and she could feel his heat.

"Do you have children hidden somewhere in your castle, my lord Dominus?" she murmured. "I have seen none in the Women's Quarters. I am certain if you desired children of these women you would have had them already."

"None of the women I take for my pleasure remain long," he admitted. "I do not want children with them and so they are given an elixir each day under the watchful eye of my sister, Sirvat, which they take to prevent any mishaps," the Dominus explained.

"Since I have come you have not lain with any of the three," Lara noted.

"Will you give me a child if I send them away?" he asked her, nipping the nape of her slender soft neck. Her fragrance taunted him.

"I will not give you a child if you do not send them away," Lara replied. "But first, my lord Dominus, we have other issues to solve. I must try to lift the sorcerer's curse from the men of Terah. I cannot do that if I am distracted by jealous women, or a child in my belly. The choice is yours to make."

"I will consider your suggestions," he told her, releasing her breasts, turning her about and then pressing her back against the stone wall. He began to kiss her face while his hands yanked up the skirt of her gown. He loosened his own garment and then, cupping her buttocks, raised her up to impale her upon his manroot. He smiled, satisfied at her gasp as he entered her. The walls of her love sheath closed about him tightly, hot and wet and eager for him. "I told you the first day I saw you, Lara, that you belonged to me," he growled in her ear as her arms encircled his neck, and she kissed his mouth.

"And I told you that you would belong to me," Lara said, her legs wrapping about his torso. "But you will never have that which you desire most from me while there are other women for you to share pleasures with in this house." Then she kissed him again, fiercely, her tongue doing battle with his as he opened the doors to paradise for them.

"I love your tightness," he groaned against her mouth. Her strength excited him.

"I love your bigness," she admitted. Her head was spinning with pleasure.

They rocked back and forth until the sweetness between them crested and drained away, leaving them both weak and satisfied. Her legs fell away from his body, but she clung to him tightly as her gown fell back to cover her.

"I will have Sirvat arrange it while we are away," Magnus Hauk said to Lara. "Will that please you, my faerie lover?"

"I want only what is best for you, my lord Dominus," Lara murmured with false meekness.

He chuckled. "You are the most delicious witch. Were you not, I should throw you over this wall into the fjord below as soon as look at you."

"But like Dasras I might sprout wings and fly away from you," she teased him. "Would you not miss me, my lord Dominus?" Lara purred. His robe was open, and she bent her head to lick at his nipples. "You taste salty," she said. "I like salt!"

"Faerie, cease your torment," he responded, closing his robe. "You will shock my servants. Besides, I am now hungry for my supper. Come to the Great Hall with me."

"Not tonight," she said. "I would rest before we begin our journey tomorrow. Besides the men in the hall always look slightly unnerved to hear my voice. I will return to my own chamber. With my lord Dominus's permission, of course." Her green eyes twinkled with mischief even as she spoke the words.

He pressed against her, the palm of one hand against the wall by her head. His other hand played with her long golden hair. "Have you cast a spell on me, faerie witch, that my hours without you seem empty no matter how busy I am?" He lifted up a lock of her hair and kissed it. "That the elusive fragrance you wear follows me wherever I go?" His hand cupped her head. "That you unleash in me feelings of incredible power and weakness in equal measure?" His lips brushed hers very, very softly.

Her eyes were closed as his smooth deep voice spoke to her. His words amazed and surprised Lara. But most of all they excited her, for she sensed in Magnus Hauk the man who was her equal. Her true equal. Could she fall in love with him? He was falling in love with her, she knew. Was she really capable of that kind of all-consuming love? Did she dare to be? Sometimes, Lara thought, she wished she was just a simple woman without a destiny. Without responsibilities. But that was not her fate.

His mouth closed over hers, and just for a moment she gave him what he desired, but only for a moment. Then she was smiling into his turquoise eyes, her hand caressing his face tenderly. He smiled back at her. "You will break my heart," he told her in a rare moment of candor.

"Not you, Magnus," Lara promised him softly. "Never." Then she slipped from his embrace and hurried from the little garden.

He watched her go. A tiny sigh escaped him. But

catching himself, he called a servant, and sent him to his sister asking her to join him at first moon rising. He would keep his promise to Lara, and send Uma, Felda and Alcippe away. They had begun to bore him of late anyway. One woman was more than enough for him—provided that woman was Lara. He realized with sudden clarity that he had waited all his life for her.

He repaired to his Great Hall for the evening meal. He would not tell even his closest associates that Lara was going to attempt to remove the sorcerer's curse. If she failed to find the answers she needed, there could be hard feelings toward her, or even toward the Dominus himself.

As the first silvery moon rose over the castle Sirvat joined her brother. She brought with her a dish of candied cherries she knew were his favorites. She sat down amid the pillows. They were in his garden, for the night was warm.

"I want you to find husbands, good husbands, for Uma, Alcippe and Felda," he said immediately. "A well-to-do man for Uma, for her family is of that station, and she would accept no less. A learned man for Alcippe, for she would be bored with any other. And for little Felda, perhaps a rich farmer's eldest son, but one with a good heart, for I can see Felda is a sweet girl. And see that the dower is very generous. Linens, down pillows and comforters, silver plate, a wardrobe to suit each bride, and a silk bag with fifty gold pieces each. And any jewels I have given them are theirs to keep. Is that generous enough, Sirvat?"

His sister nodded her head vigorously.

"Lara tells me that you speak, and it is the men's ears that are stopped up to the sound of our women's voices," the Dominus said.

Sirvat nodded, and smiled.

"We are riding out tomorrow to the Temple of the Great Creator. Lara says if she can find the words to the original curse she may be able to undo it so we may hear you."

Sirvat nodded again.

"Do you like her, Sister?" he asked.

Sirvat nodded, and pointed to him questioningly, smiling slyly.

"Aye," was all he would say.

Sirvat threw back her head, and her mouth opened wide, but her laughter was silent to him. Still, he could see she was laughing. What did her laughter sound like? What did her voice sound like? Suddenly he very much wanted to know.

"I long to hear your voice, Sister," he told her.

Sirvat pointed to him, and then back to herself again.

"You sound like me?" he replied.

Sirvat made a gesture with her thumb and finger.

He understood. "A little?" he said, and she nodded, smiling.

"Are you ready for a husband, Sister?" he asked her.

Sirvat shook her head vigorously in the negative.

Magnus Hauk chuckled. "If I know you as well as I believe I do," he said, "that means you would choose your own husband, eh, Sister?"

Sirvat nodded in agreement.

"Who is he?" he teased her. "Who has stolen your heart, Sirvat?"

The young woman smiled a mysterious smile at him, and then blushing turned her head away from his gaze.

"If Lara can lift the curse, will you tell me?" he asked her gently.

Sirvat nodded her assent, and passed him the bowl of candied cherries. The Dominus took a handful of the sticky fruit, and began to eat them one by one. Sirvat arose, and blew her brother a kiss as she prepared to leave him in his moonlit garden.

"A moment," Magnus Hauk said. "Send Uma, Alcippe and Felda to me, Sister."

Sirvat bowed to her brother, and hurried away. If only Lara could lift the curse. Then she would tell her brother that it was Corrado she loved and wanted for a husband. She had known him all of her life. They were distant kin. And she knew he wanted her by the looks he sent her when he thought no one else was watching him. But Sirvat also knew that Corrado was a modest man, and he would not aspire to the Dominus's younger sister for a mate. Still, he had not yet taken a wife.

Entering the women's quarters she found her brother's three Pleasure Women in their own garden enjoying the soft night air. She could scarcely wait to tell them of the Dominus's plans for them. "I have news," she said to them. "Where is Lara?"

"In her chamber," Felda said.

"Fetch her, for she must hear this, too," Sirvat said.

Felda arose and ran off, returning a few minutes later with Lara.

"What is it?" Lara asked.

"Sit down with the others," Sirvat said. She might be only sixteen, but she was in charge of her brother's house, and had been for almost two years now. "I have news that concerns you all. Uma, Alcippe and Felda, the Dominus has decided to find husbands for you, and he will also dower you quite generously."

"No!" It was Uma who spoke. "I wish no man but the Dominus."

"Be silent!" Sirvat said severely. "You will do what you are told, Uma. For you it will be a man of high caste, for you came from a high caste. For Alcippe a man of intellect and wit, for she has both. And for little Felda, a land owner's heir, for she is worthy of a fine young man who will appreciate her sweetness and good nature. Your dower portions will include silver plate and gold coins, among other things. You may keep any jewelry the Dominus gifted you with, and you will each have a horse of good breeding. It is a very generous benevolence my brother shows you."

"I am more than content," Alcippe said.

"And I certainly am," practical Felda agreed.

"I am not!" Uma snapped. "And what of Lara? What plans has the Dominus for her? Who is her husband to be?"

"Lara remains here," Sirvat said sweetly. "It would seem my brother favors her above all other women. He does not feel he needs three woman to attend him any longer, Uma. But I will not argue with you. I am but the messenger. My brother will now speak with the three of you in his gardens. Go!"

Uma rushed from the chamber, followed at a more sedate pace by Alcippe and Felda, who chattered with each other as they went.

"Why did you need me here?" Lara asked Sirvat.

"I hoped by telling them the news with you in attendance they would not hold you responsible for the Dominus's decision. Did you know of it?" Sirvat asked, curious.

"I did not know what he would do," Lara answered carefully. "I did suggest to him that these women might be better off with husbands."

Sirvat laughed. "You are very devious," she said.

"Nay," Lara told her, "but if your brother wishes to share pleasures with me, he cannot share them with others. Surely the men of Terah do not keep several women for pleasure in their households."

"There are no laws against it," Sirvat said. "Some do, but most cannot afford more than one wife. The few who can prefer to keep several Pleasure Women for their own private amusement. We have more women than men in Terah. Those who cannot find husbands have little choice. Some sell themselves publicly for pleasures. Other join the Daughters of the Great Creator, a religious community of women. Sometimes I think it must be a great relief to be in a family of only women."

"Will you marry one day?" Lara asked Sirvat.

The younger woman smiled. "If I may have my heart's desire, yes," she said.

"Who is he?" Lara was curious.

"You know him," Sirvat said with a small smile. "It is Captain Corrado."

Lara smiled. "You have chosen well. He is a good man, and was most kind to me. Does your brother know?"

"Nay, but when he is able to hear me tell him in my own voice, I will," Sirvat said. "Sometimes I write things to him that I cannot communicate otherwise, but not this."

"It is not a certainty that I can lift the sorcerer's curse from the men of Terah," Lara said. *What if she could not?*

"You will find a way. I know you will," Sirvat insisted.

Alcippe and Felda returned.

"The Dominus has been most thoughtful of us," Alcippe said. "And our dowers are much more than generous. They will assure us all fine husbands."

"Where is Uma?" Sirvat wanted to know.

"Trying to seduce the Dominus into changing his mind. Perhaps, Lara, you should go to him," Felda said softly.

"Did he request my presence?" Lara asked them.

"No, but she is being so aggressive," Felda fretted.

"If he has not asked for me, I shall not go. Magnus Hauk can well take care of himself," Lara replied as Uma angrily burst into the gardens.

"I will not be parceled off like some heifer cow," she shrieked. "I will sell pleasures in the streets first! I will pledge myself to the Daughters of the Great Creator, and never offer my body to a man again!"

"If you choose such a fate rather than accept a husband, then that is your decision, isn't it? And a very poor decision, too, I think," Lara said quietly.

"You!" Uma turned her anger directly toward Lara. "This is all your fault, faerie woman! Until you came the Dominus was content with us. Now suddenly we must be sent away from the castle." Her eyes narrowed, and suddenly she flung herself at Lara.

Lara raised a single hand, her palm up, and facing Uma. "Come no farther!" she warned the angry woman.

Uma stopped, confused.

"Do you want me to call the Punishment Mistress?" Sirvat said.

Alcippe and Felda grew pale at her words.

Uma whirled now to face Sirvat. "My lord Dominus would not permit such a thing," she sneered.

"In this part of the castle," Sirvat said, "my word is law, Uma. Never forget that. Now I will ask you again. Do you want me to call the Punishment Mistress?"

"Go ahead!" Uma challenged Sirvat.

The Dominus's sister did not hesitate a moment. Clapping her hands she called a female servant to her. "Bring the Punishment Mistress here at once."

Wide-eyed, the servant bowed and hurried off. The garden became deathly silent as they waited. And then suddenly the Dominus appeared.

"Sirvat has called for the Punishment Mistress?" he said to Lara.

"It is Uma. She is angry and defies your sister's authority, my lord Dominus."

"I cannot have that," he said quietly. "I will handle this myself."

The Punishment Mistress arrived. She was a large, tall woman accompanied by two great dogs. Seeing the Dominus she bowed servilely. "I was told it was the Lady Sirvat who called for me," she said.

"I did," Sirvat said. "But my brother wishes to manage the situation. Please remain, however. He will need your aid."

The Punishment Mistress bowed. "Yes, my lady Sirvat. You have but to instruct me, and I obey."

Uma threw herself at the Dominus's feet and looked piteously up at him.

Magnus Hauk smiled down at her coldly. Then his glance flicked to his sister.

"Tell this brazen creature her wiles will not move me," he said coldly. "And tell the Punishment Mistress I want the wide leather strap with the knotted fingers."

Alcippe and Felda had grown pale with fright. This was a side of the Dominus rarely seen. They did not like Uma, but they could not help but feel sorry for her.

"Must you?" Lara said softly to him as Sirvat spoke with the Punishment Mistress. "She fancies herself in love with you, and your favorite."

"I cannot let it be said that I am weak, even with a woman," Magnus Hauk replied. "Her behavior tonight is already being bruited about the castle. I must punish her so that no others follow her unfortunate example."

"Other women?" Lara asked him quietly.

"Men or women," he answered her. "Tomorrow you will begin to see the vastness of the Dominion,

Lara. And I am its master. I must never be seen as vacillating or insecure in my rule. This is what it is to be the Dominus of Terah."

She understood him perhaps better than any of the others. "Yes, my lord Dominus," she responded with a bow. The faintest of smiles touched his lips. The moment was so brief she was not certain that she had actually seen it.

"Strip her and bend her!" Magnus Hauk said in a cold voice. He watched impassively as Uma, once again spitting defiance, was pulled to her feet, her gown drawn off, and then bent facedown, her shoulders beneath the brawny arm of the Punishment Mistress who held the woman steady. Though Uma struggled, the large woman's grip was like iron. "Felda, Alcippe, go to your chambers," the Dominus said. "You need not remain. I see the distress and fear in your lovely eyes, but you have always been obedient to my will. You need not fear me."

Each girl kissed his hand in turn and fled.

The Dominus turned to his sister and Lara. "Will you remain?" he asked them.

The two women nodded silently.

Magnus Hauk now took the wide leather strap in his hand. One end of it had been divided into eight long fingers, which had been knotted several times. The strap would burn, but the knotted fingers would sting cruelly. "You will receive ten strokes of the strap, Uma," he told her. Then raising his hand he brought the leather down on the woman's full buttocks. Uma's lips pressed tightly together, but by the third blow she was shrieking and begging Sirvat to ask for mercy.

The Dominus could not hear Uma's cries, of course. All he heard was the snap of the leather and the crack it made when it hit the woman's plump buttocks. The dogs barked furiously and strained at their tethers. He saw the scarlet marks of the whip on her flesh, and knew from her struggle, and the concerned looks on Lara and Sirvat's faces, the burning pain the knotted leather fingers at the end of his strap were causing Uma. But he would not be defied by this creature. He plied the last three blows harder to make his point.

Sirvat remained silent throughout Uma's ordeal. She was not a cruel girl, but Uma had been rude and overbearing ever since she had been brought to the castle. And because Uma was one of her brother's women, Sirvat had not felt she had the right to punish her severely. She was not unhappy to see the bold woman now getting what she considered a just chastisement. And as by the fifth blow Uma was cursing her, Sirvat felt quite justified in her silence.

Lara watched the discipline being administered impassively. She understood quite well the reasoning behind Magnus Hauk's actions. But she also remembered long ago, when she was to be sold as a Pleasure Woman by Gaius Prospero, the slave woman Tania telling her of those who gained pleasure from giving pain. Yet that did not seem to be the case here. The Dominus was severe of face, and did not look as though he was enjoying himself at all. Still she was relieved, and she could see Sirvat was, too, as the final blow fell. By this time Uma was sobbing piteously.

Magnus Hauk laid the leather strap aside, saying tersely, "Attend to her." Then without another word, he departed.

Uma's back and buttocks were covered in narrow red weals.

"I will care for her," the Punishment Mistress said in her gravelly voice. She loosed her hold on Uma but a moment, catching the woman up in her arms. "Where is her chamber?" she asked Sirvat.

"This way," Sirvat said, leading the Punishment Mistress and her dogs off.

Lara remained behind in the garden, her eyes upon the sky. There were two moons above, each in a different quarter. The other two moons would soon rise. In Terah, as in the Outlands, the moons were silvery white. She wondered why only the moons of Hetar rose in brilliant color.

Sirvat returned, and sat beside Lara. "Uma is being attended to, but to hear her cries almost brought me to tears. The Punishment Mistress is dressing her wounds with a special ointment to numb the soreness. Uma must remain on her face for the next few days until her welts are less swollen and painful. Why did you remain? I had to, as head of my brother's household, but why did you?"

"The Dominus needed reliable witnesses. Had we not stayed, I am quite certain Uma would have lied to any who would listen, and told them that she cajoled him from his purpose with her female wiles. She cannot say that now. Several people have viewed her punishment. Not just you and I, but servants watching from behind the pillars. Undoubtedly she has mistreated them, and they were glad to see her being chastised," Lara said. "If she had plied him with her charms and we were not here to observe what transpired, they would have not dared to speak. But now the servants will tell their tale with great relish."

"I will have to find a strong man to husband her," Sirvat said. "It will not be easy, but her dower will entice, and her beauty is well-known. And to be given one of my brother's women for a wife is considered quite an honor."

"Then Alcippe and Felda will be easily matched," Lara said. "But how will you choose their husbands?"

"The Dominus's desires will be conveyed to several important women. They will bring me their recommendations, and then we will discuss each prospective suitor. When we have narrowed the field we shall bring in each girl separately and discuss it with her. Then the choice will be made. Because our men cannot hear us, they do not consider how much we hear. We are almost invisible and learn a great deal that way," Sirvat said with a small smile. "It makes it easier to find out the truth about the men. It will be better, however, if they can regain their hearing and finally hear us."

"You will be able to gain equality with them then," Lara agreed.

Sirvat laughed. "I think we are already superior to the men. The disadvantage is theirs, not ours. Terahn women have always held a certain amount of power. Even when they could hear our voices we were strong.

Had we not been, one of our sex could not have overcome the sorcerer. It is true he struck back at us with his dying breath, but now your faerie magic will help us to overcome his curse."

"Have you ever been to the Temple of the Great Creator?"

"I've never left the castle grounds, and I will not until I go to my husband's home," Sirvat said.

"I cannot guarantee I will be able to lift this malediction," Lara told her friend. "And I have not said I could. I can only try. I wish you had been to the temple, and could tell me about it. We call the god the Celestial Actuary."

"How perfectly Hetarian," Sirvat responded. "You are a people controlled by your commerce. While I have not visited the temple I can tell you something about it. The high priest is called Aslak. He is very old and, I have heard, prone to being narrow in his thought."

Lara nodded. "Yes, he would be, of course. Is there another I might approach if this man is obdurate in his ways?"

Sirvat nodded. "Our mother's brother, Arik, has already been chosen to succeed Aslak when he dies. This succession is always planned in advance when a high priest reaches old age. Aslak has already lived a hundred years. It would be my counsel to approach Arik first, seek his advice, and then allow him to guide you."

"The high priest would not be offended?" Lara wanted to know.

"Not if Magnus pays his respects first. Aslak need

not know of you until you find what you seek. And if you do not, he need not know of you at all."

"How clever you are," Lara said with a small chuckle.

"It is time for change," Sirvat told Lara, "but Terah plods along as it has for centuries. Nothing will move forward until the women of this land can once again be heard. It is time we knew more of what is beyond our borders."

"We are much alike," Lara remarked. "And I agree with you. Hetar has much to offer to Terah, but Terah in turn has much to offer Hetar."

"What could we possibly offer Hetar besides the luxuries we provide?"

"It is not yet time for me to speak," Lara told her friend. "Let us first solve the problem of the curse. Then I shall tell you what thoughts swirl about in my head."

"It is, I am told, a long day's ride," Sirvat said.

"I am used to riding. I enjoy it," Lara told her. "And my own horse, given to me by Kaliq of the Shadow Princes, came this day to Terah to join me. My mother gave him wings so he might fly." She laughed. "Andraste and Verica will be happy to know this. The horse is called Dasras, and he speaks."

Sirvat's turquoise-blue eyes grew round. "A horse that converses? This is great magic, Lara."

"Sometimes when I was out riding Dasras, I would speak on the matters that concerned or troubled me. He is a good listener, and an even better advisor," Lara said.

"You are advised by an animal?" Sirvat looked dubious.

"Animals have much wisdom, and often see things we mortals do not," Lara explained to her friend. "Listening to another's opinion can be helpful."

"I should like to meet this creature," Sirvat said.

"Come with me to the stables in the morning then, and I will introduce you," Lara promised her.

"What time will you depart?"

"The Dominus has not yet said. Perhaps I should send a servant to him requesting that information," Lara considered.

"Better you let him tell you," Sirvat advised. "Actually speaking with a woman must be quite an adventure for Magnus." She giggled. "Do not let him learn too quickly that you are wiser than he, Lara. Your mission must not be compromised in any way."

"Then perhaps it is best we both seek our beds," Lara considered.

Sirvat nodded. "I'm glad our rooms are nowhere near Uma's chamber. She will be moaning and groaning all the night long, I suspect."

Finally alone in her own chamber Lara spoke with Andraste, drawing her forth from her scabbard, and laying her faceup upon the bed. Verica stood upright in a corner, and at his mistress's request opened his eyes, which only made him look fiercer.

"My mother has sent Dasras to join us," Lara said. "Tomorrow we will ride out from this castle with the Dominus." She went on to explain to her two magical companions the nature of their quest.

"It will be good to get out of this castle," Andraste

said. "We have been confined for too long. Another day and I should become as irritable of nature as Verica."

"Indeed, singer of death and drinker of blood," Verica agreed. "I shall be equally glad to feel the wind on my face again."

"As the Dominus has not told me when we depart, I can only assume early in the morning," Lara told them. "Sirvat says it is a long day's ride to this temple."

A gentle knock sounded upon the door, and opening it revealed a woman servant.

"The Dominus requires your presence, my lady," the servant said.

"I will come at once," Lara replied, and hurried from her chamber. She knew her way through the castle well now, and quickly reached the apartments of the Dominus where Magnus Hauk awaited her. Smiling, he took her hand to lead her to his bedchamber, but Lara pulled her hand from his.

"Your sister says it is a long ride to the temple, my lord Dominus. If we are to depart just before the dawn then we need our rest," Lara said to him. "If you need a woman for pleasures call Felda or Alcippe. Uma, I fear, is yet indisposed."

"You are refusing to share pleasures with me?" he said, and she could see he was surprised, and perhaps just a little offended.

"I am not a slave who must do your bidding no matter," Lara said quietly. "When we share pleasures it is because we both desire it. Do not my honest cries of delight please you? Would you have me feign my passion, Magnus? I think not. You are too proud a man for games like that, and I would not offend you by playing them. The day has been long, and I must gather my strength for what lies ahead." Then she reached up and stroked his face with a gentle hand. "And did we not enjoy each other earlier?"

He caught the hand on his face, and kissed first the palm with burning lips, and then the soft tender spot on her wrist. "I can never gain all I want of you, Lara," he said low. "There is always a little piece of you that escapes me."

"It is my faerie nature," she told him with a mysterious little smile.

"Will I ever have all of you?" he asked her.

"No man ever has everything a woman can offer," Lara replied. Then she kissed his lips. "Good night, my lord Dominus. May I assume you wish to depart just before the dawn? I shall be ready then."

He nodded, and watched in silence as she left his apartments. For the first time in his life Magnus Hauk was both fascinated and intrigued by a woman. She had dismissed him, and had any other woman done that he would have punished her severely. Yet Lara's refusal had not offended him, only surprised him. What was it about the Hetarian woman that attracted him so greatly? He sighed, wondering if he would ever really know. Then because he had no other choice, and desired no other woman in his arms, the Dominus of Terah sought his lonely bed.

Chapter 7

GAIUS PROSPERO stood looking down on the City from his vantage point in the Tower of the Celestial. It was the highest man-made structure in all of Hetar, and located in the center of the Golden District. A great flight of stairs that twisted and wound up the inner core of the structure led to a single chamber at its top. A single glass window set between the stones encircled the tower giving Gaius Prospero a perfect view of the city and beyond in any direction he chose to look. There was no record or history of who had built the tower, and if there had once been it had been lost long ago.

Five years ago, following the Winter War, the tower had been crumbling into a ruin when the Master of the Merchants had purchased it, and rebuilt it. He had replaced the pointed slate roof of the building with a copper one overlaid in sheets of beaten gold. Glass blowers had been brought with their equipment to replace the great window. Two new heavy oak doors bound in iron were bought to replace the door at the bottom of the tower, and the one at the top. A single key locked each door, and only Gaius Prospero had that key. No one came into the tower who had not been invited, and so far Jonah was the only one other than Gaius Prospero to gain entry to his master's private domain.

Now, as the sun sank away for the day, Gaius Prospero sat in a comfortable chair watching for the moon rise. It soothed him to see the pale blue moon of the Midlands slipping into the sky, the twinkle of the stars as they popped into being, one by one. He had been told that in the Outlands all of Hetar's moons were visible. Now that would be a sight to see! And see it he would eventually.

The Outlands. He needed them. The soil of the Midlands was overworked, and the population of Hetar was growing. It seemed the poor had little else to do but drink Razi and futter their women. And there were too many poor now. Not enough of them died in the winters of late. Gaius Prospero was not an unreasonable man. He knew the poverty assailing Hetar was brought on by many factors. The people were not lazy. Given the opportunity they would work, and work hard. But there was no more work for them in Hetar. They needed the Outlands.

New farms large and small could be opened up, the smaller farms to appease the Squire of the Midlands. But large farms and vineyards would employ the poor, and put more profit into his hands, and those of his allies. The Coastal Kings were filling the markets with their usual supply of consumer goods, but there was not enough coin among the people to buy. The Kings were complaining, and with just cause, although he would not admit that to them. They were too insular, and more often than not behaved as if they were not even part of Hetar. That was going to change, he decided. For one thing the factories that produced those consumer goods had to be made to run more efficiently so the cost to the people be more reasonable so more could be sold. Sooner than later he would strip the Coastal Kings, and the Midlands of their autonomy. He would solidify the power into his hands alone.

He paused in his thoughts to consider the Shadow Princes. They were even more isolated than the Kings. And given their magic, extremely dangerous. It was unlikely he could co-op them into his imperial dreams. No, better to leave them alone, keep them as allies. They would not care as long as Hetar remained at peace, and there was a market for their horses. As for the rough Forest Lords, he had already begun taking some of their lands. Now that he knew their secret—that they could not produce sons on Forest women, but had to use slave women from elsewhere—he had them in the palm of his hand. The proud Forest Lords wanted no one knowing that their vaunted racial purity no longer existed. Gaius Prospero laughed. The fools!

His facile mind slipped back to the Outlands. He had spies there already. He knew from the Taubyl Traders that the lands were rich for growing, and for grazing. He imagined the flocks and herds that would come into Hetar's hands sooner than later. And the mines in the Purple Mountains would again be his. And the slaves they would gather! Many of the men would die, of course, in the war to come. But there would be women and children to be gathered up. They would have to be careful that the slave markets were not too full lest their prices be driven down.

And among those slaves would be the faerie woman, Lara. He hated her for defeating him. Yet he desired her with a lust such as he had never known. And he would have her! Oh, yes! He would! She would be brought to him naked. And he would have her spread upon his bed, her arms and legs tied to prevent her escape. Her luscious mouth would be gagged at first to prevent her speaking any spells against him. And he would touch her with his hands, his lips, his tongue, his cock. He would rub passion lotion on her until she was afire with her own lust, and unable to help herself. Then he would remove the gag, and she would beg him for pleasures. And eventually he would concede. But not before he had kissed her lips until they were purple and bruised. Not before he had filled her mouth with his cock, and made her suck him dry. But it wouldn't be enough for her. Faerie women were known for their very, very passionate natures.

And he would make her beg again while he enjoyed a restorative. Then he would call in Vilia and Anora, and he would amuse himself watching the three women make love. Anora would be jealous. She would want to punish Lara. And they would. Together. And finally he would fuck the faerie woman until she was screaming with the greatest pleasures she had ever known, would ever know. He would make her his personal love slave. And she would use her magic for him alone. Gaius Prospero sighed deeply with his daydreams of victory, acquisition and lust. Was not such conquest all of one piece? He wondered if Lara believed herself and the Outlands now safe from him. Did she ever think of him, he wondered vainly?

At that moment he would have been disappointed to know that Gaius Prospero was furthest from her thoughts.

EARLY IN THE MORNING, before the dawn, Lara went to the stables in the company of Sirvat, who was very curious to meet Dasras. The great golden horse did not disappoint. He greeted his mistress warmly and with respect. "And this is the Dominus's sister, who I am pleased to call friend," Lara introduced the young woman. Dasras made his bow, and greeted Sirvat politely.

"Greetings, great lady," he said to her.

"He really does talk!" Sirvat squealed.

"Of course I speak, lady. Did not my mistress say I did? She never prevaricates," Dasras assured Sirvat. "You are quite a pretty young woman," he noted.

Sirvat blushed at the compliment, replying, "And you are most gallant, Dasras. I hope we will have the opportunity to speak again, but I know my brother is anxious to depart. Farewell, and a safe journey." Hugging Lara, she hurried from the stables.

Lara had not left the Dominus's home since the day she arrived, and she had seen little of Terah other than what she could view from the castle windows. They rode out together with only a small escort of armed men. The road they traveled hung high above the fjord, curling slowly up as they went. The castle, she realized, was totally impregnable. Who had built it? she wondered. The longer she was in Terah the more questions she seemed to have, and the fewer answers were available to her.

They began to move inland away from the fjord. Everywhere Lara looked, the land was green. It was a rich and lush land, yet she saw no sign of habitation, mortal or domesticated creatures. Magnus had said their villages created the goods that were traded with the Coastal Kings, but where were those villages? Was this beauty an illusion? Was there something dangerous in this land?

"Where are your villages?" she finally asked the Dominus.

"They are scattered along the fjords," he answered her.

"Why are there no villages here?" she questioned him. "This is fertile land. Is there something wrong with it not visible to the naked eye?"

"Our living comes from the goods we manufacture," he explained. "Terah is a vast expanse, as you can see. By remaining near the fjords we are able to travel back and forth more easily with our wares. Ships sailing to meet with the Hetarians sail only from the fjord below my castle. All the goods are carefully catalogued, the registers kept within the castle. I pay the villages for the commodities they make and bring me, and they receive a share of the profits when the ships return."

"But what of their livestock? Have you no cattle, sheep or horses?" she queried.

"Each village has its herds and flocks," he replied. "They are kept in the meadows around and above the villages."

"How many Terahns are there, my lord Dominus?" Lara wanted to know.

"I have never counted," he told her with a laugh.

"How many villages?" she pressed him.

Magnus Hauk though a moment. "I am not certain," he admitted. "Why are you so curious?"

"My lord Dominus, you are the possessor of miles and miles of fertile land, yet there is no one making use of the land," Lara said. "You are the ruler of this place, and yet you have no idea of how many people you rule, or how many villages exist. I find this most strange. Do you not care?"

He considered his words before he spoke and then he replied to her. "We are a peaceful land, Lara. There is no want of any kind here. All of my people have homes in which to shelter from the elements. All of them are well fed. We have a purpose to keep our hands and our minds busy. We take and enjoy pleasures with one another. What more is there to life that that?"

"In Hetar—" she began, but he raised a hand to stop her.

"We are not Hetar," he said softly.

"You are more like the Outlands," she told him. "I

was happier there than in Hetar. Yet, I see this land that if cultivated could feed Hetar, and stop the want in that land."

"You have a good heart, faerie woman," he said.

"There are changes coming," Lara said to him. "Soon you will not be able to retain your isolation, my lord Dominus."

"An ocean separates us from the world of Hetar, and only the Coastal Kings know of our existence," he said. "I do not like change."

"No one is fond of change, especially great change," Lara agreed, "but change will come, my lord Dominus, whether we want it or not. The advantage is in seeing the coming changes first, and controlling them so they do not run rampant and control *you,*" she explained with a smile.

"Can you help me to control these changes you say are coming?" he asked.

Lara nodded. "I can," she told him. "But first we must see if we can undo the curse of the sorcerer, Usi."

"The temple we are visiting was once his home," the Dominus explained. "He was one of the priests, but he was seduced by an evil spirit, and turned from the light to the darkness. Ever since, the forces of the Great Creator have eschewed magic."

"Yet you would bring a half-faerie woman into their midst?" she asked surprised. "And one whose voice they will be able to hear and understand?"

"My uncle, who has already been elected to succeed the High Priest, is forward in his thoughts, Lara. I will speak with him first. There is a guest house on the temple grounds, and you will remain there until I have spoken with Arik."

"Does the temple receive women guests as a rule?" she wanted to know.

"Aye," he nodded. "They do. Women are not denied the opportunity to worship."

"But they rarely come to this temple, do they?" There was a small smile playing at her lips. She had learned a great deal from Sirvat in the early morning.

"You know we keep our women protected because of what we have viewed as their weakness," the Dominus said. "But now and again women are brought to the temple to worship. And there is a woman's order associated with this temple."

"I know. Sirvat told me," Lara said, and then she changed the subject completely. "I cannot get over how beautiful this land is, my lord. The shades of green are infinite."

"Are not the Outlands green?" he asked.

"Aye, but not like this," she told him. "The plain of the Outlands is a great grassy expanse that seems to go on forever. Now and again there are trees in small groves, or singly. And the purple mountains bordering three sides of it." She gazed ahead. "Ah, I see you have mountains, too. Are they as deserted as your plains?"

"Nay. There are a few mines in the mountains, quarried by mountain gnomes. They are solitary folk. Twice yearly they come to the castle bringing with them their gold, silver and gemstones, some of which is tribute to the Dominus, and the majority of which I distribute to certain villages who have smiths in gold, silver and gems. I pay the gnomes in the goods they need, or simply desire. We respect the mountains, and the gnomes in turn respect the Dominus."

"So, that is where you obtain the materials for the fine goods that are sold in Hetar," Lara noted. "Where do the beautiful fabrics you trade come from, my lord?"

"Other villages. Some cultivate the worm who spins the threads for the silken fabrics. Others raise sheep for fine wool. Several villages are devoted entirely to only the design and weaving of these fabrics. Others are in charge of the dyeing. Every one of my villages has a specialty so that no hands are idle, and all have a trade."

"Do your people never leave their villages?" Lara wondered. "The Outlands clan families meet each autumn at the Gathering to celebrate, and visit back and forth."

"Only designated members of each village are permitted to leave it," the Dominus explained. "The villages each keep to themselves."

"Why?" Lara wanted to know.

"It has always been that way," he responded with a shrug.

They rode on as the sun climbed into the heavens and considered its downward descent. The society of Terah was, Lara was learning, every bit as circumscribed as that of Hetar, perhaps even more so. In Hetar one might advance by following a circumspect set of rules, but here in Terah, where you were born determined the rest of your life, and there was obviously no chance for dissent. Lara knew from her conversations with Sirvat that the women of Terah didn't like it. Yes, things had to change, but they could only do so when the voices of the women of Terah could be heard once again. Lara was eager to face the challenge in breaking Usi's curse.

As the sun began to sink behind them they saw the walls of the Temple of the Great Creator ahead. The Dominus hurried his small party ahead so that they might reach the temple before the gates closed for the night. One of the men-at-arms rode ahead to warn the temple gatekeeper that the Dominus was approaching, in order to win them a few minutes more.

Just as the sun vanished beyond the horizon, they cantered into the temple courtyard, and as they dismounted they heard the gates behind them being pushed shut for the night, the great iron bar clanging into place. A young priest hurried forward to greet them, bowing low to his ruler.

"My lord, your uncle asks that you await him in the guest house. He will join you after evening prayers," the young priest said. His eyes were wide at the sight of Lara, her sword on her back and staff in her hand. But he was either too polite or too frightened to ask the question on his lips.

"Go along, lad," the Dominus said. "I know the way."

The priest bowed and hurried off, his brown robes swaying.

"Do not speak until I tell you," Magnus Hauk said low. "That a woman has entered the temple with me is cause enough for gossip, as my uncle is the next High

Priest. They will assume it is a family matter of some sort."

Lara nodded.

"They will think you are to be my bride, and I have brought you to my uncle for his approval," the Dominus told her with a mischievous grin.

Lara bit her lip in vexation, and he chuckled. "Oh, how you want to refute that, don't you?"

Lara shook a finger at him in exasperation, and he laughed aloud. He was right, of course. The sound of a woman's voice could send the poor priests of the Great Creator into a fright. Meekly she followed Magnus Hauk from the outer yard into a large inner courtyard planted with graceful trees, and delicately scented flowers and bushes. A meandering stream opened into a small lake filled with green lily pads and flowers. The lake drained at the other end into another stream. Lara and Magnus crossed the water on elevated square stones to reach the temple guest house.

"Beautiful, isn't it?" he asked her.

Lara nodded in agreement.

"I don't want any of the priests to hear your voice yet, even accidentally. It would cause great consternation," he told her. "I would tell my uncle first that your voice can be heard by the men of Terah, and why."

She nodded her understanding as she sat down on a gilded wooden chair. From a nearby sideboard he brought her a small goblet of wine, which she sipped gratefully. They had stopped but once during the journey to water their horses and relieve themselves. Lara was hungry, thirsty, tired and sore. It had been some time since she had ridden for so far and so long.

Before long a tall slim man with an ageless face entered the chamber. Magnus Hauk arose immediately to greet him. "Uncle!" The two men embraced.

Immediately Arik Hauk's eyes went to the woman with his nephew. Her beauty was astounding. But her garb—leather pants, a silk shirt and leather vest—was odd. Stranger still was the fact she carried a sword and a staff. Weapons both, he recognized. "Who is this guest you have brought me, Nephew?" he asked.

"This is Lara, Uncle. She is Hetarian. She was sent to me by one of the Coastal Kings who thought to curry my favor," Magnus Hauk began to explain.

"You were sent a slave woman?" the priest said.

"She is not a slave, Uncle. She is the widow of a great lord, but the Coastal King involved had a grudge against her, and thought to revenge himself by attempting to enslave her and send her across the Sea of Sagitta."

"And how do you know this, Magnus?" the priest wanted to know.

"She has told me, Uncle."

Arik Hauk paled. "What do you mean, she told you?" he demanded.

"Because she is not of this land, I can hear her voice, Uncle," Magnus Hauk said.

"You can hear this woman's voice?" The priest now looked intrigued. "Could I hear it, Nephew?"

"All men can hear it," came the reply. "May I allow her to speak to you, Uncle?"

The priest nodded eagerly.

The Dominus turned to Lara, and nodded.

Lara stood, and bowed politely to Arik Hauk. "Greetings, my lord Arik, uncle to the Dominus," she said. "I have come to this great temple because I need your help."

"How is it possible that I can hear you?" the priest asked her.

"I am Hetarian born, my lord Arik. I am the daughter of John Swiftsword, the Crusader Knight, and Ilona, queen of the Forest Faeries. The curse that Usi the Sorcerer placed on Terah was not on your women, my lord, but on the men who listened to the women who helped them defeat the sorcerer. Your women have never lost the ability to speak, but your men had their ears stopped up so they could not hear the voices of Terahn females. I, however, am not born of this place, and so the curse did not extend to me."

"Amazing!" the priest said. "But you said you need my help? How can I help you, my lady Lara?"

"Magnus has told me that Usi was a member of this order who was sadly seduced by the forces of darkness," Lara said. "Did he remain within these temple precincts?"

"Sometimes, after he had gained power, he did. And he built the castle in which the rulers of the Terahn Dominion reside today," Arik said.

"You did not tell me that Usi lived in the castle!" Lara exclaimed.

"I had forgotten about it until my uncle just now reminded me," the Dominus said.

"I believe if I can find the curse he uttered against you," Lara told the priest, "that I can reverse it.

Magnus believes it could be written in the Book of Terah."

"Indeed, Nephew, that is possible, but it could also be somewhere within your own castle," Arik Hauk said.

"That should have been the first place we looked," Lara said with a sigh.

"But the castle is so public," the Dominus said. "I think it more likely Usi would have hidden his curse, if indeed he even wrote it down, here at the temple."

"Sorcerers always write their words down once they have decided upon what they will say. Each one has a book of curses, for they never know if they might not use them again," Lara explained. "He could have written these words in the Book of Terah, or he could have a separate book. Well, we are here, so I suppose it best we begin our search here—with your permission, my lord Arik."

"It is not my permission you need, but that of the High Priest Aslak," Arik said.

"You are his duly elected successor," the Dominus noted. "I have heard that Aslak has grown old and feeble. That you make the decisions for the temple now."

"Indeed I do, Nephew," Arik Hauk said. "But I always place everything before the High Priest first as a matter of courtesy, you understand. Aslak is, by virtue of having lived all but twelve years of his life here in the temple, suspicious of women. And should he hear your lovely voice, my lady Lara, he would count it magic. And Aslak hates magic. He believes all magic is evil. He learned his lessons at the knee of an ancient High Priest who had been taught by one who had been taught by one who was a young man when Usi the Sorcerer was drawn to darkness. For these men, magic was wicked."

"Magic can indeed be wicked," Lara agreed, "but most magic is good."

"Usi's magic was dark and cruel," Arik said. "But you would appear to be a creature of light and goodness. I have always believed in a balance between dark and light. This is not an opinion I share publicly, for Aslak is most tenacious in his own beliefs, but many among us believe in this balance."

"Mortals share this balance, too," Lara said softly.

Arik smiled. "You are as wise as you are beautiful, I see," he said.

"Can you help us, Uncle?" the Dominus wanted to know.

Arik nodded. "I can. But first, Magnus, you must pay your respects to Aslak, for he will already know of your visit. But how to explain you have been accompanied by a woman, Nephew? For he will know that, too," Arik said.

"We will say one of the Coastal Kings in Hetar with whom we trade has sent me the woman as a possible bride. And as she pleases me well, I have come to see if she meets with your approval as the oldest male in our family. You, of course, if asked, will say you are reserving your judgment until you know Lara better."

Arik looked at Lara's disapproving face and chuckled. "Your prospective bride does not seem happy with this explanation," he noted.

"I will agree to it as it seems the simplest and best explanation," Lara said. "But I am not of a mind to take another husband."

"So you loved your husband," Arik said.

"His name was Vartan, Lord of the Fiacre, and head of the Outlands High Council. He was a good man," Lara elaborated. "I have two children, too. A son, Dillon, and a daughter, Anoush."

"Where are your children now?" the priest inquired.

"My children are in the care of blood kin of my husband's," she explained. "My husband was assassinated on the orders of an ambitious Hetarian, Gaius Prospero. Hetar has always believed the Outlands are savage and lawless, but that is not so. I have lived both in Hetar and the Outlands, and I far prefer the Outlands."

"Would you consider my nephew as a husband, my lady Lara?" Arik surprised her by asking. His look was curious.

"I don't want another husband," she told him. "I have been told I have a destiny, and so I must be free to follow that destiny."

"But if you were free to wed again," the priest persisted. "Would you choose Magnus, my lady Lara?"

"Your nephew is too overbearing, and I too independent," Lara said. "It is better that opposites attract rather than like, my lord Arik."

"Perhaps," Arik murmured with a small smile. He liked this woman, and had decided in the short time of their acquaintance that she would make his nephew an excellent wife. She was every bit as strong as he was, and Magnus would not wear her down until she bored him. This woman would never bore his nephew.

"When should I see Aslak?" Magnus asked, breaking into his uncle's thoughts.

"He will be having his evening meal now, and we should be served ours shortly. Afterwards, and before the last prayers of our day," Arik decided.

The door to the chamber in which they were all now standing opened, and a line of servants came in bearing food. Lara grew silent again. They were seated, Arik at the table's head, and his guests on either side of him. Plates and implements were set before them. Dishes and platters were passed about by the servants. Lara accepted each dish with a polite nod of her head to the silent servants. Wine was poured. They ate their meal in silence as was the custom of the temple dwellers, and as the servants remained in the chamber, Lara knew she must not speak again until they were alone. When the meal was finally cleared away the two men arose from the table. Magnus bent to kiss Lara on the cheek.

"I will return shortly, lady," he told her, and she smiled and nodded.

"She is very intelligent," Arik remarked as they hurried from the guest house to the High Priest's dwelling. "It is long past time you took a wife, Magnus. The faerie woman from Hetar is fresh blood. And she intrigues you, I can see."

"There is time yet for me to take a wife and sire children," the Dominus said. "I am in no hurry. She is quite magical, Uncle. The sword and the staff she carries both speak, as does her horse. Lara's faerie mother gave the horse wings so he might fly across the Sea of Sagitta to join her. She claims she has killed with that sword. Such a formidable woman may not be the woman for me. I need a woman who will give me children willingly. A wife who will mother those children as a woman should, and not go off seeking a destiny. She is beautiful, and I am fascinated with her, I will admit. But I do not know if I would wed her."

"She is precisely the wife for you, Magnus," his uncle said. "The kind of woman you believe you seek to wed would bore you in a year. This is a strong female, and have you not possibly considered that the destiny that has been predicted for her may also be your destiny? Have I not told you, Magnus, that change is coming? And perhaps now is not the time for children, Nephew. One day, yes. But first you must cope with what is to come. I play the traditionalist, Nephew, but you know that I am also progressive in my thoughts and ideas. I can do little until Aslak has gone on into the next life, but when he has departed, Magnus, I shall implement my plans for the Brotherhood of the Great Creator, and for the Daughters of the Great Creator, too.

"I will do all I can to help you find the written words of the curse contrived by Usi the Sorcerer. Imagine the possibilities for the Dominion, for all of Terah, if we could once again hear our women's voices, listen to their counsel and their ideas? We have not moved forward in over five hundred years because of that wretched curse, Magnus!"

"Uncle, I am astounded by the breadth of your vision," the Dominus remarked.

Arik smiled almost sardonically. "Indeed, Nephew," he said dryly. "Some would claim I am touched by the darkness because I desire change."

"Not you," Magnus Hauk replied to his uncle.

They reached the house of the High Priest, and were admitted into his presence. Magnus Hauk went immediately to the frail old man seated in a large, well-cushioned chair, and taking his thin hands into his own big ones pressed them first to his head, then his heart and finally to his lips. "I greet you, my lord Aslak," he said, "and I thank you for your hospitality."

"You have come with a woman," the reedy voice of the old man said.

"I have, my lord. The girl was sent to me from Hetar, a gift of a Coastal King. He thought I might take her as a bride," the Dominus said easily.

"And you have brought her to your uncle for his approval?" the high priest quavered.

"I have, my lord," Magnus Hauk answered.

"And what think you, Arik? Is the girl worthier than a Terahn girl to be the Domina of the Dominion?" the tremulous old voice asked. "Must your nephew take a foreigner to wife?"

"I am, you will understand, reserving my judgment, my lord Aslak. I have only just seen the girl. She is extraordinarily beautiful, and she seems pleasant enough," Arik answered. "But of course I cannot tell on such a short acquaintance. My nephew means to remain here for a few more days so I am able to make my decision. A marriage with a Hetarian girl might prove useful to Terah."

"What should we care for Hetar?" the High Priest wanted to know. "They are good for trading with, and nothing more."

"True, too true, my lord Aslak," Magnus Hauk agreed amiably, "but there could come a day when Hetar will no longer be content to meet us in midsea to trade. There may come a day when they want to come here, and we cannot stop them. Perhaps a Hetarian wife would help me to understand them so if that day comes Terah will not be at a disadvantage. We will know more of them than they of us, eh?"

The High Priest digested the Dominus's words, and then he chuckled. "Heh! Heh! You are a wickedly clever fellow, my son. I can see the benefit in such a tactic. Well, if she pleases you, and your uncle approves, you will have my blessing, also. I will even perform the wedding rite myself."

"You honor me, my lord Aslak," Magnus Hauk said jovially.

"Bring the girl to see me before you leave," the old man said. And then his eyes closed. "I am weary," he murmured.

"With your permission we will withdraw," Arik said, "and leave you to your rest."

The High Priest did not open his eyes again, but waved a languid hand in a gesture of dismissal to the two men, who backed from the chamber.

As they walked through the temple gardens Arik said in a satisfied voice, "He is content now that he knows everything there is to know, Nephew. You played your part well. I congratulate you on your answers to him. He is old, but his wits are yet sharp although not as sharp as they once were."

"Can we begin our search tomorrow?" the Dominus wanted to know.

"Aye," Arik agreed. "I will bring the books to you so Lara will not be publicly viewed searching through them. It is better, and will keep the gossip at a minimum."

"What, Uncle," Magnus Hauk teased his relation, "are you telling me you do not spend all your time in prayer and meditation within these hallowed precincts?"

Arik Hauk chortled. "I leave prayer and meditation to the youthful members of the brotherhood who are filled with the enthusiasm of piety," he said.

"Have you no fear of the Great Creator then, Uncle?" the Dominus asked.

"The Great Creator knows my true worth, Nephew," Arik Hauk said dryly.

They had reached the square stone path leading over the water to the guesthouse. "I will bid you good night, Nephew," the older man said. "Enjoy the remainder of your evening. I think I almost envy you, but then I have not had the desire since entering the temple order to take a hearth mate, as many of my brothers do. Women can be a deterrent to ambition, and it is not my responsibility to breed up sons for our family." He hurried off into the deepening twilight.

Magnus Hauk walked slowly across the waterway. He could smell the sweet elusive fragrance of the hyacinths and water lilies that grew all around him. The guest house seemed empty. Where had Lara disappeared to? He walked into a bedchamber, and he could hear her humming somewhere near. Moving through a smaller door at the end of the chamber he found himself in a bath.

"It's wonderful!" Lara said from the water of the pool. "I have already washed my body, and my hair. Hurry and join me, Magnus."

He stripped off his garments and washed himself in the bathing recess. There was a large sea sponge, and a dish of soft soap. He used them lavishly, following her lead and washing both his body and his dark golden hair. Then he stood beneath a spouting stone fish and rinsed himself off. Finally he entered the bathing pool, taking her into his arms, and kissing her a long, satisfying kiss.

"Should we be so carnal while we are on the temple grounds?" Lara asked him. Then she nibbled lightly on his lower lip.

"The Great Creator is devoted to life, my faerie love. Does our lustful play not embody life itself?" he asked her pulling her harder against him. He loved the feel of her soft breasts against his hard chest. He could feel his desire for her growing.

Lara slipped her arms about his neck. She felt his manly length hard against her thigh. He lifted her from the water, his tongue slowly licking up the length of her torso, between her breasts and up her throat. Lara lowered her head, and whispered into his ear, "I want you inside of me, my lord. I need to feel your hardness."

He lowered her slowly back into the water and

pushed her hard against the wall of the pool. He was burning for her. His hands cupped her bottom to lift her up as she wrapped her legs about him. He struggled with himself that he not enter her too quickly, for he wanted them both to enjoy the sweet anticipation a slow entry could give them.

She was always so wonderfully tight for him. Inch by inch he pushed forward into the heat of her.

Lara cried out softly as she felt him entering her with incredible restraint. Her teeth sank into the flesh of his shoulder and he moaned. Then to her surprise he was fully sheathed and walking slowly from the pool, his big hands clasping the firm twin moons of her buttocks. Reaching a marble bench he carefully straddled it, lowering her down. Then he began to pump himself back and forth within her until Lara was almost screaming with the pleasure he offered. Twice her juices flowed over the firm hot manhood within her.

Then to her great surprise he withdrew from her, turning her about, and pushed into a place she had never again thought to entertain a manhood. Lara gasped. The entry had hurt slightly, but now he just rested, throbbing, within the tight passage while she quivered beneath him, his hands bruising the flesh of her hips. "Magnus!" she managed to say.

His big body leaned over her. "You belong to me, my faerie lover," he growled as he slowly withdrew, and then plunged back within her. "This makes you mine alone."

Lara did not bother to tell him of the Shadow Princes, who had taken her body lovingly in every possible way. She could barely remember that night for as her princely lover had told her, she had been on another plane as they taught her the lesson of complete trust. "For now," she agreed, and then he shuddered, spilling his juices within her in great and violent spurts.

He collapsed upon her briefly, finally rising and pulling her up into his arms that he might kiss her. Over and over his mouth pressed kisses on her, and Lara reciprocated. Then laughing she pushed him away at last, and returned to the scented pool. He quickly joined her, pulling her back into his embrace for more kisses.

"I adore you!" he groaned against her lips.

"Do not love me, Magnus. At least not yet," Lara warned him gently.

"If I can't love you, I will surely kill you," he whispered to her.

Lara pulled away from him, taking his face between her two hands. "No, you won't," she told him. "Trust me, my lord Dominus. I will not fail either of us."

He drew her back into his arms, and her head rested against his shoulder. "Did you blood me before where you bit me?" he asked her.

"You will be bruised, I fear, but I did not bite you hard enough to break the skin. One day I may if you continue to offer us such incredible pleasure, Magnus."

"You seek to placate me," he told her.

"Aye," she agreed.

He laughed. "Such candor is refreshing," he told her.

"I am always honest," she said softly. Then pulling away from him she stepped up from the warm water, and reaching for a drying cloth began to dry herself. "For a religious order the accommodations are quite fine, my lord Dominus. They are obviously wealthy, and no poor mendicants."

"A third of what we earn in our trade with the Coastal Kings is given to the Temple of the Great Creator," he explained. He remained within the pool cooling his ardor for the moment. She would be in his bed the night long, and they would pleasure each other again. And mayhap yet again, he considered.

Lara sat down on the bench where they had recently sported, and rubbed her hair dry with the cloth. He watched her enjoying the simple task she performed. Then she arose, and with a smile at him disappeared into the bedchamber. The warm water had relaxed him after their long day's ride. Magnus climbed from the bathing pool, and taking a fresh drying cloth rubbed the droplets of water first from his big frame and then from his thick hair. Then he padded across the marble floor of the bath and into their bedchamber. Lara was brushing her hair with her beautiful gold brush.

He took it from her, and began to groom her tresses himself. "It's like thistledown mixed with moonlight and sunbeams," he told her.

"How poetic," she said to him. "I like to have my hair brushed."

"Have other men brushed it?" he asked, an edge to his voice.

"Yes," she answered him simply.

"Who?" he demanded to know.

"Magnus," Lara told him gently, "it is too soon for you to want every detail of my history. And right now I am not of a mind to relate that history. I will tell you that both my father and Gaius Prospero considered me born to give pleasure. But what they did not consider was that my destiny has nothing to do with either my beauty, or my proficiency for passion." She stood up, and took the brush from his hand, smiling into his turquoise eyes. "Are you weary, my lord Dominus? I know that I am. It has been a very long day, and I am tired."

Taking his hand she led him to the bed that they would share.

"I am the ruler of a vast land," he said to her, "and yet you do not fear me, my faerie love. Should you not?"

"Why?" she asked him with a smile, and drew him down into her embrace.

He laughed softly. "I shall never really tame you, Lara, will I?"

"You are clever to understand that so quickly, Magnus."

He could see she was indeed tired, and their earlier bout of passion had taken the edge off his appetite for her. He shifted himself so that she was now in his arms, her head upon his broad chest. "Go to sleep, my faerie love," he told her. The morning would be soon enough, the Dominus thought, and it was always a fine way to begin a day.

But when he awoke the sun was already streaming through the windows of the bedchamber, and Lara was gone. Where? he wondered, his feet hitting the floor. She was not in the bath. He looked into the outer chamber where they had eaten last night and saw her sitting silently at the table as a servant offered her fresh fruit, cheese and bread. She was already dressed in her pants, shirt and vest, her long hair fashioned in a single braid. Dressing quickly, he joined her, kissing her cheek in greeting, but saying nothing directly to her.

"Ask my uncle to attend me when he is able," he told the hovering servant. "The lady Lara will see to my needs as the food is here."

"Yes, my lord Dominus," the servant said, and hurried out of the guest house.

"Are we alone otherwise?" Magnus Hauk asked his companion.

She nodded, but said nothing, putting her fingers to her lips in a warning, her eyes going to the left. Outside on the colonnaded porch he saw another servant sweeping.

"Good girl!" He approved her astuteness, and her caution.

Lara smiled, and began to serve him his meal. He ate swiftly, more to finish the meal than enjoy it. He was as anxious as she probably was to begin reviewing the books of Terah held by the temple. Finally Arik Hauk arrived.

"I am sorry," he said. "The High Priest had many instructions for me this morning. I believe he seeks to impress upon you that he is still competent to do his job."

"It is not my right to remove him even if he wasn't," the Dominus said.

"He has some moments of confusion although overall his wits remain sharp and clear. Still, he is one hundred and fifty. He has not many years left, Nephew, and he has been a good High Priest. May I be as excellent."

"I do not fear for the brotherhood in your hands, Uncle," Magnus Hauk said. "Now, the books. Will we view them here, or in the library?"

"I thought both," Arik Hauk said. "That way it will appear natural. The Dominus is reviewing the books of Terah for himself while he visits. You were considered a scholar in your youth, Magnus, and that is well-known. When you are in the library, for Lara cannot go there, I will bring her a book to peruse here."

For the next few days the Dominus, Arik and Lara read through the holy books of Terah, which were never finished, for each succeeding generation added to them. They reached the era in which Usi the Sorcerer had entered the brotherhood as a novice. They read of his progress as he made an assent through the various levels of the religious order. And then there came the first mention of difficulty with Usi, and the realization, too late, that he had turned from the light to the darkness. And the darkness brought Usi incredible power even after he had been expelled from the brotherhood. The sorcerer built a large army for himself, and overthrew the ruling royal family, systematically murdering them as he found them. But some escaped the sorcerer's vigilance, going into hiding.

Usi had a fierce appetite for female flesh. He kept

a great house of women for both his salacious pleasure, and to torture, for he gained more pleasure from inflicting pain than from merely copulating with a female. The Terahns began to hide their women in an attempt to protect them, but families caught shielding their wives, daughters, sisters and others were subject to great public humiliation. The women were publicly raped multiple times while their men were whipped until their backs were raw. Virgins were taken to the sorcerer for his delectation. Eventually the resistance ceased, and families took the chance that Usi would not take one of their women if they were discreet, and did not venture out too often.

All the profits from the trade with Hetar went into Usi's pocket until one of his braver aides ventured that the craftsmen and women needed something if they were to continue in their work. Tools needed to be replaced, looms and spinning wheels repaired, and nothing could be had for free. Grudgingly the sorcerer gave a minute portion of his profits to the villages, threatening them with slow painful deaths if the quality of their goods grew shoddy. It was a time of terrible unhappiness, the books of Terah recalled in great and graphic detail.

And then one brave woman, a distant relation of the former ruling family, decided that Usi's reign of terror must end. She convinced a brother to accept a place that had been offered him in Usi's court. And to her brother's apparent distress the woman, whose name was Geltruda, allowed herself to be innocently seen on several occasions by the sorcerer. But always her mien was virtuous and meek. Fascinated

by Geltruda's beauty and modesty, Usi approached the woman, but eyes lowered, she demurred and rejected his invitations in such a manner that he was not in the least offended. Indeed he was intrigued by her air of fearful respect for him while maintaining her unworthiness to be even considered for his bed.

As the weeks went by Usi's lust for Geltruda grew, but to everyone's surprise the sorcerer was patient in his quest for this woman. Finally she admitted to him that while he was her ruler, and she very much wanted to obey him, her brother must give his permission for Geltruda to go to Usi's bed. To no one's surprise the brother agreed. But what neither Usi nor his court was aware of was that Geltruda and her brother had planned it all. Usi had no heirs. The Hauk family, Terah's rightful rulers, would be restored if all went as Geltruda had planned. And it would if her brother would just play his part, and be brave.

On the night Geltruda chose to give in to Usi's lusts, her entire body, even her hair, was bathed in a fatal poison. It would take several hours for the poison to kill Geltruda, and by that time Usi would also be dead. Smelling of night-blooming lilies she entered his private chamber shyly, admiring the sorcerer's physique, worrying that his manhood might be too large for so dainty a woman as she. The sorcerer could not contain his burning desire for Geltruda, but he was a master of seduction nonetheless, and took his time with her. His lips kissed every inch of the woman's trembling body. He suckled her breasts greedily. His tongue licked and caressed her with fiery ardor.

Then, mounting her, he used her enthusiastically unaware that even as his crisis approached he was dying.

And then Usi became aware all too late of what was happening to him. "What have you done, woman?"

"I have, with my brother's help, freed Terah!" Geltruda gasped, near her end. Then the pupils of her eyes dilated, and she died.

With his own dying breath, Usi the Sorcerer laid a curse upon the people of Terah.

"Is it written there?" Magnus Hauk asked Lara, who had been reading the tale. It was evening, and they were alone.

Lara shook her head. "The curse is not here," she said.

"We are confounded then," the Dominus said.

"Not necessarily," Lara replied.

"Why do you think that?" he asked her.

"The sorcerer was not here when Geltruda killed Usi. Where was he? Most likely in the castle. Usi's private chamber is mentioned several times in the text. Where is that chamber, Magnus? That is where he would have kept his book of spells. I should have considered that before. The book would not be here at the temple, nor would those spells be written down in the books of Terah for all to see and use. No! He would have kept the book hidden in his own rooms. And a spell so potent would have had to be written before he could use it. We must return to the castle as soon as possible, and search those rooms."

"But no one will know where Usi lay his head after all this time," the Dominus said. "We will have to search every chamber in the castle, and there are many."

"Given Usi's delight in torture, his secret chamber would be someplace a woman's cries could not be easily heard," Lara observed.

"The old dungeons, perhaps?" the Dominus suggested.

"I think not. Too many of Usi's ordinary prisoners would be close by, to overhear. More than likely a tower room, where he could easily vanish if enemies approached."

"Would he not be trapped there?"

"He undoubtedly had the power of shape-shifting as many magic folk do," Lara replied. "He could always become a mouse, and slip through a crack, or a bird, and fly from the window, Magnus."

"Do you have such power?" the Dominus asked her curiously.

"Yes," she answered him. "I rarely use the talent, for it is difficult."

"Sometimes I think I should be frightened of you, Lara," he told her.

"No," she responded. "You need not fear me. I told you that my magic is used only for good."

"And you do not fear the darkness?" he asked her.

"No. I need not, for I am the very essence of light, my lord Dominus."

"I will find my uncle and tell him we will leave at first light," he said.

"Yes," Lara agreed. "I am anxious to return to your castle and seek out this hidden place. Usi's book of spells will be there. I am certain!"

"The High Priest wanted to see you before we left. I must honor that request. I will speak with Arik and arrange for it tonight before we sleep," Magnus said. He arose from the table where they had been seated. "I will be back for you shortly."

When he had gone from the guest house Lara dug into her saddlebag and retrieved a carved and gilded wooden peach. Opening it, she drew out a simple gown of pale green silk with long flowing sleeves, a straight skirt and a modestly draped neckline. She had no sandals, but her bare feet would not be considered untoward on a summer's night. Lara quickly put on the gown, brushed her hair, and rebraided it into a single plait. Then she draped a long matching veil over her head. There was no mirror in the guest house, but Lara knew she looked every inch the proper woman.

Returning, the Dominus was surprised to find her so modestly garbed. "I did not know you had such a gown with you," he said.

"Would you have me appear before your High Priest garbed as a warrior woman, my lord Dominus?" she countered.

"Your look is deceptively innocent," he remarked.

She smiled mischievously. "I believe the High Priest will find me quite suitable," she told him. "Now let us go, my lord Dominus."

Taking her arm he led her from the guest house.

Chapter
8

THE HIGH PRIEST of the Brotherhood of the Great Creator peered sharply at Lara with his rheumy old eyes. He was pleased to see that both her demeanor and her dress were modest. He had never been to Hetar, and he knew little about it. But stories he had heard in his youth declared that Hetar was a venal and licentious world. The woman before him seemed pleasant enough, but something fretted him about her. When she met his gaze for a brief moment, her emerald eyes to his clouded ones, he knew exactly what it was.

"She is faerie!" he declared in a hard and shaking voice.

"Yes, the Coastal King said she was half-faerie," the Dominus said.

"She will have magic, and magic is evil. It cannot be tolerated here in Terah," the High Priest replied. "Kill her, Magnus Hauk, and her magic will be destroyed. Hetar has sent her to harm us, I am certain of it. If you will not slay her I will have my guards do it before she infects you with her evil—if she has not already done so." He now glared at Lara with disdain.

"There is something you should know about this lady, my lord Aslak," Arik said quietly. "We can hear her voice."

The old man jumped backward with shock. "Evil!" he insisted, pointing a bony finger at Lara.

"No, my lord Aslak," Arik told the high priest. "We hear her voice because she is not of Terah, but even more amazing, she had told us that our women do indeed speak. It is we who cannot hear," he explained.

"What blasphemy is this?" Aslak demanded angrily. "The women of Terah were condemned to be voiceless through eternity."

"No, my lord Aslak," Lara said softly. "It was the men who listened to their women who were cursed. Because I am of Hetar you can hear my voice, and I have both heard and spoken with your women."

Aslak had grown pale at the sound of Lara's voice. Now he stumbled backward, clutching at his chest. His eyes began to roll back in his head, and his mouth moved but no sound could be heard. Suddenly he collapsed onto the floor.

Arik knelt, and sought for a pulse. He drew a small smooth metal square from his robes, and held it before the High Priest's nostrils. The mirror remained clear, and unblemished. "He is dead," Arik said sanguinely. "He was very old." Then rising he went to the door of the High Priest's chambers, and called out. "The High Priest has collapsed! Come quickly, my brothers!"

And there was suddenly the ringing of a bell, and the chamber filled with the men belonging to the order.

"The High Priest was just giving his blessing to the Dominus and his proposed wife when he collapsed," Arik explained loudly.

It was a reasonable explanation, and the sight of the modestly garbed and veiled woman clinging to the Dominus, her head hidden in his shoulder, certainly gave credibility to the scene.

"He was an old man," one of the brotherhood said. "All praise to the Great Creator for his goodness in taking Aslak in such a merciful fashion."

"And all hail to the new High Priest Arik," another of the brotherhood said, and the chamber echoed with huzzahs.

Arik nodded graciously at their acclaim. Then he said, "Nephew, take the lady Lara from this scene of sadness. It is not fit for her lovely eyes. My brothers, we must prepare our departed brother Aslak for his funeral pyre."

As the men of the order surrounded their fallen leader, the Dominus led Lara back to the guest house in the lake.

"This is terrible," Lara said softly to him. "I have killed the old man with the very sound of my voice."

"He died because it was his time," Magnus Hauk said. "He was very old, and narrow in his thinking. He would have been an impediment to our plans to reverse Usi the Sorcerer's curse upon us. My uncle will be a more forward-thinking High Priest, which suits me, and that will be better for Terah. There is magic here. There always was, but under Aslak's influence those who have it were forced to keep silent."

"But he was so shocked at the sound of my voice," Lara worried.

"Your voice is a beautiful one. I think it was that beauty that overcame him," the Dominus told her.

Lara laughed weakly. "What a time, Magnus, to be so gallant," she said.

"Sit down," he ordered her, and then he poured them goblets of wine.

"Drink this. It will calm you. And then you must go to bed. We have an early start."

"But will there not be a departure ceremony of some sort?" she asked him. "Should you not be there for it? He was your High Priest, and you are the Dominus."

"We do not celebrate the passing of a soul from this place into the domain of the Great Creator. Death on this side of the door is the natural course for life to take," Magnus explained. "Even as I speak to you Aslak is being placed upon his funeral pyre. Our dead are burned within the hour of their passing. That way we are able to put the past aside and concentrate upon the future. When I have seen you settled in bed I will go and pay my final respects." Then he put her to bed as if she were a child, making certain she drank all the wine in the goblet. "I will be back within the hour," he promised.

But whether he was or not Lara never knew, for she slept soundly the night long, awakening to the sound of singing birds and the promise of sunrise. Magnus lay on his back next to her, sleeping peacefully. Lara observed him for several long minutes. He was a very handsome man, but rugged, much as Vartan had been. Not at all like Kaliq, who had been almost as beautiful to behold as she was, Lara thought with a fond smile of remembrance. Suddenly she became aware of the faint scent of burning on the morning wind. Aslak's funeral pyre, she realized, as she slipped from the bed, and quickly dressed herself in her leather pants, silk shirt and vest. She was pulling on her boots when the Dominus awoke. "It's morning," Lara told him.

He groaned. "I was longer than I anticipated, and then innumerable cups of wine had to be drunk to Aslak and to my uncle."

"We could wait a day," she offered.

"Nay," he said, pulling himself from the bed. "I want to find Usi's private chamber, and the book of spells. Tell me, what does Sirvat's voice sound like?"

"Like rough yet delicate chimes. All of your women have exquisite voices. Usi's curse was a cruel one that you have been denied the sound of your women's voices. To think you never heard your mother singing to you as a child." Lara picked up the delicate green gown she had worn the evening before, and before his astonished eyes poured it back into the open half of the wooden peach. Adding the veil, she closed the carved fruit and tucked it in her saddlebag.

"If I had not seen you do that I should not have believed it," Magnus Hauk said.

"It always astounded my husband, too."

They both heard the door to the guest house open, and a wary look touched Lara's face. She fell silent.

The servant entered with the early meal and set a tray upon the table in the chamber outside before departing again.

Magnus Hauk peered into the other room. "He's gone. Let us eat, pay our respects to my uncle and then be on our way. The men-at-arms will be awaiting us."

Arik greeted them warmly, and as there had been no time the night before he listened to Lara's quick explanation of where she believed the book of spells could be found. "Send word to me when you have found it," he told them. "It should be hidden away where it can never again be used," the new High Priest said.

"If I find it, once I have reversed the curse," Lara said firmly, "I will destroy the book. Evil has a life all its own, and draws other evil to it, my lord Arik. We should take no chances."

"Then let it be as you have said," Arik replied. "I bow to your wisdom."

"Not so much wisdom as caution," Lara said with a small smile, and the two men chuckled at her observation.

Then uncle and nephew embraced. Arik turned to Lara, and hugged her, too. "Farewell, faerie woman," he said. "We will meet again, I have not a doubt."

"I hope so," Lara told him. She liked Arik.

They rode out from the Temple of the Great Creator on a glorious summer's morning, passing what remained of Aslak's funeral pyre on a nearby green hillock as they rode. The day remained fair, and by sunset they once again espied the towers and turrets of the castle of the Dominus.

"Tomorrow," Lara said, "I will ride about the castle, and see what I can see."

Sirvat was awaiting them, eager to learn what had transpired. Magnus Hauk left Lara and his sister together, asking only if husbands had been found for his three former Pleasure Women. "Tell my brother I have almost concluded negotiations for them all," Sirvat said to Lara, who repeated the message.

"Good," Magnus Hauk said. "The sooner the better. I have no wish to listen to Uma's carping once my hearing is restored." Then he stamped off to his own quarters.

Sirvat called for the meal to be served. Seeing but two places set at the table, Lara asked why.

"I cannot bear their company any longer," Sirvat admitted. "Felda is sweet, but has the disposition of a milk cow. She is too bland and placid for intelligent conversation. Alcippe's tongue is too sharp, and she is critical of everything now that she knows she is to be wed and gone from the castle. As for Uma, well, you know her nature. And her complaints haven't stopped since you left. I should rather be alone with my own thoughts than bear their company. Now tell me, what happened?"

Lara carefully outlined their journey. She told Sirvat of Aslak's demise.

"He was a cranky old man," Sirvat observed. "He always looked at me as if I were a bug or a beetle, and once he suggested I be sent to the Daughters of the

Great Creator, as my older sisters were married. I'll shed no tears for him," she sniffed.

"How well do you know the castle?" Lara asked her friend.

"I've lived here all my life," Sirvat said, "and I have explored much of it, but I've never come upon a chamber that might qualify as Usi's. I would think you could feel his evil in such a place, but I want to help you search, Lara."

"What of the marriage negotiations for the others?" Lara asked her.

"Felda's and Alcippe's arrangements are already made. They have chosen husbands from among the aspirants for them. Only Uma remains obdurate. I don't like to marry her off to someone she has not approved, but I may have no choice if she does not pick soon. I don't know what to do with her."

"Let me speak to her," Lara said.

"She hates you," Sirvat replied. "She thinks my brother was madly in love with her until you came and ensorcelled him. She won't listen to you."

"I think I can persuade her," Lara told Sirvat.

"Let us eat first," Sirvat said. "You have had a long day's ride, and you will need your strength to deal with that termagant."

Lara laughed, but agreed, and together the two enjoyed a pleasant meal. When it had concluded, and the servants had taken away the remnants, Lara arose and went to Uma's little chamber. She knocked, and without waiting for a reply, entered.

Uma was creaming her lithe body. "What do you want?" she snarled, looking up.

"Sirvat tells me you have not picked a husband," Lara began.

"Oh, I have," Uma said. "It is the Dominus, and I will not be satisfied with any other man. He loved me until you came and worked your faerie enchantments upon him." She spread more lotion along her shapely leg.

"Magnus has never been in love with you, Uma, and in your heart of hearts you know that. He is a cold and powerful man. He took women into his household for his own personal gratification, nothing more. He has never shown you anything more than his lust when you enjoyed pleasures together. It is all he offers to any woman, even me."

"No," Uma said low. "He looks at you the way he never looked at any of us."

"Does he?" Lara laughed. "If he does it is because I am unlike any woman he has ever known, or will know. I intrigue him, but it has nothing to do with magic. I am Lara, daughter of Swiftsword, and Ilona, queen of the Forest Faeries. I am widow to a great man. I travel with a horse, a staff and a sword, magical creatures all. And I am magic. But Magnus Hauk's fascination with me has nothing to do with magic. It is of his own making. I am the one woman he cannot, will not, ever tame or bend to his will. One day he will love me, Uma, and when he does there will never be another for him but me."

"He is already falling in love with you," Uma cried bitterly.

"No. Not yet. But one day. Now it is nothing more than lust," Lara told the girl. "But his lust for me is greater than it has ever been for any woman. And you, despite what your eyes and heart tell you, are being a fool. Sirvat has found several men, all more than suitable to be your husband, yet you demur, Uma. Why?" Lara reached out and yanked Uma's head up. "Look at me! Do you really believe he could prefer you over me? Do you know what he said about my hair? That it was gossamer, all sunlight and moonbeams. Has he ever said words like that to you?"

Uma burst into tears. "I…I hate you!" she sobbed.

"Then choose the man that suits you best from those Sirvat has found. Marry him, and leave the castle with honor and dignity. Be with a man who will love you, and give you children of your own in your own house. Or remain here, and watch as the Dominus falls in love with me, and you become a poor shadow ignored by all. The choice is yours to make, Uma. But in the morning you will make it one way or another. You will go to Sirvat and choose your mate. Or you will tell Sirvat you wish to remain here, wasting the rest of your days in the futile pursuit of a man who will never love you because in the end he will belong to me, body and soul. You have but one opportunity to make your choice, Uma. And once you have made it you will have to live with it. There will be no second chances for you. Be warned, for I speak to you out of kindness. I have no hate for you as you claim to have for me." Then loosening her hold on Uma's hair, Lara turned and left the stunned woman, who had begun to sob again.

"What did you say to her?" Sirvat wanted to know

when Lara rejoined her friend in the day room of their quarters.

"I quite surprised myself," Lara admitted. "It was as if my mother was speaking. I was faerie cold, and faerie cruel. But come the morrow Uma will give you her decision one way or another. She will either choose a husband or elect to remain in the castle, ignored by all. I hope her choice is a wise one that will give her happiness, but she is a stubborn creature, and foolish to boot. I did tell her there would be no second chance for her if she chose unwisely."

"I think it might help if Magnus were here when she makes that decision," Sirvat said. "With a proprietary arm about you. Let us make it clear to Uma that she has no place here within my brother's household."

Lara smiled at her friend. "I see you can be cruel, too, Sirvat," she said.

"All women have a streak of cruelty in them," she laughed. "I will send word to my brother now." Sirvat arose and took a small writing box from a cabinet. "This is how I have always communicated important matters to Magnus and the other men in our household," she explained.

"Your parents are dead?" Lara inquired.

"Our father, aye, but our mother lives with our oldest sister's family. She says the castle depressed her after our father died. Magnus was the first born of my siblings, and then our mother, who is called Persis, produced three daughters in a row. The eldest is Narda, and she is married to Tostig. They live two fjords to the west, and Tostig's family control great fields of silk worms. Aselma is our middle sister. She is wed to Armen, and his family are famed weavers in Terah. They live but one fjord to the west."

"You did not go with your mother?"

"She did not ask me to accompany her, nor did Narda invite me into her house. I was ten when my mother departed, and I was not unhappy to see her go," came the startling admission. "She was very disappointed when I was found to be a girl. She had wanted another son, so her interest in me waned quickly. Had it not been for my brother and my old nurse, I do not know what would have happened to me."

"And you have not seen your mother since she left the castle?" Lara was fascinated by this information. Magnus's mother did not sound like a warm woman.

"No," Sirvat said. "She wrote my brother that she was happily settled in Narda's home, and thanked him for letting her go there. Narda wrote to Magnus that she was happy to have the companionship of our mother once again. They are much alike, as I recall. I was six when Narda was wed, and eight when Aselma married. Our father died the year after, and then our mother went away. At first I was lonely, and not just a little afraid. So much had changed for me in two short years. But then Magnus said as he had no wife, it was my responsibility to manage his household." She laughed. "I told him I was just a little girl, and he replied that I was the sister of the Dominus, and must accept my responsibilities. So I did. Did you have siblings?"

"Two half brothers," Lara replied. "Mikhail, my father's son by his wife Susanna. He was scarcely a year when I left the City. And my mother's son by her consort, Thanos. He is a little boy, too. Mikhail is all mortal, and Cirilo is all faerie. And I stand between them."

"So like me, you have the most fragile relationship with your siblings," Sirvat noted. "As you will one day be Magnus's wife, I am glad we are to be friends."

"Who told you I would be your brother's wife?"

"He is falling in love with you," Sirvat said. "He has never loved any woman before, but I see the difference in the way he treats you."

"What can you know of love, youngling?" Lara asked her, smiling.

"I love Corrado," Sirvat said quietly. "And from the look in his eyes when he gazes upon me I know he loves me, too. My brother now has that same appearance."

"How old are you?" Lara wanted to know.

"Almost seventeen," Sirvat answered. "And you?"

"Twenty-one."

"It is a good age," Sirvat replied. "When I wed Corrado I will continue to live here, for my brother's Captain of Captains, Corrado, had his home here in the castle. So we may continue to be friends, and we will be sisters one day."

"But does not Corrado live in male quarters?" Lara wanted to know.

"Oh yes, for now. But when we are wed I have already chosen where we will reside," Sirvat replied. "I will show you tomorrow when we begin to seek out the sorcerer's chamber," she promised.

"Tomorrow is almost here," Lara told her friend

with a smile. "Look outside. The moons are all rising. Did you know that in Hetar they are each a different color, and only in the Outlands can you see all four of them at once? Finish your message to Magnus, and then go to bed." She arose, and stretched. "Good night, Sirvat."

"Good night, Lara," the younger woman called after her. Then she bent her head to her letter.

Lara reached her bedchamber to find Verica awake in his corner and irritable.

"What is the matter?" she asked the staff.

"That girl with the red hair entered your chamber and woke me," he grumbled. "Andraste frightened her away when she began to sing."

Lara turned to her sword. "You sang to her?" She was surprised. She had only known Andraste to sing in battle.

"I am Andraste, and I will drink the blood of Lara's enemy," Andraste replied.

"Did she take anything?" Lara wanted to know. "Or leave something?"

"She was scarce through the door when we caught her," Verica said. "She ran. There was nothing taken, and nothing left, Mistress."

"Thank you both for recognizing the danger," Lara told her two companions.

"The wench is your enemy," Verica said.

"I know," Lara admitted, "but with luck by tomorrow her departure will be in the making. She has a choice to make come morning."

"Humph," grumbled Verica. "Waking an old man up is not good manners."

"Go back to sleep, dear friend," Lara advised him. "We will not be disturbed again tonight," she promised, and stroked the staff as he closed his eyes. Then Lara prepared herself for sleep.

She was awakened in the dawn by the Dominus kissing her. "You are a wicked man," she told him as his hands strayed beneath the bedclothes.

"My sister said I should be here to learn Uma's decision this morning," he defended himself, fondling her breasts as he spoke. "Besides, I seem to recall you like being awakened by my kisses." Pushing her back he began first to kiss her breasts, and then he suckled upon a pert nipple. "I will have you, my beautiful faerie woman," he said low. Then he began to scatter kisses down her torso until his dark golden head was pushing between her thighs and his tongue sought out her most vulnerable spot.

"Ohh!" Lara cried softly. "Oh, Magnus!" she cried louder. "Oh! Oh!"

His teeth delicately scored the tiny nub of her sex, and she shuddered. Then he moved back up her body again until his mouth was touching hers. "Witch!" he murmured against her lips. "You want her to hear us, don't you?"

"Yes!" she hissed at him. "Yes!"

He laughed, and then entering her slender lush body began to use her fiercely. Soon they were both caught up in the passionate delights they enjoyed with each other. Lara began to moan, and her moans turned into screams of intense pleasure such as she had never known. Her fingernails raked down his long back. She bit into his shoulder and tasted blood.

The Dominus was roaring with his enjoyment as they at last reached an intense crisis. "Faerie witch! Faerie witch! How I adore you!" he howled loudly. What had begun as a cruel game to taunt Uma had turned into an ecstasy of amorousness. They rolled away from each other, spent. "Faerie woman, you have unmanned me," Magnus groaned low.

Lara could not speak for several long moments. She had flown into the stars in his arms. While she had known pleasure with several men, she had never achieved such fulfillment as she did with Magnus. That, however, she would keep to herself. He was far too arrogant yet—and might always be. She could never allow him to believe that he had the upper hand over her. "You are a fine lover," she finally complimented him. Then she sighed gustily. "I suspect all in the Women's Quarters will have heard our efforts," she said with a weak chuckle.

"I hope so. I hold no ill will toward Uma. There was a day when she gave me pleasures. But now I want no woman in my bed but you, Lara, so Uma and her companions must seek new lives," the Dominus said.

"Felda and Alcippe have already chosen," Lara told him. "It is only Uma who stubbornly remains determined not to go. I spoke most frankly, even cruelly to her last night. Now you have given proof of my words, Magnus. I pray to my Celestial Actuary, and to your Great Creator—one and the same, I suspect—that Uma will now choose to follow the wise example of the other two."

"I will eat the first meal with you and my sister," he said as he arose from the bed.

"Let me bathe you before you redress," she said, seeking out the basin and the pitcher in the coals of her small hearth.

When they entered the day room they found Sirvat and the other women awaiting them. The Dominus sat at the head of the table, and Lara rushed to serve him. Setting the plate before him she poured wine into his goblet.

"Sit," Magnus Hauk commanded the other women. Then he began to eat.

They sat, wordlessly passing the bowls and platters among themselves. Looking about, Sirvat restrained her amusement. Lara kept her eyes down the entire meal. The other three looked pale, Uma in particular. When the Dominus finished his meal, he pushed back his chair and stood, signaling Lara to stand by his side. Putting an arm about her, he bent and kissed the top of her golden head. Then he said to Sirvat, "Have the women chosen husbands, Sister?"

Sirvat turned to Lara. "Tell my brother that they have indeed chosen. Alcippe will marry with the scholar, Jencir. He was her choice, and both he and his family are well pleased with the match. Felda has chosen Noval, a wealthy farmer from her own village in the east fjord. It seems her family had been considering him before you took her for yourself, Brother. Noval loves Felda, and is very happy to have her returned to him as a wife."

Lara smiled at this, and told the Dominus. Magnus Hauk nodded and smiled at Felda. "I am glad you will be returning to a place familiar and happy for you, Felda. I thank you for your loyalty and sweetness. The pleasures you gave me were good ones."

Felda blushed, and said to Lara, "Please tell the Dominus I am grateful to have served him in my own small and humble way."

Lara spoke Felda's words to the Dominus and he nodded, pleased. Now all eyes turned to Uma. She was pale, but she stood proudly before them all. That she had slept little was obvious.

"Have you made your decision, Uma?" Sirvat asked.

For a long minute Uma hesitated. Then she said, "Yes. I will choose Lord Dodek who is of my caste. I know he seeks a wife to bear him sons, and I am my father's only daughter in a family of eight brothers. I believe I can please him, and he me."

"A most wise decision, Uma, and Lord Dodek's reputation is a good one," Sirvat said. "I am happy you have finally made your choice."

"There was no choice!" Uma burst out. "Could I stay here after what I heard this morning? Even I am not that foolish. No! Do not turn away! You all heard it! He rutted with her like a raging bull. Never did he make love to any of us like that. She has bewitched him. Even I heard him call her 'faerie witch.' Look how he keeps his arm about her now in a public display of the banked fires of his desire." Uma began to weep. "I cannot leave this place soon enough," she cried to them, and then she ran from the chamber sobbing bitterly.

Magnus Hauk looked to Lara, confused.

"She has chosen Lord Dodek," Lara said calmly. "The rest was nothing more than her anger at having been forced into making her decision at last."

"Good!" he replied. "Tell my sister I want a banquet prepared for tomorrow, and the bridegrooms and their families here to partake of it. At its end these three will be united in marriage with their chosen ones, and they will depart the castle. Have their dowers delivered to their new homes before the ceremony."

"Yes, my lord Dominus," Lara replied with a servile bow.

He laughed. "You are my faerie witch," he told her.

"Do not presume to take ownership quite yet, Magnus," Lara warned him. "Remember my destiny must first be met."

"I am part of that destiny," he told her in an assured tone. "And together we will do great things, Lara. But first you have a task to perform for the men of Terah." Magnus Hauk then turned and left the women's quarters.

Instantly Alcippe and Felda began to speak excitedly.

"You had best see to your wedding garb," Sirvat warned them, and they hurried off together still chattering. "I have no time for helping you today," she told Lara. "If all is to be in readiness by tomorrow I must begin now."

"Do you need my help?" Lara asked her friend.

"No," Sirvat said. "It is all busywork. I am used to it, and will do it more quickly alone. I must get word to Lord Dodek. As Uma did not make her decision until this morning he is the only one of the bridegrooms not presently in the castle. Fortunately his home is just several miles up this fjord. He can be here by late day. And I have a banquet menu to choose, and invitations to issue, and I must make certain the girls are packed and ready to go by the morrow."

"Do you mind then if I wander about myself?" Lara asked.

"No. Go ahead. The sooner we can find the chamber the better for all of us, but I cannot imagine where it could be. There is no place in the castle I have not explored." Rising from the table, Sirvat hurried off.

Lara spent her day poking into rooms and alcoves throughout the castle, but she found nothing. She was very disappointed. The following day Alcippe, Felda and Uma were married shortly after sunrise in a ceremony presided over by one of the Brotherhood of the Great Creator. A morning banquet, attended by the couples, their families, Lara, Sirvat and the Dominus, followed the wedding. By the noon hour the new brides departed the castle. Their dowers had been paid, and remarked upon for their generosity. The trunks containing their possessions had been delivered to their new homes. Sirvat was directing the servants as they cleared away the last traces of the celebration. The Dominus had disappeared down to the docks for one of his vessels had come in from its latest voyage, and he wanted to oversee the unloading himself. Lara sought out Dasras, and the two of them rode out into the afternoon air.

They went in the opposite direction from the

castle. The path was less steep, and led to a sunny meadow overlooking the sea. Dasras galloped joyfully across the grassy lea, slowing finally to a sedate walk. When they reached the edge of the meadow Lara dismounted, and together they strolled along.

"To think that across that water, Hetar and the Outlands lie," Lara said.

"It is a long way," Dasras said. "The wings your mother gave me did not tire, but I know I did. I actually fell asleep at one point, but the wings kept moving up and down of their own accord. Your mother said if I should ever have need of those wings again I have but to think of them, and they will sprout forth from my body. It was a bit unnerving to see them there, I must say."

"I shall want you to use them again, Dasras, but not quite yet, and not to fly over the sea. I want to explore Terah, and I think we can do it faster by using your wings than by traveling afoot," Lara told him.

"What do you contemplate?" Dasras asked her.

"I am not yet ready to speak on it, old friend," she told him. "First I must see if what I am considering is possible. Then we shall discuss it. And then I must convince the Dominus to do something he will have never considered."

"It would appear that you have great plans in mind, Mistress," the stallion said.

"I do," Lara answered him. Then turning she flung her arms about his golden neck, burying her face in his cream-colored mane. "Is it not the most beautiful day, Dasras? And is this land not fair? I have never seen a place so green as Terah."

The horse chuckled. "I cannot disagree with either of your utterances, Mistress."

"Thank you for joining me, Dasras! I missed you," Lara said.

"And I, you, Mistress. Like you I am meant for great adventures. But the child you left me with was not," Dasras said.

Lara laughed. "But I will wager my son thought otherwise."

"Aye, he did. And I would have remained as you had asked me to, but that your mother told me of your need of me here in Terah. I was only too happy to come. I have actually missed old Verica, and even the beautiful and bloodthirsty Andraste," he chuckled.

"I must find the sorcerer's lair," Lara said. "I cannot accomplish what I need to accomplish until the men of Terah can once again hear their women. No society can exist successfully unless its inhabitants can hear one another, and exchange ideas, and thoughts. Do you realize that for five centuries the men of Terah have not heard a woman's voice saying 'I love you'? Or crying out in joy, or in childbirth? How tragic!"

"But," Dasras said mischievously, "they have also not heard a woman's voice nagging at them, complaining or demanding things from them."

Lara swatted at the horse and he danced away from her, chuckling. "We had best get back to the castle," she said. "While Magnus knows I am capable of taking care of myself, he does worry when I am gone." She mounted Dasras again, and they turned back toward the castle. Riding through the meadow she was able to see the entire castle, now bathed in late afternoon sunshine. It was a magnificent structure.

And then something caught Lara's eye. She stared hard at a northwest tower. There was a small section of stones just slightly different in color than the others. Was it a trick of the light? She pulled Dasras to a stop, and stared hard. But then the tower was gone. She was positive she had seen it. The tower was suddenly there again. How had the tower disappeared one moment and returned the next? No. It had to be the light. As they moved closer, again Lara was certain that some of those stones were dissimilar from the others. The difference was no bigger than a small window opening, and yet it was there. Dasras reemerged on the path above the fjord, but Lara could not keep that northwest tower in her sight. It flickered in and out of view until Lara was forced to abandon her inspection. She would come out again in the morning, and see if she could see a variation in the stones. Stabling Dasras, she kissed him on the muzzle and bade him good-night.

When Lara reached the Women's Quarters Sirvat had just finished up with her chores. "Did you enjoy your ride?" she asked.

Lara nodded. "Aye, I did. I rode through that meadow just above the beach," she told the other girl. "But you would not know it, having lived all your life within these walls. Ah, Sirvat, there is so much beauty in Terah! I cannot wait until we may ride out together so I can show you what I have seen."

"I am more than ready for an adventure," Sirvat admitted. "And I want one before I marry Corrado and have babies of my own. Of late I find I am more irritated by the dimensions of my world. Will you teach me to ride?"

"Gladly!" Lara said. "Sirvat, I may have found something while out riding."

"What?" the other girl asked.

"It might have been the way the light was reflecting off of the stones," Lara said, "but I am not entirely certain. I must look again in the morning. There is a tiny section high in a northwest tower where the stones appear to be a slightly different shade from the stones about it. It is no bigger than a small window opening. But I could not seem to keep the tower itself in my sight. Have you been in that section of the castle?"

"The northwest section of the castle was the first part to be built," Sirvat replied. "It existed even before Usi gained his dark powers. My ancestors lived there until the sorcerer dispossessed them. Then he built the rest of the castle, which is why many credit him with the whole structure. Members of my family have added a little bit to it over the centuries, and it was they who created the terraced gardens. The northwest tower is a separate structure, not even connected to the main buildings. No one resided there for many years—I always assumed because it was colder, and the castle holds so many more hospitable places to nest."

"If Usi forced your family from their tower, it was probably there he lived while the rest of the castle was being constructed," Lara said thoughtfully. "It would have been several years in the building—unless he used magic?"

"No," Sirvat said. "He used forced labor. Many families were torn apart as their men were pressed into his service. The women had to create the goods we trade. That was when many learned to be artisans, for Usi would tolerate no decline in our commerce with Hetar."

"Then the sorcerer must certainly have inhabited the northwest tower," Lara said. "And if he was like most men, he did not bother to move himself when the rest of the castle was finished. He probably had an official apartment in the newer section, but he would go to the tower to take his pleasures with the women he stole. He would keep his workshop there, and most, except perhaps a trusted servant, would be forbidden entrance to the tower. I am certain that is where we will find his book of spells. Where did he die?"

"I don't know," Sirvat said. "I don't think I have ever heard anyone say that Usi died in any one particular place."

"What happened to his body, and that of Geltruda?"

"The story is that her brothers took the bodies to burn. Usi's ashes were taken far out to sea and cast overboard in a sealed clay jar weighted down with iron. Geltruda's were scattered to the four winds. It is said a flowering tree sprang up on the site where her pyre stood. It is long gone now, of course," Sirvat said.

"Then 'tis the northwest tower where we will find

what we seek," Lara replied. "I am certain of it now. We will go in the morning."

"Why not now?" Sirvat asked.

"It is close to sunset," Lara explained, "and I would not want to enter that tower in the darkness, haunted as it must be by the souls of those Usi tortured. No. We will go tomorrow in the bright sunlight."

"We must tell my brother," Sirvat said.

Lara nodded. "Aye. Magnus should know."

"Will you be able to reverse Usi's spell, Lara?"

"I hope so," Lara said. "I must seek my chamber now, and consider on it." She left the day room as Sirvat reached for her writing box to communicate with her brother.

Closing the door of her bedchamber Lara sat down on the bed, and reached for her crystal. *Ethne? Are you yet with me?*

I am here.

You know all, Ethne. What am I to do?

You have wisely chosen to enter the tower in the daylight, Ethne said.

It will be a place of darkness nonetheless, and the evil that took place there will have permeated the very walls, Lara replied. *Today when I first saw the tower it disappeared, and then reappeared. Or were my eyes fooling me? Even from a distance I could feel the menace. The Sorcerer may be dead, but I fear his shade is yet strong, and his magic while diminished is still potent.*

Your instincts do not fail you, daughter of the queen. Usi's body is ashes, but his spirit yet has power. It is that power you must totally destroy in order to lift his influence from Terah forever. When you have reached the tower room, Ethne advised, *smash out the bricks that fill the window, and allow the light in to protect you, my child.*

How? Lara asked her.

With your magic, of course, Ethne responded with a small chuckle. *You have but to command the barrier between the light and dark to evaporate, and for you it will. You do not use your magic enough, Lara,* Ethne scolded. *It is your greatest gift.*

I wish I could speak with my mother, Lara said.

Your mother's magic does not extend to Terah, but there is one who can aid you. The Shadow Princes are the greatest powers in all of this world, though they hide it to preserve their way of life. They are strong enough to counsel you in your dreams if you ask them.

I must call on Kaliq then, Lara resolved.

A wise decision, Ethne agreed. *Mix a small bit of sleeping draught with some wine before you sleep. Otherwise you may be too anxious to slumber deeply.*

If I can remove the sorcerer's curse on Terah, what will happen then? Lara wondered. *I do not wish to destroy their way of life.*

You will know that when you reach the proper time, the crystal spirit murmured.

Riddles again, Lara laughed. *I suppose I should be used to it by now.*

The flame in the crystal flickered, and then faded to just a pinpoint of light. Lara released the crystal, which settled between her breasts above her heart, as it always did.

Sirvat was knocking upon the chamber door. "My brother is here."

"I will come," Lara replied, and arose immediately from the bed.

In the day room the Dominus waited. "Sirvat has told me of your discovery," he said. "We will go in the morning."

"Nay, Magnus, you must not go. I will go, for I am protected from the evil that the tower will surely still contain. No mortal must be tainted by it," Lara told him.

"I am the Dominus. I do not fear the shades of the past," he replied.

"Then you are a fool, for I do. And you should. I will enter the tower quickly, closing the door behind me to keep the evil penned up all these years within it. Please trust me, Magnus. This is not about your position or your bravery," Lara said.

"Tell my brother I beg him to heed your advice!" Sirvat said.

"Your sister agrees with me. She fears for your safety, Magnus," Lara added.

"I fear for yours," he told her.

"You need not, for I am protected," Lara assured him. "And tonight in the dream world I will ask the Shadow Prince Kaliq to aid me in this endeavor."

"I do not want another man in my bed," the Dominus said.

"But I will not be in your bed, Magnus," Lara replied, "and so you do not have to worry. I must sleep alone with no distractions."

"You think me a distraction?" he said, a small grin touching his lips.

"Yes," she told him. "You are a very great distraction to my concentration." Their eyes met, and she blushed even while she smiled at him.

"Now that I have my women wed and gone, I must consider finding a husband for Sirvat. You will want no other woman of rank in the castle when we marry," he said.

"Sirvat has chosen the man she desires, and I am not marrying you," Lara responded.

"Yes, you are," he said calmly. Then, "How is it that my sister has chosen a man she wishes to wed, and yet I know not who he is?"

"Must you tell him?" Sirvat cried, distressed. "What if he disapproves?"

"Sirvat fears you will not approve her choice, but I know you will," Lara told the Dominus. "It is Corrado."

Magnus Hauk turned to his sister. "I approve your choice, little sister. He is a good man, and our blood kin. When this matter is settled I will approach him. There is no other in his life, for his duties have kept him from all but casual women."

Delighted, Sirvat threw her arms about her brother and kissed him on both cheeks.

"I believe she is thanking you, Magnus," Lara said dryly.

He laughed. "I believe she is," he agreed. "Go to bed now, Sirvat. I would speak with Lara privily."

Sirvat released her hold on her brother and ran from the room.

"Come and sit with me," he said, and took her two hands in his as they sat. "I do not like the idea of you being with another man. This Shadow Prince, was he your lover?"

"Yes," she answered him honestly. "Once Kaliq and I were lovers. It is he who taught me to give and receive pleasures, for the Forest Lords surely did not. Since you are the recipient of his teaching, my lord Dominus, you should be grateful to him," she teased him gently. "I owe much to Kaliq, Magnus, but you need not fear him. He is my mentor, nothing more, and he knows that. I need his counsel. I do not believe I can do what needs to be done without it. But if you prefer that the men of Terah continue on as you have been these five centuries past, Magnus, I will cease my efforts on your behalf."

"And when this is over you will become my wife," he said stubbornly.

"I have no desire to marry again," she said. "And my children reside in the Outlands, Magnus."

"We will bring them here," he said.

"They are Fiacre, and my son may one day lead his people. I cannot take them from what is their destiny," Lara said.

"Then I will give you other children," he insisted.

"That choice is not yours to make, Magnus. You well know that faerie women only give children to those they love," Lara said.

"You speak of your destiny, yet you are here in Terah. What if this is your destiny, Lara? I will not push you into marriage, but eventually you *will* marry me. I am your destiny. Terah is your destiny. Once we

can hear the voices of our women again, who knows
what we may accomplish? When this is finished, I
want you to consider my words."

"I will," she said. "I promise you I will." She
leaned over and kissed him softly. "Good night,
Magnus." Then rising from the pillows, she left him.
But she was already considering his words. What if
it had all been leading to Terah? What if her destiny
was to come here, and lift the curse from the men of
Terah? Was it not a good destiny to do such a thing,
and have the gratitude of a people for the rest of your
life? Where could she go from here? Back to Hetar?
To what? She had not lied when she said her children
belonged to the Fiacre. They did. They had never been
hers. They had been Vartan's. Entering her chamber
she mixed the sleeping potion she had brewed earlier
into a cup of wine, and drank it. Then she lay down
in her lonely bed to sleep. And to dream.

Chapter 9

SHE WAS SURROUNDED at first by a soft silver-and-mauve haze. The ground beneath her bare feet was solid. Lara sensed something near her, but it was not Kaliq. Then she saw a wraith of dark smoke before her, and froze.

"You will not defeat me, faerie woman," a malevolent voice snarled.

"Who are you?" Lara asked the dark umbra.

"You know who I am, faerie woman."

"If you are Usi who cursed the Terahn men, I will do my best to subdue you!" Lara cried, but her heart was hammering fiercely in her chest. "I am Lara, daughter of Swiftsword and Queen Ilona of the Forest Faeries." Her throat ached as she forced the defiant words from them.

"I will conquer you, faerie woman, and you will do my bidding," Usi's voice whispered. "Under my guidance your magic can restore me to life. If you do, I will reward you as you have never been rewarded. You will know the secret of life, and pleasure such as no mortal man can offer you. That knowledge alone can make you the most powerful woman in the world of Hetar. Even Gaius Prospero will be in fear of you. Does that not appeal to you, faerie woman? Does not the idea of destroying Gaius Prospero tempt you, Lara, daughter of Queen Ilona and Swiftsword of Hetar?"

"You have no powers left," Lara mocked him, feeling the courage seeping back into her veins. "You are naught but a specter, Usi, who can live only in the dream world. Be gone from me!" She raised a single hand, pointing at the shade, and to her surprise a small flash of lightning sprang forth from her finger. The bolt exploded with a roar as it touched the darkness.

With a horrific shriek Usi disappeared from the dream plane, his mumbled curses ringing in her ears as he fled.

"Very nicely done, Lara," she heard Kaliq say, and then she sensed him by her side, but she could not see him.

"I was afraid at first," she admitted. "He startled me, and the evil emanating from him was quite terrifying. Now show yourself to me, you wretched Shadow Prince!"

He laughed, and as he did he materialized before her eyes. "Greetings, my love. You are as beautiful as ever. What think you of Terah?"

"It's beautiful, and I have never seen a land so green. What lies beyond it?"

"On its far side is another great salt sea," he told her.

"And on the other side of that sea?" she wanted to know.

"Our desert," he said with a small smile.

"The land of the Shadow Princes?" Lara was astounded. "How is that possible? I had heard of the Sea of Sagitta that lay between Hetar and Terah, but never another sea between Terah and your desert."

"You know the Hetarians, Lara. They know what they know, and seek to know no more than that. The Taubyl Traders crossing our desert never travel near that sea, which is called the Obscura. And the Terahns never venture beyond their villages and their fjords. They sail only into the middle of Sagitta, and no farther."

"There is a great deal of empty land here, isn't there, Kaliq?" Lara questioned.

He smiled. "Aye. Far more than the peoples of these two worlds could inhabit, my love. You are considering a scheme of great proportions, aren't you?"

"Not yet, Kaliq. First I need to find the sorcerer's book of spells. But to do so I must enter his apartments in the northwest tower of the Dominus's castle. It was obviously sealed after he was killed," Lara told the Shadow Prince. "Here on the dream plane his aura was dark but weak. Will it not be darker and stronger in the place he once inhabited? I need your help and your protection if I am to succeed, Kaliq."

The prince nodded. "Aye, you will need my aid."

"His private place was at the top of the tower, but the window in that chamber has been sealed shut. It must be opened quickly to allow the light in," Lara said. "Then I must search the room for the book of spells, and take it from the tower to study it. When I have found the spell Usi used to stop up the ears of the Terahn men, then I must work a spell that will reverse the curse that they may hear again," Lara explained.

"What says your Dominus regarding the situation?" Kaliq asked.

"He is not *my* Dominus," she replied.

Kaliq laughed knowingly. "Perhaps you are not ready to accept him as such, but he is. Is he not a satisfactory lover, Lara?"

"He is a most excellent lover," she admitted, blushing, "but I do not want another husband, Kaliq. Remember my destiny."

"Why did you come to Terah?" he asked her.

"Because it was meant that I come," she answered without hesitation.

"Why?" he persisted.

"Obviously I was meant to help the Terahns, Kaliq," Lara replied.

"Help them what?" he demanded.

"Be freed from Usi's curse. When both men and women here could communicate the Terahns did great things. But since the men have been unable to hear their women they have remained stuck in place. By reversing the spell Usi placed upon them I will be able to free them," she concluded.

"And then what?" Kaliq asked her. "Will you

return to Hetar, to the Outlands? Perhaps to my palace of Shunnar?"

"No," Lara said slowly, "I do not believe Hetar will ever again be my home."

"So you will remain here in Terah. Doing what? As what? The Dominus's lover, and the Wise Woman of this land?" Kaliq said.

"I do not know," Lara admitted. "But please do not insult me by telling me that my destiny is as wife to the Dominus and mother to his children, Kaliq."

"Why should becoming his wife mean an end to your destiny?" Kaliq asked her.

"This man is not easy as was Vartan," Lara told him. "When the call comes, I shall not be able to leave him as I did my lord of the Fiacre."

Kaliq chuckled. "So," he said, almost gloating, "you have met your match, Lara."

"He is a man, nothing more," Lara insisted. "Well," she amended, "perhaps more stubborn and set in his ways than others I have encountered."

Kaliq roared with laugher. Then he grew more sober. "We cannot have you going astray, Lara, and so I will tell you this much. Your destiny will play itself out from Terah. And the Dominus will not stand in your way even if you are his wife. And as his wife, you will gain the power you need to do what you must."

"He will want an heir right away," Lara said.

"Not if you tell him the price of marrying you is to wait, but eventually guarantee him the son he desires of you," Kaliq replied. "He will agree, my love, for he recognizes in you the Domina he must have, that he needs. And he loves you, Lara."

She sighed. "But first things first, Kaliq. I need to get in and out of that tower safely. Usi's ghost will be there lying in wait for me, you may be sure."

"But I will be there too, guiding you," Kaliq promised. "Do not, however, allow the Dominus to enter the tower with you. He is too human, and could be harmed—or worse, Usi might try to inhabit him in order to regain a body."

"I will warn him," Lara promised. "And so our visit is done, Kaliq."

"Stay a while with me, and I will tell you what is happening in Hetar," he tempted her, and Lara succumbed without protest to his invitation.

"How are my children?" she asked him.

Reaching into his white robes the Shadow Prince brought forth a crystal sphere and invited Lara to peer into it.

There was Dillon. He had surely grown taller, Lara thought. And there was Noss, chasing after a laughing girl with tumbling dark mahogany curls who toddled away from Lara's former companion as fast as her little legs would carry her. *Anoush!* Lara felt her heart contract at the sight of her daughter. It had been easier to leave her son, for Dillon was old enough to know who she was. "Put your crystal away," Lara said with a sigh. "I have seen what I needed to see. My children are well and safe."

"The loss of your daughter pains you most," Kaliq said quietly.

Lara nodded. "I have already missed so much of

Anoush," she whispered. Then she asked, "Will the Outlands remain safe, Kaliq?"

He shook his head. "Even our powers cannot hold off the invasion much longer, Lara. Gaius Prospero has been elected emperor of Hetar. He has made many promises that he must keep, or lose his power and his place. Perhaps even his life. He will do whatever he needs to do to survive, my love."

"I have a plan," she began.

"I know," he said. "And you must execute it as soon as you can."

"I am not sure I can convince Magnus," Lara told him.

"You must!" the Shadow Prince said forcefully. "Make it a condition of your marriage to him, Lara. It is for our world."

"Do you still love me, Kaliq?" she asked him cruelly.

"I will always love you, Lara," he replied sadly. "But I am not your destiny."

"Is Magnus Hauk?" she countered.

"For now, aye!" he told her. "You know I speak the truth. You bloom within his arms. You flourish with his love for you."

"How can you know it?" she demanded of him.

"I know everything there is to know about you, Lara. Am I not your mentor and your friend? Did not my brothers and I teach you to know when to trust?"

Lara laughed softly at the remembrance of a single night long ago. "Aye, you taught me well," she said.

"Then unlock your faerie heart, my love, and give

it to Magnus Hauk," he told her with a small smile. "You know I am right."

"He says he will tame me," Lara murmured.

"Rather you will tame each other," Kaliq said quietly. "Magnus Hauk is a mortal upon whom you may rely, Lara. His heart is good, and he has strong principles. You will find you are much alike." He took her in his arms, and kissed her brow. "I will be with you when you enter the tower, Lara," he said to her, and she suddenly found herself slipping from the dream world into a deep sleep. How typical of her Shadow Prince, she thought. He would not say goodbye.

WHEN LARA AWOKE it was a startlingly beautiful day, and she felt more rested than she had in weeks. Slipping from her bed she looked out her window, and watched the sunrise staining the morning skies in a plethora of vibrant colors. The air was warm, and fragrant with the scent of roses. She breathed it in deeply, and realized that she felt strong. *Thank you, Kaliq,* she said silently. Then going to the bath in the Women's Quarters she bathed slowly and carefully, washing her long golden hair as well. She was drying it in the bath courtyard when Sirvat joined her.

"Did you dream well?"

"I did, and today I will enter Usi's tower," Lara told her.

"Will you let Magnus go with you? He wants to, you know," Sirvat said.

"He must not, cannot come with me," Lara told the Dominus's sister. "Kaliq has warned me that Usi could attempt to steal Magnus's body in an attempt to reincarnate himself."

"Could he not steal your body?" Sirvat worried.

"Nay. I am well protected—not simply by my heritage, but because Kaliq will be there. Besides, Usi would not want to be a woman, I am quite certain." She did not tell Sirvat of her encounter with the sorcerer's shade in the dream world. There was no need to frighten her friend. She arose. "I must dress, and then see your brother."

"You will need food for strength," Sirvat fretted.

"I will eat when I have completed my task," Lara told Sirvat. Then she hurried back to her own chamber. She dressed herself in her leather warrior's garb, strapping Andraste upon her back, pulling on her boots.

"Am I not to come, too?" Verica demanded in a testy voice.

"No male or male spirit shall enter the tower," Lara told him. "I met the sorcerer's specter last night on the dream plane. I fear he might attempt to reincarnate in a male spirit, so you must remain where you are safe, Verica. Andraste is female, and I may need her protection."

"Be cautious, Mistress," the staff warned her. "This is a very evil spirit."

"I will be," Lara promised, as she left her chamber and hurried to the Dominus's apartments.

Magnus Hauk looked her over carefully. "You are garbed for battle, Lara," he said quietly. "You know I would go with you."

"You must not," Lara said sternly.

"I know. Your Shadow Prince came to me while I slept, and warned me himself. He said he did not want you wasting your energies in argument with me," the Dominus chuckled.

Lara laughed. "He is very protective of me," she answered.

"Should I be jealous?" Magnus asked her.

"Nay. You have no cause, my lord Dominus." Her hand rested a moment upon his arm. "Let me do this thing, and then we will speak on matters closer to us both. This I promise you, Magnus." She moved away from him as he reached for her. "You must not kiss me, for your kisses have the oddest effect upon me. They weaken me, and nothing must sap my strength this day, my lord Dominus."

"How unlike you to admit to a weakness," he said with a teasing smile.

"I must go," Lara said, and hurried from his apartments. Just being with him was beginning to drain her. She walked slowly through the gardens overlooking the fjord, the sky reflecting its color into the waters. She took slow deep breaths as she moved. Perhaps Kaliq was right and Magnus was a part of her destiny. She was going to need his cooperation if her unspoken plan was to succeed. And when she reached her destiny would it reveal itself to her? Or must she continue to bumble along, following the voice within and always wondering if she was doing the right thing?

You will know it, she heard Ethne's voice reassuring her.

Lara felt the strength pouring back into her body.

Ahead of her, the northwest tower of Usi loomed dark and threatening. Even on this glorious day there was something sinister about it. She shivered but walked onward, noticing that the closer she got to the tower the more bleak the ground beneath her feet was. There was no green here, she realized, only rock and dirt. Reaching the small door that opened into the tower Lara stopped, realizing she had no key.

"Use your magic," Kaliq's voice instructed her. He was not visible to her.

"Open portal," Lara said to the door. The small door creaked open with difficulty.

LARA AWOKE, and it was a startlingly beautiful day. Slipping from her bed she looked out her window, and watched the sunrise staining the morning skies in a plethora of vibrant colors. The air was warm and fragrant with the scent of roses— Wait! Had not this all happened before? Then she realized that the dark magic of Usi the sorcerer was attempting to keep her from entering his tower. "Repel, spell!" she cried and was once more before the small door, the sound of its creaking still in her ears.

It had not been opened in nearly five hundred years. She ducked as a small black flying creature flew out of the tower, and almost shrieked as several rats scampered past her, one over her very feet. Then drawing a deep breath, Lara stepped into the tower, walking toward the stone stairs just beyond the open door—which now shut itself with a loud bang. The sound of dark laughter sent a ripple down her spine, but she realized that she was not afraid.

"You are clever, Lara. I had thought to hold you off longer," his voice said to her out of the darkness. Yet he had no form that she could discern, a fact that was very unnerving.

Ignoring him, she let her eyes adjust to the tower's darkness. To acknowledge him would only rob her of her strength, and she needed all of her strength for what lay ahead. "Torch!" she said, and a small torch appeared in her hand, casting a weak glow into the gloom. To her left was a door. "Portal open," Lara commanded. The door creaked open to reveal a flight of stairs that obviously led to a dungeon. The air was fetid and damp, and a despairing moaning issued from deep below. She quickly chanted, "Portal close!" More ghosts than Usi's lived here.

She turned back and mounted the winding staircase. The stone steps beneath her boots were worn, and now and again her foot slipped on some slick substance beneath it. She dared not lower her light to see what it was. She would not permit Usi to distract her from her purpose, which was his complete and utter destruction. Now the tower was so silent she could hear her own heart beating loudly in her ears. Her legs felt suddenly heavy. She could hardly lift her feet one after the other. Lara gained the first landing, where she saw a small door to her right. Curious, she opened it, and gasped with shock. The wall before her was hung with the bones of Usi's victims. Long hair in various hues—browns, blondes, reds and black— still clung to the skulls. Suddenly the skeletons began to dance jerkily, their bones rattling together.

Tears sprang into her eyes and she slammed the

door shut. It was then she heard the crack of a whip. The piteous screams of a woman being brutally beaten filled the air, accompanied by the maniacal laughter of the sorcerer. Lara watched, fascinated yet horrified, as from beneath the closed door a rivulet of blood began to flow out onto the landing. She quickly turned away, and began to climb the second flight of steps up the tower but the screams followed her as she struggled upward.

Good, she heard Kaliq's voice say. *Keep moving, Lara. When you give any thought to what happened in this accursed place, you give it momentary life again. Concentrate only on getting to the chamber at the top of this tower! The soul you now hear in torment long ago went to her Creator.*

Lara swallowed hard, and forced her legs to move upward. Unexpectedly a tremendous wind began to blow down from the heights of the tower. She fell onto the stone stairs, striving to get up. Her torch flickered dangerously. Suddenly angry, Lara forced herself to her feet, and tucking her head into her chest she fought her way back up the staircase. One step. Then another. One step at a time. But always forward, for she was now more determined than ever to reach the sorcerer's chamber. Just three more steps. One. Two. A shriek of rage almost sent her tumbling back again, but Lara pushed herself up the final step, crying as she did, "Portal open!"

The door opened slowly, slowly. The ferocious wind had now disappeared, but as she stepped into the chamber Lara could feel the sorcerer's evil presence.

It would remain to harm her unless she could bring light into the room. "Kaliq, help me!" she called.

"He cannot help you, Lara. I am master here, and you will soon be in my power, my beautiful faerie woman," Usi murmured, the sound so close she felt the moist heat of his breath in her ear. "Yield to me," the voice caressed her seductively. "Yield, and together we will control our worlds, and know the pleasures denied mortals."

His words weakened her. She could almost feel his hands on her, touching her breasts, her face, her pure golden hair. The darkness swirled about her, beckoning her into its deepest heart. Her strength was beginning to drain away now. She could feel herself surrendering in spite of herself. Lara gasped for breath, for it seemed as if all the air in the room was being sucked away. One breath. The second deeper, the third deeper yet, and her head began to clear. Power began flowing back into her body. "No!" she cried. "You will not defeat me. I will defeat you! Where once light flowed let it flow again!" she cried loudly, pointing to the place where the tower window should be.

She heard the crack of brick against stone. "Welcome light! Welcome warmth! Cleanse this chamber with your goodness," Lara said, opening her arms wide. "Banish evil in whatever form it may take!" A faint ray of sunshine crept slowly across the stone floor from a large crack in the wall before her. "Window open!" Lara cried with a loud voice, and the mortar and bricks that had blocked the tower window suddenly exploded, falling into the room as the golden sunlight poured into the dark space as it had not been done for centuries.

"Arrgh!"

Lara whirled to see the smoky shade of Usi writhing as the warm light began to devour him. Briefly she saw him as he had once been—tall, young and very handsome, his dark eyes compelling, his very beauty belying his cruel and wicked character.

"Faerie woman!" he gasped. "Save me!" Beautiful hands with long elegant fingers reached out toward her as Lara backed away from him. "Help me!"

"Begone, and never again return to this realm or any other!" Lara cried, pointing, and the lightning from her hand cracked, destroying the sorcerer forever.

"Well done!" Kaliq said appearing beside her. "You have banished him."

"My faerie powers grow stronger," Lara marveled.

"Only because you use them for good," Kaliq told her.

"I am so tired," Lara said, slumping against him for a moment.

"I know," he told her. "It was a difficult climb, my love, but you must find the sorcerer's book of spells before you give in to exhaustion."

"And then this tower must be destroyed," Lara replied, straightening. "It is the only way the spirits of those imprisoned and tortured here will be free again. I will plant a garden here in their memory," she told him.

"The book," he repeated.

"Help me look," she said, and together they began

to search. The book of spells was finally discovered in the rear of a high shelf. There was no other book at all in the chamber. Only vials, and jars of herbs, and seeds, and various animal parts. Lara opened the volume and began going through the pages.

"Yes, this is his book of spells," she confirmed.

"Is the hex he used on the Terahn men there?" Kaliq asked.

Lara continued to thumb through the book. Then she began to chuckle. "I have found it," she said. She pointed to a page.

Kaliq looked down, and silently read the words. *Ears that heed a woman's call, shall close and hear her not at all.* The Shadow Prince began to laugh. "It is very simple," he said. "Clever, and ridiculously simple."

"But it has been very effective for over five hundred years," Lara reminded him.

"And the reverse of the curse would be?" he asked her.

"Let us leave the tower and try my spell on Magnus, to see if he can hear his sister," Lara suggested. She picked up the book and gave it to him. "I promised the High Priest that it would be destroyed. When I am certain my spell works, will you burn it?"

He shook his head. "No. You and the Dominus must do the deed. I will, however, take the ashes, and dispose of them in several places so that the book may never be mended and used again."

Together they descended the three flights of stairs to the bottom of the tower. There they discovered that the door which had closed behind Lara was now wide-open. Retracing Lara's steps they returned to the apartments of the Dominus where Magnus Hauk awaited Lara. He was pale with obvious worry, but Lara made no mention of it.

"I believe I can remove the curse," she said. "Let us find your sister, and see if I am right," Lara said to him.

The Dominus sent a servant to fetch Sirvat, who came on a run. She looked anxiously at her brother, and then at Lara. Her eyes widened with admiration as she saw the Shadow Prince. Kaliq saw her regard and favored the girl with a smile. She was a pretty creature.

"I believe I can reverse the curse," Lara told Sirvat. "I need you here. When I have spoken the words I want you to speak to Magnus."

Sirvat nodded.

"Ears that once heeded woman's call, shall open again and hear them all," Lara said, quietly but firmly.

For a moment afterwards no one said a thing, and then Sirvat ventured, "Magnus, Brother, do you hear me?"

"You have a voice like tinkling bells, little sister," the Dominus replied, and Sirvat burst into tears of happiness, flinging herself into his arms.

"You can hear me!" she sobbed. "Oh all praise to the Great Creator, you can hear me!"

Magnus Hauk's face was wreathed in smiles. His eyes met Lara's. "Thank you."

"It worked upon you. Now I must make it work on all your realm, my lord Dominus." She turned to the Shadow Prince. "How? I cannot go from village

BERTRICE SMALL 279

to village, Kaliq. There has to be an easy way to do this."

"Gather all the men here in the castle, and see if you can undo the spell for them," the Dominus said, and Kaliq nodded in agreement.

When every man in the castle from the highest to the lowest had been brought together in the Great Hall the Dominus spoke to them.

"The faerie woman, Lara of Hetar, daughter of Swiftsword and Ilona, queen of the Forest Faeries, has bravely gone into the tower once inhabited by Usi the Sorcerer to retrieve his book of spells. Finding it, she has reversed the curse that was laid upon us five centuries ago. We believed our women could not speak all these years, but it was our ears that had been stopped from hearing them. Lara has spoken her spell to me, and I now hear my sister, and the women servants in my house. Now we will see if she can reverse the plague that has affected the men of Terah for over five hundred years. Be silent for her words!"

Looking down upon the men in the hall Lara could see the questions, and the disbelief, in their eyes. Drawing a breath she intoned loudly, "Ears that once heeded woman's call, shall open again and hear them all!"

The room remained silent, and then Sirvat said, "Good men of Terah, has your hearing been restored once more?"

There was a collective gasp, and then the men began to babble excitedly, crying that they could hear the voice of the lady Sirvat.

"It still isn't good enough," Lara grumbled. "What

of the rest of Terah? Even if I went from village to village it would take me forever to reverse the hex on all the men of Terah. Kaliq, what say you?"

"Dasras has the ability to fly when he chooses. He can take two upon his back. If you and Magnus traveled from fjord to fjord it would take you only a week or two to visit each village. Any not there when you came could come to the castle later. But most of the men of Terah would be able to hear again in a relatively short time," Sirvat said.

"And we must go to the temple as well," Lara said.

"We will go to the temple last," Magnus Hauk said. "My uncle may be forward thinking, but many of his priests still adhere to Aslak's belief that all magic is wicked. Let us prove them wrong first, and then release them from the curse last."

"He is very wise for a mortal," Kaliq noted softly to Lara. Then he said, "My lord Dominus, I am no longer needed here. But there is one gift I will give you before I depart. The northwest tower must be destroyed quickly. While Lara has banished the specter of Usi forever, the tower remains haunted by the souls tortured there. They cannot be freed until the tower is gone. With your permission, I will commence my own magic now."

"I would be grateful if you would," Magnus Hauk said.

"I would make a garden there eventually," Lara told the Dominus.

"How will you destroy the tower?" the Dominus wanted to know.

"We princes of the shadows have the ability to ma-

nipulate the weather. Even now, outside your hall a storm is gathering. When the storm has passed the tower will be no more. Let the ground there rest free of its evil burden for a year, and then Lara may plant her garden." He turned to face Lara. "Burn the book now, and I will take the ashes with me to dispose of as we discussed."

She nodded, spoke a few words, and a large covered jar appeared on the hall's high board. Placing the sorcerer's book of spells within the jar Lara covered it. She put her hand on the jar. "Book burn. Never return." she said quietly. The jar glowed deep red with an unnatural heat, but after a few minutes the color faded away. "It is done now," Lara said, and she handed the jar to Kaliq.

The men in the hall were beginning to disperse back to their tasks. Outside they heard the strong rumble of thunder, and the fierce cracking of lightning.

"I will leave you now, Magnus Hauk, lord Dominus of Terah. Treat her well, for I love her dearly," Kaliq said, and he turned to Lara. "Until we meet again, my love, farewell!" Then, the jar in his hands, he evaporated in a cloud of shadows, and was gone.

"I know I should be jealous of him," Magnus muttered.

"Nay, I said not," Lara reminded him, slipping her hand into his.

"I want to see Usi's tower destroyed," Sirvat said excitedly. "There is a spot in your apartments where we may watch the destruction. Come!"

"I see I have much to learn about you, little sister,"

Magnus said. "You are quite a bloodthirsty creature, aren't you?" he chuckled. But, Lara's hand in his, he followed after Sirvat who led them up a flight of stairs to a large tower room.

The chamber had two windows close together, and peering out of them they saw that the beautiful morning had degenerated into roiling clouds, heavy thunder and wild lightning that seemed to concentrate itself about the northwest tower. Torrents of rain poured down, obscuring everything beyond the windows but for Usi's tower, which seemed to stand out bathed in a strange light. The lightning grew fiercer, crackling and glowing with an odd greenish tint. And then suddenly it began to strike out at the structure, which crumbled and disintegrated, collapsing slowly before their eyes. A great wind came up, blowing so hard it actually shook the castle. Then, as suddenly as it had come, the storm vanished and the beautiful summer's day was restored to them. Where the tower of Usi had stood, nothing remained, not a brick, or a stone, or even a shard of mortar. The ground lay barren before them.

"I should rather have your mentor, Kaliq, as a friend than an enemy," Magnus remarked dryly as he looked out upon where the earliest portion of his castle had once stood. "He has done a most thorough job of it, hasn't he?"

"I thought he was very handsome," Sirvat said with a sigh.

"Oh," her brother remarked mischievously, "the vessel docked below is Corrado's. Shall we have Lara unstop his ears, little sister, so you may tell him of your deep devotion to him?" And Magnus chuckled wickedly.

"Of course I want him to be able to hear me!" Sirvat cried, "but Magnus, if you dare say anything to him..."

"You mean you don't want me to propose a match between our two families, little sister?"

"Magnus!" Sirvat's pretty voice now bore a decidedly aggravated tone.

Lara laughed. "Being able to hear each other has changed your relationship, I fear," she said. "Sirvat, he is a great teaser. Do not allow yourself to be taunted. Magnus, tell her you will speak properly to Corrado about a marriage between them."

He chuckled. "I see now that women stick together. Sister, I will not embarrass you. And I will suggest to Corrado that you would make him a fine wife. But first Lara must unstop his ears so he may hear your pretty voice."

A woman servant now came to tell her master that the captain in question was waiting in his day room. Magnus noted with interest that not all women's voices were the same. "Come with me," he said to them, and they descended from the tower into the Dominus's apartments where Captain Corrado awaited them. There Magnus Hauk told his friend what had transpired since he had last departed on his voyage.

Corrado looked to Lara. "You can lift the curse? Then do so, lady, I beg you!"

Lara spoke her spell.

"Corrado," Sirvat said as soon as the words had

died within the room, "I love you, and I want you for my husband."

Lara began to giggle. The look of total and utter surprise upon the faces of the two men was one she would not soon forget.

Finally Corrado spoke. "We need your brother's permission," he said weakly.

"If it pleases you as much as it does my sister, Corrado, then you have it," Magnus Hauk spoke. He looked to Sirvat. "I thought you wanted me to speak to him?"

"I did," Sirvat told her brother, "but then I thought the first words Corrado ever heard from me should be memorable ones."

"Will you always be this unpredictable?" the captain wanted to know.

"Are you going to wed me or not?" Sirvat countered.

He grinned at her. "I must think on it," he said.

"Think quickly, Captain, for I am not a patient woman. Be warned, however, that if you refuse me I shall of course be forced to kill you," Sirvat told him sweetly.

Magnus Hauk continued to look thunderstruck, and Lara was barely controlling her laughter.

"Then I must accept your proposal, lady," he said. "But first let us see how well you kiss." He yanked her into his arms, and kissed Sirvat soundly. "Yes," Corrado said. "You will do very nicely, little one."

"You have loved her all along," Lara accused him.

The captain gave her a wink, but neither denied nor confirmed her words. Then he said to the Dominus, "You know I have no family other than my old father and brother, so this matter is between us alone. Where would you have us live?"

"I have already chosen apartments in the southeast section of the castle," Sirvat said. "One day we may have our own home, but for now I find it convenient to remain in my brother's castle, don't you?"

Before the captain could speak Magnus Hauk agreed with his sister. "Aye, I think Sirvat is right. You are my captain of captains, Corrado, and too valuable to me not to be near. It will be your own home, but here. One day I will give you lands for your own."

"If you are content, my lord Dominus, then I am content," Corrado said.

"Now," Sirvat said, "we must decide when you will marry me, for I am not of a mind to wait. And if Lara is to wed my brother eventually she needs to be mistress in her own house."

"I would prefer we free all the men of Terah before any marriage is celebrated," Magnus said. "It is not right that those men here within my castle can hear our women again, but no one else can. What think you, Lara?"

"I agree with the Dominus," she replied. "We should begin tomorrow to reach out to all the men of Terah so they may be free of Usi's curse."

Sirvat pouted prettily. "I have waited my entire life to wed Corrado," she said.

"Do not be selfish," Magnus said.

Sirvat glared at her older brother. "Both of our sisters were married by the time they reached my age," she snapped at him.

"Just a few days, please," Lara begged her friend. "You will need at least several days to prepare for a proper wedding, Sirvat. There is the matter of your garments, deciding what foods to serve at the wedding feast, and there is your new home. Is it ready to receive you and Corrado yet? And your dower portion must be decided upon, too."

Sirvat considered a moment, and then she said, "You are right, Lara. I will certainly need several days before Corrado and I can be properly wed. Very well then. I agree, but I must be allowed to see Corrado while you are away."

"Magnus?" Lara's look was questioning of the Dominus.

"I will agree because I know I can trust Corrado," Magnus replied.

"And you cannot trust me?" Sirvat was most offended.

"It is not a matter of trust where you are concerned, little sister. You are young and in love and prone to your own way. I trust Corrado to see your behavior remains fitting so that there will be no gossip," the Dominus said.

"Sometimes, Magnus, you are a pompous and meddlesome halfwit," Sirvat said bluntly. And she smiled sweetly at him.

"Take her away, Corrado," Magnus told his captain, "and see if you can teach her some respect for her Dominus."

"I obey, my lord," Corrado said with a grin, and escorted his beloved from the chamber. "Come, minx," they heard him say as the door closed behind the couple.

Lara sat down heavily. She was weary with the last few days. And she found there was comfort in the strong arm that he put about her. Her head fell on his shoulder.

"I think you must rest now, my faerie woman. You have exhausted yourself in your endeavors. You were gone from me for several long hours."

"The tower was so awful," Lara told him. "And Usi's shade was there as Kaliq had known it would be. I thank your Great Creator that you were not there, my lord. The sorcerer's spirit was very strong. He would have taken you over had you been there, and I should not have been able to aid you. I needed all my strength to climb to the top of his tower. He made me hear the moans and piteous cries of those he tortured. I think I shall hear the screams of those unfortunates he destroyed for his own pleasure in my dreams forever," Lara said, and then she began to weep.

Both of his arms went about her, and she sobbed bitterly against his broad chest. After a time he said to her, "I thought faerie women did not cry."

"They don't," she sniffled, "but sometimes my mortal half overcomes my faerie half, Magnus. It was so horrible! I should not have been able to succeed without Kaliq. That evil creature would have surely overcome me."

"But he did not, Lara. You triumphed, and you have done Terah a great service. Now you must decide if you will accept me as your husband as well as your lover. I understand your misgivings, faerie woman, but I cannot live with the thought that some other man might come along one day and take you from me. I believe in my heart that we are meant to be together. That you are meant to be the Domina of Terah."

"I cannot be bound to any man, Magnus, by anything other than trust. If you trust me you will allow me to do what I must to fulfill my destiny. You will wait for a son until I say the time is right. You will seriously consider my advice and my counsel, because if I am the Domina of Terah my loyalties will lie first with Terah. None of what I ask of you will be easy for you to accept. Your pride and determination is every bit as great as mine, I fear. We will have some monstrous battles, you and I," Lara warned him with a faint smile.

"Much between us will require skillful negotiations. I will not give you an answer now. And you will not require one of me. Tomorrow we will take Dasras, and we will go to each of the fjords in turn, each of your villages in turn, and I will free the men from Usi's curse. When we return you will consider if you still want me for your wife. If you can abide by my words as my husband. And I will give you an answer if I think I can believe the words you speak to me," she concluded.

He was not surprised by her candid speech. He had already learned that Lara spoke only truth. And this was more than she had offered him previously. "I understand, my faerie love," he said to her.

"Then take me to bed, my lord, for I do not believe I can remain awake for another minute," Lara told him.

He stood, and picking her up in his arms he carried to his bed, laying her gently down. She was already asleep. Looking at her he considered how pale she was. The great task she had this day performed had taken much out of her. He prayed silently that she would not dream the nightmare of her efforts. He did not know that the Shadow Prince Kaliq had already seen to it, for he understood better than Magnus possibly could the dangers Lara had faced, and the weariness she would suffer afterwards. He also knew that in order to regain her strength Lara would need to sleep a dreamless sleep for many hours. And she would need her strength to finish the task she had only begun.

Lara slept for almost two days, awakening on the morning of the second day. She was very surprised to learn she had been asleep for so long, but she had to admit to herself that she felt very well rested, and her old self again. She was eager to continue in her efforts. She was surprised to find herself in the Dominus's bed, but then she recalled they had been in his apartments when she had lost consciousness.

"You're awake," he said as he came to kiss her.

"How long?" she asked him.

"Two days," he replied.

"Is it early?" she queried.

"The sun is barely up," he told her.

"Then we must begin our journey today," Lara said firmly. "I shall return to the Women's Quarters to bathe, and dress in fresh clothing. Meet me in the stables in an hour." She climbed from his bed. "Thank you, Magnus." Then she was gone.

When he reached the stables at the appointed time he found her already there talking with Dasras. He walked over to the great stallion, rubbing his velvety muzzle in greeting, and asked, "Are you well, Dasras?"

"I am, my lord Dominus. This is a good thing we do. I have told my mistress to put a bridle on me, but no saddle. You will both sit more comfortably without it. And you must understand that my mistress will ride first, and control me."

"I am the Dominus," Magnus Hauk protested.

"But Lara is my mistress. I answer only to her," Dasras said sternly.

"It will appear as if you are holding me, rather than I clinging to you," Lara said.

The Dominus nodded. "Very well, but as we enter each village I must appear to be holding the reins," he said.

"Agreed!" Lara told him. "Our first negotiation has been successful," she teased.

He laughed.

Dasras was bridled and led into the stable yard. They mounted the big horse, and suddenly two great white wings sprouted from his rib cage. Magnus found himself moving his legs just slightly to accommodate them. At a soft whispered command from Lara, the horse rose into the air while below the men in the stable yard watched in rapt amazement. The Dominus asked if he might direct the animal, and Lara quickly acquiesced. Dasras turned to fly up the fjord.

The Dominus's fjord had no villages, but the

homes of many of Terah's important men were located there. They stopped at each, and Lara broke the spell surrounding each household's men. Uma came out to greet them when they arrived at Lord Dodek's house. To Lara's surprise she appeared quite happy, and was delighted that her husband could now hear her. They moved on, crossing the fjord and flying across the mountains to the next fjord as the day was coming to an end. They stayed at Felda's husband's farm. Norval was not unhappy to be freed of the sorcerer's spell.

For the next few days they traveled from village to village freeing the men of Terah of the curse, flying over the mountains from fjord to fjord. And Lara was astounded at the vast tracts of land that went as far as the eye could see. As they finished in the last village the Dominus was eager to return home, but Lara begged him to let Dasras fly into the uninhabited lands as far as the Obscura.

"Where will we sleep?" he demanded of her.

"On the plain below us," Lara said.

"What will we eat?" he wanted to know.

"Faerie bread," she told him. "It will taste like whatever you want it to taste. Please, Magnus. It is important to me."

"Fly on, Dasras," the Dominus said, and the horse did. And then as the day was coming to a close Magnus Hauk saw the sea that Kaliq had told Lara was called the Obscura just in the near distance. "That is not Sagitta," he observed. "Its waters are almost the color of my eyes, they are so vibrant a blue."

"No. It is called the Obscura. Kaliq told me about

it. On its other side is the desert kingdom of the Shadow Princes. Only they know of its existence in Hetar. Now we know and that knowledge may prove valuable to us one day, my lord Dominus." She turned so she might see his face. "Your world is going to change, Magnus. Better you be in charge of that change than others."

"What is it you want of me?" he asked her astutely.

"The promise that if I marry you, you will give me whatever I desire as a wedding gift, my lord Dominus," Lara said.

"And what is that?"

"First your promise," she replied.

"If I ask you again to wed me, Lara of Hetar, I will give you whatever it is you desire as a gift, and pledge of my devotion to you. I swear it on the Great Creator," he told her.

She kissed him softly on the lips, and smiled into his turquoise-blue eyes. "Thank you, Magnus," Lara said in a soft voice. Then she whispered to him, "Have you ever swum naked in the sea, and then made love beneath the stars?"

"Aye to the first, and nay to the second," he told her.

"I have never done either," she said. "I think it is time we broadened my education, my lord Dominus."

"Only if I may be your instructor," he replied.

"Descend, Dasras," Lara said to the horse, and the animal obeyed, alighting on a low bluff overlooking the Obscura.

"Unbridle me before you hurry off to seek your pleasures," Dasras said sternly. "I shall need to graze among this lush greenery most of the night to restore my energy while you two play in the waves, and lie upon the beach expending yours." He stamped a hoof impatiently.

Lara unbridled the beast. "Then we shall both have the night we desire," she told Dasras.

He looked at her a long moment, a twinkle in his dark eyes. "Indeed," he said, and then with a snort the big stallion dashed off.

Chapter 10

"SOMETHING IS DIFFERENT," Magnus said as they prepared to depart the following morning for the Temple of the Great Creator.

"What is different?" Lara asked him as she slipped the bridle over Dasras's head.

"You," he answered.

"She has ceased debating with herself," Dasras told the Dominus, and then he took the bit in his mouth. "She will probably accede to your wishes to wed."

"Is he right?" the Dominus asked.

"Will you not let me speak for myself?" Lara demanded of Dasras. "I have not yet come to any decisions, Magnus."

"So she says," Dasras teased his mistress, and then with a snort shook his magnificent head. "Run your fingers through my mane, Mistress. The wind yesterday has tangled it." Then he addressed the Dominus again. "Do not rush her, Magnus Hauk, and you will obtain your way in the end, for she is a sensible woman."

"One of these days, " Lara muttered, "I'm going to make a spell to silence you," she threatened, but they both knew she didn't mean it. Her slender fingers worked busily through his creamy mane as she combed it.

"You can't silence me. My voice comes from Prince Kaliq, and his powers are greater than yours, Mistress." Then he stamped his hooves. "Are we ready now?"

They mounted the big horse, and he galloped several miles across the green plain before taking to the skies once again. They would reach the Temple of the Daughters of the Great Creator by midafternoon. Lara had made the decision to go there first and inform the priestesses that the curse had been lifted. The High Priestess would then accompany them to the Temple of the Great Creator in order to prove to the priests there that their hearing was indeed restored.

"I do not think I shall ever get used to riding upon the back of a horse that flies," Magnus said. "It is truly amazing, my faerie love."

"I am as awed as you, Magnus," Lara admitted. "Until my mother gave him this great power Dasras was simply a fine mount and an excellent warhorse."

"You have fought a war?" he asked.

"We called it the Winter War. Hetar broke an ancient treaty and came into the Outlands. They invaded one spring in the area of the Tormod and Piaras clan families. These people are miners of gold, silver and gems, but they are also careful keepers of their lands. If you wandered through their mountains and did not know it you would not realize all the industry that goes on there. If they take a tree, they replant a tree.

"Gaius Prospero, who Kaliq tells me has now managed to get himself elected emperor, is a man for whom commerce is everything. He sought the riches that the Tormod and Piaras dug from the earth. He enslaved their people. Hetarians have always been taught that the Outlands is a place of savagery and chaos. In Hetar the laws and rules by which we live are carefully set, and strictly enforced, more with the poor than with the wealthy, however. In the Outlands they had lived simply, each clan family doing what it did best, and keeping to its own boundaries. I believe those who ruled Hetar feared if our people could see how easily the Outlanders got on they would have wanted to make changes. Change is not easy anywhere, but most especially in Hetar."

"Greed was the sole reason for Hetar's invasion?"

"I believe there was more behind it. But when the other clan families learned of the invasion they took action, and beat the invaders back. Not a man was spared but for those who drove the carts of their dead into the center of the City. It was a nasty lesson, and they still burn with the defeat. Hetar has become overcrowded in recent years. The Midland farms can no longer grow enough food to feed the people. When they were rebuffed in their incursion into the Outlands, Hetar began to encroach into the province of the Forest Lords. And the scrubland that separated the desert province of the Shadow Princes, from that of the Forest Lords is also being taken. It is only a matter of time before Hetar invades the Outlands again. The Shadow Princes have been keeping the Outlands safe by means of their magic, but they cannot do this for much longer," Lara said.

"What will happen then?"

"Hetar, in its arrogance, will enslave as many of the Outlanders as they can. They will confiscate their lands, their herds, their flocks. They cannot be convinced that the clan families are not barbarians. They do not understand the Outlands' simpler way of life. It is complete anathema to them," Lara explained.

"I do not believe I like what I hear of Hetar," Magnus said.

"My lord Dominus, you know as well as I do that the people can be led like sheep in whatever direction you want to lead them. The people can be convinced even when their own eyes say it is not so. The people of Hetar are good folk, but their leaders, I fear, have become corrupt, and imbued with a strong sense of their own importance. Many people on both sides will be killed when this conflict breaks out."

"You say you have a destiny," Magnus said.

"Yes, I do," Lara replied.

"What is it?" he asked her quietly.

Around them a soft wind whistled as the horse galloped on through the morning air. The sun was warm on their shoulders. Some of the answer had come even as he asked the question. For weeks she had considered it, but until this moment she had not been certain. Now she was utterly and completely sure. And the scope of it amazed her.

"I cannot speak on this while on the back of a flying horse," Lara said.

"Then ask Dasras to descend, and we shall walk together for a while, and you will tell me what is in your thoughts," he said to her.

Having heard him, Dasras was already descending to the green land below. Lara refrained from remonstrating her horse for doing so without her order. Slowly, slowly they dropped down until the stallion's hooves were touching the ground, his stride slowing, finally coming to a halt. The couple quickly slid from his back and began to walk, while behind them Dasras began chomping upon the lush grass.

"I want you to hear me out, Magnus," Lara began, and he murmured his assent. "War is insanity," she said. "I know that sometimes it appears there is no other way, and perhaps sometimes there isn't. But this time I believe you and I can stop a terrible conflagration before it even starts. Here in Terah you have an overabundance of land. Your population is small. The solution is so simple. What if the Outland clan families were transported here with all their goods and chattels? Then when Hetar invaded, there would be no one to fight. Hetar is desperate to expand—the only place for them to go is into the Outlands. But they will have to kill to gain control of the region. And that kind of blood lust leads to other depravities. The survivors among the clan families will be enslaved, but many will die without their freedom, penned within the confines of the City. And it could all be avoided so simply, my lord Dominus."

"Take in these people, and all their goods? How

many are we speaking of, Lara? And what of the Terahns?"

"The Outland clan families number between ten and twelve thousand," Lara said. "But your own people need not even know that they are here."

"How is that possible?" he wanted to know.

"Magnus, look into the distance. Do you see that range of mountains? Only when you get to the other side of those mountains do you find a Terahn or a Terahn village. This vast plain over which we have traveled this morning is much like the Outlands, although far more lush. We could settle the clan families here. Other than owing you their allegiance, which would involve a yearly tribute, they would continue to govern themselves as they always have. And they would live their lives as they always have. It is most unlikely there would be any concourse between the Terahns and the Outlanders."

"What of those among them who mine?" he wanted to know.

"They will make their own peace, and their own arrangements with your mountain gnomes. The Outlanders are not violent or unreasonable by nature," Lara said. "I know that the Tormod and the Piaras could come to an equitable agreement with the gnomes. And I would negotiate for them if you would permit it."

"If I agreed to this," he said slowly, carefully choosing his words, "how could we prevent Hetar from crossing our Sea of Sagitta, and invading Terah?"

"I will enlist the aid of the Shadow Princes,

Magnus. We will transport the Outland clan families and their goods by means of magic. Nothing, not even their village structures, will remain to show they were there. They will simply be gone. Gaius Prospero will not care, as his only interest is in the profits he will reap in the Outlands, and the acclaim he will receive from the people for having kept his promises to make their lives better. But one day Hetar will come, whether you do this great mercy or not."

"I must think on it," Magnus said.

"Would you have me for your wife, Magnus?" Lara asked him.

"Aye," he responded.

"Then know this. There is a price to pay if you would make me your Domina. The first I have just told you. Help me to fulfill my destiny, and save the clan families of the Outlands," Lara said. "Help me to prevent a ruinous and foolish war."

"And the second?" he queried.

"I will give you the sons and daughters you desire, my lord Dominus, but you must wait for those children until I am certain Hetar can keep the peace," Lara said.

"I must think on it," he repeated softly. "I can refuse you, and keep you as my lover if I choose."

"Then I should be forced to disappear from Terah," she warned him. "I will not wait long for my answer, Magnus. Kaliq has said he and his brothers cannot protect the Outlands much longer. The effort will weaken them if they are forced to continue."

He caught her by the arm, his fingers digging into

her tender flesh. "Faerie witch, do not toy with me," he growled. "Will you be my wife?"

"Will you pay my price?" she boldly demanded to know.

"If I said aye, what would you say?" he insisted.

"If you say aye, then I say aye," Lara told him, her green eyes meeting his turquoise ones. "Do you say aye, Magnus?"

"Do you?" He pulled her into his arms, his lips dangerously close to hers.

Lara laughed, but she remained silent.

"Aye, my faerie witch," he murmured against her lips.

"Aye," she agreed just before his mouth took hers in a fierce kiss that left her drained, and barely able to stand upon her own two legs.

"If you two are finished negotiating," Dasras drawled at them, "I believe we had best be on our way again, Mistress, my lord Dominus. I must assume as you have not said otherwise that you wish to reach the temple compound by midafternoon as planned."

Laughing at his reprimand they mounted the big stallion again, and he galloped across the meadow, his graceful wings flapping as they arose into the sky once more. Lara leaned back again Magnus. It felt to her as if a large weight had been lifted from her shoulders. Behind her the Dominus dropped a kiss upon her golden head, a happiness such as he had never known surging through him.

By midafternoon they saw the delicate Temple of the Daughters of the Great Creator ahead of them. Dasras dropped down from the sky, his wings disappearing. It was better, the intelligent beast realized, to arrive at the temple afoot. Although Lara said nothing, she reached out and patted the animal's neck in a gesture of approval. Dasras cantered easily down the road leading to the temple, slowing his stride as they drew near to its gates.

A bell began to ring announcing the arrival of the visitors, and the gates were opened to welcome them into the temple's courtyard. Dasras came to a halt, and the Dominus slid off of him, turning to lift Lara down. One of the women, recognizing the Dominus, ran quickly into one of the temple's buildings. A moment later a tall older woman emerged.

"My lord Dominus," she greeted him, holding out her hands to him. "Your outrider brought me the news of the great blessing the faerie woman has brought us. How happy I am that at long last you can hear my welcome with your own ears." She smiled at him.

"Kemina," he said, taking her hands to press them to his head, his lips and his heart. "Do you never grow old, High Priestess?"

Kemina laughed. She was a woman with strong striking features, and eyes as blue as the Sea of Sagitta. Her hair was snow-white, but her face was youthful. She did not demur at his compliment, but rather asked, "What brings you here, and who is your companion? A faerie woman, my lord Dominus?"

"I am Lara of Hetar, half-mortal, half-faerie," Lara introduced herself. "My mother is Ilona, queen of the Forest Faeries, my lady Kemina."

"I plan to wed her shortly," Magnus told the High Priestess.

"It is time you were married," Kemina scolded him gently. "Past time. But then it was obviously not meant to be until this fair creature came into your world. But come! Let us not stand in the courtyard gossiping like old women." With a warm smile she led them into the building from which she had exited. "This is my house," she told Lara as they entered a spacious room with a fountain in its center. "Sit," she invited them, clapping her hands, and instructing the attending priestess to bring refreshments. Then she joined them in a comfortable chair constructed of leather and wood. "You do not visit often, my lord Dominus, and so I must conclude there is a purpose to this visit," Kemina said candidly. "Is it too soon for me to ask if you will share it?"

Magnus Hauk chuckled. "Direct as ever," he said. "Aye, there is a reason. It seems in our pride we men of Terah believed our women had been cursed into silence when in truth our ears had been stopped up."

"There has been a great deal of rumor flying about the countryside," Kemina said.

"Lara banished the ghost of Usi who still inhabited his tower. The cursed place was destroyed as was his book of spells so that none could ever use them again," Magnus explained. "I decided to go to the Temple of the Great Creator last, and I want you to come with us. My uncle, the High Priest, knew what Lara was attempting, but you know that many of the priests still hold to Aslak's belief that all magic is evil. Lara must remove the curse from them, and you must be there to convince them that they can once more hear the voices of females."

Kemina laughed heartily. "I will gladly go with you," she said. "I cannot wait to see the look upon the faces of some of those sour old men when they have been freed of the curse Usi placed on Terah all those centuries back. Let us enjoy some wine first, and then we must go at once. I cannot wait until the morrow, and the sun will not set for several hours yet. It is but a short distance to the Temple of the Great Creator." She picked up a goblet of wine that had been placed by her hand. "I cannot say I was sorry to learn of Aslak's death. It was time. I never knew a mind so narrow or so closed."

"It was the sound of my voice, I fear, that caused his death," Lara said softly.

Kemina looked astounded, and then she chuckled. "Let us hope a few more of those old dogs keel over at the sound of it," she said, and then drank down her wine.

"As your Dominus I must reprimand you, High Priestess," Magnus said with a wicked grin. "I am shocked by your lack of sympathy."

"Do not tell me you were sorry to see Aslak go," she cackled. "Praise the Great Creator that your uncle had already been elected to follow him. Arik is a man of vision. He will shake them all up, and move the priesthood into a more modern age."

"We can but hope," Magnus said.

When they had finished their refreshment they departed for the larger Temple of the Great Creator, Dasras again carrying two passengers. The High Priestess rode upon a small roan mare that the stallion eyed with interest. Arriving, they were greeted by a young priest and shown into the High Priest's privy chamber.

"Nephew, welcome back!" Arik greeted them. "Kemina, I greet you. Lara, I greet you," he said.

Lara smiled at Magnus's uncle and recited, "Ears that once heeded woman's call, shall open again and hear them all."

"I greet you, Arik," the High Priestess said quietly.

"I can hear her!" Arik almost shouted. He looked to Lara. "You have done the impossible, my lovely faerie woman. Thank you! Thank you!"

"Gather your priests together, my lord Arik, and I will unstop their ears, as well," Lara said to him.

The High Priest called to one of his minions and gave him quick instructions. The young priest hurried out, and shortly the sound of the temple bells ringing was heard. "I've summoned them all to the temple itself. It seems a fitting setting in which to lift the curse of Usi," Arik said. "Come along!"

They followed the excited high priest from his dwelling and into the temple. It was a large building with an open portico on all four sides. Inside, however, it was simple, and plain in decor. The roof of the temple had a great dome through which sunlight poured. The High Priest led his visitors up two wide stairs to stand before the modest marble altar. Below and around them the temple was filled with priests.

"Are all gathered here now?" Arik asked, looking about.

There was a short silence, then a voice said, "All but the sick in the infirmary, my lord Arik."

Arik turned to Lara. "Will you visit them, and free them?" he asked.

She nodded. "I will."

The High Priest turned back to the crowd, and began to speak. "Priests of the Great Creator, a miracle is about to be visited upon you." He drew Lara forward. "This is Lara of Hetar, daughter of a mortal man and a faerie queen."

A murmur began below them.

The High Priest held up his hand. "She has discovered that it was not the women of Terah who were cursed into silence by the sorcerer. It was the men of Hetar whose ears were stopped up because they listened to a woman, and let her destroy Usi."

"She lies!" a voice from the crowd said.

"Nay, she does not lie, and she has come today to lift the curse from you as she has lifted it from all the men of Terah. I could hear her from the first moment we met, for she is Hetarian. Tell them, Lara."

"I can free you, good priests of the Great Creator," Lara told them.

Surprise showed on the faces below them.

"This is magic!" came the cry.

"Magic is evil. Did not Aslak teach us that?" another voice spoke.

"There is both good and wicked magic," Arik told them. "This lady is good, and her magic is good. She will speak her spell, and lift the curse from you."

Lara stepped quickly forward. "Ears that once heeded woman's call, shall open again and hear them all!" she cried in a loud voice.

Now it was Kemina who stepped forward. "And

now, priests of the Great Creator, hear the voice of your High Priestess, that you may be convinced at what good has been done you this day."

Shocked and upturned faces greeted her proclamation, and then the voices began to exclaim with astonishment as the priests admitted to being able to hear Kemina.

Arik gave them a moment to recover from the shock of what had happened. Then he said, "There is good magic in this world, my brothers."

"Where are the sick?" Lara asked him. "I would remove the curse from them as well."

The High Priest led them from the temple area to a small house where Lara once again spoke the spell, and freed the remaining men from Usi's curse. When they were settled again in his house Arik asked her, "The book of spells?"

"Destroyed," she told him. Then she related her adventure in Usi's tower. "I dispatched the book myself within a magical clay jar. The Shadow Prince Kaliq disposed of the ashes in various places so that no one will ever again use Usi's book of spells."

Kemina had listened in rapt awe to Lara's tale. "You are a brave woman," she said when the story had come to its conclusion.

"I only did what needed to be done," Lara answered her.

"You are too modest," Kemina replied.

"You must marry her, Magnus," the High Priest said.

"I would certainly agree," Kemina murmured.

"We will wed," the Dominus answered them.

"But first we have other things that must be accomplished," Lara told them. "And Sirvat is to be married to Captain Corrado."

"What is it that is so important to you both that you would wait to wed?" the High Priest wanted to know. "I could marry you both now, and it would be done with, Nephew."

"Nay, Uncle. The marriage of the Dominus must be a great occasion," Magnus said. "And my sister is not of a mind to wait," he chuckled, skillfully avoiding answering his uncle's question. He had made a very great promise to Lara, and he would not marry her until he had fulfilled his obligations.

The High Priestess departed, escorted by several young priests, back to her own temple compound.

Arik ate the evening meal with them, and then bid them good-night. "Come and see me, Magnus, before you depart on the morrow," he said.

"I will, Uncle," the Dominus promised.

"He will want the answer to the question he asked you earlier," Lara said.

"I know," Magnus answered her.

"Perhaps it would be best if you told him," Lara advised. "I know it will surprise him, but it may be better that someone else knows what we are doing. There may come a time when we need his help. 'Tis better your uncle feel we have kept nothing from him, that we trusted him enough to share our plans with him."

"Perhaps I should go to him now. This is not something quickly told, and we do want to get back to the castle tomorrow," the Dominus said thoughtfully.

"Go and find him," Lara told him. "I am tired, and will seek my bed."

He pulled her into his arms, and kissed her a slow sweet kiss. "Then good night, my faerie love. Sleep well," he told her.

An unfamiliar feeling overcame her briefly. Reaching up she caressed his face. "Good night, Magnus," she responded. When he had left her, Lara considered what had just happened. What had she sensed? Was it some type of emotion? Affection? Caring?

Love? Ethne's voice was very clear.

"I do not know how to really love," Lara said aloud.

Perhaps you are finally learning, Ethne replied. *You had great fondness for Vartan, but you did not really love him, though he thought you did when you gave him the children he desired.*

He was good to me, Lara said silently.

This man may well be your equal, Ethne said. *We will see if he keeps his promise to you to help the Outland peoples.*

He has never really faced the duplicitous behavior of which Gaius Prospero and the High Council of Hetar are capable. He is strong, and he is wise, but he lacks the sophistication necessary to deal successfully with Hetar. Terah is totally different from Hetar, Ethne. They have lived the same sort of life for centuries, never changing, never looking forward. What if Arik convinces Magnus not to help the Outland family clans?

He won't, Ethne said with great assurance, *but it would not be unwise for you and Magnus to visit Hetar. If he saw what was happening there perhaps he would better understand your concerns. We all see different situations in different lights, my child. You clearly see the danger for the Outlands, but Magnus is a stranger. He cannot see unless you show him.*

I had thought never to return to Hetar again, Lara admitted.

Just enough of a visit to introduce Magnus to the Outland clan lords and to show him the decay and corruption of the City, of those who now rule Hetar, Ethne said.

It must be done secretly, Lara told her crystal guardian. *Will you contact Kaliq for me, and see if he can help?*

I will, Ethne promised. *Now go to sleep, my child.*

Sirvat must be wed first, Lara insisted.

Of course. Now sleep!

And while Lara spoke with Ethne, Magnus had gone to his uncle. He found Arik in his private quarters. The older man did not seem surprised to see his nephew, even just having bid him good-night. He dismissed his servants and motioned the Dominus to a seat by his fire. "I thought you might come and speak with me before you retired," Arik said quietly. "This must be a most important undertaking. Tell me what it is, Nephew."

"First I would tell you that it is Lara who feels you should be made aware of what we mean to do, Uncle," Magnus began.

The High Priest chuckled. "She is a clever and intelligent woman, for which you may thank the Great Creator."

"Several days ago when she finished lifting Usi's

curse from all but those here," the Dominus began, "we flew over the mountains to the lands beyond. There is another sea as well, Uncle. Lara says it is called the Obscura."

"You flew?" Arik's eyebrow quirked.

"Her horse can sprout wings, Uncle. It is magic. And he talks as well," Magnus admitted with a small grin.

Arik shook his head, amazed. "Go on," he managed to say.

"The lands beyond our mountains are great, Uncle. And they are uninhabited. A huge fertile plain with nary a village or cultivated field."

"And what do you intend doing with it, Nephew?" Arik asked him.

Then the Dominus explained to his uncle what he had promised to Lara, and why.

The High Priest nodded thoughtfully. Then he said, "Better to have vassals paying you a yearly tribute and making the land useful than to have it uninhabited, for an enemy or stranger to take. What is on the other side of this sea called Obscura?"

"Hetar, even as it is with Sagitta," Magnus answered him. "The difference is that Obscura's opposite shore meets the desert of the Shadow Princes."

"Then we are endangered from both sides," Arik said.

"No one knows of Obscura but the princes, for it is at the far end of their desert where no one goes, even the nomadic desert dwellers," Magnus told his uncle.

"For now," Arik replied thoughtfully. "Still it would indeed be better to have enemies of Hetar on those plains. If Hetar ever sails across that sea they will not receive a warm welcome, and we will be warned. Are these Outlanders good soldiers?"

"When it is necessary," Magnus answered. "They prefer to farm, mine and tend their herds and flocks, Lara said, but when threatened they become a strong fighting force. She has fought with them in a war she called the Winter War."

Arik smiled briefly. "A most versatile faerie woman." He paused in thought for several long moments. "You love her enough to do this for her, Magnus?"

The Dominus nodded. "I do, Uncle. She believes, and I believe, too, that it is her destiny to save these peoples."

"This is not an endeavor that should soon become public knowledge," Arik said.

"We are all agreed upon that point, Uncle," the Dominus replied.

"I am glad you have shared this with me, Nephew," the High Priest remarked. "Now, tell me. Have you spoken with my sister Persis about her daughter's wedding yet? She will be most pleased, I am certain."

"Our mother has had little to do with the upbringing of my youngest sister," Magnus said stiffly. "She will be invited to the festivities, but no earlier than the other guests. From the moment she left the castle she has shown no interest in Sirvat. She has not seen her in five or more years. Narda and Aselma were always her especial pets, Uncle. She was proud to birth me for she had then given my father an heir, but Sirvat's conception was an error, she told me when my sister was born. She said she had taken comfort in the fact that this unexpected confinement would give our father a second son. When it did not she virtually washed her hands of the infant. Sirvat cannot remember Persis even addressing her but for half a dozen occasions before she departed to live with Narda," the Dominus explained.

"I had not realized she was so distant with Sirvat," Arik replied. "Persis was always a bit cold. I was surprised when your father took her to be his wife. I always wondered what it was he saw in her."

"She fascinated him," Magnus answered his uncle. "He could never get enough of her company, her beauty, the pleasures she offered him. She knew her duty, I will say that for my mother. As Domina she was without peer, and she deferred to my father in all the things she did. My father adored her, and she was the perfect wife for him. But she was also selfish and self-involved, Uncle. Surely you understood that? You grew up in the same house together."

"I left for the temple when I was eight," Arik said. "I knew from the time I could form thoughts that this is what I wanted. When I was eighteen I returned home for my interval year as required before taking my final vows to the Great Creator. Persis was gone by then, and married to your father."

"You chose not to marry," Magnus said.

"Aye, but I am not a celibate as some are. I take my pleasures now and again as I feel the need. But a wife and children, as some called to my vocation have, would have hindered my rise in our order. I have always been an ambitious man, Nephew. I prefer power to women." Then he laughed. "But you knew that, didn't you?"

Magnus Hauk grinned broadly, and nodded. "I knew it, Uncle. But you are practical, as well, I think."

The High Priest nodded, and then he arose. "And being practical, I need my rest, Nephew. Bring Lara to me in the morning that I may bid you both farewell, and give you my blessing until the time of your nuptials."

The Dominus stood. "Good night again then, Uncle," he said. Returning to the guest house, he found Lara sleeping, a small smile upon her lips. Looking down at her, his own heart swelled. He did love her. He wondered if she had any emotions for him other than passion. Did he care? He washed himself, and lay down by her side to sleep.

IN THE MORNING, Lara and Magnus bid the High Priest farewell, and he did indeed give them his blessing, after telling Lara that she had his full support, and that the immigration of the Outland clan families would remain their secret. She thanked him, taking his hands in the Terahn fashion and pressing them first to her head, then her lips and finally her heart. The gesture brought a smile to Arik's lips.

As Dasras did not like the narrow cliff road above the fjord he unfolded his great wings and flew back to the castle, landing in the courtyard close to the midday hour. The stable men stared wide-eyed as the horse's hooves touched down on the cobbled ground. They gasped audibly as Dasras's wings disappeared completely, folding themselves into his body when he commanded them to do so. They were barely used to the horse's speech, but to see the magic he made half frightened them. Then one young boy, braver than the rest, came forward and took the horse's bridle.

"Welcome home, Dasras," he said.

"I thank you, young Jason," the stallion said as he was led away.

"Once people get over being frightened of Dasras," Lara remarked, "he has a great knack for making friends."

"A horse who talks is one thing, but one who carries on an intelligent conversation is truly amazing," the Dominus replied. "Come, let us tell Sirvat that we have returned home." Catching her hand they strolled across the courtyard toward the private apartments where Sirvat came running to meet them.

"Welcome home, Magnus, Lara," she said. "Now that you have lifted the curse from the men of Terah can we please begin the preparations for my wedding?" Then she paused, looking distressed. "Unless the wedding of the Dominus should take place first. You and Lara are going to wed, aren't you?"

"Aye, we will wed," Lara quickly replied. "But before we do, your brother and I have some other business that must be taken care of, Sirvat. So if you do not object, you will have to be married to Corrado first."

"Oh no, I do not object!" Sirvat said breathlessly.

Lara and Magnus laughed at her delight.

"I shall leave the preparations in your hands, my ladies," the Dominus told them. "The only part a man should have in his marriage day is to be there." Then he left them.

"Your uncle the High Priest sends you his best wishes," Lara said to Sirvat. "He is pleased by your choice of a husband, and will come himself to perform the ceremony so he may bless you and Corrado."

"I do not wish a great celebration," Sirvat said. "I only want to be married as soon as possible, Lara. Were you not eager when you wed your first husband?"

"I did not even know I was being wed," Lara said. "Vartan tricked me into the union," she recalled with a smile. "He had to visit his villages, and asked me if I should like to ride with him. I went, and in doing so found myself married. It seems if you spend two nights with a man of the Outlands, you are considered his wife. We did not even take pleasures of each other," she chuckled, "but I was firmly wed according to clan law."

Sirvat eyes were wide with shock, but she giggled. "He sounds very bold," she said. "Was he handsome? Was he skilled at pleasures?"

"He was both handsome and skilled," Lara acknowledged with a smile.

"I cannot wait to take pleasures with Corrado," Sirvat sighed romantically.

"Have you ever taken pleasures with a man?" Lara asked her, wondering if she would have to prepare Magnus's sister for passion.

"Oh yes," Sirvat said nonchalantly. "I have had two lovers, but only for brief periods of time. Men have a tendency to grow possessive, and so I never kept a lover for very long, not wishing to be possessed. Corrado, however, knows and understands me. We are equals, as are you and my brother. That is how I know Magnus's marriage to you is the right thing, Lara. He has never before treated any woman as an equal, or a friend. Women were just for pleasures. But not you. You are different."

"But it is your wedding we must plan, Sirvat," Lara said neatly turning the subject. "We must inform your mother and sisters of this event."

"Not right away," Sirvat said. "You and I will plan, and then at the last minute we will send to my family. If we inform them now they will come, and they will interfere. I would not ask them at all but that it would reflect badly upon me. But I am not interested in hearing them criticize me or my choice of a husband."

"Why would they criticize Corrado?" Lara wanted to know.

"My mother was a distant cousin of my father. She was proud of her claim to the Hauk bloodline. My older sisters also made advantageous matches. My husband-to-be is a sea captain."

"But he is Magnus's captain of captains," Lara reminded Sirvat.

"He has no lands, no villages. He lives here in the palace, and will continue to reside here when we are wed," Sirvat said.

"Magnus has said that one day he will give you lands," Lara said.

"And he will. And Corrado and I are content to wait. But my husband-to-be has not the fine bloodlines that my family has. He is distant kin. It doesn't matter to me. I love him. I have loved him ever since I was a child, and he first came to the palace. And my brother has judged him on his worth, and found him more than suitable. My brother wants me happy. But my mother will carp at Magnus, and she will carp at me. She will be slyly insulting to Corrado in an effort to prick his pride, and drive him away. I do not look forward to her visit. And you had best beware for she will find fault with you. I am certain she has someone in mind to be Magnus's wife. She will not be pleased to learn he has made his own decision from which he cannot be swayed."

"You make your mother sound fearsome," Lara said.

"She is not so much fearsome as irritating," Sirvat replied.

"Tell me how a royal wedding is celebrated in Terah," Lara asked, once again turning the subject away from something unpleasant. Remembering her Outlands mother-in-law, Bera, who had welcomed her, and been so loving, Lara decided stoically that one could not always be that fortunate.

"The wedding commences just before dawn," Sirvat began. "Together with our guests we watch the sunrise, the beginning of a new day and our new life as husband and wife. Next Corrado and I are bathed together with our guests in attendance. This is done to show we are both fit for marriage and for children. We are then dressed in our wedding garments and led into one of the gardens, which you and I will choose beforehand. There the High Priest will inquire if we are agreeable to the marriage. We answer, he blesses us and we are officially wed. Then a great feast is held to celebrate our union. At day's end we all watch the sunset. Then Corrado and I retire to our apartments, signaling an end to the celebration."

"How beautiful!" Lara exclaimed.

"And it is even better the fewer guests there are," Sirvat said. "More intimate, and special. At least Corrado and I will not have to visit every fjord afterwards as you and Magnus will have to do. Everyone in Terah must see the new Domina."

"Let us concentrate on your wedding for now," Lara replied. "Does Corrado have any family?"

"His father, Dima, who was once my father's captain of captains. And an older brother, Ing, who is a ship's chandler, having no taste for the sea. Corrado's mother died years ago, and Ing has never married," Sirvat explained.

"So we have two from Corrado's family, and five from yours," Lara said.

"Oh, I am certain my sisters will want to bring all their children, and I cannot avoid the laws of hospitality. And Magnus will have some he wishes to honor by asking them to the wedding," Sirvat said. "It will be far more than I would have."

"Then say no," Lara told her. "Tell your mother and your sisters that they are welcome along with your two brothers-in-law, but no more. Tell Magnus that those he wishes to honor may be honored when we wed. Tell your brother that you want a small and intimate wedding. You are the Dominus's youngest sister. There is no cause for great festivities unless you desire them, Sirvat. It is your wedding."

A look of joy came over Sirvat's face. "You are right, Lara," she said. "I want a small wedding, and by the Great Creator I shall have one!"

The Dominus saw no fault in his sister's wishes. The wedding would be discreet. Sirvat chose the gardens overlooking the fjord for the ceremony. It was late summer, and the flowers were in full bloom. Consulted, Corrado agreed with his beloved's plans. The High Priest was sent for as was the lady Persis, and Sirvat's two older sisters and their husbands. Their offspring, the Dominus ordered them, were to stay at home. Corrado's elderly father, Dima, and his oldest son, Ing, lived at the foot of the castle cliff above the chandler's shop. Their journey was one of minutes.

The night before the wedding all the guests had been assembled, and a feast was set before them. The Dominus's mother was everything Sirvat had said. Tall and still beautiful, with snow-white hair and cold blue eyes, she went to sit at her son's right hand, but Magnus warned her away.

"This place belongs to my sister, the bride," he told his mother.

"Then I will sit on your left," the lady Persis said.

"That is Lara's place," the Dominus replied.

"Nay, my lord Dominus," Lara quickly said. "I am content to defer to your mother this night," and she moved down the high board to the end seat.

"Well, at least the wench has manners," Lady Persis grudgingly said as she took her seat on her son's left.

"When you come to my wedding, madam, Lara

will be seated to my right," the Dominus said with emphasis.

His mother paled. "That is the bride's place," she replied weakly.

"Yes," he said. "Lara is to be my wife."

Lady Persis's mouth fell open with both surprise and shock. "You cannot!" she snapped at her son. "A foreigner? A Hetarian? Half-mortal, half-faerie? Have you lost what few wits you had? Your father would be horrified. If you wish to marry I can bring you half a dozen Terahn girls of good family who would make you an excellent Domina."

"Madam," he said low, but his voice was edged with anger, "if I wanted, if I had fallen in love before this, I should have taken a wife. I have not because there was never any woman who suited me. It is time this family's bloodlines were freshened. But more important, madam, I love her. I had to beg her to wed me for she is widowed, and was not of a mind to marry again. But I knew she was the one from the moment we met. It has taken me weeks to convince her to change her mind. Do not interfere, I warn you."

"Do not interfere, or what?" his mother challenged him.

The Dominus laughed. "Or I shall turn Lara loose on you, madam," he said. "She does not take kindly to interference."

"She has bewitched you!" his mother half cried, and heads around them turned to see what the commotion was all about.

Again Magnus laughed. "I suppose she has, but not in the way you believe."

"What more can you want of her? She is already in your bed," the Lady Persis said venomously.

"Her intellect is superior to any little Terahn girl you would bring me. Her counsel is invaluable. She is wise beyond her years, madam. Times are changing, and we need to look at the world around us with new eyes. And I love her," he repeated.

"Terah will never accept her," Lady Persis declared.

"Never accept the woman who freed us from Usi's curse? I think you are mistaken, madam. Although frankly I would have been glad to remain deaf to your voice. My only consolation, madam, is that you will shortly return home with Narda, and I will not have to listen to you." Then the Dominus turned to his other guests, leaving his mother openmouthed in her astonishment.

Lara had seen the byplay between Magnus and his mother. That she was the cause of their conversation she did not doubt. The Lady Persis did not like her, but it mattered not. Lara would marry Magnus Hauk because he could aid her in gaining her destiny. And perhaps, just perhaps, her heart was softening toward him. She had never considered when she was a barefooted mercenary's child back in the Quarter that she would one day be the wife of a powerful ruler. It was not a bad fate, Lara thought, but there was more to her destiny than just saving the clan families of the Outlands. That much she sensed. But what was it? And would Magnus Hauk play a strong part in what was to come? She could not love him with her whole heart if he was to be torn from her as Vartan had

been. She could not lose another child to this destiny
that never seemed to come to an end. Instinctively her
hand reached for the crystal star about her neck, and
she felt the comforting warmth of the flame within it.

Do not despair, she heard Ethne's gentle voice reassure her. *This is a man you can love forever.*

Chapter
11

SIRVAT AND CORRADO'S wedding day dawned with a glorious sunrise. The few guests invited to the quiet affair joined the couple to watch it. As she stood with Magnus, his arm about her waist, Lara thought that there had never been so beautiful a morning. The cloudless blue sky was slowly stained with vibrant colors; at first delicate pinks and mauves and palest greens that gave way to the more flamboyant golds, oranges and reds as the scarlet sphere finally crept above the green horizon, its brilliant rays spreading across the firmament.

When the sun was well up the guests escorted the bride and groom into the baths, where Sirvat and Corrado were stripped of their clothing, their bodies displayed to show both were healthy and fit to wed one another. Then before the eyes of their guests the couple were thoroughly bathed before being dressed in their wedding garments. They had chosen to wear traditional Terahn wedding clothing.

Sirvat wore a long simple sleeveless gown of cream-colored silk. The neckline was draped, resting on her collarbone. The straight skirt was a mass of narrow little pleats, and about her waist Sirvat wore a delicate gold chain. Her hair was dressed in thin braids entwined with slender bejeweled golden ribbons. She wore golden sandals on her feet. Her bridegroom wore a similar tunic that fell to his knees. The skirt was not pleated but rather fell in graceful folds. About his waist was a gold chain, and he carried no weapons.

The bride and her groom were led into the garden overlooking the fjord, where the lady Persis placed wreaths of multicolored flowers on their heads.

Then Arik, High Priest of the Great Creator, asked the simple question. "Do you, Sirvat, daughter of the Dominus Ejnar, deceased, and his living widow, Persis, and you, Corrado, son of Dima and his wife, Amala, deceased, pledge yourselves to each other as husband and wife?"

"Yes!" Corrado said.

"Yes!" Sirvat echoed.

"Then let it be so in the eyes of the Great Creator of us all," Arik replied. "You are now wed, Sirvat and Corrado. The Great Creator bless your union, and give you many children and much happiness in the years to come. It is done."

"That is all?" Lara whispered to Magnus.

"It is enough, isn't it?" he replied with a small smile. "Do they do things differently in Hetar?"

"It depends," Lara said. "The daughter of a wealthy man is wed in a great show of splendor, even if it means her father will go into debt. In Hetar how one appears to others is very important. My father, however, wed my stepmother in the Midlands where both had been born and raised. Each month a marrying day is held, and the Squire of the Midlands performs a small ceremony. But even there the bride's family holds the best feast it can. No one wants it said that they did not fully honor the couple, or the Celestial Actuary," she explained.

"In Terah, it is the same for my sister as it is for a farmer's daughter. The priest asks if the parties are willing, and then blesses them. What is important is that the couple wish to make a life together, Lara. Nothing else," he told her.

"I like it better," Lara said quietly. "A marriage is not about status or wealth. It is about love, isn't it?"

He smiled down at her. "Aye, it is about love. Was it that way in the Outlands?"

Lara nodded. "In Hetar they tell terrible stories of the Outlands to frighten bad children into behaving. Threatening a child with exile to the Outlands was sure to turn the most recalcitrant boy or girl into the most obedient of creatures. The Outlands were a wild place filled with savages who murdered, stole, raped and did every kind of violence. They were barbarians of the worst ilk. But then I entered the Outlands to discover a very orderly civilization. It was different from Hetar to be sure, but the clan families live in peace. Their lives are simpler, much like those of the

Terahs. That is why I am so certain they will cause you no difficulty when they come."

"What are you two whispering about?" the lady Persis demanded to know.

"My lord Magnus was explaining to me the marriage custom of Terah," Lara said quickly, "and I told him how it is done in Hetar."

"And how is it done there?" Lady Persis persisted.

"With much too much ostentation," Lara replied. "Having seen both I can tell you that I far prefer the elegant simplicity of Terahn custom, which dwells upon the love between a couple and not the pretentious display by their families. Marriage is a serious undertaking, and not to be entered into capriciously." She gave the Dominus's mother a small cool smile.

"Indeed," Lady Persis responded. The reputation the Hetarians had for luxury was certainly at odds with this young woman. She needed to get her aside so she might learn more about Lara, especially if Magnus was serious about marrying her. "Tomorrow you will sit with me before I return home with my daughter Narda," she said.

Lara offered Lady Persis a nod of agreement, but said nothing. The important thing in dealing with this woman was to not permit her to gain the upper hand. She now turned her attention to the wedding feast, which had been set out in the garden as the day was fair. There were roasted meats, fowl and fish; late summer vegetables and fruits; fresh breads and cheeses, as well as fine wine. And when everyone was sated, a sweet cake was brought forth for the guests to share in the newly wedded couple's honor.

As they celebrated, Lara observed the other guests, particularly the family of the Dominus. Lady Persis was a cold proud woman. That she could leave her youngest child for what she deemed the greater comfort of her eldest daughter's home disturbed Lara. But then, had she not left her own children? Yet, she had not done it for herself as Lady Persis had. She had departed the Outlands because her destiny had called her.

Lara's green eyes flicked next to Magnus's two older sisters. Narda, the eldest, was a pretty woman who seemed devoted to her husband, Tostig. Tostig was obviously in love with his wife, and deferential to his mother-in-law. The second sister, Aselma, was plump with good living, and doted upon by her husband, Armen. She appeared to have inherited her mother's selfish attitude although she was certainly pleasant enough. I shall see them rarely, Lara decided. I have a friend in Sirvat, and she is all I will need.

Corrado's family, on the other hand, drew her interest. His father, Dima, was a tall and slender old man who had had his sons late in life, but despite his advanced age he still displayed a refined demeanor. His elder son, Ing, was plump and cheerful. He had never had time for a wife, and didn't seem to miss one. Now he clapped his father upon his back, teasing him that perhaps he would get to see some grandchildren after all.

The day began to wane, and the guests came together upon another high terrace to watch the sunset, which was even more perfect than the sunrise had been. Pink clouds edged in gold and purple floated in the sky above and vibrant colors—scarlet, orange, salmon, lemon-yellow, rose and gold—flowed and pulsed one into another. The air was still and warm and perfumed with late summer roses. Slowly, slowly the sun sank into a horizon of dark violet, and then there was the tiniest flash of green, which drew applause from the spectators. It was considered good fortune to spy that small moment.

"The wedding day is now concluded," the High Priest Arik said. "Sirvat and Corrado will retire to the privacy of their apartments."

With a bow to their guests the newly married couple left the garden.

"Lara!" The voice was that of Lady Persis. "Come with me now, and we will speak with one another. Tostig wishes to depart early, and I would not keep my good son-in-law waiting. Besides I am anxious to return to my comfortable home."

"Ungrateful, presumptuous bitch," the Dominus murmured under his breath.

"I shall be with you momentarily, Lady Persis," Lara said. Then she put a gentle hand upon Magnus's sinewy arm. "I will take care of this matter, my lord Magnus," she murmured. "Would you like me to turn her into a mouse?"

"Could you?" he asked, his turquoise eyes twinkling. He sounded hopeful.

Lara smiled, but said nothing, giving him a quick kiss, and hurrying off.

She found the Dominus's mother in the great day room of the Women's Quarters. Going to a sideboard Lara poured two goblets of wine, and then brought them over to where the Lady Persis was seated. "I thought we might enjoy some refreshment while we talked," she said quietly.

"Refreshment or support?" Lady Persis asked with some humor.

"Perhaps a bit of both," Lara replied with a small smile.

"My son says he means to wed you," the Dominus's mother said.

"Yes, so he has told me," Lara answered her.

"You would refuse him?" Lady Persis was surprised.

"Nay, but I would also not be hurried. I am a widow, lady," Lara responded. "My husband was a great lord. Not as great as your son, I will admit. But a great leader of his clan family, and of his entire world."

"How did he die?" Lady Persis wanted to know.

"He was killed by his younger brother who was tempted by his foolish wife. She had been inveigled by an ambitious man of Hetar who believed if Vartan were dead, the clan families of the Outlands, a land not ruled by Hetar, would be leaderless and vulnerable to an invasion. He was wrong, of course."

"What happened to the assassin?" Lady Persis wanted to know.

"I killed both him and his wife," Lara said quietly.

Lady Persis looked first shocked, then disbelieving. "You killed them? You mean you had them executed, of course."

"Nay," Lara replied. "I killed them."

"How?" Lady Persis had eyes like her son's, and

they were now wide with a mixture of both fear and curiosity—and perhaps even a bit of fascination.

"With my sword, Andraste. I am a warrior, lady," Lara said simply.

Lady Persis was silent for several long moments. Finally she spoke. "You are a warrior," she repeated slowly. "Why have you come to Terah?"

"Because my destiny led me here, lady. I do not fully understand it myself," Lara said candidly. "But it was obviously meant I be here else the curse of Usi would not be lifted."

Lady Persis nodded. "I will admit that what you have accomplished here has been beneficial to the people of Terah," she said. "I was taught that magic was wicked, yet yours seems not to be. And my brother, Arik, is favorable to a marriage between you and my son, Magnus."

"My magic is naught but for good, lady. I do not practice the dark arts although the sorcerer Usi was a man who did. But those who use the darkness eventually fall into it, and are lost. I walk in the light."

"I have been told faerie women only give children to those they love. Is this true? My son must have heirs."

"I will give them to him when the time is propitious, lady. I gave Vartan a son and a daughter," Lara said.

"Where are they?" Persis wanted to know.

"With their father's people. I could not take them with me on this quest," Lara said to the older woman. "My son may one day be leader of the Fiacre clan."

Lady Persis nodded. "You did what was best for

them. I can see that," she replied. "I left Sirvat when she was just a little girl. I know there are those who think badly of me for it, and perhaps they are right. I loved Magnus's father, Ejnar. When he died I thought I might, too, but I did not. I went on because I was supposed to do so. But Sirvat is her father's image. Each day I looked at this child I had not intended bearing, and I found myself beginning to hate her. She was alive, and Ejnar was not. I protected her the best way I knew how."

"You left her to her brother, and went to Narda's home," Lara said. "Do you still hate her?"

"No! How could I? Magnus was a far better influence for Sirvat than I ever would have been. She is the sweetest of my daughters because I had virtually nothing to do with her upbringing." Persis laughed almost bitterly. "It would appear I lost not only my husband, but a daughter as well because I could not resign myself to my own fate. You at least gave up your children for a noble cause, Lara."

"But I cannot forget them," Lara said softly.

"Nor should you!" Persis told her. "When my son told me that he would marry you I was angered, for I thought he should have a Terahn maiden to wife, and certainly not a Hetarian. But I see now that Magnus is wiser than I ever was. My brother is right. Arik says you will help Magnus to become Terah's greatest Dominus."

"The High Priest honors me," Lara said. "If Magnus becomes Terah's greatest Dominus it will be because of his own efforts. I will take no credit for his accomplishments, lady."

Persis laughed softly. "You are very clever," she noted. "I can see you will manage my son to his best advantage. He will be fortunate in you. I give you my blessing, Lara."

"Give us both your blessing, lady. I know it would please the Dominus greatly to know you approve."

"Nonsense! He couldn't care a whit what I think," Lady Persis declared, "but I thank you for saying it. And I will follow your good advice."

Lara rose. "Then I will see you before you depart on the morrow, lady."

"You take pleasures together, of course," the older woman said.

Lara nodded as she set her goblet back down.

"His father was a marvelous lover," Lady Persis said.

"Then his son surely takes after him," Lara replied with a smile, and she left the Dominus's mother alone. They had tested each other, and Lara knew that Persis would now leave her in peace. Her original motive might have been to control her son's future, but Lara could see that in her strange way Persis loved Magnus, and wanted what was best for him. Twice she had mentioned that Arik approved of Lara. It was good to learn she had the High Priest of Terah on her side should she ever need him, as perhaps she would one day. She hurried through the castle to tell Magnus of her meeting with his mother.

She found him in his private gardens enjoying the night. Sitting next to him she slipped her hand into his. "Your mother and I have made our peace. She would give us her blessing in the morning before she leaves."

"Did you bewitch her?" he asked in an amused tone.

"She is intelligent in her own way, and it seems your uncle has much influence with her, my lord Dominus," Lara told him. "He has told her a marriage between us is for the good of Terah. We talked on many things, but they are women's things, and would be of no interest to you. Just know she will make no difficulties between us."

"I want to go to Hetar," he said, surprising her. Turning, he tipped her face up so he might look into her eyes.

"Why?" she asked, though she had herself considered taking him to Hetar.

"You want me to populate all the land beyond the mountains with Outlanders," he began. "I want to know these people before I let you bring them here. And it is always better that a man knows his enemy. Hetar, should they learn of us, will be our enemy. I want to see the City. I want to know what it is I may have to face one day."

"Do you trust me?" Lara asked him.

"Of course," he replied without hesitation, "but I must see for myself. I have given you my word, faerie woman, and I will keep that word. But let me see first. Do you understand?"

"Aye," she said slowly, "I do. You are wise, my lord Dominus. Will we wed before this journey, or after? I will leave the choice up to you."

"Before," he said. "I will take no chances on losing

you, Lara." His fingers stroked her face gently. "Will you agree?"

"You said the Dominus must wed with much pomp and show," Lara reminded him. "If you wish that then we cannot go to Hetar until the spring. I do not believe the Shadow Princes can hold back the danger that long."

"Then we will bring the Outlanders here before the winter sets in. They will be safe, and in the spring you and I will go to Hetar," the Dominus said.

"It will take a great act of combined magic," Lara told him. "I must speak with Kaliq on the dream plane once again."

"Not tonight," he said softly. And his hand began to undo her simple gown. "Tonight is for love, faerie woman. Tonight I would exchange pleasures with you."

"Would you play at being my husband then?" she teased him gently, her fingers caressing the back of his neck.

"I am your husband," Magnus murmured against her mouth, his eyes meeting hers. "We but lack Arik's formal blessing, my faerie love. I know the Great Creator smiles on our union, Lara. And before we go to Hetar in the springtime we will have a proper wedding." He undid the last fastening on her gown and it slipped to the ground. Pulling her naked body against him, he kissed her.

It was good, Lara realized. This was where she was meant to be. In Terah. In the strong arms of Magnus Hauk. Her lips softened beneath his, and suddenly their tongues were at play. She murmured softly as his big hands fastened themselves about the twin moons of her bottom. His fingers dug into her flesh, kneading it gently. She could feel the desire in his very fingertips.

He felt her yielding, felt her need. His own need was burgeoning beneath his gown. Laying her back on the marble bench he straddled her as he pulled off the long tunic he had worn that day, tossing it on the gravel path.

Lara half sat and began licking at his broad chest, nibbling teasingly at his nipples. Impatient he took her head between his hands, and began kissing her face. Her hands began to fondle his great manhood; stroking it, her subtle fingers playing with his seed sacs, rolling them in her palm, marveling at their size.

"Faerie witch," he groaned. "I want to be inside of you."

"Not yet, my lord," she whispered hotly in his ear, licking it playfully.

"Tell me what you want," he demanded.

"Know my flesh," Lara told him. "Taste me all over. I want to feel your tongue on me, my lord and my love."

She lay back again, and he began to tongue her. The dampness covered her breasts, and he blew on her wet nipples causing them to pucker tightly. Unable to help himself he suckled hard on each in turn before beginning his further exploration of her lush body. Lara closed her eyes, and reveled in the touch of his warm tongue. Slowly it roamed across her torso, and belly, and then he blew on her again causing small frissons of delight to ripple down her spine.

The tongue slipped down her leg in a single smooth motion, pushing between the toes of each foot. Then his tongue swept upwards again.

"Oh, Magnus!" Lara breathed.

Reaching her smooth pink mons he placed a long hot kiss upon it. Then his tongue sought out the purple-shadowed slit and ran down it. He was almost dizzy with the heady musk of her body. And his own desire was greater than it had previously been.

His tongue pushed between her nether lips, seeking out the most sensitive spot on her body. Her small sharp cry told him he had succeeded. His dark blond head was buried deep between her thighs. He pulled her flesh open to his sight. She was milky with her juices. His mouth fastened about the tiny nub, and he began to suck her.

It was as if she had been struck with lightning. The sharp enjoyment pulsed through her as his mouth demanded more of her than any man ever had. And to her surprise Lara found she was willing to give him what he wanted. Her mouth opened in a scream. He sucked on her flesh all the harder, and a fierce tingle surged through her, leaving her helpless to him. And then he was pulling himself up, and she was beneath him again. Slowly, slowly he pushed into her body. Lara could scarcely breathe. He was so very big, and she reveled in his size as her body opened gradually to accommodate him. She could feel herself responding almost violently to the invasion, and then he was completely sheathed. Hands captured her head.

"Look at me," he growled. "I want to see the pleasure in your eyes when your desire peaks, my faerie love. I want to lose myself in that green sea, Lara."

He filled her so full, and his lover's rod throbbed and burned within her. At first she could not open her eyes. Her lids were lethargic, as if her eyelashes weighed heavily on her cheeks. But then she managed to lift her lids, and looking into the turquoise-blue eyes staring back at her, Lara shuddered with release. Magnus laughed softly and began to move skillfully within her. Her love juices were so heavy that the bench grew wet beneath them. The small release she had previously experienced had not sated her. Indeed she felt more need than before. Her nails dug first into his shoulders, and then began to rake down his back with her insistence.

"Oh, please! Please!" she gasped.

"Faerie witch!" he panted with his own urgency. "A moment more, for you are too delicious to waste so quickly."

"We have the whole night!" she sobbed. "I will raise your lust again."

"How?" he groaned. He was close and he knew it.

She softly whispered the words in his ear. "I will take you between my lips, my lord Dominus, and I promise you that you will desire me again very quickly. I know how to stoke a man's hungers." She licked his ear.

His juices exploded forth, mingling with hers, and he shouted with the hot sweet pleasure they had just attained. For several minutes they lay panting and gasping with the fulfillment they had given each other.

Finally Lara managed to speak. "Magnus, you are crushing me."

Slowly he pulled himself off of her. He was drained. Weakened. He had never been as satisfied by a woman as he was with Lara, and he sensed that it was the same for her as well. The night had darkened, and the sky above them was studded with stars.

Magnus managed to stand on his feet. He swayed briefly but did not fall. Reaching down he pulled Lara up. "Come," he said. "We will bathe, and then you will do to me what you have promised, my faerie witch."

Lara leaned heavily against him. Then she whispered in his ear again. "Shall I suck you dry, my lord Dominus?"

"Yes!" he said through gritted teeth. "Yes!" He almost dragged her into his apartments and through to the bath. They bathed each other with large soapy sea sponges. When they had rinsed the scented foam from their bodies she knelt before him and took his lover's rod into her mouth. Her lips closed tightly about his flesh, and she began to suckle upon him. He groaned with both pleasure and surprise as he felt himself growing hard again. Her lips and mouth worked him into a fever. Her tongue licked the great pillar of flesh, and swirled about his seed sacs playfully. Before he might rethink the situation, she was sucking upon him with such insistence that he was unable to control himself, and Lara drank down his juices with such fierce relish he felt as weak as a maid.

Standing she kissed him, her tongue pushing into his mouth, and he tasted himself on her. Then without a word she rinsed them both again with the fragrant water. "Shall I sleep by your side tonight, my lord Magnus?" she asked him sweetly.

"Aye," he managed to grind out as he took her hand to lead her to his bedchamber.

He was confused. Never before had he felt himself out of control, and yet he had been in those few minutes in which Lara had pleasured him so wildly and so sweetly. He had been driven almost mad by her warm mouth, her facile tongue. He was not certain he liked being out of control, and in her care. Oh, other women had done to him what she had done. But never so completely.

"What is it?" she asked as she climbed into his bed. "Did I not please you?"

"If you had pleased me any more I should have died," he told her honestly, "but I felt I had no command of our passion."

Lara laughed softly. "You didn't," she told him. "I was in complete authority, Magnus. Did it frighten you to be dominated, my lord Dominus?"

"Faerie witch," he said looming over her. "I was not so much frightened as surprised to find myself in such a position."

"Women often find themselves in such a position, Magnus, but as confusing as it was to you, you trusted me. Trust will be the cornerstone of our love," she told him.

"Who taught you that?" he wanted to know.

"Kaliq and his brothers," Lara answered him. Then seeing the look on his face she continued, "I will never lie to you, Magnus. I do not love Kaliq, but he is my mentor. I need him, for I know I have not yet attained my full powers. I use my powers for good, and what lies ahead of me, of us, is yet shrouded even to my eyes. But I know I will need all those powers and all my strength to fight the darkness that is coming."

"And I will stand by your side to fight with you, my faerie love," he promised her. "I know I have no cause to fear or be jealous of the Shadow Prince, but I am only a mortal, Lara. Mortals are weak. They can be tempted by all kinds of emotions."

"I know," she replied, "but I will try not to give you cause to be tempted. Unless, of course, you wish to be tempted by me," Lara teased him.

"You have exhausted me, faerie witch," he chuckled, "and I am not ashamed to admit it." He pulled her into his arms so that her golden head rested upon his shoulder. "Go to sleep now, Lara. You must speak with your allies tomorrow, and we must prepare to bring your Outland clans to Terah before the winter sets in."

Lara fell asleep, a hundred thoughts whirling about in her mind. Awakening with the dawn she felt logy, and she had a headache. Rising, she found her gown in the garden and hurried back through the castle to her room in the Women's Quarters. Magnus's family would be departing in a few hours, and Lady Persis had promised her blessing. She needed to look like a woman worthy to be the Domina of Terah, and not like something spat out by the sea on the shore of the fjord.

She stripped off her gown and quickly washed her face and hands. Then she took up her brush, and brushed her long golden hair until it was silken smooth again, free of its tangles. Carefully she plaited her hair into a single thick braid, fastening the end with a small bejeweled silver band. Then she chose a gown of sky-blue from her wardrobe, and put it on along with a pair of silver sandals. She could hear the sounds of the other women stirring. She hurried from her chamber and into the day room to find the servants bringing forth food for a meal.

"Is there enough variety, my lady?" a servant asked her.

"Should you not ask the lady Sirvat?" she said, and then she remembered that Sirvat no longer inhabited the Women's Quarters. She lived in her own apartment with her husband. She blushed. "Yes, yes, there is an excellent variety," she told the servant. Obviously the servants had begun to consider her the lady of the castle. How interesting.

Lady Persis, followed by her daughters Narda and Aselma, entered the chamber calling their good mornings. Lara responded, gesturing them to take their places at the table. The Dominus's mother looked approvingly at the display of foods decorating the table. Catching Lara's eyes she nodded with a smile.

"Oh, honey cakes!" Aselma said reaching for the plate containing them.

"Will you always have that sweet tooth?" Narda said almost critically.

Aselma bit into the delicacy, a smile lighting up her face. "Yes," she said.

"Girls," Lady Persis murmured warningly. She turned to Lara. "Do you have sisters?" she asked.

"Nay, but I have two half brothers. Mikhail is my father's son by my stepmother, Susanna. He was still a baby when I left the City. Cirilo is my mother's son by her consort. He will rule the Forest Faeries one day," Lara explained. She noted that both Narda and Aselma had grown wide-eyed as she spoke. "I hardly know either of them, but my mother will rule for many years, I know."

"Your mother is a queen?" Lady Persis inquired.

"Did Magnus not tell you? My mother is Ilona, queen of the Forest Faeries in Hetar. That is where I have obtained my faerie blood. My father is a Crusader Knight."

"What is that?" Narda could not contain her curiosity.

"In Hetar the military leaders are called Crusader Knights. They command an army of common soldiers called Mercenaries. My father was a Mercenary who ascended into the ranks of the Crusader Knights at the triannual tournament for new leaders. I was sold into slavery in order that he have his opportunity."

"You were a slave?" Aselma did not know whether to be shocked or not.

"Briefly," Lara replied. "Why, Aselma, you have hardly eaten a thing, and you have a long journey ahead of you today. In fact you must leave soon if you are to reach your own home by nightfall."

Lady Persis smiled to herself. Her son's bride-to-be was clever to change the subject from herself to Aselma so easily. She watched as her daughters quickly ate their meal. Her eyes met Lara's briefly, and a small smile touched the younger woman's lips.

Lady Persis almost laughed aloud, but had she done so she would have had to explain the jest to her daughters, and they seemed to lack her acuity.

When the Dominus's mother and sisters were ready to depart Magnus escorted them down to the waterside. There in the presence of many witnesses Lady Persis gave her blessing to her son, and to Lara. She bid Sirvat and Corrado farewell, wishing them long life and many children. Her elder daughters did the same, but Sirvat was more stranger than sibling to them. Then Lady Persis and her family embarked upon their vessels and sailed off down the fjord.

"Well, I suppose I won't see her for another few years," Sirvat said sharply.

"She'll come when you have your first child," Lara assured her friend.

"She'll come before then," the Dominus said. "Do you think she would miss our wedding, faerie woman?"

"Ohh, when are you getting married?" Sirvat asked excitedly.

"Soon!" the Dominus said.

"I don't know yet," Lara said.

Corrado chuckled. "I see no meeting of the minds has been achieved between you both. But then, the wedding of a Dominus should be a grand event, and it does take time to plan such an event."

"There are other considerations," Lara murmured.

"And conditions which will be met," Magnus said.

"First," Lara replied with emphasis.

"Agreed," the Dominus promised.

"I will help you with the planning," Sirvat said. "We could start today!"

Lara laughed. "Your bridegroom is just home from the sea, and you would leave him to plan a wedding for which a date hasn't even been set?"

Together the two couples walked from the fjord quayside back to the platform that would bring them back into the castle itself. Stepping on it they were raised up by the giant whose task it was to operate the lift.

"You love him. He loves you," Sirvat said. "What else matters?"

"Go and take pleasures with your bridegroom, little sister," the Dominus said as they stepped from the platform and reentered the castle proper. "Lara and I need to talk."

He held out his hand, and Lara placed her small hand into his big one. When they had arrived at the Dominus's private quarters, and were once again alone, Magnus asked her, "Must you contact Prince Kaliq on the dream plane? Can you not reach him another way?"

"I have never attempted to call him through other means, but I could try, my lord Dominus," Lara said. He was jealous, and she knew it. Yet it accomplished no purpose to allow him to become antagonistic toward Kaliq. "My mother taught me a thought spell to bring an individual into my presence. I have never used it for I enjoy the dream plane, but if it will content you I will use it now."

"I trust you!" he said quickly.

"I know." Lara smiled. "Now take me to an enclosed chamber so none may see what I am doing. Would you like to remain?"

"No," he said quickly. Then he led her to a small windowless room within his own apartments. "I will await you outside the door," he said.

"Good, for I may seek your counsel while I speak with Kaliq," Lara told him. Then she kissed his mouth softly and entered the little chamber, closing the door behind her. Looking about she saw there were two carved chairs, and a table inlaid in mother-of-pearl. A tapestry hung upon one wall. It was obvious this place was used for conversations of the utmost privacy. She turned toward a smooth blank wall, and silently thought the spell.

Kaliq of the Shadows heed my call. Come to me from out yon wall.

Lara waited, and then just as she was considering that perhaps the spell had not worked the Shadow Prince appeared. "Magnus is jealous of the dream plane," she explained before he could ask.

"Mortals," the Shadow Prince murmured wearily. "Now tell me what it is you need of me, my love."

"You know that I believe my destiny is to prevent another war between Hetar and the Outlands," she began. "It is now time to accomplish that."

"It is," Kaliq agreed. "I told you we cannot hold back Hetar for much longer. The effort has weakened us, Lara. We must soon let go if we are to regain our strength."

"Will Gaius Prospero invade before the winter?" Lara wondered.

"Nay, there is no indication of it, and we would know if there were," Kaliq said.

"All indications are that he plans his invasion as a spring event. And he will not come through the mountains this time. He will come through the Coastal Kingdom."

"What?" Lara was shocked. "Archeron would never permit it."

"Archeron is very ill, and Arcas now rules in his name. I believe Archeron is being poisoned slowly to make his death appear a natural sickening. It is said he has never recovered from his wife's death," the Shadow Prince explained.

"Arcas is ever the fool," Lara responded. "He imperils their secret by allowing Hetarians of other provinces into the coastal lands. And that will endanger us."

"He has ordered that come the spring none of their trading vessels may set sail. And he even plans to hide the ships up the coast from the palaces of the kings so Hetar's armies may not see them," Kaliq continued. "We have our spies listening and watching."

"So Hetar will invade through the Felan lands," Lara said slowly. "It is a good plan, Kaliq. The Felan clan families are gentle folk, and as mild as their sheep unless provoked. Such an attack would be totally unexpected. Hetar could easily sweep through the Outlands through the Felan first, and then attack the Tormod and Piaras from two sides. They would wipe them out, for Gaius Prospero will certainly hold a grudge against them for the last defeat he suffered at their hands. He could set an example to all who would consider defiance by annihilating those two clan families. The rest he will enslave, and many more will die rather than suffer such a fate."

"We have the strength to move the Outlands and their people here to Terah now," Kaliq said quietly. "If we do it quickly we can spend the winter regaining our energies so we may be of use in the future. Gaius Prospero has rebuilt a huge mercenary force by promising them much when spring comes. If he does not deliver they will kill him. He has wheedled and bribed many, Lara. Hetar is close to anarchy."

"I will have to return to the Outlands to speak with the leaders of the High Council, Kaliq. I must go and come by means of magic for there is no other way as we have not much time. It is almost autumn, and the Gathering will soon be held. That is a good place for me to meet with them."

"And the Dominus?"

"We must bring him with us, Kaliq. He desires to meet the clan family lords," Lara said.

"Will he keep his promise to you?"

"How do you know he made me a promise?" she asked with a small smile.

He chuckled. "Let us just say I have my ways of knowing such things," he teased her. "Besides, you are planning to wed him, are you not? You would not have agreed to his proposal had he not agreed to your conditions, my love."

"Then you will take him with us?" she said.

The Shadow Prince nodded. "Speak with him and set a time. Then recall me, and I will transport us to the Gathering. They will resist you, you know. You may not be able to save them all," Kaliq warned her.

"I know," Lara said. "But I will save as many as I can. It is all I can do."

"He awaits you impatiently outside the portal to this chamber. Call him to us," the prince said.

Lara leaned forward, and kissed the prince upon the cheek. "What would I do without you, Kaliq?" she asked him.

He laughed almost ruefully. "Soon the pupil will outstrip the master," he said.

"Never!" Lara replied softly. Then she arose, and opened the door to admit Magnus Hauk. "Come in, my lord Dominus. We have matters to discuss."

"How do you arrive in the middle of my castle?" the Dominus asked the prince, shaking his hand as he came forward to join them.

"Your future Domina cast a tiny spell," Kaliq answered. "I will always come when she calls me, Magnus Hauk."

The Dominus laughed. "You will not intimidate me for all your magic, Kaliq of the Shadows. While magic amazes me, it no longer frightens me."

The prince chuckled.

"If you two are finished playing boy games," Lara said, "we will speak on the Outlands, and their people." She fixed them both with a stern look. The two men grew silent, but the glance they shared was one of coconspirators. Lara ignored it and began.

"Magnus, you have spoken of your desire to know the people of the Outlands. Shortly they will come to-gether for a yearly meeting called the Gathering. This

is an ideal time for us to go to them, and offer them
a new homeland beyond the mountain range you call
Emerald. Kaliq and I agree we must transport them
before the winter sets in for Hetar means to invade
the Outlands come spring.

"Archeron, the oldest and most senior of the
Coastal Kings, is very ill. Kaliq believes he is being
poisoned by his son, Arcas, who has taken his place.
Arcas has promised Gaius Prospero access to the Outlands through the lands of the Felan which border the
Coastal province of Hetar. This is a terrible betrayal,
for the Coastal Kings have always lived in concord
with the Felan. And such an attack will constitute
a great surprise to the Outlands. The Hetar Mercenaries can sweep over the lands unimpeded. And as
they reach the Purple Mountains, Hetar will attack the
Tormod and the Piaras from two sides. Kaliq is more
than aware of how the mind of Gaius Prospero works.
This emperor of Hetar will slay all the Tormod and
the Piaras for he certainly holds them directly responsible for Hetar's loss to the Outlands in the Winter
War."

"You have been protecting the Outlands since
Lara's departure, haven't you?" the Dominus asked
the Shadow Prince.

"We have," Kaliq responded, "but even we grow
weary, and need our energies restored. Our advantage has been that no one is aware of our part in the
Outlands' seeming invincibility. If we can make this
transfer from the Outlands to Terah before winter sets
in then we will have that time to renew our strengths.

We will be more than ready to stand against Gaius Prospero when the time comes."

"And you can take Lara and me to this Gathering, and return us in safety to Terah?" the Dominus asked.

"I can," Kaliq answered.

"One thing," Lara said to the two men. "No one can know I have come but for the clan lords. Our visit must be a secret one. If Gaius Prospero could subvert Vartan's brother and his wife, who knows what he has promised, and to whom within the population of Outland peoples. The clan families are not very sophisticated, and have no real idea how guileful Hetarians can be. I will not be responsible for endangering Terah. It is my hope that Hetar will never know what exists on the other side of the Sea of Sagitta. I fear for us all if they learn. And worse, if they discovered the Obscura we would certainly not be safe," she concluded.

"You do not want to see your children?" Kaliq asked her, curious.

"I will see them once they are safe again," Lara replied. "I will reveal myself only to the clan lords, but first to Rendor of the Felan. He will tell me what has happened in the year I have been gone. We must seek his wisdom before we speak with the others."

"Aye," Kaliq said, "I agree that would be the best course."

"Rendor," Magnus said slowly. "He was the lord chosen to replace Vartan as head of the High Council?"

"Yes," Lara responded. "Roan of the Aghy desired the position, but we convinced him to marshal a military force for the Outlands. Rendor has a cool head, but Roan is as hot-tempered as his red hair indicates. If it had been necessary to treat with Hetar he could not have done it. Ordinarily he is a peaceful man, but not when his people or his horses are threatened," she explained with a small smile.

"Did he desire you?" Magnus asked.

"Of course," Lara answered. "But I never desired him, my lord Dominus."

"Do all men who see you desire you?" Magnus demanded.

Before she might answer Kaliq spoke up. "Men, mortal and otherwise, will always desire Lara," he said quietly. "But if she pledges herself to you, Magnus Hauk, she will be both loyal and true to you. So you need never ask her such a question again."

Lara put a hand on the Dominus's hand, and looked into his face. "I am yours," she told him. "Never doubt me."

"I am the Dominus of Terah, descended from a royal line. I am powerful, and I am obeyed. Yet having captured my heart, Lara, you rule me, and sometimes I am afraid," he admitted in a moment of great candor.

"I have said I am yours, Magnus, but I have not heard a similar declaration from you. Perhaps it is I who should be fearful," Lara told him.

Kaliq marveled at her. She was an amazing woman. But though she might believe rescuing the Outlands was her total destiny, it was not. There was much more to come, and she would one day be more powerful than she could ever imagine.

"I love you!" the Dominus said. "I am yours! Have I reassured your faerie heart, Lara? Can you believe we are meant to be together?"

"Yes," she said simply.

"Then let us decide when it is we will go to the Outlands," the Dominus replied.

"Let me meet with Rendor of the Felan first," Kaliq suggested. "I will tell him nothing more than that you wish to speak with him privately, and that he must say nothing of it to anyone else. I will explain I fear for spies, possibly even among his own."

Lara nodded. "Yes, that would be best," she agreed. "And I do not have to call you again? You will return tomorrow on your own?"

"I will appear in this very chamber tomorrow night at this same hour," Kaliq said, and as he spoke he began to fade away into the shadows until he was no longer there.

"Now that is a talent I should like to learn," Magnus Hauk said to Lara, and she laughed.

Chapter
12

KALIQ, PRINCE OF SHADOWS, met with Rendor of the Felan on the dream plane.

"Why do you disturb my rest?" the lord of the Outlands High Council asked him.

"Because here I know we two are safe from being overheard," Kaliq responded. "There is great danger ahead, Rendor, but the Outland peoples can be spared. Lara wishes to speak with you before the Gathering. If all goes well then she will appear to the clan lords only at the Gathering. Her presence must remain a secret."

"There have been rumors from the Coastal Kings that Lara is dead," Rendor replied, "but frankly I never believed it. I do not trust Archeron's son."

"You are wise not to trust him, for he lies, and he has betrayed his father," Kaliq replied. "Come the spring he will allow the mercenary army of Hetar to invade the Outlands through the Coastal province. Lara can save you if you will let her. What say you, Rendor of the Felan?"

"Of course I will speak with her!" Rendor exclaimed. "Lara is the true leader of the Outland clan families. Is she all right? And where is she?"

Kaliq chortled, amused, but then he said, "Lara crossed the Sea of Sagitta to its other side. There exists a land called Terah. It is ruled by the Dominus. Lara will soon be his wife. Her magic has increased greatly and she has the loyalty of the Terahns, for she has lifted a terrible curse from them. Have you a place within your house where we will not be seen by prying eyes? And a time when you will not be disturbed?"

Rendor considered. Then he said, "The safest place would be the cellar of my house. There is an interior room there where we store vegetables in the winter months. If we met in the middle of the night it is unlikely anyone would disturb us, my lord Prince. How soon can we meet?"

"Tomorrow night, Rendor, for time is of the essence in this matter," Kaliq responded. "Fix the time for the first hour after midnight. We will be awaiting you."

"Agreed," Rendor said, and then he awoke to see the dawn beginning to break outside of his windows. Beside him Rahil snored comfortably. Rendor of the Felan lay upon his back, and considered if his dream had been real, or if he had imagined it. *Well,* he thought to himself, *I shall know in the hour after midnight,* but instinct told him the dream had been a truth. Because of the power of the Shadow Princes they had all forgotten that the Outlands were in grave danger. Something was changing, something important.

He arose from his bed and went about his duties, and the day that followed seemed unusually long. He mediated a dispute between two of his shepherds that could have erupted into a serious matter. He inspected the sheep that they would take to the Gathering to sell, animals now too old for breeding but acceptable for eating, or for their wool. Rahil noticed his restlessness and inquired upon it, but he assured her that all was well. He was simply anxious to set out for the Gathering. She accepted his explanation with a smile and a nod, but he knew she did not believe him. Still, Rahil did know that when he wanted to speak he would speak, and so she let the matter rest.

When the evening meal was over and the board cleared away, Rendor remained by the fire as was his custom. Rahil sat across from him at her loom, weaving. Finally she arose, kissed him, and bid him goodnight. She knew her husband's custom was to remain in his hall alone before he made his final rounds to be certain all was secure. If he desired pleasures from her he awakened her when he came to their bed. Rendor dozed lightly, but then with the discipline that was his he woke himself at the proper time. Rising he made his way through the house, making certain all was locked and barred, snuffing the lights, banking the fire. And when he had completed his rounds he took a small lamp, and made his way down into his cellar, remembering to close the door behind him.

The cellar was cool, and the earth beneath his feet had a dampness that seemed to seep through the soles of his boots. As he approached the small enclosed chamber he saw a light flickering from beneath the door. Opening it he stepped into the room. Kaliq and Lara stood there, glowing in the darkness of the root cellar.

"Rendor!" Lara came forward, put her arms about him and kissed his cheeks.

"You are not dead!" Rendor said, his voice openly relieved.

She laughed. "No, old friend, I am not dead. Is that what is believed of me?"

"Rumors from the Coastal Kingdom," he said. "Faint, but perceptible."

"Arcas has no subtlety," Lara remarked. "Kaliq tells me Archeron is being slowly poisoned."

"I did not know that," Rendor answered her, turning to glare at Kaliq.

The Shadow Prince shrugged. "What could you do to help? You will soon learn you have troubles of your own."

"Could you not save him?" Rendor asked. "He is our friend."

"You really should," Lara agreed. "Archeron is the only one of the Coastal Kings who can hold the province together. Arcas is ambitious only for himself. He will reveal their secret even without meaning to, ruining the balance of trade, and then Terah will be endangered as well. Move him to your palace before it is too late, Kaliq."

"Very well," the prince agreed. "I will leave you here with Rendor while I complete the task. My powers can only do so much from a distance these days." And then he was gone.

Rendor turned back to Lara, and suddenly realized another man, a very large man, was now standing by her side. Before he might speak, Lara did.

"My lord Dominus, may I present to you Rendor, Lord of the Felan, and head of the Outlands High Council. Rendor, this is Magnus Hauk, the Dominus of Terah."

The two men sized one another up, and then Rendor said, "I apologize for my hospitality, Magnus Hauk, but this meeting, I was told, necessitated caution."

"I understand," the Dominus responded. He then held out his hand. "I greet you in friendship, Rendor of the Felan."

"I greet you in friendship, Magnus Hauk, Dominus of Terah," Rendor replied, firmly grasping the hand held out to his before releasing it. He turned again to Lara. "Kaliq said there was great danger. That Hetar will invade the Outlands in the spring, coming through the Coastal Kingdom."

"Yes," Lara responded, "and you cannot fight them, Rendor. They will destroy all resistance, and confiscate your lands and your chattel. The women and children who survive will be taken in slavery. The Outlands as we know it will soon cease to exist. The Shadow Princes are wearied with their hidden defense of it. They need time to renew their strength for the greater conflict to come. Terah can help you if you will let them."

"How?" Rendor asked her.

Lara slowly and carefully explained, concluding with, "And all you need do is swear your allegiance to the Dominus yearly."

"And we will be separated from the rest of Terah?" Rendor asked.

"Completely," Lara told him. "The Tormod and the Piaras will have to make their own arrangements with the Mountain gnomes in the Emerald range of mountains, but they are good folk, and the gnomes I am told are likewise. As for the plain beyond, it is uninhabited, and fertile beyond anything I have ever seen."

Rendor sighed. "To leave the Outlands," he said softly.

"To continue to live in freedom," Lara replied. "And everything you possess will come with you. We will transport you by means of magic. The princes will use their combined strengths for you. We will take one clan family at a time."

"What will your people think of this, Magnus Hauk?" Rendor asked.

"The Terahns live along seven fjords, which are arms of the sea," Magnus began. "They may visit back and forth among the villages of their own fjords, but they rarely sojourn to the neighboring fjords, or beyond their own fields. They have no idea what lies beyond the Emerald mountains now, nor is it likely they will know what is there in the future. Terahns are for the most part insular peoples, and have been content to remain so, Lord Rendor. Resettling the Outlands clan families beyond the mountains will have no effect upon their lives, or their livelihoods. And your peoples are much like mine, for you keep to yourselves as do we."

"There is another sea," Lara told Rendor.

"Another sea?" He was totally surprised.

"Kaliq calls it Obscura. Its waters lap the sands of his desert as well as the shores of Terah. The landscape is somewhat different, but it would still be familiar. And the shoreline as far as the eye could see in either direction would be yours. There would be no danger from Hetar for they do not realize the princes have this sea, which Kaliq tells me is even wider than Sagitta."

"I must see this place," Rendor said suddenly. "You want me to stand by your side, Lara, before the other clan lords, and tell them that they must give up all we have ever known. I trust you, yet..."

"You need the reassurance of having seen Terah for yourself," Lara said. "I understand, Rendor, and your enthusiasm will help me more than your dutiful acquiescence. How long until you must depart for the Gathering?"

"Eight days," Rendor said. "We must go in eight days."

Lara nodded. "You shall see Terah before then, Rendor, I promise you." Then she smiled at him. "When I first saw the green plain of Terah I thought of you and your flocks. And of Roan's horses, too. The Blathma and the Gitta will grow wonderful crops in that fertile land. And Accius and his Devyn will make new songs."

"Provided they will agree to come," Rendor remarked. "You know how difficult Floren of the

Blathma can be. He has cultivated his same fields for years, and loves every bit of his land. He will be difficult to persuade."

"I can only pray he will come," Lara replied. "But if he will not then he must be left behind to face the Mercenaries of Hetar. They will rape his women, and trample his flowers into the very earth he loves."

"None of the Outlands families can be left behind," Magnus Hauk said quietly. "If this Floren will not agree to come he must nonetheless be transported with his people for we can leave no one to tell where the others have gone. Or else he must be slain. I will only do this if my own people are not endangered by Hetar."

"Agreed!" Rendor said. "We cannot allow our new life to be destroyed before we have even begun it, nor can we imperil the Terahns who will shelter us, albeit unknowingly."

Suddenly Kaliq stepped from the shadows, and back into their view. "Archeron is now resting in my palace," he said. "And I have spoken with our representatives to the High Council in the City, telling them where he is so Arcas cannot give it out that his father has died."

"Thank you!" Rendor said.

"What have you decided while I was gone?" Kaliq wanted to know.

"Rendor would see Terah and its plain before we address the Outlands Council at the Gathering," Lara told the prince.

"Fair enough, but we must do it on the dream plane," the prince said. He turned to Rendor. "We must conserve our powers for the transport," he explained. "But within the dream plane Lara can show you all you seek to see. It is easier, and less intrusive. Can you comply?"

"You will feel the grass beneath your boots, and smell the sweetness of the air, I promise you," Lara said. "My magic can do that for you."

"When?" he asked her.

"I will come for you tomorrow night while you sleep, Rendor," Lara promised him. "And my lord Magnus will be with me." She smiled as she felt the Dominus squeeze her hand. She had known his jealousy would surface unless he was included.

"I will be ready," Rendor said.

"Then we must go," Lara told him.

"Will you take your children from the Fiacre?" he asked her.

Lara shook her head. "If Dillon is to follow in his father's footsteps one day he must remain with his clan family."

"And your daughter?"

"Anoush knows only Noss as her mother. When she is older she will know who I am, but not now," Lara replied. "They are well?"

"They are," Rendor said, watching with surprise as his visitors began to fade away, and the light that had surrounded them dimmed into darkness. He was left with the small lamp in his hand casting its feeble glow about the little storage chamber, almost as if he had imagined the whole scene. But he knew he hadn't. Turning about, Rendor exited the room, closing the door behind him, climbing the stairs back up to the hall. He did not join Rahil for some time, but sat before the banked fire considering all that he had learned and heard this night.

It would not be easy to convince the others that they must migrate from the lands they had always known, across a great sea and into a new place. It would be very difficult to convince them of the danger from Hetar. The magic of the Shadow Princes in protecting the Outlands had been discreet, invisible to the eye. He could already hear Floren of the Blathma questioning whether the Shadow Princes had really been involved in their safety, or if it had all been a ruse meant to put them in their debt. Rendor sighed. They would be leaving everything they ever knew.

And then he remembered what Lara had promised. It would all be transported to the Terahn plain. Only the lands about them would be unfamiliar. Everything else would be the same. But would it? And was the land as perfect as Lara was implying? And was it safe? She mentioned nothing of weather, or wild beasts. These were things that also had to be considered. Better that which they knew than that which they did not. Could not Hetar share the Outlands with the clan families?

Finally Rendor went to his bed, and slept heavily. The day that followed seemed to go even more slowly than the one before. But at last it was night, and he was once again alone in his hall. Completing his duties he sought out his bed, and being weary with his concern he fell quickly asleep.

"Rendor?"

It was Lara's voice. The Felan clan lord opened his eyes, and found himself on a foggy plain. "I am here," he answered her.

"Good!" Lara said appearing by his side. Then with a wave of her hand she cleared the mists surrounding them, and there spread before him was the most beautiful land he had ever seen.

"It is so green," he told her, and she laughed.

"Aye, it is," she agreed.

He bent down, and pulled several stalks of grass from the earth. The ground beneath was dark and loamy. Rendor chewed on the grass. It was sweet.

"Are you making this so?" he asked her.

"I am merely allowing you to know the truth I speak of this place," Lara said.

"Show me the sea," Rendor said.

Lara waved her hand again and they were standing on a high bluff overlooking a broad beach of smooth golden sand. Beyond it stretched a turquoise sea. The air surrounding them was warm and fresh, the wind gentle.

Rendor breathed deeply. "I can smell the sea," he said.

"Yes," she answered him. Nothing more.

"The mountains?" he queried her.

Lara pointed, and Rendor followed the direction of her finger. The Emerald range was even farther away than the Purple Mountains of the Outlands. The Terahn plain was obviously larger than their own. The clan families would have more land for their flocks and herds, for cultivation. He had to admit he was impressed.

"There is no magic in what I see?" he queried Lara.

"The only magic I have used is that which allows me to show you what Magnus and I have promised you," Lara answered him. "The Terahn plain, the Sea of Obscura, the Emerald Mountains are all exactly as I have shown it to you, Rendor."

"If you can do this, then make it happen," Rendor said. "I have no need to engage in a war with Hetar, nor have any of the clan families."

"Magnus and I will come to you on the second night of the Gathering. Call a confidential meeting of the clan lords. We will present our case then," Lara said.

"Your Dominus is right. They must all agree for no one can be left behind to even hint at where we have gone," Rendor said.

"None will be. I will convince even the most difficult skeptic," Lara promised him. "It is my destiny, Rendor, to save the clan families. I was born to do this, and I will! Failure is not in my nature. Besides my magic is great now, and the Shadow Princes have not protected the Outlands all these months to see your people destroyed now. Have you seen enough, my friend?"

"I have," he told her.

"Then sleep once more, Rendor of the Felan. I will see you soon," Lara said.

And he woke up to discover it was morning. He should have felt exhausted, but instead he felt invigorated, and full of excitement. He had sensed that something was changing, and now he knew what it was. The Terahn plain was beautiful, and the people of the Outlands were going to be happy there. Happy and safe from Hetar for the first time in their history. For the next few days he worked to prepare for the trek to the Gathering. His wife, Rahil, remarked on his newfound vigor as they enjoyed pleasures together one afternoon for the first time in many weeks.

"You are like a carefree lad again," she told him, a pleased smile upon her face. "I quite enjoy it, Rendor, my husband. It is as if the weight of the world has been lifted from your shoulders."

"It has!" Rendor told her.

"How has this happened?" she wanted to know.

"You shall soon know, wife," he said to her. "But now is not the time." His fingers tweaked the large nipple on her big breast. "Now is the time for more pleasures, Rahil!" And he was suckling upon her while his fingers entertained themselves within her hot wet sheath, and she moaned with undisguised delight. And when he finally mounted her Rahil could not contain her cries of satisfaction while those within hearing in the hall nodded and murmured that Rendor was still as lusty as his finest breeding ram, and that Rahil was a most fortunate woman.

Days later they left for the Gathering, traveling across the Outlands plain to the Gathering place. Rendor was pleased to see those clan families who lived farthest away, the Piaras and the Tormod, had already arrived. Petruso, lord of the Piaras clan, now shared his authority with his eldest son, Vanko, who spoke for his father. Petruso had had his tongue torn out in the last Hetarian invasion, rendering him speechless, but he was still a fierce fighter.

Imre, lord of the Tormod, greeted Rendor jovially. "We almost have our lands restored," he told the Lord of the Felan, "but of course Petruso complains it will never again be the same," he chuckled. "For a man who can no longer speak he has become incredibly vocal."

Rendor smiled. "Surely you didn't think the loss of his tongue would render Petruso silent? He was always a vocal man, but I do regret the loss of his singing voice. Who else is here?" He gazed around the encampment.

"Everyone but the Blathma," Imre said. "You know Floren is always late because some field or another needed his final touch before the first frost. He should be here by tomorrow. Why?"

"We will need to have a secret meeting of the clan lords," Rendor said. "And until it is concluded it must be kept from public knowledge."

Imre's bushy eyebrow quirked with his unspoken questions.

"Not here, and not yet," Rendor said. "And say nothing to the others. I will speak with each of them myself, but you cannot be seen speaking among each other, my friend."

"Is it good, or is it bad?" Imre wanted to know. "At least tell me that."

"It is both, but more good in the end, I believe," Rendor answered him.

Imre nodded. "You have piqued my curiosity," he replied.

Floren and his Blathma clan arrived late that day, surprising everyone. Therefore the general meeting of the Outlands Council was held that same evening, because once the meeting was over, the clan families could begin their celebrations of the year just past. The following morning Rendor went from clan lord to clan lord, calling them to a secret meeting late that night when the celebrations had reached a point where the lords would not be missed. "A small tent has been set up on the outskirts of the camp," he told them. "Speak to no one about this, not even your wives and sons. Our very lives may depend upon your silence. I will answer no questions now. And remain sober! This is important business we have to discuss. You cannot have heads muddled by wine."

So the clan lords were careful in their eating and drinking at the evening's celebration, but no one noticed, for on this first night feast discretion was usually thrown to the winds. The Gathering was the high point of their year. The fires continued to burn high as the revelry continued late into the night. One by one the clan lords disappeared from the festivities, but no one noticed. Finally, all were gathered in the little tent. Liam of the Fiacre. Petruso and Vanko of the Piaras. Imre of the Tormod. Roan of the Aghy. Floren of the Blathma. Torin of the Gitta. Accius of the Devyn. And Rendor of the Felan, their council lord.

"What is all the mystery?" Roan wanted to know. "Why could no one know of this meeting?"

"Because our very lives depend upon this secrecy," Rendor immediately answered. "Lara, come forth."

A surprised murmur arose from the men gathered at the sound of Lara's name, and then her sudden appearance among them. She was accompanied by Kaliq of the Shadow Princes, and a tall stranger with the look of authority about him. The Outlands lords each fell to one knee at the sight of her. Their homage was impressive.

"Greetings, my lords!" Lara said. "It is good to be among you once again. I thank you for your courtesy, but please rise and be seated. You all know Prince Kaliq, and my other companion is the Dominus of Terah, Magnus Hauk."

"What is Terah?" Roan of the Aghy wanted to know.

"You have heard of the Sea called Sagitta that borders both Rendor's lands, and the lands of the Coastal Kings? On the other side of this sea is a wondrous place known as Terah. Magnus Hauk is its ruler, and I will shortly be his wife."

"There were rumors that you were dead," Accius of the Devyn said.

"Did you make up a death song for me then, Accius?" Lara asked with a smile.

"We did not believe the rumor," the lord of the Devyn bards replied with an answering smile. "You are the daughter of Ilona, queen of the Forest Faeries. Death cannot claim you yet, Lara."

"Why have you returned to us?" Liam of the Fiacre queried. "Have you found your destiny then?"

"I have found a portion of my destiny, Liam of the Fiacre," she replied. "My destiny is to keep the Outlands clan families from destruction."

"Destruction? What destruction?" Floren of the

Blathma demanded to know. "We are at peace with Hetar. What threatens us?"

"Hetar threatens you, Floren. They mean to invade the Outlands come the spring. Their mercenary armies will come through the province of the Coastal Kings into Felan lands, and from there into all of the Outlands. And when they have conquered much of your lands another attack will be launched through the mountains of the Tormod and the Piaras, thus pinning the remaining Outlands in a two-pronged attack."

"We will fight Hetar and drive them back as we did before!" Roan of the Aghy declared, leaping to his feet.

"Aye!" his companions chorused.

"Nay," Lara told them. "You will not. For a year the Shadow Princes have kept the Outlands safe for you, but even their powers have limits. They can protect you no longer. Gaius Prospero, Hetar's emperor, has raised a mighty force to come against you. They will be led and commanded by Hetar's Crusader Knights. He has expended his own monies to train and house these men, and Gaius Prospero never does anything that does not yield him a goodly profit.

"Hetar suffers from overpopulation, and an inability to feed itself. The people have grown poorer with each passing day. They can barely subsist, and what little coin they can spare goes to feed and house them. There is little profit to be made any longer, and profit is the life blood of Hetar. In order to gain his position Gaius Prospero has promised the people much. He has promised them lands to live upon, and lands that will feed them. He has promised that he will return Hetar to prosperity. He has already used his power to encroach upon the Forest Lords, and along the edges of the desert sands belonging to the Shadow Princes. But it is not enough. He needs the Outlands, and he means to have them."

"And why should we not defend our homes, Lara?" Roan asked her.

"Because if you do you will die," Lara said bluntly. "You will die, and those who survive will be sold into slavery. Your flocks, your herds, everything, will be given to those Hetarians who follow the mercenary armies into the Outlands. Is this what you desire? The death of the Outlands clan families?"

"What other choice can you offer us?" Liam wanted to know.

"I can take you to Terah," Lara replied. She turned to the Dominus. "Tell them, my good lord."

"My lands are vast," Magnus Hauk began. "My people inhabit but a fraction of these lands, and all along the fingers of the sea we call fjords. Beyond the Emerald Mountains is a vast plain much like this one. It is fertile, and it is uninhabited. It is bordered by a second sea, larger than Sagitta. I offer you these lands, my lords, both mountain and plains. I ask only that once yearly, when I come to you, you give me your pledge of fealty."

"And Hetar knows nothing of Terah?" Torin of the Gitta asked.

"Only the Coastal Kings know of Terah," Lara responded, "for Terah supplies all the luxury goods Hetar desires. But I am the first Hetarian to go to

Terah. Terahn vessels meet with Hetarian vessels in the middle of Sagitta. It is there they exchange their goods.

"The kings do not want anyone else in Hetar to know of Terah lest they lose what they perceive as their advantage. Gaius Prospero assumes the goods he deals in are manufactured by the Coastal Kings. He has never been to this province. Terah is their secret, and they will keep it."

"You are asking us to give up our lands to go to a place none of us knows," Floren said. "I will not do it! My fields are like my children. I know them well. I spend the winter months in my hall developing new varieties of my plants. The Hetarians will find me too valuable to kill, and will leave me be if I do not fight them."

"Stubborn as ever," Torin of the Gitta said. His clan family were also farmers. "Do you not understand, Floren? What in the name of the lord of Limbo makes you think that the Hetarians will leave you in peace because you do not resist them? They want the Outlands for themselves. If they were content to live in peace with us they would not be planning an invasion. They do not want to rule us—they want to annihilate us!"

"How can you know that for certain?" Floren replied.

"Stay," Torin said. "Watch while your wife and daughters are forced to give pleasures to Hetar's Mercenaries before they are killed, but in your case I suspect you would be more distressed if they cooked and ate your new plants."

"The Terahn plain is twice the size of the Outlands," Magnus Hauk interjected. "You will all have twice as much land for yourselves. One thing, however."

"Aha!" Floren said. "I knew there would be something."

Lara laughed. "There is, but it has nothing to do with you. It would concern the Tormod and the Piaras. In the mountains there lives a small race of gnomes. You will have to make arrangements with them to share the lands there, but they are a peaceable folk, and if you treat each other fairly there should be no difficulties."

"I should be more content to have eyes other than yours who have seen this Terahn plain," Floren grumbled. "Understand it is not that I do not trust you, Lara, but you are asking us to uproot centuries of our existence on rumor."

"It is not rumor," Prince Kaliq said. "Do not forget two of our own are on Hetar's High Council in the City. We know what is happening, and what will happen, Floren of the Blathma. This is but the beginning, and if Hetar is to survive what is to come, my brothers and I must regain our combined strengths—strengths we have expended on your behalf, I might add. I have seen the Terahn plain. It is all Lara says it is."

"And I have seen it also," Rendor spoke up. "The land is vast and green, and but for the native birds and beasts, uninhabited. It is well watered, and there are stands of trees even as we have here. I saw several lakes, as well. The beach edging the other sea, which is called Obscura, is sandy and wide."

"Beasts? You said beasts?" Floren said nervously.

"There was nothing I saw any different from what we have here," Rendor told him impatiently. "Cease seeking reasons not to go, Floren. If you insist on forcing your people to remain, their deaths will be on you and no other."

"It is a vast undertaking," Accius of the Devyn said slowly. "How do you propose to make it happen, Lara? Will your brothers help us, Kaliq?"

"You will be transported by means of our magic," Lara told them. "And it must be soon, Accius."

"You would put us down in the middle of a wilderness without shelters or supplies?" Floren interrupted her.

"Floren, shut your mouth!" Rendor roared impatiently. "Do you think so little of Lara that you believe she would place us in harm's way? Let her finish. Open your mouth before she has, and I will kill you myself, you bloody old woman!"

Floren looked thunderstruck at Rendor's words. He opened his mouth, and then closed it again as quickly. About him his companions were snickering.

"All that you have will accompany you," Lara continued as if nothing had happened. "Your homes, your barns and outbuildings. All of your creatures, and chattels. Your granaries holding your harvests, and supply of next year's seeds. Even the workshop where you develop your new species of plants, Floren. The climate on the Terahn plain has a shorter winter and a longer growing season," Lara told them. "You will be able to plant and harvest your crops at least twice yearly."

"Twice?" Floren looked nervously to Rendor, but he had been unable to be silent.

"Twice," she assured him.

"How would you accomplish this transfer of our people and goods?" Accius asked her. "It is indeed a very large undertaking. What songs we shall write about this!"

"We will move one clan family grouping at a time. I had thought you might draw lots to decide the order in which you would go," Lara suggested. "But before you do I would have you speak among yourselves, and then when you are in agreement I would first have you swear fealty to the Dominus who has kindly offered you these lands."

"Do you marry him to save us?" Roan of the Aghy asked her boldly.

"I marry him because I love him," Lara replied promptly, "but there is always a bride price of some sort, Roan, and this was mine. Especially when I learned from Kaliq that Hetar was planning to invade the Outlands. I am glad the Dominus loves me enough to pay my price. Be loyal to him, and do not shame me."

The horse lord nodded his red head. As much as he had always lusted after Lara he had come to realize that she was not the woman for him. He looked at Magnus Hauk, and wondered what it was about this man that had caused her to choose him.

"I see no need to discuss this further," Accius of the Devyn said. "Do any of you?" He looked about the small enclosure. "Forgive me, Rendor, for I do not mean to usurp your authority, but I know I am free to speak my thoughts. We Devyn are your poets, and the bards of our people. It matters not to us where we reside, but perhaps the rest of you need to speak more on it."

"Nay," Roan said, and to Lara's surprise the others all nodded in agreement. Even Floren of the Blathma.

"Then," said Lara producing a green velvet drawstring bag before their eyes, "it is time for you to choose the order in which you will leave. Within the bag are numbered tiles. I offer Rendor the first pick." She opened the bag just wide enough for his hand to slip inside. Pulling out the tile he showed it to her. "Eight," Lara said. "The Felan will go last. Liam of the Fiacre, chose next!"

One by one the clan lords drew their tiles. The Fiacre pulled three. The Piaras four. The Tormod five. The Blathma two. The Aghy seven. The Gitta six. The tile marked one was drawn by the smallest of the clan families, the Devyn.

"Is everyone content with their drawing?" Lara queried them.

The clan lords murmured their assent.

"When will you transport us, and how long will it take?" Rendor asked for all of them. "And what do we tell our people?"

"You will tell your people nothing," Kaliq spoke up. "I have no doubt there are some among your people who may already have been subverted by the government of Hetar. Vartan's murder was an assassination arranged by Gaius Prospero himself. There are always those among the people who can be lured by the promise of a reward they might not otherwise ever possess.

"Enjoy this Gathering, my friends. Go back to your homes as you always do to prepare for the winter season. Two weeks after your return, the transport shall begin. And within eight days your clan families will be safe in Terah."

"What if Hetarians spy upon us during the winter months, and see the Outlands devoid of people and buildings?" Vanko asked, speaking for his sire.

"Those spying upon the Outlands after you have departed will see your homes, and all that they might see if you were actually here. That is simple magic to accomplish," Kaliq said with a smile. "Only when the invasion begins will they find neither mortal nor houses, beasts or other chattel. The Outlands will be empty. And by the time they have sorted out the confusion of the invasion that found nothing to invade, many questions will need answering. I expect Gaius Prospero will, however, be quick to find answers to those questions, be they true or not," he chuckled.

"And most important," Lara told them, "we will have prevented a war, needless destruction and the deaths of many innocents."

"Once again you have saved us," Roan of the Aghy said quietly.

Lara blushed at his praise. "I have done only what it was meant for me to do, my lord of the Aghy," she told him.

"And you are certain the land is suitably fertile?" Floren worried.

"The land is fertile," Magnus Hauk said, and he gazed directly into Floren's brown eyes.

The look was somehow reassuring to Floren. "Thank you, my lord Dominus," he said, and his features relaxed for the first time since they had all entered the tent.

"Now," Lara told them, "all that remains is for you to swear your fealty to Magnus Hauk, the Dominus of Terah."

One by one the clan lords stepped forward and knelt before the Terahn ruler. Lara directed them to take his hands in theirs, pressing them first to their foreheads, then to their hearts and finally placing a kiss on the Dominus's hand containing his ring of office. Each of the clan lords repeated the same words as he did so.

"I, pledge you my loyalty, and that of my clan family, Magnus, Dominus of Terah. We will come when you call upon us to protect and preserve Terah and in return you will protect us from all enemies."

Magnus Hauk replied, "I accept your loyalty, and pledge you mine. I shall preserve your safety, and you and your clan family will serve me when I call upon you for the good of all Terah."

When all had pledged Lara said, "Then it is done, my lords. I thank you for trusting me. Remember you must keep all of this from everyone, even your wives and lovers. It is for the safety of the Outlands and its people."

They nodded in agreement.

Lara looked to Liam of the Fiacre, and beckoned him to her. "The children," she began.

"They are well!" he quickly said.

"Of course they are," Lara replied with a smile. "I know they are safe with you, Liam. I just wanted you to know that with your permission I should like my younglings to remain in your care. Dillon and Anoush are Fiacre, and must remain so. When I give the Dominus an heir he will expect me to mother it exclusively. I do not want Vartan's children neglected by any, even their own mother."

"Will you come to see them once we are resettled?" he asked her.

"Of course!" Lara told him. "They are my own, and I love them for all I cannot be the mother they should have. My magic has grown strong in Terah. I can use it to visit. How is Noss?"

"With child again," he said with a proud grin. "She wants another boy. She says Anoush is all the daughter she needs." And then he flushed as he realized how his words must have hurt Lara.

She saw the look upon his face, and laid a comforting hand on his arm. "Nay, Liam, I understand, and it is true. Anoush was still a baby when I left the Fiacre. I am glad she has Noss, and I am equally glad that Noss has her."

"How did you get to Terah?" he asked her.

"Arcas betrayed me, but it was meant to be. He thought to send me as a slave to Magnus Hauk to earn his favor. I quickly disabused the Dominus of the idea that I was a slave, however," Lara told him with a small smile. Then she went on to tell Liam of the curse upon Terah and how she had resolved it.

"Your magic has indeed grown," he said. "Your

mother visits the children regularly, you know. She is quite doting, and often brings her son with her."

"I will have Ethne tell her what is happening," Lara said. "Ethne can reach out to her from Terah, but I am not certain that I can, although I have not tried."

"Will you return to Terah tonight?" Liam asked.

"Aye. We came only to tell you what was happening, and to offer the clan families a new home. Magnus cannot leave his lands for long periods of time. His people are most dependent upon him."

"What will they say when they find us upon the Terahn plain?" Liam was curious to learn.

"They know nothing of what resides upon the Emerald Mountain range, or beyond it on the Terahn plain. I am not certain they even know there is a plain. They accept just what they see, and little else. They harvest their silk, weave their fabrics, make their jewelry, and other luxury items, which are then sent via the Dominus's trading fleet to meet with the vessels of the Coastal Kings who bring salt, and lumber, pearls, hides and furs to the Terahns."

"I cannot help but wonder," Liam said, "why the Coastal Kings have never wanted to see Terah."

"The Terahns will not permit them to come in sight of their shores. They have threatened to cut off all trade with Hetar if they violate this stricture. The Coastal Kings could not exist without the luxury goods they import, therefore they honor the restrictions placed upon them."

Liam nodded. "They are cautious men, the Coastal Kings. I would be more curious," he said.

"It is time for me to depart," Lara told him. "I can

see Kaliq is weary, and it will be well past dawn by the time we return to Terah." She kissed his cheek. "Farewell, Liam. I will see you when you have been resettled in Terah."

"Will you not send your love to Noss?" he asked her.

"Liam! Noss must not know I have been here," she scolded him.

Liam flushed, embarrassed. "I'm sorry," he said. "I forgot."

"You cannot forget," she warned him.

"I won't again," he promised her.

Lara nodded, and then walked over to Rendor. "We must leave, Rendor."

"Did you manipulate the tiles in the bag?" he asked her. "I could have sworn the tile I had was pushed into my hand."

Lara smiled. "Is it not better that the two strongest clan families go last?" she said. "I did not consider it prudent that the head of the Outlands Council go early. I thought the Devyn should go first to record the migration from the ancestral home."

"And Floren next before he could think any more upon it, or cause difficulty," Rendor chuckled. "But what if he speaks to his wife without meaning to do so?"

"By the morning all of the clan lords but you will have forgotten this meeting, Rendor. Only when they awaken the morning after their transport will they recall all that has happened here tonight. I thought it better that way. We can trust nothing to chance where Hetar is concerned."

"You have thought of everything," Rendor said admiringly.

"I hope I have," Lara responded. "Go now, and take the others with you."

He kissed her upon her cheek, and nodded his agreement. Then he moved off, ushering the other clan lords from the meeting tent. When they had gone Lara made a quick gesture with her hand, and the tent vanished. Kaliq gestured next, and was gone. Magnus turned questioningly to Lara.

"We are going home," she said, gesturing a second time, and they were back in the Dominus's bedchamber in his castle.

"All this magic amazes me," Magnus said.

"Thank you for tonight," Lara told him.

"They are good folk, your Outlanders," he replied. "They will do well in Terah. Like us they prefer keeping to themselves, but eventually the two halves of Terah must meet. Not yet, but some day. While those native born continue to produce beautiful things, your Outlanders can feed this world of mine."

"Floren would be pleased to hear such sentiments," Lara said. "How he loves the land, and all that he can grow upon it." Then she grew thoughtful. "I must remember to transport the Gathering stones to a suitable spot on the Terahn plain. Next year's meeting should be quite a celebration."

"What were you speaking to that young Outlander about?" he queried her. "That was Liam, your husband's successor?"

"Yes. I wanted to reassure him I would not take my children from them," Lara told the Dominus.

"You do not want them with you?" He found that curious.

"They are Fiacre. Dillon may one day lead his clan family. He cannot do that if he is raised as a Terahn," Lara said. "And Liam's wife, my friend, Noss, loves my daughter like her own. She has two sons, and is with child again. Liam says she wants another lad— for she has said she has all the daughters she desires in Anoush."

Magnus put his arms about her, and Lara began to weep softly, unable to help herself. His big hand smoothed her golden head. "Give me a daughter," he said softly to her. "Give me a golden-haired faerie girl, Lara of my heart. She will not replace your Anoush, I know, but we will love her nonetheless."

"Do you know," Lara sniffed, "that Vartan was disappointed at first when Dillon was born? He wanted a daughter. I knew he needed a son and an heir first, but he wanted a daughter. So I gave him a daughter three years later. She will never remember him, Magnus, nor will she remember me."

"You will visit her once the Fiacre are safely here," he promised. "And you may bring her here as well."

"She thinks of Noss as her mother, and Noss loves her as if she had birthed her. I cannot come between them," Lara sobbed. "Aye, she will know as she grows older that I am she who gave her life, but it is Noss she will love, not me."

He could think of nothing to say that would comfort her, and so the Dominus just held the woman he loved until finally her weeping ceased.

Lara looked up at him. "I do love you," she told him.

"I have come to realize that," he replied. "You do understand that I love you."

Lara nodded. Her dark eyelashes were spiky with her tears.

"And we will prepare for our marriage?" he asked.

She nodded again.

"Soon?" He was smiling.

"Aye. As soon as possible, my lord Dominus," she told him.

"And then we will go to Hetar," he said.

"Do you still want to go?" She looked troubled.

"I want to go," he said. "Before they invade the Outlands. I want to hear what these people have to say, and learn how they think. We will go quietly, just you and I. We will walk about the City, and listen. One learns a great deal just listening."

"It is wise to know one's enemy," Lara agreed. "Hetarians are great talkers, my lord, and you will learn much, though I think you will be surprised by the differences between Terah and Hetar. Terahns are content to live comfortably, with purpose to their days, and in peace with their neighbors. Hetarians are concerned with how they appear to their neighbors, and are always eager for profit and more profit."

"Why?" he asked her.

Lara shrugged. "I don't know. It is simply their way."

"How shall we travel?" he asked.

"By means of my magic," she replied. "It is easier, and quicker. We will appear to be ordinary travelers sightseeing in the City. Well-to-do farmers from the Midlands," she said with a smile.

"They will understand my language?" he asked.

"You and I speak the same tongue, Magnus," Lara told him. "We all seem to speak it."

"We shall tell my people we are taking a wedding trip to my small castle in the foothills of the Emerald Mountains," the Dominus said. "But we shall really be visiting Hetar."

"You must see the desert of the Shadow Princes as well," Lara said. "And even the realm of the Forest Lords. My mother can keep us safe there."

"I cannot wait until you are my wife, my Domina," he said huskily, and his arms wrapped about her again. "It is not enough that we take pleasures together. I cannot be content until you are mine, and mine alone!"

Lara did not correct him. It would do no good. She would be his wife, his Domina, but she would never be any man's possession. Even Magnus Hauk's. She raised her face to his for a kiss.

Chapter
13

"I MUST OVERSEE the transport of the Outlands clan families to their new home," Lara told Magnus on the day that the Devyn were to be brought from the Outlands.

Messengers had already been sent to the seven inhabited fjords of Terah, announcing the wedding day of the Dominus and the beautiful faerie woman who had lifted the curse of Usi from the Terahn men.

"Our wedding is near," he protested.

"I will be back in time," she promised him. "It is only a few days. The seamstress has already fitted and fashioned my wedding gown. I never had a real wedding with Vartan, you know—I am going to enjoy this, though I thought at first that I might not. And Sirvat is taking care of the celebration feasts. I will be here by the time your mother and sisters arrive, I swear. We cannot have the lady Persis asking questions you cannot answer," she teased him mischievously. Her mood had lightened visibly since their visit to the Gathering. He could sense the weight that had been lifted from her.

"Go then," he said. "But what if I need you?"

"Call my name," Lara told him. "We are bound together by love, and should you need me, Magnus, I will hear you." Then she kissed him, and was gone in a mist of mauve smoke.

It seemed to Lara her faerie blood was growing stronger. She reappeared in the middle of a Devyn village just as dawn was breaking. Seeing Kaliq, she hurried toward him. "Was it difficult?" she asked.

"Nay, not as difficult as it will be transporting most of the others," he told her. "Knowing Gaius Prospero's plans for invasion in the spring, my brothers and I lifted our protection from the Outlands several weeks ago so we might gain enough strength to accomplish this feat of magic."

"Shall we awaken Accius?" Lara asked.

He nodded, and together they entered the house of the Devyn's clan lord, calling to him as they reached his hall. They found him in a chair by his fire, shaking himself awake. It was obvious he had been there all night.

"Is it done?" Accius asked them.

"It is done," Kaliq replied.

"Our three villages?"

"All of them," Kaliq assured him.

Accius stood up. "I want to go outside," he said, and together the trio exited the house as the sun peeped over the horizon. Accius looked around, amazed. "It is beautiful!" he exclaimed excitedly. "You are right, Lara! I have never seen such green."

"I hope you can be happy here," she answered him.

"Only a fool would be unhappy here," he said. "I must go to the square and ring the meeting bell. I will need to tell my villagers what has happened. Then will you take me to my other villages?"

"I will," Lara said. "Kaliq must now rest, for tonight he and his brothers have the great task of transporting Floren's Blathma." She blew a kiss to the Shadow Prince as he disappeared, and then escorted Accius to the village square when the lord of the Devyn rang the meeting bell to bring forth the inhabitants of his village.

When the sleepy men, women and children had stumbled forth from their homes and surrounded their leader, he began. "Listen, my good clan folk. A great miracle has taken place in the night!" Then he went on to explain the secret meeting that had been held at the Gathering. He told them of Hetar's nefarious plans for the Outlands; of how Lara had found a wonderful land called Terah, and made it possible for them to find safety there. He related how the Shadow Princes had agreed to transport each clan family, and all that was theirs to Terah. "Last night," Accius said, "you went to sleep in our beloved Outlands. You have awakened in Terah, my good clan folk! Look about you now!"

The Devyn were thunderstruck. It was a great deal to absorb. Slowly they began to look about them. Their village was familiar to them, and yet the ground upon which their cottages sat seemed different. They looked beyond their dwellings. The land was greener than any they had ever known. Excitedly they began to speak among themselves. Finally one woman spoke up.

"This is Terah, and not the Outlands?" she asked.

"Yes," Lara answered her.

"And we are safe from Hetar?"

"Yes," Lara replied. "You are far, far from Hetar, across the Sea of Sagitta. Do you see the mountains beyond you? On the other side of those mountains are the seven fjords of Terah, where the Terahn folk dwell. Their ruler, the Dominus Magnus Hauk, has agreed to shelter the clan families of the Outlands in exchange for their fealty. The clan lords have already sworn that oath. This land is uninhabited, and so you displace none. The Terahns are insular folk. It is unlikely you will ever see them, nor they you, for they know nothing of what is beyond their side of the mountains."

"Where are the other clan families?" a man wanted to know.

"One clan family will be transported from the Outlands each night until all are safely resettled. Lots were drawn, and the Devyn were first. By this time tomorrow the Blathma will be in their new home. You were chosen to be first because you are the bards and poets of the Outlands. You will observe each clan family as it is made aware of this great change in their lives, and you will create and sing this history of your people so future generations will be aware of all that has happened in this time," Lara told him.

"Once again," Accius said, "the faerie woman,

Lara, has saved us from Hetar. We must be certain her part is well documented in our songs."

A murmur of agreement arose from the villagers.

"But now," Lara told them, "Accius and I must travel to the other two Devyn villages to tell them of what has transpired this night." She reached out and took the clan lord's hand in hers.

Accius gasped to find himself in the second of his villages.

Lara laughed. "I have grown stronger since you first knew me," she admitted. "Ring the bell now so we may speak with these folk."

Once again villagers sleepily stumbled forth from their cottages, and both Accius and Lara explained what had transpired. Again there was amazement, and relief. They moved on to the third village where the scenario was repeated for the final time. All the Devyn had been brought safely to Terah. Lara remained with Accius and his family until early the next day, when Kaliq came for her.

The Shadow Prince looked exhausted with the efforts it had taken to transport the Blathma. Given the task involved in moving Floren's people, goods and chattels, he was weary with the effort. When morning dawned on the newly transported Fiacre village Liam came from his hall in the company of a small boy. Lara cried out softly and, running toward the child, knelt to gather him in her arms. "Dillon, my son!" she said, hugging the little boy, kissing his cheeks. She set him back to look at him. "You have grown in the year we have been parted." She brushed back a lock of his hair from his forehead.

"Have you come to stay, Mother?" he asked her.

Lara sighed. "Nay," she said. "I cannot remain, but Dillon, something wonderful and magical has happened in the night." She stood up. "Liam, call the villagers of Camdene from their homes so I may tell them all. I will shortly move on to speak with the others." And when the lord of the Fiacre had assembled the people of his main village Lara told them of Hetar's plot and how she and the Shadow Princes were working to protect the people of the Outlands. Like the Devyn and the Blathma before, the Fiacre were amazed.

As she spoke Lara saw Noss standing holding the hand of a small girl. She did not need to be told it was her own daughter, Anoush. When she had finished speaking Noss came forward to greet her, but Lara could see her manner was more wary than friendly. "What is the matter, Noss?" she asked the young woman.

"Will you take the children?" Noss wanted to know, and Lara understood her concern was not so much for Dillon as it was for Anoush.

"Vartan and I gave them life," Lara replied quietly, "but they are Fiacre, and should remain with the Fiacre. Dillon will always know me, but Anoush knows only you as her mother. As she grows old enough to understand, she will comprehend that I gave birth to her, but you will still be her mother as I cannot."

Noss began to cry softly. "I am so sorry," she sobbed. "I know it is selfish of me, Lara, but I love Anoush so very much. And though I seem only able to produce sons, I have always wanted a daughter. I carry another son to be born in midspring."

"And I have given you a daughter," Lara replied. "Do not feel guilty, dearest Noss. I am so grateful that you want Anoush, and love her as you do. Vartan's children are a symbol to the Fiacre. I should never take them away from their clan family. Soon I am to marry the ruler of Terah, and I will give him children. I shall not leave them, Noss, but neither will I forget my firstborn son and daughter. I will be able to visit them in safety here, which I could not do in Hetar." She knelt, and smiled at Anoush who stood half hiding in the folds of Noss's skirts. "Hello, Anoush. I am Lara."

Anoush stared at her with large eyes, but said nothing.

"She does speak," Noss quickly said, "but I think she is shy of you."

"Yes," Lara agreed, but her heart was sore with the realization of it. "She would be, for she does not know me."

Suddenly Anoush reached out, and touched Lara's crystal star with her dainty finger. "Pretty," she said.

Lara smiled. "Yes, it is," she replied. "Perhaps one day you will have one, too, Anoush. We shall see." Then she stood up. "I must go now, for Liam and I need to visit the other villages and tell them what has transpired while they slept."

"Do you love him?" Noss asked softly.

"The Dominus? Yes, I do love him. You will meet him one day," Lara promised. "Goodbye, Anoush." Then she turned about to find her son. Together mother and son spoke in low tones for several moments, and then Lara bent to hug Dillon and kiss his cheeks once more before departing.

The Shadow Princes had divided themselves into two groups so they might keep on schedule. The Piaras and the Tormod would be easy to bring, for their mines would be left behind, and that was their greatest wealth. But the last two clan families would require great effort to transport, for their wealth was in their herds of horses and their flocks of sheep. Nonetheless when the ninth morning dawned over the Terahn plain all the Outlands tribes were in place in their new homes, and the Devyn had recorded the story of their miraculous journey.

On the tenth day the Shadow Princes and Lara brought the clan lords together at the Gathering place, whose stones had been set at its new site. Each clan lord expressed satisfaction with his new home. Floren could hardly stop rhapsodizing over the fertility of the new land to which he had already put a plow, there being no frost in the ground yet. Torin of the Gitta concurred with Floren's analysis of the land. Imre and Vanko had already made contact with the mountain gnomes, asking their permission to open new mines and work them. Negotiations were underway, and success was imminent. Liam, Roan and Rendor agreed that the grazing lands were lush beyond any in the Outlands.

"Then you are content?" Lara asked them.

"We are," Rendor spoke for them all.

"Then," Kaliq told them, "we are content knowing you are safe." He looked to Lara. "I will return to our desert. My brothers and I need to rest. Who knows when you will need our help again, and we are greatly weakened by this task we have just completed, and the months we have spent keeping the Outlands safe."

"Will you be all right?" Lara asked him anxiously.

"Yes," he assured her. "By the time Gaius Prospero and his Mercenaries are ready to invade the Outlands our strength will be restored."

"Magnus wants to go to the City and observe the Hetarians," Lara told Kaliq.

The Shadow Prince nodded. "I understand his reasoning. Keep safe, my love."

"We will," she promised him.

"Will you be his wife when you go?"

"The wedding is scheduled in just a few days' time. I must go home today, Kaliq," she told him. "There is a final fitting on my gown, and Sirvat will want to confer with me on the wedding feast, although it is actually better left to her judgment. And I must arrive before Magnus's mother, for she has sharp eyes and ears and will ask a hundred questions, some of which may have no answers," Lara said with a chuckle.

"It is time we both went," he told her. "My lords, I bid you farewell and good fortune in your new homes."

"How can we thank you and your brothers, my lord Prince?" Rendor said. "Will we ever see you again?"

"No thanks is necessary, Lord Rendor," Kaliq replied graciously. "And as to whether you will see us again, only the future can know the answer to your question. Lara, my love, goodbye!" He kissed her lips softly, regretfully, and then he was gone, disappearing into the shadows of the afternoon.

"And I must go, too, for my wedding day is near," Lara told them. "But first you must all be returned to your homes. Take your horses, and ride back the same way from which you came. You will each reach your villages within the hour. In future, however, you will find this Gathering place several days' journey away as it has always been." She turned to go.

"Wait!" Rendor called to her.

"What is it?" Lara asked him, surprised.

The clan lords gathered themselves about her, and Rendor spoke quietly. "We have all pledged our loyalty to Magnus Hauk, Lara. Now we would pledge that same fealty to you, for you are the true leader of the Outlands clan families."

Then each man knelt before her in turn, taking her small soft hands into their big rough ones; pressing them to their foreheads, their hearts and finally kissing the backs of those dainty hands as each spoke in his turn their oath of loyalty. Lara's green eyes filled with tears that spilled silently down her pale cheeks. And when they had concluded the rite they saluted her, raising a single arm in tribute to her as they cried with one voice a single word: "Domina!"

She bit her lip, and swallowed back the emotion that threatened to weaken her entirely. "Thank you, my lords," she somehow found the voice to say.

They smiled at her, and then the clan lords mounted their horses, traveling off in different directions, disappearing from her view almost instantly. Lara drew a long breath in, and then whispering a single word, "Home!" she was herself gone from the Gathering place, and quickly found herself back in the castle in her own apartments.

Sirvat was awaiting her anxiously. "Thank the Great Creator you are here!" she cried. "My mother's ship has just been sighted coming around the point into the fjord. Magnus is beside himself with worry. You were gone longer than he anticipated."

"Go and tell him I am home," Lara instructed Sirvat. "I will bathe and dress quickly so I can be ready to greet the lady Persis." She began to pull off her garments, handing them to the serving women who hurried to help her. She washed herself quickly in the small private bath that was now hers. Her hair was filthy. She soaped and rinsed it twice before wrapping it in a towel. The serving women dried her, and handed her a soft light wool gown. It had long fitted sleeves, a simple rounded neckline and a straight skirt. It was a dark burgundy-red in color, Lara sat while two women vigorously rubbed her damp hair dry with silk cloths. One of them plaited it into a single braid, tying the end with a silk ribbon to match her gown. Lara slipped her feet into a pair of delicate leather slippers as a servant clasped a dainty gold chain about Lara's waist.

Sirvat rushed into the room. "Praise the Great Creator! You are ready. She is just disembarking now from her vessel." Grabbing Lara's hand she hurried her from the room, from her apartments, and through the castle. They quickly reached the quay platform entry where Magnus Hauk was already waiting to greet his mother, along with his brother-in-law. "Here she is!" Sirvat gasped.

Lara smiled at him, and pulling her into his arms he gave her a long satisfying kiss. "I have missed you," he murmured in her ear.

"I have missed you, but I did not realize how much until this moment," she told him with another smile.

"Mother's coming!" they heard Sirvat whisper nervously.

The platform creaked and squeaked as the giant in charge drew it upwards. They saw the top of Lady Persis's head first, and then the whole of her appeared as she reached her destination. The Dominus came forward to open the gate. He bowed.

"Welcome, my lady mother," he said formally, helping her from the platform.

"I hope you have something hot for me to drink," Lady Persis replied. "I am frozen from being out on the water these many hours. Lara, beautiful as always. Sirvat, Corrado, you do not look bored with each other yet." She acknowledged them all, taking her son's arm and encouraging him to lead her to his Great Hall.

"You should have a fur-lined cape," Lara told the older woman. "Marten, I think. The warm brown of that fur would flatter your lovely complexion." She walked on the other side of Lady Persis. "It is rarely warm upon the sea, as I remember."

"Yes," Lady Persis agreed. "I should have a fur-lined cape. Why have you not given me one, Magnus?"

"Because I was not aware of your need, madam," he answered her. "But your good son-in-law should be."

"Tostig? He sees nothing but Narda's needs," Lady Persis snapped.

"You shall not leave here without a fur-lined cape," Lara promised the woman.

"Well," Lady Persis declared, "having a daughter-in-law may not be quite as bad as I thought it might be." She cast a toothy smile at Lara, who smiled in return.

They had reached the Great Hall, and Magnus was solicitously seating his mother near the fire and signaling a servant for a large goblet of wine.

"In the name of the Great Creator do not encourage her," Sirvat whispered to her friend. "She will want to move back to the castle and our lives will never be the same again! I remember her from my childhood. She is the most demanding of women."

"I do not want her here," Lara agreed, "but the truth is she was not dressed warmly enough. And where are Narda and her husband? Did they not come with her?"

"Obviously not. She has had a falling out with them. I sense it," Sirvat fretted.

Lara moved next to Lady Persis. "Are you comfortable, and a bit warmer now?" she enquired sweetly. "Where is your daughter? Did she not travel with you?"

"Narda? Nay. She and Tostig did not want to come until tomorrow," Lady Persis said irritably. "This is her brother's wedding, and she behaves as if it is just an ordinary event. I will tell you that she thought

Magnus was never to wed. I believe she even saw
her own eldest son in his place one day," Lady Persis
confided.

"Indeed?" Lara murmured. "I fear then she will be
doomed to disappointment."

"Are you already with child?" Lady Persis asked
eagerly.

Lara shook her head. "Not yet, madam, but I promise I will give my husband children in due time, and
there will be a son. Those of us with faerie blood have
the right to instruct nature in these matters."

"So you could have as many sons as Magnus
wanted?" Lady Persis asked.

"We will have as many as he and I think reasonable," Lara told her. "And now I must see to the meal.
Sirvat, come and keep your mother company." She
grinned mischievously at her friend as she passed.
Sirvat stuck out her tongue at Lara but she returned
the grin.

Over the next few days the castle was filled in
every nook and cranny with family and guests arriving for the wedding. Narda and Aselma arrived with
their husbands and children. They were irritated to
find their accommodation was smaller than the one
they had enjoyed previously. Lara smiled sweetly, and
shrugged her shoulders. They had so many guests, she
told them. After all, it was the wedding of the Dominus. That Lady Persis looked pleased at her daughters' annoyance did not help the situation.

The headmen and their families from each of the
seven named fjords arrived, bringing tribute and
gifts to the Dominus and his bride. There were bolts

of colorful fabrics, silks, satins, brocades and delicate wools. There were bowls, cups, plates and platters of gold and silver, some chased and embossed or studded with gemstones. There was jewelry for Lara: chains, rings, bracelets, earrings and necklaces. There was cattle and horses. The folk in the Light Fjord raised beautiful songbirds, and they brought their finest singers in gilded and exquisitely decorated cages. There were several braces of hunting dogs. The Dominus's three last Pleasure Women arrived with their husbands, and bearing gifts. Uma and Dodek brought a red lacquered box filled with the finest pearls: pink, black, gold and white in color. Felda and Norval brought a pair of rare Enok puppies, tiny little dogs with round faces, perky ears and long silky fur. Alcippe and her husband, Jencir, came with a beautifully illustrated and updated history of Terah that even included Lara's part in lifting Usi's curse.

Kemina, High Priestess of the Daughters of the Great Creator, came with half a dozen of her priestesses. Arik arrived with an equal number of priests from the Great Temple. Lady Persis was pleased to see her younger brother again. She greeted him effusively, leading Arik to wonder what his elder sister wanted of him.

The last of the guests to come were from the Faerie Kingdom. They arrived with the dawn, transported in from the sea in a cloud of silvery mauve mist, which set itself down upon the great terrace. Ilona, queen of the Forest Faeries stepped forth from the cloud. She was followed by her consort, Thanos, and their son, Prince Cirilo. The queen was garbed in an ethereal gown of various shades of green, and an elegant brown fur cape. Her long golden hair flowed over her shoulders, a crown fashioned of green gold rested upon her head. Despite their rather dramatic entrance Lara's faerie relations quietly took their places among the other guests.

The icy season, as the Terahns called it, had arrived, but while cold the weather was fair and without snow. The wedding guests crowded out onto the large terrace overlooking the fjord, and watched the sunrise with Magnus and Lara, who wore white fur capes and nothing else. They escorted the couple into the baths to observe their physical perfection as they were disrobed, bathed and redressed. Then the bride, her groom and their guests moved on to the great hall, now decorated with winter branches and berries.

Everyone commented favorably on Lara's gown. Of soft delicate white wool lined in silk, it was sewn all over with tiny sparkling gems that twinkled with each movement, each breath she took. Its sleeves were long and tight. The neckline fell in a graceful drape on her collarbone. The floor-length skirt hung straight and just to her ankles. About her neck Lara wore the gold chain and crystal star that her mother had given her so long ago. Ethne's flame burned softly, but steadily. Upon her feet Lara wore bejeweled white leather slippers. Her long thick hair had been styled in many braids woven with thin bejeweled chains, and each plait was fastened with a round gold or silver clip that enclosed the tasseled hair. Atop her head was a gilded wreath of leaves. All present admitted they had never seen a more beautiful bride.

The Dominus wore a simple long white woolen tunic that fell to his ankles. Each of the full sleeves was decorated with a wide bejeweled cuff of gold embroidery matching a similar design on his round neckline. About his waist was a chain made up of oval gold links and in the center of each was a sparkling blue gemstone. On his feet he wore boots of white-and-gold leather. His dark gold head was crowned with a wreath of gilded leaves matching his bride's.

Taking Lara's hand in his, Magnus led her to Arik who stood with his back to a great stone fireplace flanked on either side by carved Sea Dragons, a blaze burning brightly within. The Great Hall fell silent.

"Do you, Lara, daughter of Swiftsword of Hetar, and Ilona, queen of the Forest Faeries, and you, Magnus Hauk, Dominus of Terah, son of Dominus Ejnar, deceased, and his living widow, Persis, pledge yourselves to each other as husband and wife?" asked Arik, the High Priest.

"Yes!" Lara said.

"Yes!" Magnus agreed.

"Then let it be so in the eyes of the Great Creator of us all," Arik intoned. "You are now wed, Lara and Magnus. The Great Creator bless your union, and give you many children, and much happiness in the years to come. It is done. Greet your guests."

The bride and groom turned to face those gathered. A great cheer went up.

"Hail, Dominus Magnus! Hail, Domina Lara!" the assembly cried with one loud voice. And then they clapped their approval of the Dominus's choice in a wife.

Magnus invited their guests to partake in the feast to celebrate his marriage to Lara. Everyone found their places at the tables set up in the Great Hall, and servants quickly began bringing in the food. There were large platters of roasted meats, game and poultry. There were smaller platters with whole broiled fish on beds of seaweed. There were shellfish cooked in wine, or served raw. Bowls piled high with salad greens, wooden boards laden with breads just out of the ovens, wheels of hard cheese and rounds of soft cheese were brought forth. Baskets of winter fruits were passed about.

The wines flowed generously. The feasting went on all day, and at sunset the guests joined the bride and groom to watch the day end. But unlike Sirvat and Corrado on their wedding day, the Dominus and his Domina of Terah could not yet seek the privacy of their apartments.

Entertainers arrived. Bards sang of Terah's past and of the beautiful faerie woman who freed them from Usi's curse. There were tumblers and jugglers, little dogs that danced, and a troupe of felines who walked a tightrope and rode a large patient dog. Clowns moved among the guests, pulling coins from ears and bunches of flowers from their closed fists. The celebration went on deep into the night. And just when everyone was growing tired, a group of dancers clad in scanty silks came to dance seductively before the guests as their musicians played upon drums and reedy instruments that whined sensuously. When the dancers finally departed with the other entertainers, Magnus Hauk stood with Lara by his side. Together they thanked their guests for coming and wished them a safe journey home on the morrow. Then at last they left the Great Hall for their own apartments, where the servants relieved them of their wedding finery, dressed them in loose silk robes and finally left them to themselves.

"Was your wedding day satisfactory, my faerie wife?" Magnus asked her as he drew her into his arms. He kissed the top of her head.

"It was beautiful," she told him. "And so many gifts, my lord! Surely we needed none of it. Our guests were most generous." Why did the arms about her feel so wonderful this night? How often had he held her, and yet tonight it seemed different.

"You are beautiful," he said low. "I am surely the most envied man in Terah." He undid the tie holding the halves of her robe together. His hands slipped beneath the silken fabric and up her back even as she untied his robe. He pulled her against him, and they sighed simultaneously as warm flesh met warm flesh. He kissed her a slow and lingering kiss that seemed to have no end. His desire for her began to make itself known, but he swallowed back his lust. They knew each other well, but he wanted her to remember this night above all the nights they had already spent together, and would spend together in whatever future was to be theirs.

Lara drew her head away from his, and looking up into his face said, "I love you, Magnus, and those are words faerie women only utter if they are true." She took his face between her two small hands. Her green eyes met his turquoise ones. "You have the right to my heart, my lord husband. You are the other half of my soul."

He pushed the robe from her shoulders, and shrugged his own garment away as he picked her up, and brought her to their bed. "Without you," he told her, "I would have neither heart, nor soul." He laid her down gently.

Lara was momentarily stunned by his incredible declaration. Tears welled up in her eyes, and she held out her arms to him.

Magnus smiled down at her seeing the emotion his words had brought her to, brushing a single tear from her cheek with a finger. Sitting down next to her he said, "We already know each other, my love, and there is no rush to consummate our now formalized union. Let me offer you pleasure of a different kind."

She nodded, wondering what it was he would do. Lara watched as he reached down, and drew up a small basket of gold wire filled with alabaster bottles and jars. He rolled her onto her stomach, and turning her head she saw him debating with himself before drawing the stopper from one of the bottles. "What is it?" she asked him.

"A special lotion," he told her, and held the bottle beneath her nose so she might smell it. Then he pulled her long golden hair to one side.

"Peaches," she said, surprised.

"Peaches are my favorite fruit," he replied, pouring some of the lotion into his palm. Then using her bottom as his cushion he sat and began to smooth the liquid up her back with long firm strokes. "Close your eyes," he said. "Let the sensations take over."

Lara closed her eyes and almost immediately was intensely aware of his hands on her body. The large palms smoothed over her back; the subtle long fingers scampered along the delicate bones of her spine, up and down, back and forth. She was enveloped in the scent of peach blossoms as he massaged her round buttocks, the edge of one hand slipping between the twin moons to rub sensuously between them. As he moved on to knead each of her legs Lara began to realized her entire body was reacting with increasing heat to her husband's exciting touch. She struggled with herself to restrain her squirming.

He moved back up her body again, and she felt his teeth nip sharply at the nape of her neck. The quick pain was followed by a kiss upon the same spot. "Now, my faerie love," he whispered to her, "you will turn over for me." His tongue pushed into her ear, licking it, nipping at the lobe. He helped her into the position that suited him. She lay upon her back, eyes watching him as he chose another bottle, and poured a thin stream of golden liquid between her breasts. She could smell both peaches and honey from this bottle. He lapped at the fragrant stream with his tongue until it was all gone. Then he drizzled a tiny bit upon one of her nipples, and sucked upon it.

The liquid stung her just slightly. She could actually feel it sinking into her flesh as he suckled hard upon her to draw it out. And then an exquisite intensity began to envelop her being. He poured a tiny dollop of the golden liquid upon her other nipple, drew upon the sensitive flesh, and Lara could not stop the moan of delight that issued forth. Her breasts were both tingling with sensation, and felt so swollen she thought they might burst open. "Magnus," she breathed hotly as he sprinkled drops from the alabaster bottle over her torso, and began to lick at the flesh with his burning tongue.

Some of the honeyed mixture ran between the slit dividing her nether lips, which were already pouting slightly open with her rising desire. She gasped as it touched her lover's nub, and began to squirm frantically. His mouth was quickly on her, licking soothingly, sucking upon the nub fiercely until she was begging him to complete what he has begun. "Magnus! Please!"

In answer he bathed his lover's lance with the same liquid, putting it to her lips. "Taste it," he told her, "and then we will couple, but I need your mouth upon me as mine has been upon you!"

Lara did not hesitate, but took him between her lips, and suckled upon him. The coating covering his flesh was the most delicious flavor she had ever tasted. She could not stop licking at him, drawing upon his flesh. But then he gently pinched her nostrils together with firm fingers, and when she gasped for air he drew himself from her mouth.

"More!" she begged him. "More!"

In answer he moved himself down her fevered body, and pressed the length of his lover's lance into her body as far as he could reach. Her slender legs wrapped themselves about him in an effort to bring him deeper. Her sharp little nails began to rake frantically down his back as her passion built from a flame into a conflagration of desire. She screamed as he drew himself almost completely out of her, then thrust hard over and over and over again until their combined lusts exploded, leaving them both drained and barely conscious. When they came to themselves again, the dawn of a new day was beginning to tease at the edges of the horizon.

What had happened? Lara attempted to remember the desire that had brought them to such a weakened state. She sensed he was also awake, and wondered what he was thinking. "Magnus?" Her voice was a whisper.

"Then I did not kill you," he half groaned. "Praise the Great Creator!"

Lara laughed weakly. "Nay, you did not kill me. Did you mean to, my lord?"

"The lotions and liquids," he said weakly. "I have never used them before. Corrado bought them from one of the Hetarian traders. They call them Pleasure Enhancers, he said. He thought we might enjoy them."

"Pleasure Enhancers are used in the Pleasure Houses by the Pleasure Women. Their purpose is to encourage a lover whose interest cannot be gained by ordinary means, or who can no longer function as he did in his youth. They are not for lovers in their prime, my lord," Lara explained, half laughing.

"We will not use them again," he said.

"We do not need to use them," she replied. Then she snuggled into his arms. "Put them away, Magnus. I will always be able to share pleasures with you without such means. The mere sound of your voice renders me weak with desire. But now I find I am so exhausted that I must sleep, or fade away." She closed her eyes with a sigh. The familiar scent of him was comforting.

The Dominus grinned. He was just as exhausted as she was, but relieved he had not had to admit to it. "Perhaps I will rest a bit, too," he murmured casually.

Lara swallowed back her laughter, relaxing against her husband until she heard him begin to snore softly. Only then did she allow herself to drift away.

They were awakened several very short hours later by an apologetic serving woman. "Domina," the woman shook Lara's shoulder gently. "You must awaken."

Drawing the coverlet about her Lara sat up. "What is it?"

"The Lady Persis is preparing to leave. She insists you both come and bid her farewell. She also says she would like the fur cape you promised her. She would remind you that it is cold out upon the water."

Lara laughed, shaking her head with amusement. "Tell Lady Persis that the Dominus and I will be with her very shortly. And she shall have her cape."

"Yes, Domina," the serving woman said, and withdrew.

She turned to Magnus.

"I heard," he said with a groan.

"She cannot leave until we have bid her farewell," Lara reasoned with him.

"What about her cape?" he asked. "There has been no time to have one made. She will not leave without it, you know."

"She shall have it," Lara said, rising from their bed.

"Faerie magic?" he asked.

"What other choice have I?" she replied. "Sirvat says she is angling to return to the castle. If you want her here I will acquiesce, but I suspect she is not an easy woman to live with, Magnus, and I have little tolerance for fools."

"I would build her a house of her own before I would let her return to the castle," he said. "There would be little peace with her in the castle, and I cannot rule a kingdom if I must contend with chaos in my home."

They quickly bathed and dressed, and went to seek out Lady Persis. Lara carried a beautiful full-length fur cape over her arm. They found the Dominus's mother and her two elder daughters in the day room of the Women's Quarters.

"She would not let us depart before we had seen you," his eldest sister, Narda, said. "She has forgotten what it is to be young and in love."

"I have forgotten nothing, rude girl!" Lady Persis replied.

"I have brought you your cape, madam," Lara said coming forward, and wrapping the garment about the older woman. "You shall never be cold again in the icy season." She fastened the cloak with delicate golden frog closings. "And it has a hood," she added, drawing it up over her mother-in-law's head. "I knew that marten would flatter you, madam," Lara said stepping back to admire her handiwork.

Lady Persis fingered the thick rich fur. She examined the gold work of the closings, and saw it was perfect. There had been no time, she knew, for such a cape to be fashioned by mortal hands, and thus she knew it was faerie work. She smiled, very well pleased, for it was obvious her new daughter-in-law respected her—which was more than her three daughters did. "It is a wonderful cloak," she said. "Thank you, Lara."

Lara gave the older woman a gracious nod of her head. "I always keep my promises, madam," she told Lady Persis. "And now I will bid you a safe journey." She put her arms about her husband's mother, and kissed both of her cheeks. Then she stepped over to his two older sisters, and wished them a safe journey as well. Each woman moved on to the Dominus, and then had no choice but to step upon the platform, which would take them to the quay below, and their vessels. Magnus Hauk shut the gate, and called to the giant who operated it. "Take them down now, and gently." The platform began its descent, and then the trio were gone from their sight.

"Nicely done, wife," he complimented her. "I could see the words forming upon my mother's lips as you so neatly dismissed her and my sisters."

"So could I," Lara chuckled. "Now can we go back to bed, my lord?"

He laughed, and putting a strong arm about her escorted her back to their private apartments where they remained for the next several days isolated from the world, eating, drinking and making passionate love—but without the aid of the Pleasure Enhancers.

They also discussed the journey they would make to Hetar. It was better that no one knew of their going. They had previously discussed going to the Dominus's hunting lodge in the foothills of the Emerald

Mountains, where they would have perfect privacy. They would take no servants with them for Lara's magic would be used to take care of them, they told Corrado and Sirvat. They would go before the Snow Month, and return with the spring that immediately followed it.

"What if we need you?" Sirvat asked her brother.

"For what purpose would you need me?" he replied. "You have your husband until the spring, for our trading vessels do not go to sea in the icy season. I wish time alone with my wife, and no interference from others. Other men have this privilege when they are first wed. Why should the Dominus not be allowed the same liberty?"

"I will give you a means of contacting us," Lara reassured Sirvat, "but be certain you call us only in the instance of an emergency, not because you are bored or lonely. Your new home will be ready for you in early summer. You must continue working with the architect, and you need to speak with the craftsmen about the furnishings. And Corrado will want time to plan for the coming trading season so that the fleet's time is put to its best use. And your husband needs an heir. You will be much too busy to miss us. It is the perfect time for us to slip away."

Sirvat sighed. "I suppose you are right," she said. "And it will be fun having the castle all to ourselves."

"Just as long as you don't decide to keep it," Magnus teased his little sister, and they all laughed.

"I think I prefer being a sea captain to a Dominus," Corrado said, and he wiped his brow in a gesture of mock relief.

"And for a brief few weeks," Magnus Hauk replied, "I shall enjoy just being a man in love with his wife, without the responsibilities of a kingdom on his shoulders."

Lara went to the stables the next morning to converse with Dasras. Speaking in a soft voice that only he could hear, she told him where they would be going, and why. "Will you remain here, or would you prefer to join the Fiacre again? Sakira must surely miss you."

"It has been some time," the great stallion agreed, "since I have run with my mate, Sakira. Now that she is just over the mountains, and not across a sea perhaps it would be good to join her again. When will you return?"

"In the spring," Lara said low. "I will send for you, for I know it is meant we be together, old friend."

"Take Andraste and Verica," Dasras advised.

"Magnus and I will travel only as visitors to the City," Lara answered.

"Take the sword and the staff," he repeated. "Better you not need them and have them, than you need them and do not have them."

"Perhaps you are right," Lara replied thoughtfully. "The City can be treacherous, and from all the Shadow Prince has told me it has become more so in these last few years."

Dasras shook his great head in agreement.

"Come," Lara told the big beast, and he followed her from the stable into the courtyard. "Do not tell them where I am," she whispered to him. "Just say I will visit them in the spring. Tell my son I send him my love, and will be with him soon. Go now!" And Lara watched as Dasras galloped across the courtyard, his great wings unfolding, lifting him up into the bright morning sky as he turned above her and flew toward the mountains. She hurried back into the castle to find Magnus.

Within the confines of their apartments they held hands, and Lara with a simple spell brought them to the safety of the Dominus's hunting lodge in the foothills of the Emerald Mountains. The little hall was cold, but with a snap of her fingers she caused a fire to ignite in the hearth. He watched as she lit lamps, and put food upon the table by means of her magic. They ate, and then he showed her about the small dwelling, which was much like an Outlander's house.

As they cuddled together in bed that evening he asked her, "When shall we go?"

"Let us remain here a few days, my dear lord. Knowing Sirvat, she is bound to concoct an emergency just so she may contact us. If we cannot answer her she will be terrified, and raise a cry."

"By what means can she reach us?" he asked her.

"I gave her a small mirror. All she need do is look into the glass, and call my name," Lara explained. "I will hear her."

"Why do you believe she will call you shortly?" he inquired.

"Sirvat is curious. She will want to be certain the mirror works," Lara replied.

"Of course she will!" Magnus agreed with a chuckle. "Very well. We will remain here until she has experimented with her magic mirror."

And two days later Sirvat did indeed call Lara's name, and Lara answered her sister-in-law. "What is it you want, Sirvat?" she responded.

"There is no emergency," Sirvat admitted honestly. "I just wanted to make certain that your mirror worked, Lara."

"Of course it works," Lara said. "I made it myself."

"Having a sister who can make such magic takes a little bit of getting used to," Sirvat said. "Are you and my brother enjoying your isolation? The snows will begin in another day or two. They always come at this time of year."

"We are quite cozy here," Lara assured Sirvat. "I can light the hearth with just a snap of my fingers, and the wood never burns away."

"What are you eating?" Sirvat wanted to know.

"We eat faerie bread," Lara said. "It tastes like whatever you wish it to taste, and the lodge cellar has barrels of good wine stored. It is very beautiful here, Sirvat. We have walked down to the lake, which has just in the last day or two begun to show a skim of ice upon its surface. And it is so peaceful. I have beat Magnus twice playing Traders. My Hetarian vessels always seem able to outrun his Terahn ships to the Safe Harbor," she laughed. "And he is not the best sport about it either. Did you always let him win?"

"Much of the time, once I learned how to play," Sirvat admitted, smiling.

"Well," Lara said, "if there is no emergency you must go now, Sirvat. Please, do not call me unless you truly need me. Once we return to the castle we shall not have so peaceful a time. It is a luxury we are very much enjoying. Your brother needs this time to himself. Being Dominus is a great responsibility as you well know."

She heard Sirvat sigh. "Very well, Lara. I promise not to use the mirror again unless it is a true emergency. Corrado said I was being childish. We will see you in the spring," she replied.

"We will return home with the flowers," Lara said with a smile. "Goodbye."

"Goodbye," she heard Sirvat call.

"Now can we go?" Magnus Hauk, who had been listening, wanted to know.

"Tomorrow," Lara said, "or perhaps the next day. I must consider where to first bring us. I can hardly transport us into the middle of a public square. Our advantage is in our discretion. We must appear to be ordinary citizens of Hetar."

"You do not really wish to do this, do you?" he said to her.

"I will do it for you, but we must proceed cautiously. Hetar is a dangerous place, Magnus. You have never faced the kind of danger that breeds there. The Shadow Princes gave me Andraste because I need her. My mother gave me Verica for the same reason. Here in Terah my need for them has been little, but when I return to Hetar, my need for them will be great. I have no friends in the City. If he caught me Gaius Prospero might attempt to enslave me again. And now that he is emperor he could change the laws as easily as he changes his garments."

"Would your family not protect you?" the Dominus wanted to know.

Lara laughed. "In Hetar everyone seeks status, and how one gains it does not matter, Magnus. It mattered not that my father's skills as a soldier were great. He could not join the ranks of the Crusader Knights until he won his place in their tournament. And he could not enter that tournament, which is only held every three years, unless he looked like a man worthy of a place with them. He had to have fine garments, fine weapons, a magnificent warhorse. But he was a poor man, and the only means he had of obtaining these necessities was to sell his beautiful daughter.

"I was proud to help my father. Honored that Gaius Prospero, then Master of the Merchants, would pay such a high price for me. My stepmother and I purchased all the right materials to make my father the garments he needed to impress those enrolling the combatants on the Application Day. Now I know from where those materials came," Lara said with a small smile. "The monies obtained for me purchased my father the best armor, the best weapons, the best horse and the aid of several elderly Crusader Knights. He won his tournament, and I was proud of him.

"He, my stepmother and my half brother Mikhail were moved from their hovel in the Mercenary Quarter to a fine house in the Garden District where only the Crusader Knights live. My stepmother was given servants, and she was so proud of her new status. She and my father bid me farewell with little sentiment that I could see. They were very eager to begin their new life, Magnus. I would not expect them to endanger themselves for me. They are Hetarian, and that means guarding one's place in the world of Hetar.

There is no thought of going backward for a Hetarian. There is only one way to go, and that is up.

"I will take you to the City. I will show you the world from which I came, but your world, the world in which I now live, is a far better place. You go so that you may understand Hetar, and its people. Know that they would be your enemy if they knew of Terah and its riches. For now I think we may be safe. Gaining the Outlands will solve their problems for the interim, and perhaps even for many years to come. But I will show you more than just the City. We will travel the Midlands. You will enter the faerie kingdom of my mother in the forest so you may see the Forest Lords without them seeing us. We will visit the Shadow Princes. I will show you the Outlands so you may truly understand what has been taken from the clan families. We will see the province of the Coastal Kings before we come home again in the spring. I must restore Archeron to his place before Arcas reveals the secret of Terah. And Magnus, you must trust me without reservation. No matter what happens you must trust me to bring us home in safety. Sometimes it will not be easy, I know. You are a great ruler of a great land, but you are an innocent where the world of Hetar is concerned."

"You make it sound both terrifying and intriguing," he said.

"It is both," she answered with a smile. "And more."

"And yet I am more eager than ever to go," he told her.

"I sense that," she replied. "Give me another day

to gather my strength, and we will go. You have not yet promised me," she reminded him.

"Promised you what?" he asked mischievously.

"That you will trust my judgment in Hetar above your own," Lara said.

He took her into his arms, and looked down into her beautiful face. "While it goes against my nature as a man," he told her, "I will do my best to trust to your wisdom and experience while we are in Hetar." Then he kissed her mouth lightly.

She laughed up at him. "And you will not object if I must defend us?"

"I have yet to hear Andraste sing," he said with a small grin.

"I hope you never have to," Lara told him. "Sleep well tonight, my lord Dominus. Tomorrow I will take us to Hetar. Neither of us will sleep well there."

Chapter 14

THE AIR IN THE CITY was foul. She had not remembered such a stench. There was garbage in the streets. She did not remember the streets being so dirty. There seemed to be more people, and the noise was unending. There were beggars everywhere, on corners and in doorways. Had it always been like this? Had she not noticed because it was all so familiar then? Lara had been curious to see the City again, but now she wished she were anywhere but here.

She had brought them to a secluded area outside of the City, and they had walked the remainder of the way. They were joined as they walked by others going to the City, some on foot, others driving carts that held produce.

Arriving at the main gates they waited patiently amid the growing crowd until the sun crept over the horizon signaling dawn. The gates creaked slowly open, and they entered with the others, looking for all the world like simple travelers.

"We must find an inn so we will have a place to stay tonight," Lara said low.

"Do you know where to go?" he asked her.

"Yes," she said. "There will be an inn outside of the Council Quarter gates. Come, it is this way." Lara moved quickly through the streets, which were growing more crowded as the day advanced. Finally she saw the open but guarded gates to the Council Quarter ahead of her, and directly opposite, the inn she sought. She turned to Magnus. "You must speak for us or it will seem odd. You will be asked to show your travel papers. They are inside your cloak in a pocket by your heart. You are Master Magnus, a silk merchant from the Coastal Kingdom, and I am your wife. They will not question you. They simply wish to see the papers, but if they ask why we are here say we are newly married, and have come to see the wonders of the City."

"We are newly married," he said with a little smile, "and we have indeed come to see the wonders of this place."

"Be cautious, Magnus," she advised him. "This is not Terah. There are spies everywhere looking for information to sell. We cannot draw attention to ourselves. You wished to see this place, and so we have come. But we must not remain more than two or three days. I can already see much has changed, and it frightens me."

They entered the inn, which was called simply The

Traveler's Rest, and the innkeeper hurried up to them, smiling toothily.

"How may I serve you, sir?" he asked.

"A room for my wife and myself," Magnus said. He drew a small purse from his cloak, and hefted it in his hand suggestively.

"You have come far, sir?" the innkeeper inquired.

"The Coastal Province," Magnus replied, and then he added, "we were caught outside your gates last night. Have things gotten so bad that a late traveler cannot be admitted by that small door in the gates after they have been closed for the night? My wife has probably caught a chill."

"There are new rules in place since the emperor was elected," the innkeeper said. And then he lowered his voice. "It has made it far more difficult to do business, but once we have taken the Outlands back from the barbarians who stole them, it will be easier for us all, sir. If I may see your travel papers, please."

Magnus reached into the cloak and withdrew the packet from the pocket over his heart, handing it to the innkeeper.

The innkeeper scanned the papers, and then obviously satisfied said, "I have a fine chamber on the upper floor overlooking the garden. I am sure it will suit, sir. For how long will you need it?" He handed the papers back to Magnus Hauk.

"We will remain with you three days," Magnus said. "It is our wedding trip, and I promised my wife a visit to the City before she must settle down to the business of giving me sons." He chuckled. "But I must admit I enjoy the making of those sons with my bride."

The innkeeper grinned knowingly. "Then you will not be interested in one of our fine Pleasure Houses, sir. Very good. If you will follow me, please, I will take you to your chamber. You will not have eaten yet if you spent the night outside the gates. I shall send a serving woman to you with some food to break your fast." He led them up a staircase and down a hallway to a door at the corridor's end. Opening it, the innkeeper ushered the couple inside. "Will this be satisfactory, sir?"

Lara flicked an eyelash at Magnus.

"It will suit," Magnus replied. He took two coins from the bag he carried. "Is this enough?" he asked.

"For today, indeed sir, most acceptable. You may settle the rest of your bill when you depart in three days' time." The innkeeper bowed obsequiously, and backed from the room. "I will have your food sent right up, sir." Then he was gone.

Lara put a warning finger to her lips, and then she said in a deceptively girlish voice, "Oh, Magnus, I never expected anything this grand!" Moving across the room she put her ear to the door. "He's gone," she said. "He waited just long enough to hear me, and then hurried off. After we eat I shall show you some of the City."

"From what I have seen so far it isn't a place I particularly like," Magnus admitted. "Nor is this sudden mistrust you have developed."

"Hetar is not like Terah, my lord husband," Lara answered him. "Be skeptical of everything here, and do not put your faith in anyone you meet or anything they tell you. In Hetar, and particularly in the City, your status depends upon what you have. We travel as middle-class citizens of the Coastal Kingdom. Respectable, able to pay our way, but of no great importance. Therefore little attention will be paid to us. This is the best course for us to follow."

"You do not like being here," he said quietly.

"Nay, I do not," Lara admitted. "I sense danger as I have never before sensed it. If we should be separated, or anything untoward should occur go through the gates across the way. That is the Council Quarter. Seek out one of the Shadow Princes. They can protect you, Magnus, if I cannot."

"This is beginning to seem like a bad idea," he said wryly.

"You wanted to see Hetar and meet Hetarians, husband. It is a wise thing to know your enemy. I only caution you, for you are an innocent where Hetar is concerned. And did you hear what the innkeeper said about the Outlands?"

"Aye, that they were planning to take back from barbarians what was theirs," he answered her. "Was that land once a part of Hetar?"

"Never! But that is the story they will have put about for some time in order to whip up public sentiment against the Outlanders," she explained. "The barbarians have stolen our lands. They have killed our people. Only savages would send seven cartloads of our dead, cruelly slaughtered innocents, into the City to mock us." She laughed softly. "Oh, yes, that is what they would say. We have been attacked. Proud Hetar has been defied. They would drum up a swell of nationalistic outrage, and use it to recruit men into the Mercenaries. In Hetar, Mercenaries are but fodder to be killed while the Crusader Knights direct and lead a battle. But the Knights are on horseback and armored. Few of them are killed, but then what are the extra sons of the Midlands good for if not to be exterminated in fighting? Fewer mouths to be fed. Fewer children born. In a society like Hetar peace becomes a dangerous opiate, Magnus. Too much prosperity is not good for the masses." She bit her lip in frustration, surprised by her own outburst.

A sudden knock on the door startled them both. He opened it, and a young girl, bowed down with the weight of the tray she carried, stumbled into the room. "The master said you needed a meal," the girl said setting the tray upon a small table. Then, not even looking at them, she scampered out down the corridor. Magnus shut the door behind her.

"She seemed frightened," he noted.

"Perhaps, but perhaps she just has a lot of work to do, and this was but an extra chore thrust upon her," Lara said. "Had I been plainer her fate might have been mine." She lifted the napkin from the tray to reveal fresh bread, fruit, cheese, two hard-boiled eggs and two small cups of liquid. Picking up one of the cups she tasted it. "Frine," she pronounced.

"What is frine?" he asked her.

"A mixture of fruit juice and wine, watered," she told him. "It is refreshing. The meal is simple enough, but there is no meat. You must ask the innkeeper why there is no meat with the meal. You are a big man, and should have meat."

"You are being very deferential publicly," he said.

"It is the custom in Hetar for women to be deferential to their men," Lara explained. "And all women must have men for protectors. A woman without a male is considered the lowest of creatures. A father, a brother, an uncle, a husband, a son. But there must be someone masculine to defend and safeguard her, or she can become prey for the unscrupulous. She could be forced into one of the less desirable Pleasure Houses as a slave, and worked to death."

"Tell me about these Pleasure Houses?" he asked her.

"As I have told you, I was meant for one," Lara said. "The Pleasure Houses are owned by men, except for a rare few—women are not usually entrusted with property. Pleasure Mistresses are the ones with the responsibility of managing the houses. They see to every aspect of them. Food. Repairs. Supplies. The training of the young girls. Keeping the women in order. Knowing the desires and foibles of the men who visit regularly. They receive a generous remuneration for their talents. But it is the owner of the Pleasure House who takes the lion's share of the profits, of course," she explained. "The Pleasure Women have but one duty in life. To give and receive pleasure. Those who do it very well are much in demand. Some have even become famous in Hetar, unusual for a female. A few of the Pleasure Houses specialize in the more deviant forms of passion, but only two or three of them. Some of the Pleasure Houses service the ordinary man. Most, however, are for the wealthy whose tastes are more refined. There is more profit in serving the wealthy than the simple man." She divided the food, giving him more bread, and both eggs.

"Pleasure is not really a commodity in Terah," he observed.

"Terah," Lara said to him, "does not worship the Celestial Actuary, but rather the Great Creator. The world of Hetar is driven by profit, Magnus. Everything is judged by that standard." She began to eat. The bread was good, the cheese mediocre and the fruit had seen better days. She wondered why a respectable inn across from the Council Quarters would offer its guests such scanty fare. She would speak to the little servant girl about it.

He gulped his portion, and Lara knew it wasn't enough for him. He was a big man, and used to good meals.

"There are usually vendors on the street selling food," she said.

"Good! Master Innkeeper will have to do better than this," Magnus said grimly.

"You cannot fuss, my lord," she advised again. "Remember, we are simple folk."

"Let us hope the bed is not infested," he grumbled at her.

"Come, and I will show you the City," Lara invited.

They departed the inn, and began to move through the crowded streets. She brought him through the gates of the Quarter where she had grown up, and showed him the hovel that had once belonged to her father. There was no one now who would recognize

Lara, daughter of Swiftsword, and she was plainly dressed, a dark veil over her golden hair, which she had braided and hidden beneath a dark snood. They noted how overcrowded the Quarter was.

"It was always full, but never like this," Lara noted. "Gaius Prospero has built himself up a great army."

"To no avail," Magnus murmured low.

Lara smiled. "He has promised them the spoils of war, and there will be none. I am certain he intended to divide the land up for himself and his friends. Now he will have to give some of it away to satisfy the Guild of Mercenaries. If there is no enemy there is no need for a large force, and many of these men are sons of Midland farmers. To be given land to farm will well satisfy them even if it does not satisfy Gaius Prospero." A small chuckle escaped her. "I must admit I do enjoy seeing that man thwarted in his grandiose schemes. Ah, here is the Golden District where only the most wealthy are permitted to reside."

"Can we go in?" he asked her.

Lara shook her head. "Not unless you wish me to have the guardsmen at the gates announce me to Gaius Prospero. I'm quite certain he would be delighted to receive me, my lord, and to learn of your fine kingdom, which he would begin to consider conquering. Especially after he faces disappointment in the Outlands."

"Let us find a market and buy something to eat," he said. "I am ravenous, and those two little eggs, a bad slice of cheese, bread and a few grapes are not enough for a man of my appetites." He gazed through the open gates into the Golden District. It was almost pastoral in appearance with great trees and green lawns.

"Move along!" snapped a guardsman seeing his interest.

"Your pardon, sir," Magnus Hauk said politely. "My wife and I are from the coast, and we have never before been to the City. Who lives here?"

"The emperor and his court," the guardsman said, his tone a touch more friendly. "Come closer, and take a real look," he invited them.

Lara's reluctant hand in his, Magnus stepped nearer and gawked, as he knew he would be expected to do. He could see several fine marble mansions. "'Tis grand, sir," he said to the guardsman. "I have never seen its like before. Thank you." He bowed.

The guardsman nodded in return as they moved off.

"You have a flair for the dramatic," Lara noted amused.

"It is difficult to resist," Magnus replied. "Everyone here seems to be a cock on his own dung hill. I could tell his position was important to him. I will wager if I had talked more with him we could have gotten in to the Golden District to walk around."

"And run smack into Gaius Prospero, or his toady Jonah, who I suspect is a truly dangerous man," Lara said.

"And Gaius Prospero is not?" Magnus was curious.

"The Master of the Merchants, or I suppose I should now say, the emperor, is more interested in acquisition and pleasure than anything else. But Jonah, I believe, seeks power."

"Look, up ahead the avenue opens into a square, and I see kiosks and awnings. It is a market!" Magnus said, well pleased.

"I must buy a basket if we are to make other purchases," Lara said, and with one or two queries they found their way to a basket weaver's awning. Looking carefully Lara finally selected an open container woven from willow wands. She bargained with the basket weaver until a suitable price was agreed upon by them both. Then she turned to her husband who wordlessly brought forth the proper coin. They walked onward.

"I see here in the marketplace you are free to speak up," he noted.

"Yes, this is a woman's province. It is not odd for her man to accompany her here, but she is the one who makes the purchases, and bargains where suitable," Lara explained. She next purchased a small fresh loaf of bread, some cooked meat, a wedge of cheese that she first tasted and approved. It was all more expensive than she had remembered, and it had been Lara who marketed for her family. An old woman vendor was displaying apples, pears and grapes of a much better quality than they had been offered at the inn this morning. Lara was further shocked by the price the old lady asked.

"Why are they so expensive?" she asked.

"The spring was wet, and the blossoms did not set properly. The harvest has been a poor one," the fruit seller explained. "The trees and the vines are all old now. But when we take back the land the barbarians stole from us it will be different. We will plant new trees and vines. Food is scarce this year. It is the same all over Hetar."

"Not quite so much in the Coastal province where we come from," Lara told her. Then turning the subject she said, "I will take two apples, two pears and a small bunch of your lovely green grapes. As it is my husband will complain at me for the cost." She held out her hand to Magnus who, glowering as he was supposed to, counted out the coins for the fruit, grumbling beneath his breath as he did so. Lara handed the fruit seller the coins, and received in return the fruit she had requested. Seeing a third apple she looked at the woman questioningly.

"It's small," the old lady said. "I won't be able to sell it anyway. You might as well have it."

"Thank you," Lara said, and gave the vendor a smile.

"Well," Magnus said as the moved away, "there is one person in Hetar not interested in a great profit."

"The people are good, my lord," Lara told him. "It is those in power who are overcome by their greed." And then she stopped suddenly, for directly in her path was her stepmother, and she was staring with shock and surprise directly at Lara.

Sensing something wrong Magnus asked, "What is it, Lara?"

Lara drew a long breath, and then she said, "Susanna. You are looking well."

Her stepmother swallowed hard, and then she practically whispered, "What are you doing here, Lara?" There was a young boy at her side.

"Is this Mikhail?" Lara asked, smiling at the child.

"Yes," Susanna said. "You have not answered my question."

"I do not think a public street is the place for this conversation, Susanna," Lara replied. "We are near the Garden District. Will you not invite my husband and me there so we may speak together? Perhaps I might even see my father, if he is not preparing for the Outlands invasion." Her tone was pleasant. She took Susanna's arm and drew her out of the center of the walkway.

"No one can enter the Garden District now except those living there. You would need a special permit, and I do not see how you could get one," Susanna protested.

"My magic has increased in the years I have been gone from Hetar, Stepmother," Lara told her. "I can render my husband and me invisible. We will follow you home, and no one will be the wiser," she said.

"Our servants will see you!" Susanna protested.

"And will they be bold enough to question you about your guests?" Lara asked her scornfully. "We will be discreet, Susanna. I have no wish to draw attention to us."

"You will do it whether I say yes or not," Susanna responded. Then she turned, and taking her son by the hand, moved quickly off back into the pathway between the kiosks and open shops.

"She has not always been so fearful," Lara said

as they moved to follow Susanna. "Be careful not to bump anyone, Magnus. We are quite invisible now."

"Thank you for telling me," he said wryly as he avoided a rather plump matron.

They trailed after Lara's stepmother and young brother, following them from the marketplace down several streets, and through the gates into the Garden District. The guardsman at the gate greeted Susanna and her son politely as they walked by him.

Finally Susanna stopped a moment, and then she entered a large marble villa. It was not the house that Lara recalled her father being assigned when he first became a Crusader Knight. Obviously John Swiftsword had come up in the world. But Lara did recognize the slave man who hurried forth to welcome his mistress home.

"I shall be in my privy chamber, Nels," Susanna said. "I do not wish to be disturbed. Please take Master Mikhail to the nursery. Where is my husband?"

"He has only just arrived home himself, Mistress," Nels replied.

"Would you ask him to join me?" Susanna told the slave. Then she turned and hurried off.

Lara and Magnus followed behind her.

Susanna waited long enough to be certain they had entered her small privy chamber where she came to sit and meditate. "Are you both here now?" she asked them.

"We are," said Lara, reappearing, and rendering Magnus visible again, too.

Susanna jumped to find Lara directly next to her.

"When your father comes you will tell us why you are here. Then I want you to go as you came," she said. "Your very presence endangers my family. I don't want you here."

The door to the small chamber opened, then closed, and John Swiftsword entered the room. He stared disbelieving at first, and then a wariness crept into his face. "Lara."

"I greet you, my father," she replied.

John Swiftsword looked to his wife questioningly.

"I saw them in the open market three streets over," Susanna said. "She insisted on coming with me, but no one knows she is here. Her magic made her invisible to the guards at the gate and to the house slaves. John, make her go! If she is discovered we will be dishonored, and everything you have worked for will be taken from us."

"Sit down, Wife," John Swiftsword said. Then he turned to his daughter. "Who is this man with you, Lara?"

"He is my husband, the ruler of a great land, Father," Lara answered.

John Swiftsword look confused. "We heard you murdered your Forest Lord master, and fled to the Outlands. Then it is said you helped lead a rebellion that caused the deaths of several hundred of our Mercenaries. I saw the death carts myself. Mistress Mildred's hovel was discovered empty and covered in blood. She and her son, Wilmot, were never seen alive again. It was said you were responsible, for Wilmot denounced you before the High Council of Hetar."

Lara shook her head. "Gaius Prospero has been

quite busy defaming my reputation in order to rebuild his own," she said. "May we sit, Father? The
tale I have to tell is a long one. My husband is called
Magnus Hauk, which means Hawk. He is the Dominus of a land called Terah."

"Is this some area of the Outlands?" her father
asked.

"No," Lara said. "Terah is not the Outlands. Now
as to the stories you have been told, there is truth in
all of them. I did indeed flee the Forest Lords, for
they were brutal masters with a penchant for murdering their slaves. I was aided in my escape by the last
living Forest Giant who was also mistreated by them.
We went into the desert and were taken in by one of
the Shadow Princes. It was the Shadow Princes who
opened my mind to my faerie blood, reunited me with
my mother and schooled me to be the warrior I have
become.

"I have a sword, father." Shrugging off the long
enveloping cloak she had been wearing, Lara drew
her weapon from the scabbard upon her back. "This
is Andraste," she said. "This is my father, John Swiftsword," she told the sword.

Andraste's emerald eyes opened and she surveyed
the surprised man. "He is a great warrior, Mistress,
but you are surely his equal," she said.

Susanna screamed softly as the weapon spoke, and
her husband took a step back.

"I am considered a great warrior, Father," Lara told
him. "I slew the Forest Lord who tried to reclaim
me in defiance of our own Hetarian laws. Then the
princes paid his brother a generous indemnity. Af-

terwards, I journeyed into the Outlands where I wed their greatest leader and lord, Vartan of the Fiacre. When Hetar invaded two of the clan families' territory and enslaved the people, Vartan led a force to drive them out, and we were successful. The Outlanders are peaceful folk. It was Hetar who broke the ancient treaties." She resheathed her sword.

"Nay," her father said. "They infringed upon Hetar, and we had no choice but to protect ourselves. Those territories were annexed to prevent further encroachment."

"So said Gaius Prospero and his minions," Lara replied scornfully. "The Tormod and Piaras territories were invaded in order to rob and pillage their gold, silver and gemstone mines. Gaius Prospero made himself quite rich in those few months before we drove Hetar back behind their own borders. I saved Wilmot in that battle, and sent him to Gaius Prospero first, and then to the High Council where he was protected by the Shadow Princes and the Coastal Kings. He and his mother were transported to the desert, where they live in the palace of a prince even to this day.

"And peace was restored in the Outlands. I bore Vartan two children. But then he was assassinated at the behest of Gaius Prospero, who hoped by depriving the Outlands of their strongest leader they would be weakened. But the clan families have not been weakened. They elected a new leader and grew stronger. But I have a destiny, and it called to me once again. I traveled to the Coastal Kingdom, and from there to

Terah, where I lifted a great curse from the men of the land."

"Why have you returned to Hetar?" her father asked her candidly.

"Magnus wanted to see the City," Lara replied.

"Why?" John Swiftsword demanded.

"Because," the Dominus of Terah said, "if you will invade peaceful neighbors and violate ancient treaties, it is possible that one day you may decide to invade my lands on some pretext or another."

"Hetar is not an aggressor!" John Swiftsword declared vehemently. "We are a peaceful people. We seek only what is ours, and the Outlands belong to Hetar. For centuries we have left its indigenous folk to wander its steppes, but now we need those lands back. The City is overcrowded. The Midlands can no longer feed us. We must resettle our own Hetarians in the Outlands."

"And what will happen to its people?" Magnus Hauk asked him.

"They are savages, and must be civilized to Hetarian ways. This will be best accomplished by absorbing them into our society as slaves," John Swiftsword replied.

"I can hardly believe what I am hearing from your mouth, Father," Lara said. "I was the wife of an Outlands lord. These are not wandering tribesmen. These are people with villages, flocks, herds, ancient customs and a civilized way of life. Gaius Prospero and his minions have not lived among the Outlands clan families, but I have. Whose word is more valid in this instance?"

"Lara, you were always a difficult girl," her father replied. "Only your great beauty saved you. You could have been a famed Pleasure Woman in the City but for your intransigence. The emperor was very disappointed in you and your behavior. Whatever fate you have suffered has been your own fault."

"Difficult?" She was astounded. "When grandmother died I was still a child, but I cooked, and cleaned and mended your clothes for you, Father. When after several years you took Susanna to wife I welcomed her as a dutiful daughter should. I taught her how to bargain in the marketplace, and deal with the tradespeople. I helped with my baby brother Mikhail. I soothed your conscience when you sold me to Gaius Prospero. I was never difficult, and for you to accuse me of it now is despicable. As a Mercenary you were an honorable man, but I see that you have now become a true Hetarian in every sense of the word. You rewrite history to suit your ideas and actions. You are only interested in what you can acquire. I see you have gained a larger house than the one that was originally assigned to you. What service did you perform for Hetar to merit it?

"I should not have attempted to see you but that Susanna recognized me in the market, and I realized it was my little brother Mikhail by her side. He looks like you, Father. But your wife did not even bother to introduce me to my brother. I was foolish for wanting to know him even briefly. I have a faerie brother, you know. His name is Cirilo, and he is just a bit younger than Mikhail. He will one day be king of the Forest

Faeries. My mother welcomed me as you have not. I shall not forget it."

"Mikhail doesn't even know he has an older sister," Susanna said suddenly. "He was still an infant when you left. He believes he is the eldest of your father's children. Why would we tell him of you? A traitor to Hetar! A murderess!"

"You have other children," Lara said. It wasn't a question.

"I have given your father four sons. Mikhail, Haemon, Vili and Anyon," Susanna said proudly. "Four sons for the order of the Crusader Knights. And each child I have borne is healthy and strong. You asked what your father did to merit this house? It was not your father. It was me! Successful breeders of sons who are wives to the men of this order are rewarded with larger homes and more servants. Even now another son grows in my belly, and Anyon is not yet a year!" she said proudly.

"And do your sisters envy you now, Susanna?" Lara asked her stepmother softly.

Susanna giggled, and for a moment Lara saw the girl she had once been. "You remembered," she said. "Aye, they do envy me."

"Then you have everything you ever wanted," Lara murmured.

A knock sounded upon the door.

"I said I was not to be disturbed!" Susanna cried.

"Mistress, a messenger from the emperor is at our door," Nels called to her.

"What does he want?" Susanna asked.

"He will only speak with you, or Sir John," Nels responded.

Susanna looked to her husband, who appeared unsure of what to do.

"We will be invisible to the messenger," Lara said to her father.

"Show the messenger in, Nels," John Swiftsword called to his slave.

Several moments later the door to Susanna's privy chamber was opened, and a smartly uniformed messenger stepped through into the room. Lara and Magnus were no longer visible. They had just faded away before Susanna's eyes.

"Sir John Swiftsword?"

John nodded, and the messenger handed him a tightly rolled parchment.

"From the emperor, sir. I am to await a return message." He stood at attention while John unrolled the scroll, and perused it slowly.

"The emperor invites us to join him for dinner," John Swiftsword said. "And we are to bring our guests." He grew pale, and suddenly silent. Then he heard Lara whisper in his ear.

"Say, yes, Father! And say it now before the messenger wonders why you are near to shaking with your fear," Lara said in a hard voice that only he could hear.

"Tell the emperor we will be delighted to join him," John Swiftsword answered the messenger, regaining his courage.

"Two litters will be here at sunset to take you to the

emperor's home," the messenger said, bowing again, and then turning he left the room.

Lara and Magnus returned to their view, and seeing them her father's face grew tight with his anxiety. His daughter's magic was, he found, very unnerving.

Susanna began to moan. "We are ruined! You could not be satisfied unless you brought ruin upon us, could you? My poor children! What will become of them?"

"How did he know?" John Swiftsword wondered aloud.

Lara laughed. "His spy system is even better than I would have given him credit for," she said admiringly. "I see the fine hand of his slave, Jonah, in this."

"Jonah is no longer a slave, but a freed man. He is the emperor's closest advisor," her father told them. "He is called the right hand of the emperor."

"Yes," Lara said slowly. "He could accomplish much more as a free man than as a slave. I certainly did," she concluded with a chuckle.

"You will get us all killed!" Susanna sobbed. "Why did you have to come back?"

"A proven breeder such as yourself would not be killed, Stepmother," Lara said scornfully. "Gaius Prospero has somehow found out I am in the City. If murder were on his mind we should already be dead. No. He wants something, and he is willing to be charming in order to obtain it. Magnus and I must return to our lodging. I am certain that your emperor's litter will be waiting for us there at the appointed hour, and not here." And then she and Magnus were gone from John and Susanna's sight.

"Whatever the emperor wants we will agree to," Susanna said nervously.

"He desires nothing of us but an assurance of our loyalty," her husband said. "We would not even be asked to dine with him but that he wants Lara there. I wonder if she will go, or if she will disappear from the City. I thought she looked like her mother when she was a girl, but now the resemblance is even stronger. And she has gained much magic, it would seem. She is more faerie than mortal now," he said almost regretfully.

"This man she was with," Susanna said. "Do you think he is really her husband?"

"If it were not so she would not have said it," John replied. "Lara was never a liar, but where is the place she calls Terah? And what of the children she mentioned? Did she tell you if they were sons or daughters?"

"I know nothing more than you do, husband," Susanna responded. "Oh, what shall I wear tonight? It must be perfect if we are to dine with the emperor. Wait until I write to my sisters about that!" she cried excitedly, and hurried from her little privy chamber.

John Swiftsword sat back down again. He thought about what his daughter had told him, and was troubled, for as he had said to his wife, Lara did not lie. But several years had passed since Lara had left the City. How much had she changed? Gaius Prospero had promised him that she would be treated well, but obviously that had not happened. What was the truth behind her disappearance? She had not really said. He had met several Forest Lords, and they were certainly not pleasant men. And she had not, according to her version of the tale, murdered her master and fled. She had fled, and when the Forester had finally found her she had slain him. Why, if the year and the day allowed escaped slaves to gain their freedom had passed?

And the sword she carried! It was beautiful, and unlike any he had ever seen. Its craftsman had obviously had much magic at his disposal. It gave him a small feeling of pride to know his daughter had become a great swordswoman. He would have never considered his delicate, beautiful Lara as a warrior. But a sword could not fight for her. It could only fight with her. She had obviously been well trained, but by who? There was so much he didn't know, and so much he wanted to. He had four fine sons, but only one daughter. He realized Susanna was jealous of Lara. She always had been. Alas, it could not be helped now.

He wanted more time with Lara, but he strongly doubted that he would be given that time. The invasion of the Outlands was near, and suddenly he was troubled. In the last few years it had been said that the Outlands were really Hetarian, but John Swiftsword did not recall ever having heard that before. Now, however, everyone said it was so, believed it was so. Why would the government lie to them? The City had always been crowded. And if all the Midland farmers farmed the way his father once had, resting alternating fields each year, it would have been fine. But the

Squire of the Midlands had decreed that all the fields must be planted each growing season. The land had worn itself out. But when John suggested resting the fields to his brother-in-law, he had been scornful of John Swiftsword's suggestion.

"You do what you do best, John, and I'll do what I do best," Susanna's brother had told him. And then his wife had scolded him for trying to tell her family how to farm, for they had grown wealthy with their enormous crops. Now suddenly the land had refused to cooperate, and they could barely feed themselves. It was all very odd.

"Sir?" Nels was at his elbow. He hadn't even heard the slave come into the room. "The mistress says you must hurry and dress if you are to be ready when the imperial litter comes for you."

"Aye, I had better get ready," he agreed, and standing up he hurried from the chamber. As he went he wondered if Lara would come, or whether she would disappear.

Lara was considering the same thing even as her father thought it. "We entered the City under a cloak of invisibility," she said. "How did Gaius Prospero know I was here? He is far more dangerous than I had anticipated."

"Do you want to attend the emperor? Or shall we depart?" Magnus asked her. "In a single day I have seen enough of Hetar to know that I do not like these people or their ways. I would be happy to sleep in my own bed tonight in Terah. You always spoke well of your stepmother, but I find her self-centered and selfish. And your father may be a great soldier, my faerie love, but he is a weak man, I fear."

"I know," Lara replied. "I saw it as a girl, and I see it again now. He is a man who trusts the establishment and what they tell him. He can see no farther than the end of his handsome nose. And I have confused him, I fear, for he knows I do not lie. Yet everything I have told him is in direct conflict with what the government has told him. But do not be too hard on Susanna. She is only protecting her family."

"She is protecting her status and her possessions," he said grimly.

Lara laughed. "Yes, she is. As a mother, however, she has considered her four sons in all of this. How sad that my brothers, especially Mikhail, do not know of me."

"It's cruel," he declared. "I saw your face when she told you. The bitch hurt you, Lara, and for that she will have my enmity. Now, do we go and dine with this emperor of Hetar? Or do we return home?"

"We dine," Lara told him. "I want Gaius Prospero to see what I have become, and perhaps even be afraid. But first we must drink." And she drew two small vials from her pocket, handing him one. "Poison is one of Hetar's favorite weapons. This will protect us against anything the emperor attempts to kill us with, my husband."

Magnus Hauk shook his head wearily, but he took the vial, uncorked it and drank down the contents as she was doing the same. "It tastes like Tera berries," he noted.

"Your favorite," she said with a small smile. "Now

I must use magic to clothe us, for we brought nothing but what we are wearing. Ordinary folk do not travel with vast wardrobes. You must be garbed with dignity, but not too ostentatiously." She undid the leather belt holding her scabbard and sword. "Go into the shadows unseen," she commanded Andraste who disappeared from her hand. "There," Lara said. "She and Verica will keep each other company this evening, and anyone entering this chamber will not see them."

"Dignified," Magnus reminded his wife.

"Go and wash while I consider it," Lara told him. She considered, and then with a small motion of her hand she produced a long white tunic with short sleeves, edged in bands of purple-and-gold, along with a pair of gold sandals, which she lay upon their bed. Another gesture of the same hand brought forth a simple long sleeveless gown with a draped neckline. The iridescent gown shimmered like it had been made with sunlight and moonbeams. Lara bathed herself in the basin her husband used, and slipped the gown on along with a pair of silver sandals. Her star crystal was her only jewelry. Her hair was plaited in a single braid.

"You are so beautiful," he said. "I fear for you, Lara." He was both handsome and regal in his tunic, which flattered his dark blond hair and turquoise eyes.

"We are both protected," she assured him. "We will dine with Gaius Prospero, and tomorrow we will leave the City. We will go into my mother's world, and then to that of the Shadow Princes. Hetar may be controlled now by the greedy and wicked, but it has many good people whose voices are not heard amid the chaos. I want you to see them, too, so that should you ever have to deal with Hetar you will know there is both good and evil here as there is in all worlds, husband." She picked up her cloak, handing him his. "Let us go now, for I am certain the imperial litter is waiting for us. The innkeeper will be quite agog."

"Do you think it is that man who has betrayed us to Gaius Prospero?" Magnus asked her. He donned a cloak to cover his elegant garments, and Lara did also.

"Nay. We appeared to be just what we said we were. No. Someone in the street saw me and recognized me. I tried to hide my hair, but they must have known my face. And it was someone from the emperor's household," Lara said.

Outside the inn a simple litter awaited them. It was not a vehicle that would have drawn any attention, but they knew it was for them. Entering it they sat silently as they were borne through the streets, and through the gates of the Golden District. Gaius Prospero might have gotten himself declared emperor of Hetar, but he still lived in the same grand marble house she had come to all those years ago. The litter was set down, the curtains drawn back.

Magnus Hauk exited and extended a hand to help his wife out of the conveyance. As he turned he saw a plump man in a cloth of gold tunic coming forward to meet them.

"Lara, my dear girl," Gaius Prospero said effusively. "It is delightful to see you again." He kissed both her cheeks. "Your father and his wife have already arrived, but then they had a shorter distance to travel. You will surely remember my chief advisor, Jonah."

"Of course," Lara murmured. "And may I present my husband, Magnus Hauk, the Dominus of Terah," she said.

The emperor and Jonah looked Magnus Hauk over most carefully. They silently agreed he was a commanding figure. But how powerful? How rich?

"I welcome you to Hetar, my lord," Gaius Prospero said. "But tell me why you have come with such stealth into my realm?" He linked his arm into that of the Dominus as they walked.

"Stealth is not a word I would use to describe our visit," Magnus replied coolly, reaching out for Lara with his free hand. "I came incognito in order to observe the place from which my wife had come. I have no desire to treat with Hetar, my lord. Indeed, if Lara's stepmother had not seen her in the street we should not have made ourselves known to any."

Gaius Prospero was surprised by the answer, and not just a little offended. Hetar was the greatest kingdom ever created. No other could match it. "Hetar has much to offer, my lord," he said defensively.

"Perhaps to some," Magnus said, "but not to Terah."

Gaius Prospero was becoming intrigued. Was this lordling a fool that he did not see the advantages to being allied with Hetar? Was his own land an even greater place? Impossible! Hetar was the only kingdom worthy of the definition. Obviously this Magnus Hauk was attempting to gain the advantage by pretending disinterest in Hetar. Gaius Prospero almost laughed aloud with the thought. But instead he escorted his guests into his house and to the dining hall. "You will surely remember this chamber," he said to Lara with a smirk.

"Of course," she answered him. Her beautiful face was expressionless.

Gaius Prospero went on, turning to the Dominus, and saying, "The night I displayed Lara to the masters and mistresses of the City's Pleasure Houses she was brought naked into this room upon a silver platter. I told them she was the sweet to complete our fine dinner," he chortled, warming with the memory.

"Unfortunately," Lara said sweetly, "you overplayed your hand, my lord, did you not?" She turned to her husband. "The Head Mistress of the Pleasure Mistresses' Guild came the next day to tell Gaius Prospero that my beauty had caused great chaos among the Pleasure Houses. The women feared that I would steal their clients from them. The regular clients were threatening mayhem if they were not the first to be given one of my three virginities. So she was forced to forbid my sale to any of them." Lara laughed lightly. "I was consigned to a Taubyl Trader, and purchased by the Head Forester. Still, you made a very comfortable profit, Gaius Prospero, considering I was scarcely in your tender care for more than a day or two."

"You have become hard," the emperor told her crossly.

"As a well-tempered blade, my lord," Lara replied with a smile. "I can wield a sword now, you know.

Perhaps you were told that when we returned your Mercenaries to you several years ago."

"I was sorry to hear of your husband's death," Gaius Prospero murmured.

"I have another," she replied.

Gaius Prospero laughed, and his pudgy fingers tapped her arm playfully. "Enough of our reminiscing, my lady. Ah, here are my two lovely wives, the lady Vilia and the lady Anora. Greet our guests, my dears," he purred at them, and the two women obeyed.

They sat at the long table, lounging upon couches as they dined. Both Lara and Magnus ate and drank sparingly, a fact noticed by both Gaius Prospero and his advisor.

"Are you afraid of poison?" Jonah said low to Lara.

She turned her green gaze on him. "No," she answered. "We are protected from such chicanery. In Terah, by choice, our meals are not so rich."

"Is this land a good one?" he asked. "And how far from Hetar is it?"

"Am I a fool to answer your questions, Jonah?" Lara demanded of him.

"I am only making polite conversation," he protested.

He was as thin and vulpine as ever, Lara thought. "You seek to wheedle information out of me for your benefit first, and possibly your master's if *that* would be to your benefit," she said mockingly. "Terah is where it is. Many weeks away from the farthest borders of Hetar. My husband does not dissemble with Gaius Prospero. He had no wish to treat with Hetar.

He came to satisfy his curiosity. He has done so, and we will be gone by the morrow."

"How did you get into the City?" Jonah asked, turning the subject.

"With a cloak of invisibility," she answered him frankly. "We walked unseen past your guardsmen. Now it is my turn. How did you know we were here?"

"Aubin Prospero, the emperor's son, saw you. He said yours was a face he would never forget, for it was the first time his father had included him in his commerce. He was eight then, but now is almost grown. He was meeting someone when he spied you speaking with your stepmother," Jonah replied. "You once said you had no magic."

"Once I did not," Lara answered him.

"But now you do, and it is powerful or you should not dare to be here. You do not fear my master, or even the might of Hetar, Lara, daughter of Swiftsword," Jonah observed. "I think you could be a dangerous enemy for Gaius Prospero to have."

"Are you still so loyal to him then?" Lara asked him. "Or is it just that you have not gathered enough power to overthrow him yet?" And she laughed softly at the surprise in the dark fathomless eyes engaging hers. "Your secret is safe, Jonah. There is nothing Hetar has that I want. And I have no love for your master. Magnus has seen what he came to see. We will return home, and you will likely never meet us again. Your invasion of the Outlands should keep Hetar busy for some time to come, I think."

"You know about the invasion?" He was disturbed. She was a stranger now to the City, and yet she had already heard of their plans. How much did she know? And if she was no longer associated with the Outlands, why would she care? Perhaps he was being too wary. People spoke of the coming invasion all over the City these days. Still, he was curious. "How?" he asked her.

"My stepmother mentioned it in between her pleas for us to go away before we jeopardized my father's position within the ranks of the Crusader Knights," Lara said. Better he not know of their allies among the lords of Hetar. "Is he to lead one of the invading forces, or did she really gain her large home because she births strong sons for the order, as she bragged to me?"

Jonah laughed. "You do not like her," he said knowingly.

"When I helped her to elevate my father from the Guild of Mercenaries to the ranks of the Crusader Knights I did not realize how petty and venal she was. She had no style then, but she has improved somewhat by her association with the other knights' wives," Lara noted dryly. "But I neither like her, nor dislike her."

"You two have been chattering forever," Gaius Prospero said. "What do you speak about?"

"Politics, my lord," Lara said. "In other words, nothing at all."

A ripple of laughter erupted about the table, and then dessert was served.

Chapter
15

HIS GUESTS HAD DEPARTED back to their dwellings. Anora, his second wife, clung to his arms purring deliciously lascivious and salacious suggestions into his ear. Gaius Prospero shook her off. "Not now," he said testily. "I have other things that need attending before I come to bed."

"What things?" Anora demanded. "I see you will need my whip on your fat bottom tonight, Gaius. You have neglected me dreadfully of late." She slipped her arms about his neck, pressing against him, a hand reaching down to grasp his male member.

Again he pushed her away. "Anora, there are matters concerning Hetar that require my immediate attention. Go to your bed. I have no time for you."

"Then divorce me, and send me back to my Pleasure House!" she cried. "I cannot exist without pleasures. I am not your senior wife, Vilia, content to be ignored as long as my lofty status remains intact. I need passion!"

An unpleasant smile touched Gaius Prospero's lips. He wrapped his hand in Anora's long hair, and yanked her to him. "I have no intention of divorcing you, my pet," he said to her. Then he slapped her viciously several times. "And remember that I, too, know how to give pain. You have taught me well, Anora. Now leave me!" He flung the woman from him, and she fell to her knees upon the marble floor sobbing.

"I love you, Gaius," she whimpered, looking up at him.

Her cheeks were stained with tears, and he saw the red marks his hand had made upon her cheeks. He felt the strange satisfaction that punishing her always brought him. Then getting to her feet Anora ran from the room. She would, he knew, be waiting with her whip to punish him when he was ready for her. And then they would experience glorious pleasures together until they were too weak even to rise from the bed.

"Jonah!" the emperor called to his assistant.

"I am here, my lord," Jonah said appearing from the shadows.

"Come," Gaius Prospero beckoned. "Let us have some more wine and discuss the evening." He sat down in a thronelike chair while Jonah poured two goblets of wine for them, handing his master one as he stood by his side. "Now tell me what you thought of the beautiful Lara and this husband of hers. Shall I have him killed before they depart the City? Tonight? Then I might console the widow personally."

"Too obvious, my lord, but then you knew that before I even spoke," Jonah said.

"You know I have always desired her," the emperor continued. "Would she not make me a fine empress? How old do you think she is now? Twenty-one? Twenty-two?" He licked his lips. "To take pleasures with her would be as close to divinity as a man might come, I think."

"The ladies Vilia and Anora might not approve of such plans," Jonah said dryly.

"They argue over who should be my empress, which is why neither one of them shall ever be," Gaius Prospero said.

"The woman you entertained tonight, my lord, was hardly the girl you sent off to be sold into slavery eight years ago," Jonah reminded his master. "That girl had no magic. But this woman does have magic, and it is great magic."

"All the more reason I should have her for my empress," Gaius Prospero said. "Imagine the power that would be mine with a faerie wife, Jonah!"

"Indeed, my lord, the thought is staggering. Unfortunately the lady would not be willing, I fear. Even if you murdered this new husband as you did the last, she would not, I believe, be willingly yours."

"But soon we will enter the Outlands, and I shall find the children she gave to Vartan. I will use them to force her compliance to my will," Gaius Prospero said.

"Would not her children be with her?" Jonah asked.

"Nay, they are not. After Vartan's death, when she went to the Coastal Kingdom to visit Archeron she left them behind with their Fiacre clan family, Vartan's people," the emperor said. "Arcas told me."

"Arcas lies," Jonah noted. "First he claimed he had sold Lara into slavery. Then he said she was dead, fallen overboard from his vessel. Yet, my lord, here she was tonight, the wife of a man who claims to rule in another land. I attempted to solicit certain information from the lady Lara about this Terah, but she was not at all forthcoming, other than to say it was many weeks' travel from Hetar's farthest borders."

"Then for now Terah would not appear to be. a threat to Hetar," Gaius Prospero said thoughtfully. "But where is it? And why is this Dominus not interested in being Hetar's ally? Yet he was interested enough in Hetar to make his clandestine visit."

"I think Arcas may know where Terah is," Jonah said. "The Coastal Kings have many secrets they have not shared with you, my lord. For too long we have allowed them this isolation because of the luxury goods they constantly provide us, yet from where do those goods come? We have always assumed that the coastal folk fashioned them for us. But if that were so, my lord, why do the Coastal Kings have need of vessels to sail the sea they call Sagitta? Is it possible that these luxuries come from the place Lara calls Terah? And if they do, then the Coastal Kings are no better than the Taubyl Traders. They are middlemen. If we could trade directly with Terah, would not our costs be lower and our profits higher, my lord?"

A smile wreathed Gaius Prospero's fat face. "Jonah, my dear Jonah," he murmured pleased, "you are a treasure. How facile your mind is, and how it twists, and ferrets out the nuggets of information that will be useful to us. And to Hetar," he added as an afterthought. "I could not do without your counsel."

Jonah bowed his head in appreciation of the emperor's words. "I am grateful to serve you, my lord," he said flatteringly.

"Now let us get back to the beautiful Lara," Gaius Prospero said. "What am I to do about her, Jonah?"

"Nothing for now, my lord," Jonah advised. "Patience will prove to be a virtue in this matter, I assure you. You must not confuse yourself with too many projects at once. In another week we will begin our march into the Outlands through the Coastal province. Our Mercenary army and their Crusader Knight officers are already there. Think of the riches awaiting us, my lord. Slaves to be pressed into the service of Hetar. Beautiful women for the Pleasure Houses. Villages already built, and ready to be inhabited by those you have chosen, folk who will be loyal to you first because of your generosity. There are flocks and herds of animals that will make you richer than you could ever have imagined. The fields will be ripening with their crops ,which we will harvest for ourselves at the proper time. The City's markets will be full again with cheap produce. The people will laud you for it. And the mines will again be ours to work. With such an enlarged labor force at little cost to us we will increase our returns. Your coffers will overflow, my lord."

"It is a dream come true," Gaius Prospero gushed. "All I need to make it perfect is Lara by my side as my empress, and in my bed to share pleasures."

"It will be so, my lord," Jonah assured him. "But first we take the Outlands. Then we will force their secrets from the Coastal Kings. And when we do, the road to Terah will be open to us, my lord. We must proceed slowly and carefully if we are to succeed in this endeavor. And you will have Lara's Fiacre children in your tender care so that the faerie woman will be more amenable to your wishes. A year, or two at the most, my lord, and everything you have ever wanted will be yours."

"Yes!" Gaius Prospero breathed. "And in the meantime I have Vilia and Anora, each of them bending over backward to please me in the hopes I will make one of them my empress." He laughed, and nodded well pleased. "Once more you have clarified the picture for me, Jonah. You must help me continue to be patient," the emperor said.

"I am here for you, my lord. Only for you," Jonah assured Gaius Prospero.

"I have kept Anora waiting long enough," the emperor said. "Good night, Jonah. May the rest of your evening be as pleasant as mine is certain to be." And he hurried off to where his second wife was anticipating his arrival.

On her large bed lay the gold wrist cuffs lined in lamb's wool that were connected with a silver chain, a matching collar, a small dog whip, and a hazel switch as thick as her thumb. "You are late!" Anora snapped at him as Gaius Prospero entered the chamber. "Put on your collar, and get on your knees! Beg my forgiveness for your earlier behavior, and your tardiness," she said reaching for the switch. "Display your bottom for me immediately, Gaius," she commanded him as he hurried to obey her, smiling as she saw him wince at the sound of the hazel rod swishing through the air. "You are going to spend until dawn being punished, husband," Anora told him. "Your buttocks will be well burnished by the time I have finished with you."

"Yes, my sweet precious," Gaius Prospero whimpered, eager for her to begin. Anora's whippings always produced the most extraordinary results for him. He performed like a bull amid a herd of heifers afterwards. Vilia no longer aroused any passion in him at all. But Lara… The thought of her set his male member stirring, and then he yelped as Anora's hazel switch began to sting and burn his flesh.

Listening outside Anora's chamber Lady Vilia smiled with satisfaction. She hurried through the house, and then when she had almost reached the great hall a hand reached out, pulling her into the shadows. "Jonah!" she breathed.

His mouth found hers in a hard kiss. He forced her back against the wall with his lean body, pulling her gown up as he did. Her hands fumbled eagerly to push his own gown away. Then he was raising her up. Her legs were wrapping about him. He thrust hard into her wet heat. "Vilia," he ground out. "I thought you were not coming." His hips worked in sharp, quick rhythm with hers. "You were ready for me, you wicked bitch, weren't you?" Jonah groaned, burying his face between her big breasts.

"I had to…ahh. Make certain…ohh, Jonah!…that Anora would…don't stop, you devil!…keep him the night. Ohh, that is so good! I adore…sharing pleasures…with you, Jonah, my love."

He used her vigorously. Gaius Prospero hadn't been in her bed in several years, but Jonah knew it would infuriate him to know that his former slave was even now pumping his love juices into Vilia. He had considered seducing her, but she had taken the initiative with him even before he had bought his freedom. She was a deliciously lusty woman, and would make him a fine empress one day. A man could have many beautiful women with whom to share pleasures, but a woman like Vilia, intelligent and ambitious, was rare. Gaius Prospero was a fool to consider tossing her aside for the beautiful faerie Lara. *But I will encourage his folly,* Jonah thought as Vilia began to moan with her crisis. He kissed her again to stifle the cries, feeling her lush body shudder with release.

Her legs fell away from him. "Oh, that was good!" she half groaned.

"Was she whipping his fat bottom?" Jonah asked.

"She had just begun," Vilia laughed softly. "He cannot, it seems, become aroused anymore unless she does. But once he is stiff he works her vigorously."

"Leaving me the leisure to work you even more vigorously," Jonah said in her ear.

He took her by the hand. "Come," he said. "We will go to my chamber."

"You could have a house of your own," Vilia said to him. "Why do you persist in remaining in that tiny cubicle here in this house?"

"To be near you, of course," he told her.

"Liar," she said. "But flattering. Now the truth, Jonah."

"If I am in the house then no one else can get to him without my knowing it," Jonah said. "You and I must be his only influences, Vilia."

"Agreed," Vilia answered. "Now what was tonight all about, Jonah?"

"He was curious. Your son saw Lara in the marketplace today and came to him with the news. We tracked her to the Garden District, and an inn near the City's main gate. He desires her, but then you always knew that. But it is the man she travels with, and this land of Terah, that is of more interest to us. For now I have convinced him to keep his energies focused upon the Outlands invasion."

"Yes," Vilia said. "There is much wealth for the taking there, and it is time we put those savages under our thumbs."

They had reached Jonah's small chamber, and entering it fell in a tangle of arms and legs to the bed, pulling off each other's garments.

"What is to be done about Lara?" Vilia asked him.

"Nothing for now," Jonah said. "In time we will deal with her. She might even make us a good ally, for her magic has grown strong. But for now I think she will be surprised that we have left her alone, and perhaps it will gain us her goodwill at some time in the future."

And Lara was indeed surprised that nothing more came of the dinner with Gaius Prospero. She had set Verica to guarding their door, but they slept undisturbed. And the following morning a messenger arrived from the emperor with papers giving them free access to any part of the City. "They want something," she said suspiciously.

"What?" Magnus asked her amused.

"For one thing, that snake, Jonah, wanted to know where Terah was," Lara said.

"What did you tell him?" What *had* she told him? She had been edgy, and extremely cautious since last night.

"That it is was many weeks' journey from Hetar's farthest borders," Lara replied. "If he considers my words, he will have to wonder which borders. Jonah is a shrewd and clever man, Magnus. He will eventually find us if he seeks us."

"I think for now their invasion of the Outlands will consume them," the Dominus said wisely. "I am looking forward to meeting King Archeron at Kaliq's palace. Shall we leave the City today?"

"Nay," she said. "If we are no more seen then Gaius Prospero is foolish enough to believe we are afraid of him. He has sent us safe passage, and so I will show you more of the City today. And before we depart I will take you to the tournament field where my father won his admittance into the Crusader Knights."

"Will you see John Swiftsword again?" Magnus asked his wife.

Lara sighed. "I do not know," she said. "I am still upset that my brothers do not know of my existence. What point is there to seeing my father again?"

"Perhaps it would comfort him to know that you truly hold no malice toward him for all that has happened to you over these last years. Your words yesterday appeared to give him food for thought. And I do not believe he is a man who often thinks beyond what he has been told by those he accepts as authority."

"I will send a message to him," Lara said. "If he would see me before we leave then I will go to him."

To her surprise her father came himself to the inn that afternoon just as they had returned from walking about the City. Honored to have such a fabled member of the Crusader Knights in his house, the innkeeper invited them into his garden, bringing wine and other refreshments of a much better quality than they had previously seen. Then he reluctantly withdrew.

"What does Gaius Prospero want of you, Daughter?" Lara's father asked.

"Nothing, it would seem. He was simply curious," she answered.

John Swiftsword nodded. "Tell me in detail what happened to you from the morning you were taken from my house," he said to her.

"Very well," Lara answered him, and then she began to speak.

"You were very brave," her father noted as she told of her escape from the Forest Kingdom. "And clever to make a friend of the giant."

"I became friends with him because we were both outsiders," Lara said. "In the beginning I despaired of ever knowing happiness again. It was only when Og told me how my grandmother had cursed the forest folk, and what it was they wanted of me, that I thought to flee." She continued on with her tale, and he listened.

"The Shadow Princes are a part of Hetar, and yet they go their own way," John Swiftsword observed as she told him of her time in the desert.

"They are men of great ethic and intellect," Lara replied. "And their magic is wondrous. I believe those who rule Hetar respect that, and they are wise to do so."

"And they reunited you with your mother?" he asked.

"Yes."

"She told you all?" he queried.

"Yes," Lara replied.

"And you do not hate me?" he said softly.

"You were a boy, Father. And your nature is a weak one, I fear," Lara said.

He laughed ruefully. "Aye, it is," he admitted to her.

"Your path is yours, and mine is mine," Lara told him. "You were a good father to me while I was in your care. I love you. There is no ill will in my heart toward you." She continued on with her adventures in the Outlands. She told him of Vartan, her first husband, the great Lord of the Fiacre. "You have two grandchildren, a boy and a girl. I will not tell you their names lest you tell someone you should not," she said. "I am sorry, but the times in which we live bid me to caution."

"And then you went to Terah?" her father said.

Lara told him of Vartan's death and how she had learned it was a political assassination arranged by Gaius Prospero.

"I do not understand why the emperor would do

such a thing," John Swiftsword said wearily. Almost everything she had told him was in conflict with what he had been told, or heard, or had spent his life believing. This was his daughter, and yet she was a stranger to him. His daughter had never lied. But could this woman lie? Was she lying now? It was all very confusing to him. He was a man who functioned best in a controlled environment such as the world of Hetar had always been. Until now.

"Gaius Prospero believed in his ignorance that without Vartan, the strong union of Outlands clan families would disintegrate. It was not so, of course. But he planned even then to invade the Outlands again."

"The Outlands belong to Hetar, Lara," her father said. "We are only taking back what is rightfully ours. We will bring civilization and a better way of life to those people now living there. Hetar is a great world."

"I cannot believe you believe what you are saying, Father!" Lara cried. "You know perfectly well that until recently, nothing was said of the Outlands but that it was a savage place peopled by barbarians. Hetar needs room to expand, and they think to take the Outlands."

"Will they fight?" her father asked her.

"They are a people with a long history of independence," Lara told him.

"We will win," he said. "It will not be like last time when we were caught unawares," John Swiftsword told his daughter. Then he looked carefully at her. "Were you…" he began. "Did you…?" He could not finish the question.

"Did I partake in the Winter War? Yes, Father, I did. We killed many Mercenary soldiers, Andraste and I. She sings when she fights, you know. It can be quite chilling to hear her deep, dark voice above the mayhem of battle. The last man I fought, I spared, because I recognized the son of Mistress Mildred."

"Wilmot. I remember him. A good man. You say he and his mother are safe?"

"They are with the Shadow Princes, and very well," she assured him.

"Where will you go now, Lara?" her father asked her.

"Home to Terah," she told him. He did not need to know their travel plans. She could not be certain he was not spying for Gaius Prospero. Well, she had told him nothing the emperor did not already know.

Magnus Hauk listened to the conversation between father and daughter. He realized that he felt sorry for his father-in-law. John Swiftsword was a decent man, but as he had himself admitted, he was weak. Magnus could see that Lara's tale of her adventures had disconcerted and even bewildered him. He had trusted the daughter he once knew, but he was not certain he could trust this daughter before him now. The Dominus decided to give the Hetarian something on which he could depend.

"John," he said quietly, "I want you to know that I love Lara. I will keep her safe as long as I live. She is already beloved in Terah for removing the curse of Usi from our menfolk. You can be proud of her."

The confusion left the older man's eyes. "I am glad

my daughter has been so fortunate in her husband," he said. "Are you really the ruler of Terah?"

"I am. My title is Dominus, and Lara's is Domina," Magnus answered with a smile. "We do not keep a court, however. We are a simple people."

John Swiftsword nodded in agreement. "I do not enjoy the grandiose, although my wife would take to it if offered." He stood. "I think it best that I go now. Susanna will wonder where I have gotten to for she worries that anything should happen to me."

"What would happen to her if it did, Father?" Lara asked him, curious to learn the answer. "Is it like the Guild of Mercenaries?"

"Only partly," he said. "If I were dead she would be moved to a smaller home again, but she would otherwise live quite comfortably for the rest of her days. And our sons, too. I regret that you did not get to meet them, Lara."

"Your wife has not even told them of my existence," Lara said softly. "Not even Mikhail whom I cradled and cared for as a girl."

He flushed at her rebuke. "I am sorry, Daughter," he said.

Immediately Lara felt remorse for her words. "Nay, Father, I understand Susanna's motives. She has four sons to consider, and I am not her child."

"But you are *my* child," he said with a show of spirit.

Lara smiled at him. "In the Outlands I was called Lara, daughter of Swiftsword," she told him. "And I have always been proud to be your child." Standing on her toes she kissed his cheek. "Goodbye, Father. I do not know if we will meet again."

Quick tears filled his eyes, and he blinked them away. "Goodbye, Lara," he said.

Then he turned, and gave his hand to Magnus Hauk. "Keep her safe, my lord," he told the Dominus. "She is my only daughter, and her mother's memory still lives within me." Then turning, John Swiftsword departed the garden where they had sat.

Magnus Hauk put his arms about his wife. "He is a good man, Lara."

"I know," she answered him. "But he is Hetarian. I have confused him with my tale. Once we are parted a short time, however, he will once again believe what he is told by Gaius Prospero and his ilk, because it is comfortable to believe it. Believing it will not threaten his status, or endanger his wife and sons. His loyalty will always be to Hetar first," she said sadly. "I am glad you agreed to take in the Outlands families, Magnus. At least there will be no bloodshed, and I know my father will not die this time."

"This emperor is a wily fellow," Magnus said thoughtfully. "And he desires you, wife. Are you aware of that?"

Lara laughed. "Gaius Prospero is simply greedy for the finest that life has to offer, no matter what it is. It is his advisor, Jonah, who is truly dangerous. One day Gaius Prospero will discover that to his detriment."

The innkeeper hurried into the garden. "My lady, I did not realize that you were the daughter of a Crusader Knight," he said. "Why did you not say so when you arrived? I am honored to have you in my house.

I remember the great stir you caused several years back among the Pleasure Guilds. But forgive me— the emperor has sent a message, and a litter for you." He handed her the small rolled parchment.

"Tell the litter bearers to return to their master," Lara said as she opened the message from Gaius Prospero, and perused it.

The innkeeper stared openmouthed in surprise at her. She was refusing the emperor's command?

"Go!" Lara told him impatiently, and he hurried off.

"What does he want?" Magnus asked her.

"To see me privately on a matter of interest, he writes," Lara replied.

"You don't intend to go?" her husband queried her.

"I will go, but I will use my own means of transport," Lara told him. "I see I have not yet instilled in Gaius Prospero the proper amount of respect for who I am and what I have become. It is time that I did that. Come, my lord, I must fetch Andraste."

They returned to their chamber, and Lara changed from the simple gown she was wearing into her leather trousers and silk shirt. She slipped her doeskin vest with the silver edged horn buttons on, and then calling Andraste from the shadows put the leather scabbard across her chest. The sword with its woman's head peered over her left shoulder. Then she drew on her leather boots. "Am I suitably intimidating?" she asked her husband with a small smile.

"He lusts after you," Magnus said. "There is nothing you can do to prevent that."

"It is not his lust that concerns me," Lara said. "I

want him to be afraid of me, my lord husband. So afraid that he will consider well the folly of attempting to seek out Terah at any time in the near future." She kissed him, and with a smile disappeared from his sight in a small mist of mauve.

GAIUS PROSPERO looked up from the table where he had been going over the invoices concerning new merchandise just received in his warehouses. Lara was standing before him, observing him. "I did not hear you come in," he said. "You were not announced." He stood up and came toward her.

Lara held up her hand, and he found his progress impeded. "You will not come any closer, my lord," she said to him. "I returned your litter and came by my own means of transport, magic. I shall depart the same way. What do you want of me, Gaius Prospero?" She lowered her hand, but he found he still could not move toward her.

"You had no magic, or claimed to have none when you left the City," he said. "Now it would appear that your mother's blood flows hot in your veins, Lara." He gave her a weak smile, for the truth be known, he found himself a little nervous in her presence now. Still he could not resist speaking with her one more time. Without Jonah hovering near his elbow. Without Vilia and Anora leaning forward to catch every word he spoke to the beauteous faerie woman.

"Why have you sought to see me again, my lord? What is it you want of me?" she repeated. "Tomorrow I mean to depart Hetar. I doubt I shall ever return."

"You are Hetarian," he said. "You are everything

that is good about Hetar. You are beautiful, strong, intelligent and wise, Lara, daughter of Swiftsword. Return to Hetar, and I will place you at the pinnacle of power."

"And where is that?" she asked him mockingly.

"By my side, as my empress," he said.

Lara laughed, but it was a cold sound. "Gaius Prospero, I have power of my own. I do not need yours. I have faerie power, which is stronger than any power you could offer me. I am the Domina of Terah. I am loved by a great man, Magnus Hauk. When you killed Vartan of the Fiacre, were you driven more by your desire to annex the Outlands or your lust for me? You sought power first, and now that you have it you have decided you want me, too. Beware, my lord, for power, all power, is an illusion and illusions eventually fade away. I have a destiny to fulfill, Gaius Prospero. I do not believe you will play a great role in that destiny."

"Foolish woman, do you not realize what it is I offer you?" he demanded, and attempted to move toward her again.

Andraste began to hum softly in Lara ear. "Show him your power," the spirit in the sword told her.

Lara drew the weapon forth, holding it before her. "My magic is protecting you from your own folly, Gaius Prospero. Were you able to approach me I should be forced to slay you for your insolence. Listen, and Andraste will sing for you. It is a song usually heard only by those about to feel the kiss of her sharp blade. It was heard by those I fought and slew in the Winter War."

He could see the sword's jeweled eyes opening, and then Gaius Prospero heard the dark voice as it began to sing.

"I am Andraste, and I drink the blood of the traitor, the betrayer, the foolish who cannot see the truth! Fear me, Gaius Prospero, and pray to your god that we never meet in battle, for if we do I will sup upon your very essence!"

The color drained from Gaius Prospero's plump face. His legs felt weak beneath him. "You have killed?" he said in a terrified voice, looking directly at Lara.

"Did you not put about the rumor that I had, my lord?" Lara mocked him. "Well, 'tis truth. I took the head of Durga, once Head Forester, from his thick shoulders when through bribery he attempted to subvert Hetar's laws. He was my first kill. I slew Mercenaries in the Winter War who at your bidding had invaded the lands of the Tormod and the Piaras, enslaving its people, stealing its wealth. And when Adon killed my husband, Vartan, I slew both him and his stupid wife without mercy. Yes, Gaius Prospero, I wield this sword with skill, and I am not afraid to kill with it. I am not the girl you sold off eight years ago while complaining your profit was not enough. I am Lara, Domina of Terah, daughter of Ilona, queen of the Forest Faeries. I fear neither you nor the might of Hetar. You insult me with your suggestions. You betray your wife, Vilia, who has been devoted to you. As for that pretty creature you call your second wife, I know her not. But you do her an injustice asking me to stand by your side and be your empress. Both your women deserve better of you."

"But Lara," Gaius wheedled, "I wish only to honor your beauty with my fervent admiration."

"Lustful man! Do you want to know what it is like to take pleasures with me? I can show you within the cavern of your mind what it would be like. But if I do, be warned that no woman will ever give you satisfaction again, my lord. Are you foolish enough to seek a moment's pleasure for a lifetime of emptiness?" Her green eyes blazed.

He wanted her. He had always wanted her, but he had not taken her when he purchased her from her father because half of her value was in her innocence then. But now it was different. He burned to possess her. "Yes! Yes!" he gasped. "Show me!"

"If I do," she cautioned him a second time, "you will never know pleasures with another woman again. Oh, you will couple, but you will feel nothing, Gaius Prospero. This will be my punishment for your presumption."

"Show me!" His voice grated harshly. Suddenly he was naked and vulnerable to her. He felt her hands on him, stroking his nakedness, fondling his love rod, cupping his seed sacs in the warmth of her palm. He felt the full swell of her beautiful breasts against him; her hard nipples pushing into his chest. Felt the press of her body against his body. Yet he could not move. He was drowning in sensation as he felt her tongue licking every inch of him, sucking upon his nipples, his rod. He tasted her nipples in his mouth, and he sucked hungrily, aching as his need rose like a fever within him. He felt himself being sheathed within the hot swamp of her. Gaius Prospero moaned with his desperation, for while he felt everything a man would feel while taking pleasures with a woman, Lara stood directly before him, a cold smile upon her lips. Helplessly he savored love's rhythm as its tempo increased with each stroke of his manhood. His eyes closed with the incredible pleasure he was experiencing. Again and again he thrust, and thrust, and thrust until his crisis could not be denied. It was perfect. And then he felt himself spilling his seed in great spurts that seemed endless. He groaned, for it was almost painful. Finally it was over, and he opened his eyes to find Lara was gone. He was alone. He was fully clothed, and the front of his long tunic was soaked with the remnants of his lust. Gaius Prospero collapsed onto the marble floor sobbing.

What had he done? Her faerie magic had offered him paradise only to snatch it away. She would pay for her cruelty, he vowed. She would pay! And one day he would put her beneath him, and know in reality the bliss she had shown him this night within his mind. She would give him the pleasures he wanted from her, or he would kill her. Gaius Prospero slowly began to regain control of himself. Pulling himself into a seated position he considered the possibility of sending his guards to the inn where she stayed, arresting her and having her husband slain.

No. Her faerie power was too strong now. He would be patient, and he would find a way to destroy her power. Then he would seek out this Terah and conquer it. She would be his slave once again, and he would make her watch while he had her husband tortured and killed before her beautiful green eyes. Gaius Prospero smiled to himself. If she had daughters, he would give them to his Mercenaries and make her watch while they were violated. He would neuter her sons. And then he would bring her back to Hetar to serve him for all of her days. Faerie women lived long lives. Gaius Prospero climbed to his feet, and walked slowly from the chamber, his thoughts of revenge warming him.

Lara had watched him from behind her cloak of invisibility as he recovered himself. She sensed the darkness within and surrounding Gaius Prospero. He had always been her enemy, she knew, and now he knew it, as well. But he was unlikely to find Terah soon without help. She was weary with her efforts to punish him, and with her remaining strength she transported herself back to their room at the inn.

"I was growing worried," Magnus said, coming to put his arms about her. "You are cold, my faerie love. What has happened? What did Gaius Prospero want?"

"Me," Lara told him. "He wants me to be his empress," she said. "I punished him for his presumption." Her legs gave out beneath her.

"I will put you to bed," he said.

"Nay, we are no longer safe here," Lara replied. "Gaius Prospero can be unpredictable when denied. I have not the strength to take us away right now. We must leave the inn, however, and ask refuge of the Shadow Princes in the Council Quarter. In the morning my full strength will have returned."

"What did you do, Lara?" he asked her warily.

She laughed weakly. "I will tell you when I feel we are safe," she said. "Put me down, Magnus. I can stand now."

He set her on her feet and fetched their cloaks. Putting them on they left several large coins upon the table for the innkeeper. Andraste still on her back, Lara took Verica from the corner and they slipped from the chamber, down the darkened corridor and out onto the busy street. It seemed, Lara noted, that the City was never silent for even a few hours anymore. Across the thoroughfare the gates to the Council Quarter were already closed. A single guard slept on a stool nearby. Lara put a gentle hand on the man, and he sunk into a deeper sleep. She raised her hand to the gates, and they opened wide enough so she and Magnus could slip through. Then they closed again, and Magnus heard the click of the gates' locks behind them.

"I thought you had no powers left," he said to his wife.

"I am drained, but not completely," she told him as she led him into the building housing the province representatives of the High Council. "The Shadow Princes live on the top floor," she said as they began to climb the central staircase. Reaching the top of the building Lara knocked upon the door. It opened.

"Lothair!" she exclaimed. "Magnus, this is Lothair who was one of my teachers. He taught me how to fight!"

"I had heard you were in the City," Lothair said ushering them into his quarters, "but I had not expected to see you."

"Offer us some wine, and I will tell you everything," Lara said.

"Your companion?" Lothair pressed gently.

"Oh." Lara flushed with her embarrassment. "Lothair, this is my husband, Magnus Hauk, the Dominus of Terah."

The two men shook hands, each giving the other an amused look. The Shadow Prince settled them in a comfortable room overlooking the gardens below. He brought the wine, and sat down with them. "Tell me," he said.

Lara related the visit to the City. "I'm sure Kaliq has told you everything else," she said, and he nodded.

"So the emperor asked to see you tonight?"

"Aye. He declared he wanted me as his empress. That he would give me power such as I had never had." She laughed, continuing her tale. When she reached the point where she told them of the illusion she had given Gaius Prospero both men looked disturbed. "What is the matter?" she asked them.

"Until now you have used your growing powers wisely," Lothair said. "Tonight, however, you were possessed by the tiny streak of wickedness that lives in all those with faerie blood. You were cruel, and cruelty is a language the emperor understands all too well. He will want to repay your cruelty in kind. You have made an enemy of Gaius Prospero when you did not have to make an enemy of him at all."

"He offended me," Lara said coldly.

"He offends most people," Lothair replied, "but they do not give him the illusion that he is experiencing sexual pleasure and intense gratification only to find himself on the floor with seed-spattered garments, Lara."

"He had the choice to refuse me," she said stubbornly. "I warned him he would never know pleasures again with other women if he took the path he took."

"The fool lusts after you," Lothair answered her. "Of course he would take the path you offered him." He laughed. "It really was most inventive and wicked of you."

"I do not find it amusing at all," Magnus said stiffly. "It disturbs me to learn that Gaius Prospero believes he has known my wife."

"Magnus!" Lara cried. "He was across the room from me the whole interview. He never even touched my hand. He knows nothing of me. He only believes he does. But do not all men imagine what pleasures would be like with women they desire?"

"You are my wife. You are the Domina of Terah," Magnus Hauk said icily.

"You are being childish," Lara told him.

"And you were wanton," he snapped.

"Next you will say it is my faerie blood. That all faeries are licentious," Lara said.

The Shadow Prince quickly froze the scene in place before Magnus Hauk might say something he was going to very much regret. The poor man was hopelessly in love with his wife, and mortals had the ability to ruin their own happiness when their foolish tongues ran away with them. "Lara," he said to her knowing only she could hear him. "Apologize to your husband before this quarrel escalates into something dangerous. What you did was amusing to those of us with magical powers, but your husband cannot understand the humor in it. It was also witless. You have now made this Hetarian emperor an enemy. Gaius Prospero is not a man to forget an insult.

"He will not be content until he finds Terah now. Would it not have been simpler to kill him?" Lothair concluded dryly.

Tears filled her eyes, and he released her from the quick spell. "I have acted stupidly, but when I saw that creature who once sold me into slavery, the lust so open in his eyes, I could not help myself, Lothair."

"Apologize to your husband, and end this discord between you, Lara. We will need him again one day. He has done us a great service by taking in the Outlands clan families," Lothair said quietly. "Magnus Hauk loves you, Lara. It is a pure and true love. Do not, in your pride, fling such a gift away."

"Erase his memory of what came after he said I was his wife, and Domina of Terah," she requested. "I will apologize, and my faerie blood will not be in question."

"It is done," Lothair told her.

"You are my wife, and Domina of Terah," Magnus said icily.

"You are right, my lord husband," Lara replied. "I acted foolishly, and I regret it."

Magnus put his arms about her. "Lara, my faerie love, it is forgotten, and you will forgive my jealousy, will you not?"

"Your jealousy is rather flattering," Lara murmured, looking over her husband's shoulder at Lothair, who shook a playful finger at her.

Then the Shadow Prince said, "I think you will both be safer if I send you to Kaliq's palace in our desert realm. If the emperor sends to the inn and you are found gone he will assume your faerie power took you both away. No one saw you leave?"

"Nay. The innkeeper was busy in his taproom with the many revelers," Lara said. "Does the City no longer rest, Lothair? Or have I forgotten what it was like?"

"Once the nights were silent after the eleventh hour, but no more," he responded. "It is so crowded that people rent their beds for just a few hours at a time so they may sleep. Many lack homes to go to now. And there is a new evil among the poor. It is call Razi. When put into frine it offers dreams, some beautiful, some horrific. One never knows which will ensue, I am told. It is sold quite legally and cheaply at what are called Razi kiosks. I understand that the emperor's man, Jonah, owns quite a few of these kiosks. Dreaming helps to keep the poor from rebellion and offers them an escape from the hopelessness and drudgery of their lives. And the kiosks are open all day and all night for the convenience of their customers."

Lara sighed. "Lothair, what will happen to Hetar?"

He shrugged. "I do not know," he said.

"Perhaps now would be a good time to go," Magnus said quietly. He could see that Lara was very distressed by the state of things in Hetar. It would be best to take her away from the cause of her misery.

Lothair nodded. "I will go with you," he said. "There are no meetings of the High Council scheduled for the present. In fact, we scarcely meet at all these days. I suspect the High Council is retained only to give the appearance that everything is as it has always been. Lara, we are going to Shunnar now." And he waved his hand in a languorous fashion.

Magnus put his arm about Lara, and just briefly he felt as if his body had turned to flowing liquid. Then he found himself in a wide hallway, open on one side that was colonnaded, and had a waist-high balustrade. Lara sagged against him. She was suddenly very tired.

"I will find my brother," Lothair said.

"You do not have to," Kaliq said coming from the duskiness of the long corridor.

"Welcome to Shunnar, my lord Dominus. A servant will take you to your quarters, and in the morning we will speak. I can see Lara is exhausted. Was your visit to Hetar so hard?"

"We have to talk," Lothair said with a small smile. "Lara has tired herself in a most wicked and foolish feat. But she now sees the error of her ways."

A serving man was at Magnus's side. "If you will come this way, my lord," he invited.

The Dominus picked his wife up and carried her off. They were safe now.

"What did she do?" Kaliq asked as he and Lothair stood looking over the green moonlit valley below.

"Her powers have truly grown, Brother. But she must learn to control them better. The emperor declared himself, and offered her a place by his side.

Lara was offended for a variety of reasons. She delved into his mind and allowed him to know what it would be like to take pleasures with her, because she told him he never really would. To be fair, she did give him the choice of not knowing, and warned him that if he accepted her offer he would never again know satisfaction with another woman."

"And of course Gaius Prospero greedily took her offer, and will now suffer for it. That Hetar should be governed by such a fool!" Kaliq exclaimed angrily. "We will need Ilona to come and speak with her daughter. To advise Lara on the more careful use of her powers. It would appear her faerie blood runs stronger than her mortal blood now."

"It was cruelly done," Lothair said, and then he could not refrain from chuckling. "Can you imagine the agonies this emperor of ours will suffer over what has happened this night? It will certainly not make him any easier to control. But that she could do it, Kaliq! And she is not even all faerie, my brother!"

"Which is why Ilona must speak with her. Tonight Lara veered toward the darkness. It is the first time I have known it to happen. And it must not happen again," Kaliq said seriously. And then he, too, chuckled. "Aye, it was clever of her."

The serving man came and stood by his master's side waiting to be recognized, and when he was the man said, "They are settled, my lord Prince."

Kaliq nodded, and the servant left him. "I want to speak to Lara first," he told Lothair. "Will you remain with us? On the morrow you will entertain the Dominus, and show him our valley while I deal with our naughty faerie woman."

"Call me when you want me," Lothair said. "I will be in my own palace tonight." Then he was gone.

Kaliq found his own chamber and slept for but a few hours. In the hour just before the dawn he awakened, bathed, dressed and then called out to Ilona.

She appeared with her son, Cirilo, by her side. "Greetings, Kaliq of the Shadows," she said. "My daughter is here, I know. Her brother wanted to see her. Where is she?"

"She and her husband yet sleep," Kaliq answered. "Cirilo, my lad, go and find the giant, Og, and have him take you to the valley of horses. When Lara is awake I will have Og bring you back. I need to speak with your mother now."

"Has my sister been naughty?" the boy asked with excellent instinct.

Kaliq chuckled. "Yes, but it is not for you to involve yourself. Go to Og."

"Yes, my lord," Cirilo said. He was a handsome little boy of seven, with his parents' fair golden hair and his father's deep blue eyes. With a smile he ran off.

"Come," Kaliq said, inviting Ilona to a table overlooking the valley. "Let us break our fast while we talk." He seated her and offered her a bowl of fruit.

"What has Lara done?" Ilona wanted to know, plucking a small bunch of green grapes from the bowl.

"Her powers are increasing greatly, as we knew they one day would," Kaliq said. Then he explained to the queen of the Forest Faeries what Lara had done to Gaius Prospero the previous evening.

"He probably deserved it," Ilona said, secretly proud of her daughter.

"She must learn better to control her emotions when she uses her powers," Kaliq said. "Unless she does she could easily slip into the darkness, Ilona. You know it is always there, waiting, watching."

Ilona sighed. "That is her mortal side, I fear. Mortal souls are easily taken into the darkness, Kaliq. Her faerie powers may be growing, but she is still half-mortal."

"I cannot disagree," he answered, "but she must learn to control herself. She has made an enemy of the emperor when she might have simply ignored him."

"He would never forget her, my lord, even if she had not given him a glimpse of paradise. Gaius Prospero will always desire Lara. Only his death can end it. But then there would be a vacuum in the power base of Hetar," she said. "And it is not time yet for the change, is it?"

"Will you speak with her, Ilona," Kaliq said. "Will you teach her how to control her mortal emotions?"

"Yes," Ilona said quietly. "Now tell me of her husband? Does she love him?"

Kaliq nodded. "More passionately than she did Vartan, and the Dominus is completely distracted by his love for her."

"Is he a strong man?" Ilona wanted to know. "Or is he one of those namby-pamby mortals we faeries love more often than not?"

"He is strong, and rules over much territory. He

gave some of that land to the Outlands clan families, and with Lara's aid we have transported them in their entirety from Hetar. The armies of Gaius Prospero will be met with empty territory. No villages, no flocks or herds, no people. Even the mines that the Tormod and Piaras once worked have been sealed over with ancient growth. Hetar will find nothing but the land. They will have to begin afresh, and it will cost them the instant profits they had hoped to reap from this violation of the old treaties."

Ilona smiled as she sipped her morning frine. "And so my daughter's destiny proceeds exactly as it should," she noted. "No, we cannot allow her to be lost to the darkness, Kaliq. It is time for me to be Lara's mother once again."

Chapter
16

LARA AWOKE to find her husband stroking her naked body. "Umm," she murmured, and rolled over to face him. "Good morning, my lord."

He leaned forward, and kissed her lips. "Good morning, my love," he greeted her.

Then pushing her onto her back he kissed her again, slowly this time, his hands continuing to caress her. His tongue began a leisurely exploration of first one nipple and breast, and then the other. His fingers trailed down her silken torso, running suggestively along her shadowed slit, slipping between her nether lips to tease at the kernel of her sex. "Wicked creature, you are already wet with your lust," he scolded her, amused. Two fingers pushed slowly into her, growing still, letting her sense their denseness. "Shall this be all?" he asked softly, his tongue tracing the whorl of her ear as he whispered hotly.

"No!" she replied.

"Tell me what you want, Lara?" He tortured her gently, the fingers moving just slightly within her.

"You! Inside me!" she half gasped. The delicate sensations his fingers were engendering within her were both terrible and wonderful.

"I do not know," he said, "if you deserve my attentions, wife. I think you need to be punished for your actions last night." His lips were close to hers again.

"Magnus! I remember nothing of last night. Only that you love me," she said.

He swung his body over her, his manhood rubbing against her suggestively; watching the play of emotions across her face as she anticipated his next move. He pushed the tip of his lance just within her, and stopped.

Lara gasped a second time. She was burning with her desire to be possessed by this man, her husband. "Magnus, please," she said.

"What do you think he thought when he imagined himself where I now am?" the Dominus asked. "Was he able to enjoy the anticipation of having you completely? Or did he just thrust into you like the pig he is, and greedily enjoy his pleasures?"

"You are jealous for no reason," Lara managed to say. "He knows nothing of me. Not really. He never will!"

"Aye," Magnus Hauk's deep voice ground out. "I am jealous! But he will never have you, Lara! I would kill you first!" Then he drove himself deep within her over and over again until they were both moaning with the pleasures they were sharing. And finally they were satisfied with each other, and they lay gasping upon their backs like two beached turtles.

Lara recovered first, and leaning over him she said but two words. "Only you."

Reaching up he pulled her down so that their lips met in a burning kiss, but he said nothing more.

A small tap on the door of their bedchamber startled them both. A voice called out, "Are you awake?" as the door opened. Magnus Hauk stared in amazement at the woman in the doorway, then turned to look at his wife.

"Mother!" Lara slipped naked from the bed, and ran to embrace her parent.

"Darling Lara," Ilona responded, hugging and kissing her daughter. Then her eyes turned back to the bed. "He is most suitable, daughter," she said, her bold stare sweeping over the startled man. "And so nicely endowed, you fortunate creature."

Hearing her words the Dominus realized that all of his body was visible to this copy of his wife. He flushed, and pulled the coverlet over his tired loins.

"Put something on, Lara, we must speak," Ilona said imperiously. "Kaliq tells me your powers have grown stronger, but that you have used them unwisely. Having faerie powers entails first a sense of responsibility." Her gaze caught that of the Dominus. "Magnus, get dressed, too—I will speak with both of you on this matter. I will await you in Kaliq's dining chamber. There is food, and I would imagine you are both very hungry." She flashed them a wicked smile before closing the door behind her.

Lara laughed softly at the stunned look on her husband's handsome face. "Let us hurry and bathe. She is not particularly patient. There can be no water games, my lord."

They bathed in the small room attached to their bedchamber, dressed, and then Lara, who remembered Kaliq's palace well, led her husband to the dining area, which overlooked some small gardens. They found both the prince and Ilona there, engaged in a spirited conversation. Their host waved them to their seats, and at once servants appeared to offer them fresh bread, fruit, yogurt, cheese, hard-boiled eggs and salted meat. There was cool, freshly squeezed juice poured into their goblets, and the Dominus wondered just how it was kept cold in this very warm dry climate. He and Lara ate, waiting for Ilona to speak to them.

Lara's lips twitched with amusement, but she said nothing.

Magnus Hauk studied his mother-in-law. She might be the queen of the Forest Faeries, but he was the Dominus of Terah. Why was he nervous? Probably because she had caught him at a disadvantage, and he had seen she had enjoyed it. She looked like Lara, and yet she was different. Upon closer examination he realized that being pure faerie, Ilona's features were sharper while his wife's mortal blood made her features softer. He decided Lara was the more beautiful of the two, and when the thought entered his brain Ilona suddenly looked directly at him. Then she smiled a quick smile before turning back to Kaliq.

A boy came into the room and put his arms about Lara's neck, kissing her on the cheek. Turning her head she smiled at him. "Cirilo! Let me look at you, little brother. My, you have grown taller, and you are going to be a very handsome man."

"And you will soon outstrip our mother with your beauty, elder sister," Cirilo replied. "I have been with your giant, Og, in the valley of the horses. What glorious creatures they are! And how is your new husband?" The boy turned to look at Magnus.

"Greetings, my young prince," Magnus said, nodding his head toward the boy. "I am well."

"Do you love my sister?" Cirilo asked bluntly.

"With all my heart," Magnus answered.

"Then I greet you in friendship, lord Dominus," the boy replied. Taking a seat next to his mother he allowed the servants to fill his plate, and he set to eating.

"He's a beautiful child," Magnus noted. "Will you give me a son like that? All golden with jeweled eyes?"

"One day I will give you a son," she replied. "But as for what he will look like, that is up to the Great Creator, isn't it?"

"I am glad you have him," Magnus said. "I know it does not make up for the loss of your father's sons, but this lad is more like you than they could be."

"I did not miss the younger sons that Susanna gave my father after I left. It is Mikhail, the little boy I knew, the eldest of them that I regret. I stood at my stepmother's side and held her hand when he was born. I was there to hear his first cry. He was too small when I left the City to remember me on his own, but could not my father and his wife have spoken of me, and kept my fragile memory alive in my brother? What harm was there in speaking to him of me? It was my sacrifice that put my father on the road to his success. It is that I for which I can never forgive Susanna, Magnus."

"Foolish girl!" Ilona said. "I see Swiftsword has not changed a great deal since his youth. He was a charming fellow, a wonderful lover and a brilliant swordsman, but his will was easily led, and obviously still is. Yet it is what makes him a good Crusader Knight. He is a man who will always follow the orders of a superior. He will never question anything. Put him, his jealous mortal of a wife and their mortal offspring from your mind, Lara. It is unlikely you will ever have anything to do with them again. They have nothing to offer you. Neither love, nor loyalty, daughter. It was your father's strong seed that helped create you, Lara, but you are my child before you are his, as you have discovered in the last months. Cirilo and I love you. And your great brute of a husband loves you. You do seem to like them extra large," she noted wryly.

"I know you are right, Mother," Lara replied. "And yet…"

"Put it from you!" Ilona said impatiently. "We have important matters to discuss, my daughter. Kaliq has told me what you did to Gaius Prospero. It was very, very foolish." She shook her golden head with her disapproval.

"But wonderfully clever," Cirilo piped up, and then quickly lowered his head to his breakfast at his mother's angry and silent reprimand. His cheeks were red with her admonishment, but Lara caught his eye and winked at him. Cirilo felt much better at his sister's encouragement.

Ilona hid her smile. She was pleased to see her eldest born bonding with her youngest. That bond would one day be important to them both. Then she spoke to her daughter. "The powers that grow in you are more than most half-faerie, half-mortal beings have. This was foretold before your birth. Mortal blood runs in your veins, Lara, but you will have full faerie powers before long. But with those powers comes responsibility. You must exercise your powers only for good. If you do not you will be lured into the darkness, and your powers corrupted. The sorcerer you vanquished was like you, Lara, half-mortal and half-faerie. He was to bring greatness to the Brotherhood of the Great Creator. Instead he was drawn into the darkness, and Terah suffered cruelly under his rule. Only a creature like you, Lara, could have lifted the curse of Usi, and freed the Terahn people of his influence."

"Is that why I was brought to Terah?" Lara asked her parent.

"Partly," Ilona said. "Now promise me, my daughter, that you will never again use your powers for evil as you did the other night. I do not say Gaius Prospero doesn't deserve to be punished, for he does, but time will take care of him, I promise you. You are meant for other and greater things. You must not be corrupted as Usi was."

"Every time we meet you refer to a destiny for me," Lara said impatiently.

"First your promise, daughter," Ilona said refusing to be turned from her point.

"Of course I will promise you, Mother. I will never again allow my anger to rule my magic. Now let us get back to my destiny." Lara looked directly at her mother.

"It is unfolding in its own time and manner," Ilona said sweetly.

Lara laughed. "You will tell me no more, will you?" she said.

"To tell you would change your destiny, my dearest daughter," Ilona replied with indisputable logic.

"Very well, Mother, I shall not quarrel with you over it," Lara responded.

Ilona lowered her voice. "Your place will always be in Terah," she told Lara.

"That does not mean you will not be gone from there now and again, but Terah is your home, my daughter. Remember that. You will draw more strength from that land than from anywhere else."

"And Magnus? Will he meet Vartan's end, Mother?"

"Nay, he will not," Ilona said softly. "Now be satisfied, Lara. I have said all I came to say, and Cirilo and I must return to the forest—or what remains of it."

"What do you mean?" Lara wanted to know.

"The forest is being cut down section by section to supply wood for building. The area around the villages of the Forest Lords is being left, but bit by bit they are destroying the woodlands. It was suggested by the Head Forester that the government replant where they take trees, but the emperor has decided that it would take from his profit so he will not do it. They have not yet reached the deepest part of the forest where we live, but in a few years they will," Ilona said.

"There are forests in Terah," Magnus Hauk said. "Bring your faerie folk and live with us," he invited.

"You have your own faerie clans," Ilona said.

"If we do, we do not know them," the Dominus replied, "and they cannot have all of our forests. Can you not negotiate with them? The Tormod and the Piaras clan families have done so with the mountain gnomes for mining rights in the Emerald Mountains."

"We have always been a part of Hetar," Ilona replied slowly.

"But if your forest is gone can you still exist there?" Lara asked her mother. "Are not the trees and growing things a part of your strength and your heritage, Mother? If they are gone, then you will die. Please come to Terah."

"I will speak with my faerie folk," Ilona said, "but we are yet safe, my daughter."

"Do not wait too long, Ilona," the Dominus advised. "At least visit us, see what we can offer you and meet with your Terahn kindred."

"Terah is a very green land, Mother."

"I shall think on it," Ilona said. Then she asked, "Do your forests turn colors in the autumn season, Magnus Hauk?"

"They do," he responded.

"There are no cities?"

He shook his head. "My lands are so vast, and divided by the mountains that the people of the fjords have no knowledge of what lies beyond those mountains on the lands now inhabited by the Outland clans. Eventually the two will meet, but not yet."

Ilona nodded. "A vast green land," she said. "It is tempting, Magnus Hauk."

"Laaaaraaaa!" A great voice boomed through the palace.

"Oh," Cirilo said. "I told Og I would tell you he was waiting in the valley for you, Sister. I'm sorry I forgot."

Lara stood up. "I will go and greet my old friend then," she said. "Will you remain, Mother?" she asked her parent.

Ilona shook her head. "Nay, Cirilo and I must go home shortly. We will say our goodbyes now, my daughter." The two women embraced, and then Ilona said, "And you, Magnus Hauk, you have my blessing. Treat my daughter well."

Cirilo slipped his hand into his sister's. "I wish you lived with us," he said. "We would have such fun together, Sister. Tell Dillon and Anoush I send them my faerie blessing," the young faerie prince told her.

"I don't know when I will see them, Brother, but I will tell them," Lara said.

"You will see them soon," Cirilo told her.

Lara nodded, then she bent and kissed his smooth cheek. "I am glad you are my brother," she said softly. Then straightening up she looked to her husband. "Would you like to meet Og, Magnus?"

The Dominus rose from the table. He kissed Ilona on both of her cheeks, and shook Cirilo's hand.

Then with a friendly smile at them both he went off with Lara.

"A strong man," Ilona noted.

"He will need to be," Kaliq answered her.

Ilona nodded. "How dangerous will Gaius Prospero be, my old friend?"

"Not as dangerous as he thinks," Kaliq answered her. "And there is time for Terah. I have returned King Archeron to full health and sent him home, Ilona. Arcas will not be able to poison his father again. If he wishes power for himself he will have to take it in a more open manner, which could endanger his plans."

"Can Archeron stop the invasion of the Outlands?" Ilona wanted to know.

"Nay, it is too far gone now, and he has a large army camped on his beaches, ready to depart. I did reassure him that whatever happened, the Outlands clan families would be safe from harm, but asked him to delay the army of Gaius Prospero as much as he could without endangering himself. He trusts me, and will do his best."

"Arcas will not be happy," Ilona murmured, rising and beckoning to her son. "Come, Cirilo. I will return, Kaliq." She departed the dining chamber, and stopped to look over the balcony into the valley below. There she saw Lara and Magnus walking forth to greet Og the Giant. Ilona smiled as Og swung her daughter up, wishing she could hear the conversation.

"PUT ME DOWN, you great hulk," Lara said laughing, and leaning forward to kiss the giant's ruddy cheeks.

"My husband is a jealous man, Og, and I should like to introduce you two."

Og set her down, grinning broadly. "You have grown more beautiful, Lara," he told her. Then he turned, and held out his big hand to Magnus Hauk. "I greet you, my lord. You have my friendship, for Lara's new beauty surely comes from the love you have for her."

Magnus Hauk was a very large man, but he felt dwarfed by Og. He put his hand in the giant's, amazed at how small it suddenly looked. "I also greet you in friendship, Og, for my wife has told me of your great kindness to her, and how you saved her from the Forest Lords." To his relief the giant did not crush his hand, and the firm pressure was almost immediately released as their hands fell away from each other.

"Are you happy, Og?" Lara asked him. "Remember that where I am there will always be a home for you."

"I am happy," he said smiling down at her. "I have a fine wife, Alta. She was the largest girl among Zaki's people. She was so tall that her family despaired of ever finding her a mate for she stood higher than any man in the encampment. She is the daughter of Zaki's cousin. She is a good woman and has already given me two children, a son and a daughter. She keeps my house well, and we have come to love one another in the years we have been wed."

"Then I am content in that knowledge," Lara told him.

"And you found your destiny?" Og asked her.

"Not yet," Lara admitted. Then as they walked together in the green valley she told him of her adventures in the time since she had last seen him.

He nodded observing, "You have grown strong. You would have no need of a giant now to protect you. But then I knew that when you left Shunnar six years ago."

"Is that why you remained behind?" she asked him.

"Partly," he admitted. "But I am also not a giant who enjoys adventuring. Few of my kind do. We prefer an orderly life. I will be buried here in this valley one day. My master, Prince Kaliq, has promised it. Tell me of little Noss. Is she happy?"

"Yes," Lara said, and went on to tell him of Noss's life now.

Finally, as the sun was reaching the midday, Og said, "I must leave you now for I have my horses to look after." He bowed to the Dominus. "My lord, I do not have to tell you to take care of Lara, for I know you will."

Magnus Hauk nodded.

"I do not know if I will see you again before you depart," Og told Lara. He kissed her on both cheeks. "The Celestial Actuary guard and protect you, Lara." Then he turned and left them.

"I believe he loved you once as a man loves a woman," Magnus Hauk observed.

"Yes," Lara replied. "But it has changed now into the love between friends. I always knew, but I never let him know for I would not shame him, or give him false hope." She took her husband's hand. "Let us go back now, my lord."

ARCAS WAS NOT HAPPY. He had returned from the City to discover his father back in his palace, and seemingly in the best of health. And Archeron did not mince words with his only son.

"What have you done, you fool?" Archeron demanded. "You have brought Hetar into the kingdom, Arcas. What were you thinking of when you did that?"

"They are only using our beaches as a path for their invasion," Arcas said.

"They have eyes, fool! They have ears! What will they see? Our palaces, but no manufactories. Thanks to you, Gaius Prospero will soon ferret out the secret of the Coastal Kingdom. That we trade with a land called Terah. That they are the ones who supply us with the goods we sell to the Taubyl Traders."

"What difference does it make if they know?" Arcas said sulkily.

"What use will they have for us if they know, you fool? Gaius Prospero will leap upon the chance for new and greater profit. We have stood between Terah and Hetar, selling their goods, taking our profits. Now we will sooner than later lose that advantage to that greedy slug who calls himself emperor of Hetar. Our isolation from the City has been our salvation, Arcas, and you have thrown it away! We will become nothing more than a seaport through which Gaius Prospero builds a greater empire for himself. If I could send back those troops camping on our beaches I would. But I cannot."

"No, you cannot," Arcas sneered. "Soon enough they will march into the Outlands, father. Your friend,

Rendor of the Felan, will be the first to fall," he laughed.

Archeron stared coldly at his offspring. Prince Kaliq had promised that the Outlands clan families would not be harmed, and the Coastal King believed the prince. He had not explained further, but Archeron knew that was the way with magic. "Your mother would be so disappointed in you, Arcas," he said, and gained great satisfaction in seeing his son grow pale. "When this is over I am exiling you from the Coastal Kingdom. You are a traitor to us, and to Hetar. Now leave me!"

Arcas slunk from the chamber seething. His father had been close to death when the damned Shadow Princes had stepped into the situation and spirited Archeron off. He had had everyone convinced that Archeron was pining for his late wife. Well, let his father enjoy his last few days of glory. The emperor had promised an end to the Coastal Kings. Once the Outlands were secure they would be no more, and he, Arcas, would be appointed governor of the new Coastal province. Archeron and his fellow kings would have to accept what was happening or the emperor would have them executed. He walked down to the beach to join some of the Crusader Knights who were leading the invasion. They welcomed him, flattered him and offered him some of their wine. Arcas was an intimate of the emperor, and a man never knew when he would need a favor.

Two days later he rode with them as they entered the Outlands. They rode up from the beaches onto the plain, and it did not take Arcas long to realize he

could see no sheep grazing. The land stretched unblemished as far as the eye could see.

"How near is the first village?" the Commander
Knight asked him.

"We should already have reached it by now," Arcas
replied slowly. Something was wrong. Very wrong.

They rode on for the next three days, and in that
time they saw no herds, no Outlanders, no structures
of any kind. The Crusader Knights were becoming
confused, and the Mercenaries riding with them restless. They were deep into the Outlands now, and all
they could see was the great plain and the Purple
Mountains beyond. Where were the people? Where
were the villages? It was finally decided that the great
army would make an encampment and wait for further instructions. A faeriepost was sent to the emperor
in the City.

Jonah read the post before his master, as was his
custom. Odd, he thought. Were the Outlanders in
hiding, having been warned in advance of Hetar's
invasion? It was not impossible that they had learned
of it, and knowing they would not be able to overcome such a large force as Hetar was sending into
their territory, had hidden themselves. But if that was
so, where were the villages, and the animals? The
post clearly stated that there was nothing in the Outlands but a vast expanse of land. Jonah took the post
to Gaius Prospero, who read it and then looked to his
right hand.

"They must be mistaken."

"They have ridden for three full days, and Arcas
is with them," Jonah said.

"There is nothing?" Gaius Prospero looked slightly panicked. "No people? No herds? No planted fields of crops? We were told at least two of those clan families farmed great tracts of land, growing all manner of things. I have promised homes and slaves to our people."

"Do not agitate yourself, my good lord," Jonah said in his soothing voice. "We know there are folk in the Outlands. Perhaps they have hidden themselves in the mountains with the mining clans. Was not John Swiftsword chosen to lead that force? Before we give into our dismay, let us send him and his Mercenaries into the Purple Mountains. Hetar was there just a few years ago, and we know the villages, the people and the mines exist. I wager we will find the rest of the Outlands clan families there with their flocks and herds."

"But what of the missing villages?" Gaius Prospero babbled nervously.

"They probably burned them to spite us," Jonah reasoned.

"Yes, yes! Of course they did!" The emperor sounded relieved.

"And we will put out a bulletin for the people saying the invasion goes well, and we have yet to suffer any casualties due to the skill of our soldiers and the competent leadership of the Crusader Knights. We will say the Outlanders have fled before our armies, and will soon be in custody," Jonah suggested.

"Yes!" Gaius Prospero said. "Yes, Jonah! Do it all. Dispatch John Swiftsword, and inform our people that all goes well in our campaign to reclaim the Outlands. And do not forget Lara's Fiacre children. I want them in my custody."

Jonah bowed. "It shall be as you command, my lord emperor."

Receiving his marching orders John Swiftsword departed with his Mercenary force, and marched into the foothills of the Purple Mountains. Soon he and his small army were deep in the mountains. There seemed to be no roads, however, and he wondered how the carts of dead had traversed the steep forested sides of these mountains to reach the City several years back. The forest grew thicker and denser as they traveled. They had to hack their way through it at one point. They saw not a village. Not a farmstead. Not a person or domesticated creature. And if there were mines, they were very well hidden from his view. Finally they began to come down from the mountains, and before them stretched a great plain. John Swiftsword had his forces make an encampment on that plain directly below the mountains. Then he sent a faeriepost to the City asking for further instructions. He had not been told of the larger army's empty trek.

Jonah read the missive from the mountain army. And having read it he realized there was great magic involved. Neither of Hetar's forces had found signs of disaster, or illness, or aught that would explain the Outlanders' disappearance. As fantastic as it sounded, as incredible as it was to believe, it must be that that the entire population of the Outlands, their villages, their goods and chattels had been removed to another place. But where? He brought the faeriepost from John Swiftsword to Gaius Prospero to hear what he would say, what he might think of the situation before he offered his own thoughts.

The emperor blanched. "There is nothing? No one? No signs of the mines? But Jonah, we know that they were there. We brought out thousands in gold, silver and gemstones. If there was nothing there, then what was the Winter War all about? I did not imagine those seven stinking carts piled high with our dead."

"No, you did not, my lord emperor," Jonah murmured. "There is indeed an explanation, fantastic as it will seem."

"Magic?" The emperor grew even paler.

"Of course, my lord, 'twas magic," Jonah agreed. "It could be nothing else, and how clever of you to discern it so quickly."

"I promised the people so much, Jonah, and now how am I to keep my promises?" Gaius Prospero asked his right hand. "It will be like it was six years ago. They will blame me for what has happened."

"Nothing has happened, my lord emperor," Jonah spoke calmly. "Compose yourself, and look at what you have. You convinced the people of Hetar that the Outlands were rightfully ours, and had been stolen from us by the Outlanders, which enabled you to build a large new army of Mercenaries. The Crusader Knights have been idle for years, and welcomed the opportunity you gave them to lead us into war again. You have stemmed the restlessness that plagued us these past years.

"You said there was much fertile land to be had in

the Outlands, and there is, my lord emperor. You will be able to expand our borders without the loss of a single Hetarian life. We will take more trees from the Forest Lords, and set the Mercenaries to work building new villages for themselves, and for the sons of the Midlands who would otherwise have no place to go. It is spring, my lord emperor. There is time for those young men to open new fields and plant crops. The markets will be full by autumn, as you had so wisely planned previously.

"If there are some among the people who complain that it is not as easy as they had thought it would be, we will remind them that very little is easy in life. Then we will give them a small tract of land, exhorting them to work hard for the good of Hetar and their fellow citizens. And we will say we are fortunate that our vaunted might has frightened those dark forces that held the Outlands in their thrall these hundreds of years into fleeing before us."

"But what of the thousands of slaves I promised?" the emperor whined.

Greedy fool, Jonah thought silently. Then he gave the emperor a small cold smile. "We are fortunate, my lord, in avoiding these evil creatures. They would never have made good slaves, I fear. And they would have brought darkness into Hetar."

"Of course! Of course!" Gaius Prospero agreed. Then his eyes narrowed. "Where have the Outlanders gone, Jonah?" he asked his companion. "Where?"

Jonah shrugged. "Does it really matter, my lord emperor? We have the Outlands, and for now our problems of overcrowding and unrest are behind us.

And you will, of course, avail yourself of the best tracts of land. I think the area near the sea might be best, with its mild climate. You can probably harvest two, possibly three crops, yearly. And with your gracious permission I might take some acreage near you, my lord emperor. I have a mind to plant a vineyard there."

"Naturally, dear Jonah," Gaius Prospero replied. He was beginning to feel better now. Jonah always made everything clearer to him. "You shall have whatever you desire in the Outlands. A vineyard, you say? What a delightful idea."

"We have a great deal of work cut out for us, my lord emperor. I would advise that we visit the Outlands once all is secure. Before the winter. You should see what you have gained for Hetar, my lord emperor. I am sure the Shadow Princes will transport us with their magic, so you need not be burdened by the difficulty of travel."

"Which of the Princes is in the City now?" Gaius Prospero wanted to know.

"I will endeavor to learn that, my lord emperor," Jonah said.

"Have a faeriepost sent to my Knight Commander with the larger army telling him to remain where he is, but to send a small expeditionary force ahead to ascertain that the Outlands are completely free of those evil barbarians. They are to meet up with John Swiftsword and his group. Then send a faeriepost to Swiftsword as well telling him to stay at his encampment, and expect the smaller force to join him. When we are certain of our facts, Jonah, we shall announce our great victory over the Outlands," Gaius Prospero declared. "But I should still like to know where the clan families disappeared to, dear Jonah. We should not like them coming back, would we?"

"In time you will explore the possibilities, my lord emperor," Jonah replied. "For now you must make the Outlands secure and prosperous. It is important that your people be happy. Contented folk never rebel. Give the masses safe shelters, enough food and a purpose in life just difficult enough to keep their attention, and they are usually well gratified. Those who are not you can use to your own purposes, or dispose of, my lord emperor. But you know these things, and it is impertinent of me to remind you of them." He bowed low. "I beg your forgiveness, my lord emperor."

"Jonah, Jonah," Gaius Prospero said, his mood expanding with goodwill. "Of course I forgive you. I know that in your loyalty you but speak to aid me. You could never displease me. Only one thing disappoints me about this easy conquest. I do not have Lara's Fiacre children in my charge."

"My lord, first things first," Jonah advised. "Once you have made Hetar so powerful and so inviolate that no one will dare threaten us, you will learn all we seek to know. Remember there is this place called Terah. You shall find it, and when you do, the faerie woman will be yours. Her children will not matter, my lord emperor."

"First the Outlands," Gaius Prospero said. "Then I will make the Coastal Kingdom an Imperial province with my own governor. I had promised the position to Arcas, but he is not to be trusted. And something must be done about the Forest Lords. They have not been particularly cooperative of late. They do not send their young men for our Mercenary forces. When the Outlands situation is settled I will want to see the Head Forester, Jonah. It is past time he paid me a visit, and that I made certain of his loyalty to me. Lord Enda is a wily fellow, but I believe he has more intelligence than his unfortunate brother had." The emperor's voice grew low. "Lara killed him, you know. She admitted it to me, Jonah. Said he was her first kill. She sounded as if she had enjoyed it, Jonah." Gaius Prospero shuddered with the memory of her words.

A small smile touched Jonah's lips. "Perhaps she did, my lord emperor," he replied. There! Let the fat coward consider well the woman he coveted so greatly. *If I were emperor,* Jonah thought, *I should imprison the faerie woman, and force her to use her magic for my benefit. Gaius Prospero is guided only by his lust. All women are the same. Soft breasts, and hot, wet holes for pleasuring a man. To become ensorcelled by them is a weakness. Vilia and I understand one another.*

"I think I find Lara more exciting as a strong woman than she was as a girl," the emperor said. "And more frightening. To conquer such a creature would be a victory."

"In time, my lord emperor," Jonah replied. "First we must conclude your conquest of the Outlands."

The next few weeks brought to light that nothing remained in the Outlands but the mountains and the plain itself. All trace of the people who had once inhabited it had disappeared. There were no villages to move into, no planted fields to till and no slaves. Nonetheless a great victory was declared. The emperor proclaimed two days of celebration and opened his own private warehouses to distribute bread, meat and wine to the populace of the City. The Head Mistress of the Guild of the Pleasure Woman was instructed to open the Pleasure Houses to any who wished to avail themselves of the women within. Records were to be scrupulously kept, and each Pleasure House would be reimbursed by the emperor. No one seeking pleasures was to be turned away.

When the two days had drawn to a close, an announcement was made that those wishing land in the new province of the Outlands were to assemble in the main square of the City and be interviewed for their suitability. The sons of the Midland farmers would be given first choice, for it was important that the land be made fruitful. Houses and villages would be built for all who qualified, all who could contribute to Hetarian society. The celebrations had dulled the hum of the complaints that all was not quite as they had been promised. And now what appeared to be a fair distribution of the new territory distracted the remainder of the malcontents.

Gaius Prospero in the company of Jonah, and with the aid of the Shadow Princes, transported to the Outlands. He was astounded by its vastness and its fertility. He chose a large chunk of land overlooking the sea for his very own, and arranged to build himself a small summer palace. Jonah sought land a few miles inland for his vineyard, and made preparations for a house, and the planting of the vines. Then he and the emperor spent the next ten days riding across the plain to the foot of the mountains where the encampment of John Swiftsword was located.

"You could take some of the onus off the Forest Lords by taking lumber from these forests on the mountain," Jonah suggested to the emperor.

"Yes," Gaius Prospero agreed. "Better for now to keep Lord Enda in our camp, eh, Jonah? Besides, the forests on the mountains are thick, and we will have to take the trees down if we are to reopen the mines. We must locate them again, Jonah. They were very rich, and I should be reluctant to lose such wealth."

Jonah remained silent. It would take several years and great skill to find the mines of the Tormod and Piaras, if indeed they could find them at all. The magic that had rendered the Outlands empty of any evidence of the clan families was strong magic. The Shadow Princes would have been involved, but he would say nothing to Gaius Prospero about his suspicions. The Shadow Princes were probably the strongest power in Hetar. Only their disinterest kept them from interfering seriously in Hetarian politics. If the truth be known, the princes did not need the City or the Midlands, the Coastal Kingdom or the realm of the Forest Lords. As long as their desert was respected they seemed content to leave the rest of Hetar to itself. Until now. However they had emptied the Outlands, Jonah knew that the faerie woman, Lara, had been involved somehow. There was obviously a bond between her and the princes. Perhaps she had done them all a favor by preventing the bloodshed that would have ensued from another war. They might not have villages, planted fields, flocks, herds and a fresh supply of slaves, but they had land. And no one had perished. In time Hetar would go to war again, but with whom? Jonah shrugged. It was a puzzle yet to be solved.

And the Outlands were now open to Hetar, and the people came. Farmland was distributed with orders to plant and harvest in this same year. The people of the City needed to be fed now, and through the winter. They lived in cloth shelters while the trees were felled, and lumber cut and transported across the great plain to the sites delegated for new villages. But some of the land was found not to be good for growing. It was rocky and impossible to plow. And a means for getting the produce to the City was proving difficult as well. The Outlands had been far from the civilization of Hetar.

Gaius Prospero was not pleased. It had all begun so well, and now it appeared things were not going at all as he had planned. The autumn was rainy, and landslides occurred on the mountainsides now devoid of trees. They had not been able to find the mines yet. Winter was coming, and the markets were little better off than they had been the previous year. Even his warehouses were half-empty. The emperor found himself at a loss, and Gaius Prospero did not like being without answers to his problems. Only the icy winds and bitter weather kept the people from the streets, from the rebellion he so feared.

"Terah," he said to Jonah one afternoon after Winterfest had just passed. It had cost him half of what was left in his warehouses to give the populace their expected fete and keep them at bay a while longer. "We must find Terah. Their riches can help us recover from this debacle the Outlands has become. Find Arcas for me, Jonah. He knows something, and I want to know what he knows. Is he in the City?"

"Indeed, my lord emperor, he is," Jonah replied. "He has been exiled from the Coastal Kingdom by his father for his attempted patricide."

"Archeron was right," Gaius Prospero said. "Arcas is a fool. He should have killed the old king with a single dose of poison instead of attempting to make it look like a natural death. But he will know where Terah is, I am certain. Find him!"

Jonah sent two Imperial guardsmen to the house where he knew Arcas rented a sleeping place. "Say nothing more than the emperor wishes to see him immediately," Jonah instructed the guardsmen. "Do not harm him, but bring him quickly."

The guardsmen returned less than an hour later with Arcas, who was less than gracious to the emperor's right hand. "It's about time I was sent for," he began. "What have you been waiting for? I was promised the governorship of the old Coastal Kingdom when the emperor sent down the kings."

"The Coastal Kingdom remains as it ever was, my lord Arcas," Jonah said. "At this time it is not to the emperor's advantage to change things." He wrinkled his nose. "When was the last time you bathed? You cannot greet the emperor stinking like a cow byre. I hardly recognized you with that beard, and long matted hair. And your garments are filthy."

"My father sent me from the Coastal Kingdom with no means of support," Arcas snarled. "I earn my sleeping space and what little I can find to eat reading and writing letters for those who cannot. It is hardly a gracious living considering my status."

"You no longer have a status that matters," Jonah said, "but I can help you to regain such a place if you are willing to help me."

"How?" Arcas demanded suspiciously. "I will not betray Gaius Prospero. I am not that big a fool. I like my head where it now resides."

"The Celestial Actuary forefend, my lord," Jonah said. "You know I am called the emperor's right hand, and none is more loyal than I to Gaius Prospero. I serve him in many ways. But if you serve me, you will be serving him as well. First, my lord, let us get you bathed, and shorn, and garbed in more suitable garments." He clapped his hand, and told the answering male servant, "Take Lord Arcas to the baths. See he is properly attended to, and find some decent garments for him. He is to have an audience with the emperor shortly." Turning to Arcas he said, "Go with Lionel, and he will take care of you, my lord," Jonah told him.

Surprised yet suspicious, Arcas followed the servant from Jonah's privy chamber.

Jonah could not restrain the smile that came to his face. Yes, he had full intention of binding Arcas to him, and using him. Better the fool be loyal to him, and he would be grateful briefly for the bath and clean clothing. But Jonah intended still more. He would pay for a decent room for Arcas, and in exchange Arcas would be his ears in the City.

A man in his position could never have too many ears, Jonah thought. He went to Gaius Prospero immediately.

"I have found Arcas, but his condition was so poor that I sent him to be bathed and barbered properly before I bring him into your presence. I know how delicate your nose is, my lord emperor," Jonah said. "It would seem King Archeron has exiled him, and cast him off as a son. He has been earning his living as a reader and a scribe."

"Then he will be more than willing to cooperate with us, will he not, dear Jonah," the emperor said, pleased. "He will come before me, but I shall leave the management of his person to you, Jonah. You always know how to handle people to my advantage."

"My fate is tied to your success, my lord emperor," Jonah replied, "and I am a man who desires great success."

Gaius Prospero laughed, delighted by the admission, and Jonah withdrew to wait for Arcas to be returned to him. And while he did he gave certain orders to his own minions. Finally Arcas reappeared, and Jonah nodded, pleased. Arcas had been scrubbed so that the white of his skin shone again. His blond hair had been cut, and the barber had left just a small fringe of beard upon his pale face. He had been garbed in a simple long dark blue tunic, and new leather boots.

"There is no decoration on my gown," he complained.

"Remember, you have no status, and decoration is for men of status," Jonah reminded him. "But you will eventually regain your status, my lord."

"How?" Arcas demanded in a hard voice. His life over the last months had been wretched, and he found he did not like scraping out an existence. But he was not beaten. "And when do I get to see the emperor? Gaius Prospero owes me a debt."

"I have already spoken with the emperor, my lord. You will not return to your miserable sleeping space. You have been given a room in the mercantile district above a small shop. You will have privileges in the Pleasure House of Maeve Scarlet. In return you will continue to offer your services as a reader and a scribe. A small awning has been set up for you in the main market. The location will be given you later. And while you go about your daily life you will listen for any scrap of gossip that could be of interest to the emperor. The main marketplace is always a hotbed of gossip both important and unimportant."

"You want me to spy?" Arcas almost sounded offended. "I was promised a governorship."

"If you expect to gain that position, my lord," Jonah said quietly, "you need to show the emperor your total obedience, and just how useful you can be to him. When you are eventually returned to the Coastal province it will not be to rule in your own name, but in the emperor's name, my lord. Everything you do will be at the emperor's command. You will be a tool, and nothing more. If you choose not to accept the position currently being offered to you then you will be returned to your sleeping space, but I imagine the landlord has already rented it out by now, housing being what it currently is."

Arcas looked just briefly as if he wanted to physically attack Jonah, but then taking a deep breath he said, "And how much will I be paid in this position?" His voice dripped sarcasm, and his eyes were cold.

"You may keep what you earn as a reader and a scribe," Jonah said. "Your room and your privileges at Maeve Scarlet's will be taken care of by my office. If you should bring me a particularly juicy bit of information you will of course be remunerated for it."

He gave Arcas a quick cold smile. "Are you now ready to see the emperor?"

"I have not said I would accept your offer," Arcas responded.

"You have not said you would not," Jonah replied. He turned and walked from the room. When he heard the sound of the step behind him he smiled again, but said nothing, nor did he turn about. Domination was a game he was becoming very good at. Reaching the emperor's privy chamber he briefly knocked, and entered. "I have brought you Arcas of the Coastal province, my lord emperor," Jonah said, bowing.

Gaius Prospero was seated behind the great table that served as his workplace. He waved Arcas forward with an impatient hand. "I wish to know where Terah is," he said without any preamble.

Arcas felt a sudden sensation of doom. His father, curse him, had been right. Hetar wanted the secret of the Coastal Kings, and when they had it, the Kings would fall. But he, Arcas, would be the emperor's governor then. Curse the Coastal Kings who had

exiled him, and forced him into the dirt of the City!
"Terah?" he murmured. He wanted to enjoy this
moment. He had something Gaius Prospero wanted,
and he intended that the emperor pay for it.

"Terah," Gaius Prospero said in a hard voice.

"Is there not a price to be paid for valuable information, my lord emperor?" Arcas said smugly.

"If you do not tell me what I desire to know,"
Gaius Prospero said, "'tis you, Arcas, who will pay
that price." He clapped his hands, and two large men
in the uniform of the Torturers' Guild stepped from
the shadows. "Prepare him!" the emperor said.

The torturers moved forward far more swiftly than
Arcas thought possible, and pulled him first to his
knees, then bent him forward so that his head was
almost touching the floor. They ripped the back of
his gown open and Arcas's eyes grew round with surprise as he saw two gnomes run from beneath the emperor's table carrying a small brazier, which they set
upon the floor, and a branding iron that they thrust
into the glowing red coals. The room was silent, but
Arcas could hear his heart hammering in his chest.
He was suddenly very frightened.

"Mark one of his buttocks with my mark," Gaius
Prospero said slowly and thoughtfully. "The left one,
I think."

Arcas's mouth fell open with shock. "No!" he
cried, and the cry grew into a scream as the blazing
iron ground into his flesh. His eyes bulged from his
face, and a small bubble of foam slipped from the
edge of his mouth and ran down his chin.

"Now," Gaius Prospero said, "unless you wish a

brand on your other buttock you will answer my question. Refuse me, and I will spend the remainder of the day watching as you are slowly executed in the most painful ways devised by my torturers. After you are branded a second time there is a lovely metal dildo which is hollow, and can be filled with either coals from the brazier, or ice. I will personally shove it up your fundament, my lord. Where is Terah? I will not ask you again."

"Across the Sea of Sagitta," Arcas sobbed. He was a broken man.

The emperor came from behind his worktable, signaling the torturers to draw Arcas to his feet. His cold eyes surveyed the man. "Tell me about it," he said.

Arcas swayed on his feet. He was very, very pale.

"My lord emperor," Jonah spoke softly, "perhaps a sip of wine to restore him?"

Gaius Prospero nodded. "Give him some." Then he waited while Arcas gulped down the wine.

Able to stand on his own two legs again, Arcas shook off the hands of the two torturers. "I can tell you little about Terah, my lord emperor. Not," he quickly added, "because I do not want to tell you. Because I have never been there. None of our race has. Our vessels meet their vessels at the midpoint of the sea. Or at least what we believe is the midpoint. There we exchange our goods for theirs. They have never permitted us to come farther. It has been that way between our peoples for centuries."

"How did Lara get to Terah, then?" Gaius Prospero wanted to know.

"I gave her to one of their captains for the Dominus. I hoped to curry his favor," Arcas admitted.

"What goods do you take from them?" Gaius Prospero demanded.

"All the luxuries that Hetar loves, my lord emperor. The fabrics, the gold and silver products, the gemstones," Arcas said.

"Your people do not create these products?" the emperor asked.

"No, we trade for them," Arcas responded.

"You are no better than the Taubyl Traders then," Gaius Prospero said, and he began to laugh. "What do your people do, Arcas?"

"We fish, we cultivate what we need to eat, we compose songs, and of course we manage our trade with Terah," was the reply.

The emperor laughed a moment more, and then he grew serious. "For centuries Hetar has revered the Coastal Kings for the beautiful objects they brought to our markets, but it has all been a sham. Your people do little to justify your existence. That, however, will change come the spring. I am told by my Knight Commander who led the invasion of the Outlands that the Coastal province possesses much unused land, land that can be cultivated—and it will be. Your father has already been sent my instructions, Arcas, and he will continue to oversee the Coastal lands. As for you, you will report to my right hand, and obey his every directive. Do you understand me?"

"Yes, my lord emperor," Arcas said, bowing in servile fashion. He was too terrified to remind Gaius Prospero again of his promise that he, Arcas, would

be the governor of the Coastal province. His left buttock burned cruelly with the brand that had been impressed into his soft helpless flesh.

"Excellent," Gaius Prospero said turning away, and
returning to his seat. "You are dismissed, Arcas."

"Wait for me in my privy chamber," Jonah instructed the man.

When they were once again alone the emperor
looked to the man he called his right hand. "I am
almost sorry he cooperated," he admitted. "I should
have enjoyed shoving that dildo into him, and hearing him scream again. He thought I was weak, and
that he could manipulate me, the fool!"

"In time you will have your amusement with him,
my lord emperor. I am sure he would make a nice toy
for the lady Anora to play with, don't you think?"

"You are brilliant, Jonah! Of course that is just
what I shall do. When he is no longer of use to us,
Anora and I shall have him. She will enjoy that. It will
please her greatly. I hope he will not die too quickly."

"As long as you are patient and take your time with
him I am certain he will provide a good evening's entertainment, my lord emperor," Jonah murmured.

"But now to Terah," Gaius Prospero said. "I want
you to speak with the representatives of the Shadow
Princes when they return from the winter recess. I
would have them transport you to Terah. Your eyes
will be my eyes, Jonah. First we will open negotiations with them for trade. We will gain the goods
we want more cheaply while keeping the price in the
markets the same. We shall have a greater profit now
that it is no longer necessary for us to purchase these

goods from the Coastal Kings. And in time we shall learn the strengths and weaknesses of this Terah. Eventually we will make it a part of Hetar, Jonah."

"The High Council does not resume its meetings until the spring stars appear in the sky, my lord emperor," Jonah said. "As you have pointed out, the Shadow Princes will not return until then."

"Make haste slowly, Jonah," Gaius Prospero said jovially. "You must spend the next few weeks making plans to keep the people of the City calm and contented until I can bring this new prosperity into our world. Go now. Both Vilia and Anora are waiting for me. Both will have a litany of complaints, but I am more of a mind to listen to them now that I have gotten what I wanted this day. Go! Go!"

Jonah bowed to the emperor, and withdrew from him, hurrying back to his own privy chamber where Arcas awaited him. "Good," he said to the man. "You are ready now, I assume, to accept my offer."

"You let him mark me with his brand," Arcas said resentfully.

"Did you actually expect me to stop him?" Jonah responded. "The emperor is a hard man, and you have learned a valuable lesson today. Do not cross Gaius Prospero."

"Where is this room you have found for me?" Arcas said. "I find I am very weak."

"Lionel will take you. Go to Maeve Scarlet's Pleasure House tonight. She will see your wound is cured of its hurt. She has an excellent healer among her servants. Then relax, and enjoy pleasures with one of her women. I surmise you have not had them in many months now. It is unhealthy to bottle up one's lusts, and it clouds the judgment, as you must surely have realized after this afternoon. Rest tomorrow, and then you will find the awning designated for you next to the seller of lotions, soaps and perfumes in the main market square. He is very popular with the ladies, and women do gossip quite a bit. Who knows what bits of information you will gain there? You will report to me on the last day of each week in the hour before the sunset. Do you understand? And Arcas, do try to remain discreet. You will be watched."

"I understand, my lord Jonah," Arcas responded. Then he said, "He will not create me governor, will he?"

"For now it is to Hetar's advantage that everything remain as it has been," Jonah said. "You are alive, Arcas, and you are now taken care of. If not in the manner in which you were raised, at least comfortably. You have a purpose, and in time you will, I am certain, regain your status among us. Go now," he said, and watched as Arcas went slowly from the room. The brand on his buttock blazed bright crimson. "Lionel," he called to his manservant. "Get him another robe."

When he was alone again Jonah considered the afternoon that had just passed. So the emperor wanted him to go to Terah. That was going to present a problem, but he would figure it out in time. And he did have time. And Vilia would help him. Intelligent, she now realized her ambitions would be better served with him than with her husband. Yes, Vilia was a treasure. And while Gaius Prospero did not know it yet, she was Jonah's treasure, not the emperor's. The right hand of the emperor smiled to himself. Everything was going exactly as he had hoped.

Chapter 17

MAGNUS HAUK watched his wife playing a board game with Prince Kaliq, and he was jealous. He knew he had absolutely no reason to be, but he was. That in itself added to his anger. He knew the look of intensity on Lara's beautiful face was brought about by her concentration on the game, yet he found himself wondering if that was all she thought about.

The prince reached out with a single finger, and touched the tip of Lara's nose. "Make your move," he said softly, a hint of a smile upon his lips.

"Do not rush me, Kaliq," Lara responded as she studied the pieces. "You always do that when you think you might lose," she chuckled.

"I do not!" he denied it.

Lara laughed, and moved her game piece. "Aye, you do."

"I think you have devised some manner of cheating that I have not yet figured out," he said. "You have always been wickedly clever."

Again she laughed. "I am just better at Herder than you are," Lara told him. "Vartan and I played regularly."

"Did he beat you?" Kaliq wanted to know.

"Now and again," Lara admitted, "but women are really better at these games than men are, my prince. We are willing to wait for our reward, and are not so greedy."

Kaliq moved his next piece on the board.

"Oh dear," Lara murmured.

"What?" he demanded nervously.

"I should not have done that if I were you," Lara said, and then she moved her final piece from the board. "I win."

He grimaced. "I thought I had that piece blocked," he grumbled.

"Would you like to play another game?" Lara inquired sweetly.

"And be humbled again? Nay, my love, I believe once a night is more than enough for me," the Prince said ruefully.

"As you wish, my lord Prince," Lara replied.

"It is late," Magnus Hauk said loudly. They had been speaking as if he were not even there. "We should get some rest. I have been considering that it is past time we went home to Terah. I have been gone far too long."

"Yes," Lara agreed, not recognizing his pique. "I should pay a visit to the new Outlands to see how they are all getting on there. The rest of Hetar can wait."

"You have other duties, Domina," Magnus said sharply. "There is the small matter of an heir for Terah that should come before anything else."

"I told you that I would give you an heir when I deemed the time right," Lara responded. "I am not some brood animal, my lord Dominus."

Kaliq felt sympathy for Magnus Hauk. He was hopelessly in love with Lara, but he was also filled with jealousy. Until he could gain a mastery of himself he was going to have difficulty with her. And Lara, the Prince thought, also needed to consider that for now, and perhaps for always, she was this man's wife. Her destiny had not yet been fulfilled entirely, but neither was it going to be any time soon.

Lara, he spoke to her in her thoughts. *He is jealous, poor mortal. While you and I know he has no reason to be, he does not know that. Be patient with him.*

She looked directly at the Prince, and a flick of an eyelash told him she had heard. Rising from the game table she walked over to her husband. "You are right, Magnus, it is time we returned home to Terah. But a babe takes time to make. Before we set to work at such a pleasant duty I really should visit the new Outlands to be certain all is well. It is not just for myself, but it is for Terah. I have convinced you to introduce these new folk into your lands. I must be sure they have resettled well, and will be no bother to you, for that is what I promised you, Magnus, my husband. And, too, I have Vartan's children to see. I need to know all is well with them." She put a gentle hand on his muscled arm, and gave him a small smile.

"I promised you a son, and I will give him to you in due time."

Kaliq could sense the jealousy draining from the Dominus's heart. His turquoise-blue eyes grew misty as they looked down at Lara. His stern features softened. Kaliq almost laughed aloud, but he kept his own handsome features blank. Lara was indeed magical, especially in her ability to cajole an angry man. But Magnus Hauk had a strength that she was going to need in the times to come. She might be cleverer, and more aware where the world around them was concerned, but Kaliq could see that the Dominus of Terah was learning quickly.

Lara turned back to the prince. "We bid you a good night, Kaliq," she said.

He nodded, and bowed formally to them both. "When you are ready tomorrow to be transported I shall be happy to oblige you both," he told her, and then watched as they left him. Kaliq sighed. Tomorrow he would tell them what his spies in the City had reported to the Shadow Princes today. The emperor had forced the foolish Arcas into telling him about Terah. He wanted Jonah to be transported to Terah by the Princes in order to open up direct trade negotiations. Thanks to Arcas, the Coastal Kings had now lost their monopoly on the trade with Terah.

When the next day dawned hot over the desert outside of the cliff palaces, he saw that Magnus Hauk was in a much better frame of mind. Obviously Lara had spent the night pleasuring him, and restoring his good humor. They joined him for the first meal of the day in his small private garden. The silent servants brought in bowls of ripened golden apricots, pale green grapes, and tiny yellow bananas along with individual cups of fresh yogurt. The delicate round loaf of bread with its crisp crust was fresh from the ovens and filled with berries and raisins. A dainty silver dish held sweet butter. Another contained honey in its comb. In deference to the Dominus, who ate a heartier first meal of the day, there were hard-boiled eggs in a bowl set by his place along with a plate of meat. The servants filled the goblets with fresh mixed juice.

When the meal was well underway the Shadow Prince told them of what they had learned from their informants in the City. "What do you want us to do?" he asked Magnus Hauk.

"Can you refuse to transport them?" the Dominus asked.

"The more you refuse Gaius Prospero the more he will want to come," Lara said. "We cannot hazard that they discover the Sea of Obscura on the edge of this desert. Hetarians are not explorers by nature, but we cannot take the chance. You do not want them coming at us through the new Outlands."

"What do you suggest?" the Shadow Prince asked her.

Lara turned to her husband. "This is your decision, Magnus, but now that they know more than we were willing to tell them, they will come. But we are still in a position to control their coming."

The Dominus considered for several long minutes. Then turning to Kaliq he said, "What if you told them we knew that they were coming in the next year, but that we wanted them to come across the sea? To send word to us through the Coastal Kings when their ambassador was ready so we might meet his vessel, and escort it with due honor to Terah. Do you think Gaius Prospero would honor our request?"

"Aye, he very well might," Kaliq responded. "For now he cannot go to war with you, for he is too busy in the Outlands. And he has also discovered how much land is unused within the Coastal province. He intends confiscating it for his own cultivation, I have not a doubt. That way he can control the price of food in the markets."

"And by controlling the price of food he can control the people," Lara murmured.

"So his only interest in Terah for the interim is to open a negotiation with us," the Dominus said. "He's a wily fellow, and in the end we shall have to deal with him."

"But for now," the Shadow Prince said, "you have time to prepare your people and your defenses against Hetar."

"Could we not create a vacuum within the leadership of Hetar if Gaius Prospero were no longer there?" Lara wondered aloud.

"The difficulty with Gaius Prospero's ambitions is that they have roused the ambitions of others as well," Kaliq responded. "As long as each province was governed by its leaders and all had an equal say in the High Council, Hetar could remain at peace. But nothing remains the same forever, my friends. Ambition rises with the changing times. Hetar is overpopulated in the City and the Midlands. The rest of us have remained isolated, the Foresters because of their foolish insistence for their racial purity, the Coastal Kings because of their great distance. And we because of our magical abilities, which are not for the common folk. But all that is changing now, and we must change with it. Hetar believes it is the only world here, but it is not. And it will soon learn otherwise. Terah has known better for centuries, but there is even more here than Terah can imagine," Kaliq told them. "It is Lara who is bringing about these changes, whether she realizes it or not. Your wife, Magnus Hauk, is very important in the scheme of things."

"What is she to do?" the Dominus asked, curious.

"Exactly what she is doing," Kaliq replied, and Magnus looked confused.

Lara laughed. "It is the Prince's duty to be oblique, Husband," she told him.

"My destiny seems to unfold slowly like a bolt of heavy rich cloth. If you have told us all we need to know, Kaliq, then perhaps it is time for Magnus and me to go home to Terah."

The Shadow Prince turned to the Dominus. "When we are requested to transport Hetar's emissary to Terah we will refuse, and suggest the more formal route you have presented to us. The emperor will be impatient and irritated by the delay, but we will see he acquiesces for if the truth be known he has no other choice. And we will warn you well in advance of their request and their coming," he told them.

"Keep them from your desert, Kaliq," Lara said. "They have already encroached along its scrublands, I am told."

"No longer," he replied. "They found it too inhospitable, and besides now they have the Outlands in which to expand. It is a far more pleasant land," Kaliq chuckled. "We seemed to have an unusual number of sandstorms and ferocious heat waves in the scrubland in recent months. Those poor Midlanders could not take it. They fled back to the overcrowded farms of their families very quickly. The emperor then sent a delegation at the request of the Squire. They came back declaring the scrubland useless and uninhabitable even for goats and scorpions. The emperor will not intrude upon us again. He sees no profit in our desert, and believes we spend all our time tending to the horses we sell into Hetar. He told me himself it must be difficult work, given the sandstorms and the lack of useful vegetation."

"Does he not know of your palaces, and that magnificent fertile valley between the cliffs?" Magnus Hauk asked, surprised. "Where does he imagine you live?"

"Few in Hetar know of our valley," the prince said. "Those who have traveled our province believe we reside in the tent encampments they see scattered about the desert."

"What of the Taubyl Traders?" Lara wondered.

"We conduct our negotiations with them from magnificent tents below the cliffs," he told them. "Few strangers have ever entered our palaces, or seen our valley. And those few who have are relieved of the memory of it before we send them back. And to those to whom we have given sanctuary, like the Mercenary, Wilmot, and his old mother, Dame Mildred, they do not go out into the world again. It would not be safe for them."

"How are they?" Lara asked him.

"Wilmot was a bit restless until your giant, Og, asked him for his aid with the horses. As for Dame Mildred she is most content, and spends her time with Og's wife and children. You did not see them, did you?"

Lara shook her head. "Nay. I did not want to answer all the questions that Wilmot would surely have for me."

"Then it is time for you to go," Kaliq said.

"Transport me to the new Outlands," Lara said.

"Wife!" the Dominus protested.

"It is easier," Lara told him, "if I go now. It is the time of the Gathering, Magnus. I will be able to see them all, hear and soothe complaints and see my children. And Dasras is there. I shall ride him home to you within just a few weeks' time. Please let me do this. Come if you will, but let me go."

"I need to get back to the castle," he said. Then he sighed. "Very well, Lara, go to that great fertile plain you call the new Outlands, and reassure yourself that all is well, but then return to me."

"Before I do I would have you come to your new subjects so that they may render their tribute to you for the year," she said.

He nodded. "I will come when you want me, my faerie love."

She smiled at him, and then going to Kaliq, put her arms about his neck and kissed his cheek. "Thank you, dear friend," she said.

The Shadow Prince saw the fire blaze up in Magnus Hauk's eyes. He returned Lara's kiss and then set her back. "I shall set you down in the middle of Rendor's hall," he said, and with a quick wave of his hand he transported her.

Rendor of the Felan started as Lara materialized before his high board. Rahil, his wife gave a little scream of surprise.

"Greetings, old friends," Lara said to them.

Rendor stood up, and coming forward embraced Lara. "I know I should not be so startled, but your method of entrance always amazes me. Welcome, Lara! Come up to the board, and have some wine."

"It is morning in the palace of Prince Kaliq," Lara said. She accepted the goblet he offered her, and drank deeply of it. "Rahil, you are looking well. Now tell me how has this relocation gone for the clan families?"

"Many find it difficult to believe we are no longer on the borders of Hetar," Rendor began. "Do they now possess our old lands?"

"Aye, and they are totally confused to have found an empty land, barren of villages or creatures, when they were promised it all including the clan families as a new source of slaves. Gaius Prospero is most distressed that there are no mines to be had in the mountains. He has been forced to seek the wealth he knows is there if he can but find it," Lara chuckled. "I came for the Gathering, and to speak with all the clan families so I might see for myself that they have all settled in well. I have been with the Shadow Princes."

"Where is your husband?" Rendor wanted to know.

"Kaliq sent him back to Terah," Lara said. "He will join us at the Gathering so you may all render him the tribute due him."

"Why did you not transport to Liam's hall?" Rendor wanted to know.

"I do you honor as head of the Outlands High Council," Lara told him. "Liam is only the Lord of the Fiacre. I will see him soon enough. How soon do we leave?"

"Tomorrow," Rendor said. "You came just in time. It is amazing, Lara. Each clan family sought out the place of the Gathering this summer past, and it was there exactly where it should be. We did not know if it would be."

"The Princes and I transported everything. And we closed up the mines in the mountains, and put trees and bushes back in their stead," she told him. "Hetar's emperor has been very disappointed by what he found."

"I am sorry that Gaius Prospero did not find a scorched land," Rendor muttered.

"If he had he would have had a rebellion on his hands, and we cannot tolerate a rebellion in Hetar, old friend," Lara told him. "They would have been forced to look elsewhere for growing land. As it is they have confiscated all the empty acreage that belonged to the Coastal Kings, and they have forced the secret of Terah from Arcas."

"Then we are not safe after all," Rendor said.

"The new Outlands is safe, and so is Terah. The Sea of Obscura can only be found by crossing the desert, and Hetar has decided that the desert is an unfriendly place. They have already left the small bit they attempted to settle last year. And the Emerald Mountains separate the new Outlands from Terah proper, and another sea separates it from Hetar," Lara explained. "The clan families are safe, Rendor."

"This sea you call Obscura is not like Sagitta," he told her. "We have seen sea monsters with beautiful jewel-colored scales and great tails swimming off the shore of it. They do not come near, and they seem peaceable, but I know they have seen us as well. We are not of a mind to take a dory out onto the water. But when we cast out our nets from the beach they are immediately so full of fish we can hardly pull them to shore. We will not starve. We have only done that twice since we have been here, for we would not waste the bounty of this land. We smoked what we could not eat, and shall take some of it to the Gathering for barter or trade."

"This is a good place, then?" she asked.

"Our flocks behave as if nothing has changed," he told her.

"I will be interested to hear what the other clan families have to say about this new place you have been brought to, Rendor. Let us hope they are as content."

"It will not matter if they are not, for we cannot go back, can we?" he asked.

Lara shook her head. "Nay, you cannot," she agreed.

The next day the Felan and Lara departed for the yearly Gathering. They traveled the same time and distance as always, which was a comfort to them. And when they reached the place of the Gathering Lara was relieved to see the great stone monoliths standing at the place of the assemblage as if they had been in that particular spot for centuries, which of course they had been in the old Outlands. Before the Felan could settle themselves Lara went to join her Fiacre clan family. She was warmly welcomed by Liam.

"Where have you come from?" he wanted to know.

"I traveled with Rendor and the Felan, but I was with the Shadow Princes prior to that. May I stay with you? You know I count myself among the Fiacre."

"Of course!" he said enthusiastically. "Noss! Noss!" Liam called to his wife. "We have a most welcome guest who has come to the Gathering."

Noss's head popped from the lord's tent. Seeing Lara she let out a little squeal of delight and ran forth to embrace her. "Oh, I am so glad you are here! I have another son, Val," she exclaimed. "Have you seen Dillon yet? Dillon, your mother is here!" she called out to Lara's young son. The boy came running from the tent.

"Mother!" He flung his arms about her.

Lara hugged her child, noting that the older he grew the more he looked like his father with his wonderful blue eyes and dark locks. "You simply must stop this growing business," she told him, ruffling his hair.

He grinned up at her with Vartan's smile, and her heart contracted. Once it had been so simple, she thought, and briefly was overcome with sadness.

"I can't help it," he said. "I can ride Dasras now," he told her.

"But you cannot have him," she responded. "I sent him to you for the summer because I knew I would not be able to ride him."

"Where were you?" he asked directly.

"In Hetar, and in the realm of the Shadow Princes. I saw your grandmother, and my younger brother Cirilo who is only a year older than you are," she told him. "I hope one day that you will meet your uncle. It cannot hurt to have friends in the land of the faerie," Lara said seriously.

"My father's mother says faeries bring bad fortune," Dillon replied.

"Bera is not well in her head, and has not been since her younger son murdered your father, her older son," Lara explained.

"She says you slew Adon and Elin, orphaning my cousin Cam," Dillon responded. "Did you kill them, Mother?"

"Aye, and I would have slain Cam, too, but that I was prevented from doing so. The false blood of his parents runs in him, Dillon. Never trust him," Lara warned.

"My father's mother says we should be friends, for our fathers were not just brothers, but friends also," Dillon told her.

"Vartan and Adon were never friends," Lara said angrily. "The younger spent his life jealous of the elder and everything your father earned. Obviously her grief has skewed Bera's memories. Cam is young, but he will understand the story of his father's demise one day. And mark my words, Dillon, he will seek to avenge his parents. Do not trust him ever," she re-

peated. "There will be times when you want to trust
him, but do not! And do not trust Bera either. I know
she is your father's mother, but she will hate you for
my blood, which also runs through your heart. One
day that hatred will overcome her, Dillon, and she
will strike out at you. She cannot face the terrible
truth that one son slew the other. While I had nothing to do with it, she has come to blame me if she tells
you that the faerie world is evil and not to be coun-
tenanced. Treat her with respect, my son, but put no
faith in her words."

Noss had been listening. She could not help but
overhear Lara's words. "Your mother is right," she
told Dillon. "And she is very wise. Heed her."

"Where is Anoush?" Lara asked her old friend.

"With Tearlach and Alroy," Noss replied. "She follows them about. She stands between my older sons
in age. Dillon has little time for her, being older. You
will see her at the evening meal, Lara." Noss's voice
had a slight edge to it, and her eyes were suddenly distressed. "Do you plan to take your children back with
you when you return to the Dominus?" she wondered
nervously.

"I have told you before, Noss, that Vartan's son
and daughter are Fiacre, and will remain with their
clan family. Do you not think I am aware that after
all these months my daughter will not remember me?
That she thinks of you as her mother? I understand
that. For now we will not confuse her for she is very
little, and would not comprehend. Let this not come
between us, Noss. I value your friendship and your

kindness to my children. They are safer with you than they would be with me."

Noss's eyes filled with tears. "Lara, forgive me! I adore Anoush, and dread ever losing her. Liam cannot, it seems, get a lass on me. I have three sons now," she said with a weak smile. "Anoush is the only daughter I will ever have. I just know it."

"I know that," Lara reassured her friend. "And how fortunate Anoush is to have a faerie woman birth her, and a mortal raise her."

"She shows no signs of magic," Noss said, "but Dillon does. For all he resembles his father he is first your son. In the old place creatures came to him easily, and so they do here. He and Dasras have become good friends. He will miss him when you return to Terah and your husband."

"Have you settled in here?" Lara asked Noss.

"Oh yes," Noss answered. "The land is much greener here, and the cattle have fattened well on it this summer. The landscape is a little different, but it is pleasant. The spring was long, the summer, too. The autumn has come quickly. I wonder about the winters here. Will they be hard?" She shrugged. "We will endure whatever comes, for we are Fiacre. Our way of life continues as it ever did."

"You are a woman who gossips at the well, and listens, too," Lara said. "Have you heard any discord among the others in Camdene?"

"Nay. The only small problem is Bera. I think the death of her sons unhinged her. She avoids us all and keeps Cam close. I want to feel sorry for her, for she was very good to me when we first came to the old

Outlands." Noss shook her head. "But it is as if some inner voice were warning me away. Liam does his familial duty toward her, but even my mother-in-law, Asta, Bera's own sister, no longer speaks with her except when she must. Bera is well housed, clothed and fed. She is respected when she passes by, but no more than that."

"If something warns you from her, heed it," Lara said. "Tell me about Cam."

"Secretive," Noss said. "And not very talkative."

"Does he sport with the other children?" Lara asked.

"Sometimes, but not often. Bera hardly allows him from her sight," Noss responded. "She attempts to make Dillon play with him, but Dillon says Cam is dark, and refuses to go, more times than not. Bera has accused me of keeping the cousins apart."

"Heed your own instincts and my son's where Cam is concerned," Lara said.

"I will," Noss promised.

The word had quickly spread that Lara was among the clan families again, and the clan lords all came to pay her their respects. They each wanted her to know that this new land into which they had been settled suited them well. Floren of the Blathma and Torin of the Gitta were ecstatic in their praise of their new home's fertility.

"The grain!" both exclaimed with one voice.

"And I have never had flowers like those I grew this year," Floren declared. "I brought many seedlings with me, and lost not a one! Thank you, Lara!"

Roan of the Aghy spoke up. "My horses are healthier than they have ever been," he told her. "And thanks to your Dasras I will have at least a dozen fine new foals next spring. I hope you do not mind that he came visiting my mares," Roan chuckled.

Lara laughed. "I have yet to see Dasras, but nay, I do not mind," she said. "I am pleased that this new Outlands suits you all. Rendor's flocks have the best wool they have grown in years. I need only hear from the Piaras and the Tormod now. Have you been able to make arrangements with the Mountain gnomes to open mines of your own?" she asked, turning to the two clan lords involved.

"The Tormod have," Imre said coming forward. "And I have brought two of the Mountain gnomes with us as guests. Fulcrum is the chieftain of the Jewel Mountain gnomes. They have the magic to open a hillside without doing any damage to the landscape. They have exposed the entrances to three mines for us, and we have spent these past months digging out some of the finest gemstones we have ever seen. We will, with the gnomes' aid, sell our gems to the Terahns."

"Will you not be taking their livelihood from them if you do?" Lara asked.

"Nay. It is the gnomes who will deal with the Terahns as they always have, and they will keep a percentage of our profit for doing so," Imre explained.

"But will you not drive down the price of the gems if you flood the market with what you have mined, and what they have mined?" she inquired.

Imre chuckled. "There speaks the Hetarian in you, Lara. Fulcrum and his gnomes are old. There are fewer of them now than there have ever been, and none has been born in several hundred years. Many are not so eager to work now. But we are, and so they sell to the Terahns, and we share the profits. You will speak with Fulcrum yourself and see. It is a fine partnership."

Lara nodded, and turned to Vanko of the Piaras. "And how have your people fared?" she asked him.

"We have made an agreement with the Ore gnomes that has us mining gold in their new mines, for the old ones were worn out, while they mine the silver and copper. They continue to sell the product of our combined labors, and take a percentage of the profits for their trouble. They, too, are few in number now, and mining gold is difficult work. We are all comfortable with this arrangement."

"I am pleased to hear it, Vanko. How is your father?" Lara asked.

"Eager to see you," Vanko said with a smile. "You will come and take a cup of frine with us later, I hope."

"I will," she said, returning his smile.

Lara turned to meet the gaze of Accius, lord of the Devyn. "And how have your people fared?" she asked him.

Accius smiled. "We will be writing and singing of our exodus from the old Outlands, and our welcome to these new Outlands for years," he told her.

Content that the clan families had settled into what was now known as the new Outlands, Lara returned to the Fiacre encampment to meet with Liam. There she found her former mother-in-law with the boy, Cam. Bera, once her friend, now glared as she caught sight of Lara. She bent and whispered to the lad at her side.

"I greet you, Bera," Lara said.

"Why have you returned to the Outlands?" Bera wanted to know. "You will bring the Hetarian hordes upon us, faerie woman. You are evil!"

"There is no longer a danger from Hetar," Lara said quietly. "You are in the new Outlands, and Hetar is across a wide sea, Bera."

"Faerie lies!" the older woman snarled.

"You killed my parents," Cam suddenly said looking directly at Lara.

"Your parents killed my husband," Lara responded. "Revenge was my right according to the laws of the Fiacre."

"You are not Fiacre," the boy quickly replied. "You are faerie."

"When I married Vartan of the Fiacre I took his clan family to myself, to my heart. I was Fiacre when I slew Vartan's murderers. My children are Fiacre."

"Your spawn are half-breeds!" Bera screeched.

"They are your grandchildren, old woman, but since you disparage them I will arrange for you to no longer be bothered by them. I will not have you whispering your poisonous drivel into their ears. The treachery of your spineless younger son against your noble eldest son has disordered your wits. You are mad, Bera, and I am sorry for you, but you will not harm my children in your dementia," Lara told her.

"It is my right to be here," Bera said stubbornly.

"My son is clan lord here. He will tell you when he comes, faerie witch."

Lara shook her head. "Vartan is dead," she said quietly.

"Did you kill him?" Bera demanded to know.

"No, Adon and Elin slew him in his hall," Lara replied.

Bera looked suddenly confused, and by her side the boy, Cam, smiled at Lara.

Then Sholeh, headwoman of the Fiacre village of Rivalen, and blood kin to Vartan's family, was there. She nodded sympathetically at Lara, and putting an arm about Bera led her off. Cam followed. He had taken but a few steps when he turned, and smiled once again at Lara. It was a malevolent smile for so young a lad. Lara's eyes locked onto Cam's and held his gaze until the boy was forced to turn away, the look upon his face one of awakening fear.

"He is evil, isn't he?" Dillon was by her side.

"Yes," Lara said, and put a protective arm about her son. "Come. Let us walk together, and you will tell me of your summer here in the new Outlands." Together they strolled from the tent, and away from the great encampment out into the fields beyond.

"Have you taken a new husband?" Dillon asked.

"Aye, the Dominus of Terah. I am now called the Domina," Lara said.

"Will you give him children?" Dillon wanted to know.

"In time," his mother answered.

"Then you love him?" Vartan's eyes looked up at her.

"Yes, I do," Lara replied quietly. "You will meet him soon. He will come to accept the yearly tribute from the clan families before the Gathering comes to an end."

"Could we live with you, Mother?" Dillon wanted to know.

"If you wished it, aye, but I have always thought to leave you with the Fiacre, for you are Vartan's only son, Dillon. One day you will be Lord of the Fiacre," Lara told him.

"Nay, I will not," Dillon responded. "And I do not want to be, Mother. Tearlach will follow his father, and it will be many years hence for Liam will live to be a very old man. I believe I have your gifts, Mother, and I am not afraid."

Lara sighed. "If that is so, Dillon, then one day you must study with the Shadow Princes, for your blood is more mortal than faerie. They can help you achieve what you need to accomplish better than any." Perhaps it is better that Vartan is gone, she thought, for he would have wanted his eldest son to follow in his footprints and not mine.

"I must protect the Fiacre against Cam," Dillon said softly.

"Cam is young yet as you are," Lara remarked. "Now, tell me of your summer, my son. We will have several days in which to discuss that which concerns you. Noss says you have learned to ride Dasras properly now. I shall ask him to choose another mount for you as I must take him back to the castle when I go."

"It was a summer as any other," Dillon said.

"Dasras and I explored this land almost every day. There are wonderful wild creatures here, Mother."

"And your sister? Did you take her with you at all?" Lara wanted to know.

"Anoush is too young to ride before me," the boy replied. "Besides all she wants to do is follow Noss about. She calls Noss, Mama."

"I am grateful for Noss," Lara said.

"She is not our mother," Dillon said loyally. "You are!"

"When Anoush is older she will understand," Lara counseled him. "For now let Noss who loves her be Mama. You know who I am, and for that I am glad. Always make certain your sister knows who you are, Dillon."

"I miss you," the boy said.

"I miss you, and the simple life the Fiacre lead," Lara admitted. "This destiny of mine is a great burden, and Kaliq says I have not yet met the whole of it."

"I am here for you, Mother," Dillon replied, and slipped his hand into hers.

"Next summer if you like I will bring you to the castle, and you will view the great Sea of Sagitta, and I will teach you to sail as King Archeron taught me," Lara promised him.

"Will I like the Dominus?" Dillon wanted to know.

"I hope you will," his mother replied. "He is a good and wise man."

And that night Lara sought her husband out on the dream plane.

"I have missed you," he told her softly as they embraced.

"The Gathering will be over in five more days," Lara told him. "Will you let me bring you to join with the clan families? It is the perfect time to accept their tribute, which they have brought with them for you. They meant to give it to me, but you will honor and impress them if you receive it yourself. They will feel safer and more welcome. Tomorrow I will take Dasras and ride out to see how they have all managed. I have spoken with the clan lords, and they say they are content. The Piaras and Tormod have each made a satisfactory accommodation with the Mountain gnomes. But I want you to join me. My son wishes to meet you," she told him.

"Does he?" Magnus Hauk sounded pleased.

"He seems to have inherited my ways," Lara said with a smile.

"Your mother would be pleased, I think, that her grandson sports his faerie blood," Magnus Hauk said. "I should like to see the son you gave Vartan."

"Someday I shall send him to Kaliq to be trained," Lara said.

"Do you think of your Shadow Prince?" he asked.

She heard the jealousy in his tone. "Kaliq is my friend, Magnus, not my lover. If you are going to be jealous of every man with whom I speak, what am I to do with you?"

His dream shadow shimmered at her words. He was close to waking with his all too mortal emotions.

"When can you join me?" she asked him, attempting to relieve the tension between them.

"I will be ready in four days," he said. "Sirvat is with child."

"How wonderful!" Lara exclaimed. She touched his cheek. "At sunrise in four days' time go into our own little garden, and I will transport you from there. Be aware it will be midmorning here, my lord Dominus." She brushed her lips against his. "Farewell, my love," she told him. And then Lara awoke. Rolling onto her back she looked up at the skies above. There was a hint of dawn on the horizon, and she felt suddenly restless. She arose from her bedding, and stretched herself. It had been a long while since she had slept out-of-doors, and she was slightly stiff with the dampness.

She walked to the meadow where the horses were grazing, and seeing her great golden stallion, Dasras, she went to his side.

"Could you find no time for me yesterday?" Dasras said with a hint of rebuke in his deep voice. "We have been apart for months now."

Lara put her arms about the horse's neck, and rubbed her forehead against him. "I had to speak with the clan lords and my son first," she defended herself. "Roan tells me you have spent a rather pleasant summer amusing yourself among his mares. What does Sakira think of your romping, old friend?"

Dasras chuckled. "The Horselord does have a fine herd of pretty mares," he admitted, "but you should know that Sakira is also in foal. And she, knowing my stallion's nature, would never deny me. Now let us walk for a ways, and you will tell me your adventures in Hetar."

Anyone looking out into the field would have seen nothing unusual in Lara and the great animal walking together. And when the sun had at last risen the woman leaped lightly upon the horse's back, her hand wrapped in his creamy mane, and together they galloped off across the greensward. When they had gone for some small distance Dasras unfolded his great wings, and rose up into the clear morning skies. As he flew Lara was able to view the land below. She saw the villages of the Blathma and the Gitta. There were newly opened fields, most already harvested, and prepared for the winter to come.

They flew on, and below Lara looked on the great herds of Aghy horses and Fiacre cattle. And there were the three small villages of the Devyn set neatly in the bosom of several small hills. It was not necessary, Lara decided, to go farther. The Tormod and the Piaras were pleased with their arrangements with the Mountain gnomes, and she had no doubt their villages were as well settled as the other clan families.

"Let us go back now," she said to Dasras.

"Do you not wish to see the sea creatures who populate the Obscura?" he asked her. "I hear they are beautiful."

"Then let us satisfy your curiosity," Lara agreed, and Dasras turned toward the sea that bordered Rendor's new lands.

Beneath them the flocks of white sheep grazed contentedly, watched over by their shepherds and dogs. Not everyone went to the Gathering. Soon the great animal was soaring out over the sparkling turquoise waters, and before long they saw below them several of the creatures Rendor had mentioned. They were elegant beasts with scales that glistened, long tails, and fine heads with jeweled horns. Playing in the waves they appeared harmless. Scanning the ocean beneath her she saw the desert of the Shadow Princes curving to the south. But toward the north there was a darker land. It was not Hetar, for Hetar knew only one sea. Nor was it Terah. Obscura was a sea hidden from both lands, known only to a few.

"Return now," she commanded Dasras, and he obeyed.

Her fingers entwined within his mane, Lara wondered how large the ocean below them was. She was beginning to realize that there was much she did not know about the world in which she dwelled. From the vantage of her horse's back Terah seemed to lie upon a globe shaped body in the heavens. How was this possible? For the first time in many months she touched the small crystal star that hung between her breasts.

Greetings, my child, the dear and familiar voice murmured to her.

Ethne, the land below seems round, not flat, and yet when Dasras's feet touch it again it will be flat. How is this possible?

The world upon which we dwell is indeed circular, her guardian spirit replied. *Did you not know it?* Ethne sounded surprised.

How could I? Lara demanded. *No one ever told me.*

Well, now you know. There are many such worlds in the skies above, I have been told.

By whom? Lara wanted to know.

It is simply one of the facts I seem to possess, Ethne said. *The knowledge has always been there.*

Would my mother know? Lara queried.

I cannot say. But it does not matter, for your destiny is on this world, Lara. Ethne's flame twinkled up at her.

Reaching the place of the Gathering once again, Dasras folded his wings and galloped across the field before finally coming to a stop. For a long moment Lara remained upon his back, but then she slipped down, gave the great stallion a pat and walked away toward the Fiacre encampment, where she found Noss already bustling about. Noss, however, knew better than to ask Lara where she had been. If her friend wanted to discuss that she would. If she didn't, she wouldn't.

"Come and help me," Noss called. "You surely haven't forgotten how to cook."

Lara laughed. "Nay, and I do remember how the clan families love to eat at the Gathering." She set to work peeling the dried brown skins from a bowl of onions.

For the next few days it was as if she had never departed the Fiacre, and she was one of them again. Only the pitiful shade of Vartan's mother gave her cause for sadness. She hardly saw the boy Cam. He seemed to have disappeared altogether. Although she felt guilty for the thought, Lara wished she had slain the child with his parents. She could already see the wickedness in him, and it would only grow as Cam grew.

She prepared the clan lords for Magnus Hauk's arrival, and on the fourth morning she gathered them together within the ring of stone monoliths, transporting him into their midst with a short incantation. He appeared before them, standing next to Lara, his burnished golden hair shining in the sunlight. He was garbed in a long deep purple tunic edged with silver, black leather boots, and on his head he wore a circlet of silver-and-gold studded with sparkling gemstones.

"I greet you, my lords," he said, the deep booming tones of his voice as impressive as his appearance. His bow encompassed them all.

Rendor stepped forward, and knelt before Magnus Hauk. "In the name of the clan families, I welcome our Dominus to the Gathering. With your permission we would present the yearly tribute agreed upon."

"And then I hope you will invite me to partake in your festivities," the Dominus said graciously. "Rise, Rendor of the Felan, and let the other Outlands lords come forward so I may personally greet each one as well."

Rendor stood, bowed and then signaled the others forward. Torin of the Gitta came first, bringing with him a large flat basket of decorated breads, each shaped differently, and made from the first grains grown by his clan family in the new Outlands.

"How beautifully fashioned your loaves are, Lord Torin. I thank you." The Dominus nodded his head.

Floren of the Blathma stepped before the Dominus. He, too, carried a basket but in it, nestled among a bed of moss, were several large tubers. At Magnus Hauk's questioning look he said, "Planted in your gardens, my lord Dominus, these will grow into the finest lilies you have ever seen. Their scent is exquisite."

"I am particularly fond of lilies," was the reply.

Vanko, representing the Piaras, stepped up, and offered Magnus Hauk a beautifully fashioned small black box. He opened it to display a large gold nugget. "The first we mined, my lord Dominus," he explained.

"Magnificent!" Magnus Hauk said enthusiastically. "I have never seen better."

"So said our gnome partners," Vanko said. Then he moved aside to allow Imre of the Tormod his turn.

The clan lord of the Tormod spilled a small bag of multicolored gemstones into the Dominus's hand. "They are called Transmutes, my lord. Once set within gold or silver they change color with the wearer's mood. We discovered them this summer, and Fulcrum, who is the chieftain of the Jewel gnomes, said he had heard once of stones such as these, but never before had they been mined in the Emerald Mountains."

"Thank you," Magnus Hauk said. "It would seem that in bringing you all to Terah I have done us both a favor."

"Your Transmutes will cause a sensation in Hetar," Lara said with a smile.

Liam of the Fiacre now came, bringing with him two pairs of beautiful leather boots, and vests. He bowed. "I have had these made for you, my lord, and for Lara."

Together the Dominus and Domina examined the leather goods.

Lara looked up at Liam. "They are wonderful, my lord," she told him.

"Yes," Magnus Hauk agreed. "Your leathersmiths do fine work, my lord."

Accius of the Devyn bards now came forward. "We are the clan family whose treasure is always with us, my lord Dominus. We are the poets and singers. Tonight around the great fire we will sing for you the song we have composed in your honor. It tells of your great generosity in giving us this new land, and of our journey here."

Accius bowed low.

"I shall look forward to hearing your saga, my lord," the Dominus said.

Roan of the Aghy was next to present himself to Magnus Hauk. "In the spring," he said, "you shall have three foals sired by the great Dasras," he told him. "And you will, I hope, my lord Dominus, come to choose them yourself."

"I do not have to, my lord," Magnus Hauk said, "for I trust you to do it. And the following spring when they are yearlings, I shall take them into my stables."

Roan of the Aghy nodded. "I had heard it said, my lord, that you were wise," he murmured. "The truth has exceeded my expectations." He bowed low, and turning moved away from where Lara and her husband stood.

"Well done, my lord," Lara told Magnus Hauk softly.

And finally Rendor stepped up to present the Dominus with several fine sheepskin rugs. "'Tis small thanks for your overwhelming kindness to us, my lord," he said, bowing to their new overlord.

"The land was here as if waiting for you and your clan families," Magnus Hauk replied with a small smile. Gently dismissed, Rendor stepped back, and the Dominus's glance swept the stone circle. "And now, my lords, are we ready to celebrate?"

They shouted their approval as he led them back into the great encampment of the Gathering.

"You have put them very much at their ease," Lara told her husband. "Thank you." She kissed his cheek.

"I want to meet your son," he told her.

Knowing that Dillon was nearby Lara looked for him, and waved the boy over to join them. "This is the Dominus of Terah, Dillon," she said. "My lord, this is the son I gave Vartan of the Fiacre."

Dillon held out his small hand, and taking it Magnus Hauk was surprised by the strength he found in the boy's grasp. "I greet you, my lord Dominus."

"I greet you, Dillon, son of Vartan," the Dominus said. And then he smiled down at the boy. "Aye, I can see it in your eyes, lad. We will be friends."

"Indeed we will, my lord, for we love the same woman," Dillon responded.

The Dominus laughed heartily at the boy's words. "You are clever like your mother," he told Dillon. "One day if your people do not need you I will find a place for you myself in Terah."

"And I will come when you call," was the strangely adult reply.

Deep blue eyes met turquoise ones, and Magnus Hauk had the oddest sensation that one day Dillon, son of Vartan, would indeed be of help to him.

Chapter
18

THEY REMAINED in the new Outlands until the Gathering had concluded. Magnus Hauk realized over the next few days, as he grew to know the clan families, that he had been right to heed his wife's plea and bring them to Terah. In time, of course, the clan families and those Terahn born on the other side of the Emerald Mountains would come to know one another. If their coming together were carefully managed there should be no difficulty.

But Lara cautioned patience. "First we must see what Hetar does," she said.

"Why will they do anything?" the Dominus said. "They are across the sea."

"Gaius Prospero is already wondering where Terah is. He has forced that information from Arcas, who betrayed his own people to save his miserable life. Arcas has always been a bully and a coward. And once the emperor learns that it is not the people of the Coastal Kingdom who produce the luxury goods Hetar loves so dearly, we are in danger, Magnus. Even King Archeron will not be able to stem the tide of Gaius Prospero's greed and ambition. I was foolish to take you to Hetar."

"From what I saw of this emperor he is a careful man, Lara," Magnus said. "By emptying the old Outlands of everything, and sealing up the mines, all he thought to gain is gone. There were no easy pickings for Hetar. No new supply of slaves. Gaius Prospero will have to spend some of his own ill-gotten gains to keep the peace and resettle the old Outlands. He will be too busy maintaining his own position to be bothered with us."

"Perhaps in the short term, but not the long," Lara answered. "Terah must begin to build an army so that when the time comes we can protect ourselves, and our lands."

"An army?" he exclaimed. "We have never had an army. We have never needed one. If I tell our people we need one now I will frighten them."

"Better they be frightened now when we are safe, and can overcome that fear while we raise a force to protect us in the future from any foreign incursion into Terah," Lara responded. "Magnus, it is not just Hetar. The day I came to the new Outlands Dasras and I went for a ride. He wanted me to see the sea creatures in the Obscura, and I did. But I saw something else as well. The desert of the Shadow Princes lies across the sea, and curves around the water to the south. But to the north is yet another land. It is neither

Terah nor Hetar. As Hetar knew nothing of us, there is a land of which neither of us has any knowledge. We are vulnerable from at least two sides.

"Because Terah has never been approached by foreigners does not mean we will not be in the future. The land I saw looked dark, Magnus. The sorcerer Usi represented true evil, my husband. From where did he learn that evil? Indeed, from where did Usi originate? The magic that grows within me can only protect Terah to a small extent. Terah must learn to protect itself in future. Call the headmen from the fjord villages to our castle, and tell them what we know. Then tell them we must raise a military force, and sustain it at their expense for the day when Hetar, or the lords of the dark land, will come upon us for wickedness' sake," Lara pleaded.

"I must think on it," he told her.

Lara bowed her head with acceptance of his words. Once again she was surprised by the nature of men. Her counsel was good, but he would not take it immediately. He would consider it, and then he would argue the point with her once or twice. Then if she were clever, and could manage to keep from shrieking at him for being so stubborn, he would take her advice, and make it his own. What was the matter with men that they could not accept a woman's word in serious matters such as this? Her hand went to the crystal star between her breasts. *Is there time?* she asked Ethne.

There is some, Ethne replied.

"It is good to be home," the Dominus said.

"Aye, it is," Lara agreed. They had ridden Dasras

together over the plain, and then the mountains, leaving when the great torch of the Gathering had been extinguished that last morning. She had bid Dillon farewell, hugging her son to her chest, forcing back the tears that threatened to overwhelm her. Noss had brought Anoush to say goodbye, but Anoush was at that age when she was shy of strangers. She hid her small heart-shaped face in Noss's sturdy shoulder. "Take care of them," Lara said quietly, her hand caressing Anoush's hair.

"I will," Noss promised. "Lara, if I should need you..." Her voice ceased, but her eyes begged.

"Call my name," Lara told her. "I will hear you, Noss."

The Dominus had, along with his wife, bid farewell to each of the clan lords. Roan of the Aghy, however, had made him jealous as Kaliq did, by flirting with Lara as he always did, a final time. Magnus Hauk glowered darkly at the horse lord who pretended not even to notice.

"Take care of your stallion," Roan said as they mounted Dasras.

"Which one?" Lara teased back, and Dasras chortled.

Roan just grinned at her, and then with a wave turned to join his own people.

As Dasras galloped off, and then soared into the skies above the new Outlands Magnus Hauk seethed angrily.

"I am surprised Vartan did not slay him," the Dominus said. "Or has he only begun flirting with you of late?"

"He has always done so," Lara said calmly. "When Vartan died I think he hoped to convince me to be his wife. Roan is amusing, Magnus, and nothing more."

"Doesn't he have a wife of his own? A man that age should have a wife," the Dominus said irritably. So Roan had wanted Lara for his own? Bastard!

"He has several wives," Lara informed her spouse. "Like a stallion no one mare can satisfy him," she said with a chuckle.

"And he wanted you, as well?" Magnus Hauk was outraged.

"Stallions always long for the prettiest mares, is that not so, Dasras?"

"Indeed, Mistress, it is," the big horse replied.

The Dominus was struck silent, and remained so for some time. Finally they reached the castle on the fjord known as the Dominus's Fjord. Dasras's hooves touched down in his stableyard, and Jason, his personal groom, ran forth.

"Welcome home, my lord Dominus, my lady Domina. Welcome home, Dasras!" Jason greeted them, taking the stallion's bridle.

Magnus Hauk leaped from the horse's back, and lifted his wife down. "Thank you, Jason. See Dasras is well taken care of, if you will."

"He would tell me if I didn't take care of him properly," Jason said with a grin.

"Harumpp!" the stallion responded as the boy led him off.

Lara was eager for a bath and said so as they walked to their apartments. "Bathing is not an option at the Gathering," she observed with a smile. "I have become used to this more civilized way of living."

"I have been thinking about what you said," he told her.

"About what?" Lara pretended it hadn't been on her mind at all.

"A military force for Terah. We cannot wait until Hetar pays us a visit now, can we? Better to be ready. And I am curious about this dark land you saw to the north. Do you think it is inhabited?"

"Probably, but it is best we not investigate it, Magnus. We do not wish to attract attention. If Usi gained his powers from whoever is there we are better off avoiding the dark land for now. In time I will investigate that place."

"If you wish to remain unknown you are better served not riding that great golden stallion with his flapping white wings into the region," the Dominus said.

"Ahh, husband, there is still much you have to learn about me," Lara told him.

"What?" he demanded to know.

"In time, Magnus," she promised him.

"Why not now?" he asked her. They stood at the entrance to their apartments.

"You are not ready," she answered simply. She stepped into the entry chamber, and greeted the serving woman who came forth smiling her welcome. "Ahh, Mila, your Domina wishes a bath." Turning she kissed her husband lightly on his lips. "Do you want a bath, Magnus?" she purred at him, and her hand caressed his face.

All other thoughts fled him as she had anticipated. They had not been together as man and wife in several weeks now, and he was hungry for her. "Will you give me a child, my faerie wife?" he asked her, his arm wrapped about her waist.

"Have I not promised you that I will in time?" she answered him.

"That is not an answer," he told her quietly.

"It is all the answer I can give you, Magnus. There are for now matters of greater importance to Terah than a child," Lara said.

"An heir of my body and blood is paramount to Terah. You are a good mother, Lara. I saw you with your children, Dillon in particular, but even the shy little Anoush who knows not who you are. Your love for that wee girly surmounts your own need for your daughter, my faerie love. Your sacrifice is magnificent," he told her.

"Because of my destiny I have deserted my daughter even as my own mother deserted me, Magnus. My sacrifice is a selfish one for all the nobility of my destiny," Lara said bitterly. "I was happy with Vartan, with our children. And then with his murder, my destiny called once again. I will always wonder if I had not stayed with him, let him make me his wife, if he might not be alive today. He was a great leader of his people, and they needed him. I am happier with you, my love, than I have ever been. But when my destiny calls again and I must leave you behind, I do not want to leave another child as well. There are perilous times coming, Magnus. I sense it."

"Vartan's destiny was to be your mate for a time,

to father Dillon who is a unique boy, and Anoush, and finally to die as he did," the Dominus replied. "But I am your soul mate, your life mate, Lara, my faerie wife. If there are perilous times coming we will face them together, surmount them together. This I promise you. Now go and have your bath. I will join you shortly." Then he turned and left her while he hurried off to find Corrado.

Reaching the apartments where his sister resided with her husband he was greeted most effusively by Sirvat, who was beginning to show her belly.

"You are home!" Sirvat flung her arms about his neck, and kissed her brother.

Magnus Hauk laughed. "Aye, and it was a grand adventure. These clan family folk are good people, little sister. I like them, except perhaps for the lord of the Aghy who enjoys flirting with Lara, and has several wives nonetheless."

Sirvat laughed. "Is he handsome?" she asked. "You would be jealous of an ugly man, Brother." Sirvat had been finally told of the clan families, and was fascinated.

The Dominus nodded. "Red hair, muscles and flashing black eyes," he said.

"Ohh, sounds fascinating," Sirvat cooed.

"Where is your husband?" he asked her.

"With his father and brother preparing for a voyage. As soon as he heard you were back he hurried to Ing's chandlery to begin provisioning his vessel. He wants to do one voyage before the Icy season sets in again," Sirvat said.

"Then I will go and find him," the Dominus re-

sponded. He kissed her forehead. "Keep well, Sirvat.
Lara will probably come and see you tomorrow, and
tell you all."

"Why are you so anxious to see Corrado?" Sirvat
wanted to know.

"Because then he will not come banging at my
apartment doors this evening when I am making
love to my wife. We have not been together in weeks,
Sirvat, and I do not want my longed for pleasures
being interrupted by Corrado," the Dominus told his
sister.

His explanation made sense to Sirvat, and she
asked nothing further of him as he departed her apartments. And it was the truth, Magnus Hauk thought.
Perhaps not all the truth, but then Sirvat had asked
nothing more than why he chose to see Corrado. The
Dominus grinned to himself as he stepped onto the
platform that would take him to the fjord. "Fjordside!"
he snapped to the unseen giant who operated the platform, standing quietly as he was lowered down the
platform shaft. When his brief journey came to a halt
he stepped off the wooden platform, but he did not
go out onto the docks. Instead he turned left into a
corridor lit by round glass lamps filled with firebugs.
These creatures spent their entire life-span within
their home globes. They lived, died and mated within
the confines of the glass. There were shops located
along the corridor. Magnus Hauk nodded to the other
Terahns shopping who bowed as he passed. Reaching
the establishment belonging to Ing, the chandler, the
Dominus stepped inside.

Corrado and his brother smiled as they saw who their visitor was.

"My lord Dominus, welcome back!" Corrado said.

"My sister tells me you plan a season's end voyage," the Dominus replied.

"With your permission, of course, my lord Dominus," Corrado quickly answered.

"How long will it take you?" Magnus Hauk wanted to know.

"Eight days if the weather holds," Corrado replied.

"Will it hold?" the Dominus asked.

"At this time of year, aye. Four times yearly, at the changing of the seasons, Sagitta has perfect weather with no storms, my lord Dominus. This period lasts approximately ten days. It has just begun," Corrado explained.

"Can you go today?" his lord wanted to know.

Corrado looked to his brother, Ing. "Can I?"

Ing, a man of few words nodded to the Dominus.

"Go then," Magnus Hauk said. "Today. Return quickly. Pick up any gossip you can from the Coastal Kings. Report to me immediately upon your return, no matter the hour of the day or night."

"My lord," Corrado said slowly, then turned to his brother. "Leave us, Ing."

Ing said nothing, but disappeared into the back of his shop.

"I am preparing a new venture," the Dominus said, "and I am going to need your counsel, Corrado. I want my plans in place before the Icy season begins. That is all I choose to say to you for now."

"I trust you, my lord Dominus," his captain of captains replied. "My ship and my crew are waiting. Tell Sirvat I will see her in a few days." He bowed.

"Send Ing to her with that message," Magnus Hauk said. "I have not been with Lara in weeks now. I am going to join her in her bath, Corrado. Travel in safety." Then turning the Dominus left his brother-in-law in the middle of the chandlery.

When he had gone Ing stepped from the back room where he has been waiting. "What was that about?" he asked his younger brother.

Corrado shrugged. "If I knew I could not tell you, my brother, but I do not know. Is my ship ready to depart? The crew aboard?"

Ing nodded. "All is in readiness," he said.

"Go to Sirvat, and tell her I have, at the Dominus's request, departed. I will see her in a few days. Take Father with you. She enjoys his company. Says it shows her what I will be like when I am an old man," Corrado chuckled.

Ing barked one of his few laughs. "A romantic girl, your wife," he said. Then he and Corrado clasped hands. "Travel in safety," he told his sibling.

"It will be the will of the Great Creator that I do," Corrado answered, and then was gone from the small shop.

It was almost day's end Ing saw looking out through the single dusty window his chandlery possessed onto the fjord. Corrado was fortunate in that he would catch the late tide, which would sweep him quickly out to sea. The winds this time of year were perfect. They were neither too soft, nor too hard. He watched his younger brother board his vessel; the gangway drawn up; the sails hoisted; the ship slipped out into the Dominus's fjord, its square sails catching the breeze as it moved gracefully toward Sagitta. Ing closed up his shop and went to fetch his father, Dima. Together the two men made their way to the apartments of Corrado and Sirvat.

She welcomed them warmly. "Stay and have the evening meal with us. Corrado will undoubtedly be here shortly after he has checked the other woman in his life to be certain she is ready to travel again."

Dima chuckled appreciatively, for he yet recalled what it was to be the captain of captains for a Dominus of Terah.

"My brother has already embarked," Ing said apologetically. "There was no time for him to bid you farewell. He asked that I come and tell you."

"My brother found him," Sirvat said resigned. Then she went to the window, and looked down on the fjord where she could just make out the lavender sails of her husband's ship as it rounded the bend in the waterway that opened into the sea. "What did Magnus say to him that sent him scurrying without even a farewell to me?"

Ing shook his head. "I do not know, my lady Sirvat. I was not privy to their conversation. I'm sorry. But he did say to tell you he would be back in just a few days. It is an ordinary voyage, for all I provisioned his ship for was the usual trading journey. That much I can tell you."

"I will speak to my brother on the morrow," Sirvat said. "I would still appreciate your company for the meal." She smiled at her father-in-law. "We are having prawns, Dima, and I know how you love prawns. Especially the large ones that come from the Ocean Fjord. My cook bought them just this morning right off the boat that caught them."

The old man smiled broadly. "You know how to please a sailor's palate, Sirvat," he told her nodding. "You have mustard sauce, too, I am certain."

Yes, she considered, Corrado would look like this handsome old man one day. And he would not go to sea much longer if she had her way. She would have to speak to Magnus, Sirvat thought, and smiled back at Dima. But her smile came from the knowledge that even now her brother and his wife were taking pleasures with one another, and would create a child to be the playmate of the baby now growing in her own womb. Siruat's hands went instinctively to her belly.

BUT LARA was still not certain of what she wanted to do. The future was too murky. What if she were called by her damned destiny from Terah? Could she ignore her destiny? What would happen if she did? It was all very well and good for Kaliq, her mother and the others in the magic realm to prattle on about her destiny. What was that destiny, and was it to elude her forever? She had loved Vartan, and if the rest of her life had been spent in the old Outlands with him and their children, she could have been satisfied with that life.

But what, her sensible self asked, would have happened if Vartan had survived his assassination? What would they have done when Hetar invaded the Outlands? Could they have overcome the greater forces of Gaius Prospero's armies? She did not think so, and so many would have been killed. Vartan's death had indeed been a part of her destiny, much as she hated to admit it. His death had sent her on her way again. To Terah. Into Magnus Hauk's arms, but on her own terms. As the wife of the Dominus she had been able to save the clan families from Gaius Prospero's greedy machinations. Vartan would have approved. The emperor would be busy for some time to come bringing civilization to the old Outlands. But how long would that keep him from Terah?

They should not have gone to the City she thought for probably the hundredth time. She should not have given in to Magnus's wishes. The emperor's curiosity had been quickly engaged by the knowledge there was another land beyond Hetar's borders.

And the dark land to the north? Lara knew she needed to know more about it, but there she sensed that she yet had time enough. She must speak with the High Priest Arik and learn what he knew of Usi before she considered her move in that direction. Magnus must not know, for the interim, that she could shape-shift. Did he really think her so naive as to ride her winged stallion over the dark land? But then he knew naught of the owl's shape she could take. The eagle had been Vartan's symbol. He, too, was capable of shape-shifting. They had both taken a bird's form once, and flown together to seek Kaliq's advice. She smiled with the memory.

"What are you thinking of?" Magnus asked her as he joined her in the soaking pool. Like his wife he had already washed and rinsed himself in another part of the bath.

"Of how good it was to see my children," she lied to him, and yet it was not a lie. But then Lara quickly realized her error in bringing up the subject of her children.

"I am glad the thought of children makes you smile," he responded quietly. "It would please me more if it was the thought of our children, however." His big hand cupped the back of her head, and he pulled her into his embrace for a kiss.

He thought to seduce her, Lara knew, but it must be she who seduced him away from these thoughts. Her lips softened beneath his, the tip of her tongue slipping out to encircle his mouth delicately. Turquoise eyes met green, and each felt an explosion of lust as their gazes locked. "Magnus!" she said his name breathlessly. Great Creator, she was going to give into him. But she couldn't! It wasn't time yet.

Magnus Hauk smiled a slow smile, and he kissed her again. A sweet, lingering kiss first, and then a more demanding kiss. His mouth was hard and fierce on hers for several long moments. Then taking her face between his two hands his lips traveled from her mouth to her eyelids, her cheeks. "I love you, Lara, my faerie wife," he told her in a low voice. "I can no longer imagine life without you." His gaze encompassed her beautiful face, and Lara saw the simple truth of his words in her husband's look.

She slipped her slender arms about his neck. "I love you, too," she told him. "I did not believe I would love again after Vartan's death, Magnus. It is difficult for faerie women to love at all, but I have mortal blood, too, and I suppose where love is concerned I am weak." Lara sighed softly. "When you look at me as you are looking now I find my knees grow weak, the fire within me burns hot, and there is little I would deny you. But I don't want to make love in the water tonight. I want to be in our bedchamber." She took his hand and they stepped up from the bathing pool.

Taking a large towel from the pile upon a bench she began to dry his magnificent body off. Kneeling she rubbed each of his long legs free of water both front and back. She took each of his two feet, pushing the toweling in between the toes. She dried his hard buttocks. Then Lara stood, and taking another towel rubbed it across his back, his shoulders and his chest. She dried his belly, and gently patted his genitalia free of moisture. He was already hard with her delicate touch. His burnished gold hair was half-dry, and so she gave it but a cursory rub of the towel.

The Dominus now took up a fresh towel, and lifting her onto the marble bench holding the drying cloths began to dry Lara's lush body. His fingers seemed inclined to stray from the fabric, brushing down the insides of her thighs, along the shadowed indentation separating her buttocks, across her nipples which puckered in response. He pushed the towel between her thighs, and suddenly two of his fingers were burying themselves deep inside of her, deliberately taunting her.

"Magnus!" Her voice was tight.

"You are ready, my love, and there is no time left for niceties," he told her, withdrawing the wicked digits and laying her down upon the bench. "We will attend to them afterwards." Towering over her he sucked upon the two fingers, a look of bliss lighting his face. Then sitting between her legs he pulled them up and over his shoulders, entering her body in a single smooth stroke.

Lara's eyes closed of their own volition. She felt him within her, hot and throbbing as he forced the walls of her love sheath to expand to accommodate his incredible denseness. Every fiber of her being was attuned to him. The tip of her tongue moistened her lips. And then he began to move in her, grinding himself into her body, slowly, slowly, withdrawing only to thrust back in again. He was deeper inside her than he had ever been, and she trembled with the pleasure that was starting to overcome her. "Magnus!" she gasped. Her head spun with the exquisite sensations that were overwhelming her. "Oh, the Creator, I do love you, my darling!"

He was almost insensible with the wildness and passion overwhelming him as he ploughed her deeply. His rod burned. It was swollen to the bursting point, and yet he was not ready. Immersed as far within her as he could go, he leaned back slightly, and with the tip of a single finger began to skillfully rub the little jewel so cunningly set between her moist nether lips. The nub, already swollen to twice its size, quivered beneath his touch. Lara began to moan, her body bucking as she struggled to reach her bliss. "Just a minute more, my love," he murmured, and then they took their pleasure together, their bodies trembling as their love juices erupted and mingled together. A last shudder and he gathered her into his embrace, whispering words of eternal love and devotion to this faerie woman who was his adored wife.

They sat clinging to each other for some minutes. His manhood was still buried within her, but quiet for now until they were strong enough to make love again. Reluctantly he finally withdrew from her, and taking her hand they stood up. He led them to a basin set within the marble walls of the bath, and taking up a sea sponge bathed Lara's sex even as she bathed his. They did not speak. What had just transpired between them was beyond speech.

Together they left the bath and walked naked through the short hall between it and their bedchamber. There they fell into bed exhausted, and slept for several hours until they awoke to make love again. And they remained within their apartments for the next few days indulging their passions for one another. Magnus Hauk was not needed. There was peace in his lands, unless, of course, you counted Sirvat, who wanted to know why her husband had been sent so precipitously to sea.

"You have to speak to her," Lara told her husband after four days had passed. "You don't want to upset a woman who is with child."

"Very well," he agreed. "Tell Mila to go and fetch my sister. I will get dressed."

Sirvat came immediately, and looking at Lara said, "Have you done anything except take pleasures these past few days? Have you eaten? You look exhausted."

"Your brother's passions have been all consuming," Lara responded with a smile. "I like your belly. Being with child suits you, Sirvat. You have never looked lovelier."

Sirvat colored, pleased with the compliment. "I am going to have a boy," she said. "I just know it!"

"You will have what the Great Creator wills you to have," her brother said entering the sunny day room. "What do you want, Sirvat? I have been very busy since my return from the new Outlands." Magnus Hauk attempted to look stern.

"You have been busy taking pleasures with your wife, Brother, and I know it. Why did you send Corrado away, and when will he return?"

"I did not send him away. But since he was planning to go I asked him to go immediately. He should be back in another three or four days, Sirvat. I have great plans for Terah, and I am going to need your husband's good counsel."

"It could not wait long enough for Corrado to bid me farewell?" Sirvat sniffed.

"No," Magnus Hauk said bluntly, "it could not. I won't discuss it with you, little sister. When Corrado returns you will know what it is I am doing. And do not attempt to wheedle Lara into telling you, for she will not."

"I don't want Corrado going to sea any longer like a common captain," Sirvat said. "He is your captain of captains, Magnus, and should remain ashore to guide the other captains. Besides, he is to be a father. I don't want him several days away from me when I birth his son next year."

"I will not tell Corrado he cannot go to sea, Sirvat. If that is what you desire of him then you must speak with him yourself. You are a woman grown now," the Dominus said impatiently.

"Do you love Corrado, Sirvat?" Lara asked her friend.

"Aye, I do!" Sirvat cried.

"You love the man he is?" Lara persisted.

"Aye!" Sirvat repeated.

"Then why do you seek to change him?" Lara said quietly. "You married a man who captains a ship. A man who guides and oversees all of Terah's captains. This is who and what Corrado is, Sirvat. If you truly love him, then you must accept this."

A tear slipped down Sirvat's cheek. "But I miss him when he is away!" she sobbed piteously.

"Of course you do, but the tears you now shed are the tears every woman with child sheds over the least little thing. It will pass, Sister," Lara promised. "Why don't you go to the stables, and visit with Dasras? He always enjoys your company, and it will help pass the time for you. Corrado will be home shortly."

When Sirvat had departed Magnus Hauk said to his wife, "You are wise, Domina. You comforted Sirvat nicely. Had I been alone I might have shouted at her."

"Women carrying the unborn in their bellies have a tendency to become very emotional, Magnus. One day I will, and you had best not shout at me," Lara warned him.

He chuckled. She pleased him. Everything about her pleased him. He had never loved any woman as he loved his faerie wife. "If I shouted at you," he said, "you would only shout back at me, Lara. I thank you for taking Sirvat's woes upon yourself and freeing me from them. But she had best speak to Corrado when he returns."

Three nights later the Dominus was awakened from his slumber when Corrado returned, and came immediately to speak with him as he had been instructed.

"We caught a fresh breeze and got into the fjord before the tide turned," he told his overlord. "I bring you a letter from King Archeron, my lord Dominus." He handed the rolled parchment to Magnus Hauk. "Good evening, my lady Domina," he greeted Lara who, wrapping a robe about her, had joined the two men.

"You saw Archeron?" she asked.

Corrado shook his head. "Nay. The Hetarian Coastal King we met carried the missive to be given to me and then to the Dominus."

Magnus Hauk had broken the seal on the message, and unrolled it. When he had finished reading it he handled it to Lara to read. "Your wife has missed you. Go and be with her," he told his brother-in-law. "Come and see me in the morning two hours before the noon day, Corrado. I will tell you what is in the letter then."

Lara's eyes quickly scanned the letter from King Archeron. Arcas, as she had known he would, had betrayed the Coastal Kings. Gaius Prospero was now aware that the luxury goods Hetar so craved did not come from them but from Terah. The emperor had turned the Coastal Kingdom into a province. Archeron, however, had been chosen by the emperor to be its governor. *My son thought to have this position,* Archeron wrote, *but Gaius Prospero is wise enough to know he cannot trust the man who betrayed us into his greedy hands. But he trusts me for two reasons. The first is that I have never locked horns with him, and the second is that Arcas tried to murder me.* Lara smiled. She could almost hear King Archeron chortling. The Coastal King went on to write that Hetar had now taken over the province's beautiful empty lands, and was settling people on them.

As for the Outlands, they had not proved as profitable as Gaius Prospero had promised they would be. The Hetarians transported there for the purpose of settlement were having difficulty erecting their villages and shelters before the winter set in. There wasn't enough livestock or poultry to stock the new farms. There wasn't enough lumber for the buildings, or even food to eat. The settlers were being forced to send two-thirds of what the newly opened fields produced to the City. What remained had to feed the settlers in the Outlands, and little was being stored for winter. It was an unfortunate situation.

Now the Forest Lords were demanding control over the forests of the Purple Mountains, and Squire Darah of the Midlands, now its governor, was insisting that the farmlands of the Outlands should really be under his control. The Shadow Princes had withdrawn from the High Council, and warned the emperor that any incursion into their lands would result in disaster for Hetar. *But Gaius Prospero has no idea the riches the desert kingdom holds, and so is content to ignore what he considers a wasteland,* Archeron wrote.

The mines he has opened have yielded next to nothing. Those poor in the City without means or important friends are being swept up into slavery to make up for the clan families who disappeared from the Outlands before the invasion. I don't suppose Lara would know anything about that? Be warned, Archeron went on, *that Gaius Prospero is growing desperate, and probably dangerous. Arcas has told him what little we know of Terah, and it is indeed possible that despite the situation in Hetar, which is spiraling out of control, the emperor may attempt to send someone to Terah to investigate your riches. I have warned you not because I am disloyal to Hetar, but because I am horrified by what has been happening. It is too dangerous for me to write again. I am sending this letter by my late wife's brother who captains one of our vessels. I know he is trustworthy. The Celestial Actuary protect us all in these perilous times.*

Lara set the letter aside. "Archeron is an honorable man," she said. "He thought long and hard about sending you this message, Magnus. Now do you truly understand our need for a military force to protect Terah?"

The Dominus nodded. "I will speak to Corrado first," he said. "And then I will send to the headmen of all the fjord villages. We have seven named fjords. And there are many villages. This meeting must take place before the Icy Season sets in for it will be too difficult to gather everyone once it does."

"You have no governing body?" Lara asked her husband.

He shook his head. "I am the Dominus. It has

always been this way in Terah. Once a High Council was proposed, but it was believed that a council would be likely to get caught up in debates, and then nothing would get done. Members of a council would also be open to bribery and coercion. There are greedy and ambitious among us, too, Lara. It is better that each village has its headman, who is responsible to me. I make the decisions based upon what they tell me. I do what is right for Terah," Magnus Hauk said. "It has worked well for centuries, except for the time in which Usi ruled over Terah."

"How did he gain such control over the land?" Lara wanted to know.

"The Dominus at the time was a particularly kind man, and Usi is said to have bewitched him," Magnus Hauk replied.

"We must see that does not happen again," Lara murmured.

"It will not," the Dominus said in a hard voice.

The next morning Corrado joined Magnus Hauk and Lara. Sitting together they explained all that had happened in the last few months, and why it was going to be necessary to raise a military force to protect Terah.

"But we are craftsmen and traders by nature," Corrado protested. "We know naught of war."

"So you are content to be conquered by Hetar?" Lara said to him. She knew she would hear this same protest over and over again once they met with the headmen from the many villages located along the shores of the seven named fjords.

"Well, no," Corrado said slowly, "but is there not another way?"

"We are only proposing to defend ourselves from attack," the Dominus answered.

"We will initiate no hostilities ourselves, but we must be prepared in the event hostilities are initiated by others, Corrado. And once that happens it will be too late unless we are prepared for it. Pitchforks and hoes in the hands of farmers and craftsmen will not stop an invading force. We need weapons, and we need men trained to know how to use them. The weapons can be made over the winter months, and we can train the men then, too," Magnus Hauk said.

"Women are capable of fighting, too," Lara told them. "I will train a force of women in swordsmanship and staff."

Both her husband and Corrado looked horrified at her words.

"Magnus!" Lara glared at him. "You know I can fight."

"Aye, you can, but Terahn women have never been warriors," he replied.

"Oh really? What would you have called Geltruda, the woman who destroyed Usi? Was she not a warrior? A heroine? Women are every bit as capable as men, my lord Dominus, but if you wish to cut your fighting force in half then do so. Andraste and I, however, will fight by your side should it be necessary," Lara told him.

"Will Hetar send women warriors into battle?"

"Nay, they will not," Lara said. "Do you wish to be as stupid as Gaius Prospero who believes that women are only good for pleasures, childbirth and housekeeping?"

"We will invite women to join in protecting Terah, but we will not compel them to do so," Magnus Hauk decided, and Lara kissed her husband's cheek in approval.

"I would not allow Sirvat to join such a force," Corrado said.

"Sirvat must make her own choices," Lara said quietly. "She is a member of Terah's ruling family, and will decide where best she may serve our homeland."

Corrado raised a quizzical eyebrow. "You are Hetarian," he said.

"I am Terahn," she told him. "I could not choose where I was born, and actually I was born in the faerie realm, Corrado. My loyalties, however, are Terahn. Not because I am now its Domina, but because it is where my heart is."

To her surprise her husband's captain of captains stood, and knelt suddenly at her feet. Looking up at Lara he said, "Forgive me, Domina. I am a fool."

"But only sometimes," Lara replied with a smile, and she held out her hand to help him rise to his feet again.

Both men laughed aloud, and the Dominus said, "Let us continue to talk so we may decide what is to be done. I thought to send messengers to the headmen of all the named fjords, and to the headmen of each of the villages inviting them to the castle. When we have assembled them all we will tell them what has transpired, and what we must do to protect Terah."

"We will want Arik and Kemina at these meetings, too, for they represent the religious orders, and it is the Great Creator who will guide us in what we do now," Lara noted.

The two men nodded.

"Archeron was brave to warn us," Lara said.

"Will we have time to prepare ourselves?" Corrado wondered.

"Gaius Prospero will want to know more about us before he decides on a course of action," Lara remarked thoughtfully.

"How will he learn what he needs to know?" Magnus asked her.

"He will send someone," Lara said. "First he will ask permission for a Hetarian vessel to enter Terah. You must refuse him, my lord. Then he will request permission for his emissary to come to Terah upon one of our ships. You will send back a reply asking why he wants to send an emissary to Terah."

"Will he not become impatient with all this back and forth?" Corrado wondered.

"Nay, for it is very Hetarian to query and bargain over an important matter such as this. It will not seem odd to the emperor at all. If you simply told him yes or no and refused to negotiate further then he would find himself suspicious. But this Hetarian habit will give us all the time we need to build up a defense against our enemies," Lara said. "And since the emperor's emissary will only be allowed to visit the castle on this first sojourn, we can fortify it and the area around it so that we will look very well defended to his eyes. Eventually we will have to allow him to see a village or two, but by then we will be truly well armed and ready."

"The old watchtowers on the coastal heights," Corrado said. "They should be rebuilt, and manned. We need an early warning system."

"I had forgotten about those," the Dominus replied. "That is an excellent suggestion, Corrado. I will leave that task to you. You may have whatever you need."

"Would your headmen be frightened of small faeries?" Lara asked her husband. "I could ask my mother for a dozen or more faeriepost messengers. They use them in Hetar, and they are very useful for carrying messages quickly. We could make them a home here in the castle, and for now only we would have them although later on I believe each village headman should possess two of these tiny creatures each. You want to hold your meeting before the Icy Season sets in, and we could call the headmen more quickly if we had faeriepost," Lara explained.

"I have seen these creatures," Corrado said with a chuckle. "The Coastal Kings have sometimes used them to communicate with our vessels when we are anchored for trade. They are most efficient, my lord Dominus."

Magnus Hauk nodded. "We must use whatever advantage we have," he said. "Do whatever you need to do, Lara, and bring Terah faeriepost."

Their meeting broke up, and when Lara and her husband were alone once more she turned to him and said, "We must tell the new Outlands of what is transpiring. They should have faeriepost as well."

"Do you want the clan lords at the meeting of headmen?" he asked her.

"Just Rendor who is head of the Outlands High Council," Lara replied. "This is an ideal opportunity for us to let the fjord dwellers know there are others beyond the Emerald Mountains. The headmen do not have to know that six months ago the plains beyond the mountains were empty. You said the fjord dwellers have never gone beyond their own village lands. They cannot know who or what lies on the other side of the mountains. I had not thought to bring Terahns and Outlanders together yet, but I think now we have no other choice, Magnus.

"You can tell your headmen that the family of the Dominus has always known they were there, but that the people of the clan families have always been hesitant and reluctant to deal with others, for they are peaceful folk. They pay their yearly tribute and keep to themselves. But now, given the danger facing Terah, they have agreed to send their own high lord to your council to offer what aid they may. Dasras and I will visit the mountain gnomes as a courtesy to inform them of the coming peril, and of the fiction we have woven to protect the Outlanders," Lara concluded.

"Sometimes," Magnus Hauk said, "I wonder if you are not too clever for me, Lara." Then he smiled, and ruffled her hair. "I can hope our children will take after you."

There it was again. The subject of children. How could he think of children when they were in such jeopardy? He had been very shocked by what he had seen in the City, and yet he still did not quite fathom the deviousness of Hetar. Hetar had to be stopped. She would not allow them to insinuate their guileful and aberrant customs into Terah. There was more than one way to conquer a nation. She understood that. She worried her husband did not. She left him to his planning, and sought a quiet place where she might communicate with Ethne.

Her slender fingers caressed the crystal star hanging between her breasts. *Ethne,* she called silently to the guardian of the crystal.

I am here, Ethne replied.

Lara explained all that had happened, and what her husband was planning. Then she said, *But I need faeriepost messengers. Will you go to my mother, and ask her if I may have some? I will see they are very well taken care of here, I promise.*

I will go to her, Ethne responded, *but tonight you must meet her on the dream plane and ask for this favor yourself, for it is a great boon you seek. I know you have asked her for little in your lifetime, but Queen Ilona would consider it a great rudeness if you did not speak with her about this yourself, Lara.*

I understand, Lara said. *Please tell my mother that I should appreciate it if she would see me tonight on the dream plane, Ethne. I will tell my husband, and sleep alone.*

Wait, Ethne said, and then after several long minutes she spoke again. *It is done, Lara, and your mother will be awaiting you.*

Thank you, Lara said. Then she went and told her husband that tonight she must sleep by herself so that nothing impeded her journey to the dream plane, and her meeting with Queen Ilona. He nodded reluctantly, but understood her need. They ate together and played two games of Herder before Lara felt it was time for her to sleep.

And when she slept she was almost immediately swept up to the dream plane. It was as always misty in the beginning, and then Ilona appeared. Mother and daughter embraced.

"What is it you need of me?" the queen of the Forest Faeries asked her eldest child. She smiled at Lara, most happy to see her.

Lara explained slowly all that had happened since she had last seen her mother. She told Ilona of the Terahns' need for the small faeries who served as faeriepost messengers. "There is little if any magic in Terah that I can see," she said to Ilona. "They have gnomes in the mountains, but they seem to have no faeries, though you have said there are. I have not found them yet. The sorcerer whose shade I destroyed brought magic to Terah, but it seemed to disappear when he was vanquished, Mother."

"Nay," Ilona replied. "His magic is still here, but because it is dark magic it hides itself away from the light. You are light, my daughter, and you shine throughout Terah, so it is you who have kept this magic at bay. I will give you several dozen faeriepost messengers, Lara. I know you will see they are well cared for and protected from harm. You had best cast a safety spell upon them when they arrive so no frightened Terahn can hurt them in their own fear," the queen advised.

"I will, Mother!" Lara promised. "Thank you. Are you well? And my brother, Cirilo? And your consort, Thanos, too?"

"We are all well, Lara," her mother replied.

"Mother, I saw a dark land," Lara told Ilona. "Dasras and I were riding over Obscura, and I saw the desert of the Shadow Princes curving to the south, but to the north there was a dark land. Is Terah in danger from it, Mother?"

"There is always danger from the darkness," Ilona said, and then she began to fade slowly from the dream plane. "Follow your destiny, my daughter," she called as she disappeared completely.

Lara awoke, and her first instinct was to laugh. The mortal side of her had always resented the inscrutable, and the faerie world was always speaking to her in riddles. She saw it was growing light outside of her chamber window. A new day. She had best prepare a habitat for the faeriepost messengers today. They would quickly be here, she knew. Rising she called to Mila to help her dress, and bring her food. When Lara had eaten she went into the beautiful garden overlooking the fjord. The day was gray, and a faint mist rose from the waters below. A few late flowers offered splashes of color here and there, but the trees were almost all bare of their leaves now. Gazing about her she saw a tall narrow tower on the south side. It soared gracefully into the Terahn sky.

"What are you gazing at?" Sirvat was at her side.

"There," Lara pointed. "That tower. Who lives in it?"

"No one," Sirvat answered her. "It was once our

grandmother's quarters when our father was Dominus. She loved the tower because its windows faced south, and it was always warm. She lived to be very old." Her hands gently rubbed her belly as she spoke.

"How do you get into it?" Lara asked.

"Come, I'll show you," Sirvat said leading Lara across the great gardens. "The tower appears to be part of the castle, but it really isn't," she explained. "There is no entrance into it but from here in the garden." They had reached the tower, and Sirvat's hand searched along the stones of the structure until she found what she sought. The small door to the tower opened slowly. "There is no key," she told her companion. "The door opens by pressing a small lever beneath this stone. Mark it well."

Lara peered carefully at the location of the wall stone. "I have it," she said.

"Come then," Sirvat invited her, and together the two young women stepped into the tower. "I can still climb stairs, albeit more slowly now," she chuckled.

On the first landing was a lovely sunny small chamber. It was empty. They found identical chambers on the second and top landing of the tower. Lara was delighted.

"This will be perfect for them!" she exclaimed.

"For who?" Sirvat inquired.

"My mother is giving Terah faeriepost messengers," Lara explained. "I wanted to find a safe shelter for them here at the castle."

"Faeriepost messengers?" Sirvat looked confused.

"They are tiny members of the faerie race, and

their purpose is to deliver messages," Lara said. "Terah faeries are hidden, so you have no faeriepost."

"Why do we need them?" Sirvat asked as they descended back down the tower stairs, and exited out into the garden. Behind them the door closed.

"How much has Corrado told you?" Lara wanted to know.

"He has told me nothing, which is why I came looking for you this morning," Sirvat said. "He says I must be protected since I am carrying his child."

The two women reentered the castle, and going to the royal apartments made themselves comfortable in the Domina's day room.

"See we are not disturbed," Lara told her serving woman, Mila. Then she turned to Sirvat. "I do not know how much you know of the trade between Hetar and Terah."

"I know we have a trade with the Coastal Kings," Sirvat said.

"They are but one of Hetar's regions," Lara said. "For centuries they have traded with you for the luxury goods Terah makes. The rest of Hetar believed they manufactured these goods themselves, and the Coastal Kings never said they did not. Now, however, the emperor of Hetar has learned otherwise. Sooner or later he will send someone to Terah. Their purpose will ostensibly be to trade directly with Terah, and not get their goods through the Coastal Kings. But they will also be looking to see if Terah can be conquered by Hetar. Hetar is overpopulated and needs to expand its borders. This past spring it invaded the Outlands where the clan families live. Fortunately we had warning of this betrayal of the ancient treaties. The clan families, along with their homes, goods and chattel were removed from the Outlands, and resettled here in Terah."

Sirvat gasped. "Did you use your magic to bring them here? I assumed you did when Corrado told me of these Outlanders."

Lara laughed. Sirvat's fascination with magic always amused her. "Yes. The clan families were brought to the far side of the Emerald Mountains where the land is much like the land they left. This has been a secret, but soon we will confide in the headmen of the fjord villages. They will be led to believe that the clan families have existed on the other side of the mountains for centuries, and only the ruling family knew of it.

"Hetar has now extended its borders, but all that the emperor promised his Mercenaries was not there. No villages, or herds, or slaves to be taken. The Shadow Princes even used their powers to close the hillsides where the mines had been. Only the land existed in fact for the invaders. Gaius Prospero, Hetar's emperor, has had to expend his own monies helping to make the Outlands habitable. It is going to take them years. But he will want to recoup his losses as quickly as possible, and so he will look to Terah."

"He will want to see if we are weak, if we can be conquered, too," Sirvat said.

"Exactly!" Lara agreed.

"So we have to show this Hetarian who comes

that we are not weak," Sirvat responded. "We have to build an army, Lara."

"Aye, we do, and we are going to build one," Lara replied. "Corrado is in charge of rebuilding the coastal watchtowers. The headmen of the fjord villages will soon meet with the Dominus. Magnus will explain the situation, and then we will prepare to mount our defenses for Terah. And that is why we need the faeriepost. They will aid us in communicating quickly with each other. Each headman's village will be given a pair of faeries."

"I want to help!" Sirvat said.

"And so you shall," Lara promised her. "But I must assign you a task that will not distress Corrado. At least until after you have delivered his child."

The two women giggled conspiratorially.

"I plan to use your grandmother's south tower to house the faeriepost messengers who will live here in the castle before some of them are disbursed to the villages. There are certain things these little creatures need for their comfort, and when I have told you, and shown you, I will leave you, Sirvat, to prepare for our guests."

"I will gladly prepare for these faeries who will be the first of their kind in Terah. It is an honor to be able to serve the faerie kingdom," Sirvat said. "Tell me what I must do, and I will begin at once."

"Excellent!" Lara exclaimed. "We must work quickly, for I know now that my mother has promised us these tiny helpers they will be coming quickly."

"I'll call you when I have completed my task,"

Sirvat said getting up, and hurrying away. "And I'll keep our secrets," she called out softly.

Lara smiled. It would go well. When Hetar came to investigate Terah they would discover not only a prosperous land, but a strong one. But the dark land to the north had begun to prey on her mind, intrude into her thoughts. The unknown was always the most frightening thing of all. But she shook off her fears. One thing at a time, and for now the defense of Terah must occupy them.

The tiny faeriepost messengers arrived two days later. They had flown across the Sagitta, and were exhausted. Delighted with the accommodation made for them in the south tower they settled in to rest themselves for several days. Sirvat had taken it upon herself to personally serve them, which pleased the faeries greatly, for Lara had explained she was the Dominus's sister. That the Terahn ruler's sister would see to their comfort convinced the faeries that they were welcome, and would be content in Terah.

Lara placed a safety spell upon the faeriepost band, and seven were dispatched to the headman of each named fjord. All returned unharmed with tales of the Terahns' surprise at seeing them. But all spoke of the courtesy they had been rendered. The headmen of each named fjord had then sent to each of the village leaders to come with their wives for they were called to the castle. They would come, the faeriepost messengers reported, with all due haste. Messengers were then sent to Arik, the High Priest, at the Temple of the Great Creator; to Kemina, the High Priestess of the Daughters of the Great Creator, and to the leaders of the mountain gnomes inviting them to the castle meeting. Dasras was dispatched to bring Rendor from the new Outlands.

And when all had been assembled Magnus Hauk, Dominus of Terah, told these leaders of his land everything that had transpired. Then he surprised them by introducing Rendor, lord of the Felan, to them. The fjord dwellers were astounded to learn that there were people dwelling beyond the Emerald Mountains. Fulcrum and Gulltopp, the two gnome leaders, understood the Dominus's reasoning for telling the fjord dwellers that the clan families had always been there. They kept their own counsel and listened.

"My captain of captains, Lord Corrado, has been seeing to the rebuilding of the coastal watchtowers in recent weeks. These towers must be manned at all times from now on," the Dominus said. "And we must build a defense force to keep Terah safe."

"We are craftsmen, my lord Dominus," the leader of the Jewel Fjord said. "What do we know of weapons, and war?"

"If we are strong there will be no war," Magnus Hauk answered. "And you can learn to wield weapons as skillfully as you wield your jeweler's tools. Our armies are for defensive purposes only. They are to deter any invasion by indicating our great strength."

"May I speak, my lord Dominus?" Lara asked him.

"The Domina would speak," Magnus Hauk said nodding to his wife.

"My lords, I was born in the faerie realm, but raised in Hetar. My father, a mortal man as yourself, was a Mercenary before he became a Crusader

Knight. He is a great warrior. There are many great warriors in Hetar. If they come to Terah they will overwhelm you if you cannot defend yourselves. If we show the emissary—who Hetar will surely send us sooner than later—that we are capable of defending our homeland, they will think better of invading Terah. It is likely we will never have to fight them, but it is better to be well prepared. Each of your villages must raise a fighting force. You have no other choice, I fear. It is not a bad thing for a man to know how to defend himself and what is his," Lara told them.

"It is easy for you, Domina, for you are a woman," the headman from the Jewel Fjord said. "You do not have to fight."

"My lords, like my father, I am a warrior. I have slain men in battle," Lara told them. And she silently called Andraste to come to her.

They looked disbelieving at her, but then gasped at the sword that instantly appeared in her hand.

"This is Andraste, my weapon," Lara explained. She raised the sheathed sword above her head, holding it by the protected blade.

There was another gasp as those gathered for the meeting spied the face in the sword, and Andraste opened her jeweled eyes to look out at them.

"I am Andraste," the sword's deep voice echoed across the counsel chamber. "I drink the blood of the wicked and the unjust. I serve my mistress, the swordswoman Lara, daughter of Swiftsword. Together we have slain many. Who would doubt my word?" Andraste demanded of them.

The chamber was silent.

"Then heed my mistress's words, men and women of Terah. She walks in the light." Andraste now fell silent, and her eyes closed once more.

"Women, not all women, but some, are capable of defending Terah. I will teach those who would come to me," Lara said.

Magnus Hauk put his arm about his wife. The look on his face was one of great pride. "I will now tell you how together we can accomplish what we need to do for our own protection," he said to them. And over the next few hours he, Corrado and Lara did.

After several days, the headmen of each named fjord, the headmen of the fjord villages and their wives departed back to their own homes. Two faerie-post messengers went with each ship sailing from the Dominus's Fjord. And just as the Icy Season began, ships from each named fjord—the Silk, the Jewel, the Ocean, the Star, the Green and the Light—arrived filled with men, both old and young, who had volunteered to be trained for the new Terahn army. And Lara, using her magic, brought seven hundred young men from the seven clan families to join the others. She and Magnus had decided that this would be a good beginning toward uniting all their people.

Throughout the winter those men who had served for years as men-at-arms for the castle, and some of the older new Outlanders, taught the younger men their fighting skills. But Lara taught them swords-manship. And she called upon her old teacher, Lothair, of the Shadow Princes, to help her. He had gladly come. By the time the spring began to show evidence of coming Terah had the beginning of its first army. The fjord dwellers and the new Outlanders integrated well. The fact that there were seven named fjords and seven clan families seemed to draw them together.

Spring came, and the hills around them grew greener. Sirvat easily delivered a son, named Hali. The Sagitta welcomed ships again, and the Terahn trading fleet set out for the season. As Lara had predicted, one of their captains returned with a request from Hetar to send a ship to visit the Dominus. The answer was sent back: no. Any Hetarian ship entering Terahn waters would be sunk. Lara laughed when her husband wrote it, sealing it with the Dominus's ring seal in the hot wax.

"You are going to intrigue Gaius Prospero even more with such a fierce reply," she giggled. "He knows so little of Terah, and he so desperately wants to know more."

Several weeks passed, and then a second message was brought to Magnus Hauk. "He wants to send an emissary. Hetar and Terah will meet at the trading place, and the emissary will transfer to the Terahn vessel with my guarantee he will not be harmed," the Dominus told his wife.

"Summer is almost here," Lara said. "Let us wait a while before you reply. Then send to the emperor saying you will consider his suggestion."

In midsummer Magnus Hauk did just that, and then they waited again.

A new message arrived. The emperor appreciated the Dominus's courtesy in considering his request. He would await Terah's final answer.

"Jonah wrote that," Lara said laughing. "Gaius Prospero is fuming that you have not acceded to his demands. His curiosity is eating him up."

Finally in late summer Magnus Hauk sent to the emperor of Hetar. He would allow a single emissary to visit him. One man. Not even a servant would be allowed to accompany him. The Dominus would personally guarantee the emissary's safety while he was in Terahn hands. If the emperor would be so kind as to inform them when the emissary was coming they would make the proper preparations to welcome him. He would not be allowed to disembark from his ship until those preparations were firmly in place. Lara had suggested this tactic to delay the emissary's arrival even more.

"Proper preparations are something Hetar will understand perfectly," she said. "Manner and civility are very important to them. How they appear to others is one of their greatest concerns," Lara explained.

The message was sent. Another received saying Hetar would wait to be informed until the proper preparations were completed.

"Now," Lara said, "you will make them wait just a wee bit longer before you agree to welcome Hetar's emissary. If we time it properly our visitor will come for the briefest stay because it will be just before the Icy Season sets in again. Our visitor will want to be gone before he cannot go. And the seas will not be particularly friendly by then. It should be a most uncomfortable voyage for the Hetarian."

"I think you are enjoying all of this," Magnus told her. They were together in their bed as they spoke.

"There is a decidedly wicked streak in you, Domina."
He kissed the top of her golden head, and cupping a
single breast caressed it tenderly.

"Of course I can be wicked, my lord," Lara admitted. "All women can. Umm, that feels nice," she
purred.

"We will send our message in two weeks time,"
the Dominus said, and then he put his wife beneath
him and shared passionate pleasures with her.

Two MONTHS LATER Corrado's ship, its lavender sails
billowing in the late autumn wind, sailed up the Dominus's Fjord carrying the emissary from Hetar. The
emissary was relieved to be off of the sea, which had
seemed to him to be boiling and rolling from the
moment he set foot upon his Terahn transport. He
looked around him. There were manned stone watchtowers set on both sides of the fjords' heights as their
ship entered the inland waterway. He swore that he
saw mirrored signals being sent as they came in from
the sea. The steep hills on either side of the fjord were
greener than anything he had ever seen. As their ship
rounded a sharp bend the emissary saw a magnificent
castle ahead of them. It was worthy of a great ruler.
He was impressed.

Built of dark gray stone, the royal dwelling sprang
from the mountainside, its towers soaring upward into
the bright blue autumn skies. There were planted ter-
races that seemed to hang suspended over the fjord.
There was nothing at all like it in Hetar. Then their
vessel docked, tying up at a long stone quay. The dock

was lined on either side by armed guardsmen who stood straight and tall.

"My lord, if you will allow me to escort you to the Dominus," Captain Corrado said. "I hope you appreciate the guard of honor sent for you. Visitors are rarely welcome here." He led his passenger from the deck, down the gangway and onto the quay. The guardsmen fell into formation, half behind them, and half ahead. Corrado led the visitor into the stone entrance, and together they stepped upon the transport with their guard. "The lifts are powered by giants whose task it is to pull their passengers up, or lower them down," Corrado explained.

"Most unique," the Hetarian emissary said. There was nothing like this in Hetar.

Reaching their destination Corrado escorted his companion down a hall lit with crystal globes of firebugs. There were guardsmen stationed along its length. At the end of the corridor were two tall bronze doors. Two men at the head of the escort jumped forward to fling open the doors. Corrado never broke stride, although the emissary stumbled nervously as his eyes swept the great chamber.

It was round and topped by an alabaster dome. The floors were great blocks of marble edged in narrow bands of pure gold. The stone walls were hung with heavy ornate tapestries, and they walked upon a beautiful narrow carpet of pure scarlet wool. At the end of the carpet was a white marble dais shot through with veins of gold. Three steps led to the top of the dais. Into the bottom step was carved the word, TERAH. Into the second step was the word, DOMINA, and the third step read DOMINUS. The chamber was lit by torches that had been fitted into footed bronze stands. A great crystal candelabra hung from the very center of the dome. Censers of incense—myrrh, the emissary thought, sniffing as delicately as he could—were set about the room.

Magnus Hauk, Dominus of Terah, arose to greet the emissary. He was garbed in a brocaded gold robe sewn with pearls and sparkling gemstones. About his dark blond head was a narrow gold circlet studded with a large single ruby in its center. His turquoise-blue eyes were all the more startling for the gold he wore. "Welcome to Terah," the Dominus said.

The emissary bowed low, but his eyes were already going to the woman—also garbed in gold, with a ruby-and-golden circlet about her forehead, her gold-and-gilt hair flowing around her—who had come forward to stand by her husband's side.

"I echo the Dominus's greeting, Lord Jonah. Welcome to Terah," Lara said smiling, one elegant and delicate little hand upon the distended belly that even her exquisite robe could not hide.

Jonah smiled a weak smile in return. He sensed this was not going to go the way Gaius Prospero wanted. He could feel that Hetar was already at a disadvantage. Terah was clearly a strong land, and would not be taken easily, if at all. It was even possible that Terah might conquer Hetar if they chose to do so. He suddenly recalled the words of the prophecy, written in the Book of Hetar, in the temple of the Celestial Actuary, words that neither Gaius Prospero nor he ever wanted to speak.

From the darkness came a maiden. From the golden light came a warrior. From a distant tomorrow comes Hetar's true destiny.

He shivered. Looking at Lara, Domina of Terah, Jonah knew in his heart that this beautiful woman would indeed be Hetar's true destiny one day. But how? He could not even begin to imagine.

* * * * *

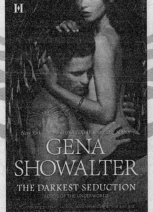

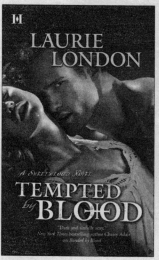

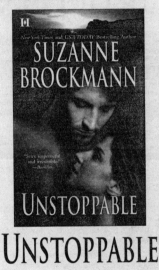

REQUEST YOUR FREE BOOKS!

2 FREE NOVELS
FROM THE ROMANCE COLLECTION
PLUS 2 FREE GIFTS!

PRESENTING...

More Than Words

STORIES OF THE HEART

Three bestselling authors
Three real-life heroines

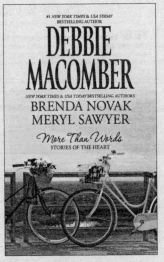

Even as you read these words, there are women just like you stepping up and making a difference in their communities, making our world a better place to live. Three such exceptional women have been selected as recipients of Harlequin's More Than Words award. To celebrate their accomplishments, three bestselling authors have written short stories inspired by these real-life heroines.

Proceeds from the sale of this book will be reinvested into the Harlequin More Than Words program to support causes that are of concern to women.

Visit
www.HarlequinMoreThanWords.com
to nominate a real-life heroine from your community.

www.Harlequin.com

PHMTW769

BERTRICE SMALL

77638 LARA   ___$7.99 U.S. ___$9.99 CAN.

(limited quantities available)

TOTAL AMOUNT	$ _____
POSTAGE & HANDLING	$ _____
($1.00 FOR 1 BOOK, 50¢ for each additional)	
APPLICABLE TAXES*	$ _____
TOTAL PAYABLE	$ _____

(check or money order—please do not send cash)

To order, complete this form and send it, along with a check or money order for the total above, payable to HQN Books, to: **In the U.S.:** 3010 Walden Avenue, P.O. Box 9077, Buffalo, NY 14269-9077; **In Canada:** P.O. Box 636, Fort Erie, Ontario, L2A 5X3.

Name: _____
Address: _____ City: _____
State/Prov.: _____ Zip/Postal Code: _____
Account Number (if applicable): _____

075 CSAS

    *New York residents remit applicable sales taxes.
   *Canadian residents remit applicable GST and provincial taxes.

HQN™ | **HARLEQUIN**®
™ www.Harlequin.com

PHBS0312BL

continued . . .

PROMISES TO KEEP

"A wonderful work of contemporary romance. With a plot ripped straight from the headlines, *Promises to Keep* evokes genuine people confronting a genuine crisis with all the moral, ethical, and emotional struggles in between."
—*New York Times* bestselling author Lisa Gardner

"Emotion, romance, realism, and intrigue. A love story that you'll never forget. *Promises to Keep* is romantic suspense at its very best, with a dynamic cast of characters, a plot that will hold you on the edge of your seat, and an ending that you'll remember long after you turn the last page."
—*USA Today* bestselling author Catherine Anderson

"The perfect blend of romance and danger. Kept me turning the pages late into the night. Kathryn Shay's storytelling grabbed me on page one and her characters held me until the very last word. A definite keeper!"
—*USA Today* bestselling author Barbara Bretton

"Shay does an admirable job with a difficult subject, writing . . . with sensitivity and realism."   —*Booklist*

"A gripping story that will haunt readers with its authenticity . . . full of sensuality and fire. If ever a label of 'sure thing' were deserved by a book, *Promises to Keep* is such a book . . . top-notch romantic suspense. Kathryn Shay adds another winner to her already impressive list of absorbing tales. Don't miss this one."   —*The Romance Reader*

NOTHING MORE TO LOSE

KATHRYN SHAY

BERKLEY SENSATION, NEW YORK

THE BERKLEY PUBLISHING GROUP
Published by the Penguin Group
Penguin Group (USA) Inc.
375 Hudson Street, New York, New York 10014, USA
Penguin Group (Canada), 10 Alcorn Avenue, Toronto, Ontario M4V 3B2, Canada
(a division of Pearson Penguin Canada Inc.)
Penguin Books Ltd., 80 Strand, London WC2R 0RL, England
Penguin Group Ireland, 25 St. Stephen's Green, Dublin 2, Ireland (a division of Penguin Books Ltd.)
Penguin Group (Australia), 250 Camberwell Road, Camberwell, Victoria 3124, Australia
(a division of Pearson Australia Group Pty. Ltd.)
Penguin Books India Pvt. Ltd., 11 Community Centre, Panchsheel Park, New Delhi—110 017, India
Penguin Group (NZ), Cnr. Airborne and Rosedale Roads, Albany, Auckland 1310, New Zealand
(a division of Pearson New Zealand Ltd.)
Penguin Books (South Africa) (Pty.) Ltd., 24 Sturdee Avenue, Rosebank, Johannesburg 2196,
South Africa

Penguin Books Ltd., Registered Offices: 80 Strand, London WC2R 0RL, England

This is a work of fiction. Names, characters, places, and incidents either are the product of the author's imagination or are used fictitiously, and any resemblance to actual persons, living or dead, business establishments, events, or locales is entirely coincidental.

NOTHING MORE TO LOSE

A Berkley Sensation Book / published by arrangement with the author

PRINTING HISTORY
Berkley Sensation edition / February 2005

Copyright © 2005 by Mary Catherine Schaefer.
Excerpt from *Someone to Believe In* copyright © 2005 by Mary Catherine Schaefer.
Cover art by Franco Accornero.
Cover design by George Long.

ISBN: 0-425-20111-2

BERKLEY® SENSATION
Berkley Sensation Books are published by The Berkley Publishing Group,
a division of Penguin Group (USA) Inc.,
375 Hudson Street, New York, New York 10014.
BERKLEY SENSATION and the "B" design are trademarks belonging to Penguin Group (USA) Inc.

PRINTED IN THE UNITED STATES OF AMERICA

10 9 8 7 6 5 4 3 2 1

To Joe Giorgione, a good friend, a wonderful man, and a true hero. Thanks for everything. I couldn't have written these firefighter books without you, and I wouldn't have wanted to.

~~~~~~~ ONE

IAN WOODWARD GLANCED up from where he sat staring out the window in the lobby of the Hidden Cove Fire Academy to see Noah Callahan stride toward him. Though Ian had been confined to a wheelchair for three years, he didn't think he'd ever get used to the fact that he'd never walk like that again—so confidently, so at ease. Noah's broad-shouldered, muscular build testified to good health and fitness. Briefly, Ian looked down at his useless legs hidden in navy Dockers, then shook off the thought.

"There you are," Callahan, his brother-in-law and HCFD fire chief, said when he reached Ian.

"Right on time." Ian's tone was dry.

"Not gonna give in gracefully, are you?"

Tired of the battles, Ian absently rubbed the scar on his left cheek. "Yeah, I am."

Noah chuckled. "Evie get you here okay?"

Ian was used to driving himself in a specially equipped van, but it was being serviced. So his sister Eve had chauffeured him to the academy today. "Yeah, but don't worry; she didn't lift anything heavy." Eve was pregnant with Noah's child.

"She'd better not." The chief got a sappy look on his face. "God, I'm excited about this baby."

Noah's awe over Eve and their unborn child softened Ian. "Me, too. I don't think I've ever seen her so happy."

"Let's go up before I completely embarrass myself." Noah nodded to the elevator across the lobby. He knew better by now than to offer Ian help getting anywhere.

The only assistance Ian accepted was from Joe Harmon, a retired Vietnam medic who'd been Ian's aide in rehab at the Westside Rehabilitation Center in Manhattan. Joe had helped Ian through the horror of ADL—learning Activities for Daily Living—then had become his private physical, massage, and occupational therapist when Ian was released. But Joe hadn't come up from New York to Hidden Cove to work with him yet.

As they made their way to the elevator, Ian thought about what had brought him back to this town from Albany, where he'd gone to live with his sister after his wife left him. He and Noah had had a hell of a fight over it . . .

"I don't believe in the old adage, *Those who can, do; those who can't, teach*," Ian had curtly told Noah.

Noah's gaze had narrowed on him. "Neither do I, Woodward. I believe that those who *can* teach others how."

Ian had slapped his hand down on the iron bars that had become his prison. "In case you haven't noticed, I no longer can."

Instead of cowering, Noah had crossed to him, leaned down, and braced his own hands on the arms of the wheelchair. "Eve says you were the best New York City firefighter she'd ever seen before 9/11. You can teach those skills and help others become the best of America's Bravest."

At the time, Ian had wondered how he could explain to Noah that the thought of involving himself in the world of fire fighting again broke his heart. Noah couldn't know what it was like to face every day what you could no longer have. What you'd loved with a passion. What had ruthlessly been taken away from you by a terrorist attack.

They'd reached an impasse that day. It was another incident—when Ian had rescued the chief's little granddaughter from a near-debilitating fall last summer—that had gotten Ian to thinking maybe he could still . . . save lives, if only indirectly. Sensing it, Noah had gone in for the kill and maneuvered him into teaching at the academy to replace an officer who'd taken an unexpected early retirement for health reasons. Since nobody had held a gun to his head to accept the job, Ian *was* trying to be gracious about it.

As they rode the elevator, Ian made small talk. "What'll we do today?"

"Meet with Jeb Caruso." Caruso was the deputy chief who ran the academy. Ian had already met him when he accepted the job. "Tomorrow you'll hook up with the other instructors."

"Do you have a schedule of the training that's going to be done these six months?" Ian had agreed to a half-year stint of contract work, which meant he wouldn't be teaching every day, only when needed. He planned to stay in Hidden Cove until Evie's baby was born.

The elevator pinged, and the doors opened. "Yeah. Caruso wants to talk to you today about your areas of expertise." Seeming a little uncomfortable, Noah headed down a long hallway as Ian wheeled himself over the vinyl floors. The walls were painted a steel blue, with prints and photos of firefighters and recruit classes gracing them, and the furniture was a speckled gray and black. Everything was spanking new because this facility had just been completed last year. Located at the edge of Hidden Cove, and under Noah's jurisdiction, it served as the Anderson County police and fire academy. All the surrounding fire departments used the facility, not just Hidden Cove, which was home to about two hundred firefighters. Noisy chatter, a phone ringing, and the smell of coffee made Ian realize how long he'd been out of the hub of activity. He'd tried to tell himself he hadn't missed it, but he had.

They reached Caruso's office, and Noah knocked on the closed door. A man yelled, "Yeah, come in." Noah preceded Ian inside. Caruso was on the phone and waved them to sit. "I promise. No. Look, sweetheart, I gotta go." He rolled his eyes at Noah. "Okay, I will. Yeah, me, too." His expression was sheepish when he hung up. Caruso was dark and swarthy, with muscles that bulged at the seams of his white chief's shirt. Ian remembered when he'd worn officer's garb like that instead of the checked blue and black shirt he had on. He refused to wear his old FDNY uniform to teach here, and he and Noah had had a hell of a fight over that, too.

Caruso rose and shook hands with Noah. "Chief." He nodded to Ian. "Good to see you again, Woodward." They shook, too.

"Sara?" Noah asked, nodding to the phone.

The deputy shrugged. "She's home now because of the baby, and lonely."

Noah chuckled. "I'll know what you mean in about seven months."

"No shit?"

"We just found out."

"Eve quitting her job?"

"No." Noah glanced at Ian, who warmed at the thought of his twin as a mom. "Takin' some time off, though. We can't wait."

Jeb chimed in with goofy-parent comments of his own. Then he focused in on Ian. "It's good to have you here, Woodward. I bumped into some FDNY guys at a conference last week. They sang your praises."

Ian had to force himself not to stiffen. He stared out the window behind the chief at the early October day. "Thanks."

"So," Caruso said, picking up a three-ring notebook. "Here's the curriculum for the training we need to provide the line firefighters." He handed the book to Ian and glanced quickly at Noah. "I wanted to meet with you about it before the others."

Sensing something brewing, Ian gripped the wine-colored binder. "What?"

"Check out the table of contents. Number four. I was hoping you'd take charge of that."

Ian opened the notebook. He scanned the first page: Basics of RIT, EMS, Confined Space Training, Terrorism . . .

His heart began to jackhammer. He had a brief flash of fireball explosions, heard the crash of bodies as people jumped from the top floors of the Tower, smelled burnt flesh. He tried to compose himself before he said, "I see." He scowled. "Is this why you wanted me here, Chief?"

Caruso's dark brows knitted. "I wanted you here to teach our guys how to be better smoke eaters. I wanted you here because an FDNY member is more valuable than some of the other instructors who haven't been on the line in a while, or been where you've been."

"I haven't been on the line in three years."

Caruso cocked his head. "You don't wanna do this, Woodward?"

Ian thought of the hours he'd spent soul searching. The discussions and debates he'd had with Lisel. She'd been instrumental in this decision, though she'd never know it. *You have so much to give, Ian. You're lucky you can still give it. Teach others, like Noah asked. Save even more lives.*

"I wanna do this. I just didn't expect to be teaching antiterrorist tactics."

The chief shrugged. "You're perfect for it. You were in the Towers. Seasoned firefighters are a bitch to have in class, but they'll respect you. They'll listen. You could save their lives someday, Woodward."

Noah had been silent. Now he leaned forward in his chair, ready to do battle. "Ian, I know you've spent these past few years researching the fire department's role in responding to terrorism. I read the articles you wrote for *Firehouse* magazine on it."

He had. He'd become obsessed with researching tactics for preparing for terrorism in the fire department. Mostly, he knew what it was like to be their victim and wanted to keep others from finding themselves in the same boat. And in some ways, he felt like he was getting even with the ones behind 9/11. For his injury and the deaths of the buddies he'd lost, something he couldn't let himself think about, had to keep buried, or he'd go crazy. Still in the dark of the night, he dreamed about Bulk, and Cortland, and the rookie under his charge . . .

Don't think about that, Lisel had told him. *Think of all the good you can do . . .*

"Yeah, okay, I'll teach this."

"Great. Let's go over what we've got in place and what suggestions you have for additions or deletions." Caruso exhaled. "God, I'm glad we got an expert on this to help out. I'm outta my league here."

By the time they were done, Ian felt . . . relieved. Despite the ambush of the terrorism content, it hadn't been as bad as he thought. He and Noah rode the elevator down in silence, staring up as the numbers blinked different floors. Finally his brother-in-law spoke. "You did good in there."

"Yeah, you could have warned me."

"I was afraid you'd say no."

"Fat chance. My sister'd do anything for you, and she wraps me around her little finger. Especially now."

"Oh, yeah? I'll keep that in mind."

"Fuck you," Ian mumbled.

"Back at you," Noah said, laughing. They reached the lobby. "Wait here while I get the car." Ian and Noah planned to have lunch before the chief went back to work and Ian returned to his condo.

While he waited, Ian wheeled over to the small sitting area where magazines and newspapers lay on a square table. Thinking about what had just happened, feeling pretty good, he glanced down at the *Hidden Cove Herald* that had been tossed there. The headlines on the front page snagged his attention. BROADWAY STAR COLLAPSES IN REHEARSAL FOR PLAY. His breath backstopped in his throat. He grabbed the paper. Skimmed the article . . .

Lisel Loring had been exhausted when she left Hidden Cove . . . hadn't recovered from her ordeal in the fire last spring . . . anemic . . . play to replace her . . . and finally . . . recuperating in an undisclosed location.

Ian closed his eyes and took a deep breath to calm himself. Okay, the good news was she was all right. Just tired. Needed rest. He'd bet it was her stomach. He figured she was getting an ulcer.

The bad news was that, more than likely, the "undisclosed location" was the condo on the lake she'd rented and subsequently bought last summer. The condo that was right next door to his mother's—where Ian was now staying.

"Damn it." He threw the paper down. How the hell was he going to deal with this? He thought of the last time they saw each other, as he was leaving Hidden Cove to get away from her.

She'd stood before him, her eyes red from crying, her face blotchy. She grasped her stomach like she always did when she was upset. He remembered she wore a red T-shirt that had advertised her play, *Longshot*. Biting her lip, she'd said, "I love you, Ian. I want a relationship with you."

"When hell freezes over."

She'd protested.

And because they'd become truly good friends in the couple

of months he'd been in Hidden Cove, he knew exactly what to say to make her go back to her life in New York. And because he'd come to care deeply for her, too, he'd said it.

It had worked, but it had killed him at the same time.

This was a fine mess. What the fuck was he going to do now, with her around all the time?

LISEL SLAMMED A box down in the living room of her condo and kicked it with her canvas-covered foot. "Son of a bitch. Goddamned men. Why, *why* do they think they can treat me this way?" First her father. Then her ex-husband. And of course, Ian. Now, her agent, Max Strong, was acting like she couldn't make the simplest decision for herself. He was furious about her leaving the play and criticized her about every little thing, like renting a van to bring her personal stuff here herself. Well, it was time to choreograph her own life, and by God she was going to do it.

From behind her, she heard, "Keep kicking that box, and you're likely to break your toe."

She turned to find Eve Woodward standing on the stoop of the condo in the propped-open doorway. Lisel's throat clogged. Eve was Ian's twin.

Still, Lisel was glad to see, her. Crossing to the archway, she pulled the other woman inside, shut the door, and gave her a huge hug. "Hi. It's so good to see you."

Drawing back, Eve smiled. Lisel's heart gave a little tug. That smile was so reminiscent of her brother's, and her gray/blue eyes were the exact shade of his. Eve's hair was a deep auburn, though, whereas Ian's was the color of ripe wheat. She'd teased him that he resembled the sexy actor, Simon Baker, from *The Guardian*. He hadn't liked the comparison. "It's good to see you, too. But what are you doing here?"

"Didn't it make the papers yet?"

"I don't know. I haven't seen today's *Herald*."

Lisel fidgeted with the hem of the long pink top she wore with jeans. "I'm, um, moving back to Hidden Cove for a while."

Eve's face showed surprise, and something else. Concern.

"Is that a problem?"

"Not for me." Eve shook her head. "But it might be for your

next-door neighbor. Ian just moved back into Mom and Patrick's condo."

The world spun for a second. Dizziness had become a problem. She had to do leaps and turns across the stage, and the dizziness was one of the reasons she'd left Broadway again.

"Lisel? You okay?"

"I've been ill. I came to Hidden Cove to recuperate fully this time. I left . . . too soon last year."

Eve reached out and grasped her arm. "I know why you left. Ian told me."

Oh, God, I hope not all of it.

"Don't worry," Eve added as if reading her mind. "He didn't go into details. He just said you wanted to take the relationship further, and he didn't."

For some reason, that made her mad. She willed back the dizziness and let her temper spark. "I told him I was in love with him, Eve."

"Oh, wow."

"And he mocked it. Said we weren't . . . I wasn't . . ." She felt her eyes mist. "Goddamn it."

Taking her by the hand, Eve drew Lisel to the taupe leather couch. They sat, but Eve didn't let go of her. "I'm sorry he hurt you." The other woman's voice got throaty. "It's just that he was leveled by what happened to him in the World Trade Center; so he closes himself off. He won't let anybody get close to him but me. And Noah, now, to a degree."

"He let us be friends."

"Because he thought a woman as beautiful as you would never be interested in him. That way."

Her laugh was full of self-mockery. "Yeah, well, I wanted to jump his bones inside of a week. I even bought a book on how to make love in a wheelchair."

Eve giggled, making Lisel smile more genuinely. She pushed back her dark heavy hair. It had gotten long and unruly. "Oh, hell, I've made a fool of myself with him and now you."

Mischief lit Eve's face as she sat back into the cushions. Wearing a loose-fitting white top and black jeans, she curled her legs under her. "Want me to tell you about how I threw myself at Noah the night I found out he was being suspended from the fire department?"

Lisel knew the gist of what had happened with Eve and Noah—she was an investigator from the Office of Fire Prevention and Control who'd come to town to incriminate the fire chief and fallen in love with him instead.

"Bet you didn't make a fool of yourself over him."

Eve twisted her wedding ring. "People in love always make fools of themselves."

"You're happy."

"Delirious. We invited you to the wedding, Lisel."

"I didn't come because I didn't want to ruin it for Ian. I wrote him a note to tell him I wouldn't be there."

"You should have forced him to deal with seeing you."

"Like you did with Noah at Hale's Haven?"

Noah had broken the relationship off with Eve, too, for her own good, but months later she'd come to the camp his department had opened for the children of slain cops and firefighters and forced him to face his feelings for her. Apparently, the tactic had worked.

"Yep." She smiled serenely, and her hand slid to her waist. "And now I got me a baby on the way."

"Oh, Eve." Lisel hugged her. "Congratulations."

"We're thrilled."

"I'll bet Ian's happy." She felt her heart turn over. "Why's he back here, Eve?"

"Noah badgered him into working at the fire academy."

"I'm glad. He has so much to give to the fire department."

"To a woman, too." She shot Lisel a knowing look. "Don't give up on him."

"It's too late for that. It's over." She had *some* pride after all.

Eve grinned. "Living next door to each other will give you both time and proximity for working things out." She frowned. "You won't leave now that you know he's living next door, will you?"

"No, I can't fathom moving somewhere else. I'm exhausted. Besides, now that I'm here, I can work more closely on the fund-raiser for the camp." Lisel had agreed to perform scenes from some of her shows on New Year's Eve to benefit Hale's Haven. She was looking forward to it.

The doorbell rang.

"That must be Will Rossettie."

"Why's the police chief coming here?"

"Some personal business." Rising, she went to the door and opened it. On the porch was the chief and another man. Tall, dangerously good looking, mile-wide shoulders, and pecs to die for. Almost as good as Ian's, who worked out religiously so he'd have as much autonomy as possible. "Hi, Will."

"Lisel. This is Rick Ruscio, the security expert I told you about." The guy's name and face were vaguely familiar.

"Ms. Loring." Raspy voice to match his looks.

"Come on in."

They stepped into the foyer. When Will saw Eve, his face wreathed in smiles like a benevolent father. Not that Lisel knew anything about benevolent fathers. "There she is." He crossed to her and gave her a warm hug. "Noah told me the news, Evie. Congratulations."

"Thanks."

"Feeling good?"

"Tired." She yawned. "This is about my nap time. I think I'll go next door and lie down while I wait for Ian to get back." She glanced over his shoulder. "Hi, Rick."

"Ms. Callahan."

"Eve, please. After what you did for Noah, formalities aren't in order."

The big man's face reddened. Lisel had no idea what they were talking about.

"Well, I should get out of here." She turned to Lisel. "But I'm coming back later so we can talk."

"Fine. Rest well."

After Eve left, they all sat in the living room. Will took the bull by the horns. "Lisel, I think Rick'll be able to help you with security in light of what's going on. Being stalked by a rabid fan is nothing to ignore."

RICK RUSCIO STARED at the beautiful woman seated in the stunning room and didn't feel a thing. Except hope that she'd hire him. At one time, the sight of a chick as hot as she was would have kicked up his testosterone to critical level. But that was before he'd lost everything. Now, most of the time, he felt like one of those cardboard cutouts used in target practice. "I want her to know up front my background. I can't get halfway into this and then have her fire me."

The woman turned huge blue eyes on him. Beneath them were smudges attesting to sleeplessness. Something Rick knew about. "Why would I fire you, especially after Will recommended you?"

"Because I have a criminal record. And I'm on probation."

"Ah, that's where I recognized you from. The papers."

"Yeah, the articles by the ever-vigilant Nick Lucas." Rick spat out the words. The news reporter had made quite a name for himself hounding Rick.

"I don't remember exactly what happened, though I know it had to do with the Callahans."

"I was kicked off the police force and charged with aiding and abetting the guy who sabotaged Noah Callahan."

Lisel shook her head. "I don't understand. Eve just said you helped them."

Will jumped in. "He did. He blew Stan Steele in and exposed the whole plot against Callahan."

"After I caused havoc in the fire department."

Will sighed with exasperation. "There were extenuating circumstances."

"Like what?"

"Steele was blackmailing him. Threatened to get him fired. And Rick needed his job to support his family."

"I broke the law."

"He was granted immunity for testifying and got a suspended sentence."

"And community service." Which Rick needed to be at in an hour. To start his new indenture. At a freakin' city preschool. God, he hated kids. He hated this do-good shit. He hated life.

The Broadway star leaned back in her chair. "Well, this is a lot to take in."

"If you changed your mind, I understand."

"Don't you want this job, Mr. Ruscio?"

His hands fisted on his jean-clad knees. At one time, everybody addressed him as Sergeant. "Yeah, sure."

"Then you better improve your interviewing skills."

Again, Will intervened. "He's perfect for this, Lisel. I know it."

"Am I your first client?"

Rick nodded, hating the fact that he was once again a rookie. "It took a while to get this off the ground." And if it hadn't been for the man next to him, the man he respected and admired more than God, Rick could never have done it. But he had to live with the knowledge that he'd let that man down, too, in the worst way. He remembered his graduation from the police academy.

I'm so proud of you, boy.

Thanks, Will. I couldn't have done it without you.

You need to believe in yourself more.

But other words taunted him, keeping him from that belief.

You stupid spic . . . you're just like your old man . . . you'll end up behind bars, not puttin' people there.

And still, he'd broken the law he loved to help the people he didn't. He *was* a stupid spic.

"I have faith in Will, Mr. Ruscio." He'd tuned in quick enough to catch Lisel Loring's statement. "When can you start?"

He glanced at his watch. "Today. But I got an appointment I gotta keep first. Can we meet later this afternoon to work out some details?"

"Do it, Lisel," Will put in. "When you got a crazy fan on your tail, you should take some security measures right away."

FAITH MCPHERSON LOOKED up from her desk as the A Time to Grow preschool administrator, Nancy, stuck her blond head in the door. "Hey, girl, he's here."

"Oh, okay. I'll be right out."

"He's gorgeous. Tall. Dark. Dangerous. Yum." Then she added, "Your daddy ain't gonna like this a bit."

Faith laughed at Nancy's comments. "Boy, we really do need men around here if one just showing up at the school turns you into melting ice cream."

"Yeah, well, I can think of a lot of things that would be fun to do with melting ice cream and this one." She ducked back out.

Faith put down her copy of *Aesop's Fables* and headed out of her room for five-year-olds to meet her newest project. Contrary to Nancy's belief, her dad had suggested she take part in this community service, and had tagged Rick Ruscio as someone she might be able to help.

She headed for the front of the building, straightening the Peter Pan collar of her pink blouse and smoothing down her skirt. Her clothes were boring. Truth be told, her life was boring. Was that really why she'd offered to take on an ex-police officer who'd gotten fired from the job for conspiracy?

Oh, she'd read the newspapers. Understood there were behind-the-scenes things happening with him, but had she agreed to this just because it was a little bit dangerous? Faith had experienced no danger, had no real tragedy—except for the death of her beloved grandpa, and then he was ninety—or even had any huge problems in her entire life.

Entering Nancy's cramped office, she saw him standing with his back to her, staring out the front window. Wow, thick head of dark curly hair. Linebacker shoulders. A nice butt. She cleared her throat. "Mr. Ruscio."

He turned. Double wow. Man, look at those eyes. Dark as sin. Striking in a rough-hewn face.

"Ms. McPherson?" His voice matched his looks. Yummy was right.

She crossed to him and held out her hand. As he reached for hers, he shook his head. She noticed he bore a little scar on the underside of his jaw. "You're gonna be my watchdog? You don't look old enough to be out of college."

"Twenty-seven and counting," she said, bemoaning her baby face, natural blond hair, and what one particularly poetic suitor had called sage green eyes.

"I don't believe it." She caught the surly tone.

"It's true. Would you like to come to my classroom? We can talk about what you'll do here. Your schedule."

"I'm on the clock," he told her.

"Excuse me?"

He fell into step beside her. "I gotta put in 300 hours. Today counts."

"Oh, fine."

"You gotta keep track."

"I think I can handle that." They walked down the corridor,

the walls of which were covered with baby animals and their
mothers or fathers. They passed a big tiger with dark stripes,
guarding its tiny cub; it reminded her of the man next to her.

At her classroom, she preceded him in and turned to face
him. He looked huge, enclosed in a room with miniature everything. He also looked scared to death. Glancing around, he said,
"Jesus."

"I wish you wouldn't swear."

He sighed. "Sorry." He jammed his hands into the pockets of
lethally fitting jeans. "Any other rules I need to know?"

"No yelling at the kids." She smiled. "Or me." Geez, she was
flirting. "No running in the halls."

"Aw, shucks, ma'am."

She chuckled. "Let's sit."

"Sweetheart, there ain't a thing in here that'll hold me."

"I've got big people chairs in the corner." She started for one.

His response was automatic. "I'll get it."

She sat at her desk and crossed her legs. Her foot bobbed
nervously, and she felt a spurt of something shiver through her
as she watched him.

He pulled up a chair across from her and straddled it like
Charlie Sheen in *Young Guns,* though his features were a lot
more rugged. "So shoot, tell me what I gotta do."

"Why don't you tell me what you want to do?"

"I wanna be in Margaritaville, lady."

She recoiled physically at his stingingly bitter tone.

"Sorry." He ran a hand through his hair. With the fluorescent
lights teasing it, the strands were the color of India ink.

"I'm sorry you have to be here if you don't want to."

"It isn't here. It's this whole community service thing."

"You don't like helping people? You were a cop, weren't
you?"

Bleakness etched into his rugged face. He said nothing.

"Cops help people."

He just stared at her, his gaze piercing.

"You can do a lot of good here."

"Truthfully, I'm surprised anybody'd let me near a school."

"Mr. Ruscio, this is a state-funded preschool. We get really
poor, really needy kids, especially for the Pre-Kindergarten

class that I teach. Their parents can barely drop them off, let alone check out the personnel."

"Why do you want me here?" he asked.

"Me personally or the administration?"

"Both."

"Well, Nancy has a checkered past, as she likes to say. People gave her a second chance, so she wants to give one to others."

"What about you? You ever done anything wrong in your entire life?"

"Why do you ask that?"

"Honey, you look like the Virgin Mary."

Her chin came up. "I've done some things."

"Like?"

"I cheated on a test in first grade."

"That bad?"

"I told the teacher right away."

"No surprise there."

"I stole black lace underwear from a department store, because my mother wouldn't let me buy it when I was in high school."

"Did you turn yourself in again?"

"Confessed like I was Jack the Ripper. But Mom bought me fancy undies after that, said she hadn't known how important they were to me."

He actually smiled. God, he had a nice mouth. Even white teeth. Beautiful lips.

"So, because of your string of crimes, you decided to help me?"

She laughed.

He stared at her for a bit, then shook himself as if he'd forgotten to be surly. "We'd better get down to business. Tell me what I'll be doing. Washing windows? Sweeping floors?"

She cocked her head. "No, you'll be working with the kids as my aide."

His whole face closed down. His hands fisted briefly. He reminded her of a picture in a Sunday school book she'd seen when she was little of a sinner condemned to hell. "No, I won't, Ms. McPherson. I will not, ever, be working with kids."

"But that's all we have here for you to do."

"Then I'll have to put in my hours someplace else." He stood and without saying a word, without a backward glance, he strode out of the room.

"Hmm," she said leaning back in her chair and staring after the enigmatic, intriguing man. "That went well."

$\longleftarrow$ TWO

IAN THOUGHT HE was prepared to see her; he'd steeled himself all the way home, while Noah made small talk, and again while Ian had chatted with his sister at the condo until the Callahans had left. He'd gone outside with them, and there she was. Seeing her was like having a ceiling cave in on him. Damn it!

She was in the parking lot, her back end sticking out of a van, so she hadn't seen them or heard the Callahans admonish him to be kind to himself before they bade him good-bye. That cute little fanny was covered in tight denims. Ian's hand curled, remembering the feel of her supple flesh the one and only time he'd touched her intimately.

When she inched her way out of the van, sliding a box to the end of the cargo area, turned and saw him, she startled. Then that lovely face, recognized by thousands, and those beautiful eyes where only *he* had seen the pain she carried in her heart, turned frosty. Her expression was in sharp contrast to the Indian summer breeze off the lake behind Cove Condos . . . where they both lived again.

She nodded her head regally, as he imagined she did when taking bows on stage. "Ian." The gesture of bravado was lost in the skeins of thick, heavy hair the color of midnight that fell into her eyes. It had gotten longer since the last time he'd seen her.

"Hello, Lise."

She literally stepped back, and it took him a minute to realize what he'd done.

Lise. *Only you ever called me that. I like it.*

Glancing over his shoulder at the lake, she wrapped her arms around her waist. At least she hadn't lost weight, something *he'd* worried about after he'd told her their relationship was going nowhere.

"I didn't know you were here," she said huskily. "I'm sorry, or I wouldn't have come back to Hidden Cove." She stared at the front door of the cedar condo. "And now . . ." She sighed with disturbing weariness. "I'm sorry, I just don't have it in me to find someplace else."

"Stop apologizing!" The snap in his voice was unintended, and caused by guilt.

She stuck out her chin. "Fine." Picking up the box, she held it in front of her like a prop. "I'll just stay out of your way."

Fat chance. Damn it, who could have predicted this? Best they *did* stay out of each other's way. Still . . . He wheeled himself back and forth on the cement, like an able-bodied person might shift on his feet. "Look, I'm sorry. This whole thing is a surprise to me. And after being at the academy today . . ."

It was like the sun coming out in a steel gray sky. Her smile lit her face and warmed the air around her. "I heard. I'm so glad you agreed to teach there, Ian. You have so much to offer."

"It was partly because of you. I couldn't forget what you said."

"At least there's that."

"What?" A car door slammed in the lot, but he was too busy watching her face to notice who it was.

"At least you didn't forget what I said as easily as you forgot me."

I haven't forgotten you. "Let's not get into that."

From her bleak expression, he could tell the absence of a denial hit her square in the ego, and the heart. How, *how* had he gotten the power to hurt her so easily? It was a power he didn't want.

"Hey, I can carry that for you." The voice drifted over from behind Ian. He angled the chair and came face-to-face with a reminder of what he'd never be again. Tall, confident, command-ing. With long legs that worked just fine and no scar on his left cheek.

He caught Lisel's brief flash of concern. "Oh, Rick. Hi. I didn't expect you so soon."

Rick took the box from her. "I finished what I was doing early." He shot an irritated look at Ian. "Should I come back?"

"No, of course not." Now she gave him her smile, the one critics said garnered her a Tony nomination for her first Broad-way play.

"Well, I'm heading inside." Ian tried not to think about her having a man in her life so soon after . . .

After what, Woodward? After you humiliated her when she bared her soul to you? It was something he was so ashamed of he couldn't think about it. As a former smoke eater, he was still good at blocking. Without saying more, he propelled his chair up the sidewalk to the front door of the condo.

"I could do all this for you," he heard Rick say. Out of his peripheral view, Ian saw them go inside her condo.

Ian could have done it, too. He could lift boxes, carry them on his lap. Unpack. Rub her shoulders if she pulled a muscle.

In his own empty condo he was assaulted by a memory of pulled muscles . . . last spring . . .

"What's wrong?" he'd asked when she winced taking muffins out of the oven.

"I wrenched my shoulder dancing." She'd had a barre and a wooden dance floor installed in her spare room and practiced ballet to stay in shape.

He'd been seated on a chair in Evie's kitchen. Since he had the use of his legs above the knees, he'd been able to spread them. "Come sit here. I'll rub it."

Eyes bluer than the frothy thing she'd been wearing twin-kled. "Ah, an offer I can't refuse. I'm a sucker for massages."

"I could send over my therapist when he visits. He's great at giving massages."

She plopped down cross-legged. He'd been immediately as-saulted by her scent—lemony shampoo and soap. He knew she also favored bubble baths.

Putting his hands on her had been a mistake. He hadn't touched a woman other than Evie in a year. Ian relished the feel of her under his fingers—slight, with delicate bones. Though she was toned all over, she could still be called dainty.

He'd begun to knead her deltoids, and she moaned.

It had taken about five seconds for him to become aroused . . . and it had felt so good to have that reaction to a woman again it practically immobilized him. In the three years since planes had flown into the World Trade Center and irrevocably altered his life, Ian had taken care of his sexual needs himself; for psychological and other reasons, he and his now ex-wife had had no intimate relationship for a year. By the time he was ready for one, she'd left him for a cop in the precinct where she worked . . .

Now, Ian realized just thinking about touching Lisel was making him hard again. "Fuck it," he said aloud in the lonely living room.

But all the cursing didn't make his reaction go away. It was intensified by the knowledge that he could have had the beautiful woman—next door with another man—in his life for sex and a million other things. But he'd rejected it, and her, preferring to live in the dusty ashes of what he'd once been than to risk the flames of a relationship again.

Ironic, he thought as he wheeled his way to the bedroom. He'd run into the South Tower and saved more than a dozen lives before a girder fell on him and severed the nerves in his legs below the knees, yet right now, he'd never felt like a bigger coward.

Dear Lisel,
I can call you that, can't I? I feel like I know you so well. I've seen every one of your plays more than once and love them all. I would give anything, do anything, to meet you. Do you ever meet your fans?

Adoringly,
Julia Madison

Dear Lisel,
Longshot was so good. I've been three times and plan to go back again. Your gown is so lovely in the second act.

Do you think it would fit me? You're soooooooooooo much prettier, but still, I'd like to try it on.

Lovingly,
Julia Madison

Dear Lisel,
That man heckling you in the third row should be shot. Pow!!!!!!!!!!

Love,
Julia

Dear Lisel,
I love you. You are so wonderful. I wish I could be you.

Jules

"Well, these are disturbing." Rick glanced up from the pile of letters his new client had given him and scowled. "Ms. Loring? Are you all right?"

Lisel turned from the window where she'd been staring out at the lake. Its surface was gilded by the sun, and it'd be a perfect setting to play some cool jazz on his sax. "Excuse me?"

"You seem preoccupied. Isn't this a good time?"

"No, I'm sorry. I had an upsetting conversation earlier."

If the shadows in her eyes were any indication, it had been more than upsetting. He'd seen her talking to the guy in the wheelchair, and neither of them looked like they'd won the lottery.

Join the club.

"I said these are disturbing. I wanna take them and study them." There were about thirty altogether. "And if you get more, don't open them. We could try to lift fingerprints off of the notes themselves."

"All right."

He stared at the letter. "This is probably not her real name."

Lisel shook her head. "It's the name of the character I

played in my first production. I was nominated for a Tony for the performance."

Rick scowled. "Creepy."

She joined him at the kitchen table. In this light, she looked even more fragile. "What's going to be the extent of this security, Rick?"

"Well, your alarm system needs an upgrade. I'd like to do that tomorrow."

"Will I need a bodyguard?"

"That's your call."

"I'd rather not, at least not now. Maybe the alarm system and trying to identify this Julia person is enough."

"Unless it gets worse." He leaned back in his chair and stretched out his legs. "You suspected someone was in your dressing room in New York."

"I did. It looked like my things were worn, my makeup used. It happened a couple of times, even after we got the locks changed." She shivered. "Will said his guys would keep an eye on the condo."

"Yeah, a black and white'll cruise by at regular intervals."

She hesitated. "Do you miss it?"

Like I'd miss my right arm. "What?"

"Being a police officer."

"Yeah." He looked around the room, trying to defuse the bomb inside him that threatened to explode any time he talked about losing his job. "Are you alone here?"

"For now. My housekeeper's coming in this weekend."

"To live with you?"

"Yes. She functions as a secretary, too." And a lot more. Lisel really depended on Mona Mincheon for emotional and physical support.

"That's good. How about neighbors? Anybody to keep an eye out for you until then?"

Her gaze strayed to the lake again. "I know Ian on that side."

She indicated the condo on the right where the guy in the wheelchair had gone. He might have been disabled, but by the looks of him, Rick figured that Ian's upper body strength matched Rick's own. "That's good."

"I don't want him to know about this problem, though."

"Why?"

When she just stared at him, Rick shrugged. "Sorry, Ms. Loring, but some prying's going to be part of this. Anything you can tell me will help."

"Please call me Lisel. We're about the same age, and I hate formalities anyway."

He gave her a weak grin and a nod. "The guy next door?"

"Ian Woodward and I were . . . I mean I . . ." Her face reddened. "We were close once; we aren't now."

"I see." He wondered if there were hard enough feelings on Woodward's part . . . shit, *Woodward*. Eve Callahan's brother. Now he remembered. The man was hurt in the 9/11 attacks. Hmm. Hero material? Or PTSD nut? Though Woodward seemed nice enough, Rick knew people weren't always what they appeared to be. Mostly, they weren't.

Lisel scrubbed her hands over her face.

Rick could see her fatigue. Besides, he had stuff to do. He stood. "I think this is a good start. Did Will tell you my fees?"

"Yes." Standing, too, she crossed to the desk and opened a drawer, removed an envelope. He followed her. Handing it to him, she said, "Here's the retainer and first week's payment."

He wondered if he could make it to the bank before it closed. His sister Pilar wanted him to take her school shopping tomorrow. He'd rather just give her the money, but his *pequeña hermanita* was a pit bull about spending time with him.

Rick took the check and left Lisel Loring in the doorway with an admonishment to use the alarm any time she was home. She looked so incredibly sad, it twisted even his hardened heart.

He made it to the bank just in time to cash the check. Then he headed for his mother's house, which had never, even in the remotest sense, been a home.

MAX STRONG, LISEL'S agent, sank back against the teak chairs she'd ordered for her patio and stretched out his legs. Even here, at seven at night, he was dressed in a chic sharkskin suit. His graying hair was so perfectly styled, it wasn't bothered by the light breeze that drifted in from the lake. He sipped his Manhattan thoughtfully. "Nice and dry."

"Well, you made it." She took a taste of the pinot grigio he'd brought. She wasn't supposed to drink because of her ulcer, but she wanted to be polite. "This is good, too."

"For my best client."

The lake rippled on the shore; Indian summer had come to Hidden Cove, and Lisel was dressed in a lightweight, peacock blue knit outfit. The view over her fence was breathtaking. The setting sun reflected on the water. A boat whirred across it. The lake always soothed her. Especially today after her troublesome meeting with Rick, and of course after seeing Ian, the calming effect of the water was worth more than gold. But she had business to attend to.

"What's the occasion, Max? Why are you here?" Sometimes, to maintain control with this man, you had to cut to the quick.

"A deal."

"To work?"

He shifted in his seat. "Well, minimally. The Century Theatre's agreed to let you come in for Sunday matinees this fall." He chuckled. "We're going to bill it as *Sundays with Lisel*."

Anger welled inside her. Damn it, why did she have to keep fighting the same battles over and over? "You know I'm under doctor's orders to rest."

"Hell, you can do this with your eyes closed. It's great money, and it will keep you in the public eye."

"I don't want to be in the public eye."

Max's face darkened, which used to scare her. Now it irritated her. "This is no way to run a career."

"It's a perfect way to run my life."

With studied casualness—she was an actor, after all, and knew the moves—he sat back and sipped his drink. "This got anything to do with those letters and that stuff about your dressing room?"

"Some. I don't like the feel of all that."

He whipped out his cell phone. "I'll call somebody in Manhattan for a workup. Security stuff."

"I already have someone here. And I'm not going back to Manhattan, not now at least."

"When *will* you be back?"

"Maybe the first of the year. I'd like to stay in Hidden Cove for the holidays and do the show."

Max's face darkened again. He'd objected vehemently to a

free performance, even though the publicity would be good. "Lisel, baby, you're killing me."

"It's not that long to be away."

"By then, the ingenue who replaced you will *be* the role."

"There are other roles."

"You're thirty-seven."

"Don't do this, Max. I'm not coming back now."

"Promise me you'll think about it."

A heavy sigh. He'd leave if she appeased him. And already she felt the twinges in her stomach, which she'd been ignoring—like a dancer who didn't think about her bleeding toes as she performed. But she was sweaty and getting light-headed. "I'll think about it. But don't get your hopes up."

Standing, he crossed to her and lifted her chin. The intimate gesture bothered her. "I just want to save your career, love."

Her hand went to her stomach. *I just want to save my life.* "I know, Max."

Max had a late dinner with a new client; she showed him out, then headed back to her patio to enjoy what remained of the sunset . . .

. . . And startled violently when she saw a figure sitting at her table; in the shade of the umbrella, and for a split second, she couldn't make out who it was. *Oh my God.*

"What's going on?" a voice asked from the shadows.

She could barely hear the words above her thudding heart, but finally the identity of the speaker filtered through.

"You scared me half to death, Ian."

"Something's going on with you I don't know about."

That made her mad. Coming fully into the backyard, she crossed over to him. His hair was rumpled, as if he'd just awakened. And the shirt he wore had several buttons undone. She could see a sprinkling of dark blond hair on his chest. "A lot's going on in my life you don't know about." She arched an eyebrow, Katharine Hepburn style. "It was your choice."

"Don't play games with me. You know what I mean."

She sat back down and picked up her wine. "Want some wine?"

Scowling, he shook his head. "You shouldn't be drinking." When she sipped it anyway, he added, "I want some answers. I was out in my backyard using my telescope near the fence"—

the one that connected their condos—"when you came out with your shark. What's all this stuff about letters? And what happened in your dressing room?"

"Maybe I don't want to share that with you."

"Goddamn it, Lisel. I wanna know."

Her stomach twisted into knots. She winced. He caught the gesture. He'd told her once that being confined to a wheelchair made him more aware of the nuances of people and their situations. "And what exactly is going on with your health?"

That was an easy one. "I've got stomach problems. It's not uncommon for former anorexics to have them." In one of their long talks last spring, she'd foolishly shared her sordid past with him. Part of which he'd used against her. The memory knifed her.

"Is it an ulcer?"

"Yes."

"When did this happen?"

"It's been coming on since just before I came here last winter. Then it got worse when I went back to work this summer."

"You went back too soon?"

"Probably. Look, it's not your fault, if that's what you're thinking. I've had a bad stomach since I was a kid. But it's why I'm back in Hidden Cove. That and fatigue."

His expression softened. It was how he used to look at her before she admitted she was attracted to him. Before she'd told him she'd fallen in love with him. "You look exhausted."

"I haven't slept well in months."

"Tell me about the letters."

Absently, she slid her fingers up and down the stem of the glass. "I've been getting them since last fall. My housekeeper, Mona, answers most of the stuff, but she was off for a few months to take care of her daughter, and I started reading the mail. Some . . . disturbing letters came."

He drummed his fingers on the armrest of the chair. "What did they say?"

"Mostly effusive stuff—how good I was, how much this fan liked me. Then, how much she wanted to be me. We got concerned when someone started prowling around the theater, going into my dressing room. Even when we changed the locks,

she got in. I think she even tried on my clothes. It was spooky."
She sighed. "Given that and my health, I decided to come out
here. Mona insisted we alert the Hidden Cove police department, and Will Rossettie set me up with a security expert."

Something like relief flitted across Ian's face. Was he glad
she got help? "The guy I saw today."

"Yes. Apparently he was a cop and got fired for his part in
what happened to Noah."

"Ah, now I know why he looked familiar. He helped out
Steele initially because he was being blackmailed, but then he
blew the whole case out of the water with the email he sent to
Eve telling her how to get into a website that would incriminate
Steele."

"I know. Still, he lost his job. Will said the job meant everything to him."

He stared hard at her.

"You'd know that feeling, I guess. Is teaching at the academy going to help?"

He glanced out at the lake and grasped the wheels of his
chair, running his palms over them. She noticed he'd removed
the fingerless black gloves he always wore when riding.
"Maybe. Might be harder, though."

"Because you have to confront what you can't ever have,
ever do, again?"

"You always understood."

She gave him a smile. "I did. I still do. Maybe we can be
friends."

His gray gaze narrowed on her. Then, unexpectedly, explo-
sively, he hit the iron arm of the chair with the flat of his hand.
"I can't watch out for you, protect you."

Lisel didn't say anything. He was partly right about that, and
if there was one thing she knew about firefighters, they were a
protective lot. Something like this would kill Ian with his inability to help.

"I'd settle for a friend right now."

"No."

"No?"

"It's too risky."

"For who, you or me?"

His eyes widened. Then he said, "You won't get a declaration from me that way."

It was too much. Seeing him again for the first time today. His rejection. Being tired. Max. The letters and Rick. Tears burned behind her eyes. Abruptly, she stood, turned, and headed for the house.

He reached her before she opened the screen. She'd always been shocked at how facilely he could manipulate the chair. Gently, he grasped her arm. When she didn't turn, he tugged hard, and she found herself pulled onto his lap. Startled, her gaze snapped to his face. He lifted his hand, brushed his knuckles down her cheek. "This has been too much for you, hasn't it?"

Emotion clogged her throat. She shook her head. But tears still leaked out. He removed the armrests of the chair and dropped them to the ground. Then, tenderly, and with the kind of care she'd rarely known in her life, he pulled her head to his chest. She wanted to resist because he'd kicked her out of his life so callously, but she couldn't. Instead she curled into him, knees locked to her chest, like a child needing coddling.

His hand went to her hair. Smoothed it down. "I'm sorry things are so bad for you right now. I'm sorry I've had a part in them."

She nosed further into his chest. Inside the open collar of his shirt. "I miss you."

"I miss you, too."

"We got close in those six weeks."

"I know."

"I'm sorry I blew it with . . . with what I told you about how I felt."

"Shh, let's not talk about that right now." He kissed her hair. "Let me just hold you for a minute." His voice was like sandpaper scraped across steel. Somewhere in Lisel's heart, she knew he cared about her. Wanted her.

"All right."

As she listened to the water lap on the shore and the crickets warm up for their nightly chorus, she wondered how she could ever convince this man to let himself love her.

THREE

"CAN I GET it now, Ms. McPherson?" Little Johnny's black eyes were huge with anticipation.

"Yes, you may, but be very careful."

"Because your granddaddy gave it to you."

"Uh-huh."

Faith watched as the young boy raced to the bookshelf and slid her copy of *Aesop's Fables* out of its slot. With the care of a priest holding a chalice, Johnny crept back to her and reverently handed her the volume. The big-eyed fox on the front made her smile. Memories of Papa flooded her. *Life is like a fable, little one. There are lessons to be learned from everything.* Each night, when he'd lived with them, he'd read to her. Her throat ached just thinking about it.

The fifteen kids in class jostled each other and squirmed as she joined their circle on the floor. Once she was comfortable, and they'd settled down, she opened the book. She paused, letting them know attention was required. "One day a mouse met up with a lion who was asleep in his lair." She proceeded to read the story of how the big cat awakened, caught the little mouse, and was about to eat it, when the mouse talked him out of it, promising if the lion spared him, someday he'd return the favor. The lion thought it ridiculous that the mouse could ever help him, but he let the rodent go anyway. Sure enough, not long afterward, the lion was caught in a hunter's net, and the mouse chewed away at the rope and freed him.

Faith smiled as she looked at the children. "Now, everybody close your eyes. Think—but don't say—what lesson we can learn from this."

A churchlike quiet filled the classroom.

After a moment, she asked, "All right, who has an idea?"

Hands went up. She called on Jamal, a frequent participant. "Don't think nobody can help you."

"Hmm. Good. Who else? Matt?"

"Small guys can beat up big guys."

She chuckled. Matt was a big fan of pro wrestling.

Little Molly, always quiet in the corner, slowly lifted her arm. "Mol, what do you think?"

"Throng people need help from little people." Molly's lisp was endearing but often caused her problems.

Faith smiled. "That's a great one, Molly. No matter how big and strong you are, other people can help you if you let them." For some reason she thought of Rick Ruscio.

Why don't you tell me what you want to do?

I wanna be in Margaritaville, lady.

Shaking off thoughts of the troubled man, she checked the clock. "All right, it's almost time to go home." Some groans. "Let's pick up after ourselves."

After delegating jobs, she turned and caught sight of the entry to the classroom. And there was the lion himself, not looking terribly happy, either. "Oh, you startled me."

"Sorry." He glanced at the class as if they were rattlesnakes ready to bite. "I thought they'd be gone by now."

"Almost." With a weather eye on the kids, she crossed to him. In the two days since she'd seen him, she'd forgotten how big he was. His shoulders, encased in a denim shirt, practically filled the wide span of the doorway. He smelled like heaven. "I'm surprised you're here."

His already black walnut eyes darkened. "Got no choice."

"Excuse me?"

"Ms. McPherson, can I put that away?" Jamal had approached her. "Hi, mister."

Rick literally stepped back. His face showed a brief flash of panic before he blanked it. He said nothing, just stared down at Jamal as if he weren't there.

She handed the boy the book. "Here you go, buddy."

"I'll be careful."

"I know you will."

Nancy materialized in the doorway behind Rick. "We're taking the kids outside to wait for their rides." She glanced at Rick. "Hi. Thought you weren't coming back."

Rick shook his head. "I, um, I'm here."

The administrator's look was amused. "Yeah, I can see. I'll take these guys," she said, motioning to Faith's class. "Susie and Tim are out there, so we'll be fine. Stay and talk to Mr. Tall, Dark, and Handsome."

"Sorry," Faith said after the kids bade her good-bye and the room was quiet. "Nancy's totally irreverent."

Rick had crossed to the wall while Faith finished up and was staring at the illustrations of Aesop's fables painted there. "Life isn't like this, you know."

She folded her arms over her white blouse with a lacy ruffle up the front. She wished she'd worn something a little more flashy. "Well, I guess that's a matter of opinion."

"I listened to you read today. I know the fables, anyway. They're bunk." He shook his head. "Life isn't fair, slow and steady doesn't win the race, and honesty certainly doesn't pay."

Curious, she watched him. He had the most incredible face . . . so many hard angles. Wondering briefly if any woman ever softened them, she glanced down at his hand. No wedding ring. Not that the absence of a ring necessarily indicated marital status, but she'd want her husband to wear one someday. Bemused by the direction her thoughts were taking her, Faith walked over to her desk and perched on the edge. She said directly, "What happened?"

"I saw my probation officer this morning. He says I got no choice about the community service here." Rick shifted from one sandaled foot to the other. She studied his face, which was grim. "Isn't there something else I can do?" He nodded to the empty desks. "Besides work with them."

"I asked Nancy. She said we need an aide to help in my class. No money for it. You're it, or we take someone who will do the job as community service. She isn't inclined to make up things for you to do."

He drew in a heavy breath. "Shit."

She looked away. She wasn't a prude, well not really, but cursing in the classroom wouldn't cut it.

"Sorry, you said no swearing. All right. Look, can you, like, minimize the contact?"

"What happened? Why don't you want to work with kids?"

"That's none of your business."

She arched a brow. "I think it is if you're going to be in my classroom."

"I . . . there was . . . I could have prevented . . ." She saw sweat bead on his brow and his chest rise and fall a little faster. He turned his back to her. "Something happened when I was a cop. I blew it. I should have been able to do something, and I couldn't." He faced her again. "Look, no charges were filed. Nothing legal or in the department happened."

"You just feel guilty."

"Like a felon."

"I'm sorry."

"So was I." Raking a hand through his hair, he shook his head. "I never talk about it."

Well, that was nice. He shared something with her he hadn't shared with others. She liked the idea, so she gave him a big smile. "Thanks for telling me, then." She indicated the desk. "Shall we hammer out a schedule?"

By four, they were done. His nearness had unsettled her, though, *her*, Faith, who her dad teased would be calm and collected during the Apocalypse. But Rick's smell—could it be any more male? Any more sexy?

He stood when they finished and jammed his hands into the pockets of indecently fitting jeans. "Fine. I can handle this. Though if the security job I got changes and I need to be free sometimes, can we regroup?"

"Of course."

He nodded, his face still somber. "I'm outta here." He started to walk away, without saying good-bye. She touched his arm to hold him back. His skin was hot. "Rick?"

He drew in a breath and turned. "Yeah, Miz McPherson?"

Understanding the meaning behind his use of formality, she smiled. His gaze—dark and dangerous—dropped to her mouth. "If you ever want to talk about what happened to you, I'm a good listener."

"Don't."

"Don't what?"

"Get any ideas in that pretty little head of yours. I'm not somebody you want on your social roster."

"Still, if . . ."

"No, never."

Her stubborn McPherson chin jutted out. "That's what you said about working here."

"I mean this." With that, he turned and strode out.

Like a big, brawny, and very unhappy lion caught in a metaphorical net.

SHE WAS SO incredibly beautiful, it made Rick's heart constrict. How was he ever going to protect her? "You gotta be kidding me," he said gruffly when she came out of the dressing room in a pink slip of a thing designed to make men's mouths water. "They can't really let you wear those things to school."

"Ri-ck. I'm seventeen years old."

Remembering what he had done with girls at seventeen, Rick shook his head. "No."

Her dark eyes snapped at him, and she reached up to the neckline of her dress. The charm bracelet he'd bought her when she turned sixteen, and had kept adding to, jangled with the action. "Please."

"No, *querida.* It's too sexy."

"You've nixed the last three dresses." She tugged on the bodice. "It's not that bad."

Crossing his arms over his chest, he stared at her like he used to rookies under his watch. They'd certainly cowered more than his baby sister. "No."

"I'll buy it with my babysitting money." She mumbled the threat as she headed back to the dressing room.

"I'll find it and burn it," he yelled after her.

Leaning back, he scrubbed his hands over his face. He knew he was being unreasonable. But if somebody had gone shopping with Anita, seen she went to school, spent time with her, she wouldn't be a high school dropout in a dead-end diner job where she couldn't even support herself.

"Rick? Is that you?"

He glanced up. Oh, great. Just what he needed. Little Miss Pollyanna. She was dressed as she'd been at school earlier, in a pretty white top with a ruffle and pants cropped at the knees. Her honey-colored hair was disheveled, and her green eyes lit up. Again, she looked about fifteen. "Miz McPherson."

Someone came up behind her. Her sister, obviously. Same blond hair, styled similarly. Green eyes the color of Faith's, like newly mown lawns. And dressed in similar clothes.

"Mom, this is Rick Ruscio, the guy who's going to be working in my classroom. Rick, this is my mother, Pearl."

Holy hell. Her mother. The woman looked about thirty-five. Good genes, he guessed.

Then he noticed there was no rancor on the mother's face when she found out his identity. That was odd. Maybe she didn't know who he was, know the situation. He stood and took her outstretched hand. "Nice to meet you, ma'am."

Faith watched him curiously. "What are you doing here?"

"Shopping with—"

"All right, I swear Ricardo, if you deep-six this one, I'm going home." As she came out of the dressing room, Pilar caught sight of the McPhersons. "Oh, hi." She glanced at Rick and blushed. "Sorry."

Faith smiled warmly. "Hi." She darted a curious look at Rick.

"Um, this is Faith McPherson and her mother, Pearl." He smiled at the teenager. "This is my sister Pilar."

Pilar shook hands with both women. "Hi." She grinned at Faith. "Are you a friend of Ricardo's?"

"I hope so," Faith said sweetly. "Nice dress."

"Oh, God, don't tell her that."

"Yes, tell me. He nixed every outfit so far." She stomped a foot like she used to when she was little and he wouldn't let her cross the street. "I thought the point of this shopping trip was to buy school clothes."

From his peripheral vision, he saw Faith's grin broaden. It made her look even younger. And angelic. Pure.

"It is, *niña*. But geez . . ." He nodded to the dress. "It's too low cut."

She jutted out her chin, and he knew he was in trouble.

"I've got an idea." Faith stepped in between Rick and Pilar. "I saw some tank tops over there. If you put one underneath, it won't be so daring for school." She leaned over and whispered something in Pilar's ear. His sister giggled. "Come on, I'll show you."

"I'll stay here and keep Mr. Ruscio company."

Uh-oh, here it comes. Mothers had been trying to run interference on his contact with their daughters for as long as he could remember. He decided to head it off at the pass.

After the girls left, he faced her squarely. "I'm sorry Faith got stuck with me in her classroom, Mrs. McPherson. I won't . . ." What, corrupt her? "I've done some things in my life I'm sorry for. I'll stay out of her way as much as I can." *So I don't influence her. Taint that obviously innocent core.*

Pearl McPherson laughed and took a seat next to the chair he'd been sitting in. He dropped down, too. "There's no way you'll ever stay out of Faith's way, Mr. Ruscio." She looked after her daughter, and for a second, Rick was overwhelmed with longing. His mother had never, ever looked at him that way. Worse, she never looked at Pilar like that. "My daughter's a pit bull when she wants something. And she wants you."

"Excuse me?"

"She wants you in her classroom. She wants to help you."

Leaning over, he linked his hands between his knees. "You know my background."

The woman's unlined brow furrowed. "Of course. Faith wouldn't do something like this without discussing it with us."

He shook his head. "Most parents wouldn't want their daughter working with a criminal."

"You weren't prosecuted, although the papers were exceptionally hard on you, I thought." Reaching out, she touched his hand. "Everybody deserves a second chance, Rick."

A shadow fell over them. He thought it signaled the return of the girls. Glancing up, he saw a tall, good-looking, smiling man standing over him. "Well, should I be jealous?"

Rick's gaze dropped to the guy's neck.

"No, of course not, dear. This is Rick Ruscio; remember he's working with Faith in her classroom." Pearl stood and kissed the man, then faced Rick. "Rick, this is Faith's father David."

He couldn't drag his eyes away from David's neck. Because around it was a white collar.

Jesus Christ, Faith McPherson's father was a minister!

"SHE'S A DOLL." From the table they'd commandeered by the window of The Pizza Place, Faith sat and watched Pilar play a video game with her mother and father. "You love her a lot."

Rick was seated across from Faith, staring at her with hooded eyes. Tonight he resembled a jaguar, not a lion. Who'd nonetheless, been caught in a net. This time it was of her father's making . . .

"We're going for pizza," her very friendly dad had said to the Ruscios. With a minister's intuition for those in need, he smiled benevolently. "Join us?"

"No, I don't—"

"We'd love to."

Pilar and Rick spoke at the same time.

"Pilar, I have work to do after this."

"*Por favor.*" She'd taken her brother's hand and kissed it. "*Deseo pasar tiempo con una familia verdadera.*"

Faith knew from elementary Spanish, Pilar wanted to spend time with a family; she also heard the underlying loneliness in the girl's tone.

At his sister's pleading, Rick had turned to mush. It was fun to see.

"She can be a pain," he told Faith now, but the comment was without starch.

"How old is she?"

He gave her a pointed stare. "Not much younger than you."

"She's still in high school!"

"Speaking of which, what did you say to her about the tank top?"

The devil inside her surfaced. "Only that she could wear the dress without one on a date."

Running a hand over his face, he sighed. "She doesn't need encouragement."

"She's a young, healthy girl, Rick. Let her spread her wings."

"And nosedive when the first hawk comes along? No thanks. I did that once."

"What do you mean?"

He sat up straight. "My other sister didn't have her wings clipped, and she's a high school dropout, goes from guy to guy and can't support herself."

"You take care of her?"

He shook his head. "How did we get on this conversation?" Frustrated, he raked a hand through his hair. "And how the hell did I end up here?"

"God's will," she said, smiling.

His eyes turned flat. It was chilling to watch. "God's forgotten about me and my family." The words were wrenched from him.

Immediately, she covered his hand with hers. "Oh, no, Rick, God never forgets about anybody. I promise."

"This another one of your Aesop's fables?"

She took offense at that. "Don't mock my faith, please. It's important to me."

His face got even grimmer. "I'm sorry. I shouldn't even be sitting here with you."

"Why?"

I'm not worthy. He didn't say the words, but they were etched on his face. Her parents and Pilar returned just then, precluding comment. Soon, the pizza arrived, and everybody dug in.

Faith kept casting surreptitious glances at Rick, who tried to remain aloof, but couldn't do it beneath her father's on-slaught . . . "Will Rossettie's a good man . . ."

Her mother's gentle coaxing . . . "Tell us about your security business . . ."

And Pilar's bragging . . . "Ricardo was first in his class at the academy . . ."

Faith liked hearing about his life.

At one point, Pilar said something to him in Spanish that made him smile. Faith was mesmerized by it—the flash of white teeth in a somber-beyond-his-years face, the light in those inky eyes.

The moment was lost when four people entered the pizza parlor—two men and two women. Rick's pleasure died like a doused candle when he caught sight of them—and they headed for the table.

A pretty blond woman spoke. "Reverend McPherson, nice to see you."

"You too, Detective . . . what is it now, still Hale or did you change it to Malvaso?"

"I kept Hale." She smiled at them until she noticed Rick. Then her expressive face darkened. "Rick, I didn't see you."

"Detective."

"Megan, to everybody please. Do you all know Jake Cavanaugh? And Carla Lopez?" Detective Hale made introductions to everybody but Rick, who of course needed none. He was face-to-face with his former colleagues. It hurt Faith's heart to see his shoulders tense and his mouth turn into a grim line. She wanted to ease his pain and the discomfort of the moment.

Interesting, though, it was Pilar's reaction that was most remarkable. The young girl bade hello to everybody but the younger female officer. Who said, to cover the awkwardness, "Hello, Pilar."

Without responding, Rick's sister slid from the bench and darted away. Rick watched her go helplessly. After a brief hesitation, Faith said, "Excuse me," and practically crawled over her parents and hurried to the women's room. Inside she found Pilar blotting her face with water. "Are you all right?" Faith asked.

Staring in the mirror at Faith, she shook her head. "I'm sorry if I was rude. I'll apologize to your parents."

"You don't have to apologize to them. Tell me what upset you."

"It's that woman. Lopez. She's responsible for Ricardo . . ." Faith waited.

"I don't know exactly what. She was his partner on the police force." Pilar fingered her charm bracelet like a talisman. "Something happened when he was on duty. He's hasn't been the same since."

"How do you know it was Officer Lopez's fault?"

"I overheard them talking right after it happened. I was stay ng at Rick's apartment. She said it was her fault, he shouldn't blame himself."

"What did he say?"

"That he'd go to his grave never forgiving himself." Big fat tears formed in Pilar's eyes. "What could he have done, Faith, that was so awful? It wasn't the thing with Noah Callahan; this happened before that."

"I have no idea, honey." She pulled out some tissues. "Here, dry your eyes. Maybe you should talk to him about it."

"I tried. He got almost as mad as Papa used to when he hit—" She broke off abruptly. "I'm talking out of turn. Please don't tell Ricardo I said anything."

"Pilar, are you in danger in your own home?"

"No!"

"Does your brother hit you?"

Her face was incredulous. "Ricardo? Oh, God, no. He treats us all like china dolls."

"Does your father hit you?"

Again, her beautiful eyes shadowed. "I haven't seen my father in years."

"Really? Why?"

Angling her chin in a gesture Faith recognized as one of her own, Pilar said, "Because he's in prison."

≈ FOUR

IAN PULLED HIS van into the academy's parking lot—in a handicapped spot, which he hated to use but had to in order to have
room to lower the vehicle's ramp; he shut off the engine and sa
there for a minute staring at the big building. The Anderso
County Fire Academy facilities were top notch, with a huge, four
story office building near the road, which housed the fire and po
lice offices; out back were four football fields worth of concret
for the rigs to practice maneuvers, a training building with bay
and a circular tower, and a three-story concrete structure, whic
was "a smoke house" used for simulating fires in training.

He tried to look forward to this meeting with the other in
structors, but he couldn't get his mind off Lisel and her situa
tion. And how she'd felt in his arms last night. He wanted t
make love to her so badly he'd practically punched the wal
when he finally left her. But more so, he was worried about thi
stalker thing. Christ, what the hell was going on there?

Ian was startled by a knock on the driver's window. Outsid
stood a woman dressed in the white shirt and navy pants of a
officer in the HCFD. Over it she'd tossed a light nylon jacke
Through the glass, he heard, "Hey, hi."

He rolled the window down.

The tall blond woman asked, "You the new guy?"

"Yeah, Ian Woodward." He held out his hand to shake.

"Olive Hennessy. I'll be working with you." She eyed the van. "It gonna insult you if I ask if I can help?"

"I can manage on my own, thanks."

"I'll wait and go in with you, if it's all right."

"Sure."

Ian rolled up the window and pushed the remote to extend the ramp. Then he backed up his chair, wheeled out to the ramp, and lowered it. When he was outside, he sent the ramp back into position and locked the doors with his remote.

She watched him. "Nice equipment, Captain."

"Ian will do."

"Olive, too."

"You been with the department long?" Ian asked, making small talk as they made their way to the entry.

"Twenty years." She smiled. "Took me a while to get in, but I stayed. I'm shootin' for BC."

"Good luck. We need more women in that role." He traversed the blacktop, avoiding the loose pebbles. The October morning was warm, yet there was the distinct feel of fall tinging the air.

"That's right, your sister made it up the ladder." Olive smiled. "And then blew it by marrying the chief."

"Blew what?"

"She could have been state commissioner someday."

"She's happier than a pig in shit."

Olive laughed. "I guess that's all that matters in the long run. Me, I wanna be at the top."

"As I said, good luck."

They reached the building's door. She hesitated before it. "Look, Ian, I'm not sure of the protocol here. I been dealing with discrimination in the fire department all my life, and I don't want to offend you. So I'll ask. How much help do you want?"

He liked Olive for that. Most people were overly solicitous or else they ignored disabilities and pretended he was whole. The worst were people who literally scooped their kids out of the way when they saw him coming. As if he were dangerous.

Few tackled the situation head on. He appreciated her being up front. "Doors can be a problem, though I see there's a button here for electric opening. But you can do it for me. It's not a big deal." As he said the words, he remembered the first time somebody jumped to open a door for him. *Jesus Christ, I can get a goddamned door.* Well, in three years he'd made some progress.

A lot, Lisel had said when they were still friends and he'd foolishly taken to confiding things like that in her.

Once inside the academy they rode the elevator together.

"Why you here in training?" Not everybody was cut out to be a teacher, and many line guys hated their stint at an academy. Ian had been one of them. He'd craved the action and adrenaline rush of the line. Sometimes, missing it snuck up on him like a blast of fire and burned him badly.

"Well, first, I need academy experience to get promoted. But I like it, actually. I got a teaching degree."

"Why didn't you go into that?"

"My dad and brothers are smoke eaters. They didn't want the baby girl of the family to do it, though. So I took the safe route, then said, fuck it, I'm gonna do what I want."

They reached the fourth floor. "How'd they take it?"

"Better than my ex."

He didn't say anything.

"Long story."

"Exes usually are."

They went the rest of the way in silence, reaching a huge room with a sign that said, Training Office. Beneath it were names, and for a second, Ian was startled to see the list: Lt. Quinn Frazier, Lt. Richard Gerhard, Capt. Olive Hennessy, Lt. Haywood Jenkins, Capt. William Underwood, and Capt. Ian Woodward.

His throat felt tight. At one time, he'd taken his title, rank, and position in the fire department for granted. Like a lot of things.

"Woodward, you okay?"

"What? Oh, sure. Just surprised to see my name in lights."

"You're one of the team."

He tried not to let that feel good, but it did. As did seeing his desk and nameplate as one of the six flanking the perimeter of the room. It had been so long since he'd been important to anything.

Suddenly, he was besieged by an image . . . it had been a structure fire in the city; kids were trapped on the fourth-floor walk-up apartment. He'd been the only one to make it there, and the aerial had helped rescue the kids. He'd carried a baby out . . . and the look on her mother's face when he handed the kid over was etched in his memory.

Hennessy was talking. "Hey, guys, meet Ian Woodward."

Three men looked over from where they were drinking coffee and shooting the shit. Hennessy introduced them as Frazier, Underwood, and Gerhard. "Where's Jenkins?" she asked.

"Dunno." Frazier was small for a firefighter, but looked like he was in top shape. His easy smile said he was a nice guy. "Glad to have you aboard, Woodward."

Ian nodded.

"Can use your expertise." This from Underwood. He was bigger with dark hair, a moustache, and bushy brows, fitting the smoke eater image more than Frazier. Ian wondered briefly if Lisel would find Frazier attractive.

"Looks like you got experience here already," Ian said.

Gerhard was a big bulk of a guy with hands like baseball mitts. "You gonna do the terrorist shit, right?" In contrast to the others, this man's tone was not friendly.

"Yeah."

"Fuckin' murderers."

Hennessy said, "We waiting on Jenks?"

"No." The voice came from the doorway. "You're waiting on me." Jeb Caruso entered the Training Office. He took a minute to greet Ian. Then he said, "I got a problem."

"What else is new, Chief?" Frazier asked.

Hennessy sat on the edge of her desk. "Shoot."

"Jenks is sicker than shit."

"Damn," Frazier said.

Gerhard cursed, too. "Hell."

Then Underwood asked, "What're you gonna do?"

"We gotta regroup. In"—he glanced at his watch—"exactly one hour, thirty veterans are showing up at our door, guys."

Ian cocked his head. "You got training scheduled *today?*" Most people didn't realize that veteran firefighters took refresher classes and did practice sessions called evolutions to keep up their skills and also to learn new things. Ian hadn't been aware that anything was going on at the academy this morning other than their meeting.

"Yeah," Caruso said, "starting at ten. That's why we asked you to come in so early." He ran a hand through his dark hair. "But our classroom instructor is pukin' his guts out." He surveyed the room, taking a bead on the instructors.

"Don't look at me." Gerhard backed up a step. "I'm workin' with the bomb squad today."

"I'm committed, too, chief." This from Frazier, who was scheduled already to teach a lesson in confined space training.

Underwood shrugged. "I can't do this, Chief. You know my background's EMS."

Hennessy held up her hands, arrest style. "I got the morning off after this. Remember? I gotta take my kid to the doctor's. I'll be back for the evolution this afternoon."

"Fuck," the chief said. "I got a meeting with the mayor all the rest of the day, so I can't do it."

Gerhard looked at Ian. "Don't suppose you got any RIT experience."

Everybody stilled. The air was charged like it got just before flashover. RIT stood for Rapid Intervention Techniques. The procedure to rescue a downed firefighter.

Finally, Hennessy said, "Gerhard, you got no class."

"What?" He looked at Hennessy. Then the light dawned and he cast a sheepish glance at Ian's wheelchair. "Jesus."

Ian drew in a breath. He hated awkward moments like this. He used to seethe about them, but he'd learned if he could defuse them, he was better off. So he tried to ease the tension in the room. "Nobody's got more experience with trapped firefighters than me, I guess. From inside, anyway."

Frazier asked somberly, "How long were you in the towers?"

Ian could remember vividly the feel of the beam crashing down on his legs. Being pinned. Knowing he was going to die. Wondering what happened to his men. "Almost an hour."

"The tower hadn't fallen yet, right?"

"No. I was in Tower One. They got me out just before it came down." He rubbed the scar on his cheek. "One of the lucky ones, I guess."

Ian looked to Caruso. He'd thought being a firefighter had been crushed out of him by that beam. He'd thought being part of a team had been taken away by suicide pilots. But he'd apparently thought wrong. "More to the point, I did a stint at the Rock"—New York City's famous fire academy—"and I did RIT training." He said wryly, "Several times."

Crossing to him, Caruso held up the binder. "Think you can handle this?"

He took it from the chief. Leafed through it. "Yeah, it's the same curriculum, updated, though, from what I used." He scanned the manual. "You got the scenarios on Power Point?"

"Yep." The BC focused in on Ian. "You wanna do it?"

"Why the hell not?"

"Sort of baptism by fire."

"I guess," Ian said. What did he have to lose?

IAN HAD FORGOTTEN what it was like to be in a room full of smoke eaters—the banter, the razzing, the testosterone permeating the air, though there were a few women included in today's training. He recognized some of the people as Eve and Noah's friends.

One approached him. Mitch Malvaso. "Hey, Ian, nice to see you." The captain of the Rescue Squad's dark eyes were quizzical. "Noah told me that you were gonna be working here, but what are you doing in this training?"

"I got roped into this session by default this morning."

"You're *teaching* this class? Great!" He actually meant it. The notion startled Ian.

Mitch's family—Grady and Jenn O'Connor and Zach and Casey Malvaso—also came up to say hi, then everybody sat when Jeb Caruso asked for quiet. "All right, ladies and gentlemen, you know what we're here for. RIT, or in other words, an incident within an incident. Haywood Jenkins was supposed to run this class, but he's on his knees with the flu and the other instructors were busy."

Ian heard a distinct mumble in the crowd. "Least it's not Gerhard."

"So, we got the best of the best to train you clowns. Captain Ian Woodward is at the academy at the request of his brother-in-law, Noah Callahan, to do some teaching for six months."

"Poor guy . . ."

"What'd he have on ya, Woodward? Musta been blackmail."

"Ian's done RIT"—Caruso glanced at Ian—"from both sides, as you all probably know. So listen up and learn something from him. And be nice, for a change."

Ian expected polite silence, maybe a few welcomes, but instead, he was shocked when somebody started clapping. A slow, loud putting hands together. Then others joined in. All firefighters had gotten accolades after 9/11, but this, from his brothers, choked him up. He didn't know exactly what to do. It went on for a long time, then ended with some embarrassed coughs, mumbles, and quiet again.

To cover his emotional response, Ian thanked them quickly, then dived in and put up the first slide. It was entitled, Rescue Operations, and listed all the goals of the training session . . . when to call a Mayday, the Personal Accountability Roll Call, Steps in RIT, SCBA Use, Radio Use, Incident Assessment, and last, the Evolutions where trainees would actually perform a rescue in the smoke house using a dummy.

Quiet filled the room as the veterans watched the screen; Ian broke it. "Let's start with when to call a Mayday."

As soon as he said the words out loud, they echoed in his brain, Mayday, Mayday, I'm trapped. Location second floor. Huge beam . . . He could feel the heat, smell the burning, and hear crashing outside. He later learned the crashes were made by jumpers from upper floors.

He hoped he covered for the flashback when he managed to say, "You need to call right away, as soon as you think you're in trouble or your buddy is. Anybody know why one of us wouldn't call?"

Mitch Malvaso lazed back in his chair. "Pride."

Somebody yelled out, "You jokers on the Rescue Squad would know all about that."

"Ego," Zach Malvaso added.

His wife—of only a few months, if Ian remembered right—added, "If the shoe fits." But Ian noticed she smiled intimately at her husband, who locked his hand on her neck and whispered something in her ear.

"Get a room," his sister Jenn quipped.

"Denial," another female firefighter added. "It's like guys getting lost and refusing to ask for directions."

Ian chuckled as the men ribbed her about her driving. God, he'd forgotten how good this camaraderie felt.

For a while, he let them go, then picked up the thread. "The first step is training in RIT, so we can practice what to do now, instead of when the critical situation happens. That's why you're here. As Caruso said, we have 'an incident within an incident' and it's gotta be practiced."

He talked further about the Mayday, specifically when somebody like a partner calls it in. The group got into a heated debate whether or not to use the name of the downed firefighter over the radio—fearful that lay people's scanners would pick it up.

Shit, Woodward's down. Repeat, Woodward's down.

How did he tell them that at the moment you think, "I'm gonna die," nobody in his right mind cared about privacy or embarrassment.

"Captain Woodward?" Mitch asked. "You gotta have an opinion on this."

"You won't give a shit then and neither will your men. Use names."

People nodded—as if he had some authority in this. It took him a minute to realize he did.

"Let's talk about locating the victim. You got survivor lights?"

"What are they?" a rookie asked.

"Guess you don't. Some companies have lights to pin on your turnout coat for just this purpose."

A paramedic named Joe raised his hand. "There are these glow-in-the-dark stick lights some companies have . . ."

After he finished, somebody razzed Mitch's group again. "You guys on Rescue got the juice. See if you can get us some lights."

A crude expletive followed the teasing.

Then they went on to talk about the PASS alarm, Personal Alert Safety System, which every firefighter carried on his shoulder, and which would go off if he was inactive for thirty seconds, or which a smoke eater could activate himself when he was in trouble. "Okay, the job of the PASS alarm is to locate the downed firefighter."

The blare was deafening . . . like the alarm on an emergency exit door. It seemed to sound in Ian's ear forever.

He said to the group, "For God's sake, turn the damn thing off when you find the guy."

They all chuckled, knowing instinctively that what sounded routine became a whole different ballgame when in an emergency situation. A downed brother brought even more heightened emotions to the scene.

He picked up the SCBA Caruso had provided him. "Now, let's talk about getting your brother some air." He held up the Scott pack. "We found in the FDNY that putting the pack on the victim's chest is more effective than trying to remove his old pack and replace it with this. Just strap it around . . ." He hefted the SCBA. "Attach it with . . ."

Hurry up, get this on him. The second tower fell . . .

Instruction finished just in time for lunch. Afterward, they'd conduct the evolution. Ian didn't have to stick around for that . . . but, as he wheeled out next to the Malvasos, who were going to go pick up subs and asked if they could bring him something, Ian decided he'd stay and see what was going on.

IAN HADN'T FELT this good in a long time. As he maneuvered the streets of Hidden Cove and headed out to the lake, he was running on high from his successful instruction and from being on the *fireground* again. Though it was just simulation, the experience had been exciting.

He'd forgotten how much smoke filtered out of a building when it was on fire, though in training they used mist-based smoke. Still, surrounded by it, he remembered the adrenaline rush he felt when he was part of knocking down the red devil. And there was the cacophony of noise—the officers talking into the radios, the staticky reply of the men inside, the rig idling loudly, even the water dripping from the bottom of the pumper. Briefly, it reminded him so much of his former life that the loss almost overwhelmed him; but he'd battled it back and let being part of a team make him feel good.

And, Ian thought as he pulled the van into the parking lot of the condo, all the trainees had been effusive in their praise of him. "Great job, Captain. Lucky to have you, thanks for filling in. You got a great style of teaching . . . real personable. We'll see you for the terrorist shit, right?"

Ian had no idea he'd be a good teacher, nor had he realized the satisfaction that came from imparting knowledge. Maybe Noah was right, maybe he'd like this.

Sitting in his van, he stared at the condos. Was Lisel home? He wanted more than his still-macho soul cared to admit to share what had happened today with her. It's what he'd missed most when he'd left her. But craving that connection with Lisel was what had gotten him in trouble in the first place.

The door to his condo swung open. Shit, he'd forgotten! Out swept his mother . . . there was no other way to describe her entrances and exits.

Next to Lisel, Lila Cunningham was the most feminine creature Ian had ever seen. She kept her blond hair short, but it fell in soft folds over her forehead—her relatively unlined forehead for a woman of sixty-two. Today she wore a lime green outfit of silk, he'd guess. As she came toward him, he noted that gold graced her throat and ears, neck and wrists. He buzzed down the window.

"Hello, darling." Her Lauren Bacall voice revealed no annoyance, only pleasure at seeing him.

"Hi, Mom. I forgot you were coming."

"That's all right. We just got here." She smoothed his hair back and rested her hand on his arm.

He loved it that she still treated him like her "boy." He covered her hand with his and squeezed.

She studied him. "You look . . . different."

He grinned. "I had a great day." Her eyes widened. He understood the reaction. He hadn't had a lot of good days in the last three years.

"How wonderful." She frowned. "I worry about you."

"Mom, I—"

"Lila? Is that you?"

Ian hadn't heard the car pull in next to him. It was a black Mercedes, and out of it had climbed two of the beautiful people.

Both were tall and striking. The man had on a meticulous suit—Italian he'd bet—and the woman dressed in the kind of clothes his mother wore. The two looked vaguely familiar.

"Jude?" His mother seemed surprised; he knew her well enough to know it was not pleasantly. "Oh, my, what are you doing here?"

"We've come to see my daughter."

The couple circled the front of the van, and Jude gave his mother one of those air kisses. The man shook her hand. "Is Patrick with you?"

"Yes, he's inside."

"Inside?"

"My son lives here. In 444."

"Really? Lisel is in 446."

Ah, Ian got it. The parents. The withholding, overbearing parents who'd caused an insecurity in Lisel that few knew about. Ian disliked them on sight.

He had no idea his parents knew the Lawrences, though both his stepfather and Lisel's father were Wall Street men.

Lila turned to Ian and smiled warmly. "This is our son, Ian Woodward."

Both of Lisel's parents greeted him warmly . . . until he opened the door, lowered the ramp, and they caught sight of his wheelchair.

It happened all the time. The subtle shift . . . to pity, to condescension, to maybe even a little bit of fear. He called it *telethon mentality*. Ignoring it, he rolled out of the van, secured it, and crossed over to the sidewalk. "Nice to meet you," he said politely to the Lawrences. Then to his mother, "I'll go inside and say hello to Patrick."

In his living room, he found his stepfather, the multimillionaire, watching TV in Ian's favorite recliner. He was tall and thin and fit looking. "Hey, buddy," Patrick said, rising and coming over to shake hands with Ian. "Hope it's all right we came in."

"Sure, it's Mom's place."

"We want you to think of it as yours."

It was hard not to. When they'd bought the site to build the condo, just before Evie came to Hidden Cove, they'd given it state-of-the-art handicap accessibility—lowered kitchen cabinets with no cupboards underneath, hardwood floors, a bathroom in the spare room with a roll-in shower, pedestal sink, extra-wide doorways everywhere.

"I know. I appreciate it." That gratefulness was all too true. From his volunteer work in rehab after he dragged himself out of his funk, he realized that he was one of the lucky ones to have a place like this; though Evie had made adjustments to her home in Albany, this space was clearly designed for him.

They were making small talk about the baseball game Patrick was watching when Ian's mother came back in. "Oh, dear." She was frowning. Ian and Patrick exchanged an indulgent look.

"What is it, love?" Patrick asked.

"The Lawrences asked us to have dinner with them." She looked to Ian. "I said no—Jude is not my favorite person—but I'm afraid I couldn't get out of drinks." She glanced at her watch. "They said to come right over. It would give you a chance to meet your neighbor. From what I hear, she's a lovely girl, even though she's a big star. I had no idea she was living out here. Do you mind terribly, dear?"

Did he mind? He shook his head. Life sure did have a way of conspiring against you. "No, Mom, I don't mind."

"DARLING, WHEN ARE you going to learn to make a decent martini?" Lisel's father had taken one sip of his drink, grimaced, poured it out into the wet bar on the glassed-in porch that faced the lake, and began to mix his own. Everything Allen Lawrence did was with flair, like he was the star of the show.

Lisel's hand went to her stomach. Already it was cramping. Great. She shot a glance at Ian, whose eyes narrowed on the gesture. He didn't look any happier than she was to be having these cocktails. Bad enough she had to deal with her parents' visit. But for Ian to witness their relationship—she was mortified. Not that she hadn't already told him about it. Still, for him to see her weaknesses staged and acted out was more than unpleasant.

Patrick Cunningham intervened. "Me, either, Lisel. I never did get the hang of fixing one of those."

She smiled at the older man who, according to Ian, had married his mother ten years ago and made her deliriously happy.

"You have a lovely place, Lisel," Lila said.

Ian's mother was absolutely gorgeous. Ian had her eyes, her facial features, but there was a delicacy about Lila that neither Ian nor Eve possessed. She sat close to her son, her hand frequently touching his arm or his shoulder.

"You've done something different to it," Jude noted, surveying the porch where they sat, nodding back into the rest of the house. The lake, through the expanse of windows, rushed up to the shore in time with Lisel's accelerated heartbeat. "Yes, I made some changes before I left last summer."

"Widened some doorways, didn't you? And got new flooring? And new furniture."

She'd made the place more handicapped accessible. She'd replaced the carpet to make it easier for Ian to maneuver, gotten a table he could wheel under . . . things like that.

"Isn't that recliner like the one you have, Ian?" Lila asked.

"Yeah." His mouth thinned. "Amazing coincidence."

Well, she'd planned and ordered all the changes before he'd cut her out of his life. In one of their more intimate conversations, he'd talked a lot about getting out of his chair and how the recliner, which had built-in massage, felt like heaven. She'd wanted to please him.

She saw Lila and Patrick exchange a look. They got it. Her own parents hadn't. Hopefully they wouldn't. She couldn't imagine what trouble they'd stir up.

Right now, they were ignoring Ian, and it made her mad. "So, Lisel," Lila Cunningham asked. "Are you out of *Longshot* for good? We hadn't gotten to see it."

Jude's face darkened. "No, of course not. This is just a hiatus." She elbowed Allen, like this was some stupid sitcom with the doting husband and the pampered wife.

He said, "Max called us. He told us about the Sunday thing. We think it's a good idea."

Ah, so that's why they'd come. She saw Ian grip the edge of his chair and his mother lean in close to him, probably at the tension invading his body. He put a hand over hers. Lisel remembered his words from last night, *You don't have to do this just because others want you to.*

"My doctor doesn't agree, Mother." Lisel could hear the whininess in her own voice. *Just say no to them,* she told herself.

Jude's shoulders stiffened. "Not a good idea to drop out altogether, darling. Especially at your age."

"What are you, Lisel, all of thirty-five?" Patrick asked.

Jude sniffed. "She's thirty-seven."

Ian edged his chair back and forth. "That old? You're almost over the hill," he teased. But Lisel caught the underlying frost in his tone.

Her parents didn't. Jude threw back her shoulders. "Well, we're hoping we didn't bring you all this way for you to throw it away because you're tired."

"She has an ulcer." Everybody looked at Ian. Lisel closed her eyes, wishing he hadn't revealed that little piece of information.

"How would you know that?" Allen asked. "Have you met before today?"

"Yes, of course, Father. When I lived here last summer." She smiled at Ian, hoping he'd support her. "We became friends."

"An ulcer, dear?" This, not from either of her parents, but from Ian's mother.

Jude brushed imaginary lint off perfectly fitted silk trousers. "Nonsense. You've always had a finicky stomach."

Ian's gray eyes got stormy. "As a trained EMT, I can tell you an ulcer is stages beyond a finicky stomach."

Allen's eyes narrowed on him. "You're an Emergency Medical Technician?"

"I used to be. I'm not a firefighter any more, for obvious reasons."

"What exactly do you do, Ian?" Jude asked coldly. Her mother was clearly pissed at Ian's defense of her.

"Not much."

"Ian owned an electronics company before 9/11," Lila said impulsively. "And now he's teaching at the fire academy."

No reaction. No "9/11, wow," or "Thanks for giving your legs to helping others." The Lawrences instead looked uncomfortable.

"Well," Allen said, regrouping. "If Lisel does indeed have an ulcer, that's a good reason to cancel this fund-raising thing for New Year's Eve." He shook his head. "God, Lisel, I can't believe you allowed yourself to be roped into that."

Lisel felt her stomach clench into Girl Scout knots. Sweat beaded on her brow. So she ignored the dig that they gave every time they saw her. "I'll go check on the hors d'oeuvres." She stood and headed for the kitchen. Once there, she grasped onto the countertop edge.

Take deep breaths. Don't let it get to you. Reaching up into a cupboard, she found the medicine that the doctor had given her for attacks, then fished a spoon out of the drawer. But her hand was shaking so badly she dropped it. Biting her lip, she bent to pick the spoon up. The action made her stomach pitch, then clench. For a moment, she stayed doubled over.

"Lisel, what . . . Jesus Christ." She looked up to find Ian had come to the kitchen.

"I'm all right."

"The hell you are."

Taking deep breaths, she managed to stand. "I just need to take some medicine."

His eyes dropped to her hands. Without saying anything, he wheeled over and removed the spoon and bottle from her fingers. Then he made quick work of pouring out some of the pink liquid. "Here," he held it up. Bending, she licked it off the spoon.

Then she leaned against the counter and closed her eyes, willing her stomach to settle. Finally she said, "I'm embarrassed."

She expected anger, for her sake, but anger nonetheless. "Don't be." His tone was soft, soothing. "You're nothing like them."

His kindness brought on the threat of tears. She battled them back. He picked up her hand and squeezed it between the two of his. Her fingers were ice cold, and warmed with his touch. "Do you have to go out with them tonight?"

"Yes."

"They invited us. Mom got out of it. But we'll come, if you like."

Moisture pushed harder to get out. "You'd do that for me?"

"Slay your dragons, you mean?"

She smiled.

"Sure. How bad could it be?"

"Bad. They'll harp on me about the play."

"We could head it off."

"No, I don't want all that played out in front of your parents." His smile was so tender, it made Lisel wish for so much from him. "My mother's a natural born nurturer. She'll jump right in and probably not even realize what she's doing."

"She's wonderful."

"I know."

"No, thanks, though. About dinner."

"You could refuse to go."

Resting her head against the cupboard, she shrugged. "I wish."

"Just go in and say you're sick."

"You think?"

"We could stick around for that. They'll probably be better behaved if you do it in front of us."

"They'll just come back. Do this again."

"Well, in the meantime we'll figure out another strategy to get them off your back. Let's just deal with tonight." He reached out and placed a hand over her middle. "I don't think your tummy can handle them now, honey."

"It would be heaven not to have to endure that. I love them, Ian, but they won't stop ragging on me, even now, about my career." She threaded back her hair. "Jesus, I'm thirty-seven, and I still can't stand up to my parents."

"None of us can. My mother gets Evie to do all those girly things she hates. And she wraps me around her little finger. It's just that's she's a nicer person than your parents."

He understood so well.

"Come on," he said, still taking her hand. "Let's go beard the lions."

She held on tight to his fingers. "Thanks."

"You're welcome."

Dear Lisel,
Where are you? I've been to the theater several times, and you're not there. And the newspapers say you won't be back for an unknown period of time. I hope you're not sick. Enclosed is a card. Howwwwwwwwwwwwwww can I find you?

I love you,
Jules

THE HOUSE ON Eighth Street always smelled the same. Like week-old mildew. Stale cigarettes. Booze. And especially like desperation. All his life, Rick had battled against succumbing to that desperation. As a teen, he couldn't wait to get out of the place.

And look what you did with your life, hotshot.

Maybe some things couldn't be overcome. No, he wouldn't think that way. Mostly because it would mean Pilar would end up like his mother and sister Anita.

He'd eased open the front door and stood in the entryway, staring at the scarred staircase, the dirty rug that he knew Pilar tried to keep clean but couldn't. Taking in a deep breath, bracing himself, he crossed into the living room.

And there she was, sitting in front of the snowy TV, watching some show on Telemundo. Despite the fact she said she hated "spics," she seemed fascinated by his father's culture.

"Hi, Ma."

Dolores Ruscio didn't even glance up at him. She wore a dirty red shirt and nondescript black pants. Her graying hair was pulled back into a messy knot. At her elbow was a beer; for some reason he thought of Pearl McPherson and her pink capris and white shirt. Dolores took a drag on her Marlboro and said, "Ricardo. Did you bring money?"

"I came to talk to Anita. She in her room?"

Dolores grunted. He took that as a yes. Turning, he hurried away from the evidence of what he'd come from and took the stairs two at a time. He made a note to call the landlord about the banister. It was rickety. Anita's door was ajar. Some sexy salsa played inside. From the doorway, he watched her. She perched in front of a cracked mirror, doing something to her almost orange hair. Her face was caked with makeup. She was in a black lace slip.

"Hi." He walked in and crossed to the bed. Picking up a bathrobe, he handed it to her. "Here, put this on."

She rolled mascara on her eyelashes. "Why?"

"Ever hear of modesty?"

"Not in my vocab, big brother."

He cleared a space on the bed by sweeping a pile of clothes to the floor. The room was filled with the scent of some cheap perfume. "Where you going?"

"Lennie's." She peered in the mirror at him. "You? You look great."

He glanced down at his gray slacks and long-sleeved gray shirt. "I got a birthday party."

"And I'll bet your little *lady* is gonna entertain you in her birthday suit." She laughed at her joke; it was an unpleasant sound.

He ignored the comment. "Where's Pilar?"

"At the library."

"Ah."

"Yeah, the little Virgin Mary's got nothin' better to do."

Rising, he crossed to his sister and grasped her arm. The action caused the inky black makeup to streak her face. "Hey, watch it."

He held on to her. "Don't you ever talk about your sister like that. She's got values, and she believes in things. I won't sit by and let you put them down."

"Who the hell are you to talk? You didn't get booted off the police force for your upstanding ethics. You're just like him, you know."

Bingo, she hit the mark. He felt the familiar roil in his stomach, the drumbeat in his heart. Looking down at Anita, he wondered if, in reality, he *was* like her, like his drunken mother, like his criminal father.

Unable to rectify the thought, he dropped her arm and turned away. "I'm outta here," he said and headed for the door.

She caught up with him at the bottom of the steps. "I'm sorry, Ricardo. Please. I need to ask you something."

He drew in a deep breath, his back to her.

"I need some money."

"Now there's a surprise."

"I wanna take a hair stylist course at a shop in town. It starts soon."

Pivoting, he faced her. "Can you do that and work, too?"

"Yeah."

"What's the place called?"

"Maxima's. Will you give me the money?"

"When do you need it?"

"Two weeks."

"I'll check it out first. How much is the course?"

"A thousand dollars."

"Jesus."

"I can get a real job then, not some stupid-ass job."

"Waitressing's honest work, Anita." He thought of some of the jobs he'd had in his life—working on the docks had been the worst. Waitressing was high up on the scale from that.

She slid her arms around his waist and laid her head against his chest. "*Por favor,* Ricardo."

For some reason, he couldn't stand up to her or his mother. It had always been that way. He smoothed down her hair. "I'll let you know."

From the living room, he heard his mother's too-many-Marlboros voice. "Aren't you gonna leave me some cash?"

Stepping back, Rick jammed his hands into his pockets and felt for a bill. He handed it to Anita. "Give this to her." He opened the door. "I'll be in touch."

Outside he could breathe again. He looked up at the stars sprinkling the sky and took in the clean air. It didn't help. He always felt dirty when he left here. He stared at the heavens.

God's forgotten about me and my family.

Oh, no, Rick, God never forgets about anybody. I promise.

Little Miss Innocent was wrong about that one. Let her stick to her illusions about God and Aesop and life being good. He glanced back at his house as he made his way to the car. Here was living proof that God sure as hell didn't watch out for everybody. Rick's only hope was, if He was up there, He would take time for Pilar.

"HEY, GIRLFRIEND, WHERE are you?" Dressed in baggy sweats, Nancy was sitting on Faith's couch in front of a half-devoured pizza, sipping a glass of merlot. She'd have a cigarette in her hand, but Faith wouldn't let anybody smoke in her house.

She nodded to the TV. "Watching *Third Watch.* I think Bosco's cute even if he is tough."

"You're vaguing out."

"No I'm not."

"You thinking about *him?*"

"Who?"

"Mr. Tall, Dark, and Handsome. God, he looked good in those black jeans today."

Faith had thought so, too. The sight of Rick Ruscio's tight butt and muscular thighs had sent her pulse spinning. She hadn't admitted she was attracted to him before this. But you'd have to be dead and buried not to be turned on by the sight of him this afternoon. Truth be told, she'd been drawn to him since Day One.

Wouldn't you know he'd showed up just in time for another Aesop's fable. It had been one of her favorites—"The Good and the Ills of the Earth." At one time they'd walked equally among mankind. But then, through man's foolishness, the Ills multiplied and threatened the Goods. So God—or Jupiter, the book said—advised the Good to stay with Him, and go one at a time to earth when He could watch them. "And that's why there's so many trials and tribulations coming people's way, but the goods come one at a time," she'd told her class.

He brought it up after the kids got busy drawing pictures of the goods and ills of the world. "You don't really believe that, do you?" he'd asked. She'd wanted him to mingle, but he'd stayed near the back bookcase, which somebody had just donated.

"Of course I do."

"You're something else."

"I hope that's a compliment."

He grunted and folded his arms across his chest, staring at the kids as if they were convicts ready to revolt.

"Rick, you've got to help with the children. They're all staring at you. They want your attention."

His Adam's apple had worked convulsively. "Could I watch, and clean up afterward? Just today. I'll do something with them on Monday."

"Promise?"

"Scout's honor."

She agreed, and he gave what passed for a smile . . .

"You-hoo. McPherson. What are you smiling about? The blond just dumped your guy there, and he feels terrible. You shouldn't be grinning."

"Sorry."

"You are *so* thinking about him."

Faith sighed. "He's an enigma. He's Mr. Tough Guy across the board, but you should see him with his little sister. He's mush." She told Nancy about their impromptu dinner earlier in the week. "She's lovely and she wraps him around her finger. It was cool to watch."

"He just breathes, and he's cool."

"I know."

Nancy stared at her. "Heard from Sam lately?"

"Sure, he calls almost every night."

"He coming home soon?"

"I don't know. He's got a real overload this semester. He wants to finish in January."

"So you can get married?"

Shaking her head, Faith stared at the TV, not really seeing the hunky cops and cute firefighters. "I don't know, Nance. You and I talked about this. Things aren't right with Sam."

"He doesn't flick your switch."

"Not like I think he should. Hell, we've known each other since kindergarten."

"He's gonna be a preacher like your daddy. He's your

brother's best friend. And he's a nice guy. I'd think twice before I ditched him."

"I'm not planning to ditch him."

"Well, he said he wanted an answer when he's done with seminary. He'll ditch *you*, girl, if you don't commit."

Faith didn't say anything.

"You slept with him yet?"

"Nancy!"

"All right. I'll stop prying. Let me just say that might make a difference." She stood. "I'm going outside for a smoke."

"It's bad for you."

"Yeah. Yeah." She angled her head to the TV. "Concentrate on Bosco and Jimmy while I'm gone. Thoughts about Mr. Bad Boy aren't good for *you*."

Faith watched the show, thinking none of the cops' shoulders were quite as wide as Rick's, their faces not as angular. When Nancy pulled open the door five minutes later, Faith glanced up.

"Well, look who the cat dragged in." Nancy's tone was teasing, but there was a note of worry in her voice.

Faith's gaze slid past her, where Pilar Ruscio stood—her hair disheveled, her eyes red, a white islet nightgown peeking out from underneath a raincoat.

And a huge bruise spreading across her cheek.

"THERE YOU ARE." Casey Malvaso stood in the doorway of her mother-in-law's den and smiled at Rick. Her hair had gotten longer, and she wore a black skirt with a ruffle along the bottom. He was still stumped by the transformation of tough-guy Brennan since she married Zach Malvaso. "Can I sit?"

He'd come in here to get away from all the . . . affection at the party. "You better not. Last time your hubby caught us alone, there were fireworks."

Casey grunted. Malvaso had good reason to hate him. Rick hadn't known when he'd slept with Casey last spring that she was in love with Zach. Their hookup had caused a big rift between the now happily married couple, but Zach still looked at Rick as if he was one of America's Most Wanted.

"I'll take my chances." She came in and dropped down onto a chair. "Will was worried you might not come."

"I wouldn't miss his birthday party." He sipped the beer he was nursing, picturing Will's broad smile and the huge hug he had given Rick when he arrived.

Casey stared at him. "He watched the door until you got here."

"Don't bullshit me."

"He loves you like a son. Why can't you accept that?"

"I let him down." He stared at the TV where the *Third Watch* guys were saving the world. "In the worst way."

"Yeah, well join the human race, Ruscio. We let down people we love, it's part of being alive. You gotta forgive yourself for the dumb stuff you do and concentrate on the good."

"You sound like a damn Aesop's fable." Which he'd been hearing way too much of lately.

"I know from whence I speak."

"Jesus, Brennan, you really have changed."

"Yes," came a voice from the doorway. "She has."

Rick looked up into the unsmiling face of Zach Malvaso.

Casey laughed. "Down boy."

Zach scowled. He held up the phone. "You got a call, Ruscio."

Immediately, Rick felt for his cell phone in his pocket. Damn, he must have left it in his car. "Who is it?"

"Don't know." Zach strode in and gave Rick the phone; he grabbed Casey's hand and tugged her to her feet. "I'll take my woman back now, thank you." With that he started to drag her off.

Casey called over her shoulder, "We'll talk later. You're going to help at the camp cleanup next week, right?"

Rick didn't answer. Shaking his head at the retreating couple, he spoke into the phone. "Ruscio."

"Mr. Ruscio, this is Ian Woodward. Sorry to bother you at the party—I needed to get in touch with you and took a chance that you were with Eve and Noah at Chief Rossettie's party."

"It's cool. What's up?"

"I've got Lisel Loring with me. She tried reaching you on your cell. Something's happened with this fan thing I think you should know about."

"Tonight?"

"I'd feel better talking to you about it in person."

"Sure. I'll leave right now."

After a quick good-bye to Will and a promise to try to return, Rick drove like he was in a squad car again and was ringing Woodward's doorbell twenty minutes later. The man checked through the glass, then opened the door. "Thanks for coming."

"Where is she?"

"Right here." He wheeled back and let Rick in.

Lisel sat on a couch off to the left, wrapped up in a lap blanket. Pink satin peeked out from beneath it. He crossed to her. "Are you all right?"

"I'm sorry to ruin your evening."

"That's what you're paying me for." He sat down. "What happened?"

She nodded to the letter on the table. "I got back late tonight from a trip to the city about my play. While I was there, I picked up my mail from the theater. My housekeeper's coming tomorrow, and I wanted her to deal with it." She nodded to the letter. "That was in it. I opened it, then realized what it was. There's several more in the stack."

Gingerly he picked up the note. Skimmed it. He knew he was frowning when he said, "This isn't any worse than the rest of them, Lisel, although we might get some prints off it."

"It wasn't just the letter." This from Woodward, who'd wheeled over and sat as close to Lisel as he could get.

Rick raised a brow.

"Tell him, honey."

"I got phone calls. Three of them. The person hung up after I answered." She nodded to the note. "Given what that says, I was afraid this fan had found me."

"Hmm. Maybe so. Could be crank. But it's best to be safe."

"When I couldn't reach you, I came over here."

Rick patted his shirt where he'd remembered to put his phone. "Sorry, I left my cell in my car."

As always, he'd been distracted by visiting his house. Some security expert he was. He looked at Woodward. Something about the guy's attitude niggled at Rick. It was possessive, protective. He wondered if Woodward was as innocent as he seemed tonight. He could have made those calls to lure her over here.

"Well, I can stay the night out here if you want. We can talk to Will tomorrow about where we should go from here legally and decide some options for your protection."

He saw Woodward grip the armrests of his chair. A quick glance told him the guy's jaw had tightened. Was this interfering with his plan? Yet he'd called Rick.

"I wish Mona—my housekeeper—had come today. I'm sure having her with me will calm my skittishness."

"This is not just skittishness. It's valid concern." Woodward sounded angry. He faced Rick. "I think it's a good idea if you stay with her."

Lisel's soft look focused on Woodward. "I'd rather stay here with you, Ian."

Though the guy shook his head, his body language and the heat in his eyes said he wanted the exact same thing.

Rick stood just as his cell phone rang. "Sorry. Must be my night." He flicked open the phone. "Ruscio."

"Rick?" The voice sounded familiar.

"Yes."

"This is Faith. McPherson. Your sister's here with me. I think you need to come over to my place right away."

PILAR RUSCIO SANK further into the cushions of Faith's couch and wiped her eyes. "I'm causing so much trouble."

"Nonsense," Faith's mother told her. "You did exactly the right thing by coming to see David." When Faith's parents hadn't been home, the young girl had seen a light on in the carriage house behind the parsonage where Faith lived and come back.

Pilar gazed at Faith's father. "You said if I ever needed anything . . ."

"And I meant it, Pilar. Anything. Any time."

"I was afraid to call Rick." She touched her cheek and winced. An angry red welt marred the perfection of her skin. "You don't know him. He'll lose it over this."

Faith tucked back a strand of Pilar's hair, which was the exact color of Rick's. "Honey, we had to call him."

When her parents had gotten home, Faith had phoned them and explained the situation. Her dad said Rick needed to be notified.

"Are you afraid of your brother?" David asked gently.

"No! He's got a terrible temper, but he wouldn't ever hurt me, if that's what you mean. This will just cause him more problems, and he already has enough to deal with in his life." She sighed. "He'll want to take me out of Ma's house."

Faith had begun to wonder why he hadn't insisted on that sooner.

"We don't need to discuss this now," David said. "Would you like to tell us what happened or wait for Rick?"

"Can I just wait?" she asked sniffling.

"Of course."

Nancy came in from the kitchen and handed Pilar a mug. "Here sweetie, drink this."

Pilar had finished her hot chocolate when the bell rang. She jumped at the noise.

"Shh, it's okay." Her mother soothed the young girl like she used to do for her own kids, while Faith got up to answer the door. She swung it open.

Rick stood on the stoop, his face more ravaged than when she'd told him he had to work with kids. Faith reached out and touched his arm. "She's okay."

For a minute he just stared at her. Swallowed hard. "Good."

"Come on in."

He stepped inside and froze when he got a good look at his sister. "Son of a bitch."

No one spoke. He crossed to Pilar. Kneeling down, he took her hands in his. "Are you all right?"

The tears came again then. Pilar had been strong since she'd arrived, just a little weepy. However, as soon as she saw her brother, she threw herself into his arms. Held on. Sobbed. He held on, too, tight, uttering nonsense words. Crooning assurances. "Shh. *Querida.* It's okay. I'm here. I'll take care of you."

Finally Pilar pulled back, and Faith's mother handed her tissues.

Rick took the cushion on the other side of Pilar. "What happened?" When she didn't say anything, he looked to Faith.

"She hasn't told us yet."

David said, "We can leave you two alone, if you like."

"No." Pilar's gaze was pleading. "He won't get so mad if you're here."

"I won't get mad, *niña.* I promise."

"Yes you will."

Rick said gently, "Who did this to you?"

"Anita's boyfriend. Lennie."

"*What?*"

"He was hitting her, Rick. In her room. I heard it. I couldn't just let it go on."

"Oh, God. I've tried to get her away from that guy a thousand times. I can't stand the thought of him hitting her."

Pilar's chin jutted out. "Me, either. So I went in and jumped on his back."

Rick's chest rose and fell heavily. But he said nothing.

"It gets worse."

"Tell me."

"Anita . . ." Pilar's eyes teared again. "She yelled at me. She told me to mind my own business." Her eyes widened. "She sided with *him.*"

"Battered woman's syndrome." Rick looked to Faith's father for confirmation.

"Yes, it is."

"It kills me to think of her in that situation." He turned angry eyes on Pilar. "And now this. What did he do exactly?"

"He hit me."

Rick's face, which he'd struggled to keep composed, reddened. "*Hijo de una perra. Lo mataré.*" His swearing and desire to kill Lennie charged the already tense atmosphere.

"I was afraid, Ricardo. Of what he'd do." She drew in a breath. "Of what Anita might let him do. To me."

Faith watched Rick bite back the deadly anger simmering in his eyes. They were as black as onyx now. "Well, this clinches it. You're moving in with me."

"I hate to leave Ma."

"*Sí, bebé.* But I can't let you go back there."

"Your apartment's tiny."

"I'll sleep on the couch."

"You're gone all the time. You might have to do night surveillance for this new job."

No answer for that one.

"The parsonage is huge." This from David, who Faith saw exchange a smile with her mother. "And since Peter went to divinity school in New York and Faith moved out here, we have a lot of room." He looked at Rick. "For someone to stay with us."

Pearl literally beamed. "I would love it." She reached out and squeezed Pilar's hand. "We still have Faith's room all set up. It has a white canopy bed. David works right next door at the church." She smiled at Rick, and Faith knew he was dead meat when her mother effected that tone. "Pilar talked to us the other night about attending services."

"That's a whole lot different than moving in with you, Mrs. McPherson."

"Pearl, please."

David said, "Perhaps Rick and I can speak privately for a minute." He stood. "Let's step into the kitchen."

Like a man going to purgatory, Rick stood and followed her father to the kitchen.

Pilar's innocent gaze swung to Faith. "What's he going to say?"

Biting back a chuckle, she smiled down at the young girl. "How Rick has to put his ego aside and do what's best for you. How my parents can take care of you. You're as good as moved in, kid, lock, stock, and barrel."

Nancy, who'd stood by and watched the McPherson family dynamic unfold, gave Faith a knowing look. "Yeah, and it looks like our Bad Boy will be hanging around here a lot, too. Isn't that interesting?"

Damned if Faith didn't feel herself blush.

OUTSIDE, IN THE crisp October night, trying to contain his emotions, Rick jammed his hands into the pockets of his gray slacks. His rage had been murderous, but Reverend McPherson's firm yet gentle coaxing had quelled it. "Come on," he said to the preacher's daughter. "I'll walk you back to your place."

"Okay." Faith started down the path to the carriage house from the parsonage, where they'd gone to settle Pilar. "She's going to be fine with my parents."

"It's an inconvenience." And Rick hated asking for favors.

Faith stopped walking. The moon and low-level lighting on

the ground illuminated her skin. It glowed like shiny pearls. "Of course it's not. They love helping people."

Rick turned to her. "I never met anybody like your family."

"It's who we are, Rick." They started walking again. "What did Dad say to you in the kitchen?"

It wasn't so much what the Reverend McPherson had said to Rick. It was his . . . expectation that Rick would do the right thing. The guy's mere presence had to give the devil a run for his money. "How I had to put my own need to protect Pilar on the back burner and do what's best for her."

Faith smiled. "Sounds like my dad."

"She can't stay here forever." He'd said the same thing to David.

I think we should put that in God's hands and just work this out one step at a time.

They kept walking; crickets had come out and were chirping. The air smelled like fall leaves. It had gotten nippy, and Faith hadn't thrown on a jacket. Wearing only a long-sleeved T-shirt that said Union Divinity School, she shivered. Rick whipped off his sports coat and slid it around her shoulders. "Thanks. What will your mother do, Rick, about this?"

"Nothing as long as I keep paying her rent." He swore under his breath. He hadn't meant to reveal that.

"It's nice of you to support your family."

"I do it for Pilar and Anita, though I'd like to break my other sister's neck right now."

"Still, it's nice." She was quiet as they neared the house, then she added, "Beneath that gruff exterior, you're a nice guy, Rick Ruscio."

He stopped again. "No, Faith, I'm not."

She smiled up at him. God, she was little; he loomed over her. Then she shocked the hell out of him by reaching out and brushing a hand down his biceps. "This gray shirt looks terrific on you."

After a moment, he grasped her fingers. "Don't do that."

"What?"

"Get any ideas."

She chuckled. "You don't pull any punches do you?"

He ignored her comment. "I'm bad news."

Her lovely green eyes rolled with exasperation. "Spare me."

"In reality, little girl, the lion eats the lamb."

"I can't help it if I find you attractive." She lifted her hand to rub his jaw. Jesus, it felt good. "You don't scare me, Rick."

He gripped her arms and said silkily, "I should."

Again she grinned. Shit, he didn't know what to do about her. She was coming on to him and she wasn't listening to his warnings. Well, maybe he'd just have to show her his true colors.

There were shadows under the tree to the left. Rick dragged Faith over. Without warning, he slammed her body against his. His jacket fell from her shoulders to the ground, as he lifted her up. Then he took her mouth. Carnally. Roughly. Like the man he was.

Only . . . in seconds, against his will, he found himself gentling the kiss. Her arms encircled his neck and, like a courtesan, not a preacher's kid, she wrapped herself around him. She had curves, a lot of them. His hands grasped her waist. It was supple, causing his fingers to flex on her. And her scent, fresh and sweet, filled his senses. She tasted wonderfully erotic and innocent at the same time; the combination made his head spin. He moaned and sank into her. She moaned and inched closer.

This wasn't what was supposed to . . . oh, God, her tongue, shit what was she doing . . . her fingers inched down into dangerous territory . . . he dragged his mouth away and tried to push her from him. "Faith, stop . . ."

She fitted herself even closer, shook her head, and went for his mouth again; he felt like he was drowning, but his hand slid to her bottom and pressed her up and against him. Holy hell . . .

A voice broke the silence. "Faith, is that you out there?"

Nancy, from the preschool. Thank the Lord the woman hadn't gone home.

Finally Faith drew away. "Yeah, it's me."

The moon came out from behind the clouds. Rick looked down at her and was poleaxed by the sight. Her hair was messy from his hands. Her lips swollen from his mouth. His entire body responded to the sight.

And then Nancy said, "Faith, come on inside. Your fiancé's on the phone."

SIX

PUNCH. PUNCH. PUNCH.

Ian hit the leather bag mercilessly, letting the frustration drain out of him in increments. When he'd been injured and realized his legs would be useless the rest of his life, his rehab therapist, Joe Harmon, had suggested boxing as an outlet. It had saved Ian's sanity. They often sparred when Joe was with him; the man had become his physical therapist and a lot of other things.

Since Joe didn't get to Hidden Cove until tomorrow, Ian had taken on the bag. He'd opened all the windows and let the cool breeze from the lake and the water's gentle lapping envelop him. The clock in the living room clanged twelve times. He hoped it didn't wake Lisel, who slept in Eve's old room. Though Ian hadn't wanted her here, when Ruscio's sister had gotten in trouble, the security expert had to leave.

His hands began to hurt, so he drew back, threw off the gloves, and turned to the bars behind him. He'd set up a gym of sorts in here so he could work out. Right after he was injured, he'd learned he needed, in addition to a carefully planned diet and a lot of good sleep, the upper body strength of Hercules to

manage his life. He glanced down at his legs, encased in sweats.
And to exercise his useless limbs. Though he did stretches and
strengthening exercises every single day, and Joe really worked
him out four times a week, Ian's calves were still thin. Embar-
rassingly so. Something he wouldn't want any woman to see,
least of all Lisel. Fuck! Why was he even thinking along these
lines?

He spent another hour exhausting himself. Then he wheeled
into the bathroom, rolled into the shower, and transferred himself to the built-in shower seat by lifting himself on the grab
bars. He pushed away the chair, then slid off his sweats.

As he looked down, a vision of his legs, hairy, sinewy, full of
life, superimposed over the shriveled limbs. He and his ex-wife
had been hiking in the Catskills. She'd slipped, and he'd braced
himself on those legs to catch her. He'd strained one calf, and
bitched about it.

Little did he know.

Turning on the water as hot as he could stand it, he let it
pummel his face; reaching up, he fingered the scar on his left
cheek. The first time Marian had seen it, she'd cried. It was less
red now, only a couple of jagged marks that faintly resembled a
Z, but he was marred there, too. Maimed and scarred.

Lisel had said innumerable times that she didn't care. But
Ian cared. He always would. And yet . . . he'd felt guilty about
moping because so many brothers had given the ultimate sacrifice. How ungrateful. So, he'd done some volunteering at the
rehab center and worked himself out of the worst of the funk.
He'd gotten on with his life.

It just wouldn't include Lisel.

Finished with his shower, he dried off, stuck another towel on
the chair, pulled it close and transferred back. He wheeled into
his bedroom, removed pajama bottoms from one of the draw-
ers—he wouldn't sleep naked tonight—and slid them on. He remembered when just the act of dressing had exhausted him.

He brushed his teeth, used the john, then wheeled himself
back to his room and transferred to his bed. Shutting off the
light, he lay against the cool brown sheets, linked his hands behind his head and stared up at the sky, visible through the two
skylights. It was starry tonight, like it had been that night he'd
broken it off with Lisel. Mostly he tried not to think about that

time, but with her sleeping just a few feet away, his mind refused to cooperate. Hoping if he rehashed his original reasons for alienating her it would give him strength, he let the ugly images come . . .

He'd been sitting on her back porch on the floor, playing Scrabble with her. They were laughing, drinking wine. She'd made a word, and his eyes narrowed on it. *Virile.* He didn't say anything, but three words later when she'd made *sexy* and *sinew* and *cute,* he'd stared over at her. She'd held his gaze, drew him in with her cobalt blue eyes.

Finally, he'd asked, "What's on your mind, lady?"

"You," she said simply.

He hadn't expected that. He'd thought she'd tell him about a new boyfriend and had braced himself to hear about her and another man.

"Got me confused with somebody else," he mumbled and stared down at his letters.

"No, Ian. I don't. I've felt this way for a long time, waited for you to pick up on the signals, but I'm tired of waiting."

His heart catapulted in his chest. "Well, redirect those signals, will you? To somebody whole."

She'd swept the board clean with her arm, shocking him with her anger. "Don't ever say that again. You're more whole, more of a man than any I've ever met."

"Look," he'd told her, panicking. "If I'd thought for one second you'd ever see me like that, I'd never have let myself be friends with you."

"We're more than friends. I love you, Ian. I want a relationship with you."

He'd brutally ignored her precious declaration. "When hell freezes over."

She had the audacity to come up on her knees and inch over to him; she was wearing a yellow gauzy sundress that looked dynamite on her. Leaning in close, she put her lips on his scar. "I don't care about all this. Except for how it hurts you."

Roughly, he'd grabbed her arms. "I care."

She'd sat back on her haunches, the action pulling the dress tight across her full breasts. "How can you think so little of yourself? You dragged more than a dozen people out of the

World Trade Center before you got hurt. You've made a wonderful recovery physically. You're an attractive man, Ian."

"Don't do this to me. That part of my life's over."

"No, no, don't say that." He'd never expected what came next; she'd crawled up on his lap and wound her arms around his neck. "Please."

He tried to push her away, but her grip was strong.

And then it happened. He felt himself go hard.

She felt it, too.

In his ear, she whispered, "Looks like your body didn't get the message that that part of your life is over." She'd settled into him, making him moan. "Share this with me. Share yourself with me."

"We're not playing *Beauty and the Beast*, Lise. Life with a gimp is hell."

"I hate to hear you talk like that. About the man I love."

"I don't love you, Lisel."

She stiffened, but that lie wasn't enough to discourage her. "All right. Let's just have sex."

"I don't want sex with you."

"Because you're not man enough?" She squirmed on his lap, making a mockery of his words. "There's evidence to the contrary."

He had to do something fast. Finally, he said, "No, because you're not my type." Callously he added, "*You're* not woman enough for me."

He'd known exactly what he was doing. In a close moment, she'd confessed to Ian that her ex-husband had been a son of a bitch and knew her insecurities about her weight, her problems with eating. When she got too skinny, he'd taunt her with the exact accusation Ian had just hurled her way.

Consequently, his insult had hit the bull's-eye. She'd slid off his lap and stood, but not before he'd seen the tears in her eyes. He felt like an asshole. His hands itched to reach for her. But he'd controlled it and she'd left. He'd saved her from himself . . .

"Ian?" Her voice came out of the darkness. For a minute, he thought he was still in the past. Then, the light from the moon glinted off the icy pink pj's she wore.

"Lisel?"

"Can I come in?"

Fuck! "Sure."

She crossed to the bed. He sucked in a breath at how lovely she looked with the silk molding to her body, her hair messy like his hands would make it.

"What's wrong? Can't you sleep?"

She sat down on the edge of the mattress, her dancer's posture slumped tonight. "I was out cold for a while. I just woke up and couldn't go back to sleep."

"Your old nemesis." They'd shared insomniac stories and even sat together on some early summer mornings when they both couldn't sleep. "Did you take a pill?"

"Uh-uh. I left them next door."

"Want me to go get them? Or I have over-the-counter stuff."

"No thanks. That's not what I need."

Don't ask. "What do you need, Lise?"

She raised her hand to push the thick waves of hair out of her eyes. He saw it was shaking. "Can I . . . can I stay here with you a little while?"

"Here?" Oh, God, why tonight? When he was feeling raw. And aroused just by the sight of her.

He started to say, "That's not a good idea," but she clasped her hands tightly in her lap, probably so he wouldn't see she was shaking. Shit.

Sliding over, he patted the mattress. "Come on, climb up."

Her eyes widened, then she clambered onto the bed, stretched out and sank into him as if she'd done it her whole life. He let himself savor the sensation of having her curled up into his side. Nothing, *nothing,* had ever felt this right.

The scent of her hair filled his head. The softness of her curves against the hard planes of his body was indescribable. He'd missed touching a woman in general, but the feel of Lisel . . . that was heaven.

"You feel so good," he whispered in the darkness.

"You've never once held me, except that day I threw myself into your lap."

Darkness was dangerous. It called forth confidences best left unsaid. "I was just thinking about that."

She didn't say anything, but nosed into his chest.

His lips brushed her hair. "I'm sorry I hurt you that night."

"I'm glad you're sorry."

He rubbed his palm up and down her arm. "I haven't changed my mind, honey."

"I know. I'm sorry about all this. About coming back to Hidden Cove in general."

"It's not your fault."

"I know. Still. Once Mona gets here, once we settle on the extent of the security with Rick, I'll stay out of your way."

He didn't want her to. It took all the strength he had, all the stoicism he'd cultivated since 9/11, to keep that thought to himself. "Let's just get through tonight."

She burrowed into him. It felt good, as if he could really protect her. In just minutes, she relaxed. He heard the soft rise and fall of her breathing. His own eyes started to close. But for once, he fought sleep. He wanted to luxuriate in the feel of her. Treasure holding her against him.

Because he never planned to do it again.

HIS FEET HIT the ground along the shoreline with stunning force. It was cold for October, but he didn't care. The wind whipped his hair, reddened his cheeks; he basked in the freedom of a simple run. Pound, pound! His toes squished in the sand; a few little stones dug into his flesh. Each and every muscle in his calves began to ache, and Ian reveled in all the sensations. By some miracle he could use his legs again, feel them again, be whole. He kept running, let his breathing escalate, make his heart pound. He was Superman. He could do anything.

She was up ahead, dressed in ice pink pajamas. The wind molded the silk to her, and as he neared, he couldn't wait to get his hands on her. She was laughing as he reached her, scooped her up, held her over his head—because he *could*—and felt the weight of her strain his arms.

"I love you," she said on a giggle. "But put me down. You're making me dizzy."

"I love you, too," he admitted freely, for once not hiding his emotions. He let her slide down his body, reveling in every inch of her. His hand rested on her stomach. "How's my little one?"

"Wonderful." Her face glowed. "He's going to look just like you. Be as strong, as masculine as you."

"Damn right," the man he used to be said.

And then . . . everything changed. Lisel was in the water, and the waves were crashing around her. She was gripping a little child's hand. It looked like Noah's granddaughter, Abby, but he knew the child was his. "Help us, Ian," Lisel shouted from the water.

"Daddy . . ."

He wanted to race in and rescue them, like he'd rescued so many in his lifetime, but as he lurched forward his legs wouldn't move. And then he glanced down. They were shriveled again. And useless. He shot a panicked look out to the lake; the water was rising above his son's head.

"Nooooooooooooo," he yelled.

He awoke with a start. He sat up in bed, covered with sweat, breathing hard. Gray dawn was peeking through the skylights, and he recognized the outline of his room in the condo; the wheelchair stood guard next to his bed. What was that doing here? Then he remembered his reality, and that he'd only dreamed about being whole.

He used to dream all the time he was healed, but he hadn't in a long time. In the dream, he could feel what it was like before the accident; the worst part was waking and the disorientation that came with the awareness of what his life had become. He wondered why the dream had come back tonight.

And then something moved on his bed; he glanced to his side and saw Lisel, sleeping next to him. Ah, now he got it. Now he knew why he dreamed he was whole.

THE LAKE WAS rough at seven A.M., crashing violently against the shore. He'd parked his chair beyond the break wall where he could watch the waves batter the stones and encroach upon the sand. Tugging his jacket closer, he forced himself to blank his mind. Not to think. Not to feel.

"Ian?"

He angled the chair, and there she stood. He tried to shut down immediately but he couldn't. What it had felt like to hold her all night filtered in and out of his mind, his body. It had made him want more, so much so he'd dreamed about it. And wanting more could kill him. "You shouldn't be out here." He nodded to the pink pajamas peeking out from under one of his coats. She wore the white canvas sneakers she'd had on last night when she'd come to his house, scared and embarrassed. "It's cold."

"Are you all right?"

Swallowing hard, he stared out over the lake. "No."

"I . . ." From his peripheral view, he saw her toe some gravel out of the way, as if she was garnering courage. The wind caught her hair and played peekaboo with the silky strands. Some of it obscured her face. "I missed you when I woke up. I was dreaming about you."

He snorted. "I had my own dreams."

"Tell me."

He watched her for a minute. "Come here." She moved in close. He took her hand, linked their fingers. "We were together. Out here on the lake. I was running after you."

"Oh, Ian."

"You were pregnant." His voice caught on the last word. "With my child." He swallowed hard, remembering the impotence of what happened next. "Then you were drowning. With my son. I couldn't save you because my legs wouldn't work."

Her eyes darkened. Midnight shadows chased through them. "Oh, no . . ."

It was the hardest thing he ever had to do, but he was going to do it. He kissed their joined hands. "Lisel, do you really love me, like you said last summer?"

"Of course."

"Then you have to do something for me."

"Anything, Ian."

"You have to stay away from me. No more spending the night together. No more closeness." He stared hard at her. "Don't tempt me to take this further, to let you in and then have to deal with things like in my dream." He summoned strength from God knows where. "Don't make me want what I can't have. It hurts too much."

She squatted down and faced him at eye level. Softly, she whispered, "You can want me, Ian. It's all right."

"No, you just don't know, you just don't understand. After 9/11 I've taught myself not to want anything."

"Please don't do this to us. You care about me. I know you do."

"I have to do this." He hit the chair with his fist. "I can never be happy burdening you with my disability. It would destroy me."

"I—"

His fingers went to her mouth. "Do it for me. If you really love me. Just stay away."

He saw the tears then and knew he was right. He kept hurting her, and he almost couldn't stand it.

She rose and wrapped her arms around her waist. "All right, Ian, I'll do what you ask. But I think you're making a terrible mistake."

"No, the mistake would be in changing my mind from what I decided last summer."

Finally, she nodded and turned away. He watched her walk up the grassy slope to her condo then looked back out to the lake and breathed a sigh of relief. He'd done the right thing again, protected her from life with a cripple.

He wondered if the grinding ache in his heart would ever go away.

"YOU KNOW," JOE Harmon barked to Ian as the therapist hammered away at his back with a series of karate chops, "you could have resisted the Cong's interrogation."

"I had a good teacher at the rehab center." Joe and a nurse named Sunny were the only good things that he could remember about those days. Harmon especially had helped him begin to deal with his limitations.

Harmon snorted. From where he lay on the massage table, Ian raised his head and opened one eye. Joe would never say how old he was, but from what he'd told Ian about his war experiences, Ian figured him to be in his late fifties. He had swarthy skin, a grizzled mane of hair to his shoulders, and a beard. His body was honed from years of workouts. "What do you want to know?" Ian asked, just to torque him.

"For starters, whose pink lace socks were on the floor by your bed this morning."

Shit. "I don't kiss and tell, old man."

Harmon worked his back muscles without responding. Finally, he said, with gentle gruffness, "My impression was you didn't kiss at all, buddy."

It was the brotherly tone that got him. Like always. Joe was the only one Ian talked to about his disabilities. "I didn't. Somebody spent the night, but . . . shit, I don't wanna talk about it, Joe."

Joe's hands kneaded the base of his spine. Ian moaned at the easing of the tension there. "It was her, wasn't it?"

"Yeah."

"What's she doin' in Hidden Cove?"

"She's sick again. She moved back in next door."

"Fucking son of a bitch. You know about this when you took the job at the academy?"

"No."

"She's bad news. It took me weeks to get you outta the blues when she ditched you last summer."

Ian hadn't been totally honest with Joe. He knew if he told his friend the truth, Harmon would ride his ass about his decision to forgo a relationship with Lisel. So, Ian had been vague about what had gone on between them, and Harmon had drawn his own conclusion. "Like I said, I made a mistake. Won't happen again."

"Yeah, and I got a bridge I'd like to sell you." He worked his way down Ian's legs, reaching the useless parts. He massaged there, too, then went through the exercises to maintain muscle tone. "You been doin' these? Your legs are stiff."

"From the knees up, it's been a piece of cake. For the rest, I've been trying with the machines." He grunted. "Took you long enough to get out here. By the way, where's your stuff?"

"I ain't stayin' with you."

Ian raised himself off the table onto his elbows and glanced back. "Why? That was the agreement."

"Nope, it's what you wanted. I got no desire to see your ugly puss twenty-four/seven."

Ian knew that in many ways Joe was a private man and needed his own space. "You're not going to drive up from New York four times a week, are you?"

"Turn over," he told Ian before he answered. As Ian completed the maneuver, Harmon began some range-of-motion exercises on his legs. "Nope, I'm staying across the lake in the main cabin of Hale's Haven."

The camp Noah's firefighters had started. "Why's that?"

"They just framed in two more cabins. I said I'd do some inside work if I could live there for free. With what you're payin' me, I'm gonna be a rich man."

Ian guessed that it was Joe's way of donating to the camp more than anything else. Everybody who lived in Hidden Cove or came here seemed to form quite an attachment to the place. Churches were doing fund-raisers, there was a massive cleanup effort next week, which Eve had roped him into helping with, and even Lisel was doing a benefit show on New Year's Eve.

"Noah never mentioned that you'd be staying out there."

"Will Rossettie suggested it."

"You know the police chief?"

"War buddies," was all Harmon said.

Settling back down, Ian was thoughtful. He'd been hoping Joe would be staying at his condo as company, but also as a buffer to keep him away from Lisel. Well, Mona Mincheon, her housekeeper, was due in today, too. She'd at least be some kind of chaperone. Thoughts of Lisel made him wonder what had been decided about the fan letters. And how she was doing, after yet another rejection from him.

"What's wrong man? Your muscles just tensed like a tightrope."

"Nothing. Did I tell you what I'm gonna be teaching at the academy next week?"

Harmon hesitated, then allowed the change of subject. "No. Fill me in."

As Ian launched into a description of his first lesson on terrorism, Joe was successfully distracted from talk of Lisel.

Ian wished he could turn off his mind as easily.

FROM THE SUNNY kitchen's alcove desk where she was sorting the mail, Mona eyed Lisel like a mother who knew her daughter had been in the backseat of a boy's car the night before. Remembering what it had felt like to be in Ian's arms all night, Lisel hid her face in the fresh flowers Mona had brought her.

Finally, Mona broke the silence. "What's he doing here, Lisel?" Mona had arrived just as Lisel left Ian this morning on the lakefront and had witnessed how upset Lisel was . . . again.

"Ian?"

Mona sniffed. It was so . . . motherly. With her graying hair pulled back in a bun, no makeup, and a modest dress, she was the epitome of Lisel's maternal image. "Yes, of course."

"He's teaching at the fire academy. Neither of us knew the other had come back to Hidden Cove." Mona riffled through the mail but didn't comment. Her shoulders were stiff, and she reminded Lisel of the disapproving nuns from Catholic schools she'd attended. "You're upset he's here."

Her friend stopped and looked up. "Only because of how devastated you were in July when you unexpectedly came back to New York."

Carefully, Lisel removed the flowers from their green cellophane. "Have I told you how wonderful you were to me then?"

"Many times." She gave Lisel an indulgent smile.

Lisel remembered Mona's loving care. "Your daughter's a lucky woman." She retrieved a hand-painted, blue ceramic vase, crossed to the sink, filled it with water, and began to insert the flowers in an arrangement. She found the homey ritual soothing. "Did Jenny like having you stay with her up in Rochester?" Mona's daughter was a nurse in upstate New York.

Shadows crossed her friend's face. "I think so. I worry about her, though. Sometimes I think she turned out just fine, and other times, she's so distant. I wonder if it's because I wasn't home enough when she was growing up."

"You did the best you could under the circumstances."

Mona had been a single parent and raised a child by herself. "Maybe." She took a bead on Lisel. "I worry about you, too."

"Well, this fan thing is really getting to me."

"That's not what I meant, but tell me about it."

Lisel filled her in, stopping to smell the pink carnations she loved, forcing her mind away from Ian. But the feel of his arms around her in bed all night long wouldn't go away.

"Lisel, dear, are you all right? You look flushed."

"I'm fine, I—"

The doorbell rang. Lisel jumped. Then she remembered Rick Ruscio was coming over today. "It's probably the security expert."

Mona shivered. "I don't like this newest thing."

Lisel walked by Mona on the way to the door and squeezed her arm. "We've got help, Mona. We'll be fine."

Checking the viewer first, Lisel opened the door. She was surprised to see Will Rossettie with Rick. With a very rumpled Rick. He looked like he'd had a wild night. Oh, dear, she hoped he was responsible enough for this job. "Hi. Nice to see you, Will."

The men entered, and she introduced Mona. "Glad you arrived," Rick said gruffly. "Lisel was anxious for you to get here."

"Really?" Mona frowned. "I would have come sooner, had I known."

"You needed time with your daughter." Lisel let the men in, and they all sat.

Will took over. "Rick showed me the newest letter and the stack of others. He also told us about the phone calls. There's nothing we can do about those, and unless we monitor your phone, we can't trace future ones. First, you need to tell us who has this number."

"Well, a lot of people. My parents, my agent, the theater . . ."

"That's enough." Rick shook his head. "We won't get anything from checking the phone. The fan could have gotten it in a lot of ways, particularly if she's associated with the theater. You need to call the phone company Monday and cancel this phone. Use just your cell phone. Get a new number for that, and don't give it out."

"But how will people I know reach me? My parents? My agent?"

"You'll have to call them occasionally. Just until this is settled."

The idea of being cut off was chilling.

"The main thing about this, though, is if the fan had the house phone number here, she might know where you are."

Lisel thought about that. "Well, it wasn't a secret last summer that I came out here. But we kept it out of the papers this time." She shrugged. "Then, of course, the fund-raiser's here. Anybody could have put two and two together, I guess."

Deep grooves formed in Rick's face. He didn't look like he'd slept much last night. "In any case, we should assume the fan knows where you are."

"All right. What do we do next?"

"Will thinks if I stop in a few times a day and the cops

cruising by like they are should be enough daylight surveillance. I'd like to watch the house during the night for a while, though."

"Really?" This from Mona. "I hadn't expected that."

"Lisel was frightened enough to spend last night next door." Rick's tone was concerned.

Damn. Mona's gaze whipped to hers. Lisel felt an urgent need to explain herself. Again like the kid in the backseat of the car. "I was spooked. I'm sure with Mona here, things will be fine."

Rick shook his head. "Could be. Just to be safe, I'll park outside the next couple of nights. Keep watch. If nothing happens again, we'll suspend that."

"If you think that's best. Mona and I were planning to go to the Catskills for a few days at the end of the week."

Rick stood. "That'll be all right if things settle down. If they don't, we'll have to regroup."

Will stood, too. The men bade them good-bye, and Lisel and Mona walked them to the door. They'd just stepped outside to the connecting front porch that she shared with Ian when his door opened.

A big, burly man exited Ian's house, laughing. "Yeah, you too, buddy."

Ian was behind him, smiling broadly. His happiness and infrequent smile startled Lisel, who was feeling like an abandoned spouse this morning.

The man stopped, turned, and his lined, weathered face darkened when he saw Lisel. But it wreathed in smiles when Will came into focus. "Rossettie."

Lisel was surprised when the two men hugged. "Good to see you, Harmon."

Ah, this was Ian's friend and therapist. She hadn't met him last summer.

"Get settled into the cabin?" Will asked.

"I'm on my way there."

"Want some help?"

"Sure. You free?"

"Yep." The men said a final good-bye and walked away.

Rick turned to Lisel. "I'll be going now." Again, the shadows in his eyes concerned her. Then she remembered what had happened the night before.

"Rick, I'm sorry I didn't ask. I was distracted and forgot. Is everything all right with your sister? You look . . . upset."

"My sister's just fine. It's . . ." He shook his head. "I didn't sleep well last night. I guess I am worried about her. I'm gonna go see her now, but I'll be back tonight."

When he left, Ian, Lisel, and Mona were alone on the porch. Lisel said, "Mona, this is Ian Woodward."

Mona's whole demeanor was frosty. "Mr. Woodward."

Ian frowned, but said, "Mrs. Mincheon. Lisel speaks highly of you. I'm glad you're here."

"Really?" She angled her chin. "I can't say the same for you." She nodded to Lisel. "I'll be inside." Then she left.

Ian edged the chair back and forth.

"I'm sorry. She was rude."

"Joe was rude to you."

"They're both protective of us."

"Yeah, I know." Ian nodded after Rick. "What did Ruscio say?"

She filled him in.

"Well, sounds like a plan."

"You don't have to worry that I'll show up on your doorstep again."

He swallowed hard, but said nothing.

"I'm going inside to get Mona settled." She turned away.

"Lise?"

That nickname. Damn him. She halted, but didn't turn back.

"I'm sorry . . ."

Without facing him, she whispered, "Yes, so am I."

MY DEAREST LISEL . . .

Dear, darling Lisel . . .

Oh, Lisel, how could you . . .

Pushing away from the computer, Jules stared at the screen then pressed delete. Nothing was coming out right tonight. Nothing had been right since she'd been unable to see Lisel on stage, communicate with her, at least from a distance. She stood and crossed to the mirror. Mmm. Yeah, this was good. She pushed a lock of dark, thick hair off her forehead, as Lisel had in *Longshot,* in the scene where her mother dies. Leaning closer to the glass, Jules examined her blue eyes. One reviewer had called Lisel's cobalt. Hers were, too, right?

Oh, she hurt so much. Yearned. Back to the drawing board . . .

Dear Lisel,
It isn't fair that I can't see you. Do you know what that does to your loyal followers? You might do 'Sundays with Lisel,' right? At least I could see you then. Please, please, please do that. Why are we being punished just because you don't feel good? Reconsider.
For your own safety.

Lovingly,
Jules

SEVEN

IAN WHEELED OVER to the closet and switched on the light.
With the bars lowered to eye level, it was easy to choose his
clothes. He rifled through the shirts, looking for something
moderately dressy. But his hand stopped on one specific garment. It was white, crisply pressed, smelling faintly of starch.
An emblem on the left shoulder faced out. Closing his eyes, he
thought of the man responsible for bringing it to him . . .

"This is fucking cruel," he'd told his brother-in-law when
Noah entered the condo and Ian saw what he carried on the
hangers.

"You are such an asshole." Noah held up the uniform. "This
belongs to you. You should wear it when you teach."

"I'm no longer a firefighter."

"It's like being Catholic, Woodward. Once a firefighter always a firefighter."

He'd gulped back emotion, replaced it with ire. "Where'd
you get it?"

"From your BC in New York. He was thrilled to send it out
to me."

They must have had it specially made . . . this one was new and unworn. Reaching out, he ran his finger over the patch sewn onto the shoulder. 927. His badge number. Still against his will, he slid out the shirt. Captain Ian Woodward was engraved in the little metal name tag.

His throat tight, Ian remembered the day he was made. His wife, his parents, his sister, everybody he loved had come to the ceremony. He pictured himself striding, tall and confident, over to the podium to receive his stripes. Striding back, cocky as hell, thinking nothing could take him down.

He couldn't have been more wrong.

"Stop it," he told himself. "Think about your buddies . . . Cortland . . . Bulk . . . Sorenson . . ." God, there were so many who hadn't made it out of the tower. Ian had wished for a long time that he hadn't either.

He didn't wish that now. He was glad to be alive, even if, after three years, he still experienced rock-bottom bouts of depression. And as always, he felt guilty for the bitterness he still drifted in and out of. Now that he was back in Hidden Cove, he thought about going back to the trauma survivor's group he'd attended last summer.

Lovingly, like a father stored his son's picture or a mother carefully tucked away her daughter's baptismal gown, he replaced the uniform in the back of the closet and pulled out another shirt. It wasn't until he was fully dressed and on his way in the car that he realized the blue gauzy shirt he wore with navy dress pants and polished loafers was one that Lisel had bought him when she insisted he accompany her shopping one rainy afternoon . . .

"What's this for?" he'd asked when she picked it out.

"For coming shopping with me today. I know you're bored."

Watching her try on slinky skirts? Hardly. "You don't have to do this."

"Let me." She'd held it up to him. "It makes your odd-colored eyes a steely blue."

"Is that a compliment?"

"You betcha."

Thoughts of that day led to thoughts of Friday night and how he'd held her all night. He growled at the direction his mind was going. As he pulled into the academy, exited the car, and made his way upstairs, he shook off the memories. "Think of something else."

Terrorism. That was, after all, the topic of the day. He'd planned his lesson over the weekend, from an article he'd done for *Firehouse* magazine and the curriculum outline Caruso had provided. The content had been grim, but the preparation had been satisfying. He wondered, if he hadn't fallen in love with fire fighting, if he'd have made a good schoolteacher.

He was reviewing the notes in his head when he reached the fourth floor and met Jeb Caruso by the office. "Want some coffee?" Jeb asked.

"No, actually, I'd like to go right to the classroom. Get my stuff ready."

"Good. The guys are filing in. They look nervous as hell."

Ian knew his audience consisted of probies from outside HCFD's jurisdiction. "You said they hadn't had the kind of preparation Noah's guys got, so to go basic." He patted his briefcase. "I went basic."

"That's good." They found the classroom, where Ian had given his RIT training. "One of the reasons we built this interdepartmental training facility is to reach outlying areas where they don't have a lot of money or expertise to do sophisticated training. Though truthfully, our own guys need constant refreshers."

"Yeah, I'm doing some on WMD soon, right?" Weapons of Mass Destruction had become an important part of fire department training on terrorism.

"Uh-huh. For the seasoned guys. The ones you had for RIT. By the way, nobody could sing your praises loud enough about the class you taught. They appreciated your . . . *perspective*." Caruso hesitated on the last word.

"Jeb, you don't have to walk on eggshells around me." He hit the bars of his chair. "I know one reason I'll be listened to is because I was in the towers. It gives me a special connection to RIT and to terrorism."

"It doesn't bother you to be a poster child?"

"Truthfully, it does. But I've come around—with Callahan's ass kicking—to think that if it'll save lives or beat the bastards responsible for this, so be it." He didn't realize how much he meant the words until he said them aloud.

Caruso stopped. "Noah hinted you might be touchier about this."

"With good reason. During tragedies, people are worst to those close to them. He's taken shit from me." Ian thought about the uniform. "I'm doing better with it."

Jeb pulled open the classroom door. "Well, he got you to us. I'm grateful."

By the time all the guys were seated, Ian had his papers out, his computer set up for Power Point, his pathway to maneuver the front of the room cleared, and was ready to be introduced. He looked out at the audience.

These guys were so fresh-faced, so much different from the firefighters he'd trained in RIT. They reminded him of Jimmy Jones, the rookie on Ladder 4 whom he'd been training when 9/11 hit. The kid had never completed his stint. Thinking about it made Ian seethe inside, but also renewed a resolve that had been forming since he came to Hidden Cove. No more wallowing in self-pity. *Doing something* should be his focus, and he'd begin today.

"All right, guys. In front of you you'll find a blank sheet of paper. If you'll look at the first slide on the screen, I want you to answer these questions. No names on the papers, but do it without help. I wanna see what you know."

Very nervous grumbles.

Ian called up the first slide he'd created in his presentation. Listed were questions that would lead to the objectives the fire department had for this lesson. The curriculum was well planned with goals and activities, though Ian had made the material his own and tailored the information with his insights based mostly on research.

Ian gave the group some time to write, then asked them to share their information in pairs. The private discussion broke the tension in the room, the fear of being embarrassed in front of their colleagues, and made those who knew little, less self-conscious.

When they'd done the sharing in pairs, he called up the goals of the session on the screen and told them the information was all in handouts, so just to pay attention. "Hopefully by the end of today, you'll have a clear definition of what constitutes a terrorist attack, the history of terrorism in this country and some recent attacks, what are the weapons of choice for those bastards, and what procedures you should follow if involved in an incident."

Ian turned away from the slide. "First, let's toss around what the fire department's role is in a terrorist attack. Why are we doing this training?"

A plump, jowly guy raised his hand.

"No need to raise hands," Ian said. "Just tell me your name and give us your thoughts."

"Jack Close. The fire department and EMS personnel are gonna be the first ones on the scene in a terrorist attack. They say we need to know what to do, and what not to do."

"Yeah," his buddy next to him put in. "Tom Smith. We mitigate the incident; we're not there to try to stop one."

It was obvious he'd been reading up on the subject. "Great point, Tom. Mitigate means what?"

"To assuage it."

Even probies would only take so much. "Jesus, professor, what the hell does that mean?"

The guy blushed. "To relieve it. To take the edge off it."

"Specifically," Ian added, "to deal with those involved and bring them to safety. The main point is nobody expects first responders to stop a terrorist incident, just deal with it."

"Bad enough," somebody growled from the back. The guy looked to be about forty; it was real common in fire departments today for rookies to be older.

"Do you have something to say?"

"Yeah, look, I'm not complaining, but seems to me the fire department keeps bein' asked to do more and more. We fight fires. Then we took on car accidents. Then EMS calls with defibs, and intubations, and all that shit. Now I gotta know about Weapons of Mass Destruction? When's it gonna stop?"

Ian had heard the concern before. In his own eyes, it was valid. "I don't know . . . ?" He waited.

"Guy Shumaker."

"Guy. And in some ways, it sucks that we keep adding to the department's responsibility. But if there's an anthrax scare or a bombing, you're gonna go. No two ways about it. So you probably want to know what to do."

"Yeah, 'course."

Ian turned back to the screen. "Okay, ladies and gentlemen, here's the official definition of a terrorist incident. Can everybody see it, or should I read it aloud?"

"Read it," a young woman said. "Sometimes I'm not sure all these clowns know their ABC's."

Since they had to pass a Civil Service exam to be firefighters, that was highly unlikely. But when the rest chimed in, he read the definition. "Terrorism is defined by the FBI as the unlawful use of force against persons or property to intimidate or coerce a government, civilian population, or any segment thereof, in the furtherance of political or social objectives." Ian paused, then said, "What are the key words here?"

It took some waiting, but they finally contributed . . .

"Illegal use of force."

"Action intended to intimidate or coerce."

"The attack supports political or social objectives."

"Great," Ian said. "The criminal component of intent is the key."

Ian went on to ask about recent terrorist attacks. He didn't need the slides that listed them, the group knew so much, but he put them up because he had pictures of the buildings or the bomber or the damage done, and the graphic depictions were sobering.

When he was sure he had their interest, he continued. "Let's talk about specific WMD's and how to deal with them. Terrorist weapons can include these things: nuclear weapons, radiological material, and chemical and biological agents. Which is the least probable that a country would use as a terrorist weapon?"

The rookies shouted out answers . . .

"Nuclear."

"Why?"

"Because they're too hard to get."

"Right, however, the other three are relatively easy to obtain and pose a greater threat. Since both availability and impact are high, and have potentially devastating effects, most fire departments are concentrating on those. It'll be our focus, too. Next time."

Ian went on to give them information on why weapons of mass destruction would be used: easy availability, requiring small quantities of the agent, difficulty to recognize, easily

spread over large areas, strong psychological impact, and the
overwhelm resources like the fire department. The studen
shifted in their seats, so he threw them a bone. "On the oth
hand, effective dissemination is difficult, delayed effects ca
detract from the impact, and they're potentially hazardous t
the terrorist."

"Where do terrorists get this shit?" Guy asked.

"Good question. Let's pause and brainstorm that."

A really young-looking man said, "I read where some Ru
sians just ordered smallpox from a lab here in the States."

"Unfortunately, some of the obtained weapons are from ou
own facilities. Some can be produced at home—a likely sourc
for chemical and biological agents. Then there are foreign mil
tary sources. And medical/university research."

One of the females in the group raised her hand. "What
likely to be attacked, Captain?"

"Well let's brainstorm that, too. What do you think?"

Eventually they came up with a pretty good list: enclose
spaces, large crowds, critical facilities, materials in storag
symbolic or religious targets, and ports or ships.

As the morning wound down, Ian felt good about the lesso
"Let's wrap this up now by reiterating what we learned this tim
around."

Ian was in the middle of his summary, when Caruso showe
up at his door. He looked at the deputy. "Am I running over'
he asked.

"No. But you gotta see something." He strode into the roo
and flicked on the TV, which was nestled overhead in a corner

A female reporter was on-screen; behind her was Hidde
Cove Library. "We're here, in front of the east wing of the ol
library, where a fire was allegedly started this afternoon by
group of boys smoking in the abandoned wing. Books sti
hadn't been cleared out when a stray match ignited a whole wa
of them."

"This isn't live coverage," Caruso said as the came
switched to the building on fire. It blazed so hot Ian could a
most feel the heat, smell the burning wood.

A voice-over continued. "All the boys were dragged out, b
a firefighter from Quint 7 became trapped."

A picture of Quint 7 firehouse appeared on-screen. "A RI

eam was called in, the Rescue Squad, which is headed by Captain Mitch Malvaso, who we were able to interview. We're pleased to announce that the team successfully freed firefighter Casey Malvaso, who'd been pinned by a beam."

"Holy shit ... those are the guys ... the group ..." Ian looked at Jeb.

The deputy beamed. "That you trained just last week."

Mitch appeared on-screen—sweaty, his face covered with grime. He'd removed his air pack, helmet, and turnout coat and faced the camera with obvious reluctance. The female anchor seemed mesmerized by him. "Captain Malvaso, the rescue of the downed crew member went well?"

"Yes. Though at the time, we didn't know it was my sister-in-law. But we've been trained in this, so my group went in."

"Aren't all firefighters trained in RIT? That means Rapid Intervention Team, doesn't it?"

"Yeah, that's what it means, and no, not everybody's trained. Our department's doing more than most." He looked out at the camera. "As a matter of fact, we owe this particular success to Captain Ian Woodward, a new staff member at the Anderson County Fire Academy. Just last week he ran us through these drills. Ironically, there was a similarity in the training to this rescue that we'd just discussed and hammered out." He smiled. "Good training's essential in departments."

"So you're heroes once again," the woman said, a little flirty.

Mitch's eyes twinkled with humor. "Nah, not us. I'd cast my vote to Captain Woodward, though."

Caruso turned off the TV, patted Ian on the back, and faced the rookies. "Remember this, people. Remember how important our training is." He shot a grateful look at Ian. "And what our experienced staff have to teach you."

Stunned and inordinately pleased, Ian just stared at the group.

HALE'S HAVEN LIVED up to its name. Even now, on this Saturday morning in October, and because it was the seasonably warm Indian summer, the lake lapped lazily in tune with this benign place. This place of sanctuary. From the dock, Ian sat watching the water, the sun warm on his face, the breeze teasing

his hair. While others gathered in the kitchen for doughnuts an
bagels, he wanted time out here to think.

"Penny for your thoughts." His sister's voice came from be
hind him. He peered over his shoulder to see her in baggy jean
and a green checked flannel shirt covering a middle that wa
thickening, she'd told him, so much she couldn't wear all he
clothes anymore.

He asked, "What was it like, Evie, when the kids wei
here?"

She rested her hands on his shoulders and began to knea
there. Through the navy blue sweatshirt, he could feel he
strong fingers loosen the muscles, tight from his morning worl
out with Joe. "Oh, Ian, it was wonderful. We had twenty kids, s
the cabins were crowded. But they had a ball. The older one
took care of the little ones, since they were in forced proximity

He glanced back at the two shiny new cabins built since Jul
for next year. "You're gonna have more kids next summe
right?"

"Yes, we're expecting twice as many, but we're also havin
two sessions." She hesitated. "I was hoping you'd be around
take part."

Automatically, he started to ask what he could do for kie
from the iron prison that confined his life. He used to be pret
good at the basketball they played, the rope climbing they di
and relay races they conducted. Staring out at the lake, h
sighed. He'd also enjoyed water sports. "Remember how w
used to water ski? Dad's captain used to take us out, and yo
and I would try to outdo each other."

"Yeah, you always won."

"Hey, I was a guy."

She chuckled, leaned over, kissed his head, then continue
the massage. "You didn't answer my question."

"I know." He reached behind him and grasped her han
"I'm tired of not being like other people."

"I would be, too."

"I want a more normal life."

"Teaching at the academy's a good start."

"I know. I like it."

"I heard about the RIT training."

He shook his head. "It felt so good, Evie. I felt so whole."

"Oh, Ian, don't say you aren't."

"No, it's too nice a day for morbid thoughts."

"I agree. They're taking sign-ups in the pavilion for next summer."

"They are, huh?"

"Yep, Jenn O'Connor is over there with the baby." He saw his sister glance to the pavilion where Jenn sat with her new son in a carriage. She was talking to her mother, Sabina. Ian knew that Jenn was working half-time for a while, still in charge of the camp, though she'd taken the RIT training from him, too. "Go see the kid," he told his sister. "Get some practice holding him."

"Want me to sign you on?"

"I'll think about it."

When Eve left, he turned and wheeled up the path. Now, everybody was busy. He caught sight of Joe Harmon raking leaves with Chief Rossettie. They were joking good-naturedly. In back of them were some people Ian recognized from the academy sawing off ragged tree limbs. The leaves were turning now, and vivid yellows, reds, and greens ringed the perimeter of the camp.

He sighed. What could he do? Then he saw the Malvaso brothers and their wives at the newest cabin. They were painting. God this was hard, he thought as he watched them stretch and strain on ladders, watched their muscles bulge with exertion. Still, he wheeled over. When he reached them, he waited a minute. "Hi, all. Is there something I can do here?"

Mitch turned and smiled broadly. "Hey, Captain, how you doing?"

"Just fine."

Casey Malvaso was on a ladder, but trundled down quickly. She strode over and held out her hand. He shook it. Cool blue eyes stared down at him. Without preamble, she said, "I got caught on some wiring in the library; they were using it to tie things up in bundles. It was, you know, like I was wired down. Remember how you told the guys to do that to the dummy in the smoke house?"

"Yep."

"You saved my life."

His smile was genuine. "I'm glad." He nodded to the cabin. "What can I do?"

"Know how to caulk?" Mitch asked, coming up behind him.

"A bear shit in the woods?"

Mitch and Casey laughed. "Go help Zach. He's like a wounded lion today; maybe he'll be nice to you."

"Why's he upset?"

Megan joined them. She looked fresh and young in a camp T-shirt and jeans. "Leave my favorite brother-in-law alone." She slapped her husband on the fanny. "He's still reeling from Casey's close call."

"Yes, ma'am."

Warmed—and truthfully jealous—of the couple's closeness, Ian nodded to Zach. "I'll go over." He started away when Casey called out, "Ian?"

He glanced over his shoulder. "Yeah?"

"Thanks."

Smiling, he continued on his way. When he reached Zach, the man was concentrating so hard he didn't look up. "Zach?"

"I said to leave me the fuck alone. I got a right to be grumpy."

Ian laughed and Zach whirled on him.

"I guess you do."

Zach scrubbed a hand over his face. "Sorry. I thought you were Mitch."

Fatigue lined Malvaso's handsome features. He was clearly a man who hadn't slept well.

"You okay?"

"Hell, no." He stared over Ian's head. "I'm having trouble dealing with what almost happened to her."

Ian remembered that Zach had been in the trauma survivor's group Noah had taken him to and that he'd attended while he was in Hidden Cove last summer. "Ah." He shook his head. "Symptoms come back?"

Zach's head whipped to Ian. Awareness dawned in his eyes. "Yeah. Full-fledged. I puked this morning when I spilled coffee on the burner."

Ian knew smells triggered a physical response in trauma survivors. "Loud noises like the crashing at the towers do it for me."

"Yeah?"

"You still in the group?"

"Not lately." Zach ran a hand through his black hair. "Maybe

I'll go back, though." He studied Ian. "You gone to any since you left here?"

"Nah."

"You doing better?"

"In some ways."

Zach was distracted by a laugh. Ian tracked his gaze and saw Casey holding Jenn and Grady's baby. The kid had his fists tangled in her thick black hair.

"I don't know what I'd do if—" He broke off then focused on Ian. "You saved her life, Woodward."

Ian said, "I just helped give you the tools to do it."

Shaking his head, Zach said, "Same thing in my book." He swallowed hard. "Thanks, man. You saved my life, too." Then, embarrassed by emotional display—typical of smoke eaters— Zach nodded to the cabin. "Wanna help?"

Ian looked at the building then scanned the whole camp. He said, "Yeah, I wanna help."

LATER THAT NIGHT, Ian sat once again before his closet. So many emotions swirled inside him—satisfaction for how the lesson had gone yesterday at the fire academy, surprise at Mitch's public praise on television, pure pleasure at the Malvaso family's reaction to him today at the camp. Reaching out, he slipped a hanger off the bar; from it, he removed the white shirt.

It felt different tonight than it had yesterday morning.

Slowly, he stripped off his blue shirt. He stuck his arms in the white one, then buttoned up the front. It took him a minute, but finally he wheeled to the mirror.

And for the first time in over three years, Ian saw a firefighter looking back at him.

EIGHT

RICK FELT LIKE he'd gone a couple of rounds with a fleeing suspect. Every single muscle in his body ached, and his eyes were gritty as he drove downtown. He'd left Lisel's condo this morning when all seemed well after three nights of surveillance, gone home, and caught a few hours of sleep. Not enough. He'd showered, but it didn't help. He hadn't done all-night stakeouts since he was in his twenties, and he couldn't quite grasp the routine. If he needed to do it again, he'd have to hire some help.

Especially since he had to go do his time in the school today. With the kids. With little Lolita.

Shit. He still couldn't believe he'd kissed her Friday night. He struggled not to think about how she'd kissed him back—actually she'd taken the fucking thing to a whole new level. He did *not* want that on his mind. Nor the bombshell her friend had dropped—that Faith was engaged to another man. Wonder if *he* knew who was masquerading inside that innocent facade.

After Nancy's announcement, Rick had stalked away before Faith could say what she'd opened her pretty little mouth to tell him. Then he'd managed to avoid her when he picked up Pilar on Saturday and Sunday afternoons.

Pilar, who, in just two days, was flourishing like a hothouse flower, finally given the environment she needed, she deserved, in the household of the good reverend and his wife. His sister seemed happy, relaxed, and . . . at home. Rick would put up with the torture of the damned, if he had to, so she could have that.

And it *was* torture . . .

Mrs. Pollyanna. "Stay and have supper with your sister, Rick."

Her father. "Care to attend services, tomorrow, Rick? I'm told I don't put too many people to sleep."

Oh, yeah, sure, that's all he needed. Lightning would probably strike the steeple if he dared to walk into a church.

And then Faith's room, which Pilar had naively thought he'd love to see . . . a white islet canopy bed, freakin' pink carpet . . . and pictures of her at all ages. Even some with the fiancé—who was as young and fresh-faced as she was.

Rick was even more on edge when he reached A Time to Grow. He parked next to her little purple Saturn and headed inside. He noticed a car across the street with someone inside, and wondered briefly who it was. Dismissing the thought, he climbed the steps. There was only one thing that could make him feel worse today, and it was going to happen right now.

I promise, I'll work with the kids next week.

When he reached the classroom, he found them all seated in a circle on the floor. Pollyanna was in the midst of them, quietly strumming a guitar and talking with the kids. She glanced at the clock and frowned. "Well, let's get started. Looks like . . ."

"He's here," Jamal said enthusiastically. "Mr. Ru . . . ru . . ." How do you say it again, Miz McPherson?"

"Mr. Ruscio." She glanced up at Rick and smiled sweetly. "Hi, Mr. Ruscio. Welcome."

Her manners called forth his own. He'd seen it with criminals, too. If you spoke quietly, formally to them, they often mirrored your tone. "Sorry I'm late. It was . . . work."

"No harm done. Join us?"

He trudged to the circle. Jamal immediately scooted aside. "Sit here, Mr. Ruscio."

Rick dropped down onto the carpeted floor. He tried sitting with his legs stretched out, but that made him look like Gulliver among the little people. He tried crossing his legs, but that was nearly impossible. Finally he hiked up his knees, spread them some, and draped his hands in between.

Faith hid a grin at his attempt to get comfortable. "We won't be on the floor too long. Just to sing the song and brainstorm." She scanned the class. "All right, who wants to tell Mr. Ruscio where this song comes from and how we use it?"

Matt raised his hand. "It's from *The Sound of Music*. That's a movie."

Faith nodded to a little girl. "Molly, tell him about the song."

"The little kids sthing it when they're sthcared. It makes 'em feel better."

Faith asked, "And what do we do?"

Jamal answered. "Every Monday, we sing it and draw our favorite things."

Faith smiled again and started to play the guitar. Pilar loved *The Sound of Music*, but Rick hated it. Along with shows like *The Brady Bunch*. Real life wasn't like this. Should we be teaching our kids that it was?

But it was hard to be grumpy in a room full of five-year-olds all singing the wrong words, off key and giggling. Faith laughed right along with them, though, and kept strumming the guitar, repeating chords and helping them with the words. She played well and sang like an angel. As good as Julie Andrews. Shit, she probably sang in the church choir. With her fiancé.

When the song ended, she faced Rick. "Now we divide up into small groups and draw our favorite things." She addressed the kids. We'll sit at tables today, so Mr. Ruscio will be more comfortable." With an arch of her brow, she added, "You have to draw something, too, Mr. Ruscio."

"Now there's a surprise." He joked, but inside he was churning. What would he draw? What was his favorite thing?

His badge.

A badge that had been stripped from him. A badge, and what it represented, which he loved more than anything except Pilar.

Damn it, could this get any worse?

AS FAITH DREW her favorite thing this week, she cast surreptitious glances at Rick. His hair was damp and slicked back off his face. Today that face was drawn and tired. She knew from Pilar that he'd been on surveillance for three nights. He was probably exhausted. Dressed in khaki cargo pants and a black shirt rolled up at the sleeves, he looked dark and dangerous.

He was. The kiss they'd shared beneath the trees Friday night was anything but safe. It made Faith think that her heart, perhaps even her life, was in jeopardy. She knew that intellectually, but emotionally she couldn't forget how it felt to be in his arms, to have that mouth take hers with a passion and possession she'd never known in her life. One simple kiss . . . that was anything but simple.

"What are you drawing, Miss McPherson?" one of the kids asked.

She looked down. Lips. His. Damn. "Oh, I'm just doodling—remember that's how we can find an idea. Sometimes, it takes a while to discover what you like and don't like." She glanced at Rick. *And sometimes it doesn't.*

As she went back to her drawing, she continued to steal quick looks at him. His knees were wedged under the table, and he was concentrating on his drawing as if he were reading ancient scripture. The kids kept trying to talk to him.

"Whatcha drawin', mister?"

"What do you like to do?"

"See my folder. It's already got things in it. By the end of the year, Miss McPherson says we'll have them full of our favorite things."

Faith had to give Rick credit. He was trying. He studied Jamal's folder, made a comment, then went back to his work.

After the allotted time, Faith called for everybody's attention. "All right, we're going to share now. Because Mr. Ruscio has trouble sitting in our circle on the floor—"

"He's as big as Hulk Hogan . . ." Matt said.

Everybody laughed but Rick.

"We'll share from our tables. Who would like to go first?"

Jamal raised his hand. "This is my doggy. My mom got him for me last night."

Smiling, Faith said, "I didn't know you were getting a dog."

The boy beamed as he talked about Spot.

Several kids contributed, then Faith showed her drawing. "This is my bed. It's one of my favorite things, because my grandpa made it for me." It was crafted with a beautiful mission-style headboard and footboard made of warm oak. "I feel safe here."

She saw Rick's eyes narrow. And was dying to know what he was thinking. For a brief minute, the image of him and her bed merged. She shivered. "Mr. Ruscio, your turn."

His face paled, and his expression was fierce. But he held up his drawing.

"It's a horn," one of the kids said.

"What kind?" Faith asked.

"It's . . ." he cleared his throat. "It's a saxophone."

"You play it, mister?"

"Ah, yeah. When I have time." He looked so uncomfortable, Faith started to intervene.

"Will you bring it here and play for usth?" Molly asked shyly.

His look said, *Not on your life.* His answer was, "Maybe." He glanced at the clock.

Faith did, too. "Well, will you look at that, it's already time to go."

The end-of-the-day flurry took place. She was following the kids out the door, but turned back to Rick, who looked ready to bolt. "You have another half hour," she said nodding to the tables. "I was hoping you could help me move some things."

He watched her like a cornered suspect. "Not today."

"Yes, today. I'm afraid I'm going to have to insist."

"Fine."

"I'll be right back." She got the kids on their way and when she returned, she found him leafing through the folders of the kids' favorite things. "It's a good exercise," she said, closing the door to her room.

He glanced up. "Whatever. What do you want moved?"

"I lied. I don't want anything moved."

"Your daddy wouldn't like you to lie."

Ignoring the comment, she focused her gaze on him. "I'm not engaged."

"Look, lady, makes no difference to me if you're married with three kids."

That stung. Not that she really believed it. She crossed her arms over her chest. "Your actions Friday night say otherwise."

"Forget about that."

"I can't."

"You better."

She came in closer. This near to him, she could see the red rimming his midnight eyes. His mouth was bracketed with lines of fatigue. "You were trying to scare me off by kissing me."

"Obviously *that* didn't work."

"Because it backfired."

He stepped to the side and tried circling around her. She blocked his way. "I don't know what you mean," he hedged.

"Like hell."

"Hey, no swearing in the classroom."

"You meant to scare me off, but you got involved in the kiss."

"You're wrong. I'm not into little girls."

Holding her ground, she stared hard at him. "You're really afraid, aren't you?"

"Of what?"

"Of me, of what that kiss meant."

"It meant nothing."

"Have dinner with me tonight, Rick. At my place. I want to get to know you better. I'll cook for you."

His eyes blazed. She recognized anger there. But it was mixed with other powerful emotions. "The guy on the phone the other night won't like that."

"He's not my fiancé. It's complicated what he is. I'll explain it at dinner."

"No."

"Please."

He drew in a breath and threw his shoulders back. He grasped her arms, but not roughly. She stared at the little knick under his chin he must have gotten from shaving. She wanted to kiss it. Make it better. Make him better.

"Look, lady, nothing's going on between us. What happened Friday night was a mistake. Any . . . *any* thoughts you're having along those lines are detrimental to your health and welfare."

"I'll take my chances."

"Over my dead body." Reaching down to her desk, he picked up her drawing. "See this? This safe bed you love so much? It wouldn't be so safe with me in your house."

With that, he stalked off.

* * *

AT SEVEN THAT night, Rick pulled up to the parsonage to visit his sister. He stared hard at the white rambling house and wondered how the hell he'd managed to get tangled up with a minister and his family.

Swearing with intentional crudeness, he exited the car and covered the brick path to the front door in big strides. No answer when he rang the bell. Pilar had known he was coming. He rang again, then was attacked—by a huge dog. The mutt had scurried around the side of the house, and jumped on Rick. It was a beautiful Irish setter. In spite of his determination not to get sucked in by this family—Jesus, they were all treating him like the prodigal son—he bent down. "Hi, girl. You're a beauty."

"Yes, she is."

He looked up. "Hello, Mrs. McPherson."

Faith's mother smiled warmly. "Rick. I told you to call me Pearl. We've been waiting for you." She motioned to the back of the house. "Decided to get yard work done tonight. Sorry you missed dinner."

"Uh, yeah, me, too." He wasn't. The last thing he'd wanted was to sit across from this woman's daughter for another meal. All this family shit had to stop, now. "How's Pilar?" he asked as they rounded the path, passing bright yellow mums planted randomly along the walk. Oak and maple trees scattered their leaves on the sloping grounds. It was the kind of setting he'd once dreamed of growing up in.

Pearl was as small as her daughter and had to look up at him to answer. "I think she misses your mother and sister. Have you seen them?"

"I called several times to talk to Anita about that jerk who did all this. But nobody was home, and she won't return my calls." He ran a hand through his hair. "It makes me crazy that I can't get through to her on this."

"We called. Left a message with Anita about Pilar's whereabouts."

"How'd they take that?"

"Well, David used his best minister persona, and it's hard to get around him."

Yeah, Rick knew that. He only hoped he himself would be spared any more of Reverend McPherson's persuasion.

He stopped halfway to the back and pulled out his wallet. "I've got some money for Pilar's room and board, here." He held out a check.

Faith's mother looked at it, then at him, with sympathy. Though she was slight, he felt a little like Goliath facing David. "We won't take your money, Rick. Pilar's staying in a vacant room, and she doesn't eat much. Even if we were spending money on her, I wouldn't take yours."

"I *want* you to take it."

"Of course you do. Then you won't feel indebted." They began to walk again and reached the back of the house. The dog ran ahead. Rick watched as she raced over to Faith, who was raking leaves like the rest of them into a huge pile. Tonight Faith wore skin-tight jeans—thanks, God, for that particular punishment—and a sweatshirt. Pearl, David, and his own sister were dressed similarly. The dog bypassed Faith and jumped right into the leaves in front of her.

She dropped her rake. "Geez, I just . . ." Then she was tackled from behind. By her father. She fell into the pile and came up sputtering. Rick caught a glimpse of his sister, who watched the interchange with such yearning on her face, it hurt to look at her. He was about to go to her when he saw Faith say something to her dad, and then they both stalked toward Pilar, who laughed aloud and started to back away. Too late. They caught her; David took her shoulders, Faith took her feet, and they picked her up bodily. They crossed to the leaves and began to swing her back and forth. "One . . ." Swing, swing. "Two . . ." Swing, swing . . . "Three . . ." Unceremoniously, they tossed her into the pile. Girlish giggles—one of the best sounds Rick had ever heard—echoed through the maple trees and sprawling lawns.

Pearl called out, "David, don't hurt your back."

They turned toward Pearl and him.

"Rick!!" Pilar yelled, climbing out of the leaves and jogging toward him. As if he'd been away at war, she threw herself into his arms and held on tight. She smelled like the outdoors. He soothed her hair, which he found full of leaves. *"Niña."*

David and Faith joined them. The minister held out his hand to shake. "Rick, good to see you."

"Hello, Rick." This from Faith. Her hair was a mess, strewn with dried leaves. Her eyes sparkled with mirth, and her cheeks were rosy. It was nippy out, though he guessed her color was due to exertion, not the cold. He wondered if her light complexion reddened during sex.

"Hi, all." He turned to his sister. "You doing okay?"

"Yeah, of course. Want to help finish the leaves with us?"

No. "Sure, if that's what you want."

"We're having pie à la mode afterwards," she said, grinning.

"Oh, well, I can't stay for that."

Her face fell. "You have to, Ricardo. I made it." She smiled at Faith's mother. "Well, Pearl and I did."

Sucked in, he thought as he looked at the perfect family. He was getting sucked in big-time.

Before he could answer, someone from behind said, "Yo . . . I'm lookin' for the McPhersons."

Everyone turned toward the voice. David stepped in front of his family, and Rick automatically went to his side. David said, "I'm Reverend McPherson."

The guy was thin and sleazy-looking, with watery brown eyes; he wore a wrinkled suit and what passed for a tie. He held out a paper. "This here's for you." He glanced behind David. "You Pilar Ruscio?"

Rick stiffened and saw Faith move in close to Pilar. "Yes," his sister said.

"This one's for you."

Rick intercepted the envelope.

"What are they?" Pilar asked.

"Ah, notice that legal action's gonna be taken. Read 'em and weep." Rick was reminded of one of those poor imitations of a private investigator on TV.

He crossed to Pilar and gave her the envelope. David opened his as she did hers. Rick read over her shoulder, "Notice . . . return to legal dwelling . . . minor . . . runaway . . ."

He caught the drift.

Pilar frowned deeply. "Ma took legal action?"

Rick doubted that. The man who delivered these didn't look like anybody a court would send out; besides, he seemed familiar. And the wording of the document suggested it didn't come from the courts.

David shook his head. "It looks like they're just warning us to send you back."

Pilar gripped Faith's hand. "Can they make me go back, Ricardo?"

"In some cases."

"Not this one," David said. "Not if we contend you aren't safe there."

"Are you sure?" Pilar asked.

"No. Which is why I'll call Jackson Graves right now."

Rick stepped forward. "Who?"

"A member of our congregation. He's a judge."

"Can you call him now?" Pilar's eyes were bright. "It's late."

David smiled. "Of course."

Rick shook his head and started to dig into his pocket for his keys. "I'm going over to the house."

David grabbed his arm. "I'd rather you waited until I talked to Jack."

"She just wants money. I'll give it to her, then she'll leave us alone." He ran a hand through his hair, guilt smothering him. "I should have gone over there before. I was just so mad . . ."

Pilar began to cry.

He turned and drew her close. "Aw, *bebé.*"

Pearl put a hand on Rick's arm. "I wish you'd wait, Rick. Come inside with us. We'll call the judge and make decisions from there. Rash actions aren't going to help your sister."

His heart was catapulting in his chest. The need to protect and defend coursed through him. It was one of the things that made losing his star so hard.

David said, "It's for the best, son."

Son. Rick couldn't swallow.

Finally, he managed to say, "All right, I'll come inside."

A simple statement, but one Rick suspected was going to wreak havoc in his life.

STEAM CURLED OUT of the top of the apple pie, like smoke escaping a chimney. Pilar smiled as she sliced through her masterpiece.

"Smells great, honey," Faith said, like a big sister. Though if that were true, her feelings for the grim man sitting at the table next to Pilar would be totally sinful.

"Yeah, I'm hungry again." She looked to Faith's father like he'd just walked on water. "Thanks so much, David."

"I told you Jack would know what they can and can't do."

Rick shifted in his chair. "I still think I should hire my own lawyer to take care of all this."

"Why? Martin Bell's one of the top guys in Hidden Cove."

"Then I should pay him."

Pearl and David exchanged an indulgent look. "He's doing it pro bono," David said. "It's all arranged."

By Judge Graves, who Faith knew had had big-time problems with his youngest son, and David had worked miracles with the kid.

Pilar frowned. "Ricardo, please . . ."

Rick settled back into the chair like a chastised child. He shook his head; Faith guessed he was shaking off the mood. "All right, for now, I'll leave it." He eyed the slice of pie, and Faith's heart warmed at his obvious attempt at pleasing his sister. "I'll have a bigger piece than that one, kiddo."

They all ate with relish. Faith helped keep things light, making jokes, talking about school and the kids with Rick.

"I didn't know you played the sax," she said around the taste of tart apples and cinnamon.

He stilled.

"He's super," Pilar told them. "He used to play at Jazzie's downtown."

"Jazzie's is a great place." This from Pearl. "When you play again, we'll all come hear you."

"I don't play there anymore."

Pilar said, "Not since . . ."

Rick said something to her in Spanish. Faith suspected it was spontaneous use of their language as opposed to keeping the rest of them out of the communication.

In hopes of easing the tension, Faith guessed, Pearl changed the subject. "Did you talk to Sam, dear, about the fair?"

Uh-oh. Not exactly soothing content. "Yes. He isn't sure he can make it home. He has an exam the next day."

"Sam is Faith's boyfriend," Pilar told Rick.

"Is he?" Rick eyed Faith, something unpleasant sparking in his gaze.

"He's been her best friend since they were little. Both of them were born and raised in this church." David smiled benignly. "He's in Divinity School, with my son, Peter."

"All in the family," Rick mumbled around his coffee cup.

"I think it's romantic." Pilar's expression was dreamy.

"What fair?" Rick asked.

"The church's annual Fall Festival. It's in a couple of weeks. It's a fund-raiser. This year the money's going to Hale's Haven." David winked at his wife. "We asked Pilar to be in the kissing booth."

Rick spit his coffee all over the table. The McPhersons laughed, and Faith handed him a napkin.

With pretended innocence, Pearl shot a quick glance at Rick and then addressed her husband. "Well, if Sam doesn't make it, we need to get somebody to man the basketball throw."

"I think it'd be wise to replace him." This from David.

Rick stood, like a man avoiding capture. "I gotta go. I've got some surveillance things to check out at nine."

Faith glanced at the clock. "I should leave, too. Would you mind walking me back to the carriage house? I wanted to ask you something about school."

He looked like he was about to object. Pearl said, "Go ahead, dear. We'll clean up here."

"Come with us and say goodnight, *niña*," Rick said to Pilar.

Instead, bless her heart, the girl rounded the table and hugged her brother. "I can't. I told Marcy I'd call her at eight-thirty." She held on to Rick's arm. Faith saw him smooth her hair down again, the gesture tender and brotherly.

It zinged its way right to her toes.

Outside, the air was cooler. Once again Rick whipped off his nylon jacket and placed it around Faith's shoulders. "Don't you ever wear a jacket?"

Like the last time, she wrapped herself up in his coat. His scent encompassed her, and she breathed it in, closed her eyes to savor the experience.

His hands fisted at his sides. "Don't do that!"

"Why are you so cross tonight?"

He sighed. "I'm being a jerk, I know it."

She touched his arm. "Because of the legal thing with Pilar? You're entitled to be worried."

"All they want is money, Faith. I'm going to just give it to them, and they'll leave us alone."

"Do your really think that's the best way to handle this? They're blackmailing you, Rick. With Pilar's situation."

"They've been blackmailing me for years."

"How?"

"Emotionally." He ran a hand through his hair. "They can't take care of themselves. I can't let them suffer."

"Pilar told us Anita works."

"Yeah, and spends most of her money on clothes."

"She'd spend it on rent, if she had to."

He stopped. "Wouldn't you help Peter or your mother, if your dad wasn't around to do it?"

"Yes, but . . ."

"I can't let them want for stuff."

"Pilar says your mother drinks."

"My *pequeña hermanita* needs to stop talking out of school."

"I'm sorry, we don't mean to invade your privacy."

He sighed as they reached her porch. "No, I'm sorry. You're helping Pilar in ways I can't. She was on cloud nine about a little apple pie."

Faith grinned. "It *was* heaven."

Rick smiled. She reached up and touched his lips. "That's nice to see."

He grasped her hand and pulled it away. "Faith, don't do this." His tone was gentler than the last time. "I'm bad news, but even if I wasn't, your life is all set. And it's so different from mine. You got everything you could ever want. Don't jeopardize it by flirting with danger, by walking on the wild side. When it's over, you'll go back to your real life, anyway."

Temper sparked inside her. "Is that what you think I'm doing, dallying with you to get some kicks?"

"Forbidden fruit, so to speak."

Without thinking about it, she grabbed his arm. "I can't remember when I've been more insulted."

His look was startled. "Insulted?"

"Yes, that I'd play with you just to get my rocks off."

"Watch your language."

"I'm not your sister, Rick. Don't treat me like a child. I'm a grown woman who hasn't, as far as I know, ever toyed with a man in her life."

He didn't say anything.

"I resent your accusation that I'm doing it with you."

"You don't know what the hell you're doing with me."

Well that was true. "Look, maybe that's true, partly. All I know is that I'm attracted to you, a lot. That you make me feel things that nobody ever has."

"Not even Sam?"

She sighed and sat down on the steps. "Sit, please, just for a minute."

She could tell he didn't want to. But eventually he dropped down. "My relationship with Sam is complicated. Everybody expects us to get married. We've dated, though not exclusively, for years. It's just that he doesn't—"

"Faith, I shouldn't be hearing this."

"I don't think we feel what we should for each other, physically." She hesitated and decided to go for broke. "Not what you made me feel from the first day I saw you . . ."

"Faith . . ."

"And especially when you kissed me." Reaching over she took his hand and was surprised he didn't shake her off. "I've dreamed about you every night, Rick, since then."

"Aw, geez, don't tell me that."

"It's true. I'd like to date you, to get to know you, to see if this is real."

"Oh, it's real. It's real sex, and it's dangerous. You're being tempted to the dark side."

That hurt her heart. "You're not the dark side, Rick."

"Yeah, honey, I am." He raised her hand to his mouth and kissed it. "And I'm flattered, really I am, but this is *so* not going to happen." He stood and looked down at her. "Let's just leave it at this. Civilly."

"What if I refuse?"

"Then I won't play nice, Faith. I mean it."

She just watched him, falling a little bit more for him as each side of him was revealed. He had real integrity; he was trying to protect her.

When she said no more, he stood. "Did you really want to ask me something about school?"

Peering up at him, she shook her head.

"I didn't think so." He watched her, then leaned over and kissed her nose. "Goodnight, little girl. Don't forget this conversation." With that he turned and strode into the night.

He was out of sight before she realized she still wore his jacket. She opened her mouth to call him back, but stopped herself. Instead, she burrowed into it and thought about the man who'd just left her.

And into the night, she whispered, "You're wrong about a lot of things, Rick Ruscio." She smiled as a thought struck her. "Especially Aesop. Slow and steady does, really, win the race."

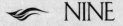 NINE

IAN LOOKED OUT at the battalion chiefs, deputy chiefs, and the top guys, four fire chiefs, from surrounding areas whose attention he'd kept for a full three hours with his lesson on Domestic Preparedness and the role of those in charge. "Let's end this session with a review of what we've covered. I'll take volunteers."

Used to being in control, several chiefs raised their hands.

He called on one from a small department south of Hidden Cove. "We read the Open Letter to Tom Ridge, which was published in *Firehouse* in April 2002, asking for help in certain areas."

Ian had begun with that missive because it was so good and because, in the intervening years, some of the fire service's needs had been met, some had not: It dealt with radio use in high-rises, turnout gear that is more suited for terrorist attacks, better PASS systems, and tracking devices and several things for the FDNY because of high-rises.

"Let's go to the four areas we covered that you as incident commanders need to do. These also have to be taught to your officers."

Noah tackled this one. "Recognize and identify that we have

an incident." This was not always immediately obvious, Ian had told them, citing both the first and second WTC attacks where it was suggested in the initial few minutes that these were freak accidents.

"Incident stabilization," someone else called out.

"Which includes?" Ian asked.

Jeb Caruso read from his notes. "Actions that will preserve and protect lives, reduce casualties, limit expansion, and maintain order."

"No cheating, Caruso. Can't you remember anything?"

"Nah, he's too tired," a battalion chief joked.

Someone else teased, "That'll teach you to have a baby after forty."

"Decon," someone suggested for the third point. "First-arriving companies need to recognize a problem exists and take the appropriate actions to ensure their safety and the safety of the victims." This meant, Ian reiterated, immediately initiating activities like rapid application of water via hand lines by firefighters.

They finished up with the PPE, personal protective equipment, which caused a heated, twenty-minute debate of the pros and cons of what the department had now and how long guys should stay in a hot zone—the contaminated area—in their goods.

When Ian ended the session, the chiefs clapped.

Damn good for his ego!

Noah approached him as the others filed out. "Great job," he said about the lesson.

"Thanks."

"And that's good to see."

Ian hadn't had a chance to talk to his brother-in-law beforehand, so Noah hadn't said anything about the fact that Ian had worn his uniform. It felt strange, but good.

To downplay the event, Ian shrugged. "Yeah, well, don't make a fuss."

Noah stopped at the front of the room and glanced out over the retreating brass. "You did a good job today." The chief's eyes narrowed on the empty classroom seats. "Sometimes, it's hard to believe we're doing this. Like, where will it all end? I think about my daughter Becca's unborn baby, mine and Eve's, and Abby. What kind of world are we leaving them?"

Ian shook his head in silent commiseration. "Speaking of which . . ."

"Papa!" The childish screech came from the door. In the archway were Eve and Noah's granddaughter, Abby. Whose eyes widened when she got a glimpse of Ian. "Ian!" The screech got louder. The child broke away from Eve, raced down the side of the room, and threw herself into his lap. If he hadn't had the brake on his wheels, the chair would be halfway across the room.

"Hey, sweetheart." He kissed Abby's hair. He had a special bond with this little girl since rescuing her last summer from a fall. Abby burrowed into his shirt.

He mumbled something to her, but looked up when he heard Noah say, "Evie, love, oh my God, what is it?" Noah strode to the back of the room.

Where Evie was leaning against the doorway, tears coursing down her cheeks. Her emotions had been close to the surface since she'd gotten pregnant, but oh, dear Lord, please don't let anything be wrong.

Ian held his breath as Noah placed his hand on her stomach. "Is it something with the baby?"

She continued to stare at Ian. "Huh?"

Noah's voice rose a notch. "Eve. Why are you crying? Is it the baby?"

Coming out of the trance, she looked up at her husband. "Oh, no, I'm sorry. Honey, no." She hugged Noah. "The baby's fine." She nodded to her brother. "I never thought I'd see you in that shirt again."

Holding Abby close, Ian smiled. "It's time, don't you think, sis?"

Her grin was watery. "Past time."

Noah had wilted against the doorjamb. For a brief minute, Ian wondered what he'd feel like if a woman was pregnant with his child. Would he worry about every little nuance? He pictured sparkling blue eyes and long black hair and considered what a little girl of his and Lisel's would look like.

He caught himself. It didn't matter. That particular scenario would never be.

Abby was talking to him. ". . . my birthday party."

"Of course I plan to be there."

Eve came farther into the room. More composed, she perched on the edge of a desk and gestured to his shirt. "So what brought this on?"

"Long story."

She gave him a knowing-twin look. "You like teaching, don't you?"

"I did some good here, I think. I wasn't sure I still could." He kissed Abby's blond head. "I thought maybe saving this munchkin last summer was a fluke."

"It wasn't."

"Guess not." He scanned the room. "I like being at the academy."

Noah joined his wife. "I hope you feel the same next month. We got the hardcore smoke eaters coming for training on the new sensor machines we got with a HazMat grant." Ian knew the fire department had been writing grants to get the technology that would help them cope with a WMD attack. "Especially Ed Snyder."

Ian smiled. "Always did like a challenge."

"Want to come to dinner with us?" Eve asked.

"No, Joe's coming over at five for a PT session. I gotta get home." He grinned. "You look great, kiddo." He winked at Noah. "Even if you are getting fat."

"I think she's beautiful."

"You would. You've turned into a lovesick sap."

Abby jumped off his lap. "Hungry," she said and launched herself at her grandfather.

Ian bade good-bye to his family and wheeled down the corridor to the Training Office. He stopped outside of it when he heard, "Jesus Christ, Gerhard, do you *try* to be a prick or does it just come naturally?" It was Olive Hennessy's voice. He'd spent some time with the female captain writing curriculum and eaten lunch with her a few times. He liked her. And he picked up real soon that *nobody* liked Gerhard.

"What? I just said if I was a gimp, they'd listen to me, too. I know what those guys did, but I'm sick of all this hero worship shit after 9/11."

Somebody else jumped in. "I can't believe you. He's a great teacher. Why you got a burr up your ass about it?"

"The line guys love Woodward and hate Gerhard." Olive again. "Simple as that."

"I don't need no shit from you." Ian heard a drawer slam. Before he could roll away, Gerhard reached the exit to the office. And stopped cold. "Fucking son of a bitch," he growled and stalked past Ian down the hall.

Olive and Frazier came to the door. "Oh, no," Olive said.

"It's all right. I met guys like him before." Ian shook his head and rubbed the bars of his chair. If they only knew the cost of that hero worship.

Frazier's expression was sincere. "Sorry, Woodward. We value what you can do here. Gerhard's got a chip on his shoulder the size of Mount Rushmore."

"Forget it."

Frazier left, but Olive stayed behind. "You really wanna forget it?"

He wheeled inside and over to his desk. "Yep."

"Suit yourself."

He grinned up at her. "You're okay, Hennessy. No shit, no games. I like that in a woman."

"Yeah?" She'd gone to her own desk and looked at him over glasses slung low on her nose. "You got one in your life, Woodward?"

"What?"

"A woman."

He thought of Lisel. He'd had to use every ounce of his willpower to keep memories of her at bay. "No. I . . ." He glanced down at his legs. "I'm not into relationships right now."

"Yeah, me either. My ex did a number on me." She ran a hand through her short hair. It was a pretty shade of blond. "I miss doing stuff, though. With men."

He smiled, remembering how the texture and scent of a woman was one of the finest pleasures in life. "Me, too. With women."

She cocked her head. "You wanna get something to eat with me? Said ex is with my kid tonight."

Though the idea was appealing, he hedged. "I got a physical therapy session at five."

"We could meet after." Her face lit up, her brown eyes

warming. "Or I could cook for you at my house." Her smile died. "Damn, it's not wheelchair accessible."

He rubbed the scar on his cheek. "It's okay. Maybe this isn't such a good idea, anyway." He started to wheel to the exit.

She stepped in front of his chair, successfully halting his escape. "I could cook at your place." She shrugged. "I'm not asking for a commitment here, Woodward. Not even any funny stuff . . ." Her face reddened. "Hell, I don't even know if you can . . ." She let out a heavy breath. "Man, am I blowing this, or what?"

Her honesty made him chuckle. "I *can,* Olive. But I'm not looking for any funny stuff, either."

He watched her blush, and felt almost as good as when he put on his captain's shirt today. Actually he felt pretty good all around. It made him say, "And you know what? A home-cooked meal would be great." Pivoting the chair, he wheeled over to her desk and scribbled his address on a notepad. "Here." He handed it to her and winked. Geez, he was flirting. "See you about seven, Captain?"

"Yes, sir, Captain. I'll bring the food."

"You're on."

He was whistling on the way home, when he was hit with a blast of sanity. He had a date! Guilt crept inside him like insidious smoke. What was he doing? How could he do this to Lisel? But, hell, he wasn't doing anything to her. She should be dating somebody else, too. Besides, she was away with Mona at the Catskills till the weekend, so she wouldn't even know about him and Olive. Maybe this was just what was needed all around.

"I'M SORRY. I didn't mean to spoil our getaway."

"You didn't spoil it, Mona. We had a perfectly good trip." And just what Lisel had needed. She'd wanted some distance from Ian after what happened last Friday, and she and Mona had spent a lovely three days in the mountains.

"Are you sure you'll be all right?" Mona's motherly concern warmed Lisel. "I'm worried about Jenny, or I wouldn't even consider leaving."

They walked out the front door to Lisel's rented van. A light breeze picked up the strands of her hair and played with them. "Mona, I'm a grown woman. I can stay here by myself."

"Maybe we should call Mr. Ruscio."

"No. You go ahead and get started. Rochester's several hours from here. I'm glad you're taking the van."

"Thank you so much, dear." Mona opened the back door and tossed in her bag. "She probably just went away with a new boyfriend or something."

How much to say? "It's not like her to miss work, though, without calling. It's right for you to drive up."

"I know."

"Are you sure you don't want me to come with you?"

"No, dear. It wouldn't be good for your health."

She gave Mona a hug. "Good luck. And call me on my cell when you get there."

"Yes, I will. Good-bye, Lisel."

Lisel stood on the sidewalk watching Mona drive away. Tugging her sweater closer to her chest against the October wind, she shook her head. Jenny Mincheon was not a good daughter. Lisel had spent time with the twenty-two-year-old on several occasions and had often wished for a sister like her. But the girl wasn't attentive enough to Mona. If the older woman were Lisel's mother, she'd take much better care of her. If, if, if . . . If Mona were her mother, if Ian loved her . . . if Lisel herself was stronger and could work instead of sitting idly around, wondering about Ian . . .

She tried to block what it had felt like to sleep in Ian's arms last week. The way he held her all night . . . what it could have been. The memory haunted her like the lines of a script that kept echoing through her mind.

A snazzy, copper-colored sedan pulled into the parking space Mona had vacated. Lisel had never seen the vehicle before. Nor the woman who climbed out. Tall, willowy blond. Muscular, but feminine. Dressed in a pretty skirt with a ruffle on the bottom. Realizing she was staring, Lisel smiled at the woman, said an innocuous hello, and turned to go back into her house.

She heard behind her, "Oh, damn."

Lisel pivoted around. A bag the woman had taken out of the

trunk had broken, sending the contents onto the pavement. Hell, maybe this was a new neighbor who could use a friend as much as Lisel. She scooted back down to the sidewalk. "Let me help." Bending over, she gathered a can of tomatoes, fresh green peppers, and a box of rice. The woman picked up a bag of frozen shrimp and some spices. They stood. "Hi, I'm Lisel Loring."

"Oh, hi. Yeah, I recognize you now."

"I, um, I'm spending some time at the lake."

"Oh." She smiled. "I'm Olive Hennessy."

"Do you live out here in the condos? I don't think I've seen you before."

"No, I'm cooking dinner for a friend." She shrugged at the bags. "I hope he likes shrimp cheese."

Lisel smiled a little wistfully. She wished she had plans tonight. She wished she could cook for Ian. "Want some help getting these things inside?"

"No thanks, I'm going right there."

Lisel's gaze tracked hers. To number 444. Just as the door opened and Ian wheeled out. She noticed three things about him as he came toward them. His face was purposefully blank. She'd seen him effect the look enough to know it was hiding intense emotion. He'd obviously just showered—his hair was damp, he'd shaved, and his skin glowed. Finally, he was dressed in beautiful light wool navy pants and a sexy-as-hell shirt—that she'd bought him.

Lisel's heart clutched at the implication of what she was seeing.

"Hi, Ian." Olive rolled her eyes. "I'm a klutz. I dropped this stuff and your neighbor helped pick it up."

"Hi, Olive." Ian cleared his throat. "Hello, Lisel."

"Ian."

He reached out to the bag she held. "Here, I'll take that."

Numb, her mind whirling, Lisel just stared at him. "Oh, sure." Dumping the bag on his lap, she glanced from him to the pretty woman. Who shifted uncomfortably.

Well, Lisel wasn't an actress for nothing. And she had *some* pride. Assuming her best stage presence, she tossed her head back regally. "I won't keep you. Enjoy your evening."

Ian halted her getaway with a comment. "I thought you were staying in the Catskills till the weekend."

Ah, so that was it. He thought she was away and wouldn't find out about his little assignation. Not that he cared that much about her feelings if he was dating someone else. "Something happened with Mona's daughter." *You fucking bastard.* "We had to come home; Mona just left for Rochester."

He frowned. "You staying alone?"

"Yes."

"Call Ruscio, then."

"I'm fine, Ian."

The woman was clearly picking up vibes. "You could join us."

Ian's face drained of color. Lisel wanted to die. "No thanks. I've got a workout planned, then a long bath with a glass of pinot grigio to keep me company. Enjoy your meal, though. Looks like you've got a great evening ahead of you." She knew her voice cracked on the last statement.

Ian just stared at her as she turned and made her way to her house. Resisting the urge to slam the door, she closed it quietly and leaned against the wood. Her eyes immediately filled with tears. He had a date tonight with another woman. She was absolutely stunned.

That part of my life is over, he'd told her when she said she wanted a sexual, physical, romantic relationship with him.

The dirty rotten liar.

Well, she told herself, *you aren't going to sit here moping. Change, get to the barre, take your bath, and have your glass of wine.*

Have several, if you want. Staying as numb as she could, she locked the dead bolt, punched in the security system, and headed for the spare room.

"THIS IS GREAT, Olive."

"Are you sure? You're not eating much."

"I'm sure." He smiled over at her, unable to banish the image of Lisel's face when she realized who Olive was. What was going on here tonight.

He'd tried to tell himself this was for the best. Maybe, if Lisel thought he was just another man lying to her, using her, she'd keep her distance. It fit right into one particular lie that he'd told last summer . . . *You're not my type, sweetheart. You're not woman enough for me.*

The thought sliced his heart into ribbons.

"So what's it like to live next to a big star?" Olive asked after biting into a juicy shrimp.

Excruciating came to mind. "She's a nice woman."

"I hope she's all right."

Ian swallowed intentionally, so he didn't choke on his food.

"She seemed upset. Why didn't you think she should be alone? Because of what the papers said—she's been sick?"

"Yeah, that and a couple of other things going on with her."

"She's stunning, but she looked pretty tense."

With good reason. He wondered how her stomach was doing.

They made small talk as they finished their meal. Then they went to the kitchen to clean up. He gestured Olive to the table. "Sit. You cooked, I'll do this."

"Fine by me." Olive crossed to the table and sat down, staring out at the backyard. "Ian, is that a telescope?"

He scraped plates into the sink, which had been specially designed without lower cabinets so he could wheel under it. "Uh-huh. I like to look at the stars."

"So does my son Jeremy. He's such a fanatic, I've taken to it, too."

"Let me finish up here, and we'll go outside." He grinned at Olive. She was a good companion. If he could block out Lisel, he'd be having a great time. But he kept wondering what she was doing. What was she thinking?

He completed his tasks quickly, and Olive packed up everything and stored leftovers in his fridge; they donned light jackets and went out back. There, they spent a fun half-hour checking out the heavens.

At ten, Olive yawned. "Well, I'd better get going. I have to be to work early in the morning." She cocked her head. "Are you coming in tomorrow?"

Ian was doing contractual work, so he wasn't required to be there every day.

"No, not tomorrow."

"Oh, well, then." She nodded to the path that went around

the outside of his condo. "I think I'll just go that way." She grinned at him. "Walk me out?"

"No can do, sweetheart."

It took her a minute. "Oh, God."

They both laughed.

"Come on, I'll see you to your car."

They headed around the end unit and reached the parking lot. He wheeled over to her car and took her keys. Like any able-bodied man might, he unlocked the door and opened it for her to get in.

"Thanks, Ian." She accepted the keys and stood by the car. "This was fun."

"Yeah, it was."

"And not too heavy." Leaning over, she brushed her lips against his. "Just a friendly goodnight, buddy," she said, then slid into the front seat. He backed away and watched her as she pulled out and waved, then swung the chair around.

And saw Lisel standing in the shadows on the front porch that connected their condos. "Have fun on your date, Ian?" she asked.

LISEL SHOULDN'T HAVE had that last glass of wine. She'd done exactly what she'd planned: worked out till her muscles ached, taken a bath, drunk some white wine, and tried not to feel bad about Ian next door with another woman. But when she'd been munching on a supper of brie and bread on her enclosed porch, and heard them come outside to look at his stars, she'd fallen apart. She'd taken another glass of wine into the living room so she wouldn't have to listen to them, and drank that in the darkness.

And then she drank another one. It didn't help, though, because while she was in front of the house, Lisel saw Ian escort his date to her car. And she saw pretty Olive Hennessy kiss the man Lisel loved.

The man wheeling toward her right now. She pushed off from the house and met him halfway down the sidewalk.

"What are you doing out here?" He glanced at the cherry red lounging pajamas she wore. "You'll freeze in those."

"Did you have a good time?" she repeated.

He wheeled nervously back and forth. "Look, I thought you were away for the weekend. I didn't . . ." He shrugged.

"And that's supposed to make this all right?" She tried to quell the emotion in her voice. "That you had a date tonight?"

"Not exactly a date. I work with Olive now."

"She's a firefighter?" Oh, great, everything Lisel wasn't.

"Lise, look, be rational about this."

"Rational? You want me to be rational, when I'm in love with you and have to watch you kiss another woman?"

Like most men, when backed into a corner, Ian tended to strike out. "Were you spying on me?"

"No, I kept trying to get away from you two. Everywhere I went, I caught a glimpse of you." She shook back her hair. "Damn you, I sound like a jealous shrew."

"No, not that."

"Don't patronize me!"

He rolled in closer. "Lisel, how much wine did you have?"

"None of your business."

"Oh, that's mature."

She drew in a calming breath, like she might before she went on stage. "You're right, this has the disgusting overtones of high school. I'm going back inside." She turned and headed down the path to her condo.

Ian let her go. He was thinking it was for the best, for them to be on bad terms, when all of a sudden, he heard a rustle in the bushes. From the shadows a figure emerged. It darted toward Lisel, who had almost gotten to the porch. Ian headed for her, too, and just before the person reached her, he levered himself out of the chair and brought Lisel to the ground with him.

FLASHING LIGHTS SPUN around the yard. Ian held Lisel down, covering as much of her as he could, until he heard, "I'm Officer Lopez. We were cruising by like Rossettie told us to do and saw somebody dressed in black on foot heading to the condo. Are you hurt?"

"No, we're fine." He kissed Lisel's head. "Aren't you, honey?"

Her face scrunched into the grass—thank God they'd done a

lateral move and not ended on pavement—she whispered, "Yeah, I'm okay."

Another officer rushed up to them. "No one's around."

"Still, let's get them inside."

Ian rolled off Lisel to his back. "Take her first, I need a minute."

"Want some help?" the young cop asked when the other got Lisel up and into the house.

Because he was shaken and because he wanted Lisel safe, he accepted the rookie's assistance into the chair. Ian took stock of his body. His arms were sore, and his shoulder ached like a bitch.

Lisel was seated on the couch, talking to the policewoman when he went inside her condo. He crossed to her; he'd never seen her more fragile—her beautiful complexion was ashen, marred with a dark red bruise on her cheek; and she was shivering. He took a blanket from the back of the recliner and managed to swing it around her shoulders. She was gripping her stomach. "S-somebody actually tried to, what? Hurt me? Kidnap me?"

Lopez exchanged a look with the young cop, whose tag said Clemens. "We think so." She turned to Ian. "What did you see?"

"Somebody came out of the bushes and headed straight for her. It was dark, so I didn't get a good look at him. Or her."

"Why did you tackle Ms. Loring?" Clemens asked.

Ian stared at him a minute, gripping the chair. "I'm easy to overpower in this thing. I thought if I got her to the ground, covered her, I'd be more useful in stopping whoever it was."

"You didn't get him?" Lisel asked shakily.

Lopez said, "No. I'm sorry. He got away. Call it in, Clemens, and contact Rossettie. He wanted to be notified if anything happened out here."

"We should call Rick Ruscio. He's on this case." This from Ian.

He noticed the female cop shift. "Fine. Do that, too, Clemens." She faced Lisel. "Ms. Loring. We know your situation. Why were you outside at ten at night when you've got security problems?"

Lisel looked up. She glanced from Lopez to Ian. "I, um, I saw . . . oh!" She winced then, grabbed her stomach, and bolted upright. She raced out of the room.

Ian whipped the chair around. "Damn it." He followed her.

The bedroom had a wide doorway he could wheel through. He went inside; the bathroom was accessible, too; he maneuvered the chair behind Lisel, where she bent over the toilet bowl. And wretched violently.

Coming in close, he held back her hair. Soothed her scalp. "It's okay, it's okay . . ." He said nonsense things, but his heart was racing. With concern and guilt. When she finally finished, he backed away and went to the sink. Wetting a cloth, he wheeled back, and found her sitting against the wall, her head back, her eyes closed, her knees bent. He couldn't get close enough to bathe her face, damn it. "Here, this will help."

She opened bruised eyes, took the cloth, and blotted her cheeks and forehead. "I'm sorry."

"Don't, honey. I'm just worried." He nodded to the toilet. "And I'm sorry for being partly responsible for this."

"Officer Lopez was right. It was foolish to be outside." She closed her eyes. "Foolish to have had the wine. I know I can't drink more than one glass."

Ian's heart was breaking. "This is my fault. I—"

She held up her hand. "Please, don't make excuses. And don't lie. It was obvious what was going on."

"Lise, I—"

The doorbell pealed. Lisel said, "Ian, please. I need to handle all this. I don't want to get into an analysis of your love life." She stood like a colt on shaky legs. "Thanks for helping me outside. But I don't want anything more from you." Tossing her head back, she sidled around the chair and left him in the bathroom.

After he tidied it up, he went out to the living room and found Rossettie and Ruscio on the couch. Lisel was talking quietly with them. Something about the scenario struck him; finally, it crystallized. Lisel was really in danger. Anything could happen to her. The thought scared the shit out of him. And, conversely, sobered him.

Life was full of danger. He looked down at his legs. He knew that only too well. You could either hide in the closet and not face it, or you could live the life you had well.

And for the first time since 9/11, Ian admitted which side of the line he'd chosen. Thinking about all his buddies that died, his choice made him very ashamed.

⤚ TEN

RICK LEANED AGAINST the wall in Lisel Loring's glassed-in porch and folded his arms across his chest. There was a show that was going on here. Lisel was the main player, but it was the supporting actors who were most interesting.

"I ain't sure that's such a hot idea," Joe Harmon said, keeping his post close to his charge, Ian Woodward. "I got a job. Two really."

"Both part-time." Will Rossettie frowned at his friend. "And you got the experience."

Only this morning had Rick learned that Woodward's therapist had been a Special Ops medic in Vietnam.

"I could do more at the camp."

Dressed in a dark blue one-piece thing, Lisel brought herself up to height. "Wait a second here, I have some say in this, don't I?"

"Well, yeah, sure," Will told her. "But you should take the advice of experts. Ruscio and I talked. It's time to go round-the-clock. Somebody tried to get to you. We don't know what they'll do next."

Woodward swore under his breath.

Rossettie faced Harmon. "Pitch in here, Harmon. As a favor to me."

Lisel stiffened. Sometimes she was made of fluff, and sometimes real backbone surfaced. A lot like Faith McPherson. "I wasn't aware I needed favors, Chief Rossettie. I was under the impression Mr. Ruscio could take care of this."

Raising bushy gray brows, Will gave her a shrug. "He can do 24-hour surveillance, if you want him living in your house. Otherwise we need a team to do duty from outside."

Turning his face away, Woodward gripped the wheels of his chair. The man's possessive streak was showing. He wondered if Lisel sensed it. Truthfully, she seemed pissed off at the guy today. Woodward said, "I don't think it's a good idea for Ruscio to move in here."

She tossed him a Queen of England look. "I wasn't aware your opinion on this had been requested."

Yep, definitely pissed. Rick wondered what the poor schmuck had done.

"It concerns me if Joe goes to work for you. I hired him to come to Hidden Cove to help me out."

She faced Rossettie, frustration making her slender shoulders slump. "Is no one else available?"

"You don't want Joe?" Will asked.

Vulnerability flashed across her pretty features. "It's obvious he doesn't want to do this."

Harmon straightened. Rossettie had been sending him covert messages of the you-owe-me sort. Rick knew his mentor had been in Nam with Harmon and wondered about the relationship. Will was one of those guys who couldn't talk about his war experiences.

The therapist said, "All right, I'll do it." He glanced at Woodward, an expression Rick often saw Will bestow on him. The guy cared about Ian.

Woodward sighed. "Fine by me." He wheeled toward the back exit. "Hammer out the details and fill me in when you're available for therapy." He left the house in a huff.

"I wanna talk to you out in the kitchen," Harmon said to Will.

When the old friends disappeared through the archway, Rick crossed to his employer. "Lisel, this can be handled another way. Harmon doesn't have to work for you, if you don't want that. I can cover 24/7 until we find somebody else to take shifts."

She faced him, her expression ragged. "No, that's not fair. You've got a life."

Actually, he didn't. "Not one that would interfere with this job."

"Rick, there's no reason for you to watch me every minute. Joe Harmon can take some night duty; besides, you've got a sister you're obviously concerned about, and you have that community service to do."

"I might be able to get that stint postponed if it interferes with starting up this business."

She studied him like he was a character in one of her plays. "You don't like doing community service, do you?"

"The person supervising me is a real pain in the ass." As soon as he said the words, guilt hit him like a rapid round of bullets. "No, that's not true. She's just so perky . . . and persistent."

"She wants more from you than you're willing to give."

His spine stiffened. He hated when people could read him so easily. "I hardly know her."

"I study characters, and people. I can tell . . . something's going on." She shrugged. "Besides, I sense something in you. Like with . . ."

When she didn't finish, Rick nodded to the back of the house. "Like with Woodward?"

Her eyes clouded.

"Look, I'm sorry if I'm out of line. It's just obvious with that Harmon thing that a lot's going on under the surface here."

"I'm not Joe Harmon's favorite person."

"Why? What'd you do to him?"

"I have no idea."

"You have a history with Woodward."

"It's pretty apparent, I guess."

"Anything I can do?"

"No. Thanks." She wrapped her arms around her waist in a gesture that would call forth any red-blooded man's urge to protect. "You're a nice guy, Rick."

You're a nice guy, underneath that tough cop exterior . . .

"Why does everybody keep saying that to me? It's not true."

Lisel smiled. Before she could comment, Rossettie returned with Harmon. "We're all set," Will told them.

No surprise there. Will could break hardened criminals. "Here's the schedule of when Joe can work."

Harmon just grunted.

Rick went over time frames with them—they planned to have some police coverage, too, freeing up Rick, certainly enough to do his community service and spend some time with his sister. He sighed as he agreed and sighed again as he headed over to A Time to Grow.

When he arrived at the school, they were outside for recess on the playground. Again, the familiar anxiety, brought on by what he'd done, triggered when he saw their happy little faces. Faces like . . .

"What's the scowl for?"

He turned to find Faith behind him. Today she had her bangs pulled off her face with clips, making her look even younger. She wore pink again, a shirt and pants. The outfit didn't look warm enough for a cloudy October afternoon.

"Just enjoying my job, ma'am."

Her pretty, unlined brow furrowed at his sarcasm. "Well, you said you weren't going to play nice."

"You got it, sister." He scanned the area. "What am I doing out here?"

"Supervising." She nodded to a group of boys with a dodge ball. "Or you could play with the guys."

His heartbeat kicked up. "Do I have to?"

She grasped his forearm in a firm grip. He remembered how she held on to him that Friday night under the trees. "No, of course not. You can just watch them."

His sigh was heavy. "Where?"

She surveyed the playground. This close, he could see her eyes were the exact color of the trees behind her. "Over there, where the girls are building a sand sculpture." She mumbled under her breath, "Maybe you can handle females *their* age."

His ego challenged, he started to say, "I can handle you, baby . . . ," but bit it back. "I'll go over."

His stride heavy, he crossed to the sandbox. Three little girls were inside the six-by-six area, marked off with railroad ties;

they were building something he couldn't make out. He crossed his arms over his chest and watched.

"That's dumb. It doesn't look like a castle." This from a red-headed leader type.

Another girl chimed in. "Yeah. It looks dumb."

The littlest one, with wispy taffy-colored curls, stuck her sandy fingers in her mouth.

"You're a baby." This from the first girl. The two of them stood. "Let's go swing," she said to the other, purposely leaving the third kid out.

When the girls left, Rick watched the effect of their bullying. Big fat tears welled in the eyes of the one left behind. He glanced around to see which of the teachers were available. Nancy was playing dodge ball, and Faith was now on top of the monkey bars. The two aides, Susie and Tim, were running a hop-scotch game. *Aw, shit.*

The little girl just sat there, staring down at her shabby jeans. *Damn it, son of a bitch.* Rick swore to himself as he climbed into the sandbox and squatted in front of her. "Hey, *niña,* what's wrong?"

She wouldn't look up.

"What's your name?" he asked.

Nothing.

"Tell me," he coaxed.

Finally, she said, "Molly."

"What you building, Molly?"

Tiny, thin shoulders shrugged. They were covered in a dirty jeans jacket.

"Molly?"

"A ca-sthel." Then she peered up at him, and Rick knew he was dead meat. Her dismal gaze sliced his heart. "Can't do it."

"Sure you can."

"You know how to build casthels?" she asked hopefully.

"I got two baby sisters. When they were your age, I used to take them to the park." *To get away from their father's fists.* "I got pretty good at this."

Sinking down onto his knees, he plunged his hands into the sand. It was cold and gritty. "Come on, let's start with the base of the castle. Then we can do the fancy stuff."

"'Kay."

He worked quickly and tried to get little Molly to talk . . .

"Got any brothers or sisters?" She did. Three. All younger. Geez, the kid had to be four or five herself.

"Where do you live?" Near the school, in the center of the city.

"What do you like to do?" She didn't answer this one.

By the time recess was over, they had a pretty decent castle and a fairly good turret. Turrets had always been his favorite; he remembered vividly making the girls, eyes go wide with his skill in the sand. Faith approached the sandbox—with all the kids in tow. "Oh, my goodness, this is a work of art. Who did it?" She smiled broadly at Molly. "Is it yours, honey?"

Molly's face flushed, but she looked up. "Uh-huh."

"It's wonderful." Faith turned to the side. "Susie, could you run in and get my camera out of the desk. We have to preserve this beautiful thing for posterity."

The little girl stabbed a bony finger at Rick. "He did most of it."

"Nah, I just helped. Little Mol here's a great architect."

There was a flurry of oohs and aahs. Rick stole a glance at the bullies. They were standing off to the side, scowling. It made him smile. He stood and brushed the sand off his pants.

Peering up at him, Molly held out both arms. He had a flash of Pilar making that baby gesture, so he leaned over and scooped Molly up. Her weight felt good in his arms, solid. Whole.

After pictures were taken, they headed back into the school. Molly didn't scramble to get down until another girl came up and asked her to play. Then they ran ahead, giggling.

Faith fell into stride with Rick. "Thanks for doing that for Molly."

He grunted.

"She's an angel. I wish the other kids wouldn't pick on her."

He didn't want to get involved in this.

They reached the doorway to the school. "Anyway, I liked your castle, Prince Charming."

He shook his head and stole a glance at her. "That is *so* not me, Miz McPherson."

"Yeah, you keep telling me that." Her eyes shone with something he wouldn't identify.

He grunted again and went inside.

ANGRY AT MOLLY'S two little tormentors, Faith headed for the schoolroom, searching for a way to end their bullying. Kids tended to pick on Molly because she was poorer than most and had a lisp. She'd already dealt with this twice and it was only October. Tonight she'd have her dad help her figure out what to do. Meanwhile, she'd use Aesop to set the stage. When they were seated in a circle, she chose the "The Eagle and the Beetle." "Once there was an eagle who pursued a hare. The hare went to the beetle and asked for protection. Despite its best efforts, the beetle was not able to protect the hare, and the eagle ate it up." Faith went on to tell how, from then on, the beetle destroyed the eggs of the eagle, even tricking Jupiter to achieve his goal. She ended with the moral, "The weak will find a way to avenge insult, even when it's with the strong."

After she finished the story, the two girls looked rightfully chagrined. When the kids left for the day, Faith turned her attention to Rick. In the back of the room was an eight-foot wooden shelf somebody had donated; she needed to clean it up and get some of her books out of storage. She tried to tell herself tackling that job today wasn't just an excuse to be with him. He had to stay anyway to get in his hours. But since she was thinking about him constantly, her internal protests didn't ring true.

"Could you help me fill the shelves in the back of the room?" she asked sweetly after the students left.

He'd withdrawn, in the hour since recess. He had a lot of trouble opening up, especially to the kids. From what Pilar had told her about his background, she could understand why he didn't let people in. Right now, with traces of sand on his blue Dockers and polo shirt, he looked as forlorn as Molly.

"Yeah, sure. What do you want done?"

"I'm going to clean those shelves. I want to put some of my books that are in the storage closet down the hall on them." She whipped a set of keys out of her pocket. "Here. There should be a cart in there to haul them back."

He took the keys without looking at her. When he left, she slid the CD from *Phantom* into a player she kept in the room, rolled up her sleeves, and went to work. She managed to dust all the lower shelves easily, but the others were too high for her to reach. There was no ladder near, so she climbed on the bottom shelves to get to the top ones. She was humming with Michael Crawford when she heard the crack. Then the wood began to sway. "Ohhh," she yelled when she realized the bookshelf was unstable.

And coming down.

She fell backward, but instead of hitting the floor, she felt strong arms catch her and scoop her out of the way. There was a loud thump, like something hitting a wall, and then she and two hundred pounds of male flesh landed on the rug. Rick took the brunt of the fall just before the entire shelf crashed in a big, heavy heap about a foot away. It was thunderclap loud.

Her heartbeat galloped in her chest.

So did his. "Are you all right?" he asked gruffly, his arms in a viselike grip around her. It felt great being sprawled on top of him.

Nodding, she asked, "You?"

"Yeah, sure." He looked up at her, and without meaning to, she'd guess, he pushed back her hair and left his hand in it for a few seconds. "You scared the shit out of me."

She winced at her foolishness.

"What the *fuck* did you think you were doing?"

"Rick please . . . not that language."

He shook his head. "I don't believe you. You practically kill yourself, like some half-witted blond, and you scold me for my language."

"Half-witted blond? That's so lame."

"Get up."

"Huh?"

"You need to get up."

"Oh." She scrambled to her knees and stood, offering him a hand. Bypassing it, he rolled to his feet. And cringed with the action.

"What's wrong?"

He gripped his shoulder. "An old injury, then the bookshelf clipped it on the way down."

"Oh, dear. I'm sorry. I could rub it for you."

An exasperated sigh escaped his lips. "Not on your life." He nodded to the shelves, which lay in a heap on the ground. "What possessed you to climb on that?"

Thoughts of you clouded my good judgment. "It was stupid. I'm sorry. I wasn't thinking."

"Yeah, you're good at that."

"What?"

"Acting without thinking."

She was getting sick of him treating her like a child. "If you're referring to last Friday night, I knew exactly what I was doing."

"Sweetheart, you don't have a clue." He turned away from her, so she let the comment go. He pointed to the shelves. "I don't think that's salvageable."

"No, probably not."

"In any case, it won't be safe."

"Darn, I needed new shelves."

"Metal ones are pretty cheap."

"I know, but I love wooden stuff. My grandpa used to make me things out of wood."

"Like the bed?"

"Yeah, and a doll's house for my room, and a hope chest."

"What happened to him?"

She smiled and leaned against a nearby table. "He died three years ago. Just went to sleep one night and didn't wake up. My dad said God loved him too much to let him suffer, but wanted him back now."

Rick's eyes, just for a brief flash, clouded. She remembered what he'd said once. *God's forgotten about me and my family.* "Rick, about . . ."

He stepped away. "No, sermons, little girl." He faced away from her. "Look, what do you want done with those boxes?"

"We'll stack them in the corner. Rick—"

But he walked away. Faith felt bad, helpless, really. And it wasn't just because she was attracted to him. He was so troubled. She wished she could do something for him. Maybe she'd talk to her dad about that, too.

* * *

RICK HAD TWO hours before he was on surveillance duty. He agreed to meet Pilar for pizza before he drove out to the lake. She wanted to go back to The Pizza Place so he pulled into the parking lot at six; he said he'd pick her up, but she told him Faith would give her a ride. He entered the restaurant, anxious to see his sister. He caught sight of Faith on the other side of the room with people from the school. Damn, he didn't know she'd be *eating* here. Ignoring her, he crossed to the booth where Pilar sat.

"Ricardo." She looked up. Her eyes were bruised. "Hi."

"What happened?" he asked, sliding in next to her and encircling her shoulders with his arm.

She nodded to the other side of the room. He tracked her gaze and saw his sister and mother at a table, throwing nasty looks at them. Rick said, "Come on, we're leaving."

"But I already ordered. You said you were in a hurry."

"I'll get it to go." He stood, tugged her up, and handed her his car keys. "Go wait in . . ."

"Not so fast." At the touch on his arm, he spun around to see Anita behind them. She wore a skimpy black top that bared some belly, obscenely tight jeans, and more makeup than Marilyn Manson. "I wanna talk to you."

"All right," he said to Pilar. "Go outside."

Instead, Pilar turned hopeful eyes on her sister. "How are you, 'Nita?"

"Not that you two care," she said, arching a brow. "I'm okay. But Ma's not feeling good."

Pilar's face blanched. "What's wrong with her?"

"Who knows? She didn't go to the doctor's because we don't have insurance."

"What happened to the policy I set up for you?"

"Ma let it lapse."

"What . . . I gave her . . ." Hell. Now he remembered. Rick had been embroiled in the scandal with Steele when a couple of payments were due; he'd just given the money to his mother to pay the bill. "She spent it on booze."

"Look, I dunno what she did. Speaking of which, I need the grand for my beauty school."

"What beauty school?" Pilar asked innocently.

"Like you care. You abandoned us."

Pilar's eyes filled with tears. "No, no I didn't. 'Nita, Lennie attacked me."

"Oh, don't be such a baby."

Rick watched the dynamic, paralyzed like he often got when Anita or his mother went on a tirade. He felt his stomach clench, sweat bead on his brow. But even when Anita's voice rose, he couldn't move.

He felt somebody at his elbow. "Come on, Pilar, come outside with me." It was Faith.

Pilar said, "Huh?"

"Come on, honey. Let's go outside and let Rick handle this."

"She ain't your sister, you know."

Faith faced Anita and gave her an angel's smile. "I know, Anita. She's my friend. You could be, too, with our whole family. Why don't you come over sometime? Visit with me and my mom and dad."

For a minute, an odd emotion flicked across Anita's face. "Oh, yeah, me and a preacher. That'll be the ever-lovin' day."

"David's a wonderful man, 'Nita." Pilar's voice held so much hope, it made Rick's throat tighten. "You'd like him. Why don't you come and see us?"

"Us?" She snorted. "Us? You aren't part of them, *pequeña muchacha*. They're•slumming with you." She gave Rick a disgusted once over. "Both of you. Look, all I want is some money."

Rick swallowed hard, smothered by the situation. Mechanically he reached in his back pocket.

Faith put her hand on his. "Rick . . ."

"Please, Faith, just take Pilar outside." He could see everybody in the place witnessing the scene. He was embarrassed for Pilar.

With a brief squeeze of his arm, Faith led Pilar outside. Pilar, who was crying openly now. Taking a deep breath, Rick took a check out of his wallet, bent over the table, and wrote it out. Then he straightened and faced his sister. "Here's the money for the course. And to see a doctor. I'll take care of the insurance myself."

His sister smirked. "Thanks, big brother." She turned and called over her shoulder, "Don't forget the rent's due next week."

Slowly Rick shook his head. "Anita?" She stopped and

looked back. "Faith's right. You could go see the McPhersons. They're nice people."

"No way. I chill with my own." She gave him another scathing look. "Best you remember that, *hermano mayor.*"

Rick was struggling to get his emotions under control—for Pilar—when he reached the van. The two women were inside. He pulled open the driver's door.

Faith slid out of the seat. She closed the door for privacy. "You're not okay. What can I do to help?"

Leaning against the van, he ran a hand through his hair. "I . . . I don't think I can face pizza with Pilar right now."

"Fine, I'll take her home. Make some excuse to her, though. I'll go back in, get the pizza, and tell my friends where I'm going."

Relief, and warmth that someone cared enough for him to do this with no questions asked, flooded Rick. He squeezed her arm, went around to the other side of the car while Faith hurried into the restaurant. Rick opened the door. "Come on, *niña.* You're going with Faith."

His sister climbed out of the car and into his arms.

"We lost some time. I had less than I thought, anyway, so I gotta be on surveillance soon." He held on tight. "You okay?"

She nodded. She knew, of course, that he was making an excuse. They'd been through this kind of thing before, where Anita's antics leveled Rick. But he wasn't together enough to keep his emotions from Pilar. He had an hour before he had to head out for the lake. Maybe he could run this off.

"Sure, I'm fine. You?"

"I'm all right, honey." He kissed her head. "I'll call you later."

Faith returned, got Pilar in her own car, then faced Rick. "You're not all right."

"No, but I will be." He swallowed hard. "Thanks for doing this."

"Rick, let me . . ."

"Please, Faith, just take care of my sister. That means more to me than any other comfort you could offer."

"Okay." Standing on tiptoes, she kissed his cheek. "We're here for you, too. Me, dad, mom."

"Just go," he managed to get out without his voice cracking. "Please."

"All right."

He watched them drive away, then got in the car. He put his head down on the steering wheel and tried to take in another breath, tried not to be affected by what had just happened, by the evidence of the muck he lived in.

He couldn't do it.

LIGHTS FLASHED FROM the oncoming cars into Faith's face; the glare made her blink, and sent a message to her brain that she was crazy to be heading out to the lake at ten at night. *What* was she doing? Glancing next to her in the front seat of her Saturn, she thought, *Bringing food to the hungry?* Well, that was kind of true. Rick had called Pilar about nine, and Faith had been in the room with her, doing her hair to distract the young girl, who'd let Saul cuddle on her lap for comfort.

She'd only heard Pilar's side of the conversation . . .

"You haven't eaten, have you . . . do you at least have coffee . . . I hate it when you don't take care of yourself, Ricardo."

And so when Pilar finally crashed, Faith had heated up the rest of the pizza, baked some brownies, made coffee, and hopped in her car by ten. She knew he was on surveillance until midnight, when somebody else would take over. Pilar had told her where he was working. He'd be outside the Cove Condos in the parking lot.

She pulled in right next to his green van. Scooping up the food, she got out of the car and came around to the driver's side. He buzzed down the window. "I don't believe this."

She held up a picnic basket. "Aren't you hungry?"

He scrubbed a hand over his face. Doubt curled inside Faith. For the first time, it hit her she might be bothering him. Oh, Lord, she hated the idea.

"Look, I'll just leave this with you. It's heated-up pizza, some brownies, and coffee. Take it. I won't stay."

"Brownies?" he said like a little boy.

"I made them."

"For supper?"

Her face colored. She shook her head.

"You made brownies just for me?"

"With chocolate chunks. Rick, I don't want to pester you." Well, she did really, but not tonight when he was raw. "Take this, and I'll go."

He shook his head and pressed the locks button. "Don't go. Get in while I eat and tell me how Pilar is."

Grinning, she scooted around to the passenger door and climbed inside. When she handed him pizza, he said, "There's a whole half left?"

"My parents were out. Pilar and I could only eat half."

His eyebrows furrowed. "You didn't leave her alone, did you?"

"No, Dad came home."

Rick ate hungrily. "You tell him?" he asked around mouthfuls of the pizza.

"Yes."

"He must really think I'm a loser."

"Why do you do that? Surely, you don't think Pilar's a loser, because of your family."

"Of course not. But . . . never mind. Let's not ruin my supper."

She reached out and squeezed his shoulder. She gave him time to finish off several pieces by telling him about Pilar, then asked, "What happened there with them tonight, Rick? With you?"

He didn't pretend to misunderstand. Laying his head back on the seat, he sighed and closed his eyes. "It's always the same way." The words were wrenched from him. She waited. "I freeze. I can't . . . I've never been able to stand up to them. Two puny little women . . ."

"Hey, puny women can be tough."

"Oh, yeah, you're hard as nails."

She giggled. "It's all right that you care about them."

He just stared ahead, his chiseled jaw accented by the lights from the parking lot lamps. She could see a growth of beard—dark, sexy, masculine.

When he didn't say anything, she asked, "Are you really helping them by enabling their behavior?"

"Sounds like a preacher's comment."

"Dad has great insight into people."

"Who the hell knows? I'm not rational about them."

"Your childhood was rough."

Faith was surprised he took the opening. "Same old same old. Dad drank. Knocked everybody around until I got old enough to stop it. Landed himself in prison before too long. Where he currently resides."

"Do you ever see him?"

Rick swallowed hard and gave a shake of his head.

Reaching into the basket, she pulled out the coffee thermos, poured them both some, then got the brownies out and set them on the divider between them. "You're what? Thirty-six?"

"Yeah, age wise." He thumped his heart. "In here, I'm a lot older." He glanced over at her. "It's like you, Sunshine. Your body's twenty-something, but the rest of you is still a babe."

She didn't take offense. "You're twenty years older than Pilar."

"Yeah, believe it or not, Ma had me at fifteen, and her at thirty-five."

"Wow. With Anita in between."

"Crazy. The whole family is." He sipped his coffee. "Sometimes I wonder if the whole world's fu—"—he rolled his eyes—"screwed up, then I look at you." He reached out and soothed a hand down her hair. "How'd you get to be so . . . good?"

"Loving parents. And grandparents. They made my world wonderful, so I believe the world is that way. Dad and Mom married early, too. They were madly in love, mom skipped college to marry him, then supported him through divinity school. They had me when she was twenty-two and Peter two years later."

"Peter's younger than you? I thought he was a big brother."

"No, though he tends to act that way."

He cleared his throat. "How about Sam? How old is he?"

She didn't want to talk about Sam. "My age. He got a master's degree in psychology before he decided on divinity school. Now he's finishing faster than Peter."

"You love them both."

"Of course. But Rick . . ."

He reached up and covered her mouth with his fingers. They

were callused. The touch sent shivers through her. "Shh, none of that tonight. I'm whipped."

And he couldn't take more conflict. She yearned to reach over, take him in her arms, and pull him to her breast. Her whole body longed to feel him close. But he needed something else from her.

"Okay." She fished out the brownies. "Taste one. They're sinful."

He chuckled and took a sweet. "Oh my God, Faith. These are great."

"Nancy says they're orgasmic."

He choked, gave her a sideways glance—and ate several.

She stayed until he devoured all the food. "Well, I'd better go."

"It's getting late." He gave her a long, searching look. "Thanks for doing this for me."

"Couldn't let you go hungry."

"I didn't mean the food. I feel better."

That made her heart sing. "I'm glad."

He reached out, picked up her hand, and kissed it. "Thank you."

"You're welcome."

Dropping her hand, he grabbed the steering wheel. "I'm going back to not playing nice next week."

She laughed. "Okay, I'm forewarned." She grabbed the door handle.

"Call my cell when you get home. I want to know you're all right."

"Yes, sir." Then she leaned over and pecked him on the cheek. "Good night, Rick."

HE DIDN'T KNOW what the fuck he was doing here, for the second afternoon of the weekend. He cursed himself for following through with this stupid idea. But the thought invaded his brain after Faith left Friday night—and it wouldn't leave him alone. He told himself he was just grateful to all the McPhersons for helping out with Pilar, to Faith for her intervention at the pizza place, and then for her impromptu visit to the lake, which meant more than he cared to admit. This was something he could do for them. For her. So Saturday morning, he'd called a buddy of his to help with what he didn't know how to do, enlisted Pilar for some grunt work, and here he was at five on Sunday at a freakin' preschool, holding a paint brush, staring at his handiwork.

I love wood . . . my grandpa made things for me . . .

The bookshelves he'd built were simple but pretty enough for Faith. About ten feet wide, and not tall enough so she might hurt herself climbing up them, they were also bigger and sturdier than those that had collapsed—and scared the life out of him when he'd seen her falling. His buddy had sawed a curved curly cue to go along the top. The rest of the shelving Rick had bought precut, so they'd gotten it together in a few hours. He and Pilar had stained them a light oak—like Faith's bed—and now he was putting on the polyurethane. After some fast talking, Nancy had been convinced to let him in to do all this.

It was just a gesture of thanks, he told himself again as he applied the topcoat. It had nothing to do with the feelings he was having for Miz McPherson. Of course not. Okay, so he found her attractive. Okay, so she made his pulse leap when she walked into a room. He'd wanted women he couldn't have before. He'd live through this. Just so long as he stayed away from her romantically, he'd be fine.

Sure he would.

"Rick?"

Aw, shit. Without turning, he continued to apply the clear coat on a shelf. "What are you doing here? Pilar told me you had Bible study."

"Nancy called me. She said to come to the preschool right away. Something about I shouldn't wait until Monday morning to see this."

Thank you, Nancy. He hadn't planned on being around when she got her present. He just grunted and kept working.

"Rick, what . . . why . . ." Silence. Then sniffles. Son of a bitch! "You did this for me?"

His back still to her, he barked, "Don't go all weepy on me. I wrenched my shoulder saving you from the other bookcase. I just wanted to make sure you didn't kill yourself. Or me."

More sniffles. Quiet. Then he felt a hand on his shoulder. "Don't minimize this. What a lovely, lovely thought. I can't believe you did this for me."

He straightened and pivoted sharply. "Faith, don't make this out to be—"

He stopped short; he could feel the paint drip from the brush onto the floor, hear the sound of traffic outside, but he couldn't move. She was dressed in a plain navy jacket and pants, her hair held off her face by a velvet band; but she was looking at him . . . as if he'd hung the moon, just for her. As if he could climb mountains, fly, find the cure for cancer, if any of it would please her. And he was more frightened than he could ever remember being—more than the time he'd been held at gunpoint by a dopehead on crack, more than the time he'd been shot and lay in a dirty alley bleeding, more than the time he'd realized his actions with Stan Steele had ended his career. He was petrified that this woman was going to change his life forever.

Self-preservation told him to be mean. To put her down in some way. He should do that. He would. As soon as he could breathe again. It was just that right now, he could barely take in air.

Reaching up, she wound her arms around his neck. Standing on tiptoes, she buried her face in the crook of his shoulder and nestled in there. Of its own accord, his free hand came up to caress her hair.

And though he knew he didn't deserve her, would never ever deserve her, for a few minutes he just held on.

                                    ∾   ELEVEN

IT FELT SO good to be onstage, even if it was just to practice in
the small auditorium at the fire academy for the New Year's Eve
fund-raiser. The real show would be in the Civic Center downtown, but Lisel was partial to small spaces. They reminded her
of when she was starting out on off off off Broadway.

    She thought about those days as she adjusted her black,
filmy dance skirt, which she wore over a leotard, tights, and leg
warmers, for her practice later—she was doing several pieces
from her past shows. Funny how she'd achieved every single
one of her career goals, and she still wasn't happy.

    Stop it. You sound ungrateful.

    She fixed the lights to suit the monologue she was rehearsing
and dragged a stool out to center stage; perching on it, she closed
her eyes. In minutes, she was Jacey Long, high-priced call girl,
standing over her mother's casket in what was supposed to be a
darkened funeral home. On Broadway in the current hit *Longshot*, this scene had garnered its share of tears. As always, Lisel
pictured her own mother when she began the soliloquy.

    "I was one, and you weren't there. They say babies can't re-
member anything that young, but I do. The room was dark and

dirty. I was in a crib, and you left, just for a little while, you told me. I don't know how long I cried. Finally, a neighbor called the police, and child welfare came. Child welfare and I were on intimate terms my whole young life."

Here, Lisel bolted off the stool, effecting the demeanor and body language of a five-year-old. "Mommy, please, don't leave me here."

She stepped to the other side and stared down. Straight posture. "Jacey, please. Don't make a fuss."

Other side, same little-girl mannerisms. "I don't wanna stay with them."

Back on the stool. "When I was fourteen, I had sex with a pimply-faced senior named Jack. I wanted to talk to you about that, but you were passed out drunk with your own boy toy."

Jacey sighed. "You know, if I'm ever a mother . . ."

Lisel continued the monologue for about five minutes until the small auditorium door opened. Someone walked in and down the aisle. In the corner of the darkened auditorium, her current watchdog, Joe Harmon, stood to see who it was.

"Ms. Loring? It's me, Quinn Frazier. I'm in charge of your New Year's Eve fund-raiser."

She nodded to Harmon. "Yes, of course. We have a meeting today at one."

"I thought it was at twelve."

Shrugging, Lisel said, "Either way is fine. I can practice afterward."

By now he'd made it down to the end of the aisle. He was a good-looking man, about five-ten, slim but muscular—guess all those firefighters stayed in shape—with light brown hair cut short, and a very kind smile. He reminded her of a younger Ed Harris. "I can come back." He glanced at his watch. "I'd have to rearrange a class . . ."

"No, of course not." She descended the few steps. "Can we meet here, or should we go to an office?"

"Here's fine." He held up his briefcase. "I brought the brochure proofs. Your agent said you have to have approval."

She rolled her eyes. "I don't, Lieutenant Frazier. Max is fussy about things like that, but I'm not."

"Yeah, well, I'd just as soon not cross him. He scared the life out of me."

Lisel laughed and took the brochure. "Max can be intimidating." She sank onto a cushiony seat, and he dropped down next to her. The brochure was nicely done—the front covered with stars, in keeping with the slogan "New Year's Eve with a Star." She opened the brochure and scanned the inside. "So you decided to go with a hundred dollars per ticket?"

"Yeah. We could've gone higher because we're just about sold out, but Megan Hale thought we should keep it down so people from Hidden Cove could attend."

"I see I'm autographing afterward." There was to be a reception after the show with champagne and desserts, where Lisel would sign the program for a hundred of the ticket holders, drawn in a lottery.

"Is that still all right?"

"Yes, of course. I think it's a nice touch."

Frazier hesitated. "I read where you haven't been feeling well. Are you sure you're up to this?"

"Of course. I want to do something for the camp." She smiled. "Actually, I'm on the volunteer list for next summer."

"Me, too." He grinned. "Must be my lucky day."

She liked his easygoing manner, and he was charming. "What do you do at the academy?"

"I'm in charge of confined space training and other operations like that. I work with Olive Hennessy."

Ah, Ian's *date*. "I met Olive."

"Really, where?"

She glanced to the back of the auditorium and wondered if Harmon could hear them. "She was out at the condos where I'm staying."

"Olive's one terrific lady."

Yeah, she'd bet. For a brief flash, she had a mental image of Olive Hennessy and Ian having sex. It made her stomach cramp.

"Are you all right? You went pale."

She gripped her middle. "Yes. I just haven't eaten today."

He glanced at his watch. "I have an hour. The academy has a small cafeteria. We could get something to eat while we finish this." He grinned. "Have you seen the academy? It's a new facility."

"No, I haven't."

"I could show you around. It'd be a good excuse to spend more time with you."

She looked at Quinn Frazier, thinking how she always thought Ed Harris was attractive. "I'd love to, Lieutenant Frazier."

"Make it Quinn."

"Then call me Lisel." She nodded. "Excuse me for a minute while I talk to someone who's with me."

He looked confused. Then disappointed, when he spotted Harmon. "Your friend could join us."

"No, thanks. It's a long story why he's here. He won't be joining us." She rose and walked to the back of the auditorium. Joe Harmon sat slouched in the corner, reading a magazine. He looked up when she reached him.

"I'm going to the cafeteria to get something to eat with Lieutenant Frazier."

His look darkened. "Fine. I could use some coffee. Stay where I can see you."

For the life of her, she couldn't understand the man's hostile attitude toward her. "All right." She knew she shouldn't, but she asked anyway, "What did you think of the performance?"

He stood. "You're good."

Hell, Lisel thought as she walked away. He was about as effusive as Ian Woodward.

"WHAT THE HELL are you doing here, Harmon?"

Ian's therapist looked up at him from the magazine he was reading and snorted. "My turn to babysit," he said dryly. Then he nodded to the other side of the room.

Ian tracked his gaze. His heart stumbled at the sight. Lisel was there with Quinn Frazier. He'd heard Frazier say he had a meeting today about the fund-raiser Lisel was doing, but Ian didn't know it was with Lisel herself, or here at the academy.

Sighing, he watched her. She was smiling broadly in between bites of her sandwich. Her face was rosy, and she looked good.

"He's putting the moves on her." This from Joe.

"Really? How would you know?"

"Acoustics are good in the auditorium."

"The auditorium?"

"Yeah, she was practicin' her skit when Frazier came in."

"Only *you* would call a sellout show on Broadway a skit."

"Some namby-pamby shit about a daughter blaming a mother for everything." He sipped his coffee. "She's stunning, though."

"Pretty big word for macho you."

"Fuck you."

Ian watched her. She was telling Frazier something, and her delicate hands were gesturing all over the place. "I've never seen her perform."

"Oh, I don't know. I think she's actin' all the time. Comes off as real fragilelike with men, makes them jump through hoops, when she's really a barracuda." His gaze narrowed on the couple. "She had him eatin' out of her hand in minutes."

Maybe she'd start dating Frazier. He was a nice guy. Good-looking. Ian liked him.

Joe said, "I hate women like that."

To change the subject, Ian took a bead on Joe. "There been a lot of women in your life, buddy?"

"Scores. Went through them like water in my young days. Me and Will . . ." He trailed off when Lisel and Frazier stood, as if they were about to leave. They were headed toward the exit when Lisel caught sight of Ian. At first her eyes widened at him; it took him a minute to realize she was staring at his shirt; she'd never seen him in uniform. And just for a second, her expression was so profoundly proud, it humbled him. Then, her face closed down and all that beautiful animation he just witnessed evaporated like thin white smoke. She assumed the same demeanor as she had the night she saw him with Olive. She was mad at him all right. But it was better left this way. With Joe thinking she was some kind of femme fatale. With her thinking Ian was a cad.

Interesting how things could appear so much different from what they really were.

IT WAS CRAZY to be here; it clearly wasn't in his best interest, Ian knew, but he just couldn't help himself. He had no idea his willpower was so weak. After 9/11, and what he'd been forced to do if he didn't want to live life as an invalid, he thought he was stronger, capable of resisting anything.

But he'd just taught a lesson on decontamination that disturbed him. Usually, studying ways to combat terrorism, and now teaching it to others, strengthened his resolve.

Yet . . . she was getting under his skin. Permeating his brain. The feel, smell, taste of her lingered in his consciousness like a dream you couldn't shake the next day. And so he wheeled in through the door, which for some reason had been left open, to the back of the academy's small auditorium. He spotted Harmon sitting four rows back from the stage; he was glad Joe couldn't see him. Despite his hostility to Lisel, the old man was watching, too. You'd have to be made of stone not to be mesmerized by the sight.

She glided across the stage in some free form modern dance that reminded him of the play *A Chorus Line,* which Ian had seen with his mother. Lisel's lithe body stretched, the leotard revealing every curve and supple muscle in her torso. A torso he wanted to explore. Caress. Grasp onto as he emptied himself inside her.

A leg came up, revealing beautiful calf muscles. He couldn't believe she could get her leg that high, that straight, where her knee kissed her cheek. She bent, with the leg still almost parallel to her body, and he held his breath that she'd keep her balance.

Across the stage again . . . then she leaped into the air. He'd swear she sprouted wings, swear she stayed up there like a graceful heron might.

Lisel saw him hovering in the back of the auditorium, so she danced, just for him. Arm out, bend, stretch. *Let your body feel, Lisel. Feel my body, Ian, think about the texture of my skin and these muscles that are straining.* She stopped and executed a series of quick turns. *Think, Ian. Your heart would pump as mine's doing now if we made love. Stroke me,* she called to him. *Possess me.*

Fury bubbled through her and came out in a series of staccatto punches in the air. How, *how* could he think he wasn't enough of a man for her? How dare he make that decision for her?

She slithered on the floor, then arched her back into a *U,* hands and feet anchoring her. Her body pulsed with energy and need. *Don't do this to us, Ian, don't.*

When the music ended, and she collapsed into a heap on the stage, Ian had to grip his hands together to keep from clapping. To keep from racing to the front of the auditorium, picking her

up, settling her into his lap and promising her they could be together. Instead, he stayed in the shadows, where she couldn't
see him. Where she couldn't sense he wanted her with an intensity he'd never known before. Mind, body, spirit.

You could have her, asshole.

He knew that, which made him sad. And angry. For the last
three years, he'd had to do a lot of things he didn't want to do.
And he was tired of it. Tired of not living like other men.

So stop the pattern. Tell her you've changed your mind.

No, not that quickly. He'd need time to think this out.

"She's something else, isn't she?" Ian looked up into the
face of Quinn Frazier.

"Yeah, she is."

The lieutenant puffed out his chest, and a sloppy grin spread
across his face. If he wasn't such a nice guy, Ian could hate him.
"Can't believe she agreed to go out with me."

"She did?"

"Yeah, we're having dinner tonight. And maybe take in a
movie." He socked Ian in the arm. "Geez, who would have
thought?"

"Go for it." Ian moved his chair back. "I have to be somewhere," he said and wheeled out.

As he rolled down the hall, he realized that maybe he didn't
have the time to think this through.

Ironic. He, of all people, should know that.

THE APARTMENT WAS dark, but Julia didn't turn on the light until she drew the shades and made sure her presence here wouldn't
be visible to any nosy neighbors. Then she sat down at the desk.

Dear Lisel,
I miss you so much. I miss seeing you onstage.
Communing with you. You know how we had this special
bond every time you performed and I was in the auditori-
um. You felt it, too, I know you did.

She stopped and fingered the red satin pajamas she'd put on.
Brought the sleeve to her nose. It was Lisel's scent. She'd
smelled it before. She examined Lisel's vanity, where she was

writing the letter. Her black-as-night hair needed brushing. She picked up Lisel's brush . . . ooooooooooh, how intimate . . . and ran it through her curls. Then she went back to her letter.

> *I haven't heard anything more about Sundays with Lisel. I told you that you needed to do them. I just can't wait till New Year's Eve to see you.*

Bored now, Julia signed the letter. She'd leave it under the door, as if someone had slipped it there from outside.

Then she hit Lisel's makeup.

Then the lingerie drawer. Pulling on a sexy red thong, Julia smiled.

RICK JUST HOPED he could stay awake during the movie that Lisel had picked to see with the firefighter. He wondered briefly what Woodward thought about her date. The guy was head over heels about her, even though he tried to pretend otherwise.

You recognize the signs, I guess.

Rick wasn't head over heels about Faith. He wasn't. So they shared some things—some significant moments. He'd tried not to do that, but he couldn't stop himself, so he'd ended up spending time with her family, depending on her to help out with Pilar, building those damn shelves.

Still, it didn't mean anything. He could keep his distance from her emotionally. Settling back, he wished like hell the movie was something he'd be interested in—like *The Terminator.* He liked Arnold. He'd wanted once to save the world just like the cyborg from the future. Instead, Lisel had chosen a chick flick that was part of a classic film festival with old movie stars.

But not until the opening credits did Rick realize that this was a Doris Day film. He remembered watching those movies with his mother when he was little. She loved the innocent Doris, who brought worldly men like Rock Hudson and James Garner to their knees. What was it about women that made them relish films where men groveled?

The title came on, then Doris's melodic voice singing "Young at Heart." Though he didn't remember this particular movie, the star's voice catapulted him back . . .

His mother, telling him to turn on the TV then shushing him with soda pop and candy. Sometimes she'd let him cuddle next to her on the couch. He remembered how safe he felt curled up next to her; it was one of the few times she'd let him get close. A police department psychologist told Rick once that he had trouble letting women in because he'd tried to be close to his mother and she pushed him away, so he didn't try with any woman as an adult.

Faith would have a field day with that one. She was so sentimental. He could still see the fucking tears in her eyes when she realized he'd built her some simple wooden shelves. He was ashamed to admit he'd let her snuggle into him like she belonged right there in the crook of his neck.

Focus on the movie, asshole.

But then Doris came on screen. Son of a bitch, he forgot she was blond, light-eyed; a rosy innocence just like Faith's bloomed there in her cheeks in full living color.

Ten minutes later he was swearing vilely to himself. Old Blue Eyes, Mr. Sinatra himself, was the no-good hero of this stupid film, the man who didn't deserve Doris. Somebody else did. Gig Young—a good guy, a real hero; he loved Doris and wanted to marry her.

Just like Sam. Faith had told him she and Sam were just friends, they both didn't think there was a future together romantically, but Rick didn't believe that for a second. Who could not want Faith that way? Even though she was too pure for him, he wanted her with an intensity that made his forehead sweat and his hands shake when he was around her.

He didn't deserve to lay a finger on her.

For fifteen minutes, Rick tried not to take the movie in. He tried to ignore Doris's falling for Frank, and Frank, the bastard, letting her do it. He hated Frank for that, just like he'd hate himself . . . no, no, he wasn't Frank. Faith wasn't Doris.

Abruptly he stood. He couldn't stand this, couldn't sit still. He walked down the aisle, out to the concession stand, and got a coke. When he came back in, he didn't take a seat. Instead he leaned against the wall, kept a weather eye on Lisel and her date, and tried not to watch Frank ruin Doris's life.

He tuned out the rest of the movie, but on the drive home, Frank's inability to resist Doris, his weakness in letting her sacrifice her life for him, bugged Rick. The selfish bastard. In a moment of weakness, Rick prayed to Faith's God. *Please, don't let me do that to her.*

He felt more composed when he reached Lisel's condo, just behind the firefighter guy's Bronco. He got out of the car before they headed for the house. "Hi," he said to Lisel.

"Hi, Rick, this is Quinn Frazier."

"I recognize you," Quinn said coolly. Not an unusual reaction from America's bravest and finest.

"Yeah, well . . ." He looked to Lisel. "You tell him?"

She sighed. "Yes."

The guy touched her arm. "Let's go inside."

"I'd like to check out the place first."

At Lisel's worried look, he squeezed her shoulder. "Just precautionary. Humor me."

He approached the door first and stopped dead in his tracks. Gingerly, he removed the letter that was stuck in the crack, so as not to disturb the prints the cops would look for.

Lisel reached him. "What is it?"

He held up the envelope. "Somebody left you a present."

LISEL'S HANDS BEGAN to shake. "That means the fan does know I'm here."

"Yes." Rick nodded to her and Quinn. "Stay back. I want to check inside."

He turned and opened the door, felt for his gun, and switched off the alarm, which had begun to buzz. He made quick work of scouting out the interior, then let Lisel and Quinn inside. Once they were seated, Rick slid rubber gloves out of his pockets, brought the letter to the table, opened it, and read it aloud.

"God, this is so creepy." Lisel wrapped her arms around her waist, but it didn't make her less cold.

"You need to look around, see if there's anything wrong in here."

"But the alarm was on. No one . . ." Her eyes widened. "Do you think someone might have gotten inside?"

"Not necessarily. This is precautionary."

Lisel checked the house, and Rick followed her. "It looks okay in the living room and kitchen." She frowned.

"What?"

"I don't remember leaving the chair pulled out. I haven't used the desk recently."

"Check the rest," Rick told her. He trailed her into the bedroom.

She stopped. "My underwear drawer. It's open."

Purposely, Rick gentled his tone. "You could have done these things, right?"

"Of course. I just don't remember. I'm spooked, I guess."

Rick put his arm around her. "With good reason, I'd say." He reached for his cell phone and punched in a number. "This is Ruscio, Will. Somebody's been at Lisel's apartment." He listened. "We found a letter at her door. The person's been here. Maybe inside." He clicked off. "Will's coming out. Sit tight while I check and see if neighbors saw anything."

He saw a flash of something in Lisel's eyes.

"I'll be right next door," he said to her. "Checking both sides. Then I'll canvas the rest of the area while the police are here. We'll reset the alarm; you'll be safe."

"It's not that."

"What is it?"

"I don't want Ian involved in this."

"I'm sorry. He may have seen something." Rick squeezed her arm. "It'll be okay. If you don't want him here, I won't let him come over."

"I don't."

"All right." Again he gave her a reassuring squeeze. "Things will be all right, Lisel. I promise."

She didn't believe him for a minute.

IAN SLAMMED HIS fist into the bag so hard he moaned in pain. Still he didn't stop. Covered with sweat, shaking with muscle depletion, he kept going. Punch, punch, punch, punch. It was the only thing that kept him from thinking about where she was tonight, that she was with another man. And that the whole thing was his fault. Had he said the word, she'd be with him.

Quinn Frazier was a nice guy. So be it.

The doorbell rang, dragging him out of his haze of misery. Could it be her? Like the last time? No, he sincerely doubted that. She was pissed at him, still, for his date with Olive. Again the bell. What if she was in trouble? Hell, Ruscio was with her. But if something had happened . . .

Without removing his gloves, he wheeled out to the front of the house and whipped open the door. On the stoop was Ruscio.

"What's wrong?" Ian asked.

"There was another letter. Tucked into Lisel's front door. She's not sure that somebody wasn't inside."

Ian looked beyond him to Will's car, which had just pulled up. Flashing lights illuminated the front of the condos, and he could hear the buzz of radios.

"We're checking the neighbors to see if they saw anything. Did you?"

Only in my mind. Her, out with another man.

"No." He glanced over his shoulder. "I been working out in my bedroom, which faces our backyards."

"For how long?"

"The last hour."

"Yeah?" Ruscio scanned his sweat-soaked shirt. "What monkey's on your back?"

"Take a wild guess."

Ruscio tried to hide a smile. "Hear anything earlier?"

"No. She wasn't home, was she?"

"No, she was out on a date. I was with them."

"You think somebody got inside?"

"I don't know. The alarm was on. I'll change the code, just in case."

Ian felt his hands fist. He lifted the right glove and pulled the strings with his teeth, then edged the glove off. He removed the other. "I want to see her."

"When she knew I'd be interviewing the neighbors, she specifically said she doesn't want to see you."

That hurt. "Tough shit. I'm going over."

"You'll have to get through me, first."

"Rick?" Will Rossettie stood behind him. "I need to see you."

Ian shut the door on Ruscio and Rossettie, wheeled around, and headed for the back of the house. By the time he took a shower, the cop cars were gone. Was Frazier? Would he stay with her? Not that she slept around, but would she let another man comfort her like Ian had the last time she got scared. As he climbed into bed, Ian vividly remembered the night she'd come over. She wasn't going to come to him anymore. She'd left instructions with her bodyguard to keep him away.

Well, it was exactly what Ian wanted, for her to leave him alone. *Be careful what you wish for,* he thought, closing his eyes and willing himself to sleep.

But slumber was long in coming.

≈ TWELVE

RICK TOYED WITH his pasta, rolling the cheesy strands on his fork to avoid looking at Will Rossettie. They were seated at Taylor's, a downtown restaurant with a bar that turned into a twenty-something dance joint after nine. Faith said her friends often hung out here, so he'd be sure to be gone by nine. Rick's old cronies often hung out here, too, when they weren't at Badges.

Badges, a place run by a retired police officer and his brother, a former firefighter. A place where Rick used to feel welcome.

As if reading his mind, Will said, "We shoulda gone to Badges." He glanced around at the wooden walls and peanut-shelled floors. "This place reminds me of the seventies."

Rick said nothing; he stuffed a forkful of pasta into his mouth, not even enjoying the alfredo sauce, which he used to love.

"But you won't go there, just like you won't help out with the camp."

"The camp's closed," Rick finally said.

"There's work to be done this fall and over the winter, as well as fund-raisers like the one Lisel's doing."

"Look, Will, I've done enough damage to the camp."

"Because of you, nothing happened to Hale's Haven. That fucker was going to torch it. You stopped him."

"I *helped* him."

"He blackmailed you. And you needed the job to support your mother and—"

"Will, don't." It made his stomach queasy to talk about how he let Steele use him. He'd found out something Rick had done and said he'd get him fired if Rick didn't help him sabotage Noah Callahan. Though Rick had eventually blown Steele in, he was still guilty as hell. He set down his fork and sipped his beer.

"Hell," Will said, like a father noticing the gesture of a child. "Eat. We'll change the subject."

So Will wouldn't feel bad, Rick picked up his fork and ate. He'd already caused the man enough grief.

"No prints off the letter Lisel got, right?"

"Zilch." He chewed a bit, then asked, "Where should we go with this, Will? I can't keep her under surveillance forever."

"The fan will screw up. They always do."

"Don't we all?"

Rick didn't realize he'd said the words aloud until Will rapped his glass down onto the table and some of his beer sloshed over the side onto his hand. "Jesus Christ, boy, I hate when you do that to yourself. You made a fucking mistake. You paid for it. Get rid of the hair shirt you're wearing."

If only it was that easy. But Will didn't know the worst of his sins. Nobody did, except Carla Lopez. And Stan Steele, whose incarceration was deep and permanent. "How's Carla doing?" he asked Will.

"Good. She misses her old partner, I think."

"Yeah, I miss her, too." They'd been friends before they made the mistake of heating the sheets together. Sex really messed things up.

Come over to my place tonight. I'll fix you dinner. I want to get to know you better.

Faith thought she wanted more than dinner, though. Suddenly he was bombarded by the feel of her in his hands the night he'd kissed her under the tree. He coughed to dissipate the sensation.

"Speak of the devil." Will's words brought him back to reality.

Faith was here? His head snapped up. No, it was Carla with a couple of other female cops. She stumbled a bit when she saw him, said something to her friends, and approached their table. "Hi, Chief. Rick."

"Carla."

"Hey, Car," he said. "How are you?"

"You said you'd call," she blurted out.

"I know. Sorry. I been busy."

"Buy me beer out in the bar before you leave?"

"Sure."

"Promise."

"Yeah, I promise."

An hour later, Will extracted his own promise from Rick. "Stay in touch, boy," he said gruffly as they stood.

"Yeah, sure."

"And think about helping at the camp."

"Okay."

"And about forgiving yourself."

He had to smile. "Yes, Dad."

When Rossettie left, Rick went out to the bar and spotted Carla downing shots. She was alone now; her friends must have left. He approached her. "Hey, girl. Hittin' the hard stuff?"

"No reason not to."

"You drive?"

"Nope, Macy did."

"How you getting home?"

She pivoted then, and leaned her elbows against the bar. The action pulled her skimpy top tight across her breasts. "I was hoping you'd take me, lover boy."

He watched her. She was lovely, with her smooth olive skin, black eyes, and curly brown hair. He tried to remember what *she* felt like when he touched her, but he couldn't. Jesus. He'd lost count of the number of times he'd slept with her, yet he couldn't recall the feel of her. Whereas he'd only kissed Faith . . .

No doubt about it; he'd been too long without a woman. He

glanced down to where Carla's top had ridden up from her jeans, to reveal a pierced belly button and taut muscles. He wondered what Faith's stomach would feel like. Muscular, but soft, he bet.

Disgusted by the direction of his thoughts, he made a decision. "I'll take you home, Car. Order me what you're having first, though."

Her eyes sparkled with sexual promise.

Too bad it did nothing for him.

Still, he gave it his best shot. He stayed with her, though he just had one Cutty Sark and a beer. They talked about nonsense stuff, which became more nonsensical the drunker she got. Finally, he straightened. "Time to take you home, girl. You're hammered."

She giggled. They left the bar arm in arm, though he was bearing most of her weight. Outside, she shivered in the cold air. He tugged her close. "My car's right there."

She lay her head on his shoulder. "I'm tired," she said.

"Mmm." He practically dragged her to his van. When they reached it, before he could get her inside, she slid her arms around his neck and kissed him.

What the hell? he thought. He kissed her back. And felt nothing. "Get inside," he told her when he pried her off him.

"Anything you say." Her words were slurred; she waited till he opened the van. Giggled when he assisted her in. Kissed him again before he could get the door closed.

He pivoted to circle the back of his van and looked up from his keys. Right into eyes so green he could see their color in the glow from the parking lot lights.

They were full of hurt.

"HELLO, FAITH." RICK'S voice was raw. His expression was startled.

"Hi." She looked past him into the car. "Officer Lopez have too much to drink?" Damn, her voice was tinged with a hurt she had no right to feel. One she felt, nonetheless. Rick was with another woman.

"Yeah. I'm taking her home." A myriad of emotions played tag on his face.

She shifted from one foot to the other. "I didn't know you were dating her."

"You keeping track of my social life?"

"No. I—" Oh, God, she could feel tears clog her throat. She fought them back. "Pilar chatters on about you, is all."

From behind her, Nancy coughed. "Come on, Faith, the others are meeting us inside." Nancy's tone was cold.

He stepped back. "Go ahead."

Just then the window rolled down. Carla's words were slurred when she said, "Come on, big guy. I wanna get laid."

Rick winced. Nancy swore, and Faith just stood there. Upset over a guy who was routinely screwing other women. "Um, I won't keep you."

She pivoted fast and caught up with Nancy, who'd gone several feet before she waited for Faith.

Rick called out from behind her, "Faith?"

She stopped and glanced over her shoulder. He looked so handsome standing there in a thermal red chamois shirt with his bomber jacket over it. His hair was messy. From the other woman's hands? "Yes?"

He stared at her for a long time. "Nothing. Have a good night."

"Sure. You, too." She cursed the fact that her voice cracked on the last word.

Nancy grabbed her arm and pulled her away. "Get it together, girl."

She bit her lip so hard she tasted blood.

Nancy dragged her around to the entrance, inside but instead of going into the bar, she pulled her into the bathroom. "Sit and put your head between your knees. You look like you're gonna faint."

Faith shook off the upset. "I'm not. I was just . . ." She walked over to the sink, wet a paper towel and blotted her face. "I was just surprised. I didn't know he was still dating her."

"Still?"

"Yes. She's his ex-partner. Pilar said they were hot and heavy once." She choked on the last word. "Oh, God."

"Faith." Nancy was next to her. "What's happened between you two to make you so upset? Last I knew you said you wanted to play footsies with him and he wasn't buying."

"He isn't buying. It's just that we shared some things. I thought he was opening up to me."

"He's bad news. He's going to hurt you, girl."

Faith shook her head. "No, don't talk about him like that."

"He already has. Look at you, tonight."

She didn't need to stare in the mirror. She knew she'd blanched. Felt sick when she saw another woman kiss him. Was he going to sleep with Officer Lopez tonight?

"I'm a jerk. I thought I was making progress being his friend at least. Hell, I wanted more. But it was all in my mind. He said he wasn't going to play nice."

Nancy leaned against the counter. "Well, he's been giving you mixed signals. Like with the bookshelves."

And the tender hug afterward. Though he'd been distant all week, she'd hung on to the fact that he cared enough to build her the shelves. "My fault, though, really. He said he didn't want anything to do with me that way."

In an uncharacteristic move—Nancy was tougher than female prison inmates—she reached out and smoothed a hand down Faith's hair. "His loss. Come on, let's go out and meet the rest of the gang. And dance."

Faith followed Nancy out to the bar and sat down with her friends. She had a glass of wine, danced some, chatted with everybody. By ten she was feeling better. Okay, so he was dating—screwing—other women. Obviously he'd meant what he said about not being interested in her. When she thought about how he'd kissed her, asked her to stay with him in the van that night she brought him food, and then built the shelves, she told herself that she'd made those things into more than they really were. He hadn't actually given her much encouragement. It was all in her mind.

Which was why when she'd just finished dancing with Tim, she was shocked to feel a tap on her shoulder, stunned to turn around and find Rick behind her. "Can I cut in?" was all he said.

RICK PULLED FAITH into his arms when another song began. "Don't say anything."

"Okay."

"I shouldn't have come back."

"No?"

He drew her even closer.

"Why did you?"

"It's complicated."

She laid her head on his chest.

The music swelled around them. It was a jazzy blues, something Rick had played on the sax but couldn't remember the name of. His chin rested against Faith's hair and its flowery scent, innocent and alluring all at once, wafted up from the wheat-colored mass. She'd curled it tonight and it looked sexy as hell. Other guys had noticed, too; he'd been inside by the door for a while, watching her dance with them.

He'd been right—he shouldn't have come back; he shouldn't have asked her to dance. He shouldn't be holding her like she was his. Briefly, that image, of Faith belonging to him, of spending mornings with her, dinner with her parents, picking her up from work—all the ordinary things ordinary men did—assaulted him. He sighed with it and tightened his grip on her. Those things were never meant to be.

Tonight he'd convince her of that.

When the song ended, she drew back and smiled up at him. It was an angel's smile. With a hint of mischief. "So, what now?"

"Did you drive here?" He knew she didn't. He'd checked the parking lot for her sassy purple Saturn.

"No, Nancy picked me up."

"I'll take you home."

She touched his arm like a lover would. "All right. Let me just tell Nancy."

Who was throwing daggers with her eyes at him. Faith crossed the room; she had on a cute little black and pink skirt, and a tight pink sweater. Not her usual style. Both hugged her curves, accented them.

He moved to the back of the dance floor and watched Nancy shake her head, glance venomously at Rick, touch Faith's arm. Faith kissed her cheek, and headed back to him. She wore shoes with a high heel, so she was a little taller tonight, and they did great things to her hips when she walked.

"Let's get your coat."

"I didn't wear one."

She needed a keeper. "It's mid-October."

Leaning into his arm so her breast grazed his biceps, she whispered, "You can keep me warm."

"This isn't what you think, Faith."

"No?" They exited Taylor's and headed to the parking lot. The wind picked up and played peekaboo with her skirt. He caught a glimpse of thigh and groaned.

He groaned even louder as the pretty ruffled hemline hiked up to kingdom come when he helped her into the van. He rounded the front and climbed in. "Don't talk, okay?" he said as they headed for her house.

"Whatever you say."

Reaching out he hit the CD button. The Rippingtons came on and the jazz soothed him on the way back to the parsonage. When they hit the driveway, passed the main house, and pulled up to the carriage house, she reached for the door handle.

"No, don't, I'm not coming inside."

Exasperation etched itself out in her features, visible from the porch light she'd left on. "Rick, if you think I'm letting tonight end without talking about why you came back, you're crazy."

He ran a hand through his hair and expelled a ragged breath. "I am crazy."

Her hand covered his where it rested on the steering wheel. "Why *did* you come back?" Her tone was so soft, so enticing he bet she could melt a hardened suspect in interrogation better than he could.

He had to tell her the truth. Make her understand the rest of it. "I couldn't . . . Faith, I . . ." He turned to her, taking both her hands in his. "Honey, your face, when you saw me and Carla, you were hurt. We gotta talk about that. You can't get attached to me like this. You can't let me hurt you like that."

"Did you sleep with her?" She glanced at the dashboard. "You had time."

She was so innocent. "I'm not going to answer that."

"You didn't. I know." She smiled, and his heartbeat speeded up. "You wouldn't have come back if you did."

"Oh, baby, that's where you're wrong. I've done a lot worse things than that."

"I don't care what you've done, Rick."

"You have to." He swept his hand to encompass both of them. "This is getting out of hand."

"What is?"

"Us getting closer. Spending time together. Doing things for each other."

She shook her head.

"I don't want the power to hurt you, Faith. Christ, we've only known each other for a few weeks." What would happen if it continued? "I'm going to ask for another community service placement."

"You already did that."

"I'll push harder."

"If God wants this thing between us to happen, Rick, you're not going to be able to stop it."

"God would have to be out of His mind to want this to happen."

"He works in mysterious ways."

"No. Look, *querida,* you were *hurt* tonight when you thought I was with Carla. And I hated—" He caught himself just in time.

"When you found out about Sam."

He hit the steering wheel. "Your fiancé."

"He isn't."

This wasn't working out like he planned. His voice rose a notch in frustration. "Well he should be."

"Rick, you can yell at me all you want, it doesn't change the fact that you've come to care about me, about my feelings. Or you wouldn't have built those shelves for me. You wouldn't have come back tonight."

"If I led you to think those things, I made a huge mistake." He nodded to the door. "You can go in now."

She giggled and shook her head, sending blond silk into her eyes. Before he could unscramble his brain, she surprised the hell out of him by throwing herself over the gear shift, and straddling his lap. She only fit between him and the steering wheel because he needed the seat as far back as it could go for leg room.

Rick was bombarded by sensation. She was heavier than she looked. Her weight settled into him, her crotch nestled right into his. Of their own accord, his hands went to her waist, found it supple and taut and so female he was stunned by his reaction.

A reaction she was privy to. Leaning over, so her breath fanned his ear, she whispered, "Unless you have wonderful recuperative powers, you didn't sleep with the lady cop."

"Faith."

Her mouth still near his ear, she coaxed, "Tell me, please, at least that."

He tried not to answer. But her scent, the feel of her, seduced him. "I didn't. But I'm not going to sleep with you, either."

"I'm not ready for that yet." She tongued his ear, and he jolted into her. His hands gripped her even tighter. "I just wanna neck in the car some."

"Don't do this. Please."

"You came to me, Rick."

"I can see now what a stupid move that was." But he didn't let her go.

She kissed the small scar on his cheek. "Tell me how you got this. I want to know everything about you."

"No, no you don't."

She brushed her lips over his. "Yes, yes, I do."

How wrong could she be? If she knew about him, she'd never look at him like this again. Never let him hold her like this again . . . if she knew.

And suddenly, in the dim light of the car, Rick himself knew that *that* was the way to end this. Not with some misconceived notion of picking her up, erasing the hurt he'd caused, and sending her on her way. He'd tell her what he never told anybody before and be done with it.

Now she was nibbling on his neck. It felt so good, his hand went to her head and cuddled her close.

She inhaled him, like she had that night he'd given her his jacket. "I love the way you smell." She ran her hands over his pecs. "The way you feel. I want to touch your bare skin, Rick."

He'd stop her in a second. He would. And tell her. But just for a minute, he'd let himself hold her. This one last time.

And then her mouth closed over his.

Faith could only feel. His lips were soft and met hers with gentle pressure. She weaved her hands in the hair at his nape and leaned farther into him so her breasts brushed his chest. His arms banded around her waist. She cursed the sweater she wore until his hands slid under it. She moaned at the feel of his callused fingertips grazing her, learning her. Her own fingers went to his shirt. Fumbling, she unbuttoned it and slid her hands over his bare skin. His chest was sprinkled with coarse hair and felt so male, had so many hard planes and indentations, that she knew she could spend forever exploring him, just like this. All the while, their mouths melded. His tongue was inside now, causing live sparks to shoot through her. She squirmed on his lap, eliciting a groan from him so loud it made her smile.

His mouth left hers, found her neck, and sucked. Hard.

She startled. "Ohh, God, Rick . . ."

"Me vuelves loco . . . bebé . . . " His hands, which had been roaming her back, slid to the hem of her sweater and pulled it over her head. Cool air on her heated skin made her shiver. He buried his face in her breasts, nibbled at the black lace there.

"Take my bra off, Rick. I want to feel your skin next to mine.

Expertly he undid the hook, dragged the lace away, and yanked her to him. Skin meeting skin . . . male to female . . . nothing had ever felt more right in her life. She told him that.

Suddenly, she was enfolded in his arms, snuggled to his chest, stopping all his movement and hers. "No more," he said.

Still fueled by heady passion she'd never experienced in her life, she said, "No way." She tried to break free of the tender imprisonment that kept her from moving.

"Mi amor, calm down. Stay still for a minute."

"I don't want to."

"You have to." His voice was ragged. "I don't know what happened here, but it's got to stop. I need to tell you something."

Drawing in a steadying breath, she rested her face on his chest. "Okay. Only if we can we go back to this afterward."

"You won't want to."

She pulled away, and his gaze dropped to her breasts. He swallowed convulsively, and she knew with a woman's heart he wanted to touch them, take them in his mouth. She tossed back her head and let him stare. "I'll make you a deal. I'll stop, and you can make this big confession; then, if I want to go back to this, you have to do it."

"All right. But you won't want to." He gulped. "Please, get dressed. I can't stand this."

She laughed, hugged him hard, and reached for her sweater. She slid it over her head.

"Let's go into the carriage house."

"Why?"

"I want to see you clearly when I tell you this."

Her heartbeat speeded up. She didn't like the sound of that. "All right."

"Give me a minute, here. Okay. Go open the door and get inside."

"You won't leave?"

"No, I'm going to do this. It's the only way."

Shaking her head, she climbed off him—loving the way he groaned again—and exited the car. Shivering in the cool night air, she let herself into her house. He joined her a few minutes later, definitely looking more composed.

Which was not at all what she wanted. She wanted him wild and needy, like he'd been minutes before. Well, they'd get back to that.

WHEN RICK HAD to tell Will that he'd succumbed to Stan Steele's blackmail, he thought he'd faced the worst confession he'd ever have to make in his life.

He was wrong. Telling the lovely innocent woman sitting on her tapestry couch, looking up at him with such shining acceptance in her eyes, what a horrible man he was didn't hold a candle to meeting with Will that time. Rick could barely breathe. He felt a pain so deep in his heart, he was afraid he was going into arrhythmia. *Just start, idiot.* He jammed his hands in his pockets, wanting to bolt like a purse snatcher, knowing he was going to steal a part of her innocence now. She thought she cared about him. She was in for a rude awakening.

"I'm just gonna spit it out."

"Okay." She patted the couch next to her. "Come sit."

And have her run away from him like she'd been burned when he finished? No way. "Here's okay." He drew in a breath. "Faith, I did something horrible."

"With Stan Steele. I know about all that."

He laughed, a raw, ugly sound. "No, worse than that. Though this thing led to the stuff with Steele."

Her brow furrowed. Curls fell onto it, but he could see the puzzlement. "Just tell me, then."

"Things . . . they'd been happening to me. Last spring, my life was spinning out of control. I was hitting bottom, I knew it, and couldn't stop it. On top of all this, that day I had a horrible fight with Will."

"Whom you love like a father."

His throat ached so badly he thought he might choke on it. He just nodded and forced himself to continue. "I was on duty with Carla Lopez."

Something flashed in her eyes. Dislike, and a bit of fear.

"I was a sergeant. I wasn't on beat. She was partnered with me, though she wasn't at my level. Some stupid training pilot program. It was a mistake to take her on."

"Why?"

"We'd slept together before. Meaningless, convenient sex, Faith. That's what I'm into."

"Maybe in the past." She said it so confidently he wanted to shake her. He was *so* not the man she saw when she looked at him.

"Anyway . . ." His hands fisted. He'd loved the law so much. It was hard to admit how he'd blasphemed it. "I drank on the job that day. It was the first time."

"Something really bad must have happened."

"The man I am would do that, Faith. Carla and I took a late lunch. We went out to a park on the lake. Bought a six-pack. We'd had a couple beers and she got . . . hot." He could still see the park, shaded by trees like the ones that grew in the parsonage, hear the rush of the water on the shore, smell the seaweed. "We fucked right there in the squad vehicle." He remembered the feel of raw sex in the car. It was so empty. "I know you don't like that language, but it's what we did."

Her face shadowed, but she nodded. "Finish the story. That can't be the worst of what happened that day. It's not good that you drank on the job, but it wouldn't put this albatross around your neck."

"Oh, it gets worse." His voice clogged. "A lot worse. We got a call. But our radios were in the backseat with our clothes, and we were too far gone to fish them out."

"You were on lunch break."

"We were close to the incident. Dispatch knew it. They called us to go."

"Still, you were off duty."

He felt his eyes sting. "Don't do this, Faith. Don't rationalize what I'm telling you. Just listen to it."

"All right."

"When you're on duty, lunch breaks are fair game. We didn't go." He scrubbed a hand over his face. "We didn't go."

"Finish the story."

"When we were . . . done, I realized there'd been a call. We got dressed fast, checked in, and headed over to a house on the lake. It was about a mile down from Hale's Haven . . ."

His heart had catapulted in his chest when he realized what had happened. He'd shirked his duty. He stuck the light on the top of the car and hit the road with unwise speed. Tires screeched as he rounded a corner, and the back of the car fishtailed. He stared ahead. *Please God, don't let us be too late.*

They pulled up to the cottage ten minutes after they finally got the call. Black and whites—fucking rookies—arrived at the scene before he did. He leaped out of the car with Carla behind him. One fresh-faced cop was waiting for him. Another was off to the side puking. And in that instant, Rick knew that of all the mistakes he'd made, this was going to be the worst.

"It's too late," the young cop said.

Rick drew his gun anyway.

"They're all dead."

"They?"

"The parents. The kids." The young boy's eyes teared.

Rick said, "You're sure?"

"We heard the shots just as we pulled up. Went in to investigate."

Rick's first thought was, *I could have stopped this if I got here sooner.* He told Carla to wait there and forced himself to go inside. The smell hit him first. There was nothing like the sickly sweet scent of fresh blood.

It was all over every surface in the kitchen—splattered on the walls, pooled on the floor. A woman lay sprawled on the marble tile, her face missing. Brain matter oozed from her skull. The man was next to her . . . dead, but holding her hand.

Then Rick turned around. And swallowed back the bile. One child was facedown in his Rice Krispies, a bullet having blown off the back of his head. Another child was next to him; her head was to the side. Her taffy-colored curls were streaked scarlet. She looked like Molly from the preschool.

But it was the last that got him . . . the baby in the high chair . . .

"Rick . . ." Someone was grasping his shoulder. "Look at me."

It took him a minute to realize where he was. Faith's house. Telling the story. He must have paced, ended up at the fireplace, gripping the mantle, his back to her like the coward that he was. "Rick." Then he felt arms slide around his waist, and her cheek against his spine. "Rick," she said for the third time.

Finally he straightened. He'd face her if it was the last thing he had to do on this earth. He needed to see the revulsion in her eyes, even if it wasn't in her words or her actions. He needed to see that he tainted her with his weaknesses and his lack of willpower. He knew that would make her stay away from him, make her keep her hands off him.

Slowly, he turned around. And froze.

Faith's cheeks were streaked with tears. Some still leaked from her eyes. Eyes that held not a whit of revulsion. Quite literally he didn't know what to do. He stood there dumbfounded.

She didn't. Once he turned, she stepped close and wrapped her arms around his neck. Still he didn't move. She whispered, "I'm so, so sorry, Ricardo."

It was the name that did it. His real name. He felt moisture well in his eyes. Rick had only cried once before in his life. When he'd lost his badge.

Now, again, he was powerless to stop the flood. "It was my fault, Faith. I was drinking, screwing around. I could have gotten there in time. I let those kids die."

She didn't say anything, just held on tight, soothed his back. Ludicrously he realized she had to stand on her toes to hold him like this. He gripped her around the waist and picked her up. Held her close.

And cried into her hair.

When he finished, he put her down and stepped back. She

didn't say anything. But when he looked at her, there was still no anger or animosity in her face. He didn't get it.

"Come over here." She took his hand and led him to the couch, like she might have one of her five-year-olds. She sat and pulled him down with her. Cradled his hand in hers. "I'm so sorry," she repeated. "I read about it in the papers, of course. My dad went to help out. I didn't know you were involved."

He didn't say anything.

"Rick, the *Herald* said the man had been treated for a bipolar disorder. He was a sick individual."

"I know."

"Are you sure you could have stopped him?"

He looked up at her. "I could have tried. If I wasn't drinking, screwing around . . ."

"Was the timing that close?"

He nodded.

"Then I'm even more sorry. It must be horrible to live with something like that."

He scrubbed his hands over his face. "So now you know."

"Know what?"

"What a scum I am."

She cleared her throat. Here it came. He braced himself.

"All I know is that you're a good man who made a mistake."

Emotion rose in him. "Why does everybody keep saying that? I've made two *huge* mistakes in my life." He looked at her squarely. "You won't be my third."

Ignoring that statement, she said, "What was going on in your life at that time? You said you'd hit bottom."

Might as well tell it all. "First, I helped screw up somebody's life I cared about." He thought of Casey Brennan and how he'd almost ruined it for her and Zach. Again, for just a quick lay. "Then stuff happened with my family. My father . . . he's in prison. He got in some trouble that could have messed up his parole. We needed another lawyer." He drew in a breath. "Then Anita got pregnant again. She had an abortion."

"Where did you get all the money to do this?"

"Stan Steele gave me money to help him make Noah Callahan look bad. But after a few incidents, I refused to go along. Until . . ."

He shook his head. Why was he telling her all this? He'd never made excuses for what happened to him.

She leaned forward. "Please, don't hold back. Tell me everything."

He stared at her silently.

"It's public record that he was blackmailing you. He found out about you and Carla that day, didn't he?"

"All right, yes."

"How?"

"He got Carla drunk, and she told him."

"Damn her."

He smiled weakly at her cursing. "Don't blame Carla. She was young and inexperienced. As senior officer, I took the blame for the delay in getting to the scene. Thankfully, she just got a reprimand after it all came out."

"You did the right thing in the end, though, with Steele. Why?"

"He wanted me to set fire to Hale's Haven."

"*What?*"

"He was sick, Faith, and wanted to torch the place because Noah Callahan cared about it. Anyway, I emailed Eve Woodward. I knew how Steele had done the sabotage. He talked when he drank, too. I let her know anonymously. Later I confessed everything to Will."

"Why?"

"I was guilty. I didn't deserve to defend the law. I gave them enough information to put the guy away."

"And that's why they didn't prosecute you for your part in this."

"Yeah, I was granted immunity. There's still a civil suit filed by one of the rookies that got hurt by something we did. The case hasn't been decided yet. But nothing could be worse than losing my badge."

"Which meant everything to you."

"I didn't deserve it after what I did."

"I'm not sure I agree with that. But it's water under the bridge."

"So," he said, glancing over at her. She was so pretty it hurt to look at her tonight. "Now you know."

"Now I know. Maybe sharing it will make it hurt less for you."

"I don't want to hurt less. But I had to tell you."

"Yes, I can imagine why." He didn't say anything. "You think this will push me away for good, don't you?"

"Of course it will. That's the only reason I told you."

"Then you wasted your breath."

For a second, he didn't know what she meant. Finally, it sunk in. "You gotta be kidding me."

"Rick, good men make mistakes."

He gripped her hand. "I'm not a good man."

"Good men are sorry for those mistakes. Suffer over them. Try to atone for them."

Panic flirted with the edges of his consciousness. This was the last thing he expected. "No, Faith. No."

"I think you should talk to my father about this."

"Why?"

"He's a psychologist, too. He can help you accept what you've done."

"I'll never accept what I've done." He stood abruptly. "We're through here, Faith." He had to force himself not to touch her. "And you and I . . . about what happened in the car . . ."

She stood then, too, and sidled in closer. Ran her hands up his chest. "Yeah, the car. Let's pick up where we left off."

Dios mío. "No."

"We made a deal."

"We did?"

"Yeah. We'd go back to where we were"—she kissed his breastbone, and he felt it all the way through his shirt—"if I wanted to after your big confession." Huge green eyes stared up at him, sucked him in like a sexual whirlpool. She whispered, "I think you had my sweater off."

He gripped her arms, hard. "No way."

"You promised."

Truthfully he didn't even remember the deal, she'd messed up his mind so much. "I lied."

"Not good enough." She was crawling up him now.

Forcefully, he set her away. "I'm getting out of here."

She laughed. It wasn't girlish at all. It was sultry and sexy and made him hard in seconds. "Is the big macho guy running away from little ole me?"

"This isn't funny, Faith."

Stepping back she folded her arms over her chest. "Do you honestly think that after what happened in the car earlier, I'm going to simply walk away?"

Deadly serious, he said, "No, I honestly thought, given what I just told you, you'd run for the hills."

Her eyes teared. "What you told me made me hurt for you. But it doesn't change how I feel about you. I'm not running, Rick."

Staring down at her, he realized he was in deep trouble. "Then I am."

"What?"

"Running away."

"You can run, but you can't hide."

"Emotionally I can hide."

"I don't think so, not after what we shared tonight, both emotionally and physically."

Of all the things she'd said to him, that scared him the most. Stepping back, he circled around her and made his escape. He strode outside, slammed the door, and reached his car without her trying to stop him. At the van, though, he stopped and leaned his forehead against the cold steel.

What the hell had just happened in there? What had he done?

 # THIRTEEN

FROM THE BACK of the academy auditorium, Lisel had sat and watched Ian give a lesson on the possible threats terrorists might employ. She'd been dumbfounded as he discussed biological, chemical, and radiological agents that could be used against the United States. It chilled her when he discussed another plague and other diseases that could be unleashed on the U.S. population.

"He's a pretty good teacher, isn't he?" Rick commented to her just as the presentation ended.

"Um, yes, he's very good." Actually he'd been brilliant. She was mesmerized watching him work the audience. Especially when the guys had gotten nervous about the subject matter. She'd been right, he could help save the world with his knowledge.

Rick nodded to the stage. "Sorry you were usurped up there." Someone had gotten room usage mixed up, and when Lisel arrived for rehearsal, Ian had been teaching his class in the auditorium.

"I didn't mind."

"Yeah, I could tell that."

She turned in her seat to face Rick. He was really a handsome man, especially when he was smiling mischievously, like now. "Are you making a comment here, Mr. Ruscio?"

He laughed. "Yeah, Ms. Loring, I guess I am." He shook his head. "Your feelings for that guy are written all over you face."

"Oh, Lord, I hope not."

"He's gotta have a screw loose not wanting what you're offering."

She chuckled. "Thanks." She studied him. He looked tired. "Is the young teacher you're assigned to at the preschool making you lose sleep these days?"

Briefly, he closed his eyes. "She's scrambled my brains is what she's done. You know, I don't get women."

"Well, I don't get men. Maybe we can enlighten each other." Again a grin.

"What's she done?"

"She hasn't a clue what's good for her."

"You want a relationship with her and she isn't buying?"

"Hell no."

"Ah, just the opposite." Lisel scowled. "Why aren't you buying, Rick?"

"She's Little Miss Innocent. I'm The Big Bad Wolf."

"How old is she?"

"Twenty-seven."

"Old enough to know her own mind."

"Tell me about it. I just get her where I want her, and she pulls the rug out from under me."

"You know, you and our instructor up there are a lot alike."

"How?"

"He thinks it's in my best interest to stay away from me, too." She stared hard at Ian. "I'm in love with him."

Rick whistled. "I didn't know it had gone that far."

"And I'm pissed as hell at him."

"I could tell that. What'd he do?"

"He started dating someone else after he told me he wasn't interested in dating at all."

"She must not mean anything to him, then."

"Why do you say that?"

"She's probably safe, so he can enjoy her company and not worry about getting involved. *You* probably terrify him."

"Does Little Miss Innocent terrify you?"

The humor left his face. "Yeah, she scares the shit out of me." He glanced at the stage. "He's coming down here. Want me to head him off like I did the other night?"

"No." She stood. "I think I'll go scare the daylights out of him."

Rick laughed, and Lisel sidled out into the aisle.

Ian rolled up to her. His captain's shirt stretched across his chest, outlining his gorgeous pecs. She loved seeing him in uniform. His color was high, flushed with success. "Lisel, what are you doing here?"

"Don't worry, I'm not following you around. I was supposed to use the stage for my rehearsal."

"I know you're not following me." He glanced back at the stage. "They shuffled me in here because of the number of requests the academy got for this session."

Without thinking, she reached out and squeezed his hand, where it rested on the chair. "That's wonderful, Ian. I knew you'd be good." She nodded to the stage. "I watched some. I thought you were brilliant."

"That's quite a descriptor." His eyes twinkled. "I saw you dance the other day up there."

"I know. I got a peek at you in the back here." *And danced, just for you.*

"Now, *you* were brilliant." He smiled, and it made her heart clutch. "But you've been called that before."

"Reviewers." She rolled her eyes. "Are you coming to the New Year's Eve show?"

"Yeah, Noah got us tickets."

"Ah."

He scowled. "I heard about the letter at your door. And that possibly somebody got inside."

She wrapped her arms around her waist. "It was scary." She sighed. "Combined with that incident outside my condo the other night, it looks like the stalker's stepping things up."

"I'm sorry. Is there anything I can do?"

"No." She looked up and saw Olive Hennessy walk onto the stage. The good humor between them evaporated like mist off the lake. "You're girlfriend's waiting for you."

Again, he glimpsed over his shoulder then back at her. "She's not my girlfriend, Lisel. It was just a date."

She knew hurt flashed in her eyes. "Well, I guess you'v
changed your mind about letting a woman in your life."

"I . . ." He ran a restless hand through his hair. She though
she saw a chink in the armor of his steely determination to no
let her in. He wheeled back and forth. "I . . ."

Two things happened at once. Olive came down the aisle
And Quinn Frazier entered the auditorium and headed towar
them. "Guess you have other commitments right now," he sai
tightly.

Her gaze narrowed on him. When he said no more, sh
thought, *Fuck him.* Rick was wrong. He didn't look terrified a
all.

"Well, I will. I'm inviting Quinn for dinner."

He grabbed her hand before she made her escape. "You'
inviting him, as in you haven't yet?"

"That's right, Ian. I don't have to beg Quinn to spend tim
with me, so he'd come on a moment's notice. And it feels real
good." She shucked off his grip, said, "See you," and walke
away. Her stomach cramped, but she held her head high, lik
any good actor worth her salt.

Rick caught up to her before she reached the back of the au
ditorium. Leaning over, he whispered in her ear, "Definitely te
rified, Lisel."

She shook her head. "I think you're wrong, Rick. But thank
for caring."

BY THE END of her rehearsal, Lisel's stomach was definitel
churning. Rick was a lot of fun, though, watching her, clapping
whistling now that she'd finished. Sharing their male/femal
problems had seemed to lighten him; she also suspected, de
spite what he said, that Faith McPherson was having an effec
on him. A good one.

He stood and made a formal bow to her when she came dow
off the stage. She touched his arm. "You're good for my ego."

"You're a star."

"You have to go, don't you? Joe Harmon's picking me up."

"Yeah." He glanced at his watch. "I've got a date with you
know-who's father."

"Really?"

"Uh-huh. I hope he doesn't have a shotgun."

"You're kidding, right?"

"He's a minister, Lisel."

Looking past his shoulder, she saw someone in the back of the room; she could tell from the outline of his sturdy build that Joe Harmon had arrived. She wondered briefly how long he'd been there. "Looks like you're sprung."

Rick tracked her gaze. "Looks like."

Impulsively, she reached up and hugged him. He hugged back. Just as Harmon approached them.

The substitute bodyguard's expression was more fierce than usual. Lisel was still puzzled by his animosity toward her. Not once, in the several times he'd guarded her, had he been friendly. Maybe he was just the surly type. But she had a hunch it was more than that. And, as always, her stomach clenched in his presence.

Today he seemed even more angry. "Am I interrupting something?"

"What do you mean?" Rick asked.

"Hugs and kisses aren't usually a bodyguard's style."

Rick scowled, shook his head at Harmon, then faced Lisel. "I hope everything goes well. I'll be back on at nine." With a last look at Harmon, he left.

Lisel faced Joe. Damn him. Damn these men! "What's wrong, Mr. Harmon?"

"Not a thing, Ms. Loring."

This time the use of the formality was not friendly at all.

"Like hell."

He stared at her. "All right. I guess I'm just curious. How many do you need?"

"How many what?"

"Men."

Her hands covered her stomach. "Men?"

"Yeah. Notched in your belt. Isn't it enough you got all of Broadway at your feet?"

"What is this about?"

"You tryin' to seduce Ruscio. He's got enough problems without your prima donna antics."

"You're way out of line."

His bushy gray brows raised. "You asked."

Her stomach cramped again, so she assumed a haughty role she knew would get her through this. "My mistake. I'd like to go home now."

Without speaking, he preceded her to the truck. The ride to the lake was thicker with tension than an opening night. Lisel tried to figure out why Joe Harmon saw her as such a man-eater, but she couldn't.

He was driving fast, taking corners too sharply for her tender stomach. "Could you slow down a bit?"

"Used to winding men around your little finger?"

"What does that mean?"

"Forget it."

He slowed down, though; the silence became deafening.

Then they hit some construction. "Shit," he said, maneuvering the cones.

Then they traversed an unpaved road.

Lisel jolted. Her stomach heaved. "Could you please take it easy?"

"Even you can't control the highway, Your Highness."

That was it. "Pull off."

"What?"

"I said pull off."

"I don't need this shit."

"Me either. Pull off the road."

He found a small rest area and swerved the truck onto it, somersaulting her stomach. She wondered if he did it on purpose.

She faced him. "What exactly do you have against me?"

"You gotta be kidding me, lady."

"I'm not. I have no idea."

"You really are a bitch."

"You can't talk to me that way."

"Oh, yeah, I can. After what you did to my boy, I can. You know, I don't need somebody like you in my life. I'm takin' you home, and I'm done with bein' your babysitter."

Her stomach heaved. But some of his words stuck. "What did I do to Ian?"

"Just about broke his heart." He grabbed her chin. "Do you have any idea what it's like for him? How hard it is for him to face the real world, never mind lettin' a woman in, especially after his wife left him because he got hurt. No, of course you don't. You play palsy-walsy with him, make him fall for you, then dump him."

His hand hurt on her chin. "Let me go."

He did. "Gladly."

She clutched her stomach. Tears clouded her vision. "You have your facts confused. I didn't dump Ian; he dumped me."

"My ass."

"He did. I told him I loved him, and he sent me away." She swallowed hard.

Harmon snorted. "You're a good actress, I'll give you that. I almost believe you."

"I'm telling the truth."

"Then he's lying. He told me otherwise."

"Why would Ian do that?" Her stomach, in sync with her brain, questioned, too, and revolted. She reached for the truck door and bounded out.

Kneeling on the side of the road, she vomited.

She was weeping when Joe came over. Drawing in several breaths, she wiped her mouth with her sleeve and looked up at him. "I love him, Joe. I didn't dump him. When I told him how I felt, that I wanted to be more than friends with him, he sent me away."

Harmon's hard eyes watched her. Finally, he said, "Shit. I'm gonna kill him."

He got her in the truck, and they drove home in silence. By the time they pulled into the condo, her stomach had settled, and she was stronger. She said, "Do you believe me?"

"Yeah. I—" He hit the steering wheel. "It even makes sense, now that I've thought about it. Ian's mind frame . . ." He gave her a searching look. "I was wrong. I'm sorry."

She nodded and smiled weakly. Drained, she slipped out of the truck.

Unfortunately, Ian pulled in just as she did, in tandem with the arrival of Mona's car. She watched Joe get out of his truck and stand on the sidewalk, hands on his hips. He wore jeans and a denim jacket; with his hair wild, he looked like an older Rambo. Lisel stayed by the truck as Ian got out of the van, and Mona exited her car.

Ian was smiling when he approached Joe. He held up his hand for a high five. "Hey, buddy."

Joe just looked at him. "You fucking son of a bitch. I ought to knock your block off."

"Well, that's a friendly greeting."

Leaning over, Joe braced his arms on the wheelchair, effectively trapping Ian. "I been treatin' Lisel like shit because of what you told me. Now I find out you're the bastard here. You know, maybe you're right, maybe you don't deserve her."

"I didn't lie. You drew your own conclusion."

He pushed the chair back with the force of his straightening. "It's the same fucking thing." Joe pivoted and started away. He reached Lisel, who was staring at the unfolding drama, just as Mona approached her from the other side of the walkway. For the first time, Lisel noticed that behind Mona was her daughter Jenny.

"Leave her alone, you creep." This from Mona, who at half a foot shorter than Joe, didn't measure up to her threat. Jenny came and stood beside her mother.

Joe stepped back. "I'm sorry, Lisel. Really." He glanced at Ian. "I gotta get away from here before I break something in half. I'll pull the truck over to the other side of the lot where I can still see your place."

She squeezed his arm. When he was gone, Lisel pivoted at the sound of Ian's voice. "Lise, I need to talk to you."

Rounding on him, she grabbed her stomach. "How could you do that to me?"

"It wasn't intentional. I had no idea you'd have any contact with him."

She shook her head. "Maybe you're not the man I think you are."

"Clearly, he's not." Mona grasped her arm, and Jenny flanked her on the other side. "Let's go in, dear."

Lisel left Ian sitting there in the late fall afternoon sunset, staring after her.

Mona opened the door, and they went inside. After disposing of the alarm, she turned to her daughter. "Jenny, go into the living room. I need to talk to Lisel."

Jenny's light brown eyes widened. She pushed blond bangs off her forehead. "I'm not a child, Mom. I can help."

"This is private, honey."

"Lisel's like my sister." She transferred her gaze to Lisel. What did it matter? "It's okay, Mona. She can stay."

They went to the back porch; Jenny sat close to her on the couch. Lisel had often wished she did indeed have a sister like Jenny, though she hadn't felt particularly close to the girl. "Not that I'm not glad, but why are you here, honey?"

"She had a few days off from the hospital, but they lost the leave form. She'd gone to Niagara Falls with her boyfriend. By the time I tracked all this down, she was back, with another couple of days to spare, so she came home with me."

"I hope it's okay," Jenny said.

"Of course it is. You're always welcome here."

"What happened with Ian?" Mona asked.

"Oh, Mona. He lied to Joe. He said I dumped him."

"He's not a good man."

She ran a hand through her hair. "Maybe not. I'm confused." She grasped her stomach.

Mona caught the gesture. "You've been ill."

"Yes."

"Let's get you to bed."

"Truthfully, I'd like to lie down out here, if it's all right."

"Sure. We'll go get Jenny settled." Mona and Jenny stood.

Lisel stretched out. "Open the glass doors, okay? It's warm out, and I like to hear the lake."

When the Mincheons were gone, Lisel closed her eyes. She had no idea Ian could be so cruel. She turned on her side, and tears slipped out onto the pillow. Maybe Mona was right. Maybe he wasn't the man she thought he was.

"GET THE FUCK up."

As dreams went, this wasn't a good one. Ian burrowed into the pillow and willed the voice away.

His upper body moved. Like someone was shaking him. "I said, get the fuck up." This time the voice was louder. And not happy. It sounded like Harmon.

It was. Ian opened one eye and saw his friend standing beside his bed. Joe's hair was more wild than ever, he wore fatigue pants, a green sweater, and a scowl on his face that used to shut up even the surliest of patients at the rehab hospital where they'd met. Ian buried his face in the pillow this time and gripped it tightly.

Joe stripped the covers off of him.

"Jesus Christ, what the hell's going on?"

"We're takin' a trip. Get up, shower, and get dressed."

His eyes closed, he didn't look at Joe. "Like hell."

A silence. Ian knew he didn't win—Harmon always won, which was the very thing that had gotten Ian through rehab—so he waited for the fallout. "If you don't get up now, and come with me, I'm goin' back to New York for good. If you don't care about your own sorry ass, you better care about that poor woman you're treatin' like shit being left without protection."

Ruscio could watch Lisel. But it would be a problem. Besides, though he knew Joe was pissed at him, Ian didn't want his therapist, his friend, to go away.

"All right. At least get me some coffee."

Joe headed for the door. "When hell freezes over."

Man, he *was* sore. Ian thought about why as he showered, shaved, and dressed. Truth be told, he did feel guilty about misleading Joe. And his reasons for cutting Lisel out of his life were getting harder and harder to defend. He got his own coffee and something to eat—he was religious about his diet, because it enhanced his ability to take care of himself—and they were on the road in a quick hour.

Ian sipped his coffee and glanced over at Joe, who had insisted on driving the van. There was a replacement driver's seat, and the passenger side had a lift, too, but it was a pain in the neck to reorganize the whole interior; Joe must have really wanted to play pilot today.

"So, where we going?"

"You'll see."

"Look, I know you're pissed. I'm sorry for not telling you everything."

"Shut up. I don't wanna talk to you yet."

They headed for the city; a tense hour and forty-five minutes later, they pulled up to a building on the lower west side of New York. Staring at the two-story brick structure on Twenty-Eighth Street catapulted Ian back more than three years ago. Westside Rehabilitation Center. He hadn't been down here in two years, and now it brought a flood of emotions that he'd felt when Eve and Marian first took him here: fear, hopelessness, shock. Though his stay in this place had saved his life—figuratively—and he'd volunteered at the center with Harmon until he moved to Albany, Ian could barely contain the wash of recollection.

Instead of being sympathetic, Joe barked, "Good."

"Good what?"

"You're rememberin' what it was like here."

He stared at the building, rubbing the scar on his left cheek. "I'll never forget what it was like here."

"Yeah, well, seems to me your memory needs joggin'."

"Is that what this is about?"

"This is all about you feelin' sorry for yourself."

"I don't feel sorry for myself." He had, though, when he'd gotten to rehab on that dreary September day. He'd signed on to learn the skills he'd need to live the rest of his life, but when they'd left him alone that night, he'd been consumed by anger and bitterness; those emotions were his constant companions for months.

Joe exited the van, and Ian used the car's remote to follow suit. He wheeled slowly behind Joe, who, at the entrance, let the door slam in Ian's face. Jesus.

Inside, they were greeted at the front desk—Joe still worked here one day a week—though Ian didn't recognize the new receptionist. Following the old man, Ian rolled down the hall. He remembered banging his fist on this wall enough to bruise his knuckles. He also recalled that by the time he left rehab, he'd been racing one of the other guys down this very corridor.

They reached the adult male ward. As soon as they entered the large room, Ian was assaulted by the smell. The place was kept as clean as humanly possible, but paraplegics and quads, who made up most of the clientele, had catheters and bowel bags, and the odor was impossible to dispel.

He remembered a guy—Tony—who wore a halo and could barely move . . . "You don't know, Woodward, what it's like to not be able to take a shit, or a piss on your own."

There were more beds ringing the perimeter of the room now. As he stared at the men in them, Ian remembered a survey somebody had done on spinal cord injury victims. When asked what ability they wanted back most, the men said first, the use of their hands, second and third, their ability to urinate and defecate on their own, fourth to be able to sexually perform, and finally, to walk. Ian had been shocked, since the last was the only thing he couldn't do. The notion had sobered him and brought him a long way out of his depression.

A nurse approached them. "Hey, handsome, what are you doing here on your day off?" She kissed Joe in the middle of the sentence.

"Makin' a wake-up call." He nodded over his shoulder, stepped aside, and glowered at Ian. Then he said, "I came to see how one of my guys was doin'. He drove down with me." Nodding to a bed, Joe started over to see the guy he was using as an excuse.

"Oh my God, Ian?" Sunny Stockwell had been Ian's nurse for his two-month stay. Nurses and aides—Joe had assisted her—were everything to patients: caregivers, confidantes, psychologists; they also ran family interference when necessary. Ian remembered many late nights when Sunny coaxed him to talk. He teased her that she must be using truth serum on him because he'd been introverted and quiet for much of his stay.

Sunny threw her arms around Ian and hugged him tight. He remembered her smell, too—Jean Naté bath splash. When he'd left the center, he'd asked Eve to buy a bottle of the splash, on the pretense of sending it to Sunny. But instead, he'd opened it and smelled it, and it gave him such a sense of security that he kept it. For a long time, when he was feeling particularly low, he'd sought the bottle out.

Like a pervert.

"Hey, babe. You're as beautiful as ever." She wasn't. She had a hawkish nose and shoulders like a roller derby queen, but to him she'd always look like an angel.

"Yeah, tell me another one." She ran a hand over his shoulder. "Geez, you look even bigger." He was—his chest had gone from 38 to 42 inches thanks to his grueling workouts.

Her look turned quizzical. "Why are you here? You gonna start volunteering again?"

"Um . . ." He hedged. In many ways, he wished he hadn't stopped working in rehab. One of the volunteers who had helped *him* the most had been in a wheelchair, and Ian believed the guy could actually understand what he was going through. "I got a job."

"Yeah? Where?"

"At the fire academy in Hidden Cove."

Her eyes warmed, like a mother whose child had just brought her wildflowers. "Oh, Ian, I'm so glad." She hugged him again. "You know, we opened a facility in Oberlin, about ten minutes from Hidden Cove."

Ian knew the town. He had firefighters in his classes from there. "No, I didn't know that. They need volunteers?"

"Of course." She nodded to Joe, who was at a young man's bedside. "What's really going on?"

"He thinks I need a kick in the butt."

"Do you?"

"Maybe."

"What'd you do?"

"It's what I haven't done. Joe's trying to show me how good I got it compared to these guys."

"We talked about that, Ian. Just because you're better off physically than most of them doesn't mean you don't have a whole lot of shit to deal with."

He wheeled back and forth. "I know. Man, remember how it was the inactivity that got to me the most."

"Why wouldn't it? Being a firefighter was a physical job. Suddenly you were stuck in that thing."

"Joe got me to box."

Folding her arms over her chest, she chuckled. "Yeah, I was afraid you two were going to kill each other." She watched Joe talk to his buddy. "Is it still the inactivity?"

Ian shrugged. "It's a woman."

"Ah. Your last stumbling block."

Though he'd been married during his stay here, he'd been volunteering when Marian left him. By then, he wanted his wife to take advantage of the family support groups they offered, but it was too late. He'd quit volunteering at rehab and moved to Albany to be with Eve. "Yeah, I sure burdened your soul with all that shit."

Sunny leaned over and kissed him. "Nah, I had to pry it out of you."

He laughed.

Someone called out from a curtained bed. "Oops, gotta go. As long as you're here, make yourself useful. There's a cop in bed three who's never going to walk again. Go see him."

The idea of doing some good appealed to him.

Two hours later, he and Harmon were in the van again. Ian was quiet, thinking about how far he'd come from rehab, even from when Marian had left him. Which, of course, had been the old man's purpose.

Might as well give in gracefully. "Okay, I got it, Joe."

Joe didn't say anything. He kept driving downtown.

"Did you hear me? I said I got the point."

"I don't think so."

Ian scowled. "What are you up to now?"

"You'll see."

Ian closed his eyes. "I'm tired. I want to go home."

"After this." His voice was gruff but held a tender tone that Joe had used in the rehab center in the middle of the night when he'd been on duty and Ian couldn't sleep.

Ian saw why when they pulled up to the site.

Joe faced him, but Ian just stared ahead at the empty air where the World Trade Center had been. Emotion welled in his throat as he remembered: the panicky radio calls, the sound of bodies crashing from jumpers, the suffocating loss of air, and finally the weight of the beam that forever changed his life.

He spent a lot of the three years since his injury not letting himself remember, or feel. Especially what it was like when he was told half of his company—including the rookie under his care and his best friend Bulk Baker—never made it out.

Instead, though, today, in the safety of the car, with Joe next to him, he let himself talk about it. Once he started, he couldn't stop . . .

"First there was the disbelief. When reality sunk in we just did what we had to . . . the chief knew his brother wasn't coming back. They hugged and said good-bye before the kid went in . . . I kept calling for Bulk when the beam fell . . . he'd been right behind me. I think he pushed me out of the way . . ."

A half-hour later, when he finally ran out of steam, he leaned back against the seat and closed his eyes. He felt a hand on his arm. It grasped him tightly. "You didn't die, son. Let yourself live; your brothers'd want you to."

"I know." Tears clogged his throat. He knew his face was wet.

"I'll take you home now."

"Yeah." He took a deep breath. "You know what, though? I'd like to make a stop first."

"You hungry again?" His friend was trying to lighten the mood.

"No. I'd like to stop at the firehouse. Some of my old company's still there."

Joe knew Ian had never been back to Ladder Four.

"Yeah, sure." He started the van.

Ian stayed his arm. "Thanks, Joe. For kicking butt. I needed it."

"Any time," Joe laughed. "Any time."

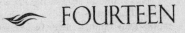 FOURTEEN

EVEN THOUGH HE wore a light cotton sweater, instead of the clerical collar, David McPherson looked every inch the minister as he sat behind the desk in his huge office. The room was a showplace, with floor-to-ceiling bookshelves made of light oak, huge windows, and a desk the size of a lake. Saul, their dog, lazed in the sunlight. "Nice place," Rick said as he took the seat David offered. He felt scruffy here in jeans, a long-sleeved black thermal shirt, and scarred boots.

"The church wanted the office redone a few years ago. I thought we should do something else with the money, but they won." David smiled. "I liked it as it was before because it reminded me of when Peter and Faith were little. They'd come here, curl up in a corner, and play while I worked. It's a pleasant memory."

Rick wanted to ask what kind of kid Faith was but didn't.

"They were different as night and day, those two," David said as if reading Rick's mind. "Peter was a scaredy-cat most of the time. Faith got him into more hot water." He shook his head. Once again Rick was astounded by the yearning he felt—to have had a father like David. "Faith was a risk taker."

"Risks aren't always good."

"No, they're not." Green eyes the color of hers narrowed on him. "I trust my daughter, in most things."

Ah, Rick got it now. What this meeting was about. His heart did a little crash and burn with the knowledge that David wanted to warn the unsuitable suitor away, but at the same time he was glad he'd have an ally in protecting Faith from herself.

"She needs your guidance, now; I know that, David. I welcome it."

The good reverend's brows furrowed. "What do you mean?"

Huh? Damn it, he didn't think this guy would play games. Rick said bluntly, "Look, I appreciate your taking in Pilar. I can't ever repay you for what you're doing for her. I won't ruin that by . . ." Hell, this was uncomfortable.

"By what, Rick?"

"By . . . by . . ." He blurted out the rest. "Spending too much time with Faith!" When David didn't say anything, Rick added, "I know you wouldn't want that."

"Why wouldn't I want that?"

"For obvious reasons."

"Not ones obvious to me."

"Are you for real?"

"What do you mean?" When Rick didn't answer, David sat back in his chair. "Is that why you thought I asked you to come here? To tell you to stay away from Faith?"

"I will, I promise."

"Faith's an adult, Rick. She makes her own decisions." He sighed. "In any case, why do you assume I see you as a bad influence on her?"

"Of course I am."

David shook his head. "You think so little of yourself. I wonder why. I know about the thing with Steele, but Rick, you redeemed yourself there."

"No, I haven't. I've done awful things." That could still come back to haunt him with the civil suit. "Anyway, it's not just that."

Faith's father rose and came around the desk. He took a chair opposite Rick. "Want to tell me about it, son?"

You should talk to my dad about this. He's a psychologist. He went out to the lake to help that night . . .

Linking his hands between his open knees, Rick bowed his head. "I can't."

"I'm a man of God, Rick. I won't judge you."

Rick wanted badly to confess his sins to David. He really did. But if he told him, and the man forgave him, there wouldn't be any barriers between Rick and Faith. And right now, he needed some; he needed backup to stay away from her. "I know that. But I can't tell you." He looked up. "I do need some help, though."

"With what?"

"Your daughter . . . she seems to want . . . she refuses to see me as who I am. She thinks . . ." He stood then, and crossed to the window. Outside, hanging from a tree, was a swing. To give him courage, he pictured Faith as a sunny child, swinging on it. He pivoted to face her father. "She seems to think she wants a relationship with me."

"What kind of relationship?"

"You know"—he jammed his hands in his jeans pockets—"a romantic one."

"Ah, I see." David folded his arms across his chest. Rick couldn't read the look on his face.

"David, you gotta help me change her mind about that."

And then McPherson, the good and holy minister, did something that shocked Rick. He didn't curse. He didn't show understandable outrage. He began to laugh. Rick stood by the window dumbfounded and just watched him. When the mirth subsided, the man got up and crossed to Rick. He clapped him on the shoulder. "Sorry. If you only knew . . ."

"I'm confused."

David glanced out the window. "Maybe I can clarify. See that oak tree out there?"

It was huge, with thick limbs and branches, swaying in the October breeze.

"It was big, even when Faith was little. She begged to climb it. We forbade her to."

"Of course you did."

"She tackled it one weekend when her mother and I were away and neighbors were watching her and Peter."

"What happened?"

"She fell and broke her arm." He chuckled. "We also

wouldn't let her take her training wheels off her bike as soon as she decided she was ready. She took them off herself—again one day when her mother and I were out."

"She fell, right, and got hurt?"

"Sprained ankle that time."

David proceeded to tell him about her other escapades— driving alone with just a permit, going out for the boy's hockey team, several other examples where Faith wouldn't listen to them. In most cases, she regretted it.

"Well, this proves my point. Faith doesn't know what's good for her."

"No, sometimes she doesn't. As it happens, though, this also proves my point."

"Which is?"

"I couldn't stop Faith from doing all those things when she was little. She's a grown woman now. I can't stop her from pursuing you, if that's what she wants."

Rick swallowed hard.

David stepped closer and put his hand on Rick's shoulder. "Even if I wanted to, Rick. Which I don't."

"David, you don't get it. I'm bad news. I'll hurt her."

"Somehow, I think you'd slay dragons before you'd hurt my little girl."

"All right, not intentionally, but it would happen. That's who I am. That's what's inside me."

"God made you good, Rick. That's what's inside you."

He shook his head. "I don't get you people."

David smiled. "Then you'll just have to stick around and figure us out."

This wasn't going at all as he expected. "Why did you ask me here, then? If not to warn me away from Faith?"

"I want a favor."

"Sure, anything."

"I want you to take over the basketball throw at the fair this weekend."

Shit, more contact with this family. Still, he couldn't refuse, after all they'd done for Pilar. "You want me to do Sam's job? David, that doesn't bode well."

David clapped Rick on the shoulder. "God works in mysterious ways, boy. If you'd come to church . . ."

Rick held up his hand. "Whoa. Don't go there. I'm not going to this church or the Catholic one I was raised in. I'll do the fair, sure. But I won't go to church. Don't ask me to."

David nodded. "All right, I'll put that on hold." A car door slammed outside. David glanced out at the driveway that connected the church to the parsonage. "Uh-oh. Our little femme fatale is here."

"Don't joke about this."

"Sorry."

Clatter in the outer hallway. The dog roused and barked. Then Faith came to the doorway. She wore denim overalls and a checked shirt underneath. She looked about fifteen. "Dad, is that Rick's—" She broke off and her face wreathed with smiles. "Rick, hi." She glanced at her father. "Did you come to talk to Dad? I'm so glad."

He shook his head. "It's not what you think."

Her gaze went to David.

"I asked Rick here to coerce him into working at the fair."

An even broader smile. "Did you get him to do it?"

"Of course."

"Super."

Like a drowning man, Rick grabbed for emotional purchase. "I gotta go."

"All right." David clapped him on the back again. "Remember what I said, son."

He just nodded. When he reached the doorway, Faith blocked it. "I'll walk you out."

He was about to say, no, he didn't want her to, when she turned her head. Rick noticed a red mark, just below the collar of her shirt. Vividly he remembered putting that mark on her. It made him speechless.

"I'll be right back, Pop."

"Take your time, princess." David's voice was tinged with amusement.

Rick strode out of the office and down the hall ahead of her. But since she followed, he opened the front door and let her accompany him to the car. "Okay, you walked me out," he said when he reached his van.

"You didn't tell Dad about the night at the lake?"

"No." He looked out over the car's roof at the church. It

gleamed white and pristine in the afternoon light. Pure. Holy.

"Why?"

"I couldn't get the words out."

"You told me."

He just watched her.

Reaching out, she ran a hand down his arm. "I've got to talk to Dad about the fair thing for a while. But stay. Let me cook you dinner at my place."

"Faith, please, don't do this. Nothing's going to happen here."

She lifted her chin. "It already happened."

Reaching out, he skimmed a finger inside her collar. "I did this," he said huskily.

"Uh-huh."

"I'm sorry I was rough."

"You were wonderful." She grasped his hand when he started to pull it away. "I dreamed all night about you. About us together."

"Don't tell me that."

"I'm not giving up on you."

He thought about the stories David told. *Dios,* he wasn't sure he had the strength to fight her. But he could run. "I'm going."

"All right. I'll let you go. For now." Her face softened. "Promise me something, though."

Anything, he wanted to say. Geez, this family could wring blood out of him. "What?"

"You'll think about telling Dad what happened at the lake that day."

"All right, I'll think about it." He reached in his pocket for his keys, but his cell phone rang so he snatched it out. "I gotta get that."

She leaned against the car. "Okay."

Shaking his head, he clicked on. "Ruscio."

"Ricardo, this is Manny. Morales. From Jazzie's."

He turned his back to Faith. "Manny. How's it going?"

"I need help. My sax player broke his leg today. I gotta get a filler for tomorrow night."

"Aw, shit, Manny. You know I don't play anymore."

"Just this once, *amigo.* I'm desperate."

Rick remembered when the thing broke in the newspapers

about Steele. Though Nick Lucas had come down hard on Rick, Manny hadn't withdrawn Rick's contract to play at Jazzie's. Instead, he'd encouraged Rick to stay on. Rick had made the break. "Maybe just this once. What time?"

"Ten."

"I'll be there." He clicked off and turned around.

"You're playing your sax somewhere?"

Fuck, that's all he needed. To share *that* with her. "No, I'm not."

"You're lying."

"I gotta go." He fished his keys out and started to turn; she grabbed his arm, stood on her tiptoes, and kissed his cheek.

It was a chaste kiss. It was almost a friendly peck. But it was so normal, so sweet, it took on a raw intimacy that rivaled what had happened in the car last night.

And, once again, Faith managed to scare the shit out of him.

AS FAITH DROVE through the streets of Hidden Cove to the beauty salon to get her hair trimmed, she frowned. She was making progress with Rick, especially after what had happened two days ago. But things weren't going well with Sam. The phone call last night had been upsetting . . .

"I can't come home for the fair." He sounded upset, which was atypical for him.

"I know, Dad told me. I'm sorry." She was, more than he would know. She really needed to talk to him. Though everything she'd told Rick about her relationship with Sam was true, she knew she owed it to him to tell him she was falling in love with someone else.

"I miss you," he said softly. "A lot."

"I miss you, too."

"Faith, I want you to come down here. To the city."

Yikes, she thought, *this wasn't like him.* "Oh, well, that would be fun."

"Peter's going away the weekend after the fair on a retreat. So the apartment will be ours. Come then."

She didn't think that was a good idea. "I, um, there's a lot going on here."

"Damn it. Don't I have any priority in your life?"

"Of course you do. Sam, what's going on?"

"I'm lonely, and sick of this limbo. I want you down here. We've got to get some things settled."

She hadn't liked the sound of that. "All right, I'll come to New York the weekend after the fair."

Something was different about his attitude, though. She could tell. And it worried her.

She reached Maxima's and parked in the back lot. Hurrying inside, she found her stylist busy with someone else. "Be right with you," Margaret called out.

"No hurry. I'm going to peruse the *Star.* I never get to read it."

Margaret smiled. She'd been doing Faith's hair for years and was a member of the church. Faith was busily reading about all the movers and shakers and how they were getting face-lifts. Around her, Mary Lynn, the pretty blond owner, talked about reusing Glad bags, Margaret told her customers about her daughter's new swimming pool, and young Heather discussed how short to cut a guy's hair. Lulled by the familiar routine, Faith didn't recognize right away the girl who came out of the back room carrying a load of towels. It was Rick's sister, Anita.

"Where do you want this?" Anita asked.

"In the cupboards under the sinks," Mary Lynn told her. "Hey, thanks for pitching in today."

"I like being here." She turned then and noticed Faith. She stopped briefly, nodded, then went to the back of the shop. On impulse, Faith followed her. She found the girl in the washroom, folding more towels.

"Hi, Anita."

Anita's eyes, the exact color of Rick's, flashed with pique. "What do you want, *gringa?*"

"To get to know you better."

She said something else in Spanish that Faith didn't understand.

"Talk to me, Anita. Really, I'm interested."

The girl rounded on her. She looked menacing in black jeans, a dark sweater, and boots. "In me or what my big brother has in his pants?"

"Why would you be so crude to me?"

"Spare me. I saw the way you looked at him. I watched your phony interest in Pilar."

"It isn't phony. I'm coming to love Pilar like a sister."

The other girl's eyes flared hotly. "She's not your sister. She's mine."

"I know." Reaching out she touched Anita's arm. Anita drew back immediately. Still, Faith said, "Rick worries so much about you. There's room for you in all this."

"In what? You dicking around with Rick's head? You slumming with Pilar? No thanks."

"I care about both of them, Anita. And by association, I care about you."

"Forget it. You'll have to seduce my brother all on your own. Not that it should be too hard." Brushing past Faith, she headed for the door. Over her shoulder, she scanned Faith's green corduroy dress. "He'll screw anything in a skirt."

Twenty minutes later, Margaret was cutting Faith's hair, when a woman with two infant car seats entered the shop. Faith had never met her, but the woman was obviously distressed. "Hi, Margaret. My husband had to work, so I had to bring the twins."

"No problem." Margaret smiled at the babies. "They're adorable."

Everybody in the place oohed and aahed over them.

They slept until, just as Faith finished her haircut, and the mom sat in the chair to have her hair washed, one baby started to scream. Anita, standing by the sink said, "I'll hold the baby if you want, while you get your hair cut."

"Oh, that would be great," Margaret told her. "You can take her into the break room in the back."

As Faith was paying, the second baby began to cry. She grinned. "I could watch him."

The woman's eyes filled. "I can't ask you to do that. It's just so hard with two . . ."

Margaret stepped in. "Lonnie, I can vouch for Faith. This will only take ten minutes, and you need to take a breather."

"If you're sure."

"Are you kidding? I get to hold a baby?" Faith picked up the little boy. He was a soft bundle of smells and feels—baby powder, fleece, duck's down skin. As she walked him, he quieted. She caught sight of the back room. Hmm. "I think I'll take him back there, with Anita and his sister."

Margaret mouthed "Thank you," and Faith headed down the

hall. At the end of it, in a small room with a couch and a couple of chairs, she found Anita sitting down, crooning to the other twin. She looked up when Faith entered. Her soft expression turned hard.

Faith said, "Babies are the best, aren't they?"

Anita looked away. Her hand brushed down the tiny girl's cheek.

"Do you want to have kids someday?"

A bleakness she saw in Rick's eyes all the time filled Anita's. God, she'd forgotten. Rick had told her . . .

"I had two abortions," Anita said nastily. "What do you think?"

"I think maybe you felt you had no choice."

"Tell me a preacher's kid approves of that kind of thing."

"It's not for me to approve or disapprove. I can offer my sympathy. It must have been hard."

"It didn't hurt that much."

"That's not what I meant."

The baby Faith held began to fuss, so she stood to walk him.

"What's in all this for you?" Anita asked.

"By *all this*, I assume you mean befriending your family. Nothing but what I told you."

She snorted. "You know Rick likes experienced women. Worldly ones."

Faith touched the place on her neck where his mouth left red marks. "Why are you trying to hurt me? What have I done, Anita? Maybe I can make up for it."

"Are you for real?"

She chuckled.

The twin Anita held began to cry, so she stood and began to walk her.

Faith said, "Rick asks me that all the time."

"You're probably bothering him."

Now that hurt. Because Faith worried about that very thing. She tried to focus on the facts: He kissed her like a passionate lover would; he told her about the lake incident; he couldn't seem to send her away for good. Still, Anita kicked into her insecurities. "I hope not, Anita."

An exasperated sigh. Faith recognized it as one her students used when she'd managed to make them feel bad for doing something wrong or making a comment that hurt someone else. She hid a smile in the baby blanket. Like Rick, Anita had a soft spot she tried to hide.

"There's a fair at our church this weekend. Why don't you come. Bring your mother."

"A fair. Like with booths and games and stuff?" She snorted. "A little too tame for me."

"Still, Pilar's working at a booth. So's Rick."

"My macho brother at a church fair?"

"It's for Hale's Haven."

She shook her head. Just then Margaret appeared at the door. "Lonnie's done. Thanks so much for helping with the babies. She's running in circles most of the time."

As they were ready to leave, Faith touched Anita's arm. "If you change your mind about seeing us, you know where to find me. Or my family." When Anita said nothing, Faith added, "At the church and parsonage on Graystone Lane." She squeezed Anita's arm—this time the girl didn't back off—and left.

On the way home, Faith thought about the Ruscios. She wanted to help all of them. But Anita was right, she had an ulterior motive with the male among them. A very ulterior motive.

God would understand, though. He always had.

THE COOL BLUE notes of his sax floated in the air at the hip club with its exposed pipes and slate floor. The sound resonated with emotion—this was the one place Rick could let it out. In truth, he couldn't keep it in when he blew his sax, which was why he rarely played in public anymore.

But not tonight. Tonight his feelings were out there like a neon sign. The riff of sound shouted his longing, his desire, his need. So he vented. This was the last of the set they'd done; his solo was the finale until they went another round at midnight. Closing his eyes, Rick lost himself in the melody.

The clapping brought him to reality. Even in the dim light, Rick could see the club was jam-packed, and people were standing, whistling, yelling, and calling for more. Manny approached the microphone. "Isn't my man tight?" he asked the audience. More yelling. "Rick Ruscio, on the sax. It's nice to have you back, *amigo*."

Rick smiled. It was nice to be back.

"He'll be up here in thirty, gang." Manny turned to Rick. "Come on, I'll buy you a Molson's."

"Sounds good. Just let me . . ." He scanned the back of the stage, searching for the case he'd dropped there, and his gaze was snagged by something off to the side. A pink sweater. One he recognized. Jesus Christ, it couldn't be.

It was. He stood stock still, staring at her. She was partially obscured by someone near her table, but when the guy moved to the bar, Rick got a good look at her.

She was wiping her cheeks. Reaching into her pocket, she pulled out a tissue and blew her nose. And then she looked up at him. She didn't smile. She didn't turn away. She just stared at him with such profound emotion on her face he was frozen by it.

"Ricardo, you cool?"

"Huh?"

Manny grabbed his arm. "What's up, man?" When Rick still said nothing, just locked eyes with Faith, Manny tracked his gaze.

"Holy mother of God, buddy, who's the babe?"

"Just somebody I know."

"Yeah, I can tell." He socked Rick in the arm. "Go on over, lover boy, and I'll bring you the beer." He shook his head. "She's a little young, but she's a looker."

Summoning anger at her intrusion here, he put away his sax and came off the stage. He was stopped a few times by people praising his music, but he finally managed to get to Faith. When he reached the table, she peered up from where she sat. Intending to rail on her, he simply stared back down.

She broke the silence. "I have never in my entire life heard anything so special."

He swallowed hard. "That's an ex—"

"No!" Her voice rose a notch, and she shook her head vehemently. "I won't let you diminish your play." She nodded to the stage. "It was mesmerizing, engrossing, moving." She swiped at her cheeks again. He could see they were still wet. "I wasn't the only one choked up."

God, he couldn't do this. He couldn't push her away with surliness about something that meant so much to him. He just couldn't. "Can I sit?"

She nodded, and he straddled a chair. Picking up her red wine, she sipped it. "How long have you been playing?"

"Since I was eight. My father played, and when he left, he didn't take his sax." Rick sighed, thinking about those days after Gus Ruscio took off. "I taught myself, then took lessons in high school." He remembered the instrumental music teacher telling him how good he was. "After, when I got a job, I had enough money to keep them up."

"When did you start playing clubs?"

He sighed. "Never mind that. How did you figure out where I was?"

She blushed. It was a perfect opportunity to make her uncomfortable. He didn't do it. "I heard your conversation yesterday out at the van." He nodded. "Then I remembered you said you played at Jazzie's. I looked up their website on the Net, and saw Manny Morales as manager. You called the guy on the phone Manny."

"How'd you know it was tonight?"

"Pilar said you stopped by all dressed up." She scanned his black pants and gray shirt. "You look yummy, by the way." Her eyes darkened. "You had that on the night you first kissed me."

Manny brought his beer. After meeting Faith, his friend left. Rick lifted the bottle and took a long draw. Setting the drink down, he just watched her. Frankly, he had no idea what to do about her.

He saw her hand grip the stem of the wine glass. "Rick, will you tell me the truth about something?"

"Why stop now, sweetheart? I got no secrets from you, it seems."

"Am I bothering you, truly? Pestering you?"

Something about her tone. There was an insecurity there that kicked him in the gut. He wanted to reach out, drag her off her chair, and pull her onto his lap. Instead he grasped her hand. It was so soft, unlined, delicate. "I've told you to stay away from me."

"I know, for my own good. That's different. Am I, like, being a nuisance? Chasing you?"

"Yeah, baby, you're chasing me, all right."

He looked into her eyes and saw hurt flash there.

I think you'd slay dragons before you'd hurt my little girl.
No, not intentionally.

"Faith, you're not a nuisance. You're not pestering me. I'm flattered by your interest. It's not that." Her eyes were huge green pools of wariness. "I don't want to hurt you. If we act on this attraction between us, I'll drag you down. I know I will."

Moisture welled now in those eyes again.

"What? What'd I say?"

She cleared her throat. "That's the first time you admitted you were attracted to me."

He chuckled. Reaching over, he outlined the scoop neck of her sweater. "What do you think the other night in the car was all about, *querida?*"

Now she bit her lip. "I thought I knew. Then Anita told me today I was probably bothering you."

"You mean Pilar."

"Uh-uh. I saw Anita today at Maxima's. I was getting my hair trimmed, and she was working there."

"She hurt you."

"No, she just kicked into something that's been nagging at me. I can be persistent, stubborn. I don't always listen to what other people say."

"No, really?" he said with a smile.

Her grin was thousand watt and it made its way into his heart, settling there with a soft sigh. "I just want to be sure I'm not misreading the signals here."

Letting go of her hand was one of the hardest things he ever had to do. "Honey, what I said doesn't change anything. I still don't want a relationship with you."

Hurt again shadowed eyes he suddenly wanted to make darken with desire, blur with need. Sexual need. She moved in the chair, and her sweater pulled up. He saw a midnight black thong peek out at the waist of her jeans. Jesus.

"Let me rephrase that," he said huskily. "I want a relationship with you more than I want to breathe. But it ain't gonna happen."

Her look changed now. It said, *That's what you think.*

Fearful that he was losing ground, he sought another topic. "How'd you get here?"

"I drove."

"I don't want you leaving a bar in this part of town alone. You'll have to wait till I'm done with the next set. I'll walk you out. Follow you home."

Her eyes did a little two-step.

"Don't get any ideas." He stood and scraped back the chair. "I gotta go."

Still, her gaze locked on him. "Rick?"

"Hmm?"

"You're really, really good. That sax, it gets inside my soul. In my blood."

He closed his eyes. Because at that moment, he realized he was falling in love with this beautiful, precious woman before him.

FIFTEEN

"IAN, WHAT'S GOING on with you tonight? You've been unusually restless since your father and I got here."

"Sorry, Mom." His mother had just come in the living room
and found him staring out the front window of the condo. He
covered the hand she'd placed on his shoulder. "I was looking
for someone."

"Do you know how many times you've gone to that window
in two hours?"

Damn, he was behaving like a high school boy with his first
crush. He peered up at Lila. She looked stunning tonight in a
teal blue silk thing that flowed around her. "Did I ruin dinner?"

"No, of course not. Dinner was wonderful. I love seeing Eve
and Noah and you all together." His sister had brought supper
over when their mom and stepfather had called to say they
wanted to come to Hidden Cove to see their children.

Turning away from the window, Ian faced her. He could hear
Noah and Patrick and Eve's quiet conversation coming from the
dining room. His mother's expression was so full of warmth
and understanding, it made him feel like he could scale mountains. Metaphorically, of course. "Come sit over here," he said,

indicating the couch and leading her there. When Lila was comfortable, he faced her squarely. "It's a woman."

Lila's eyes widened. "Oh, my goodness. Oh, Ian. Oh, I'm so glad."

"Yeah, well, it hasn't been easy sailing. I screwed up. I'm not sure I'm going to be able to fix it."

"Tell me."

He stared at the ceiling and blew out a heavy breath. "She's been interested in me since the summer. I refused to pursue the relationship."

"Why?"

"Because of my disability. I felt I couldn't stick her with this." He slapped the bars of the chair with an open palm. "Hell, I was afraid she'd get tired of it someday and leave me."

"Oh, honey, any woman would be lucky to have you interested in her."

"That's what she said. It's taken me months to get around to that way of thinking." He wheeled his chair back and forth. "Now I've decided I want to see if this can work out, but I can't *find* her."

"What do you mean?"

"She's been gone for two days."

"Gone?"

"Yeah, out of town." He nodded to the window. "I've been watching for her to come back for forty-eight hours." And it had driven him nuts. He could barely sleep thinking about her, and, other than tonight, he wasn't sure if he'd touched any food at all.

"Watching for her." Lila smiled. "It's Lisel Loring, isn't it?"

"Yeah. The actress. Who would have thought?"

"The very troubled actress."

"What do you mean?"

"She's got issues with her parents."

"Tell me about it. Did you remember that from the time we got her out of that dinner with them?"

"No, I saw her last night."

"Last night? Where?"

"At Allen Lawrence's sixtieth birthday party. He and Jude celebrated it in the Hamptons. It was quite an affair."

So that's where she was.

"There were more than a hundred people attending, but not

enough to keep them from bullying Lisel. Along with that horrid Max Strong, who seemed in on the whole thing."

His hands fisted on the wheels. "What'd they do?"

"They announced to everyone that Allen wanted, as a birthday present from his only daughter, for her to do 'Sundays with Lisel.'"

"Damn." His heart twisted in his chest. "She didn't agree, did she?"

"She was very gracious. She said something about considering a show or two. But she was troubled, I could tell."

"I wonder if her stomach was acting up."

"I talked to her a bit. She seemed mostly sad."

"Hell." He ran a nervous hand through his hair. "I tried calling her and Ruscio on their cell phones. They didn't call back."

"He was there, in the background. Her father didn't like it."

That drove Ian's blood pressure up. "What's with them, Mom? How can parents be so callous with their own kid?"

"I don't know, honey." Reaching out, she brushed back his hair. "I could never do that to Evie or you. Though I've wanted to give you a kick in the pants a few times these last three years."

Ian chuckled. "I've been hard to live with."

"Not that. I hate seeing you think less of yourself because of your injury. You're a real hero, Ian."

He thought of his buddies who died in the towers. "Well, I'm alive." He thought of the guys at rehab. "And more whole than a lot of people I know. I'm ready to move on."

"With Lisel."

"If she'll have me."

Lila laughed, the feminine sound tinkling through the living room. "She may make you grovel a bit, but she'll have you." His mother squeezed his arm. "How could she not?"

Car doors slammed outside. Ian pivoted fast and wheeled to the window. Sure enough, Lisel was exiting Ruscio's van.

"She's home."

Lila stood. "You'll want to go over."

"Yeah."

"Go ahead. We'll finish chatting with Noah and Eve—mostly about my new grandchild I suspect. Then I plan to talk Eve into going to the new spa in town that just opened. We'll let ourselves out if you're not back when we're ready to leave."

"Mom?"

She stopped halfway to the kitchen. "What, dear?"

"Thanks."

"For talking?"

"No, for always being who you are."

"Well, that's one of the nicest things anyone ever said to me." She winked at him. "Talk like that to Lisel and you may not have to beg too much."

Ian was frowning as he let himself out of his house and wheeled over to her door. He hadn't considered any of this groveling stuff. Hmm. He was about to ring her doorbell, when a hand grabbed his shoulder. "Not so fast, Woodward."

He sighed. "What is it, Ruscio?"

"She doesn't want to see you."

Pivoting, he faced the big guy. "Look, you're her bodyguard, not her father. I need to talk to her. Now, I may be in this thing"—he grasped the bars of the chair—"but I work out and I box. I could give you a run for your money."

Ruscio folded his arms over his chest. He stared at Ian a minute, then glanced at the door. "Suit yourself. It's worth a try, I guess." And as he walked away, he thought he heard the other guy say, "We're a pair."

Ian rang the bell. She didn't answer. He rang again. Finally the door opened. She had her cell phone at her ear. "It's okay, Rick. Yeah, I'll take care of this. I will." Clicking off, she tossed her head back like she was playing the Queen of England deigning to give audience to a subject. "What do you want?"

You. "I'd like to talk to you." She was dressed in a long one-piece thing made of pink satin. It outlined all her curves. His mouth came damn near close to watering. He couldn't wait to get his hands on her.

"Not tonight." She rubbed her eyes with her thumb and forefinger. "I've had a wretched couple of days. I just want to go to bed."

She could go to bed with him. He hated seeing the fatigue and lines of stress on her face. He'd take care of her.

"You might want to hear this."

She just stared at him.

"It's important."

Sighing heavily, she let him in, led the way into the living room, sank onto the couch, and picked up a mug. He could smell hot chocolate. She didn't offer him any. "What is it?"

"I, um . . ." Christ, he'd been planning for two days what to say to her. Now he was as tongue-tied as a rookie facing a reprimand from the chief. "I've been doing a lot of thinking these past few days."

Still, she watched him.

"Joe got on my ass about some things. Rightfully so. He helped me to see . . . he took me . . . I . . ."

Another heavy sigh. "Is this *going* somewhere, Ian?"

Damn. "Yeah, it is." Reaching out, he took her hand. Until she snatched it back.

"What? Just say what you have to say. If it's more of this 'we can't be together for my own good crap,' I got the message. You don't have to convince me anymore. I'm done with you."

Man, he didn't expect that. "No, that's not what I want to say, sweetheart. It's just the opposite."

"The opposite?" Her voice was wary, and she didn't look very happy.

Maybe she didn't understand. He was botching this bad. But he was nervous now. "I've been wrong about us. I want to see where this relationship between you and me can go."

"Why?"

"Why?"

"Yeah. You've been pushing me away for months. Why now?"

"I told you Joe helped me see some things."

She waited a beat. "So what is it that you want? Some sex?"

"Well, yeah, I want to make love." God, he was dying to touch her intimately. "But not just that. I want to spend time with you. Be with you. See where our feelings for each other take us."

"Where do you want go, exactly?"

He shrugged. "I don't know. I hadn't gotten that far."

Her face flushed. She uncurled her legs, leaned over, and slammed the cup she held down on the table. The loud crack made him jolt. "You don't know. How nice. I told you I loved you, I told you I wanted a life with you, and you come over here tonight to say, 'Oh, gee, I think I've changed my mind. I think I want something with you—sex, yeah, but I'm not sure what else.' What do you expect, Ian, that I'll fall at your feet, jump onto that chair, into your lap and say, 'Thank you, Ian, for wanting to see if we *have* something together.'"

Yeah, he'd pictured a scene like that. But he knew better than to say it aloud with the mood she was in. A mood he'd never seen before. "Um, Lisel, I . . ."

She stood then and folded her arms across her chest. "Well, forget it. I'm sick of you, of my father, of Max, of all the men I know trying to bully me, bend me to their will. I'm done with it."

"It's not really fair to group me with them."

She started to pace. "Fair? Fair? Has it been fair what you've been doing to me? Flaunting other women in my face. All this push-pull, stay away. Well, forget it. I'm not playing any more."

"Sweetheart, I'm not playing."

Her chin came up. "How do I know that?"

Damn, he wasn't used to this. Before his accident, before he was married, women always seemed to be at his beck and call. "I guess you'll just have to trust me."

"Well, I don't trust you. Or any man right now." She glanced out the window. "Except maybe Rick." Leaning down, she picked up the phone and punched in a number. "Hi, Rick, it's me. I'd like Ian to leave now."

"What the hell?"

"Yes. Come in and make sure he does."

He reached for her. "Lise, honey . . ."

Again she shrank back from him.

Ruscio opened the door. "Is there a problem here?"

Lisel looked at Ian. "Not if he leaves. I'm tired, and I want to go to bed."

"I can't believe you're doing this."

"Well, think about it, Ian. See if you can come up with some rationale here." With that, she turned and walked out of the room.

He was staring after her when he heard Ruscio say, "Didn't go so well, did it, pal?"

"Guess not." Hell, his mother had been right. Looked like he was going to have to grovel—big-time.

Problem was, never having done it, he didn't know where to begin.

* * *

"THANKS FOR DRIVING me to the rehearsal, Joe. I appreciate it." Lisel smiled at the older man who sat across from her in her rented van. Wearing jeans and a Nam sweatshirt, he looked fit and healthy. And younger, now that he wasn't scowling at her all the time.

"Least I can do." He swerved into a parking space in front of the condo. "I feel bad about what happened . . . you know, how I treated you." He glanced over and winked at her. "Besides, I get to watch a star dance for free when everybody else has to pay a hundred bucks."

"This star isn't shining very bright today, I'm afraid."

"You tired?"

"I'm not sleeping well."

They exited the van and were on the sidewalk heading to her place when Joe stopped. "Wait for a minute."

Lisel's heart began to pound. "What is it?"

"There's something in front of your door."

Just what she needed. She was still reeling from her father's and Max's badgering for two days, then Ian's unexpected about-face, and now something more from the stalker. Damn it all. Why couldn't people just leave her alone?

She watched Joe approach the box as if he were picking through minefields. When he got up to the door he crouched down, leaned over, reached in, and drew something out. A card, which he read. And began to laugh. He called out to her, "You can come over, Lisel."

Can't be too bad then. She covered the sidewalk quickly. "What is it?"

"It ain't from that kook who's stalkin' you."

"No?"

"Nope, it's from the kook next door."

"I don't understand."

He handed her the card. It said simply, "I'm sorry. Please, give me another chance." It was signed, "Ian."

Looking down, she saw what she guessed were flowers wrapped in green tissue paper. Joe picked them up and brought them inside. In the kitchen, he lifted them out of the box, and Lisel tore off the paper.

The arrangement from Arena's florist was breathtaking. It was made up of tiger lilies, giant sunflowers, huge irises, and a jungle of greens. Lisel had gotten bouquets from countless fans, a senator once, and a diplomat. But none were ever as lovely as these. Or as precious. She brought her face down and breathed in their sweet scent.

"You're jerkin' his chain, aren't you?"

Uh-oh. "No, no, Joe."

"Hey, it's fine by me. He deserves a hard time after what he did to you."

"No, after what he's gone through, he deserves nothing but good things. I overreacted last night, I guess, but truthfully, I am wary. What if I let him in and he rejects me again?"

"That's a risk. If I were you, I'd make him work for it." The older man's brown eyes gleamed with a mischievous sparkle. "Just to show him how important you are to him."

"I'm surprised you'd say that."

"Sometimes you gotta be cruel to be kind."

"Paraphrasing Shakespeare, Mr. Harmon? I had no idea . . ."

"Ah, girl, when you flirt . . ." He glanced at the flowers. "Woodward's dead meat. Still, I'd keep him danglin'."

She laughed as her cell phone rang and was chuckling as she answered it. "Hello."

"Did you get them?" a sexy-as-hell voice said. A purposely sexy-as-hell voice. Seemed Ian Woodward had a few tricks up his own sleeve.

"They're lovely, thank you."

"Can I come over?"

"No."

"Aw, baby, come on. Let's at least talk."

She looked at Joe. He shook his head.

"No, not today. I need more time to think about this."

"What's to think about?" There was impatience in his voice. She could picture him wheeling back and forth in the chair.

"Whether I can trust this new you."

"You can. I'll convince you."

"Maybe." For Joe's sake, she fluttered her eyes. "Still, I want some time." She hung up. "He's not happy."

"Well, long as he will be, eventually, that's what matters."

She knew what he was asking. "I love him, Joe."

"That's enough for me." Straightening, he crossed to her and kissed her forehead. "Ruscio should be here any minute. Good thing. Bet our boy is in the mood for some boxin' right now."

Lisel laughed.

THE NEXT DAY, another delivery arrived. This time, Rick was watching the house, and he intercepted it. He was chuckling when he brought it inside. "I didn't read the note, but I'm guessing it's not from the fan. Open it in front of me, anyway."

She opened the card attached and read, silently, "I want to see you in that big tub of yours. Using this when you bathe. Think of me as the water . . . stroking your bare skin . . ." She began to blush.

"It's from him, isn't it?"

"Yes." She ripped open the package to find a very expensive bath oil, soap, a loofah, and even a bath pillow nestled in a white wicker basket. She loved this particular brand and had lotions from their line.

"He's groveling pretty good."

"Yeah." She looked to Rick. "Should I give in?"

"I'd hold out one more day. It'll make your point real strong."

She took a bead on him. "How are you holding out?" she asked. "With Faith."

"I'm going under for the third time."

"Would it be so bad, Rick?"

He swallowed hard, and his dark eyes got bleak. "I just don't want her to get hurt."

"She'll be hurt more if you don't even give your relationship a try."

"You think?"

Lisel glanced at the bath stuff. "I know."

ON THE THIRD day, Lisel was alone in the condo, as Mona and her daughter had met in New York City to see a show. More gifts arrived . . . DVDs delivered from a store in town—the complete anniversary set of Doris Day films; a box of Swiss chocolates, dark, like she liked them; a leather-bound book of love poetry. There was a note inside it. "Please see me. Talk to me. I have so much to say to you. It won't be in fancy words like this book, but I'll mean every one of them."

Hell, Lisel thought as she read the inscription. Three days had to be enough. She picked up the phone. He answered on the first ring. "Lise?"

"Hi."

"I saw you come home."

"All right, I'll talk to you. When?"

"Now. Come over here."

"I've got to take a shower." She smiled into the phone. "Or a bath, maybe."

"Darlin', you're killing me."

"I am ready to talk, Ian."

"Thank God. An hour?"

"Yes, an hour." She hung up the phone, went into the bathroom, and started the bath. Looking in the mirror, she whispered, "Please God, let this work out for us. Please."

MAN, WAS HE nervous. It was worse than his first date, worse than the first time he did the nasty with a girl in the backseat of his 77 Chevy, and worse than his jitters the night before his wedding. Women had a way of turning your life upside down. He stared at himself in the mirror. The lightweight gray wool pin-striped suit was new—clothing he'd owned before his injury was too small, given how pumped up he was because of his work-outs. He'd asked Noah to go shopping with him yesterday . . .

Got a hot date? his brother-in-law had asked.

I hope so.

Noah's eyes had showed deep emotion. *About time, buddy.*

It *was* about time. Now that he'd decided to risk this thing with Lisel, Ian wondered how he'd stayed away from her for so long. And regretted, a lot, how much he'd made her suffer. Maybe he could make up for it tonight.

When the doorbell pealed a half-hour later, he was ready for her. Or so he thought. She came inside, shed her coat, and made his jaw drop. "Hi," she said, tossing back hair fluffed and curled and begging to be touched. She was dressed in black lace—a short cocktail dress scooped at the front; it skimmed knees covered with misty black silk, and hugged her fanny like a dream. Without a word, he wheeled close and tugged her between his legs. His hands went to her hips, circled around, and flexed on her fanny. He buried his nose in her breasts. She jolted from the intimate contact. He inhaled. "You smell like a garden of wildflowers."

"It's . . ." She cleared her throat. "It's the bath oils you sent."

"I can't tell you how much I want you. How much I want to be inside you."

"Oh, God." She gripped his shoulders.

He tugged her onto his lap. "Give me a kiss. I've got dinner planned, but I need to taste *you* first."

She was breathing hard. "Ian . . ." She cupped his face with her hands. "I can't believe this is happening."

"Believe it."

Before he could lower his head, she bent close and brushed her lips over the scar on his left cheek. He sucked in a breath.

"Shh," she said and kissed it again. "Shh."

And then he took her mouth. It was a deep, wet, tongues-mating, teeth-scraping kiss. Carnal and needy. "Lise . . ." he said against her lips. And kissed her—deeper, hotter, and wetter—again.

"You'd better get up," he said as she gripped him tightly and buried her face in the crook of his shoulder and neck.

"In a minute."

They managed some semblance of sanity when the doorbell rang. "What's that?" she asked, sliding off his lap.

"Dinner. I ordered it from Michel's." He wheeled to the door, let in the delivery boy, who took the lobster, asparagus, and Caesar salad to the kitchen, then left with the fee and a hefty tip.

"Are you hungry?"

"Yes." Her eyes said, "For you."

He grinned, crossed to the sideboard in the living room, poured her some champagne, and handed it to her. "Just a bit."

She sat on the couch. Clinked her glass with his.

"To us," he said simply. "You and me, Lise. I mean it."

"I hope so." She drank the Cristal. "It's wonderful."

Given the state of his body, he was surprised he could carry on a lucid conversation. But they chatted like normal people during dinner. "Hmm," she said, sinking her teeth into the succulent lobster. "This is so good."

He bit into his own but watched her mouth, watched her lick the butter off her bottom lip. "Is it?"

She smiled seductively.

The rest of the meal passed in a blur. They cleaned up minimally, then he grabbed his coat, bundled her up in hers, and led her outside. He wanted to be romantic, to do romantic things for her. Moonlight and twinkling stars seemed appropriate. She sat on his lap and cuddled into him while he pointed out constellations. It felt right.

When they got cold, he brought her inside to the living room and put on a CD—Doris Day's *When I Fall in Love*.

She smiled, but her look was puzzled.

He shrugged. "I never did this. You know, since I was hurt, but I read about it." He held out his hand. "Wanna dance?"

Tears glistened in her eyes. "Yes, of course."

She went to him and eased onto his lap again. His erection, which had subsided somewhat during dinner, raged heartily once again. She giggled and snuggled into it. He moaned, but held her close enough so her hair tickled his nose.

"How?" she asked.

"Put your arms around my neck." She did. Her breasts crushed his chest. He encircled her waist with one arm, like an able-bodied man might do. And then he simply moved the chair. Back and forth, to the right, then left. Halfway through the song, he got the rhythm, and was able to close his eyes and pretend that things were normal. He hadn't realized how much he'd missed simple things such as dancing with a woman.

When the song ended, he whispered, "Look at me, Lise."

She pulled back; her eyes were smiling, though somewhat dazed.

"That song?"

"Mmm." She kissed his jaw. "I love Doris."

"I want you to know something, before we head in there." He nodded to the bedroom. "Which we're gonna have to do asap, or I'm gonna die here."

She chuckled.

"That song. *When I Fall in Love?*" He cradled her cheeks in his hands. "I have, sweetheart. I've fallen in love. With you. I've felt it for a long time." He kissed her nose. "When you told me, in the spring, you loved me? I knew how I felt about you then," he finished huskily.

Briefly, she closed her eyes.

"I'm so sorry I hurt you. I thought it was best."

"I know you did. Please, never do anything like that again, Ian."

"All right."

"Promise?"

"I promise."

Sighing, she lay her head on his shoulder. "Now, take me to bed."

SHE'D DREAMED ABOUT this so many times before . . . she was cuddled up to Ian, in bed, and he was holding her. Darkness cloaked them, cool night air sneaked in from the crack in the window, and the lake's whoosh matched the tempo of his touch—slow and easy. His clever hands glided over her skin, raising goosebumps. He played with the lacy black bra strap (and matching thong), which he told her to leave on for a while.

Smiling, he nipped the lace with his teeth. "Your skin feels like watery silk," he whispered, his voice husky and unguarded. "I could touch it all night."

"I love your hands on me."

There was nothing between them in the darkness. No fear, no caution, no baggage from his injury or her illness.

"Here, honey, lift up . . . mmm, yeah, that's it. Oh, God, Lise, I've wanted to touch you here forever." He cupped her. She bucked; his palm ground into her. "Ian . . ."

A very male chuckle. "You like that?"

"Oh, God."

"Ride it."

Restlessly, she shook her head back and forth on the pillow. "I want you inside me."

"I will be. Not yet. I've waited too long . . ." He eased down her panties and then brought his hand back to her.

Her skin was flush and flashed heat. "Ian. There. Oh,

yes . . ." She went rigid and erupted into his hand. She called out his name, twice. It lasted a long time.

Leaning back, he pulled her to his chest. "You are so lovely when you're aroused. Needy."

She smiled and nosed his chest. His skin was clammy now, and his heart thundered beneath her cheek. He was a solid wall of muscle. "My turn," she whispered.

"How could I ever have denied myself this?" he asked as she pressed him back into the mound of pillows and explored his naked chest; he was so sculpted really, like a statue cut from stone. She licked his nipples, making him jerk. She tongued his navel. He tasted salty. Her fingers trailed down his ribcage, his stomach, lower to encompass his steely length. His erection was hard and hot and heavy—*glorious.* He allowed the ministrations for a bit, then eased her to her back.

"I want you inside me."

"Now, then," was all he said.

"How do we do this, Ian?"

"Lay on your side." She did. Bracing himself on his elbows, leaning over her, his biceps bulged as he took her mouth. The kiss was deep, consuming, as if he was trying to absorb her.

"Scissor your legs, love." Again, she did what he told her.

And then he slid inside her. Gently, coaxingly, tenderly.

For all of thirty seconds. "Oh, God," he bit out. "Lise. I . . . it's been so long . . . I've wanted you so long . . ."

He began to move, slow, faster, fast; then . . . thrust . . . hard, harder. "I can't, I want to wait . . . Lise . . . God, Lise . . . Yes . . ."

He came then, exploded really, in a series of moans and groans, which were the best chorus she'd ever heard.

Afterward, they lay together like husband and wife, Adam to Eve. She buried her face in the crook of his shoulder and neck. His arms were protective and gentle as they encircled her. "Want to sleep, love?"

"No, I just want to savor this."

"Me, too."

"I just want to savor you. I love you, Ian."

"I love you, too."

* * *

THEY DID SLEEP, though, dozing in each other's arms, wrapped up in each other's limbs, luxuriating in the feel of skin against skin, heartbeat next to heartbeat. Once, Ian woke her. She was face-down and pressed into the pillow. His chest grazing her, he stroked her naked back and buttocks. Lingering there, he leaned over and kissed her spine.

"Ian," she mumbled into the sheets.

"Shh. Just relax."

"What . . ."

His hand slid between her legs. She was wet from before, and the scent of their lovemaking surrounded them. "Shh. Lift up. Let me."

She did. He listened to her breathing escalate as he found the little nub that would send her spiraling. She grabbed the pillow, moaned into it, and let him bathe her with pleasure.

A while later, he didn't know how long, he awoke with a jolt. Only her outline was visible in the moonlight streaming in through the blinds. She was straddling him. Her hair was wild, her shoulders thrown back. She might have been a modern warrior riding into battle.

Instead she rode him. "Lisel . . . what . . . oh fuck . . ."

She increased the tempo. Her bare bottom slapped against him, and she braced her arms on his chest. The increase in speed, the sound of her kicked him up to near flashover.

When he burst inside her, the world exploded in his head, piercing light streaked through his brain, and his heart seemed to shatter into a thousand pieces.

He lay awake afterward, just holding her as she slept, promising silently that he'd make this work between them.

And because he was awake, and because he'd left the window slightly ajar, he heard something—or someone—prowling outside.

Dear Lisel,
What are you doing *with that gimp? I can't believe it. You*
need to be with somebody whole, somebody deserving . . .

Jumping up, Julia walked away from the portable computer. Fuck! Her hands were shaking, she was so angry, and it made it hard to type. Crossing to her briefcase, she pulled out some pictures. She always carried them no matter where she was. Smiling, she traced Lisel's beautiful mouth, eyebrow, classic nose.

Putting the relic away, she went to the window and stared out at the water, thinking about what had happened earlier. She'd been careful; she'd parked her car at the other end of the complex and hiked to Lisel's condo. It was dark, so she'd circled around back.

The house looked so empty she'd gotten concerned. She'd waited, then she heard them, outside of Woodward's condo, looking at the stars. She'd tracked them after that. They'd gone to the bedroom and while Julia prowled outside, horrified at this turn of events, the cop had shown up. She'd dived behind a nearby tree, curled into a ball, making herself as small as she could.

The police were watching Lisel because of her. Which was totally crazy. Julia would never hurt Lisel. Nope, *now* she'd save her. Now she had a mission. Something she could do for her idol.

Back at the computer, she began to type again.

Dear Lisel,
He's unworthy of you. You deserve somebody like Ansel in Longshot. *You have to stay away from that guy. If you don't, he'll be sorry . . .*

Love,
Your ever-watchful Jules

SIXTEEN

SATURDAY DAWNED CRISP and sunny for the end of October, just perfect for the church's Fall Fair. Rick stared out at the fellowship hall and shook his head. He'd done the same thing when he'd donned the shirt he wore—a forest green T, lettered in bright yellow with "Help provide their haven." On the back was scripted both the fire and police department insignias, and in front, Hale's Haven's prominent logo of a rainbow with a pot of gold at the end. Trying not to think about how out of place he felt in this setting, Rick was lining up the basketballs in his booth when someone spoke from behind. "Hey, handsome."

Pivoting, he smiled at Lisel Loring. She was radiant today in loose blue jeans and a pretty red angora sweater. He glanced beyond her shoulder, where Joe Harmon and Ian Woodward surveyed the fishing booth.

Rick arched a brow. "So it went well the other night?"

Her whole face glowed with suppressed sexuality. "It was wonderful." She nodded to the next booth over, where Pilar and Faith were setting up to do face painting. "The water's great. Does your presence here mean you're wading in?"

"I told you, I'm drowning." It didn't feel too bad, though.

After Friday night when Faith listened to him play the sax, he knew he wasn't going to be able to keep her at arm's length anymore. "But it's okay."

Reaching out, she squeezed his arm. "I'm glad."

Woodward and Harmon approached them. Ian's gaze narrowed on Lisel's hand on Rick, and he said with amusement in his tone, "Back off from my woman, buddy."

Damn, the sucker had it bad. But the way Lisel stared at him, the way he tenderly took her hand, made Rick's cast-iron stomach go to mush. He held up his arms arrest style. "No problem."

A bundle of energy zoomed over to them. Noah's granddaughter, Abby. He saw the chief had just arrived, too, with his wife. "Papa says come quick, Ian. They got darts."

"Darts?" Lisel asked.

Even to Rick's male eyes, Ian's smile was flirty and sexy. "Just one of my many talents, babe."

"Ride me over." Not waiting for an answer, Abby jumped on Ian's lap. They started to wheel away.

"I'll be right along," Harmon told them. "Stay in sight." When the three of them were gone, he faced Rick. "I heard about what happened last night."

"The police didn't find anything. The beat cop who was on for a few hours before I came back said he was checking the rear of the house. He thinks Woodward heard him nosing around."

"Don't sit right with me."

Since gut instinct had saved Rick's life a time or two on the streets, he asked, "What would you do?"

"I don't know. Just keep the guard on her, I guess." He nodded to the dart booth. "Ian don't look like he's gonna leave her side any time soon, so we got another man around her at least."

When Joe left, the basketball booth got busy. After an hour, Rick noticed a couple of men had been lingering around for a while; he recognized one as Nick Lucas, the reporter who broke the story on Stan Steele. He approached Rick when there was a lull. "Strange seeing you here, Ruscio."

"Yeah. You wanna play?"

"No. Just wanted to get a glimpse up close and personal what you were scamming this time."

"I'm not scamming anything."

"Yeah, sure, like at the preschool."

"What about the preschool?"

Another guy who'd been hanging around came up behind the reporter. "Looks like you got a customer." Lucas walked away, smirking. Rick wondered what he meant about A Time to Grow. But the other person distracted him.

The man looked familiar, but Rick didn't think they'd ever met. "Hi. Ready to play?"

Blue eyes, hooded and suspicious, focused on him. "I'm Peter McPherson."

"Oh, hi." Rick held out his hand, and Peter hesitated a minute then shook. "Rick Ruscio."

"I know who you are. My sister can't seem to talk about anybody but you." In contrast to David McPherson's implied blessing last week, the brother's comment held a note of warning.

"She dotes on Pilar, that's probably why."

Briefly, Peter's gaze swung to their booth, then back to Rick. "She always wanted a sister."

"I don't know, she speaks highly of her brother."

No smile. "You seem to know her pretty well." Again, displeasure in his tone.

"I—"

"Hey, Peter Piper. How you doing?" Faith had approached them. The green T-shirt she wore was loose enough, but she had on eggshell-colored jeans that would snag any red-blooded male's attention.

Rick wanted her with an intensity he'd never known before. And, God help him, he was close to taking her.

Big brother slid an arm around her shoulders. "I'm doing great." He kissed her forehead and glanced meaningfully at Rick. "I wish Sam could have come."

Rick felt his insides tighten, like he'd done too many sit-ups.

"He misses you, princess," Peter added.

"Yeah, I talked to him last night." She reached for Peter's hand. "Come on, I'll introduce you to Pilar." She winked at Rick as they walked away. "I'll be back."

He watched her leave with her brother. Peter was about half a foot taller, and their hair was the exact same color. His broad shoulders dwarfed hers, but his arm kept her close. This was a tight family. How could they ever accept him? As he fell headlong into caring about Faith, Rick had begun to think maybe things could work out, but seeing her in her element, hearing the first sign of distaste from her family . . .

Please stop putting up barriers, she'd said after he followed her home from Jazzie's. He refused to go inside the carriage house, but she'd insisted he walk her up to the door.

Weakened by her wholehearted acceptance, he'd leaned against the porch. *Maybe I should.*

She'd practically leaped into his arms, and by God, he couldn't let her go. He'd kissed her senseless and promised to think about them having a relationship.

The fellowship hall got more crowded, and Rick turned his attention to the game. After a while, Megan Hale and Mitch Malvaso stepped up for some not-so-friendly competition. Mitch's kids and mother, Sabina, were with them.

"Come on, Dad," Bobby said, hooking an arm around Mitch's neck. "Make us men proud."

Sabina smiled and mumbled something in Italian.

Trish muscled her way in. "No way; he never beats Megan when they play in the driveway."

"I do, too." Mitch's tone was wounded, as he fit the ball to his hands. Rick heard him lean over and say to his wife, "If I win, you gotta do whatever I say."

"What else is new?" Megan whispered back. She picked up another ball and held it while she watched him. Ten minutes later, a line was starting to form, so Mitch was forced to capitulate.

"Good going, Megan," Rick said.

Her family started away, but Megan stayed back. "Nice to see you here, Rick. I mean it." He just looked at her, the woman who had everything he'd lost. "I hope you'll volunteer next summer at the camp."

His glance strayed to Faith, who was painting Pilar's cheek. "Maybe."

It was fun, working the booth, chatting like a normal man with townspeople. Except for the reporter who never came back, and of course Peter's disapproval, nobody shunned him, nobody seemed to be gossiping about why a guy like him would be here.

Rick took a break and approached the girls' booth. Pilar had gone to the ladies' room, so Faith was alone.

"Ah, there he is." Faith leaned over and grabbed his chin. "Want me to paint a bull on your face, buster?"

"No way, lady."

He heard behind him, "I'd like a unicorn on mine."

Stunned at the softly spoken words, Rick whirled around and saw Anita standing behind him. "What . . . what are you doing here?"

She blushed. She was dressed simply tonight in jeans and sweater underneath her denim jacket. And she wore almost no makeup. "I, um . . ."

Faith came around the outside of the booth before Anita said any more and hugged her. "I'm so glad you came."

Anita rolled her eyes, but her tone revealed something much more than what her gesture indicated. "I feel stupid."

Rick stared at her. "I don't understand."

"Faith invited me. Don't worry, I just wanted to see Pilar."

"Why would I worry? It's great that you're here."

"It is?"

Reaching for her, he hugged his sister. "Yeah." He added, *"Te amo, pequeña hermanita."*

"Oh, my God. Nita?"

Rick let Anita go just in time for Pilar to throw herself at her sister. "Nita, you came. Faith told me she asked you. Can you stay? You could help in our booth. You could sleep over, in my room, I mean Faith's old room." By now, Pilar's eyes were moist.

Anita smiled weakly. "Let's just take this one step at a time. I want a unicorn on my face."

"Okay, I'll do it. Come on inside." Pilar led her sister through the roped-off area to a seat near the paints. When Faith started to follow, Rick grasped her arm. "Wait a sec." She halted and looked up at him. He drew her away for some privacy off to the side of the booth. "How come Pilar knew about this and I didn't?"

"I wasn't sure she'd come." She cradled his cheek in her palm. "You expect so little out of life, I didn't want to disappoint you."

"I'm stunned."

"I told you I saw her at the beauty salon."

"Yeah, but I didn't know you said any more than hello."

"We talked after I got my hair done. Then I brought her supper over there one night. We talked more."

He grinned down at her. "You're something else, Sunshine."

She smiled at the name.

"Later," he said and walked away.

While he still could.

"HERE SWEETHEART, LET me show you how to fix the pole." Ian took Abby's line and put a magnet-type hook on the end of it.

"Will the fishies like it?" she asked. "Papa said they only eat worms. Yuck!" She finished by putting her fingers in her mouth.

Ian kissed her head. He'd always been affectionate with this child; she'd broken through his barriers right away, but today he felt like hugging everybody.

He pivoted, and Lisel came into his view. She was throwing rings onto a pole, giggling like a schoolgirl when she scored. Just one night with her and he felt like a schoolboy himself again. They'd made love and it was fantastic. But the intimacy of sleeping together, waking together, whispering in the dark and in the morning light was what meant the most to him. How had he resisted her for so long?

Jenny Mincheon, who'd arrived at about two with her mother, came up to Lisel and asked her something. Lisel hugged Jenny. Looked like his woman was happy, too.

"Mr. Woodward." Mona had approached him from behind. "May I talk to you?"

"Please, Mona, no formalities."

Mona crossed her arms. "Lisel didn't come home last night."

The housekeeper and her daughter had been in the city, but she could probably tell when she got back to the condo that Lisel hadn't been there.

"Did you talk to her about it?"

"Not much. She's been with you most of the day."

"Is there something you'd like to ask me?"

"No, there's something I'd like to tell you."

He straightened as much as he could in the chair. Damn it, he liked it a hell of a lot better when he could tower over people and intimidate them. "All right."

Mona shifted, blocking his view of Lisel. "Don't hurt her."

"I don't intend to, Mona."

A cough behind Mona. Ian looked up to see her daughter had joined them. "Is this your daughter? I don't think we've formally met."

The girl's eyes were hard, like her mother's. "I'm Jenny Mincheon."

"Ian Woodward. Lisel speaks highly of you."

"Yeah, whatever. Come on, Mom, I want to show you something."

Jenny pulled Mona away, and frankly Ian was glad. The older woman made him uncomfortable, and it seemed the daughter was following in her footsteps.

"What's the scowl for?" He looked up to find Lisel next to him. Now that he let himself, he was awed by her beauty. Her face was flawless, her eyes the oddest color of blue. The smile that had charmed thousands was now aimed at just him, and it took his breath away. She looked after the Mincheons. "They giving you trouble?"

"Yeah. Seems they don't like me."

Lisel came to the back of the chair and circled her arms around his neck. He hadn't admitted to himself how much he'd missed physical contact like this with a woman—one leaning on him, her head on his shoulder. Because he was in a chair, none of that happened anymore. "They're just protective of me. Like a mother and a sister."

He grabbed her hand and kissed it. Even her smell—something very feminine and floral—encompassed him. "They're afraid I'll hurt you."

"You won't, I know it."

"Lise . . ." Doubts still lingered in his mind. In his heart. But he battered them back. "Never mind." He nodded to the food court area. "Wanna try the fried dough with me?"

Still touching him, she smiled intimately. "I'll try anything with you, Ian."

He chuckled. Pulling her head down, he whispered some-

thing naughty in her ear. She giggled, drawing the attention of
Mona and Jenny, who were still close enough to hear her laughter. Now, *they* scowled. Well, as long as their animosity didn't
bother Lisel, he wouldn't let it bother him. Taking her hand, he
pulled her around. With his other, he managed to wheel the
chair over to the food section without having to release her.

Despite what the Minceons thought of him, he didn't intend to ever let her go.

IT HAD BEEN a successful fair, Faith thought, as the last of the
people filed out around six. They'd made tons of money. Combined with the other church fall festivals around the city, it
would be a nice chunk of change for the camp. She left Pilar
and Anita—thank you God for letting her come today—to close
up their booth and went to help Rick with his. He was just about
to dismantle the net when she said, "No fair. You were supposed
to show me how to do a free throw."

He pivoted and a grin split his face at the sight of her. Did he
have any idea how much his expression gave away his feelings?
"Well, it's a tough job, but somebody's got to do it."

She hopped up on the counter, threw her legs over to the
other side, and smiled flirtatiously. "I need help getting down."

"Help my ass." But he crossed to her anyway, spanned her
waist with his hands, and let her slide down his body. He
couldn't quell the groan that escaped him. Then, or when she
hugged him. He held on for a minute. "Thanks again for what
you did with Anita."

She kissed his cheek. "You're welcome." She grinned. "I'm
pretty persistent, when I want to be."

"No, really?" Shaking his head, he gave her an extra hug.
"Thanks." Then he checked to see that no one was around, and
patted her fanny. "Come on, I'll teach you how to wield a basketball."

It was fun. She missed the first shot, so he showed her where
to hold the ball and how to extend her arms. In the process, she
let her breasts graze his biceps.

He did a little of his own groping. Placing his hands on her
hips, he rubbed them up and down. "Just adjusting your stance,
baby."

Backing up, she leaned into him. "You can adjust my stance any time you want."

They laughed. Finally, when he could apparently take no more teasing contact, he dragged her into the shadows of the booth, behind a partition that partly obscured them from view. He plastered her up against the wall, and she went for his mouth. When he finally came up for air, he held her arms on either side of her. "Wait a sec."

She pouted, and he took a quick nip out of her lips.

His look changed from flirty to profound. "I need to talk to you. About us."

"Oh, Rick."

"You win," he said huskily, meeting her forehead with his. "I—"

"Faith, love, is that you back there?" The voice was like getting doused with cold water on a blistering hot day. Faith felt her body go rigid. "What . . ."

"Faith, it's me, Sam. Are you there?"

"Oh, God."

Rick sprung back as if he'd been shot. She stepped out so Sam could see her, but not Rick.

"There you are." He vaulted the booth. "Come 'ere, woman." Sam pulled her into his arms. "There now, that's better." His mouth came down on hers in a crushing, intimate, long, and totally carnal kiss.

Faith wanted to die. She managed to pull away just as Rick inched out of the shadows. His face was totally blank, but she could see the stricken look in his eyes. And his usually ruddy complexion was pale. When Sam drew her even closer, she said, "Sam. Someone else is here."

"So I see." He didn't let her go. Instead his hands dropped to her hips, grasped her there. "Sorry, love. Can't fault a man for dying to get his hands on his fiancée."

Rick went stone still. Only his eyes moved when he looked to her, then back to Sam.

"Rick . . ."

Sam held out his hand. "Sam Dalton."

Rick stared at it a minute, then shook. "Rick Ruscio."

Sam said simply, "Yes, I know who you are."

* * *

DON'T THINK. DON'T think. Don't think. Just get the fuck out of here. Rick could barely breathe as he stumbled out of the fellowship hall and headed for the parking lot. He was bombarded with images . . . Faith, in the arms of another man, who touched her with a clear "Mine" written all over it.

Can't blame a man for dying to see his fiancée . . . Sam really misses you.

What had Rick been thinking?

His car was across the lot. The wind had picked up and slapped him in the face as he headed toward it. Hurrying, he'd just about reached it, when he heard, from two spaces down, "Son of a bitch."

Looking over, he saw Joe Harmon bending over Ian's van. "Shit."

Rick couldn't think straight. Just then Harmon looked up.

"Somebody slashed Ian's tires. Why the hell would anybody want to vandalize a handicap vehicle?"

Rick couldn't answer. He knew he should do something, say something, call somebody, but he kept seeing Faith, with Sam . . . and hearing his own conscience say, *That's where she belongs.*

"Ruscio, you okay?" Joe stood. "God, man, is there pain somewhere?"

Fuck, he must look really bad. "Pain?"

"You're not all right, Rick."

"No, I'm not." He stared blankly at the tires. "Joe, I can't handle this now. Could you call Will?"

"Don't have to." Joe looked over Rick's shoulder. "He's right behind you."

Turning, Rick caught sight of Will striding toward them. "What's going on here?" He glanced at Rick. "Rick, son, what's . . . you all right? Is it your heart?"

"Yeah, it's my heart," he said. "I gotta go."

"Wait, I'll come with you."

"No, no, Will. I need . . . I need . . ." He swore again, vilely. "Just help out here and let me alone a while."

He got in his car, blanking his mind; but he dropped the keys beneath his seat. Fishing them out, he came up with something else. Black lace. Faith's bra from that Friday night. The image of touching her, the memory of kissing her, sliced him in half. She was engaged, and she'd let Rick . . . "Fuck!" He threw the garment to the floor.

He tore out of the parking lot, away from the church, and most of all, away from Faith.

She'd lied to him. They were engaged. And sexually involved. Sam Dalton's actions said it loud and clear. And the guy knew what he was doing. He knew who Rick was.

For what seemed like hours, Rick drove around. It calmed him and lulled him. All right, all right, this was it. This was the end of it. That was for the best. What had he been thinking that a man like him could fit with her?

Fuck! He'd been thinking that because she told him so. Pursued the hell out of him. It didn't make sense. Why would she do that? Faith wouldn't intentionally hurt him like that. He couldn't figure it out. He was tired of trying to.

He kept glancing at the bra on the floor. He needed a drink. He drove by Badges and caught sight of a sporty black Camaro outside in the parking lot. Carla was at the bar. *Fuck it,* he thought, pulling in. He could use some liquor and some female company. He didn't even care that he never went to Badges anymore.

Two hours later, he and Carla stumbled out of the bar; Rick was drunk enough not to care what he was doing. Drunk enough not to feel guilty. Carla was his own kind, and he'd convince himself of that tonight.

To hell with Faith McPherson.

THERE WAS NO reasoning with him. Faith sat on her couch and stared at the Mr. Hyde that Sam had turned into. "Tell me where this came from, at least."

"Your brother called me this morning. He knew I was concerned about you. He told me about that guy." Sam paced, taking up the carpet with his long strides. "I caught the next train out."

"Peter had no right."

Sam stopped abruptly. His deep brown eyes, a shade darker

than his hair, were incredulous. "No right? You're falling hook, line, and sinker for a criminal, and your brother had no right to alert me? What's gotten into you?"

"Now, hold on here. Rick Ruscio is no criminal."

"Come on, Faith, I know his background. Your dad told me."

"Dad?" Oh, please don't let her father be in on this.

"When I got here, I went straight to him. He told me the guy had been caught helping somebody sabotage the fire chief."

"Dad did? I can't believe it."

"Oh, he couched it in forgiveness terms and told me not to get too upset about it. This Rick was a good man."

"That's more like Dad."

"Damn it, Faith, *are* you involved with him?"

She stood to face him squarely. "Yes."

"What about us? We've been together for years."

"We've been friends for years. I can't believe what you made it seem like to Rick." Her heart hurt. What must he be thinking?

"We're more than friends. The last time we talked about this, I told you I wanted to move on or break it off as soon as I was done with divinity school."

"Either/or, Sam, that was the deal."

He threw up his arms. "I *love* you."

"I love you, too, but not like that. I love you like a brother."

"Don't say that."

Rising, she crossed to him and grasped his arm. "Sam, if that's not the case, why haven't we ever made love? Our relationship has never been sexual."

"You wanted it that way."

"I thought you did, too."

"I don't know what I wanted."

"I don't think you do now, either. I think you're just scared."

"I am. You've been a part of my life forever. I can't lose you."

"I'm sorry, Sam. If you mean it as a lover, a fiancée, or a wife, you *have* lost me."

He stared down at her. "You're in love with him, aren't you?"

"Yes."

"He's not good enough for you."

"That is so un-Christian. When you calm down, you're going to regret saying it." She frowned. "And you'll regret misleading Rick."

"Tough." He gave her his back.

"Sam, you don't mean what you're saying."

He shook his head.

"I think you should talk to Dad about this."

"I don't know, maybe."

"Come on, let's go find him. We'll both talk to him."

"All right."

Thank God, Faith thought, as she led him out of the carriage house. She'd stay with Sam as long as she needed to, but she couldn't wait to find Rick. She knew in her heart this misunderstanding had to be killing him.

~~~ SEVENTEEN

RICK WAS PASSED out on the couch when the doorbell rang. Waking to a fuzzy TV screen, he roused himself, shut off the television, and belted his navy terry robe tighter around his waist. By then, the buzzer had rung two more times. "Hold your horses." Jesus, it was midnight. And his head felt like baby elephants were dancing in it. His mouth tasted like day-old shit. He reached the door, none too happy. Whipping it open, he barked, "This better be good."

"I think it is." She stood there like a vision in her green T-shirt and no coat. Her eyes were red, as if she'd been crying.

Tough shit.

He leaned insolently on the door. "What do you want, little girl?"

"I have to talk to you."

Belligerence fit him like an old shoe. He looked past her. "You and your fiancé?"

"He's not my fiancé, Rick."

"Get real. Isn't there an Aesop's fable with the 'fool me once, shame on you' moral?"

"I didn't fool you before. Can I come in?"

"I wouldn't if I were you. I'm not in the mood for games."

She slipped past him and ducked inside.

"Fuck," he said, on purpose, to offend her, as he slammed the door. Rounding on her, he found her standing a few feet away. And knew in his heart she was going to try to convince him what he'd seen, what he'd heard, wasn't real. Well, he knew how to deal with her. The lion and the lamb. He stalked toward her.

"We aren't engaged."

He came closer.

"Peter called him. About you. Sam panicked."

Another step. He grabbed her arms.

She jolted at the jarring, but continued. "He came to the fair with the express purpose of scaring you away."

He shook her, and her eyes widened. "Well, Sunshine, it worked."

"Rick, please—"

He squeezed her hard enough to leave bruises. "Don't lie to me."

"I'm not lying."

He snorted. Gripped her tighter.

Her eyes teared. "You're hurting me."

"Well, then we're even." Fuck, he hadn't meant to say that. Still, he loosened his hold on her.

"Sam and I haven't been involved like he implied."

"He kissed you, damn it, like a lover. He grabbed your ass."

"He did that out of desperation." Tears were streaming down her cheeks now. She grasped his arms. "He admitted that to Dad. We stayed and talked to him, that's why I didn't come sooner. Sam and Peter just left for New York."

He shucked her off as if she was scalding him. "No, I'm not falling for this again."

"Rick, I didn't lie. Sam and I aren't engaged. We're not involved sexually. How could you think I'd let you touch me if I was involved with someone else?"

Because he knew her core, he knew what her standards were, he couldn't answer that one. So he turned his back on her.

She placed a hand on his shoulder. "Rick, please. Look at me."

God must have been with her. Something made him turn and

face her. He peered down into misty eyes full of feeling. For him. "I love you, Ricardo."

His heart thudded in his chest. He didn't want to believe her. Didn't want to fall into her trap again. But he did believe. And he fell, again, hard.

This time, when he grabbed her arms, it was with the utmost gentleness. "Faith." His throat clogged. "I thought . . . I thought . . ."

From the corner of his eye, he saw his bedroom door open. Then it creaked. Hearing the noise, seeing he was distracted, Faith turned.

"I hope it's okay, I borrowed a shirt. Mine's ripped . . ." Carla's words trailed off. "Oh, sorry, something woke me, but I didn't know anybody was here." She looked at Rick and asked silently, *What's going on?*

But it was Faith who drew his attention. She stepped back and clapped a hand over her mouth. She scanned Carla from head to toe. Then her gaze swung to him. "You . . . oh, God . . ." She stared at him with those wounded eyes.

And before he could react, she bolted for the door. It took him a few seconds to follow her out of the apartment, down the stairs, and outside. He found her in front of the old house he lived in, barfing in the bushes. "Faith, oh baby."

A voice in his mind kept chanting, *Look what you've done to her.*

"Sweetheart, I'm so sorry." He held her hair back, feeling helpless.

"Oh, God." She threw up more.

When he thought she was done, he drew her up. "Come on inside."

Leaning against him, she was as weak as a kitten. "I can't. Please, don't make me go back in there, with her."

"Faith you don't understand. I have to explain all this to you." The wind picked up, toying with the flaps of his bathrobe. He glanced down at himself. "I need to get dressed. Then we'll talk."

She took in his state of *un*dress and looked like she might get sick all over him. But she said, "All right" and nodded to her Saturn. "I'll wait in there for you."

He helped her to the car. "Promise me, you'll just wait here."

"I promise." She laid her head on the back of the seat.

He flew into the house, brushed off Carla's comments, whipped on pants, a shirt, and sweater, and was scuffling into his shoes as he walked outside.

He found the driveway empty.

She'd broken her promise.

SHE COULDN'T STOP crying. She sat on her porch, outside in the cold, hoping it would chase the tears away. Shivering, she wrapped her hands around her elbows and tossed her head back. He'd slept with Carla Lopez. He'd probably been sleeping with her all this time. That realization only made her cry harder. How could she have been so foolish? Nancy warned her. Sam had left saying she was making a big mistake. Her brother wouldn't speak to her.

They'd all been right about Rick Ruscio. He did indeed break her heart.

A cat prowled out of the darkness, shocking her with its loud meow. She recognized it as one she'd fed before. "Go away," she yelled to it. "I'm done with strays. I'm not feeding you again."

It just stared at her.

"I don't care what happens to you. I don't . . . I don't . . ."

When the cat stayed perched where it was, she got up to chase it away. She had to go halfway down the driveway before it scampered into the trees. Which was why she wasn't close enough to make it into the house when a big gray van pulled into the parsonage. Still, she made a run for it.

Behind her, she heard a door slam and Rick call out, "Faith, wait."

She kept running. She reached the front door, whipped it open, and was in the foyer of the carriage house when he caught her from behind. She kicked his shins, pummeled the hands that vised her around the waist. "Leave me alone. You bastard, leave me alone."

"No."

"I'm done with you."

"Too bad. I tried to end this whole thing before it got started, and you wouldn't let me. Now I won't let you. I'm calling the shots in this relationship for once."

She kicked again. He groaned when she hit his shin dead on, but pulled her closer.

Booting the door shut, he growled, "I'm gonna have my say, Sunshine. Then if you want me gone, I'll go."

She shook her head and felt the tears return at the nickname. "How could you? How *could* you?"

Holding her close enough so she could hear his heart pitch in his chest, feel his breathing against her cheek, he said simply, "I didn't."

She stilled. "What does that mean?"

"I didn't sleep with Carla."

"Damn it, Rick, she was coming out of your bedroom, half naked."

"I dumped her there when we got back to my place."

"You brought her home."

"Yeah. I was gonna fuck her."

Faith gasped. She struggled some more; he subdued her.

"But I didn't."

"Why, were you too drunk to get it up?"

"No, I don't think so. I don't know exactly because when we ripped our clothes off and she crawled on the bed, I was so disgusted with myself, I grabbed my bathrobe and left. She passed out in there." He nuzzled Faith's ear. "I passed out on the couch, crying over you."

"You expect me to believe this?"

"I believed what you said about you and Sam."

All the fight went out of her. She went as limp as a rag doll in his arms. Only then did he circle her around. She peered up at him and whispered, "Please, don't tell me this if it isn't true. I can't bear it."

"It is true, *querida*. I swear. I wanted *you*. I couldn't do it with anybody else."

"Even though you thought I was lying about Sam?"

"Even then."

Oh, God, what to do?

The answer came quick. *Trust him.*

"I don't know what to say."

"Say you believe me."

Though he looked like a criminal with his unshaven jaw, mussed hair, and bloodshot eyes, she saw only truth in that face she loved. "I believe you."

"Tell me how you feel about me."

"I love you."

He kissed her forehead. "Say you'll go to bed with me, right now."

"I'll go to bed with you, now, any time."

He pulled her close. Clamped her against his heart. "*Gracias a Dios.*"

Smiling, she nosed into him. "I thought you didn't believe in God."

"Hush." He drew back and lovingly caressed her cheeks. "Are you sure this is what you want, Faith? I come with so much baggage."

"I love you. I don't care."

He sighed. "All right." He glanced back at the parsonage. "Anybody comin' after me with a shotgun?"

"No, like I said, Peter and Sam left. Dad and Mom went to bed hours ago."

"Good." He drew back, picked her up, and cuddled her to his chest. "Let's go, love."

HE SWORE TO a God he didn't believe in that he would, tonight and always, treat her with tender care. They reached her bedroom. Inside, he found everything that suited Faith—dark pink walls, a raspberry carpet, a huge spindled bed with a patchwork quilt of pinks and reds. Surprisingly modern paintings graced the walls. "This room is you." He placed her on the mattress, against the mountain of multicolored pillows. His heart constricted. "You look exhausted." It was his fault.

She swallowed hard. "It's been quite a night." Her eyes darkened again. "I thought you . . ."

Sitting on the edge of the bed, he rubbed his thumb over her lips. "I know. I wanted to die when Sam claimed you."

Gently, she reached up and soothed a hand down his hair.

He said, "Thank God you came over to my place."

"Thank God you came here. I didn't know what to do."

Pulling her to him, he held her close, relishing in the feel of her. She hung on. Her hair smelled like the outdoors.

He knew what *he* smelled like. They'd both had a long day—and she'd gotten sick. Drawing back, he smiled. "I need a shower, sweetheart, before we do this." He swiped a hand down his cheek. "And a shave. I don't want to give you any brush burns. You got one of those little pink razors with daisies on them?"

"In the medicine cabinet. There's extra toothbrushes in there, too." She smiled weakly. "I'd like to shower, too, but before either of us does, I have to talk to you about something."

His heartbeat escalated. "Something bad?"

"No, no." Still, she clenched her fingers together. "Rick, about our lives before tonight?" A blush rose from the scoop of her neck to her cheeks. She glanced away as if afraid to say something.

He got it. "Honey, it's okay. If it's about . . . me . . . my sexual past, I'm clean. I haven't been with a woman since May. I've had a checkup between now and then." He kissed her nose. "And I've got condoms."

She chuckled, but it was a nervous sound. "It isn't that."

"What then?"

She bit her lip. "Promise me something first."

"What?"

"That you won't change your mind about us. About doing this."

"About making love?" His laugh was deep and from the belly. "No way, sweetheart. The die is cast." He watched her twist her hands in the quilt. "Faith, if this about your being with some other man—even though you didn't sleep with Sam—you can't possibly think I, of all people, would hold you to a double standard."

"In a sense it's about being with another man." She rolled her eyes. "Or *not* being with another man."

"I don't understand."

"Oh, Rick." She took his hand and kissed his knuckles. Her lips were soft and brushed his fingers like silk. "I've never done this before."

"Done what?" He waited a beat. "You don't mean, you've

never . . . you haven't . . ." The thought boggled his mind. "Faith, you haven't had sex before?"

She shook her head.

His jaw dropped. "Faith."

"Don't let it change your mind."

Briefly, he closed his eyes. *Please, make me handle this right.* "Of course it doesn't change my mind. I just . . . I'm surprised." And pleased, he realized. Utterly, stupidly pleased. He felt so primitively possessive, he was embarrassed by it. How could this woman's innocence mean so much to him? He was a man of the world and had associated only with women like himself.

Maybe that was why.

But there were some things he needed to know. "Why, Faith? Why haven't you done this before?"

She lifted her chin. "I wanted to wait until I fell in love."

"You love Sam."

"Not like this. It's not what I feel for you. This is what I've been waiting for."

Hell, it was a huge responsibility. Could he handle it? Looking into her eyes . . . young, yes, and vulnerable now, he realized some things: This was a woman who knew her own mind, lived by her values, stood up for who she was.

And he was in love with her.

Pulling her close, he held her tight to his heart. "I'm honored, honey, really, really honored."

Shyly, she nosed into him. "I hope so. This is very special to me."

"To me, too." And if it was the last thing he did, he was going to make tonight memorable for her. When she looked back on her first time, no matter where she was or who she ended up with, she'd think of it with joy.

He sensed she was ready, so he drew back. "Why don't you shower first?"

"We could, together."

He rubbed a knuckle down her throat. "No, not this time. If I see you wet and naked, I won't be able to control myself." As it was, he wondered about his ability to pleasure her. "And your first time isn't going to be standing up against a shower stall."

For a minute, mischief replaced the innocence. "It'd make a good story to tell our daughter."

Jesus. "Let's take this one step at a time."

While she was in the shower, he left the bedroom and rummaged around in her kitchen, then the big cupboard in her dining room. He found what he wanted, made a stop at the stereo system, and returned to the bedroom. Things were ready when she came to the door.

She scanned the room. "Oh, Rick."

Distracted from what he'd done, he just stared at her. She wore a deep pink robe that matched the walls. Her hair was a little damp and her skin glowed from the hot water. "You're beautiful. Like something out of a Victorian novel."

She gestured to the room. Her voice was a soft caress when she spoke. "Thank you for doing this."

"I raided your kitchen." He slid off the bed and picked up the champagne he'd poured and put on her night table. "I hope you weren't saving this for anything." She shook her head. He brought the bubbly to her, along with his own. When she took it, he clinked their glasses, the sound an accompaniment for some soft, mournful jazz sneaking in from the living room. "To tonight," he said and kissed her gently before they both sipped the wine.

In the candlelight, he could see her pleasure at his words. She tasted the gold liquid. "To forever," she whispered.

"Go sit on the bed, love. I'll only be a few minutes." That way, she could have some wine to relax her, let the vanilla scent of the candles soothe her and the sexy music set the mood.

It did. By the time he took a scalding shower, swiped a razor over his face, and came out, she was lying back on the pillow, one long luscious leg peeking out from the robe. The champagne glass on the nightstand was empty. He sipped his own for a minute and watched her. Silly to be overcome by her beauty. Inner and outer. Silly to be thrilled that she'd chosen to give him this gift of herself. Silly to cherish tonight so much. Cherish her. He only hoped he could do this right. At times, he could be a bull in a china shop.

But not tonight.

She must have sensed him watching. Her eyes opened. "Wow," she said easily. "You're beautiful."

"Uh-uh. *You* are."

Crossing to her, he put his glass next to hers. Slowly, he

reached up and ducked a finger inside the vee of her robe. "Something occurred to me in the shower. I . . . I won't hurt you, will I? I know women today use tampons and stuff."

She giggled. "And stuff."

"I just want to be sure this is good for you."

She smiled as if she knew something he didn't. "No, Rick, you won't hurt me. I promise."

"Well then." He ducked a hand inside her robe.

She sighed when his palm closed over her breast. She was full and supple, and her nipple pouted against his hand.

He parted the satiny material. "Ah, Faith. I couldn't see much in the car that night. You are so lovely." *And mine,* he thought as he cupped her, kneaded her.

Mine, he thought as his fingers trailed down her ribcage, caressed her flat stomach.

Mine, he thought as he covered her curls and pressed.

Her eyes turned slumberous. "That feels so good."

Leaning over, he let her scent from the bath—lemony and clean—encompass him. "You've felt this before right?" God, it was awkward, but he needed to know. "This kind of pleasure?"

"Yes." She clutched his shoulders. Then whispered, "But not from a man."

He'd been aroused since he carried her in here. Now he went rock hard, at her words and at the realization that he'd be the first person to bring her to orgasm.

With that knowledge, he gently took her to the brink of the first peak—and then watched her fall over into a soft meadow of pleasure. As she did, he captured her moans with his mouth.

Sensation flooded Faith in the aftermath of her climax. She became aware of the scent of Rick, clean from the shower, and the feel of his skin. Reaching out, she ran her hand over the wall of his chest. His muscles leaped at her touch. He said, as gently as a summer breeze, "That was the most beautiful thing I've ever seen."

She smiled at him and grasped the waistband of his shorts. His stomach contracted involuntarily. "I want to see you."

He stood and shucked off his boxers. He was beautiful all over and deeply aroused. He was long and as hard as granite. Blue veins pulsed, the tip of his penis throbbed. Instead of frightening her, it thrilled her. She reached for him, but he stayed her hand and sat down on the bed. "No, baby, not this time. If you touch me, I'll go off."

"I could . . . do what you did to me.".

"No, I want to be inside you." His voice was gravelly. Snagging a condom from the nightstand where he'd put them, he slid it on then sat back on the bed and stretched out. "Come here," he said, patting the space between his powerful legs. She inched into the cradle of his thighs, bending her knees on the bed. His arms went around her, and he pulled her tighter. She could feel his restraint, his heart thunder. He buried his face in the crook of her neck and nipped her there. After a moment, he set her back a bit. Brought his hand between them. Rubbed her with his thumb. Pressed. Rubbed some more. Sliding a finger inside, he made her jolt.

"Hurt?" he asked.

She brushed the scowl from his face. "No. It feels wonderful."

He touched her, learning her, readying her. She began to squirm. "Now, Rick. Please."

He positioned himself. Inched in. A groan escaped him. More inches. He was firm and full and stretched her. Nothing had ever felt more wonderful. "Oh, Rick . . ."

"*Querida*," he mumbled again. Then he said, *"Te amo, Fe."*

The physical sensation of having him inside her was increased a thousandfold by his words. Her throat closed up. "Rick . . ."

He smiled and pushed harder. She felt the first tingles of orgasm begin. He thrust harder, and in seconds, the tingles exploded into a powerful rush of feeling. She grabbed onto his neck, and his arms banded around her. More thrusts. More. Suddenly the world burst into colors and sights and sounds she'd never seen or heard before.

Just as she came back to reality, his grip tightened, and he called out her name, gripped her shoulders . . . and exploded inside her. Afterward, he didn't let her go, kept her cocooned in his embrace. They were as close as two people could get. She stirred, and his grip tightened. "No, don't move. Stay right where you are. Just for a minute."

She did, relishing the smell and feel of his big, hard body against hers. Inside hers.

Then he drew back. And for as long as she lived, she knew

she'd never see such powerful, naked emotion on anyone's face again. He stared down at her. "Thank you. I've never been given a more precious gift."

"I love you," she told him. Then caressing his face, she asked, "Did you mean it?"

"Yes, I meant it."

"Say it again, in Spanish."

"Te amo."

"Te amo," she whispered reverently. "Do you have any idea how that makes me feel?"

"I know exactly how it feels." He smiled.

She smiled.

Then he arched a smug brow and thrust forward. Aftershocks flooded her. "Oh."

Now a smug smile. "So, how was it?"

She hid her face in his shoulder. "You know it was wonderful."

He caressed her nape. "I'm glad."

"Better that the vibrator in my nightstand."

He stilled. "What did you say?"

"A few years ago, Nancy took me to a store in New York to buy a vibrator."

"Holy shit, Faith."

"It's all right. Mom said it wasn't a sin."

"You told your *mother* Nancy bought you a dildo?"

"Of course. Wanna see it?"

"God, no."

"You know," she said, inching closer. "I can do it as many times as I want with that."

"Faith, stop!"

"How, um, long does it, like, take *you* to recover?" Already she could feel him respond.

"With you apparently not very long."

She grinned. And he began to move. Getting back his equilibrium, he said, sexily, "Let's see if I can do better than that little device in your nightstand."

As Faith held on to him, he did.

$\backsim$ EIGHTEEN

IT WAS THE week before Thanksgiving, and for the first time in three years, Ian was looking forward to a holiday. Lately, he'd been embarrassed by what his attitude had been all this time, by the fact that some of his brothers hadn't had the time he got after 9/11 or others hadn't had his quality of life. It had taken him a while to get his head on straight, but he was there finally. Lisel was the reason.

As was the fact that he felt so *normal*.

He was running late because of that normalcy. Like an ordinary man, he'd overslept, with her by his side. Disabled people needed an inordinate amount of time to accomplish the same daily living tasks as able-bodied people—it was one of the things that had been so damn hard to get used to. Waking up with only an hour to get somewhere was cutting it close.

Lisel had scooted over to her house to dress to go to New York with Joe. She had a meeting with her agent, and his therapist-turned-bodyguard had volunteered to drive her. Ian suspected Joe had a king-size crush on Lisel these days.

Ian had showered, dressed, and was left with only a half hour to get to the Quint/Midi 7 fire station where he was doing some WMD in-house training. He had to eat, though, something he was vigilant about. So before he left the bedroom, he took his cell phone out of his uniform pocket and called Mitch Malvaso to say he might be late.

In the kitchen, eating his oatmeal, he could't help but smile over his life these days. Yesterday had been normal, too. Man, he'd missed living like other people. He and Lisel had spent a regular Sunday together, reading the paper and watching some CNN news and sports on TV. She'd fixed a huge brunch, and in the late afternoon, he suggested they play some ping-pong together in the community hall of the condominium complex. They'd donned coats and gloves and headed over to the recreation center. He could still see her in blue jeans and one of his old FDNY sweatshirts diving for the ball, paddling it back to him as hard as she could, giggling when she scored a point.

Then they'd gone back to her place—Mona wouldn't return from her day off until tomorrow—and without warning, right there in her living room, Lisel had knelt between his legs and initiated one of the most sensual, sexual, blow-the-top-of-your-head-off lovemaking sessions Ian had ever experienced. Even now, he felt the stirrings of arousal just thinking about it.

And that wasn't all that had happened. He finished up his juice, rinsed out his dish, and headed for the closet to get his windbreaker. As he locked up, he remembered the events after the sex . . .

"Ah, Lise," Ian had moaned from his chair. "That was . . . mind-boggling."

She'd given him a siren's smile. "Yeah, well, I want payment."

"Sure, let's go to the bedroom . . ."

"No." She was still kneeling between his legs. In a tender gesture so contradictory to her earlier ministrations, she laid her head in his lap.

His hand came up to caress her hair. "What is it?"

"I want you and me to take a bath together."

He stiffened. "Honey, no."

"Why? My bathroom can accommodate this." She rubbed the rim of the chair. "If we're careful, we can get you into the tub."

"That's not it."

"What?"

He glanced down at his skinny, useless legs, which were easier to ignore when they were covered with clothes or concealed by his dimly lit bedroom when they made love. He peered over at the beautiful woman he held in his arms and wanted to be whole for her.

"It's because of what your legs look like, isn't it?" Kneeling up, she leaned in and kissed the scar on his cheek. "It's the same reason you don't like me touching this."

He'd felt cold inside. Swallowed hard. And nodded.

"We can't go through our whole lives without my seeing your legs."

"It's too soon."

"No!" Her voice rose a notch. "I want that intimacy with you." When he just stared at her, she whispered, "Please. I love you. I think you're the most attractive man I've ever met."

So for her, for all she'd done for him, he'd agreed.

And it hadn't been half-bad. After the first awkwardness, and once in the tub, he'd pretty much forgotten about his deformity and lost himself in the sensation of cradling her wet, naked body into his, lazily caressing skin made even more silky by the bath oils.

He was out the door of his condo and heading to his van, whistling, before he noticed the drizzle. Preoccupied, he hadn't thought to get an umbrella, though he knew it had rained last night. He and Lisel had listened to it pound on the roof as they lay in bed together. Maneuvering a chair in the rain could be dicey. Hell, he thought, wheeling to his car, he felt like Superman today. He could do anything.

He was within three feet of the van when his chair stalled. What the hell? This had never happened before. Scowling, he looked down and tried to wheel ahead. He couldn't. He was stuck. In a puddle? That didn't make sense. On closer examination, he could see that the puddle was deeper than he thought. Murkier. Reaching down, he managed to stick his hand in the water. It was cold, and something else. Slimy. He lifted his arm and was shocked to see his fingers were covered with black greasy stuff. Some kind of oil. He brought it to his nose. Or tar. Holy hell, how could that have gotten here, right at the exact spot where the van's ramp would be lowered by the remote?

Again, he tried to rock the chair back and forth. His muscles strained with the effort. It took him five minutes to realize he was good and truly stuck, and couldn't get out.

"Fuck," he said aloud. He scanned the parking lot. There were only a few cars here. Reaching into his uniform pocket, he felt for his cell phone. He was going to have to call somebody.

But his phone wasn't there. Shit. As a disabled man, he was careful to keep it charged and with him at all times. Where the hell was it? Mentally, he retraced his steps of the morning, and pictured himself calling Mitch from his bedroom. Distracted by thoughts of Lisel, he must have left the phone on the dresser.

Sighing heavily, he shivered as the light rain fell onto his head and began to soak through his jacket. He had no idea what to do. He swore some more. The impotence of the situation rose up out of a darkness as deep and murky as the water, threatening to overpower him. Frustrated beyond measure, he could only sit there. Some Superman.

And then, the heavens opened up.

"MR. RUSCIO'S HERE." Jamal screeched the words, causing everybody's head, including Faith's, to swivel to the doorway.

Rick noticed she was dressed in plain navy slacks and a red fuzzy sweater. Her hair was curled and fluffy and kissed her cheeks. She said, from where she sat in a circle with the kids, "Hello, Mr. Ruscio. Welcome."

"Miz McPherson. Sorry I'm late." He'd had a meeting with his lawyer about the civil suit filed by the rookie who'd been hurt by Steele's sabotage. He pushed the still-unresolved issue away and concentrated on the woman before him. Joy surged inside him at just seeing her today.

"Have a nice weekend?" she asked with a flirty smile.

"The best." He'd spent much of it with her, though he refused to stay the whole night at her place or let her come to his apartment and sleep there.

Out of respect for your family I'm drawing the line, doll.

She'd pouted, but it had only earned her a searing kiss.

Molly left the circle and approached Rick. Since the incident on the playground, he'd become her hero. The little girl took his hand; this time, he didn't shrink away. "Wanna sthit with me?" Molly asked.

Molly's tormentors from that same day, "the sandbox girls," Rick now called them, sniggered. He knew Faith had spoken to them about their behavior. She told them she wouldn't tolerate any taunting of Molly. Bending down, Rick scooped up the little girl and crossed the room. One-handed, he dragged out a straight chair, joined the circle, and sat down with Molly on his lap.

"Baby," one of the girls quipped so everyone heard.

Faith stood then and approached Rick. "Here." She held out the book. "Read them a story."

He watched her as she turned, went to the two girls, and stood before them. "You're coming with me, ladies."

"We'll miss the story."

"Yes, you will."

"We didn't do nothing."

Faith raised her voice, not a lot, but enough to make a point. "Now."

Heads down, the girls followed her out.

Rick watched Faith go, chuckling. She had grit when she needed it. Ever since they slept together, she'd asserted it. *Stay all night . . . let's try it this way . . . of course we're going out together to the movie, did you think I'd hide my relationship with you?*

He was still worried about all that, about her reputation being tainted by her association with him, but there didn't seem to be anything he could do about protecting her, short of not seeing her, which wasn't going to happen anytime soon. He was enthralled by her. Charmed. And deeply in love. *What would be,* he thought, opening the book, *would be.*

He found a fable that reminded him of her. They'd been skimming a copy of Aesop she kept at her house, and she said this was one of her favorites.

"One day," Rick began, "The North Wind and the Sun were having a disagreement over who was the strongest. 'I am, of course,' the wind said, 'I can overpower anything with my strong breath.'"

"The sun just smiled benevolently at him. 'There are many kinds of strength.'"

" 'We'll have a contest,' the wind decided, nodding to a traveler along the road below them. The sun sighed heavily, but agreed. 'Whoever can make the man remove his coat wins.'"

Rick laughed as the North Wind—was there a comparison here to him?—blew hard. The traveler pulled his coat close to his chest. When the wind blew harder, the man hugged his coat tighter. Alas, the North Wind failed. Then, the Sun had her turn. All she did was beam down on the traveler, silently, slowly, benignly. And sure enough, the guy took off his coat.

"What's it mean, Mister?" Jamal asked.

"It means," Rick said, grinning at Faith, who was now poised in the doorway. "That gentle persuasion, patience, and goodness win out in the end."

Faith grinned at him. He grinned back, feeling like he could conquer the world. "Thanks," she said, taking the book. "That's my favorite."

"I know, Sunshine." He glanced around. "Where are the girls?"

"In with Tim. He does time-out." She studied the class. "Let's sing our song now and draw our favorite thing."

Rick was at a table with Jamal and Molly sketching out his favorite thing, when Jamal leaned over Rick's masterpiece. "Hey, it's a girl." Faith's head snapped up from the table where she sat with several kids. "You got a girlfriend, Mr. Ruscio?" Jamal asked.

"Yeah, kid, I do." Looking directly at Faith, Rick's gut burned with raw, sexual intensity. "What's your favorite thing today, Miz McPherson?"

Smiling, she held up her drawing. Pink carnations.

He'd come over Sunday afternoon with a bouquet of those, and she'd been moved by the gesture.

At mid-morning snack time, the two aides came in to feed the kids while Faith took a break. "Let's go outside. You can push me on the swing."

"It's raining."

"We'll sit in the pavilion, then."

"Do you at least have a coat?"

He wore dark tan corduroys and a green faux suede shirt. In lieu of a coat, he'd thrown on a dark green blazer.

"Yeah." She shrugged on a light jacket. He pushed up the collar of it as they headed outside. "This isn't warm enough."

Grinning, she took his hand, and they dashed for the pavilion. They were laughing when they hustled inside. Sometimes, when he was with her, he felt fifteen again.

"Did you sleep well?" she asked innocently when they were seated on the picnic table.

He stared out at the drizzle. "Not hardly." He'd tossed and turned for hours, then when he did doze off, he found himself awakening and reaching for her.

What would he do when it ended?

"Why so sad?" She picked up his hand. "Didn't you have a good weekend?"

Since he'd spent it with her, she knew he had. "It was okay."

"Okay?" She punched his arm. "Just okay? Great sex. Wonderful home-cooked food, and that backrub last night. Just okay?"

He turned toward her. Her face was flushed, her eyes sparkling with feigned outrage. He was planning to tease her some more, but was suddenly so overcome by feelings for her, he caressed her cheek. "Someday, I'm going to look back on all this and know it was the best time of my life."

Faith scowled. "I don't like how that sounds."

"What do you mean?"

"Like you expect this between us to end someday."

He shifted away from her, dangling his linked hands between his knees. "Let's not get into that now."

"Rick, I . . ."

His cell phone rang. Despite the respite from her comment it provided, he frowned. "This can't be good. Anyone who knows me, knows I'm doing my community service. Ruscio," he said, clicking on the phone.

"Rick, it's me, Ian. Can you come and get me? It's an emergency."

"Sure. Where are you?"

"In front of the condos by my van."

"Woodward, don't you know enough to come in out of the rain?" Silence. Rick thought maybe they lost the connection. "Ian?"

"I can't come out of the rain." The strain in the man's voice was marked. "I need some help."

"I'll be right there." He hung up. "I gotta go. Ian Woodward needs me—it sounds weird." He stood, glanced around quickly, and then kissed her on the nose. "I'll be back in touch as soon as I can."

Faith watched him dash through the rain. She frowned after him. His statement worried her. He'd said he loved her, but nothing about a future together. Common sense told her not to push him, that he'd made huge strides letting her into his life. But she wanted happily ever after and she intended to get it.

"Faith?" Nancy appeared at the back door. "Are you out there?"

"Yes," she called out. Draping her jacket over her head, she dashed through the now-heavy rain and to the building. Once inside, she faced her boss and friend. "What is it?"

Nancy held out the morning newspaper. "Something you need to see."

Faith unfolded the paper.

"It's the editorial, by Nick Lucas, at the bottom."

Nick Lucas. He was a native of Hidden Cove. Faith had grown up with him. She scanned the editorial.

COMMUNITY SERVICE, OR JUST ANOTHER LOOPHOLE?

Recent developments in the judicial system have this reporter concerned. Plea bargaining for reduced sentences is a fact of life in our legal courts. Not always a good thing, but the needs of the many prevail over punishing one. However, when these criminals are allowed back into the community and worse, corrupt our youth, someone has to take a stand.

Case in point . . . it has come to the newspaper's attention a recent offender is now working at one of our city-subsidized preschools. What is this world coming to?

"Oh my God." Faith looked up from the article.

"Bastard," Nancy said under her breath. Nancy had made it clear she was wary of Rick and Faith's relationship, worried that Faith would be hurt by it.

"Nancy, I'm sorry if this is going to cause problems here at the school. But it isn't Rick's fault."

Nancy's dark eyes narrowed. "I meant the reporter, Faith." She shook her head. "I don't trust lover boy not to hurt you, but he doesn't deserve this." She searched Faith's face. "It's gonna get to him, honey."

"I know." She sighed. Nancy had no idea how much.

THOUGH A MISTY gloom filled the air from the recent downpour, Lisel spotted Ian's van immediately when she and Joe pulled into the parking lot of the condos. "I wonder why Ian's van is here. I thought he was going to be gone all day."

Joe's hand tightened on the wheel. "Don't have the foggiest. I hope nothin's wrong."

"Me too." They swerved into a space, just as Will Rossettie's police car pulled in beside them. "What . . . Oh, Joe." Lisel bounded out of the car and circled the van; from the driver's side, Rick Ruscio stood up. They hadn't seen him because he'd been bending over a puddle. "Rick, what are you doing here?" She grasped his arm. "Is Ian all right?"

Rick's eyes were troubled, his mouth tight. "He's fine, physically, though chilled. Mentally, he's a wreck."

Her heart racing, she nodded to Will, who'd stopped to talk to Joe. "Why did you call the police?"

"Let's go inside. I think Ian should tell you."

Biting her lip, she began to shiver in the thin raincoat she wore. She greeted Will, and all of them proceeded to Ian's condo. The door was ajar; obviously Rick had left it that way. He went in first. "Ian?" he called out.

After a moment, she heard Ian's gravelly voice come from the bedroom. "In here. I'll be right out."

Lisel started across the floor. Rick grabbed her arm. "Give him a minute."

"Then you tell me what's going on."

"It's not good. He got stuck in the parking lot and couldn't get out of it by himself." Rick's voice was raw, full of feeling. Lisel could tell he was upset for Ian.

"Stuck? I don't understand."

"I have some suspicions." He glanced at Will. "I found this in your door. Again." Obviously it was another letter from the fan.

"What does it say?" This from Ian, who'd come to the doorway of his bedroom. He was dressed in flannel pajama pants and a white T-shirt. His hair was slicked back off his face. His eyes were blank. And every muscle in his body was tense.

Lisel flew to him. Dropping down to her knees, she grabbed his hands. "Are you all right?"

He glanced away. "Yeah."

"Ian, what happened? Rick said you got stuck. I don't understand."

He glanced at Rick, then looked over at her. "I was getting ready for work this morning. I was thinking about you"—here he brushed his knuckles down her cheek—"and I was distracted. I left my cell phone on the dresser."

"You never do that. You always make sure you have it."

"I know. I was just about at the van when it started to drizzle. Then . . . I got stuck." His voice caught on the last word.

"In what?"

"There was a puddle. The wheels got mired in it. Some kind of oil spilled, or tar came off the blacktop. I really don't know what it was. I just . . . couldn't get out."

Tears formed in her eyes. She battled them back. "And you didn't have a phone, couldn't call anybody."

He shook his head, his eyes bleaker than a February dawn.

"How long before anybody found you?"

"About a half hour. Then this little old lady from the end unit . . ."

"Mrs. Larson."

"Yeah. She finally came out to walk her dog. She rushed over, of course, but there was nothing she could do to help. So she brought me her cell phone and an umbrella."

Lisel swiped at her cheeks and kissed his hand. "I'm so sorry. You called Rick?"

"Yeah, you and Joe were in New York. Rossettie was on a case. Noah and Eve took that little jaunt together. I knew Ruscio's schedule, so I called him."

"Hey, man, no problem," Rick said.

"Oh, Ian." She hugged him, but when he stiffened, she drew back. Then she stood. "Still, why the police?"

Ian nodded to the letter Rick held. "It must be because of that. Where did you find it? What does it say?"

"On my way out to check the puddle—the whole thing was odd to me—I found it in Lisel's door. I read it and called Will."

Ian wheeled forward a bit. "It's from the fan, right?"

"Yeah." Rick nodded to Lisel and Ian. "You both need to read it." He crossed to them and gave it to her. "I'm sorry, Lisel."

Ian grasped her arm. "Bend down so we can read it together."

Lisel did. They scanned it. "Cripple . . . gimp . . . not worthy . . ." The obscene words made her eyes tear again.

Ian finished reading it, then crumpled the paper in his fist. "Fuck!"

Joe Harmon crossed to him and took the letter. He straightened it out and read it. His gaze snapped to Will. "The slashed tires at the church fair. The puddle outside. They're related to this, aren't they?"

"That'd be my guess," Will said.

Lisel wept softly, until she felt a hand on hers. Tugging her. She tumbled into Ian's lap. And cried against his shoulder.

His whole body was stiff. But she felt his hand at her neck soothing down her back. "Shh. It's okay. This letter's shit. And it was just a little rain."

It was a whole lot more than that. Knowing how fiercely independent he was, the impotence of it all must have killed him. Lisel said, "I'm sorry."

"Baby, it's not your fault."

"I . . . I . . ." She began to cry harder.

"What?"

"I don't want this to make you change your mind."

"About us." It wasn't a question.

She gripped the soft cotton of his shirt. "Yes."

His hand clasped her neck. He held her close. For a long minute, she could practically feel his internal struggle. Then he said to Joe behind her, "What's your guess, Harmon? If Al-Qaeda terrorists couldn't take me out, you think some piddly little fan can do it?"

Lisel deflated like a balloon losing air.

Will chuckled.

Rick said, "Way to go, man."

Joe smiled and quipped, "Not on your life, boy."

AT FOUR THAT afternoon as he drove to Faith's house, Rick was still thinking about Ian Woodward and the courage it took to rise above what had happened to him this morning.

The guy had been leveled when Rick had gotten to his condo about ten. Sopping wet, shivering, and impossibly embarrassed, he'd briefly explained the situation to Rick . . .

"What can I do?" Rick had asked, his heart going out to the guy. Firefighters were as tough and independent as cops. Woodward had had his share of humbling experiences, making what happened even more shitty. Rick knew if he'd been in that predicament, he'd punch whoever came close to him.

"You'll have to carry me inside." Ian's voice had been gruff. "If you bring the other chair out, so I can transfer myself, it'll get wet and then I'll have no wheels."

And so Rick had struggled—the guy was solid muscle—to maneuver Ian out of the chair and get him inside. He'd brought Ian into the bedroom, positioned the spare chair, then left to go fetch the other one and check out the situation. Had the fan been around then, Rick would have beaten the crap out of her.

Still, Ian had class. He'd raged alone—Rick had heard him pummeling the punching bag when he brought the first chair in—but when Lisel showed up, he'd put her welfare ahead of his own. He hadn't made a federal case out of what had happened. Hadn't used it to distance Lisel, like Rick would have been tempted to do. Rick admired his courage more than he could say.

He arrived at the carriage house and was surprised, when Faith pulled open her door, to see her father behind her. Instead of the searing welcome she promised him when he'd called, he accepted the quick peck on the cheek and let her pull him inside.

"Hi, David." He glanced to Faith. "What's going on?"

"I wanted Dad here for reinforcements."

"For what?"

"Sit."

He crossed to the couch and sat. "All right, what's going on?"

David rose from the chair across from Rick and handed him the newspaper. "Read this." He looked at his daughter. "There's no better way."

Rick looked at the editorial. When he saw Lucas's name, he stiffened. When he read the first paragraph, his heart began to pound in his chest. When he was done, he tossed it to the floor and covered his face with his hands. Ludicrously, he remembered an Aesop's fable about the fox and the pheasants—its moral was that trouble often came when people least expected it.

He felt a hand on his arm. "Rick?" Lips kiss his head. "I'm so sorry."

"Yeah, me, too."

David leaned against the chair, his arms crossed over his chest.

Rick looked up at him. "This will embarrass you and your family."

"Like hell."

He was surprised at the minister's curse. "I'm going to cause you grief, like I knew I would."

"No." Faith held on to his arm.

David spoke softly. "If there is any backlash, and you take any grief, we'll stand by you."

"There's more. There's a pending civil suit. I expect some decision on it soon."

Faith looked sad that he hadn't told her about the timing. What was he doing to these people that he loved? Rick shook his head. Then Faith crawled into his lap. And he was reminded of the scene he'd witnessed that morning. Of a man he couldn't respect more. Of a man who had lost more than Rick ever had. Again, ludicrously, he thought of another Aesop's tale, the boasting traveler whose moral was, "Actions count more than words."

Did Rick want to be the man he'd always been, who flew off the handle, who raged against the world, yet didn't change the status quo? The man who didn't take—and keep—what he cherished? Or did he want to be like Ian Woodward and have the courage to withstand even more blows to his pride and ego for the woman he loved.

Sighing, he pulled Faith close and kissed her head. "Thanks

both of you. I appreciate the support. I promise I won't let you down."

But deep in his heart, Rick wondered if he had the courage, like Woodward, to keep his promise.

⌒ NINETEEN

SOUTH HAMPTON COUNTRY Club was teeming with activity when Ian pulled his van into the parking space reserved for the handicapped. Patrons paraded like dignitaries into the clubhouse banquet room. Glancing over at Lisel, Ian bit his tongue in order not to complain about this . . . *summons* from her parents to come to Thanksgiving brunch; he was concerned because he knew the Lawrences would badger her, and he'd have to sit by and watch it happen. The only saving grace was that they were leaving by noon to get to Eve and Noah's, where his family holiday gathering was planned at three.

He could tell Lisel was dreading this appearance, too, so he reached over and squeezed her arm.

She sighed heavily. "I don't want to go in there."

"Then don't." This from Joe, who sat in the backseat of the van; he was Lisel's bodyguard for the day. Ian was glad he was going to get to spend the holiday with his friend.

"I have to."

Ian glanced in the rearview mirror.

Joe's eyes were narrowed, his brows forming a vee. "Wouldn't let her do this if she was my girl."

"It's not Ian's fault. I dragged him here." Which was true. But he'd never have let her come alone.

"It's only two hours, sweetheart. How bad can it be?"

"Bad." She drew in a breath. Today she looked every inch the Broadway star in a long suede skirt and jacket in a soft cinnamon color. With it she wore dressy brown boots. Her hair was curled and hanging in waves down her back.

His heart went out to her. He loved his mother so much, and he'd been crazy about his father; dreading dinner with them on Thanksgiving Day was about as foreign to him as running from a burning building. Maybe this was the time to suggest something he'd been thinking about, something he knew would cheer Lisel up.

"Let's go in," she said resignedly.

"Wait, I want to ask you something." Again, he glanced in the rearview mirror. "Joe, remember how we were talking about this fan thing last night, after Lisel went to bed?"

"Uh-huh."

"I decided to do it."

"Good."

"Could you, um, wait outside a second, so I can ask her?"

The old man smiled. "My pleasure."

When Joe exited the van, Ian reached over and grabbed Lisel's hand. He said simply, "When we get back tonight, or tomorrow at the latest, I want you to move in with me."

"What?"

"I want you to live with me, Lise."

Her face, instead of wreathing in smiles, got even sadder. "You want me to move in with you because of the fan thing."

Ian kissed her hand. "No, love, I want you to move in with me because I love you. Because I want to be with you. I just seized on the fan thing as an excuse."

"Oh, Ian." She turned toward him, and he pulled her head to his chest. Kissed it. "This means so much to me."

"It means a lot to me, too." More than she knew. It was a gargantuan emotional step for him. Ian just held her. After a poignant moment, he asked, "Think you can hold on to that while we beard the lion in her den?"

She leaned back and kissed his cheek. "I think I can do anything right about now."

Which was exactly what he wanted her to be feeling before she tackled the session with her parents.

They exited the car. The day had dawned crystal clear, but crisp. Outside, Harmon leaned against the van. "She say yes?"

"Of course," Ian told him, cockily.

"Good." He jammed his hands in his navy trousers and nodded to the clubhouse. "I ain't comin' in there."

"Why?"

"Cuz I don't want to." He glanced around. "It's nice out. I'll hang here, catch the Jets on the radio. Lisel's with you, and I can see comings and goings. She's safe enough."

Lisel asked, "Want us to bring you something to eat?"

"No, I'm gonna have Evie's cookin' in a few hours." Impulsively, Ian could tell, Joe leaned over and kissed her cheek. "Don't let them push you around, girl."

"I won't."

As they made their way down the sidewalk to the handicap accessible entry, Lisel put her hand on Ian's shoulder. "Thank you for making this easier for me."

He grinned smugly. "What do you mean? I was trying to catch you at a weak moment. After all, I'm gonna like having you cook and clean for me."

She giggled.

Stopping briefly, he peered up at her. "I'm looking forward to being with you, Lise. All the time."

"What about after the fan thing is over, Ian?"

He squeezed her arm. "Then we'll talk some more. Let's try to enjoy the good that comes out of this mess."

"Okay, handsome."

He chuckled as they resumed their progress.

"You do look handsome in that suit."

"Thanks."

"It reminds me of the first time we made love."

"Stop, or I'll embarrass myself in front of your family." She leaned over and kissed his head just as they reached the doorway.

"Lisel, is that you?" A deep male voice came from behind them.

Ian glanced over his shoulder and saw a tall, dark-haired,

slim, sophisticated man had reached them. He surprised the hell out of Ian by kissing Lisel's cheek. "Hello, darling."

"Edward, hello."

"You look sensational. Jude said you might be here today."

"Yes, we came to have brunch with my parents." Reaching out, she again placed a hand on Ian's shoulder, but this time it was a possessive gesture. "This is Ian Woodward. Ian, this is my ex-husband, Edward Carrington."

Ice was warmer than the look in good old Edward's eyes. "Yes, hello. You're the firefighter." He glanced pointedly at Ian's legs.

Ian resisted the urge to squirm. "Yes, I'm the firefighter," he said, surprised by the pride that sneaked out in his tone.

"Good to meet you."

"Are you alone, Edward?" Lisel asked.

"No, I'm meeting some people from the club."

"Well, nice to see you again." She reached for the door.

"Here, let me get that." Before Ian could react, Edward stepped jauntily in front of him and yanked open the door. Ian stifled his resentment, and graciously wheeled through after Lisel. They entered the large dining area.

It was a breathtaking club, with a panorama of windows facing the golf course, still-green lawns rolling and dipping and curling around ponds and brooks. The interior was dotted with tables bearing linen and crystal. A monstrous buffet lined the perimeter, and the smells of cooked meat and bread wafted from it. Ian was grateful to Patrick, who'd taken them to places like this on occasion, so he didn't feel totally out of his element.

He saw Jude waving them over. Her smile for Lisel was stiff. Her glance down at him told him why. Well, he'd expected this. "Let's go." He squeezed Lisel's arm. "And remember what Harmon said."

They headed for the table. Uh-oh. Snag number one. The carpet here was plush, of course. It was difficult to maneuver his wheels through it. Their trek was slow, causing people to stare at them. It probably wasn't that they weren't used to seeing disabled people, but when one was dating a star like Lisel, it was noteworthy. He pasted a smile on his face.

When they reached the table, Jude gave Lisel an air kiss on

both cheeks, and Allen stretched out his hand to Ian. "Nice to see you again, Woodward." His tone implied it wasn't.

"You, too."

Jude parroted that phony sentiment. "Let's sit." Her mother blushed, looking at Ian. "Oh, dear, I'm sorry."

"No need." He turned his chair to the table. Snag number two stared him in the face. "But you need to remove a chair."

Allen snapped his fingers, and a young waiter came running. "Take one of these chairs, Marcus."

"Yes, Mr. Lawrence."

When they were situated—Lisel between her parents and across from him—the inquisition began. "What do you drink, Woodward?"

He glanced at his watch. "Nothing now, thanks."

"Nonsense. We'll all have champagne." Again he signaled the waiter. Champagne was delivered and a toast made. "To all we have to be thankful for."

"As they sipped the wine, Allen didn't waste any time pouncing on his daughter. "I hear you declined, officially, 'Sundays with Lisel.'"

"Yes, Dad, I did. But I've made a compromise. For you."

Ian quelled a scowl. She'd discussed this with him, and he had made his displeasure clear, but since she decided to do it, he'd support her.

"I'm doing a holiday special on December fourteenth. Two performances of *Longshot*."

"Fine," her father said coldly. He picked up a menu and handed it to Ian. "You'll want to order off this, I imagine."

Ian stiffened. "No, thanks. I can maneuver the buffet."

Allen gave him a sideways glance. "Fine," he said again.

Jude began chatting about people they knew and committees she was on at the club. As if it just occurred to her—Ian doubted it—she gave her daughter a simpering smile. "Since you've got so much time on your hands, you should work on the charity bazaar with me." She shared a look with Allen. "You'll move back down here, while you recuperate, and we'll do it together."

"Thanks for the offer, Mother, but no. I won't be moving back down here." She smiled at Ian. "I am moving in with Ian."

"What?"

"What?"

Her parents spoke simultaneously.

"Ian and I are moving in together."

"This is rather sudden."

"It's because of the fan thing, isn't it?" As if he just remembered, Allen scanned the dining room. "Where is your watchdog, anyway?"

"Joe's outside. He didn't want to come in."

"Well, I hope he stays inconspicuous. I wouldn't want people to talk."

Ian felt the fire inside him spark. What the hell was wrong with these people? "Lisel's safety is our priority, Jude. If anybody notices Harmon, it's a small price to pay." He nodded to the other patrons. "I'm sure some of these people have employed bodyguards before." He winked at Lisel. "Now, I'm starved. Shall we serve ourselves?"

It was after the meal when Ian went to use the restroom that snag number three happened. Really, it was more of a stumbling block purposefully thrown in his way. He'd left the men's room and was behind a partition that faced a hallway when Lisel's father and a man whose back was toward them came into view.

"Jesus, Allen, how can you allow this?"

"I can't control her any more than you could, Edward."

Ah, the ex. "What will people think?" The guy ran a hand through his hair. "First quitting Broadway."

"She's taking a hiatus; she hasn't quit."

"Whatever. Then she moves to that hick town. Now she's hooking up with a cripple."

"I know," Allen said. "It's all very embarrassing. I can hardly field the questions from my golf partners."

"I wonder how . . . functional he is."

Ian wanted to turn tail and run. He wanted to hide. But, damn it, he wasn't going to let these snobs—this man who'd destroyed Lisel's confidence with his arrogance and this father who never had her best interest at heart—get off scott free with what they said.

So he wheeled out from behind the partition and over to them. "I'm fully functional," Ian pronounced, giving the ex a withering look. "Seems I'm capable of keeping her happy. I wonder, Edward, why you couldn't." Then he faced Allen. "I'd think *you'd* be more concerned about her emotional and physical well-being than what people think. That's what fathers do, you know."

With that he turned in the chair and wheeled away with his head held high.

"WHAT TIME WILL they be here, dear?" Pearl McPherson stirred the hot applesauce at the stove and addressed Faith, who was cutting up vegetables for a snack. Usually they ate Thanksgiving dinner early in the day, but they'd delayed it to mid-afternoon so the Ruscios could have breakfast with their mother. Dolores Ruscio steadfastly refused to celebrate Thanksgiving Day with the McPhersons. It was still up in the air which of her children, if any, would come.

"I told you, Mom, Rick might stay with his mother." But she was praying he'd come for dinner. She glanced down at the pretty peach-colored sweater and skirt she'd put on just for him.

Pearl smiled. "I think your young man is beyond letting his mother manipulate him." She sighed. "I don't understand how a parent can treat a child like that."

Impulsively, Faith rose and went over to kiss Pearl. "Not every kid's as lucky as Peter and I are to have a mother like you."

"It goes both ways, honey."

"Did I hear my name out here?"

They turned to see her brother enter the kitchen, rolling up the sleeves of his red plaid flannel shirt. He'd been out back with David, bringing in firewood.

"I was just saying how lucky we were to have parents like ours."

Peter crossed to Pearl and hugged her from behind. "We sure are." He sniffed then glanced around the kitchen. "How come dinner isn't further along?" He checked his watch. "It's noon."

"We're eating later," Pearl reminded him. "I told you that."

"I forgot. Why are we, anyway?"

"To wait for the Ruscios."

Her brother's face hardened. He crossed to the refrigerator and pulled out a beer. "Ah, yes, the Ruscios." Uncapping a Molson's, he took a long gulp from the bottle. "Isn't it going to be awkward when the Daltons get here?"

Pearl looked up at her son. "Your father explained that the Daltons wouldn't be eating with us this year, didn't he?"

David came through the door just then. "No, I was just about to when I got a call." He crossed to Faith and kissed her head, then casually glanced over at Peter. "Sam and his parents decided not to come today."

"Well, no surprise there." Peter's big shoulders were stiff as he sat down across from Faith and drank more of his beer. "What time they getting here?"

"We're not sure." Her father was hedging.

"It's a long story, Peter." Faith eyed him squarely. "Rick's mother—"

"Hello, everybody," she heard from the foyer. Pilar's voice rang out through the house, interrupting Faith's confession. Briefly Faith closed her eyes and asked God that Rick and Anita be with her. Pilar entered the kitchen wearing a cheerful pink parka, with a pink sweater peeking out beneath it. Behind her was Anita, in black, but with a smile on her face.

No one followed Anita. Faith's heart constricted in her chest.

"Happy Thanksgiving, everybody." Pilar handed a bouquet of sunflowers to Pearl and kissed her cheek.

Anita had carried in a couple of bakery boxes. "Happy Thanksgiving," she said shyly.

Introductions were made. Faith almost couldn't quell the disappointment she felt. She tried, though, clearing her throat. "Rick decided to stay with your mom?" she asked Pilar.

The young girl's brow furrowed. "No, he's getting stuff out of the car. He said to send you to help him."

Angel choruses sung in Faith's heart. She threw back her chair and raced out of the kitchen. She'd just reached the front door when it opened.

And there he stood in his black leather coat with a checked black and red sport shirt beneath it. "Hey, there you are." Leaning over as if it was the most natural thing in the world, he kissed her cheek. "Happy Thanksgiving."

She held on, despite the fact that his arms were laden with a basket full of holiday things like nuts, and berries, and fruit. He also carried a small gift bag.

"Happy Thanksgiving." She drew back, and he placed the packages on the foyer table. "Let me have your coat." As he removed it, she smoothed her hand over his shoulders. "How'd it go with your mother?"

His eyes flashed with sadness. "Same old, same old. She hardly ate any of the breakfast we cooked. She drank vodka and orange juice all morning. And she was just about passed out on the couch when we left."

"I'm sorry."

"Yeah, I know." He grasped her neck and pulled her to him. "She got in her digs about us abandoning her."

"But you came, anyway."

He nodded. "Yeah, I thought Pilar was going to cave, then I didn't know what I'd do. But Anita saved the day, blatantly telling Ma she had choices, like we did." He held Faith close to his heart, and she could hear its steady thump. "I felt bad leaving her there, but good in a way. Freer." He was silent. "Does that make me a bad person?"

"No. You had to stop enabling her sometime." She hugged him close. "I'm so glad you're here."

"Me, too." Though Rick had just seen Faith last night—he'd forced himself to leave her bed at ten—his whole body, his whole *being* responded to her closeness. He was into this whole thing deeper than a cocaine junkie. There was nothing he could do about it. Nothing he wanted to do about it. He looked around and took note of the small den to the left of the foyer. "Come in here a second with me."

Her eyes danced with sexual promise. "Want a little hanky panky, big guy?"

"Hush, not in your parents' house." He grabbed the small package off the table. Inside the den, he closed the door and leaned against it. Before he could say anything, she threw herself at him for a searing kiss. When he could manage to ease her off, he chuckled. "Faith, stop. Come on, we're in the parsonage."

Reluctantly, she pulled back. "Okay." But she didn't stop touching him. He loved that about her, how she petted him, soothed him, as if he didn't outweigh her by seventy-five pounds and wasn't half a foot taller. "Why we in here?"

His hand shook when he held up the bag. "I got something for you."

"A present?"

"Hmm. A Thanksgiving present." To show her how thankful he was she was in his life. And to show her a few other things.

"Oh, Rick." Her beautiful green eyes shone the color of polished jade. She took the bag, drew out the long, skinny velvet box, and opened it. There was total silence as she stared down at the necklace. Then, reverently, her hand came up and fingered the charm on the end. "Oh."

He placed his hand at her neck. Bent over and kissed her head. "I found it when I was shopping for a charm for Pilar's bracelet; her birthday's next week." His voice pitched lower of its own accord. "This spoke to me."

Slowly she raised her head. Her eyes were moist. "What did it say to you, Ricardo?"

He smiled. "You know."

"Tell me."

Staring down, he studied the miniature twenty-one-caret gold book with the five letters raised in deeper gold. "It said 'I believe.' "

She clutched the charm to her chest. "I'll never take this off." Her gaze locked with his, she whispered, "I love you, Rick. I'm glad you believe."

Damn, if he wasn't choked up all over again, like when he'd bought the thing. "I love you, too, Faith." Taking the necklace from her, he undid the clasp, slipped it around her throat, and closed it up. Then he picked up the charm of Aesop's book, kissed it, and tucked it in her sweater. "Happy Thanksgiving, love."

"I'D LIKE TO propose a toast." Noah lifted his wine glass and captured Eve's gaze. "To my wife, on our first Thanksgiving together. Thank you for all you've given me."

Eve smiled. "I love you, Noah."

Lisel's eyes misted at the poignant sentiment. She glanced at the other women seated around the Callahan's big teak table. Lila, next to Lisel, was wiping her eyes at seeing Eve so happy. Noah's daughter, Becca, grasped her husband's hand and buried her tears in her Tom's shoulder. From the other side of her, holding Abby on his lap, Ian looked over and clicked his glass with Lisel's. His look said *I love you* clearer than words. It was an emotional moment all around.

"All right, everybody," Eve told them, "dig in."

Abby climbed off Ian's lap and onto her own chair. "Can I go play with Paulie when I'm done? They already ate."

Tom ruffled his daughter's hair. "If somebody's watching you."

"His sister will."

"How old is she?" Becca asked.

"Twelve."

Noah nodded. "I think it's all right, Bec. There's a lot of daylight left."

Abby shoveled food into her mouth and was out the door before anyone else was done. Ian set down his fork and scowled. "I'm gonna go check on that. She can be a pistol."

Becca started to rise. "I can go."

"Sit." He wheeled away.

Joe Harmon kept glancing toward the door until Ian returned. "Something wrong?" he asked gruffly.

"No." He scowled. "The sister's out there."

Lisel watched him. Something more was going on. He looked like he was worried. She was distracted from Ian's concern by the turn the conversation took—a boisterous discussion of the upcoming babies: Eve was due in six months, and Becca in three. Lisel resisted the urge to place her hand on her stomach. She wanted Ian's baby so much. They were careful, of course, to always use protection, and Ian had made such strides she didn't want to upset the balance. But she longed for his child.

After dinner was cleaned up, he caught her hand as the others headed for the desserts, set out in the kitchen. "What were you thinking?" he asked her pointedly. "At dinner?"

She shook her head. "Nothing. Just how happy I am."

"You were thinking about babies, weren't you?"

"Um . . ."

"Am I interrupting?" Harmon came through the doors.

"No." Lisel sighed at being saved from the interrogation session.

Joe leaned against the table. "What was going on with the kid? You checked on her twice now."

Ian shook his head. "I don't know. I had a bad feeling about her playing out there alone."

"She all right?"

"Yeah, I guess." He shrugged. "I just got a special connection with her. Something felt amiss when she left."

"Pa-pa!" They heard the shriek after a door banging.

"Well, she's here." Lisel straightened. "Let's go get dessert."

They all proceeded into the kitchen, a huge square with a big center island and an eat-in area. The aroma of baked pies and cookies filled the air. From the garage entrance, Abby rushed across the room and hurled herself at Noah. She carried a manila envelope with her. "This is for you."

Noah took the envelope and scowled. "Where'd you get this, sweetheart?"

She stuck her hand in her mouth and said something garbled. Noah removed her fingers so she could speak. ". . . lady gave it to me outside."

Becca frowned. "You didn't talk to any strangers, did you?"

"Nope. She gave it to me, said to give it to Papa, then left. I didn't say nothing."

"What is it?" Harmon asked, going to stand behind Noah.

Noah looked up. "Actually, it's addressed to Ian."

"Me?"

Noah shook it. "Feels like papers." He looked to Harmon.

Joe took the package. "I'll open it." They were beyond tracing fingerprints from the fan. Not one communication had them.

With a scowl on his face, Joe ripped open the envelope and slid out the contents on the kitchen table. They were photographs.

"It's Lisel!" Abby quipped.

Both she and Ian circled around the table to sidle in next to Harmon. Lisel stared down at the pictures of her.

The first was a publicity photo she'd had done with Mel Gibson when he'd starred in a play on Broadway and Lisel had a walk-on part. Though he wasn't a large man, he seemed tall and looked big next to her.

The second was a picture of the leading man in her fourth play. Jamie Connors was built like Schwarzenegger, and his stance reflected it. He, too, towered over Lisel.

"That's Scarface," Abby said of the third picture.

A current Hollywood sensation in superhero movies had been Lisel's friend when they were both upstarts, playing off off Broadway.

As each picture was uncovered, Ian sat stock still. When she placed her hand on his shoulder, it was granite hard.

The last photo was of Ian, in the wheelchair. He looked small and fragile, compared to the bulk of the men before. Over his jeans, someone had pasted the withered legs of a polio victim. On his picture was scrawled, "You don't deserve her."

Lisel gasped when she saw it. Eve came to stand by Ian and put her hand on the other shoulder.

Abby stared down at the photo. "Those things are scary," she said, pointing to the pseudo legs. Then she traced the letters. "What's it say, Papa?"

Noah took the offending photo out of view. "Nothing of importance, honey." He looked to his daughter. "Take her into the living room, Bec."

Both Tom and Becca stood to escort Abby out, when Harmon said to Rebecca, "Wait a minute." Joe went over to the little girl and squatted down in front of her. "Abby, what did the woman look like who gave this to you?"

Abby stuck her fingers in her mouth. Her gaze sought out Ian.

"Tell him, honey," Ian's voice was like sandpaper on steel.

Abby scanned the rest of the adults. Then she pointed to Lisel. "Like her. The lady looked just like her."

RICK RAN A hand down Faith's naked body and watched her shiver. "You're so pretty." He stopped at her breasts, squeezed gently. "Here." He cupped the curls at the juncture of her thighs. "And here." Leaning over, he brushed her stomach with his lips.

She sighed, a woman contented. Satisfied. And in love. Rick's heart swelled with the miracle that made this woman love him. Reaching up, he traced the charm he'd given her.

Turning toward him, she kissed his hand. "I want to tell you something."

He grinned and swept the hair out of her eyes. "What?"

"First, reach into the nightstand."

He glanced over his shoulder at the offensive furniture. "Where you keep the vibrator? No thanks."

She grinned into the pillow. "I haven't used it in ages."

He scowled at her. "Look, if you got some other things, like for us, you know, I'm not much into sexual aids."

She laughed. "It's not that. Though I can't believe a big tough guy like you is afraid of those things."

"I'm not afraid." He tried to sound offended.

"You're not a very good liar." She leaned over him, opened the drawer, and drew out a small square package. "I've had this wrapped and ready to give to you when I thought you could accept it. I think it's safe to do it tonight. On Thanksgiving night." She grasped onto her necklace. "After this."

He drew in a breath, but took the present.

"Open it."

His hands fumbled with the plain tissue paper. Inside it, he found a note to taped to the box. It was addressed to her. "What is this?"

"It's from my grandpa. Read the note."

Frowning, he unfolded the sheet of paper. It read, "Dear Little One, Enclosed is something I want you to have when I'm gone. It was mine, and I kept it close to my heart always, like I kept you. But this isn't for you. I want you to give it to the man you decide to share your life with. I trust your judgment, so look at this gift as if it's my blessing on the two of you." Then in a postscript, it said, "To Faith's young man: Take care of my girl."

Rick's eyes moistened. He couldn't speak, couldn't get past the golf ball–size lump in his throat.

"I wrapped it up for you weeks ago," Faith told him when he didn't move. "I didn't do it just because of this." She held on to the charm around her neck.

He cleared his throat. "So you said."

"Open it."

He did. Inside was a heavy St. Christopher's medal on a man-sized chain.

Faith smiled fondly at it. "My grandma gave it to Grandpa when he was in the military. He never took it off."

Finally Rick could look at her. "Faith, shouldn't this go to Peter?"

"No, Grandpa wanted done with it what he said. Peter got his gold pocket watch. My cousins got other things."

"I don't know what to say."

"Say you'll accept it."

He knew what she was asking. Did he have the courage to accept the responsibility her grandfather was giving him? Once again he thought of Ian Woodward and how he'd overcome his own demons for Lisel. "I'll accept it," he said reverently. He ducked his head. "With honor."

Lovingly, she slid the chain around his neck. "Grandpa would have loved you. I wish he—"

Loud knocking on the front door interrupted her. They'd left the bedroom door open, since no one was expected at ten on Thanksgiving night. Anita was sleeping over with Pilar, and everybody was pretty worn out by nine when Rick and Faith had come back here.

"Faith . . ." Some muffled words.

Rick said, "Who is it?"

"It sounds like Peter."

"Oh, Christ."

"Don't swear." She kissed him on the cheek. "He sounds drunk."

"He is drunk." He'd been drunk since dinner. And he'd shot barbs at Rick whenever he could. David finally pulled him aside to talk to him.

Getting out of bed, Faith donned a bathrobe.

"Shit, Faith, put some clothes on."

"No. This is my home. I'm twenty-seven years old. Peter has to learn to back off. I'm not hiding what we were doing from my baby brother."

Rick closed his eyes.

He heard her leave and grasped the medal in his hand.

The door wasn't thick enough to block a brother's outrage . . .

"Damn it, Faith, he's in your bedroom . . . you're fucking him?"

She chided Peter about swearing, too. Then she said more gently, "We didn't fuck, Peter. We made love."

More swearing. "He doesn't deserve you."

"How would you know? You hardly know him."

"I know all his secrets. I went online and downloaded the articles about him. There's a pending civil suit against him. Do you know the grief that could cause Mom and Dad?"

Rick slid out of bed and began dressing. He was expecting some resolution to the civil suit this week. His lawyer seemed to think it would be dropped.

The shouting got louder. Rick hurried and reached the living room, his shirt still unbuttoned. He went to stand beside Faith. "What's going on out here?"

"Nothing. I've handled it." She looked like a little general pissed off at her troops.

Peter weaved as he stepped closer. "Oh, yeah . . . you're handling your life just fine . . . you're . . ." He stopped and squinted at Rick. Outrage covered his face. "Goddamn it, Faith. You . . . you gave him Grandpa's medal."

"Yes, it was mine to give." She reached out to touch her brother's arm. "I love him, Peter. I want a life with him."

"Over my dead body," Peter said, just as he bent at the waist, and like a linebacker making a tackle, lunged for Rick.

TWENTY

JOE HARMON SWERVED Ian's van into the parking lot of Quint/Midi 7 and shut off the engine. Turning, he faced Ian, who was about to exit from the passenger side where he'd ridden in his chair. "I'll be here by ten to get you," his friend said gruffly.

They'd fought over this. After the humiliation of the pictures the stalker had sent—and opening them in front of everybody he cared about—Ian had been in a sour mood, which he allowed to show only when Lisel wouldn't witness it. Like now.

"I don't need a babysitter." Harmon had insisted he drive Ian in to the firehouse. Lisel was with Ruscio, but Joe had to meet them so Rick could run some errands.

"Damn it, boy. We ain't goin' through this again. You gotta be watched with the fan on the loose."

"The fucking fan can go to hell."

Joe shifted and drummed his fingers on the steering wheel. "She's steppin' this up, I can feel it."

Grabbing the iron bars of his chair, Ian strove for calm. "I'm so pissed off about all this I can hardly stand it."

"I know," he said. "And you're doin' a good job of keeping it from our girl."

"I'm trying. Sometimes I feel like I'm going to explode, though."

"We can box later, if you want. And remember, the police are on it big-time cuz threats to you have been made."

"Yeah."

Joe reached out and squeezed his shoulder. "Hang in there, boy."

"All right, see you at ten." With the remote, he opened the door and activated the lift. Outside, a light snow had fallen and the pavement was slick.

"Be careful out there, it's slippery."

Ian grunted, lowered himself to the blacktop and wheeled himself to the firehouse. A door had been propped open. Once inside, the smell of smoke, oil, and gasoline hit him. The trucks—a Quint, a Midi, and the Rescue rig—stood guard in the bays, looming like chariots waiting to take off. Firefighter boots and bunker pants stood like soldiers waiting by the rigs for a call. He hadn't realized how much he'd missed this atmosphere. Other than when he'd gone to see the guys at Ladder 4 in New York, he hadn't set foot in a fire station since 9/11.

"Hey, Captain, hello." Mitch Malvaso had walked out of his office and found Ian daydreaming in the bay. "Thanks for coming."

"I'm happy to. I haven't done night training since I was hurt."

Mitch shook his head. "Must be hard. To be back in a house."

"Yeah, it is. But it feels good, too." He nodded to the hallway. "They back there?"

"Yeah, and in a mood, I'll tell you. Grady and Zach are at odds over something to do with Jenny. The guys from Engine 17 are here razzing the Rescue Squad. And Ed Snyder, who used to work with us, is ragging on Zach's wife, Casey. As always."

"God, I miss it."

Mitch chuckled.

They wheeled down the corridor to the kitchen where several men and two women sat around a huge table. Training on WMD was required of certain squads at regular intervals to comply with government statutes passed since 9/11. If training wasn't done, the department could be sued in the event of an in-

cident. Careful records were kept. Ian knew the HCFD tried to
balance fire academy training and in-house training. Usually,
in-house was more relaxed and full of firefighter humor.

Most of the crew greeted him when he entered the room. For
a minute, he was startled by the sight of them, all in navy
T-shirts, sipping coffee, picking on each other. A longing to be
one of them socked him in the gut.

"Hey, guys," he said easily. He nodded to the several instruments that were already laid out on the table. "I'll bet you're really lookin' forward to this."

"About as much as a root canal," somebody joked. Others
chimed in, and soon it became a contest of who could think of
the worst scenarios . . . changing a kid's diaper . . . wading in a
basement full of shit . . . dinner with the mother-in-law.

Ian laughed along with them. He noticed a space had been
left for his chair. He wheeled over to it. Casey Malvaso stood.
She was an attractive woman, with black hair and blue eyes like
Lisel. "Can I get you coffee, Captain?" she asked.

"Oooh . . . eee . . . Brennan's acting like a girl." This was
said teasingly by another smoke eater.

"Shut up, LoTurco. The guy saved my life."

"Too bad," somebody else mumbled. This was not uttered in
a jocular tone.

Zach Malvaso came halfway out of his seat before Grady
O'Connor held him back. "Say one more fuckin' thing about
my wife, Snyder, and you'll be eating your teeth."

"Yeah, and who's gonna make me do that, Malvaso?"

Mitch stood. His shoulders stiff, he braced his hands on the
table and leaned in. "We have a guest tonight. If I hear one more
nasty thing come out of your mouth, Snyder, you're outta here."
He faced his brother. "And if you can't ignore his stupid shit,
you're going, too."

Zach sat down.

"Ah, it's good to be back," Ian quipped, lifting his briefcase
and taking out papers. He dived right in. "State standards say
you need refresher courses to review the equipment you carry
and some of you have used before. So we'll do that first. Then
I'm gonna tell you about that baby down there." He nodded to a
TravelIR, which was the most recent piece of equipment that

Noah had written a grant for and gotten. "There's only a few departments in the state that have one. You're lucky to get it."

He began with the Arearae. It was a rectangular black box that was used to monitor an area where an outbreak occurred to determine the quality of air. "Who knows what this tests for?" Ian asked. He'd rather not lecture and knew some of these guys were pretty smart.

Grady O'Connor answered. "Chemical saturation, biological agents, or radiation. We'd go into the site in Level-A suits"—the typical white alien-looking gear—"and determine if evacuation is needed."

"Show off," somebody grumbled.

"You're just jealous, Greg," Grady quipped.

Wholesome-looking Greg swore back at him good-naturedly.

When they finished reviewing that device, Ian started with another. "Let's look at the new Drager Tube Kit." Drager tubes had been around a long time but weren't commonly used until after 9/11. "This is the new Drager CDS kit." It consisted of a pack that plugged into a five-pronged tube holder. "What five things does this test for?"

Grady sat back in his chair and crossed his arms over his chest, obviously reluctant to be center stage again. Mitch jumped in. "Nerve agents, blister agents, lung agents, blood agents, and nose and throat irritants."

Briefly Ian reviewed how to break open the tubing and pump the handle. It was easy stuff, but there were a few new guys here who hadn't had the training at all.

"Now let's get to the crème de la crème." He pointed to the TravelIR. "We already know this is for use in the hot zone"—where contamination was expected—"and this will be in the HazMat truck, but you'll take it out into the open. Why?"

"Don't want to contaminate the truck if it's a real thing." This from one of the guys Ian didn't know.

"Right. Anybody know what the testing will do?"

"It has the definitive ability to identify the unknown," Grady said, seemingly unable to stop himself. "We won't have to go into a full-blown HazMat Level-A entry if it's just sugar we're dealing with."

Ian demonstrated its setup. He took all the components from

the case and connected the power box to the foot-high machine. He demonstrated how to connect the plug to the power source. "I used this in an incident once in New York," he told them. He installed the monitor bracket in the top of the machine as he talked. "Okay, this is the monitor that will track the agent. But the useful information will come on the laptop." He'd already connected that to the machine. It would give the entire composition of the chemical found. "Pass me that sugar." Ian pointed to the glass jar on the table.

He took a sample and placed it on the flat circular surface that would hold the agent. "Then you take this pin," he said, pointing to the needlelike thing that would touch the agent and transmit the information. Ian screwed it in and watched the lights come on the monitor, telling them it had enough of the sample. He said, "Okay, watch the laptop. It'll come up with the composition."

"What happened in New York when you used this machine that time, Cap?" Zach Malvaso asked.

Ian warmed at the affectionate nickname. He hadn't heard it in a long time. "We took a sample of white powder the guy thought to be anthrax, given him by a homeboy who turned on him. Turned out to be talcum powder. But the good thing is that guy would have had to wait days to get an answer from the lab before we had this baby. There'd be talk of quarantine, possible panic from neighbors. This device saves a lot of shit."

They talked for a while longer about the TravelIR, then some other technology O'Connor had read about. Before Ian left, the group thanked him for his expertise and interest in doing their training. Casey Malvaso came up to him and gave him a hug.

At ten, Mitch walked Ian out to the bay. "Listen, sorry about that crap in there. Snyder's an ass."

Ian smiled. "I had a guy in my group once like that. Nothing you can do except step on them from time to time."

"That's why you handled him so well."

Ian's chest expanded with pride. "Thanks."

"The lesson was great, Ian." Mitch stopped at the bay door. "You sticking around Hidden Cove?"

Ian shrugged. "I don't know. I accepted this assignment for six months. I'll probably stay in town until Eve's baby is born."

Mitch smiled. There was something about it . . .

"What?"

The guy glanced around, a goofy grin on his face now. "It isn't public knowledge, but my wife, Megan is pregnant."

"Hey, congrats."

"Well, it was a bit of a surprise. We haven't been married long. Megan's always wanted a baby, but we were going to wait a while."

Ian chuckled.

"Anyway, back to you. All the guys are hoping you'll take something permanent at the academy."

"Hmm." Ian had considered it. Caruso had mentioned it. Noah had brought it up a couple of times lately. He thought of Lisel living with him in Hidden Cove. "Maybe." He held out his hand. "Thanks, Mitch."

Mitch nodded to the parking lot. "Need any help? That light snow we had earlier made the blacktop slippery."

"No, thanks. I'll be fine." He didn't want to advertise that Harmon would be picking him up.

Instead, as he wheeled himself out of the firehouse, he thought about babies. And no matter how he tried not to, an image of Lisel came to mind every time the subject was raised. Ian had seen her face as Noah's daughter and Evie gushed about their pregnancies. She'd confided innumerable times before they were involved that she'd like to have a child. And he wanted one, too. His ex hadn't been able to get pregnant, but it hadn't stopped Ian from wanting a kid.

That would certainly throw off her career, he thought, waiting under the overhang. He could just picture Jude and Allen's reaction. What he'd overheard at the country club still rankled him. He hadn't told anybody about what her ex and her father had said; he was considering going back to the trauma survivor's group tomorrow night to talk about it. Hell, he should table any ideas he had about a baby. They hadn't even discussed marriage.

It was dark outside, but the parking lot was well lit. He noticed no cars in the visitor spaces. He glanced at his watch. Harmon wasn't here yet. How odd. Joe had been rabid about being his escort. Should Ian go back inside? Turning the chair, he tried the door to the firehouse and found it locked. It was cold, and he shivered, pulling his leather jacket closer around him.

He was just about to ring the bell, when he was jerked back suddenly; someone yanked on the handles of the wheelchair.

What the hell? He started to turn around, when he felt the chair move. His heart thunderclapped in his chest. The chair was dragged away from the firehouse. It thrust forward.

"Hey, what are you—"

The person pushed it harder. Faster.

"What are you doing?"

"Shut up!" The voice was female. "I told you to stay away from her. You're not worthy of her. She deserves somebody whole."

"You're the—"

The person must have started running, because the chair picked up speed, cutting off his sentence. Wind whipped his face raw, and the chair teetered. Ian forced himself not to panic. He glanced around. The parking lot was deserted. But he yelled anyway, "Hey, somebody help me!" He jammed his hand inside his coat and grabbed for his cell phone.

A blow landed on his head; pain streaked from his skull to his neck, throughout his entire body; his stomach roiled. The lights in the lot dimmed.

His eyes closed, but he grabbed the chair and forced them open. Just in time to see himself headed for the brick fence that surrounded the parking lot.

The impact was brutal.

PULLING HER SCARF tighter around her face, Jules watched him bounce off the wall. The chair crashed, too, with a loud metallic clanging. A head injury of serious contusions would result from that contact. Combined with the rap on the skull she gave him with the club she'd brought just in case, he was going to be out of commission for a while.

He was thrown from the chair, of course, and landed facedown on the hard pavement with a satisfying thud. Pathetic, that's what he was, curled up on the blacktop like some bum. Quickly, she took out her camera and snapped a picture. Lisel could see for herself how pitiful he was.

A shout from behind her. "Hey, what's going on there?"

She took off at a dead run. Having made sure she had a route of escape, she rounded the corner of the firehouse and slipped through the gate of the chain-link fence in the back.

But she was careful to keep hold of her evidence. It nestled like a precious gem in her pocket. She couldn't wait for Lisel to see it.

LISEL WAS SHAKING so hard her teeth rattled as she flew into the ER with Joe Harmon behind her. She'd slipped once in the light snow and fallen. She hardly felt the cold wetness of her jeans and the jacket she'd thrown on when Mitch Malvaso had called them.

Harmon had been ruthlessly calm, but quiet. Lisel knew he was worried. Mitch met them at the ER entrance. "He's okay," Mitch said soothingly. "Some contusions and a concussion. Nothing broken, though."

Thank God. How would he manage in a wheelchair if he'd injured his arms?

"Lisel, hi."

She looked up at Rick Ruscio; the sight of him big and brawny in a bomber jacket caused anger to rise in her. She didn't try to hide it. "How could this happen when you were with him?"

Rick's brows formed a vee. "I wasn't with him." He glanced over her shoulder at Harmon. "You were covering tonight."

Joe said, "We got a call from the dispatcher at the firehouse that you'd shown up there and didn't need us to come back for him. Lisel was watching a movie with Mona. Her daughter had just called and upset her, so Lisel was glad to stay. I—" He ran a hand through his hair. "I didn't think twice about it."

Will Rossettie, behind Rick, shook his head. "The stalker got to him."

"You sure?" Harmon asked.

Mitch nodded. "He came to on the ride here. Said somebody ambushed him, pushed him into the brick wall at the end of the parking lot."

Lisel swayed. Joe and Rick grabbed for her. "Oh, God. He's unconscious?"

"In and out," Mitch told her.

"Are you sure it isn't serious?"

Mitch said, "Let's go see."

They all trekked through the ER doors and made their way in silence to Ian's cubicle. He was lying in bed, stretched out, with his arm at a ninety-degree angle resting on his forehead. A bandage was taped over his left eye, and there was one around his wrist. Lisel's stomach lurched at the sight of the man she loved broken and bruised in the bed. Damn it, she thought bitterly. Hadn't he been through enough?

"Hey, boy." This from Joe.

Ian turned his head toward them. Rick gave Lisel's arm a squeeze, which propelled her forward. She gasped when she got up close and saw the cuts and black and blue marks on his face. "Oh, Ian." She tried to be strong, but couldn't control the moisture that welled in her eyes.

"Shh. I'm okay." He winced when he reached out his hand. She grasped it, noticing the back of it was scraped, too. "This was nothing like being pinned under that beam, sweetheart."

"You don't have to try to make me feel better. I'm just glad you're okay."

"I am." But his voice was raw. She suspected he was hurting.

"Did they give you anything for the pain?"

"No, I wanted to wait until I saw you."

She turned to Mitch. "Can you call the doctor? He needs to have something now."

"Sure." Mitch slipped out of the room.

Ian looked past her. "You can come in, guys. I'm not dying here."

Lisel bit her lip.

Joe, Rick, and Will came to the bed. Ian held Lisel's hand tightly. "How'd it happen?" he asked.

Vaguely, she heard them explain. All she could focus on was how battered he was. His hands. His strong arms. His beloved jaw—with the scar that testified to how much he'd already suffered.

She came back to the conversation when she heard him say, "Can I see my girl alone now?"

"After the pain medication," Lisel heard from the doorway. A young man stood there with a syringe. "Glad to see you talked him into this. He's got to be sore as hell."

Lisel cringed. The others left, and she sank down into a chair at the side of his bed and pulled it close. He moaned when he rolled to his side. "Ian, don't move."

"Shh. Come here." He tugged her over and drew her head to his chest.

Gingerly, she nestled in. "I'm so sorry."

"It isn't your fault."

"The fan's after me."

"The fan is deranged. She's sick, Lisel. You're in real danger."

"So are you."

"That's obvious. I'm stunned at her viciousness."

"Did she say anything, Ian?"

He hesitated. She sat up. "Tell me. Please don't keep anything from me."

Brushing back her hair, he shook his head. "She said I don't deserve you. You should have somebody whole."

She gasped.

He lifted his chin. "She's wrong. I do deserve you." He ran fingertips down her cheek. "I might've wavered before about that, but no more. She isn't going to win. We are."

"Oh, Ian." Lisel began to cry.

He kissed her head. "Don't cry, baby. Please."

She couldn't stop.

Until he said, dryly, "So, when are we going to make this official?"

She stopped. Abruptly. "What . . . what do you mean?"

"I mean, when are you going to marry me?"

FOR THREE DAYS, Ian could barely contain his frustration and fury. The only person he let down with at all was Harmon, who seemed to understand his rage and his need to protect Lisel from it. They couldn't even box, because Ian's injuries had necessitated bed rest, and he had to wait even to get to the trauma survivor's group. So he'd seethed, much as he had after he was first injured.

On the third morning after the incident, he approached the group meeting, with Ruscio behind him.

"I'll wait out here," Ruscio said gruffly as they reached the door.

Ian remembered something. He pivoted in the chair. "Why don't you come in with me?"

Ruscio's face blanked; Ian recognized the tactic masked inner pain. "Me, why?"

"You were here once before when I was."

Ruscio shook his head. "I left that day." He jammed his hands in his pockets. "I can't talk to a group like this."

"It's fucking tough, I know."

Hank Harrison, the police and fire department psychologist, came down the hall and spotted them. "Ah, guys, hello." He shook hands with Ian and turned to Rick. "I knew Woodward was coming, but not you, Ruscio. Welcome back."

"I'm not coming in." He glanced away, down the corridor. "I'm helping out Woodward." He walked to a chair across the way and dropped down into it. "I'll be out here."

Harrison waited a beat. "If you change your mind, come inside."

Ian and Hank entered the room. Today, the conference area was filled with nine men and a woman. Zach Malvaso was among them. Ian wheeled over to him. "This space taken?" he asked.

Zach smiled. "No. Glad to see you back." He looked around the room. "I hate this, though."

"Me, too."

"Hi, everybody. Since those expected are here, let's start." Harrison asked them all to identify themselves. Then he suggested they talk about the kind of week or month or, in Ian's case, the kind of months they'd had since they'd last been to the group, which was meeting every week. Ian listened sympathetically to the guy who'd lost a buddy in the Sinco fire, a cop who'd shot somebody. And now that he knew him, he was most interested in Zach's problems.

"I haven't been here in a while," Zach said. "I got married and thought my problems were over."

Somebody snorted. "Just beginning, man."

"The PTS symptoms were gone." He shrugged. "Until she almost bought it in a rescue. Now they're back with flying colors. Fuck it," he said, running a hand through his hair.

Harrison talked to the group about how trauma survivors

were susceptible to triggers. Casey's safety was a big one for Zach. Others contributed what seemed to set them off.

Then it was Ian's turn to talk. "I didn't say much when I was here before, but I gotta get this out now." He hit the arm of the chair as rage welled up inside him. "I was just getting used to this, getting beyond it, I guess, and thinking of myself as a man and not a cripple, and something happened."

"What, Ian?" Harrison asked.

"Somebody's doing her damnedest to make me feel like a useless gimp." There were gasps from the others. Malvaso, next to him, swore again. "And I'm pissed. She isn't going to win." He looked around. "But I need help." His gaze locked on Harrison. "This is private, right?"

"Yes, nothing leaves this room. It's safe, Ian."

"All right. Let me tell you about it."

➤ TWENTY-ONE

YOU SHOULD TALK to somebody about it.

Rick sat staring at the door where the trauma survivor's group was in session, remembering Faith's words. He should be in that room. But he couldn't make himself go. So much good was happening in his life. He tried not to think about the negatives—really an avalanche of bad things that threatened to bury him—but it was hard having your nose rubbed in it.

First, there was the newspaper article, which forced Nancy Hendricks to fight for his community service at the preschool. She'd won, but he knew he'd put them in a bad position, and he hated owing anybody. He'd discovered that Nick Lucas, the reporter, had come from a family of cops that he was really proud of, which explained his interest in a bad one.

Then, there was Peter McPherson's rage at Rick's relationship with his sister. Nothing had been able to smooth that over. Rick's gut clenched, remembering Peter's drunken tackle. He hadn't been hurt, except for his pride and for how upset the encounter had made Faith. The pain in those grass-green eyes had knifed Rick, knowing he'd caused it.

And finally, this morning, he'd met with his lawyer. The civil suit that had been filed by the rookie who'd been hurt at the academy was coming to a head; a decision was expected this week. Damn it! He'd thought, with Faith, things would be different.

Faith. The love of his life. He stretched his legs out, crossed his arms over his chest, and thought about her. Yesterday, he'd gone to her church to hear her and Pilar sing . . .

They'd both trekked up to the front of the sanctuary like angels doing God's work. Dressed in a navy blue skirt and jacket, with a little pink blouse peeking out, Faith had picked up her guitar and begun strumming. Soon, her rich alto combined with Pilar's beautiful soprano, and Rick had been . . . moved by their music. And by the words of the Psalm: Blessed are the lowly ones, for they shall inherit the earth . . . Blessed are those who seek peace, for they are the children of God . . . Rejoice and be glad, blessed are you, holy are you . . .

And, there in church, Rick had begun to think maybe he had a chance at salvation. Could he really believe, really rejoice in what he had?

Standing, because in the stark light of day the question disturbed him so much, he paced. Damn, he hadn't planned on this . . . on believing in anything again. But he did! He would! He scrubbed a hand over his face, sick of the seesaw. To distract himself, he snagged the *Hidden Cove Herald* off the table. Absently, he leaned against the wall and scanned the front page, then opened to the second.

And there it was . . . in black and white . . . his answer to how far he'd come—or hadn't. An article dominated the local section—another by Nick Lucas; the headline read, "Civil Suit against Former Police Sergeant to Be Decided This Week."

The text dredged up all the sordid details of the sabotage case of Stan Steele, mentioned that other people had been implicated, but for legal loopholes hadn't been prosecuted.

That would be Rick.

The article went on to say that civil charges could, however, balance the scales. *Great objectivity, Lucas,* Rick thought. He read further.

> The young rookie, Jason Keller, who was hurt in a rope-climbing accident at the academy earlier this year, has sued Stanley Steele, former councilman,

now an inmate at Richmond Penitentiary, and Ricardo Ruscio, a police officer at the time, since suspended. The suit charges that the overt sabotage of rope equipment has caused Keller's inability to work in the fire department. He is suing for personal injury and emotional damages, as well as loss of income. A judgment is expected this week.

As Rick read the text, he was mortified. Here it was, the muck he lived in.

He looked at the door where the group was meeting.

Talk to someone.

Talk to Dad.

Okay, Ruscio, push just came to shove. You gonna trust, or you gonna book like you usually do? Once again he thought of Ian Woodward's courage, not in 9/11, but during this latest onslaught to his pride and masculinity by the stalker.

It took Rick several minutes, but in the end, he whipped out his cell phone and punched in directory assistance. When he got the number he wanted, he waited nervously. Never in his life had he depended on anybody. Never asked for help. As the phone rang, he heard his father's voice, *Don't trust nobody, boy. They'll do you in.* And his mother's drunken comments, *Women are better off without men. They just fuck you up.*

But then he summoned the Psalm. *Blessed are the full of sorrow, for they shall be consoled. Rejoice and be glad . . .*

His thoughts were interrupted when the phone was answered at the other end. "David McPherson."

"David, this is Rick Ruscio. I need to talk to you."

WITH A HEAVY heart, Rick entered the church and headed toward the pastor's office, thinking of David's unconditional response to Rick's phone call. "I read the article in the newspaper, son," David had said. "Come talk to me. Any time today. I'll make myself available." The earliest Rick could get away was four. Harmon would cover both Lisel and Ian, who were having dinner with Mona. Rick suspected that Joe was getting to like Mona Mincheon. The thought made him smile, as he took the steps down through the fellowship hall to David's church office.

The door was open. He stopped just before the entryway, when he heard a harshly uttered comment. "Reverend McPherson, you have to listen to us." Rick didn't recognize the voice.

"Under no circumstances will I listen to this attack on one of God's children." The ice in David's tone was also unfamiliar.

"He is a blight on your family."

"Martin." David gentled his voice. "That is so un-Christian."

"Faith is an innocent young woman being tainted by that man."

Rick's heart lodged in his throat. *Tainted.* His word.

"She cares about him. So do I."

Someone coughed. "It was obvious, from her behavior after church last week, your daughter is enamored of that man." Rick remembered how Faith had hugged him in front of the whole freakin' congregation. "All the more reason to cut him out of your family."

"And what do you suggest I do about his sister? Kick her out of my home, too?"

"No, of course not. She's innocent."

"How do you know Rick isn't?"

"The paper said so."

"Lucy, even you can't believe everything you read in the paper."

He heard a chair scrape back. "I'll be taking this to the elders." The first speaker again.

"Do what you have to, Martin. But I'm not backing down."

"Excuse me?"

Rick turned to see an older man with kind eyes behind him. "Can I help you?"

Stunned, Rick just stood there staring. Then David appeared at the door. "What's going on . . . oh, Rick." He put his hand on Rick's shoulder. "How long have you been out here, son?"

"Long enough." He looked at the three people now watching them. "They're right. I'm *tainting* you. And Faith. I knew it all along."

David's face flushed. "I will *not* allow this." His voice rose a notch, and he grabbed Rick's arm with a strength Rick didn't know the man possessed. "I'd like the rest of you to leave. I need to counsel this young man."

"Very well," the woman said, sniffing.

The man in the office accompanied her out. The new guy frowned. "I'm sorry, David. I couldn't get here sooner."

"I know you tried," the reverend said. "I'll phone you."

The other man squeezed David's arm, while Rick stood by like a little boy on the playground waiting for his teacher. "I trust your judgment, David. Know that." With a nod to Rick, he left.

"I should go."

"No." David's face was still flushed, and somewhere in his mind, Rick marveled at this new, angry David who'd risen up out of the mild-mannered minister. "Inside. Now. Sit."

Rick obeyed, taking a chair opposite the desk. David sank down next to him. "Those two people are gadflies in the church. They constantly look for problems. I've about had it with them."

"I *am* a problem."

"No, you're not." He took a bead on Rick. "God wants us to forgive each other, Rick, and help each other be better people. He never wanted us to judge."

"David, I can't cause problems for your family. You've been too kind to me and my sisters."

A fatherly brow arched. "You'll give my daughter up that easily?"

Rick's hand went to his chest, where Grandpa McPherson's medal hung. "I'd do anything for her. Anything. Give my life. Give her up."

"I won't allow it." He linked his hands between his knees. "Tell me about this suit."

Rick went cold. How could he admit his worst flaws to a man he'd come to respect so much? "I . . . I . . ." He couldn't get the words out.

"Tell me." The tone brooked no argument.

"I . . . Stan Steele ordered me to tamper with some of the equipment the department ordered from Anderson Ropes."

"Did you do it?"

"Once." He shook his head. "Not at the academy. Not when that rookie got hurt."

David looked confused. "I don't understand."

"I did it once on a rescue squad rope. Casey Brennan almost got hurt."

"Almost?"

"Yeah. She didn't, thank God."

"What happened at the academy?"

"I don't know. Steele asked me to meet him there and told me to sabotage the ropes. I wouldn't do it."

"So you aren't guilty of hurting Jason Keller."

"Not of that, no. But of other things."

David stood. "I'll talk to him."

"Who?"

"Steele. I've been doing counseling at the prison. I see him frequently."

"It doesn't matter, David. Your church members won't forget."

Again, his face reddened with righteous anger. "We are a family of God. We don't turn against our brothers. I won't head a congregation that does that."

Rick swallowed hard.

"I'll be in touch."

Before he could object, David was out the door.

Rick stared after him, then made his way out of the office and headed up the steps. He passed the narthex, off of which was the sanctuary. Something drew him. Slowly, he went down the hallway, opened the door, and entered the holy room. He slid in the back pew, sank down onto the oak bench seat.

And buried his head in his hands.

IT TOOK A lot to make Faith angry, but as she climbed the stairs to Rick's apartment, she felt the emotion well inside her. Accompanying it was hurt, which she tried to ignore. On the third floor, she pounded on the door to number 4. He hadn't given her a key, of course. Another distancing maneuver, which she was good and tired of. She waited for him to answer, thinking of the phone message she'd gotten earlier.

I won't be able to make dinner tonight. I'm tied up. I'll call you. His voice had been strained, his words clipped, as if he was trying to contain what was inside him. She understood, but wouldn't tolerate being cut out, which he was obviously doing.

She pounded again. And again. Finally the door swung

open. He stood before her, his face lined with exhaustion, dripping with sweat. His tight muscle shirt and gym shorts were damp, and he was breathing hard. "Faith? What are you doing here?"

Lasering him with a look, she said tightly, "This is what tied you up. Working out?"

"Um . . ."

"Don't lie to me. You just didn't want to be with me." She held up the *Hidden Cove Herald* she'd brought. "Because of this." Brushing past him, she stalked into his apartment. She heard the door close, then pivoted to find him leaning against it. He seemed bigger, more dangerous. "Do not *ever* do this to me again."

"Do what?"

"Close me out like this."

"I . . ."

"You don't shut people out when they love you. You let them help."

He stared at her, as if she was speaking a foreign language. His bewilderment almost softened her. Almost.

She rapped the paper on her knee. "I'm sorry about this. I knew there was a suit pending, but you should have told me everything."

He swallowed hard. "Don't you want to know if I did what the kid says?"

"It doesn't matter. You've made mistakes, Rick. Things happened in the past I know you're not proud of. But you've changed, and that's what matters."

"I . . ." There was pounding outside again. "Jesus."

"Don't swear."

Shaking his head, he turned and pulled open the door. Faith was surprised to see her father standing in the archway. "I need to talk to you," her dad said.

"Join the party," Rick quipped dryly.

David entered the room with a question in his eyes. When he saw Faith, he smiled. "Hi, princess, I didn't know you were here." He glanced at Rick. "Something wrong?"

"I'm pissed at him."

Rick gave her a sideways glance, probably at her use of a curse.

"Well, I have good news, so it might help all this." David crossed to the couch and sat. Everybody followed suit. "I went to see Steele. He's experiencing a lot of guilt and admitted you had nothing to do with this incident at the academy."

Rick looked shocked. "Wow, you're a miracle worker."

"He also agreed to tell this to the judge who's making the decision on the case this week. My friend Judge Graves is getting in touch with him tonight. This mess should be cleared up within hours."

Faith sat watching them; her anger was fueled by the interchange. Rick had confided in her father, not her; he turned to her father. She'd wanted that, but it hurt that he cut her out.

"So, you can relax." He nodded at his daughter. "And not give up the love of your life."

Oh, great, just great!

"What about the church members who came to see you this morning?"

"I'll take care of them."

That did it. She stood and let the anger bubble out like heated mercury. "I can deduce what's happened here. Thanks, Dad, for your help." She turned to Rick. "*You* can go to hell." With that she stalked out.

HE FOUND HER at Taylor's. He was frantic by then—he'd gone to her house, to the parsonage, and finally to Nancy's, where her friend said some of the people from the preschool were going out to dance. By the time he located her, Rick was none too pleased with her disappearing act.

Standing by the entrance, he saw her at the bar, by herself. Dressed in tight jeans and the infamous pink sweater—he'd go to his grave remembering the first time he took it off her—she was talking to a guy he didn't recognize as one of her crowd. It took him a minute to realize the jerk was hitting on her. Jesus. Rick strode over.

"One little dance, sweetheart."

"No thanks."

"Aw, come on—"

"The lady said no, lover boy."

The guy looked up at Rick. He was the thin runner type with no muscles. He eyed Rick's. "Who're you?"

"Her boyfriend. We had a spat. She came out. I'm here." God, it sounded like the dialogue from a grade-B movie.

Wisely, the man left, and Rick dropped down on the stool he'd vacated. She peered over her glass, half full of red wine, and gave him a frosty look. "What do you want?"

"You."

The cool facade slipped. Then she shook her head. "Sure, you want me until things get rough. Then you run. Or you're ready to."

Because he knew he hurt her, he said only, "I'm sorry."

"You told Dad you were breaking off with me because of the civil suit in the paper today, didn't you?"

"Yes."

Anger flashed, making her eyes the color of fire. God, she was pretty like this. "You'd give up on us so easily?"

He wanted to defend himself, tell her the suit thing was a big deal. "No, not quite. I went to see your father, to talk to him, like you suggested."

Her face softened.

"But church people were there. I overheard them say I was bad for you. For your family."

No tears. More anger. "How dare they?"

"Like father like daughter," he mumbled under his breath.

"Rick, you can't let other people affect us like this. You can't, or your feelings for me aren't as strong as you say they are."

"*Disculpa.* I'm sorry."

She sniffed. "I don't get over my anger that fast."

"I've never seen you mad." He bit back a grin. "It's daunting."

A smile broached her lips. "I'm no cream puff."

"I can see that now."

She looked directly at him. "Don't do this again. Decide to leave me for my own good. For my family's good."

Sucking in a breath, he knew in his heart agreeing to her command was a huge commitment, even more than making love, even more than telling her he loved her. He grasped her hand. "I won't." He kissed it.

"Promise?"

"I promise." He stood just as "Lady in Red" began to play. "Come on, dance with me. I want to hold you."

Her eyes narrowed, as if trying to decide.

He leaned over and kissed her ear. "I love you, *querida*. And I'm new at this relationship stuff. Be patient with me."

"As long as I have your word that you won't decide the fate of our relationship based on what you think is best for me."

God, this woman thought so much of him—she'd take his *word* on this; it made him want to be a better person. "You have it."

Quietly he led her to the dance floor and took her in his arms. As they swayed to the music, he thanked God—who he'd prayed to today—for the reprieve he'd gotten.

He only hoped he could live up to his promises.

ON HIS WAY to pick up Ian Woodward, Rick stopped in at the parsonage to see Pilar. He found her, Faith, Pearl, and David in the kitchen. "Hi, everybody," he said as Faith opened the back door.

Looking cute as hell in green corduroy jeans and a bulky sweater, she threw herself at him and hugged him tightly. For a minute, he was overcome by her warmth, by the fact that she loved him. "Hi."

Pilar grinned over at them. He'd had a talk with her weeks ago about the progression of his relationship with Faith, and his sister had been thrilled. He hadn't shared his own misgivings.

"What's going on here?" he asked.

"David's pouting," Pearl told him. "It's Girls' Night Out— Anita's going, too—and he doesn't have anything to do."

Coming fully into the kitchen, Rick stood across from David. The good pastor feigned a pout as the women fussed over him. In the week since the civil suit—which had been dropped by what he understood was a very disgruntled Jason Keller—Rick had spent time with David McPherson. They'd played racquetball once, had lunch, and caught a Knicks game on TV together. Just like his feelings for Faith, Rick was afraid he was coming to care for the man too much. Still, he grinned at

David. "Why don't you come with me and Ian? We're going to check out the car show at the dome arena over in Oberlin."

"Car show?" David's gaze slid to his wife's.

"I've been after you for two years to replace that clunker of yours, dear." She looked up at Rick and smiled an indulgent smile. "What's being shown?"

"New vans. Ian wanted to go because they have a section on handicap-equipped vehicles."

Faith had been standing next to him and as usual was petting him—a stroke of her fingers down his arm, toying with his leather coat, fiddling with his fingers. He loved her ministrations. Absently he grabbed her hand and held it.

"It's slippery out," she said, leaning into him. "We're only going to the movie theater in town and the road to Oberlin has all those winding turns. Be careful, okay?"

He leaned down and kissed her nose. "Okay."

"I'm in." David stood. "If you want to get dinner first, I'll treat."

"We'll ask Ian, but I'm game."

Twenty minutes later, they picked up Ian. Mona Mincheon and her daughter were out to dinner with Lisel and Joe. The three men were on their way by six. As Rick listened to David and Ian talk, and participated in some male joking, he felt a strong sense of well-being, a belief that his life might indeed be on the right path for change.

Snow began to fall as he navigated the slippery roads from Hidden Cove to Oberlin. He remembered driving a patrol car in the winter, when a few high-speed chases had caused the car to fishtail. But he was a good driver, he thought, as he listened to Ian and David argue over the Knicks.

Still, the best driver in the world couldn't avoid the dark sedan that came up behind them on the fairly deserted road to Oberlin.

Especially when it bumped them viciously from behind and sent them in a tailspin, careening off the shoulder of the road. Rick had time only to yell, "Hang on," before they hit the iron guardrail.

* * *

HER HEART JACKHAMMERING in her chest, Faith pushed open the door to the ER and kept a hand on her mother's arm. From the corner of her eye, she saw Pilar hanging on to Pearl's other arm. No one spoke.

Please, God, she thought as they searched the waiting area. *Please, not my dad.*

She saw Ian Woodward's wheelchair first. He sat as rigid as a statue, staring out the window. She scanned the room. Rick paced over by the vending machines. Faith rushed to him. "Rick?"

His face was ravaged as he gripped her hands. "He's in surgery, like I told you on the phone."

They hadn't waited for the family to arrive. Her father's condition had been too serious.

"You said internal injuries." Her mother's voice was calm.

Rick looked to the side, where Pearl had come up to them. "Yeah. They're removing his spleen." He grasped her mother's arm.

Pilar said, "Oh, God."

Letting go of both Faith and Pearl, Rick circled them and took Pilar in his arms. "Shh, *niña.* It's all right."

Pearl straightened and reached out to run a hand down Pilar's hair. "He'll be all right, Pilar." She faced Faith. "I know it."

"Of course he will." Faith prayed her mother was right. She tried to believe, to trust God. When she felt herself wavering, she turned away from the group. And spotted Ian Woodward again alone by the window. She crossed to him. "Ian?"

His face was equally sober, his hands fisted on his knees. When she reached him, he looked up at her. "Faith." He shook his head. "I'm so sorry. It's my fault."

"Why would you say that?"

"Some crazy fan of Lisel's is after me. Long story why. Rick and I don't have a scratch on us . . ." His voice cracked here. "Your dad . . ." He closed his eyes and swallowed hard. "The person was after me."

"It was that person's fault, Ian. Not yours."

"Thanks for saying that." He didn't sound convinced.

They talked some, then she pivoted to see Rick, seated now, with her mother and his sister. Squeezing Ian's shoulder, she said, "Come sit with us."

"No, not right now. I want to stay here."

Faith approached the trio. Rick took her hand and pulled her down to a chair next to him. He didn't let go for the interminable hour they waited for news.

When she was just about to go out of her mind, a young woman in scrubs came through the ER doors. "I'm Susan Sanders, the surgeon. Mrs. McPherson?"

Pearl stood. "Yes."

"Your husband made it through the surgery fine. We removed his spleen and patched up a tear in his intestine, which caused some bleeding."

"Is that the extent of it?" Pearl asked.

"We think so, but we won't know everything until he comes to. He's been unconscious since they brought him in."

"Oh, dear, that's not good."

"We'd rather he woke up, of course." She glanced at the clock. "I'm going back in, but I'll let you know when there's a change."

"Can we see him?" Pearl asked.

"Not for a while. You might want to go home and get some sleep."

But they didn't go home. They sat in the waiting room, along with Ian Woodward, who was eventually joined by Lisel Loring and Joe Harmon, until 3 A.M.

When David McPherson woke up.

⟜ TWENTY-TWO

RICK FELT LIKE a million bucks as he held Faith's hand and dragged her down Fifth Avenue. Pretty greens decorated the streets, store windows were full of silver and gold, and chimes tinkled on the corners. Christmastime in New York City was like nowhere else in the world, and to share it with Faith was . . . precious. Hell, anything he did with her was precious.

"Having fun?" he asked, tugging her scarf closer around her neck. Her cheeks were ruddy, and she was grinning ear to ear at the sights.

"Are you kidding? To see New York at Christmastime? It's such a gift."

That had been given to them by Lisel Loring . . .

Bring Faith to New York with us. There's plenty of room in my townhouse for you two, Ian, and Joe.

She'll break my concentration, he'd said, but he wanted her with him.

You'll be miserable without her, Lisel had told him. *And I want everybody to be happy.*

Lisel had told Rick that Ian had asked her to marry him. In an unexpected twist of events, the stalker's determination to show Ian he wasn't worthy of Lisel had only strengthened his newfound confidence and his deep feelings for her. Rick wasn't sure he could have stood up under the onslaught of somebody pointing out his weaknesses. It was bad enough that Peter McPherson still refused to come around.

David was recovering nicely, which was the only reason Faith agreed to accompany Rick to the Big Apple. But Peter had been frantic over his father and raced home the day after the accident; in the hospital, he'd rounded on Rick.

This is your fault. First you corrupt my sister, now you almost get my father killed.

Faith's mother had taken control. *We'll go for a walk, Peter. I understand you're upset, but taking it out on Rick isn't helping any of us . . .*

"Oh, Rick, look. F. A. O. Schwarz. Can we go in?" Faith asked, snuggling into him.

"We can do anything you want, Sunshine."

"Hmm. We already did that this morning."

He chuckled, trying not to think of being in bed with her. Who would have thought Little Miss Innocent would have an adventurous side? *Can we do it this way? What if I touched you here? I know you don't like sex toys, but come look at this catalog . . .*

"Hush." They headed into the famous store. This close to Christmas, it was packed. But Rick hardly noticed for Faith's wide-eyed wonder.

"Oh, my God, look at the monkey. It's huge."

Rick couldn't take his eyes off *her.*

When they strolled through the doll section, Faith was mesmerized by a beautiful dark-haired, olive-skinned little baby doll. She'd picked it up reverently and cuddled it. She said, "She has your eyes." She peered up at him with a deep and shining love, brighter than the sun bouncing off the snow outside. "I want one that looks just like her, Ricardo."

Rick was poleaxed by her comment. He swallowed hard. She made these remarks all the time. *We can tell our daughter this . . . would you like to live in the carriage house . . . someday I want to go to Puerto Rico with you . . .*

He didn't call her on her remarks—to deny they had a future or to confirm it. But his silence never stopped her.

Now, staring down at her, he wondered if he was going to get to keep her after all. If, by some miracle, they were going to make it. He kissed her nose and made an innocuous comment about the doll.

Faith wandered off into the musical instrument section, and they were separated for a while. When they met up again, they left the store and headed for St. Patrick's Cathedral. As they strolled down Fifth, amidst the buzzing of the traffic, the ringing of Salvation Army bells, and light snowflakes dotting her hair, she pointed to the bright-red F.A.O. Schwarz shopping bag Rick carried. "What's in the bag?"

"A present for Pilar."

"Can I see it?"

"It's wrapped . . . Oh, look. There's that restaurant I told you about. Maybe we can have dinner there."

Suitably distracted, Faith oohed and aahed over the sights, but stilled when they reached St. Patrick's. The gray-stone monolith loomed before them like a palace, and even Rick was awed by its stature. Faith simply stared up at it; when he caught a glimpse of her face, he saw she had tears in her eyes. "It's so beautiful. Look at all those statues on the front. That grill work. God must love it."

He let her admire the exterior until she was ready to go inside. The hushed atmosphere, despite the number of people milling around the cavernous interior, was spooky. Rick noticed an alcove near a statue of St. Teresa off to the side. "Come over here a minute." He dragged her into the small space, which provided some privacy.

"What are you doing?" she asked.

"I want to give you this." He glanced around the house of a God that, in so many ways, was a part of this woman's inner core. "In here." He held out the bag.

"Pilar's present?"

"It's for you," he said. "Open it now."

Pulling the package out of the bag, she unwrapped the present like a kid on Christmas morning. Peering around this holy place, he said a quick prayer that he might get to spend every Christmas morning from now on with her.

She chuckled when she saw the doll. "Rick, this is so cool." Yet she looked up at him somberly. Sometimes the expression in her eyes belied her twenty-seven years. "But I didn't mean I wanted this doll." She rested her forehead on his chest. "I meant I want your baby."

He tipped her chin and brushed his fingertips down her cheek. And right there, in the most beautiful church in the world and in front of her God, Rick made the biggest leap of faith in his life. "I know what you meant, *mi amor.*" He whispered in her ear, "The doll is just until we have a real baby of our own."

THE CENTURY THEATRE was old-time Broadway—heavy draped curtains, ornate scrolling on the ceiling and woodwork, and red carpeting. There were the traditional viewing boxes off to the side of the balcony. Rick accompanied Lisel down the aisle to the stage for the dress rehearsal for tomorrow's matinee and night performances. Joe and Ian had an errand to run and would join them shortly.

"Feel good to be back?" Rick asked her. There was something about him these past few days. Something light, and young.

"Some." She looked around. "I love the theater. But I'm tired of it being my life." She glanced at her watch. "I'm glad Ian's here. It centers me."

"I know what you mean." He followed her backstage to her dressing room.

As they reached it, she asked, "Things are going well with Faith, aren't they?"

"Yeah. Her father getting hurt sobered us all, I think. Made us, you know, appreciate life more."

"We all should do that." She unlocked her door and startled. "Oh." Inside were flowers. Dozens of them. "How sweet of Ian."

Rick held her back. "Wait." Entering the room, he crossed to a card propped up against one of the vases. He opened it and scanned it. Looking up at her, he said, "They're not from Ian."

Her insides went cold. "What do you . . . oh, no, the fan?"

"Damn it. We had these locks changed just last week when we knew we were coming to New York."

"Maybe somebody from the theater put them in here."

"Nobody has keys."

She sighed. She didn't want this trip spoiled. Ian was having such a good time, was in such a good mood. Ian. "Rick, Joe's got to stick close to Ian. If she's here, she could try to hurt him."

"We're on top of this, Lisel. Will was in touch with the NYPD. We'll have a couple of plainclothes officers here tomorrow."

She shivered. "I'm sick of this."

"I know. I'm sorry."

"I wish Mona was here."

"Where is she?"

"In Rochester. Her daughter's gone off again."

"What do you mean?"

"She does these disappearing acts." Lisel removed her coat to reveal a black leotard, tights, and a silky dance skirt. "I really like Jenny, but I wish she wouldn't worry Mona so much."

"How old is she?"

"Twenty-something."

"Parents never stop worrying, I guess. Speaking of which, are yours coming tonight?"

"Are you kidding? They wouldn't miss it for the world." She smiled. "Ian's parents will be here, too."

"Did I hear my name?" Ian came to the door with a smile on his face that died like doused fire when he took in the interior. "Fuck."

Harmon stood behind him. "This is *so* not going to happen." He looked at Rick. "Did you call the police?"

"They're already coming tomorrow. I got a meeting at the precinct in about an hour to talk to them about surveillance. I'll mention this."

"Good." Joe sighed. "I'll stick like glue to these two."

"Not quite yet." Ian kept his eyes on Lisel. "I need to see Lisel alone." He scanned the dressing room, the flowers. "And I think this is just the perfect place to do it."

Rick headed for the door. There was an odd smile on Joe's face. He squeezed Ian's shoulder before he left and winked at him. "Go for it, boy."

The door shut behind Joe.

"Go for what?" Lisel asked.

Ian wheeled over. "Sit in my lap." He was dressed in black jeans and a black sweater, making him look even bigger across the chest.

She plopped down. "My favorite spot." She nestled into his neck, inhaling the spicy cologne he wore.

"Right now, I wish I could get out of this thing and down on one knee."

"Oh, Ian. I don't care that you can't . . ." She drew back. "What did you say?"

He slid something out of his leather jacket that was hung over the back of the chair. His big hands fumbled with the square, red velvet Tiffany's box. His eyes locked with hers as he opened it and presented it to her. The look on his face was so profound, she almost didn't want to look down. Almost.

The ring was exquisite. Its marquis cut caught the dressing room lights and made the diamond sparkle like stars. The huge stone nestled in a platinum band. "Ian," she breathed, her eyes blurring. "It's lovely."

"Nowhere near as lovely as you at this moment."

She swiped at her cheeks and looked into his eyes when he tipped her chin up.

"Will you marry me, love?"

"You know I will." She gripped his neck hard. "Yes, Ian. Yes. Yes. Yes."

Slowly, he slid the ring on her finger. It fit perfectly. A good omen. He raised her hand to his mouth and kissed her where his ring nestled. Then he pulled her to him and just held her.

She held on to him, too. Over his shoulder she could see the peach roses on every surface of the dressing room. The fan hadn't driven him away. She'd brought him closer.

"Ian?" she whispered into his ear.

"Yeah?" His hand was lazily rubbing her back.

"Remember that book I showed you I bought last summer? *Sexuality and the Disabled?*"

"Uh-huh."

"There was a chapter on making love in a wheelchair."

He laughed so hard she could feel the rumbles all the way through her own body.

She chuckled, too. "I think it's time to test that out."

"Do you, now?"

"Yep."

"If that's what you want, love." He held her tighter for a moment. "I'll do my best, Lise, to give you everything you want in life."

She drew back and held up his ring. "You already have." Then she leaned over and kissed the scar on his cheek.

This time, he didn't shrink away.

SHE LEAPED OFF her feet, almost from a stationary position, and seemed to fly into the air like a fairy. When she landed, she rounded on the audience. "There, Mother, are you happy? Do you see what you've turned me into?" Lisel stopped. "What? I didn't hear you." Another pause. "Oh, yes, yes you are responsible. If it wasn't for you, I wouldn't be in this seedy little apartment, entertaining my men. See what a mother can do."

And then she collapsed into a heap on the floor and started to weep. Even Ian, who had seen the rehearsal, was moved. From his vantage point, off to the side in the balcony box Lisel had reserved, his throat got tight as she made him believe she was really Jacey Long, the hooker who'd never had a chance. The love of his life was truly a star.

Applause swelled in the theater before intermission. Next to him, his mother wiped her eyes. She'd gripped Ian's arm during the performance, and when the lights went up, she faced him. "Oh, sweetie, she is brilliant."

From behind them, Jude Lawrence leaned forward. "Of course she is. She simply can't give this up."

Allen Lawrence grunted. "She won't. I'll see to that."

Ian considered turning around and setting them straight, but there had already been one scene today . . .

"What's that you're wearing on your finger, darling?" Jude had asked when they showed up at her townhouse. Her withering look at Ian, who had wheeled out of her bedroom earlier, had been telling.

"Ian asked me to marry him, Mother. Isn't that wonderful?"

Both of the Lawrences' faces had blanked. Ian bet they were trying to figure out how they could derail this engagement.

But Lila and Patrick had made up for it. Of course, his mother had cried, but she'd fussed over Lisel the rest of the morning.

So screw the Lawrences.

Lila sighed. "Jude, let us buy you two a drink." All four stood. "Join us, Ian."

Ian pivoted the chair. "No, thanks. I'll just sit here and read the program."

Noah stood. "I'll come. Evie?"

His twin put her hand over her stomach, which was rounded enough so she wore a satiny green maternity top. She looked cute as hell. "No, I'll keep Ian company."

After they left, Eve shook her head. "Don't let it get to you, buddy."

He was scanning the crowd. He noticed the plainclothes officers off to the right and left sides. Harmon and Rick were backstage, he knew. "It isn't. They can't stop this wedding, this relationship. I know it's going to work out."

When he heard the sniffles, he turned and saw tears in Evie's eyes. "Oh, honey."

"I'm just so happy for you."

He pulled his sister close. It was then, over her shoulder, that he noticed a woman down below taking pictures. Hmm, no photos were allowed in the theater. Still she snapped. And snapped. She moved the camera to take photos of the stage, of the audience. Then it swung up—directly at him. She took several shots. Finally, very slowly, she lowered the camera.

Wearing a red fuzzy sweater and a black skirt, she was the same height and build as Lisel. Her hair was Lisel's exact color. If he didn't know better, he would have thought it *was* Lisel. Suddenly Ian remembered some things. The letter, *I want to be you,* and Abby's description of the woman who gave her the pictures . . . *she looked just like her.*

"What's wrong?" Evie asked.

In her ear, he whispered, "Go get Noah."

Eve drew back. "Why?"

"I might have a line on the fan. Go, honey, fast."

When she was gone, and keeping an eye on the woman— who'd donned dark glasses after she finished taking pictures— Ian whipped out his cell phone. When Ruscio answered, he said, "Rick, I think she's here."

"Where?"

"In the orchestra seats, three rows back. She's been taking pictures of me."

"What does she look like?"
"Exactly like Lisel."

EVEN TO JADED New York audiences, the scene must have been surreal. Two plainclothesmen converged in the front of the theater, one from the right and the other from the left. Rick hustled down one aisle, Joe down another. The officers took up positions in the front. Pretty heavy artillery for a patron taking illegal pictures.

Rick addressed her. He said simply, "Come out of the aisle, ma'am."

Through dark glasses, the woman looked at the officers, then over her shoulder. Seeing Rick, she shook her head. "I put the camera away."

They were attracting attention now.

A police officer stepped close to the front row. "Come out of the aisle, ma'am." He angled his head. "To the left."

Rick felt for the gun in his holster. This woman was not sane. Slowly, she edged her way down the aisle, over three theatergoers who sat watching the scene openmouthed. When she reached Rick, he thought something about her looked familiar, but the glasses kept him from identifying her.

From the corner of his eye, Rick saw a little boy of about five race down the aisle; he crashed into Rick, sending him back a few steps. The kid grabbed Rick's leg to keep himself from falling. "Sorry, mister."

It was the break the fan needed. Darting around Rick and the boy, she took off at a dead run. Rick disentangled himself and headed after her. He was derailed again by an old woman in a walker. When he reached the lobby, it was packed as hell. Still, he saw the top of her head as she darted in and out of people. He also saw Harmon heading after her. Rick made his way through the crowded foyer and down a corridor. Ahead of him, Joe rounded a corner and picked up his pace. Running now, Rick caught up, just as Joe threw open the door to a room marked *Private.* They flew inside. The fan was at a window trying to tug it open when Rick shouted, "Stop!" He drew his weapon, remembering what this woman had done to Ian and David McPherson. Her back was to them. "I have a gun. I'll use it."

The woman stopped.

"Turn around."

Slowly, she did.

"Who are you?"

She shook her head.

Rick nodded to Joe, and they crossed to her.

Reaching up, Rick removed the dark glasses. "Holy shit." Then he yanked off the wig. "Jesus Christ."

Standing before him was Jenny Mincheon.

SOMETHING WAS WRONG. Lisel could feel it. She'd had to blank her mind, concentrate on the show's second half, but she knew in her heart all was not right.

The bows were long, and there were several curtain calls. As she took the ninth, she caught sight of Ian waiting in the wings for her. It only confirmed her suspicions.

She came off the stage for the last time and headed right for him. "What's wrong?" she asked as her dresser brought her a Chinese kimono to cover up her costume.

"We caught the fan."

"What?"

"She was here taking pictures. I spotted her from the balcony box. Rick and Joe went after her when she ran. We got her, honey. It's over."

Lisel's knees buckled. She grabbed on to Ian's chair. "Oh, thank God. Where is she?"

"Down at the police station. Come on to the dressing room."

They made their way down the corridor. Ian held her hand all the way. Inside, where the flowers had been cleared away, he nodded to a bench. "Sit."

She sat.

"Lise, you need to brace yourself for this. The fan . . . it's Jenny Mincheon."

"Jenny? Mona's Jenny?" She clapped her hands on her mouth. "Oh, no, please, no."

"I'm afraid so. She admitted what she'd done. She said a lot of things, even after she was read her Miranda rights."

"I want to see her."

"No, honey."

"Absolutely." She stood and whipped off the kimono. She turned and started to remove her makeup. Her hands were shaking badly.

There was a knock on the door. "That'll be your parents, and my family."

"We'll deal with them, then I'm going to the station."

It was an interminable amount of time before Lisel could free herself and head to the police department. Dressed in baggy jeans and a sweater, she felt shaky inside. Rick and Joe met them there and took her to a holding cell.

Jenny Mincheon, looking small and frail—and dressed in what Lisel recognized as one of the cashmere sweaters she'd thought she had lost—sat at a table. She peered up, and her face wreathed with smiles. "I knew you'd come."

"Jenny." Lisel crossed the room and stared down at the woman who'd wreaked havoc in her life. Lisel noted she still had in the blue contacts that, Ian had told her, she'd been wearing with a black wig to make herself look like Lisel. "What's going on?"

"I did a bad thing."

She sounded twelve not twenty-two.

"Did you write those letters?"

"I already said yes."

Lisel drew back. "And you harassed Ian."

Her lips pouted, her brow furrowed. "A cripple isn't good for you."

Lisel felt the anger rise. "You could have killed him, Jenny. They'll charge you with aggravated assault."

Rick added, "And attempted murder."

Jenny's eyes widened. "Murder, why?"

Rick's fists curled. "You drove my van off the road and almost killed a friend of mine, David McPherson."

"I didn't do that." She shot a venomous gaze at Ian. "I only tried to scare him at the firehouse that night." She looked back to Lisel. "To show you how inferior he is. I love you, Lisel."

Lisel felt her insides clench. "You hurt people—me, Ian, the McPhersons." Lisel swallowed hard. "And your mother—oh, God, what will she do when she hears this? Right now, she's in Rochester looking for you."

Jenny's face transformed right before her eyes. It became

cold, calculated, stony. "My mother will still have you, Lisel. Like always. This won't be such a blow to her."

Lisel started to shake.

Ian wheeled over to her and grabbed her hand. "This is enough, Lise. Let's go."

Inhaling deeply to keep her balance, her sanity, Lisel took one last look at Jenny, turned, and headed for the door.

When they reached it, Jenny called out, "Lisel?"

"What?"

"When did I supposedly run your watchdogs off the road?"

Lisel cocked her head. Then she remembered. "Oh, God."

"Come outside," Rick said. The four of them left. "Lisel, what is it?"

"Rick, the night you and Ian went to the car show?"

"Uh-huh."

"Joe and I had dinner with Mona and Jenny. We were with them all night."

"She's right." Joe scowled. "I don't get it. If it wasn't that wacko in there, who . . ."

Rick's face paled. He whipped out his cell and punched in a number. When he connected, he said, "Pearl, it's Rick. No, no, Faith's fine. I need to talk to David." He waited. "David, hi. Listen, we caught the fan who was stalking Lisel. She didn't run you off the road. Somebody else did that. I wanted to warn you . . ."

A silence. Then Rick's entire body sagged. After listening for several moments, he finally said, "Yes, yes, I know. All right. I won't." He clicked off.

"What?" Ian asked.

He looked directly at Ian, his eyes stricken. "It's my fault. David McPherson was hurt because of me."

"What do you mean, boy?" Joe asked.

"The police in Hidden Cove caught the person who ran us off the road. He was after me, Ian, not you."

"Who was it?"

"Jason Keller, the rookie who lost the suit. He wanted to hurt me, but he got Faith's father instead."

✧ TWENTY-THREE

DRESSED IN KNIFE-PLEATED black pants, a gauzy white shirt that
Faith had said made him look like a cover model, and a gray
tweed sports coat, Rick sipped his coffee and stared out at the
streets of New York. He hoped the strong scent of the coffee,
combined with the jolt of caffeine, would give him energy after
a completely sleepless night.

Already, at 7 A.M., the streets were crowded. He liked this
city. Good thing, since he intended to stay here.

From the corner of his eye, he saw Faith turn over in the bed
onto her side. Naked beneath the sheets, she was fast asleep because of him. He'd kept her up most of the night. Their lovemaking had reached a new level . . .

*Rick, I didn't think it was possible to be this close to
anybody* . . .

Ruthlessly, he pushed aside the notion that she'd be that
close with some other man someday; though it drove a stake
through his heart, he'd do what he had to do. Again, his mind
drifted to the night before . . .

Her smooth skin had shimmered in the moonlight, almost
matching the glow in her eyes. *Don't use a condom . . . let's see*

what happens. If I end up pregnant, we'll get married right away . . .

Nothing could have tempted him more. If he got her pregnant, then he *couldn't* leave her. But, from the McPhersons, he'd learned honesty and integrity. He wouldn't bind Faith to him with a child, so he could selfishly keep her in his life.

Promise me you'll always love me . . .

Well, that had been an easy one. He knew in his heart he'd love forever this beautiful precious woman who made him feel like he was a good person.

But he wasn't a good person. Because of him, because of his actions, a sainted man had almost died. If Rick stayed with Faith, he'd destroy her and maybe her family. Which was why he hadn't slept, and through the long hours of the night, he'd come to a decision. He reached into his shirt, clasped the medal Faith had given him, and prayed to God to give him the strength to do what he had to do. Sinking down onto a chair, he stared over at the bed and watched her sleep.

A little while later, she awoke. "Rick . . . what time is it?"

He smiled.

She was on her side, facing him. Sleep-tossed and rumpled, she looked so vulnerable it gave him strength.

"It's almost eight." Gripping his coffee mug, he stood and approached the bed.

Pushing back her hair, she sat up a little and scanned his outfit. "Wow, you look great." When he sank down on the edge of the mattress, she took the mug out of his hand and sipped from it. She winced at the bitter brew, which today suited him just fine. Her eyes narrowed. "Why are you dressed? We don't leave until noon."

"I know."

She took another sip.

"I have some things to tell you."

"Good stuff?"

"Good for you."

Leaning up, she kissed his cheek. "You're good for me."

The sheet slipped, revealing the swell of a creamy breast. He tucked the cotton around her more firmly and set the cup on the nightstand.

Taking a deep breath, he said, "I'm not going back to Hidden Cove with you, Faith."

"Is Lisel staying in New York longer?" She frowned. "But even if she was, you caught the stalker, so your job's over."

"The fan's in custody. And no, Lisel's returning when you do."

Still, her face was relaxed. She wasn't expecting this. Best to get it done, like a surgeon's knife, make the cut quick and clean so it would heal faster.

"I'm moving out of Hidden Cove. I'm staying on in New York to look for work here."

"Oh." She shook her head. "I'll go anywhere with you, of course, but shouldn't you have discussed this with me?"

"You're not coming with me."

"What?"

"I'm moving to New York alone." Reaching out, he brushed back her hair. "We're not going to see each other anymore."

Fear flashed in her eyes. "You don't mean that, Rick. You love me."

"More than I love myself. Which is why I'm getting out of your life."

"This is because of what happened to Dad, isn't it? What you found out about Jason Keller."

"Yes."

"That wasn't your fault."

"Honey, you keep saying that about everything. At some point, you have to realize all this *is* my fault—Peter's estrangement, the church people being up in arms. Christ, your father almost died because of me."

"No, Rick—"

He placed his fingers over her mouth. "Faith. Don't defend me. You're wrong in thinking Keller's actions aren't my fault, but it won't make any difference anyway. I'm not continuing this relationship with you or your family."

"You promised me you wouldn't do this kind of thing again."

He said nothing. His promises were empty.

She bit her lip and watched him. "I won't accept this."

"You have no choice."

"Of course I do. I got you to admit how you felt about me. I got you to start seeing me. This time, I'll make you see you're wrong to leave me."

"If you do, I'll hurt you. Intentionally. I'll sleep with other women, flaunt them in front of you. I know how to be brutal. Even your goodness won't be able to withstand that." His eyes stung at the thought of hurting her. "Please, Faith," he said huskily. "If you do love me, please don't make me do that to you."

Gently, she wiped the moisture from his face. Then she drew him to her and cradled his head to her chest. "Shh," she said softly. "Shh."

He gripped her shoulders. "Faith, please."

"All right. I won't."

"Promise?"

"I promise." He drew back and faced her. She wasn't crying. "But I'm going to do something else for you. For us."

"What?"

"I'm going to pray that you'll come to your senses."

He shook his head, awed by the faith this woman had in the goodness of life. "If you pray to God about us, it should be to forget me."

"I'll never forget you, Ricardo."

"Yes, you will." Slowly, excruciatingly, he lifted his arms and slid her grandfather's medal off his neck. Gripping her hand, he put it inside and closed her fist.

"Oh, Rick, no." Her eyes clouded now. "You said you'd never take this off."

"I am not a good man, Faith. I am not a man of my word." With that, he stood, leaned over, and kissed her head. "Good-bye, Sunshine," he said and walked out of her life.

This time, it was for good.

FAITH APPROACHED LISEL Loring's condo with a heavy heart. It wasn't that her belief that Rick would come back was slipping. It was just that she missed him so much she could barely tolerate his absence from her life. She hadn't seen him in a week, and she felt like she'd lost one of her arms. Lisel answered the door after the first ring. She was dressed in navy slacks and a simple white cotton sweater, and her face glowed with true joy. "Faith," she said, and hugged her. "Come on in."

Faith entered the condo. The room was filled with boxes, and the walls and tabletops were bare. "You're moving?"

"Yes. I've been living with Ian anyway, and it's time to get my stuff out of here. We're selling the condo."

"I wish Rick and I could buy it." The words slipped out before she realized she'd even thought them.

Lisel just watched her.

"Have you heard from him?" Faith asked.

"Yes. Here, sit." After Lisel removed boxes, they took seats on the couch. "He's following up on some contacts I gave him in the city." She smiled sadly. "He's the reason I asked to see you. He has to come back for a few weeks to finish up his community service at the preschool. Then he can transfer to a new placement to New York. He asked me to tell you."

"Oh." Her eyes welled. She swiped at the tears that fell. "I'm sorry. I just miss him so much."

"I do, too. I wish there was something I could do."

The front door opened then, and Ian Woodward wheeled in. Quickly he took in the situation. "Oh, sorry, I didn't know you had company. Hi, Faith."

"Ian." His face mirrored Lisel's. He looked healthy and strong in jeans and an HCFD T-shirt.

Wheeling over, he came to the couch and briefly kissed Lisel. "I was going to help you pack, but I can come back."

Desperate for information, Faith asked, "Have you seen Rick?"

His gaze traveled from Faith to Lisel. "Yes. Joe and I drove down to New York to talk to him."

"He's staying in my townhouse temporarily," Lisel added.

"How is he?"

In an uncharacteristic show of affection, Ian reached out and squeezed her arm. "Miserable."

"Did he ask about me?"

"No, honey. I tried to talk him out of his plans, but he's adamant that he knows what's best for you."

She shook her head, but bit her lip so she wouldn't cry again.

"Faith, I understand where he's coming from. I felt the same things about my relationship with Lisel."

"Yes, I know. Rick told me about it."

Lisel took Ian's hand. "So maybe there's hope."

"There's always hope." She stood. "I just have to hang on to that." She leaned over and kissed Ian's cheek, then Lisel's. "Good luck to you."

Lisel rose, too. "Faith, there's something else. Ian and I are getting married on New Year's Eve Day, the morning before the fund-raiser. We're going to do it in your father's church, and we'd like you to come, but Rick will be there. That's another reason I asked to see you today."

"Of course, I'll come." She swallowed hard. "Congratulations."

They walked her to the door. "Don't give up," Ian told her. Faith noticed he held tight to Lisel's hand. "I'm so glad *she* didn't," he said, looking at Lisel.

"I won't give up," Faith said, determined. "I won't."

DAMN IT ALL. Son of a bitch. Rick sat in his van in the parking lot of A Time to Grow and couldn't believe he was back here at this school where it had all begun three months ago. But he had no fucking choice. He hadn't seen her in seven days, two hours, and forty-five minutes, and each second had been pure torture. He missed her with a passion so great it leveled him. Hundreds of times he'd questioned if he'd done the right thing. If he should have made the break.

As he sat staring at the snow falling around him, he thought of the nights without her that had driven him out to Manhattan bars. Once, he tried hooking up with somebody else—a stacked redhead with one thing on her mind. She'd been all over him in the corner of the seedy place in Greenwich Village. Rick thought he was going to puke. The whole night was a bust, because he'd gone back to Lisel's townhouse alone, of course, and dreamed of Faith.

He'd had visitors, too. Ian and Joe, who'd read him the riot act about his decision . . .

Don't do it, boy, Joe had said. *This one tried the same thing with Lisel and only caused everybody heartache.*

Speaking from experience, Ian agreed. *You know what I learned, Ruscio? That you don't have the right to make that decision for her.*

But he did have that right. Rick believed it firmly.

He began to waver, though, when Faith's brother, Peter, had shown up on his doorstep . . .

Well, this is a surprise. If you wanna take a punch, save your strength.

The younger man, who looked so much like Faith, had reddened. *It's not why I came. I was home last weekend. Faith told me what happened. I just wanted to say if I had anything to do with your decision, I'm sorry. Faith's miserable, and Dad's mad at you, which is about as rare as the Red Sea parting. If I caused some of this . . .*

No, Peter, I caused it. But thanks for coming here.

You love her. I can tell.

Yeah, I do. But it doesn't matter.

And with the wisdom of his father, Peter said, *Of course it does. In the end, it's all that matters.*

There was a knock on the window of his van. Rick looked up, praying it wasn't Faith. It wasn't, it was Nancy Hendricks. He buzzed down the glass. "Well, if it isn't the long-lost sheep."

Looked like David wasn't the only one that was mad at him.

"Hi, Nancy."

"You're a stupid son of a bitch, you know that?"

He sighed.

"She loves you. And she's twenty-seven years old. Old enough to know her own mind." Nancy stepped back. "Men!" she spat out and walked away.

Finally he got out of the car. Time to face the music. He entered the preschool, and as he found his way to her room, so many memories flooded him. The hallway with its mama and baby animals, and her teasing him about the lion . . . stealing a kiss after hours in the break room . . . and her classroom, which he approached with dread. He came to the doorway and froze.

There she was in the middle of the kids on the floor sharing their favorite things this Monday morning. She wore a baby pink skirt and fuzzy sweater to match. Chaste. Innocent. "What's that, Jamal?" she asked.

"A sax. I'm gonna get one and play just like Mr. Ruscio."

Little Molly at her side frowned. "I misthe him."

Her two antagonizers chimed in. "So do we. When's he coming back?"

In the doorway, he shifted, causing Faith to look up. Her

gaze locked with his. He almost lost it when he saw her eyes fill. She cleared her throat. "Right now." She nodded to the entry to their room. As a group, the kids bolted up and rushed to him. They all talked at once.

"Welcome back."

"We misthe you."

"Read us a story."

Finally, they quieted. Faith called them back. "All right, get on your mats. It's time for a fable."

As they took their places on the floor, she approached him. She looked wonderful, if a little thinner and tired. "Hi." She reached out and squeezed his arm. Her voice was thready. "It's so good to see you."

His eyes stung. "You, too."

Jamal came over and tugged on his hand. "Here, Mr. Ruscio, read us the fable." He held a book.

Rick looked to Faith.

"Sure. I've got the page marked."

They sat on the floor, with Rick taking the only chair. He opened to the marked section and began to read. "Once there was a water snake who befriended a swan. They were both young, and met accidentally, with no other animals around, so they didn't know they shouldn't associate. All summer long, they played together and became fast friends. Until their parents caught them. And told them snakes killed swans and ate them up. They were fated to be enemies.

" 'But I won't do that,' said the snake. 'I love her.'

"Still, their parents kept them apart, and they grew up separated. One fine morning, years later, the snake was swimming and came upon one of his brothers about to attack his old friend, the swan. The first snake rushed through the water and stopped the other snake.

" 'What are you doing?' the second snake asked.

" 'You can't kill her,' the first snake said, 'she's my friend.'

"The other snake replied, 'Stick with your own kind,' and slithered away.

"After that, the snake and the swan became friends again, and despite the rules of nature, they lived happily ever after."

Rick peered up from the book right into Faith's eyes. Her

look told him she picked this story intentionally. When she didn't say anything to the class, he felt Jamal tug on his arm. "What's it mean?" the boy asked.

Rick unlocked his gaze from Faith and looked down at Jamal. "What do you think it means?"

"You shouldn't let others influence who you're friends with," Faith said. Geez, she never preempted the kids. "Some relationships were meant to be."

"The snake could have eaten the swan in a heartbeat," Rick replied, watching her carefully.

"The snake didn't, because he loved her."

"Still, he might destroy her someday."

"No," Molly said forcefully. "He won't."

"I don't think so, either." This from Jamal.

Just then Nancy came in. "Time for your break," she told Faith.

Faith said to Rick, "Buy you coffee?"

He had to be alone with her sometime. So he followed her to the break room, trying to ignore the soft slope of her shoulders and the gentle sway of her hips in the pretty pink outfit. She preceded him inside and closed the door. She fixed his coffee with cream and no sugar. When she handed it to him, their hands brushed. "How are you?" she asked. "You look exhausted."

He couldn't help himself. He reached out and brushed fingertips over the smudges under her eyes. "My fault."

"Yes." She grabbed his hand. Kissed it. "I miss you."

"This is for the best."

"No, it isn't." She stepped back and turned away from him. She crossed to the pot again, but he saw her swipe at her cheeks. "So, is New York going to work?"

Nothing's going to work without you.

"Yeah, looks like. I got a job with a security firm. Lisel's recommendation helped."

"Oh, good." She turned around. "They're getting married."

He didn't say anything.

"He loved her enough to work things out."

Still, no answer.

"I don't know what else to say to you." She turned back around. He could tell she was crying.

He crossed to her and grasped her shoulders. "I'm sorry, honey."

"I know." She shook her head. "I promised myself I wouldn't do this. But seeing you . . ." She cried in earnest now.

He circled her around and pulled her to his chest. Nothing in his life ever felt as good as holding this woman in his arms.

She cuddled in, like she'd found her home again after days of being away. "I miss you so much," she repeated.

"I miss you, too." He waited. "Faith . . ."

The door flew open, and Tim and Susie burst in.

Rick stepped back, not exactly sure what he had intended to say. Well, at least he'd dodged that bullet.

FAITH DRESSED CAREFULLY Christmas Day in a green velour dress and a black velvet headband. They'd begin the day with a church service and then open presents and share family time.

The Ruscios were joining them for dinner. Pilar and Anita had talked Rick into spending Christmas Eve night in their childhood home. Today, they'd have breakfast with their mother, then the three siblings would head over here for the afternoon and evening. *We're family,* Pilar had said. *We want to be with you, too.*

"Ready, dear?" Faith heard from the doorway.

"Yes." Her smile was forced. "You look nice, Mom."

"You don't have to pretend to me, Faith. I know this is hard for you."

She smiled sadly and changed the subject. "How's Dad feeling today?"

Pearl shook her head. "Oh, his injuries are healing just fine. But I've never in my life seen him in a mood like this. He's furious with Rick."

"I feel bad about that."

"Don't. Maybe he can help."

"He's still recovering. He doesn't need to worry about this."

Pearl crossed the carpet and watched Faith in the mirror. "We all miss Rick. We each have to deal with it in our own way."

"I know." She glanced around the room where she'd slept last night. "Who would have thought things would turn out this way?"

"God wouldn't like to see you waver in your trust about this, dear."

"I know." She held her mother's gaze. "It's just so hard to believe."

"Well, come on. Let's go to church. That'll help."

It did. It renewed Faith's resolve, and she asked God, like she used to when she was little, for just a small sign that Rick might change his mind.

That sign came at two in the afternoon when Pilar burst through the doorway ahead of her family. Without removing her coat, she flew to the kitchen where Faith and her mother were cooking. "Oh, God, Faith. Pearl. My mother came with us."

"*What?*"

"My mother's here. We asked her again to come to dinner, and she said yes. She said she hated being alone Thanksgiving Day, and she wanted to be with us. She's changing Faith, I know it. Rick's so pleased. For the first time in so long . . ."

Thank you, God, Faith thought.

They all gathered in the living room where David and Peter had come in to greet the Ruscios. Pearl took Dolores's hand. "Mrs. Ruscio, I'm so glad you came today with your children."

Dolores looked to Rick. He nodded. "They asked. Hope it's all right."

"It's wonderful." David stepped up and squeezed her arm. "We love your children like family and appreciate getting a chance to spend time with you." He gave Rick a look that said, *Even if they are jerks sometimes.*

Rick averted his gaze.

Faith greeted her last. She stared at the woman who had given birth to the man she loved. There was a resemblance in the slope of her cheek and the shape of her mouth. "Hello, Mrs. Ruscio."

"You're Rick's Faith?" the woman asked.

She raised her chin. "Yes," she said firmly. "I'm Rick's Faith."

The afternoon went surprisingly well. Peter was nice to Rick, Pearl found a common interest with Rick's mother in a cooking channel, and Pilar and Anita talked Faith and Peter into playing *Malarkey*—the game the McPhersons had given them for Christmas.

Rick was still shell-shocked by the events of the morning as he watched the four of them gather at the dining room table; they'd asked him to play, but he declined. He kept darting glances at David, wanting to talk to the man, not knowing what to say. The good pastor had greeted him stiffly and hadn't addressed any comments to him since then. Rick pretended to watch TV when he noticed David get up and leave the room.

Without analyzing what he was doing, Rick followed him. He found David in his home office, staring out the window. His arm was still in a sling. He was dressed casually in black pants and a striped sweater Faith had bought him in New York. "David?" Rick said.

David didn't turn around. "I don't think it's a good idea to come in here now, Rick."

"Excuse me?"

"I don't think you should be in here with me alone."

"Why?"

Faith's father whirled around. "Why? You ask me why?" He raised his eyes to the ceiling. "Arrgh, God give me strength." Then he lasered Rick with a contemptuous look. "How can you ask me that? How can you not know how much you've hurt all of us?"

"I know I hurt Faith. I'm sorry."

"You hurt us *all*. Pearl loves you." He swallowed hard. "I think of you as a son. And my daughter, who has hardly ever spent a miserable day in her life, has been inconsolable for two weeks."

"I . . ."

"Don't say you're sorry. It's not enough."

"What would be enough?" Rick asked, feeling more intimidated than if he were facing down a mugger with a knife.

"Come back to our family. Be a part of it."

"It's not best for Faith."

David kicked the wastebasket next to the desk; it tumbled over, spilling papers onto the floor. "That's for Faith to decide."

"Faith doesn't know what's best for her."

"With God's guidance she does. And never for one moment has God abandoned her in this whole thing with you." He drew in a breath and stepped back. "I'm leaving. It's Christmas, and I shouldn't be having these feelings I have for you right now on Christ's birthday."

He brushed past Rick, but Rick grabbed his arm. "David?"

David stopped and glanced over his shoulder.

"I . . ." He choked back the emotion. "I love you all, too."

David's gaze softened. "You don't desert people you love, Ricardo."

The rest of the day passed in a blur. He barely remembered the dinner. Afterward, because the Daltons arrived with their son Sam in tow, Rick decided it was best to take his mother home.

So he was in his apartment, alone, at ten on Christmas night, removing his jacket, when he felt something in the pocket. He drew out a prettily wrapped package. Reverently, he took off the paper and lifted the lid. His eyes blurred when he saw what was inside.

It was Grandpa's medal.

ON NEW YEAR'S Eve morning, Rick was slipping into his suit coat to go to Lisel and Ian's wedding. It was a small affair, just family and close friends, but Lisel wanted him there. He'd had words with Ian about it, but in the end he'd agreed to attend.

So, he'd see Faith today. It had been almost a week since he'd laid eyes on her. She hadn't been at work for his last three days of community service at the preschool. Nancy said she was sick, and he'd worried so obsessively, he finally called Pilar.

What's wrong with her?

As if you care. You're leaving us. His little sister was angry that Rick was moving out of town.

Niña, I need to know.

The flu.

And Pilar had hung up.

Rick had stood there, stock still, staring at the phone. All he could think of was Faith's comment *Don't use a condom . . . let's see what happens. If I end up pregnant, we'll get married right away . . .*

He'd used one, of course. Every single time. But they weren't foolproof. What would he do if she was pregnant? His heart leaped at the thought. And deep down, he realized as he knotted his tie, he *wished* she was pregnant. So he could have her back.

He was contemplating that thought when the doorbell rang. What now, he wondered as he opened the door?

Dios mío.

Before him stood a hunched man with completely gray hair, slightly balding, an unshaven face, and bloodshot eyes. He smelled of stale booze and sweat.

"*Feliz Año Nuevo, mi hijo,*" his father said.

"Pa. What . . . what are you doing here?"

"I been sprung. I came to see my kid." He shrugged. "That woman wouldn't let me in. *Maldición de Dios élla.*"

Ma? That was odd. His mother always took his father back into their house. They drank like fish, then had a fight to rock the roof. As a child, it used to scare him. Now, he was just disgusted.

"Can I come in?"

Rick stepped aside. "I'm going out."

Gus Ruscio looked around, then scanned Rick. "Where, all dressed up at nine in the morning?"

"To a wedding."

His father's face was incredulous. "*Jesús Cristo.* Not yours?"

As if it was unthinkable. "No."

"Oh, good. You and me, we're alike, boy. Women ain't no good for us."

Faith was good for Rick.

Gus spotted the sax that rested against the wall. He crossed to it and took it out of its case. "I haven't seen one of these in years."

"It's yours, Pa, you can take it with you if you want."

"Nah. I don't know how to play no more." He stared at his son. "Have a beer with me before you go?"

"It's a little early."

"Don't tell me you gone straight on me."

I guess I have. "I don't drink in the morning."

Gus sighed. "Make an exception."

"No." He glanced at his watch. "I gotta go."

"Skip the wedding. I haven't seen you in months. We'll have a brew, talk. Just like old times."

Rick didn't want it to be just like old times. "No, Pa. I can't." For some reason, he added, "I've changed."

His father's laugh was ugly; he pulled a pack of Marlboros

from his pocket and lit up. "Nah, you haven't. Leopards don't change their spots."

Rick thought of Aesop's fables, where animals performed all kinds of miracles.

"Well, I think they do. Anyway, I gotta go."

Gus blew out smoke. "Can I crash here? Stay with you a while?"

Rick thought about that. Thought about all the damage his father had done to him and to his family. He studied the man he had believed, for a very long time, that he himself had become. And staring at Gus Ruscio in the cold light of day, Rick knew in his heart he couldn't be more wrong. He was not his father.

"No, Pa, you can't stay here." Still, this was his flesh and blood. Rick reached inside his back pocket, pulled out his wallet, and removed all the money he had—a few hundred dollars. "But take this. Get a room for a few nights and decide what you're going to do."

Gus Ruscio's eyes lit at the bills in his palm. "*Santa madre de Dios!*" He regarded his son. "*Gracias.* But when this doesn't work out . . . this change, I'll be around."

Rick shut the door behind his father and leaned against it; he closed his eyes and sighed.

It felt good to know he wasn't his father.

It felt right.

THE CHURCH WAS still decorated for Christmas with holly and greens and banners that proclaimed hope and renewal. Rightfully so, Ian thought, as he sat next to Noah near the altar. Ian smiled over at Evie, who stood with her husband as the second witness, and at David McPherson, who was performing the ceremony. His gaze went to the congregation—his mother and Patrick were off to one side. Lisel's parents had flown to Belize for the holidays and were "unable to get back for the wedding." Ian felt bad for his soon-to-be wife, but she was doing all right with it. His gaze lighted on the McPhersons. Faith sat next to her mother. Interestingly, Max Strong, Lisel's agent, had come and was behind them.

The only blot on this sunny scene was the absence of Mona Mincheon. She'd left Lisel's employ after everything came out about Jenny and her psychotic jealousy of Lisel. Jenny was under psychiatric care, and Mona was staying with her. Lisel had been crushed by the whole thing, but was dealing with that, too.

Ian was distracted from his negative thoughts when Joe Harmon appeared in the back of the sanctuary; he'd never seen his friend in a suit before, and he looked natty.

Then Joe reached out his hand—and there she was.

A vision—in a cream-colored dress that flowed around her like a dream. It was simple, with some lace and beads; she wore flowers in her hair, which tumbled casually down her back. Ian couldn't take his eyes off her as he watched her come down the aisle to the accompaniment of "Ode to Joy." Though she'd picked the song, it fit him, too. Never in his life had he been so happy. He met her at the front of the sanctuary and took her hand. Joe went to sit with Ian's parents.

David smiled at the attendees. "Welcome to the marriage of our good friends Lisel and Ian." He faced the couple. "Lisel, Ian, you are about to enter into a sacred union, and from talking with you these few weeks, I know you're ready. This is something you both want and that God wants for you. You've written your own vows, which I understand you haven't shared with each other. Let's say a prayer of blessing first, then you can exchange them."

David asked for God's help in making their marriage a true partnership, a happy one, but Ian knew it would be. He smiled at his bride, and she smiled back, and he could practically feel God grinning down on them.

She went first. She picked up his hand and held it tightly. "Ian, my love, I wed you today willingly and gladly. I promise to support you in whatever you need to do in life to be fulfilled. I promise to be kind and loving and try my best to make you happy. If we disagree, I promise to listen to your side, and consider all the options. I hope to give you children and raise them in a caring home. Because I love you, Ian, more than life itself."

He was choked up. Big tough firefighter that he was, he had to clear his throat. "Lisel, love, I can't wait to be your husband. This is the happiest day of my life. In the past I haven't always been honest with you. But today, I promise to tell the truth in everything, to always let you know my inner feelings, and never to presume to make decisions for you. I promise to support all your choices, even if I don't agree with them, to take care of you and the babies we'll have, and to love you to the best of my ability."

Tears clouded her lovely eyes. His, too.

David asked for the rings and did the pronouncements. Ian held Lisel's hand through the entire thing; when they were husband and wife, and David quipped, "You may kiss the bride," Ian pulled her down into her favorite spot and kissed her thoroughly. As he held her close to his heart, he thanked God for giving him this wonderful woman to love and cherish.

FAITH WAS SNIFFLING at the end of the ceremony, so her mother fished out a handkerchief. "It was lovely," she said.

Pearl put a hand on her shoulder and squeezed. She knew Faith had hoped to be planning her own wedding, but there was nothing to say to make this better. Faith turned to exit the pew. And froze.

She thought Rick hadn't come. But he stood in the back of the sanctuary looking as handsome as sin in a gray wool suit he'd worn in New York. Her heart clutched at the sight of him, tall and imposing in her father's church.

"I, um, I'm going out the side, Mom."

"Why? There's a gathering in the Fellowship Hall."

"I'm pretty raw. I don't think I can face another rejection from Rick without dissolving into a puddle of tears. And I don't want to do that to him."

"All right." Pearl kissed her cheek. "Go lie down in Dad's office for a while."

Faith slipped out the side door and made her way to her dad's office where she'd wait until she was sure Rick had left. She'd already made a fool of herself six ways to Sunday. She needed to stop that, and she'd start now, on New Year's Eve.

Her father's office was dim in the gray, last-day-of-December morning. She didn't turn a light on, but instead crossed to the window and stared out at the snow, at the barren trees, at the rolling grounds of the church. She'd hoped hers and Rick's kids could climb those trees, frolic in that yard, surrounded by all the love she'd had as a child. He'd be a wonderful father.

Sick at the thought of him fathering somebody else's child, she crossed to the couch and dropped down. Her eyes closed. *Think of something else. Of the pretty dress you bought for the fund-raiser tonight, of Dad feeling better every day, of the preschoolers who always make you smile.*

"Are you sick again?" His voice came from the doorway, smooth as whiskey and just as intoxicating.

"No, I'm not sick." She placed her hand on her middle. Her tummy was churning just from the sound of his voice.

He crossed to her and stared down at her hand. "Did you really have the flu?"

"Yes, of course." She'd caught a nasty bug from one of the kids because her resistance was down from not sleeping or eating.

For a minute he watched her, then sat on the edge of the couch, his leg resting against her hip. Immediately she was assaulted by the sexy smell of his aftershave. Reaching out, he covered her hand where it still rested on her stomach. "Are you sure, honey?"

The endearment caused emotion to choke her throat. When she didn't answer, he asked, "Faith, are you pregnant?"

"No! Where did you get that idea?"

"Pilar said you had the flu. I was thinking maybe you were pregnant and keeping it a secret. Until you decided what to do."

"If I was pregnant with your child, I'd shout it from the rooftops."

"You'd tell me?"

"Are you kidding? I'd get you back any way I could. I know I can make you happy." She sighed, and started to sit up. "But I promised I wouldn't do this." He stayed her movement. "Let me up."

Instead he pressed her back down into the pillows. "I know you can, too."

"What?"

"Make me happy."

"Rick, why are you doing this? It hurts to hear you say how much you care about me, then turn around and walk out. You can rest easy, I'm not pregnant."

"I wish you were."

"Oh, that's just not fair. Don't tell me these things when you're going to leave me again."

He drew in a deep breath. She looked so lovely lying there in her long-sleeved, black velvet dress, which swirled around her knees and scooped at her neck. He could see the charm he'd given her nestled near her heart. He loved her so much. Reaching out, he ran a knuckle down her cheek, thinking of her father's words . . . *You don't desert people you love.* Of *his* father's words . . . *Leopards don't change their spots.* Of the wedding ceremony . . . *I promise . . . never to presume to make decisions for you . . .*

Ian Woodward had taken a risk Rick himself was too cowardly to take.

Or was he?

Staring out the window across the way, he went with his heart. "What if I don't leave this time? Or ever?"

She was silent so long, he had to look at her. Her face was full of feeling, and she was biting her lip. "What are you saying?"

"I love you, *querida*. And I think I made the wrong decision a few weeks ago."

"You do?" Her eyes were wide and luminous.

He picked up her hand. "I . . . I want to be with you, Faith. I want to marry you"—he pressed a hand to her stomach—"and give you babies and try my best to be the man you think I am." He leaned over and kissed her lips. "Forgive me, again. I love you. Take me back."

Without a moment's hesitation she flung her arms around him. "Yes, of course, yes."

He held on tight, awed by her unconditional love. He let himself bask in it for a few minutes, until she stirred.

"There's a lock on the office door, you know," she whispered sexily.

"Faith . . ."

"I missed you so much." Reaching down, she cupped him through his dress pants. "I want to make love, right now."

He thought of the stories her dad told about the oak tree, the bicycle. She did *not* always do what was best for her. "No way, lady, are we doing that with all those people right over in the Fellowship Hall."

"Please."

He chuckled. "No! We're going to get up, get out of this room, and go wish the newlyweds good luck."

"All right."

He took her face in his hands. "And then I'm going to take you home and make love to you. Today, tomorrow, and always."

"It's a deal."

"I'll make you happy, honey. I promise."

"I know that, Ricardo. I believe it with all my heart."

And, for the first time in his life, with this woman, in the house of God, Rick Ruscio also believed it, believed in himself. But just for good luck, as they rose and headed for the door, he pressed his hand against his chest, where the St. Christopher medal hung, and said silently, "I'll take care of your girl, Grandpa. I promise."

⤳ EPILOGUE

DRESSED IN A raven black tux, Mitch Malvaso escorted his wife, Megan, to the center of the stage. Megan wore a sequined slip of a thing that Mitch heartily appreciated. Holding hands, they faced the audience at the Civic Center with smiles. "Hi, I'm Captain Mitch Malvaso, and this is my gorgeous wife, Detective Megan Hale—the brains behind Hale's Haven. Thanks for coming tonight to this fund-raiser. Before Lisel's performance, we'd like to show you Hale's Haven and what your money's going to."

The lights dimmed. "Next year, we'll double our enrollment of campers." He spoke as a video began, focusing on the sign for Hale's Haven—a big white rectangle with black letters identifying the camp; the logo included a rainbow with a pot of gold at the end.

"This is our lake," he said as the camera panned the cove. The video was made in the summer when the sun gilded the water and the trees were green as jewels; you could almost smell the scents of seaweed and earth. Children dived off a dock Zach had installed thirty feet out into the cove. The kids who'd been stunned by the death of their father or mother laughed now, in camaraderie with others like them.

The next shot was of the new cabins built this year. On the video, Mitch and Megan stood in front of the white vinyl-sided, black-shuttered buildings, dressed in camp T-shirts, smiling. Megan said to the camera, "These are new cabins, built over the summer with last year's funds."

Mitch's voice came over the mike. "Tonight's fund-raiser will go toward a common area where indoor activities will be held."

The video showed Jenn O'Connor, still in charge of the camp, on the spot where the cavernous, high-ceilinged pavilion would be. It would sport a kitchen area, a rock-climbing wall, a huge floor for dances and performances, and comfortable sitting areas for informal talks. Her husband, Grady, was with her, holding the sketches, which the video focused in on. "We're planning to rough this out over the summer and do the inside the following winter." Mitch smiled at the audience. "We appreciate your money, but if anybody wants to work from the ground up, my sister-in-law Casey"—who came on the video with Zach, holding a clipboard—"will take volunteers tonight."

Mitch continued, "We'll also use some of the money for activities such as these."

The camera panned the kids riding go-carts and playing softball; it caught Noah Callahan shimmying up the ropes and Will Rossettie refereeing a basketball game. It ended on the two chiefs coming together in front of the sign and thanking everybody for making the camp a reality for the offspring of America's Bravest and Finest.

Mitch's voice came over the mike, again. "We'd like to thank everybody who's made Hale's Haven a reality. Keep up the good work, give generously with your time and money, and help us help the kids of our fallen heroes."

The stage went dark. "And now, for the star of our show, Ms. Lisel Loring."

Ian sat off to the side in the front row as his bride of just a few hours walked on stage in the hooker outfit—which made his mouth water—that she wore in *Longshot*. He was mesmerized, watching her act. For two hours, he was captivated. He made sure he was back in the wings after she took several bows.

She smiled as she came off the stage, dripping wet. He handed her a robe. She slipped it on. "Thanks."

"I gotta take care of my wife," he said, grasping her hand and leading her to the dressing room that had been set up for her.

"I love the sound of that, Captain Woodward." She used his title because just that afternoon he'd agree to take a permanent position at the fire academy as head of the WMD training.

He stopped inside the door. "I love *you.*"

"Excuse us?" They looked out into the hall at the smiling face of Rick Ruscio. On his arm was Faith McPherson. The reluctant hero wore a dazzling black tux, and Faith was stunning in a sequined, slinky dress. Ian had seen them briefly after the wedding this morning, but hadn't gotten a chance to talk to either of them privately. Since they were holding hands, he figured things had turned out well.

Lisel smiled at them. "It's nice to see you two together."

Faith leaned into Rick. "The wedding did it."

"Yeah?" Ian rubbed Lisel's hip, keeping her close.

Rick shrugged. "Yeah." He looked to Lisel. "Thanks for all you did for me in New York. The place to stay. The contacts. But, I'm not moving after all."

"No?" Lisel couldn't keep back her grin.

"Nope. We want to stay near our families."

"I know a condo on the lake that's for sale," she told them.

"Hey, that's a great idea." Rick smiled. "We'll let you get changed." Leaning over, he kissed Lisel's cheek, and shook hands with Ian. Faith kissed them both.

Ian watched them walk away. "That's nice."

"Hmm." She leaned into his embrace. "Almost as nice as us."

He held her close. "Nothing, love, is ever going to be as nice as us."

"Well, when we have our babies. That'll be as nice as the two of us."

"Oh, yeah." He glanced at his watch. "How long do we have to stay at this shindig?"

"I have to sign some autographs. But I should be free for the turn of the New Year."

"It's a date," he said, kissing her thoroughly. "I want you alone when the clock strikes twelve."

And, just before midnight, she met him at the exit door,

where he kissed her again, took her hand, and led her out into the lightly falling snow. "Look, over there," Lisel said to Ian.

By his van, Rick and Faith were kissing.

Checking his watch, Ian grabbed her, and tugged her onto his lap. He rolled over to his own van, where, not to be outdone, he kissed her again. "Happy New Year, love."

"Happy New Year."

Ian held her tight, close to his heart, and looked up at the sky. Since 9/11, he'd never considered himself a lucky man, but tonight, with Lisel in his arms, he thanked the stars, and God, and whoever else was listening for giving him back a job he could be proud of and for bringing him the wonderful woman in his arms.

Across the way, Rick Ruscio was doing the same thing.

AUTHOR'S NOTE

PEOPLE OFTEN ASK me, of all my books, which is my favorite. Although it's a little like choosing which of your children you like best, I'd rank *Nothing More to Lose* right up there in the top three. The reason for this is the fact that both heroes in this book have lost everything dear to them—or at least they think they have—and they must decide whether to go on from there. For me, Ian's story was the hardest to tell. He was one of America's Bravest who ran into the Twin Towers on 9/11 and never walked out. For the entire book, he sits in his iron prison, a wheelchair. As I wrote his story, I cried. I didn't want him to be in that situation. I wanted him to be whole. I wanted him to have everything back that he'd lost in his attempt to do the most heroic of things—save others' lives at the expense of his own. It was so unfair! But I, along with Ian, had to come to terms with the fact that he'd never be what he was before that day and he needed to reinvent himself. As I became more resigned to this, so did he. As I became optimistic, so did he. Thank God. I was emotionally overwrought writing the first half of the book. My heart also went out to the second hero, Rick Ruscio, a guy nobody wants to love. He hates himself and the world. He, too, thinks he has lost everything. But beneath his gruff exterior lurked a good heart, and, in the course of the book, I had to find it, just as he did.

Of course, creating women who won't take no for an answer, who insist on helping the heroes out of their funks, was particularly enjoyable. I love strong heroines, and because both women are unlikely matches for their guys, that made the entire book fun to write. I particularly loved Faith's *joie de vivre* and her unflagging trust in God to help her make the right decisions. As for Lisel, she never gave up on Ian, as I was tempted to do.

The focus of this book is the fire department's response to terrorism. Though I've written many books about firefighters, I'd never researched the topic of terrorism. So I went back to my buddies at the Rochester Fire Department in New York and they were very willing to help. Rescue 11 invited me to ride with them again and also had me attend some presentations on the fire department's response to terrorism. One snowy December night, they booted up the HazMat truck, took out all the instruments available to check for weapons of mass destruction at a site, showed me how to use them, and explained everything in detail so Ian could do the same in one of his lessons. I also went back to the Fire Academy, which is exactly like the one in the book, and the HazMat guys there talked at length to me about the potential threats by terrorists and about what Ian might be going through as a disabled firefighter. They provided me with texts, such as *Emergency Response Guidebook* and *The U.S. Coast Guard's Weapons of Mass Destruction and First Responder Awareness*, PBS videos on dirty bombs and bio-terror, and Power Point presentations on domestic preparedness. They also let me attend a RIT training session, which turned out to be remarkably like the one Ian teaches. I truly had no idea what these brave men and women had added to their rescue responsibilities since that fateful day in September.

I also went back and worked at the camp this trilogy is based on. I got to experience, once again, all the amazing things these people do, and it was fun walking around the site—this time, I could picture my characters in the boathouse, on the ropes course, and in the cabins. As before, my thanks go to Camp Good Days and Special Times for its role in this setting for all three books.

Last, a special thanks to my favorite firefighter, Joe Giorgione. He not only engineered my attendance at all fire-fighting sessions, but once again invited me to dinners at the firehouse and to ride with the guys. Incidentally, Joe accompanied me to the signings for the first two books, and I think the fans lined up to see him and not me, as he was his usual charming self!

As this is the last in the trilogy, I'm sad to leave my friends at Hidden Cove. Thanks to all of my readers who have written to me about them. Please stay in touch and let me know what you think about this final installment. You can reach me at kshayweb@rochester.rr.com or snail mail me at P.O. Box 24288, Rochester, New York 14624. Also, be sure to visit my website at www.kathrynshay.com.

Turn the page for a special preview of
Kathryn Shay's next novel

SOMEONE TO BELIEVE IN

Coming soon from Berkley Sensation!

 PROLOGUE

"LADIES AND GENTLEMEN of the jury. Have you reached a verdict?"

"Yes, Your Honor, we have." His face somber, the foreman crossed to the judge and handed her a paper.

As he did so, District Attorney Clayton Wainwright scanned the courtroom. It was like a morgue. And he just didn't get it. He'd proven his case and he was sure the perpetrator would be convicted. So why was Sandra Jones, the judge, glaring at him, the jury looking as if it were about to sentence Christ to crucifixion, and even his own assistant acting like Clay had betrayed God?

He stole a glance at the defendant. Hell, she looked about sixteen, not twenty-five. Long, dark hair, porcelain skin. Even a few freckles if you got up close. Her appearance just didn't fit with the image of the worldly anti–youth gang specialist that she'd made a name as. Maybe that was why, right from the start, this case had put a sour taste in everybody's mouth. Truthfully, he'd had some moments of self-doubt. But it was his job to prosecute her and was in keeping with his tough-on-crime, particularly juvenile crime, stance.

Her face blank, the judge handed the verdict back to the foreman. The foreman read aloud, "The jury finds Bailey O'Neil guilty of Accessory After the Fact."

Clayton was far from elated, but she deserved the outcome. She was guilty as hell of harboring a criminal, in this case a teenager, knowing he'd committed murder.

He heard a gasp and saw O'Neil grab on to her lawyer; her complexion turned ashen. A hush came over the courtroom.

Then the foreman spoke up. "The members of the jury have a statement I'd like to read, Judge Jones, if that's all right."

"I object," Clay said, bolting out of his chair. "This is clearly out of order."

"Objection overruled. Sit down, Mr. Wainwright. You got what you wanted." The judge turned her attention to the juror. "Go ahead, Mr. Foreman."

He read, "While we recognize the error committed by Ms. O'Neil, and acknowledge that the evidence is substantial, we strongly recommend a light sentence. Ms. O'Neil has kept kids out of gangs, as shown by the defense presented, and she's saved lives doing it. We applaud the good she's done and believe she can do even more to stop youth gangs, given the chance. The requisite fine is acceptable, but the two-to-five-year imprisonment is not. We advise a suspended sentence."

Clay was on his feet again, but before he could open his mouth, the judge held up her hand, palm out. "Mr. District Attorney, do not object. I've heard your arguments. I will take the jury's wishes under consideration. The defendant is to remain in custody until Monday of next week, when I'll render the sentence. Court is adjourned." The slap of the gavel echoed like a gunshot in the too-silent courtroom.

What the hell was going on here? If the defendant received a suspended sentence, it would send the wrong message to people in general and kids especially. To them, it would say, "Adults will protect you when you break the law." Clay snapped his briefcase shut. He noticed no one congratulated him, not even his assistant. He looked over to the defense table; O'Neil's attorney held her in his arms. She cried softly. Clay felt an unwarranted spurt of guilt.

But what else was he supposed to do? A young man had been murdered, and this newly convicted woman had harbored the killer. When the punk been caught, and questioned, it slipped out that he'd hidden in the office of his "guardian angel," who was Bailey O'Neil, and that he'd told her what he'd done. Still, she'd lied to the police when they questioned her about his whereabouts. The boy later contended the murder was committed in self-defense, but that was yet to be determined.

As soon as Clay left the building, he was surrounded by reporters sticking microphones in his face and flashing cameras at him; backdropped by busy traffic sounds on the street, a crowd had gathered on the courthouse steps. "Mr. Wainwright, does this case affect your throwing your hat in for the senate race this year?" one reporter asked.

Straightening his tie, he cleared his throat and swallowed his doubts. "Why would it?"

"It's no secret Bailey O'Neil has the sympathy of people in this town."

"The jury found her guilty. I did my part in upholding the law, which she broke. As you know, I'm running for the senate on a Zero Tolerance for Crime platform, in concert with the Republican Party's stance, particularly for teenagers. I believe the voters want a safer city, state, nation."

"Don't you think this is a little like Goliath attacking David?" another reporter shouted.

"No, I don't." And he didn't. He fully believed he was doing the right thing. Even if watching Bailey O'Neil was tough to take. In some ways, he bought the defense's theory that hers was a knee-jerk reaction to protect a kid by a young and innocent do-gooder. Her lawyer had called her a street angel in his closing statements.

Well, the Street Angel was going to be caged, he guessed. It was the right thing to do. He just hoped this case didn't haunt him the rest of his career.

~ ONE

Clay Wainwright slapped the morning's *New York Sun* down onto his desk after reading the inflammatory letter to the editor. "What the hell does that woman want from me?"

"Calm down, Senator." Usually as patient as Job, his press secretary, Mica Proust, sighed with weary exasperation.

"I'll calm down when our little Street Angel has her wings clipped once and for all." Hell, Bailey O'Neil was still using the name she'd gotten during the trial more than a decade ago when he'd prosecuted, and won, a case against her.

"Thorn's coming right up."

"Yeah, well, he won't like this one." Loosening his tie, Clay unbuttoned the collar of his light-blue shirt. He'd already shed his suit coat; his temper had heated his body—and caused his blood pressure to skyrocket.

Mica gave Clay an indulgent look, like the ones his string of nannies had used on him. He didn't particularly appreciate the comparison. "I'm continually amazed at the effect that woman has on you. You face the Senate Majority Leader down without a qualm, and I've seen you handle angry constituents without breaking into a sweat. But her . . ."

He gave the older woman a self-effacing grin. "I know. She turns me into a raving maniac. Maybe because she got off practically scot-free for Accessory After the Fact."

"A year behind bars is not scot-free." Slick and tidy, Jack Thornton, his chief of staff, entered Clay's office, housed in the Russell Building on Capitol Hill. Thorn took a seat on one of the two leather couches in the mahogany-paneled room, propped his ankle on his knee, and shook his head. "The Street Angel's at it again, I take it."

While Mica filled Thorn in, Clay pushed back his chair, stood, and began to pace. He ran a frustrated hand through his thick crop of hair as he covered the carpet. When Mica finished, Clay started to rant again. "I have not lost my edge. I have not caved to politics. I am not *retro*. Who the hell does she think she is, suggesting I should retire to my country home and play golf, for God's sake?"

"More than likely she's pissed at you now for blocking the funding for Guardian House in the Appropriations Committee. And for writing those memos to the governor and her local senators about that interactive network she's got up and running at ESCAPE." Thorn's voice was neutral as he studied his notes.

"ESCAPE!" Her anti–youth gang operation. "I'd close it down completely if I could."

"And she knows you'd do that."

"It's a menace to society. The police should deal with gang intervention. Not a social agency that coddles young criminals."

It was an old debate, one they were all well versed in.

Thorn said, "What happened eleven years ago also remains between you."

"That woman's only gotten worse in the last decade. Guardian needs to be stopped. The last thing we should be funding is a shelter for gang kids. The money from Stewart's new bill should go to poor, underprivileged kids who didn't choose a life of crime."

Mica said, "Hey, you're preaching to the choir here."

His press secretary glanced at his chief of staff. Thorn added, "I just found out she's throwing her weight behind Lawson."

"What?"

"Publicly. She told the *Sun* she'd be volunteering for the young councilman's campaign bid for the Democratic primary for senator next year so he can run against you in the November election."

"Oh, this is just great." Clay scowled. "Get the governor on the phone."

"Clay." Mica spoke gently from where she'd gone to stand by the heavily draped window that overlooked Delaware Avenue. "You can't afford to antagonize him again about this. He likes Bailey O'Neil."

"The only reason that woman has his ear is because she helped his niece when the girl was being lured into that gang."

Clay saw Mica and Thorn exchange frowns this time.

"Okay, okay, I know. She's done some good. She's saved a few kids. But she broke the law to do it once that we know about, and God knows how many times she's broken it since then. She should be brought up on Negative Misprision." Not reporting a crime when a person knows that one has been committed was illegal.

"You already sent her to jail once." This from Thorn.

"I don't like your semantics. I didn't send her to jail. She went to prison for Accessory After the Fact. For a crime against the United States of America." He cocked his head. "If I needed vindication, which I don't think I did, the kid she harbored was found guilty of the murder."

"The whole thing only made her a martyr. Groups fought to get her out early. Even the former governor was torn." Thorn paused. "Look, Clay, you've got to get a handle on this public feud with O'Neil. We can't let that old case endanger your chances of reelection. And of being considered for the vice presidential nomination."

"That's over a year away."

"Close enough to watch everything you do now. In any case, your feud with O'Neil was negative publicity eleven years ago, which you overcame by concentrating on what you'd done to stop youth gangs as well as other juvenile crime as a DA. Then we effectively buried it in the last election. You can't let the case resurface and get out of hand for the next one. You've got to make peace with Bailey O'Neil now."

"Hell, it'd be easier to sell her the Brooklyn Bridge."

"I think we should set up a meeting with her. Better, you should call her. Ask nicely for once."

He struggled to be rational. "When am I due back in New York?"

Whipping out his Palm Pilot, Thorn clicked into Clay's schedule. "Thursday. You have a late meeting with HEW on Wednesday afternoon so you can fly out at dinnertime." He fiddled with some buttons. "You have a window of time that morning before you do the ribbon cutting for the women's shelter. I could have Bob set up a breakfast."

Taking in a deep breath, Clay shook his head. "No, I'll call her, like you said. And ask nicely."

His phone buzzed. Mica crossed to his desk and pressed the speaker button. "The senator's son is on line one."

Clay's steps halted. Jon rarely phoned him. And almost never at the office. He felt the familiar prick of loss shift through him. "We done? I'd like to take this in private."

Thorn nodded. "Sure."

His staff left and Clay tried to calm his escalated heartbeat. *Fine commentary on your life, Wainwright, when a simple call from your son affects you like this.* Dropping down in his chair, he caught sight of the picture that sat on his desk of him and Jon, taken last year when his son went off to college. Same dark blond hair. Same light brown eyes. Both broad shouldered. But they were as different as night and day. At least now they were.

Clay picked up the phone. "Hello, Jon."

"Dad." The ice was still in the kid's voice, though a bit thawed. "How are you?" Pleasantries at least. Better than the accusations the last time they talked . . .

You know, I may not even vote for you. That bill you cosponsored shortchanged the environment across the board.

That bill provided needed funds for shelters for battered women.

Yeah, the token bone, tacked on to get guys like you to vote for it.

Pushing away the bad memories, Clay asked, "How are you, son?"

"Whipped."

"Anything new?"

"Uh-huh. I'm in charge of the fund-raiser for our Earth Environment group." Jon attended Bard College as an environmental engineering major. He'd gone up to school in mid-July with some other students to plan the year's activities for their organization. Jon coughed as if he was about to do something unpleasant. "The dean asked if you could come to the event we're sponsoring to kick off our fund drive. He thought maybe you could give a talk to the students who'll be here for orientation and community members who always want to hear their senator speak."

Ah, so the kid wanted something from him. "If I can. When is it?"

Jon named a date and time. "I already checked with Bob, to see if you were free. Congress will be on recess."

So you didn't have to ask a favor for nothing. "Well, then, let's set it up. Can we do something together, just you and me, while I'm there?"

A long pause, which cut to the quick. "Like what?"

"Go into the city. Have dinner. See a show."

"I guess."

At one time, Jon issued the invitations . . . *Let's catch that Knicks game . . . I want you there, Dad, at my debate . . . I need to talk about a girl . . .*

When on earth had they lost that? During the long campaigns when Clay wasn't home much? After all the school events and baseball games he'd missed? In the midst of the messy divorce from Jon's mother, who, Clay suspected, badmouthed him on a regular basis?

Because he wanted badly to mend their fences, he said with enthusiasm, "Okay, then, we're on. I'm looking forward to it."

"Yeah, me, too. It'll be a great fund-raiser."

Not what he meant, and his son knew it. Clay wondered if Jon distanced him on purpose. Angered by the thought, he tapped a pencil on his desk, and let the frost creep into his own voice. "I'll talk to you before then."

He put down the phone, thinking of a time when conversations had ended with *I love you.* Because the fact that they no

longer said those words automatically hurt, he tried to focus on
something else. Absently, he picked up the paper. And stared at
the Letters to the Editor page. Now Bailey O'Neil was aligning
herself with the man who was after Clay's seat in Congress.

Hell, he didn't want to lock horns with her again. Grabbing
his phone again, he said to his assistant, "Joanie, get me Bailey
O'Neil in New York, would you? I think we have her work
phone on file." Gripping the receiver before the call was
punched through, he said aloud, "Okay, sweetheart, time for another round."

So, who are you? The words scrolled across the screen of
Bailey's computer, like so many others, uttered casually.

You know who I am or you wouldn't have come to my site, TazDe-
vil2. Bailey was unfamiliar with the screen name.

No response.

So she typed, I'm the Street Angel. And I can help you.

Yeah, sure.

Why don't you tell me why you came to my site. It's just us two.
She grinned in the empty office. And I won't tell anybody else. *No
matter what the good senator from New York does to me.*

Chill out a minute.

Bailey waited. Kids needed time to take this big step. As she
drummed her fingers on the table, she scanned her messy office.
ESCAPE, her organization that helped kids find a way out of
gang life, needed more space. They'd grown so much they
needed three offices on this floor, and still she shared hers with a
coworker. But she'd rather direct the funds to programs, instead
of spending it on overhead. When they moved, as they did every
few years to maintain their anonymity—much like shelters for
battered women—their space probably wouldn't be much larger.

Her private phone shrilled into the silence, making her star-
tle. She wondered if she should answer it while the newest visitor to her interactive website garnered her courage. Or got
interrupted. Bailey winced. Once, she'd been on the phone hot-
line with a boy and he cut off abruptly. Bailey later suspected
he'd been caught and killed. A body had turned up with ear-
marks of the teen she'd been talking to. *Don't think about the
loss.* To avoid it, she picked up the phone. "Bailey O'Neil."

"Ms. O'Neil, this is Clayton Wainwright."

Oh, shit. "Senator, this is a surprise."

"Is it?"

Ah, he saw the letter in the *Sun*. "Hmm."

"I was wondering if you'd make some time for me on Thursday of next week. I'll be in New York." His voice was deeper, huskier than she remembered.

"Um, I'm pretty busy."

"You have to eat. How about breakfast?"

Okay, enough dancing. Not only did they have a history together, but she despised his politics and the damage he'd done to social agencies like hers. No way was she going to see him in person. "Look, Senator, we don't have much to say to each other. You disagree with how I choose to help kids, and I think you're conservative and backward and that you've copped out on the potential you showed early in your career. We're never going to see eye to eye."

"Humor me."

"I don't think so."

"I'm afraid I have to insist."

"Are you for real?"

"What does that mean?"

"That you can insist all you want. It has no effect on me." Time to take the gloves off. "I'm furious with you for your two latest tricks."

"Tricks?"

"Blocking my funding for Guardian at the federal level. At least so far. And then for writing memos to the state officials about ESCAPE."

"They weren't—"

The instant message chimed, indicating the teen had posted. "Look, I've got to go. Thanks for the invitation, but no." She hung up before he could respond, and read the message.

TazDevil2 was back on. Maybe I'm thinkin' this is jackshit.

You don't have to be tough with me. Tell me about your situation. A pause. I got me a set. The Good Girls.

Literally, Bailey froze. The Good Girls had been the worst girl gang in New York City in the eighties. Swallowing her reaction, she typed, That gang doesn't exist anymore.

Yeah, dude, they do. We been calling ourselves that for a few months. Used to be the Shags. Decided to reincarnate that other gang cuz they was so tough.

Uncomfortable, Bailey toyed with the picture of her son, Rory, on her desk. I know.

How?

I was close to somebody in the GG's.

Hey, you got the tag right.

Yeah.

Who was it?

My sister. She was one of the original members.

Fucking A! You kiddin' me?

I wish I was. I saw firsthand what the GG's did to girls.

No comment.

How old are you?

Seventeen.

How old were you when you got in?

Fourteen.

The same age as Moira. Beautiful, troubled Moira, whom Bailey had loved unconditionally, despite the problems her half sister had caused in her family.

That her name?

Yeah. Did you jump or train in?

Jumped. I ain't no boy's slave. Bailey knew training into a gang, by fucking several guys fast and in a row like train cars, was the preferred method of gang initiation over jumping in, which consisted of being brutally beaten by the members. Except if you trained in, you were treated like scum afterward.

What happened to her?

Moira? She died.

No answer.

Again, Bailey glanced at the phone. Moira had died in prison, where a young DA, much like Clayton Wainwright, had put her. Bailey herself had been partly responsible, too.

You sad about it still?

Every day of my life.

You got more family?

I do. Four brothers. Me, my mom, and dad.

How come she join a gang if she got family like you?

Because dad slipped up and had a kid with another woman.

Long story. Since the girl seemed to want to talk, she asked, What's your name?

Tazmania. I go by Taz.

Tell me about yourself.

A pause. Maybe later. Gotta jet now, Angel. Ciao.

Ciao. And then Bailey added, Stay in touch. Please. I'm on tomorrow night.

No answer.

For a moment, Bailey just watched the blank computer screen. Sighing, she leaned back in her rickety chair, eased off her scuffed loafers, and propped her feet up on the desk. Idly, she noted that her jeans were threadbare and almost white at the knees. She plucked at the frayed cuffs of the oxford cloth blouse she wore. Geez, she needed new clothes. But hell, who had time or the inclination for shopping?

Shutting her eyes, linking her hands behind her neck, she tried to center herself. She became aware of the quiet. It had gotten late, and the day-shift workers had left the office. The hotline/website night crew would be in soon. But for now she was alone. With her memories of Moira. With the pain that twisted her heart like an emotional vise whenever she thought about her half sister; it had dulled, but never really gone away. She was alone with her now-rabid zeal to save kids, which she knew was excessive. That quest had taken over her life until Rory came along. And it was still too important to her. But she couldn't help it. She was going to make a difference.

She thought of Clayton Wainwright—her nemesis since his district attorney days. Though she didn't blame him for prosecuting her—she was guilty, after all, of harboring the kid when he'd told her he'd committed a crime—she did hold Wainwright in contempt for his continual vigilance over her organization, and his attempts to keep her funding at bay. Her efforts had been stalled considerably, more than once, just because of him. His latest target had been Guardian, and she was still fuming over what he'd done. Now, however, a new battle would ensue; there was money available from the government in a new bill initiated by a senator from Massachusetts and passed by Congress for both social agencies and law enforcement. Bailey wanted some of the funds. Wainwright was just as determined not to give them to her.

If he only knew what was really what. But he lived in an ivory tower, with a silver spoon in his mouth, so he could never conceive of what street life was like for kids. Partly because of that, he was dangerous. Best to keep her guard up. With a man like him, you needed your guns poised and your belt full of ammunition; she couldn't hand him any bullets to stop her with, no matter how nicely he asked.

"Beware, Senator Wainwright," she said, glaring at the phone. "I'm gonna win this round. The Street Angel is not giving up."

From award-winning author
KATHRYN SHAY

On the Line
0-425-19710-7

When investigator Eve Woodward comes to
Hidden Cover looking for clues in an arson case, she
uncovers something completely unexpected—a
handsome fire chief and a burning attraction.

Trust in Me
0-425-18884-1

As teenagers, they were called the Outlaws.
Now these six friends will find that yesterday's
heartaches are part of the journey to
tomorrow's hopes.

Promises to Keep
0-425-18574-5

A high-school principal resents the new
crisis counselor assigned to her school.
But Joe Stonehouse is really an undercover
Secret Service agent. Will the truth temper the
attraction that threatens to set them both on fire?

BERKLEY SENSATION
COMING IN MARCH 2005

Mr. Impossible
by Loretta Chase
When a reckless rogue and a beautiful scholar set off
to foil a kidnapping, tensions flare—and so does love.

0-425-20150-3

Ashes of Dreams
by Ruth Ryan Langan
In 1880s Kentucky, Amanda Jeffrey is a young widow,
left to raise a family and run a farm alone. But when
she enlists the help of an Irish immigrant, she finds
her long-dormant passion is rising from the ashes.

0-425-20151-1

Total Rush
by Deirdre Martin
New from the bestselling author of *Fair Play*, a story
of a new-age girl and a fireman. They couldn't be
more different—or any more in love.

0-425-20111-1

For Pete's Sake
by Geri Buckley
Meet Pete. She's a modern-day Southern belle trying to
hold her dysfunctional family together, while keeping
her love life from falling apart.

0-425-20153-8